I0666011

THE KEY TO THE KINGDOM

THE KEY TO THE KINGDOM

Book III of The Bard's Heresy

Justin D. Bello

Copyright © 2025 Justin D. Bello
All rights reserved.
First Edition

NO AI TRAINING: Without in any way limiting the author's exclusive rights under copyright, any use of this publication to "train" generative artificial intelligence (AI) technologies to generate text is expressly prohibited. The author reserves all rights to license uses of this work for generative AI training and development of machine learning language models.

ISBN 13 (Print): 979-8-9900597-8-8
ISBN 13 (Digital): 979-8-9900597-9-5

CONTENT WARNING: The following work of fiction is set in a fantastic, but quasi-historical world, and contains graphic violence, sexual content, and language that is intended for mature audiences. Readers should be advised that much of the mature content is based upon realistic situations that were part of an extremely violent period of human history. Potentially disturbing scenes include vivid descriptions of battle, blood and gore, murder, torture, implied sexual assault, and violence involving animals.

To the victims of tyranny and injustice—
May your oppressors receive their just rewards.

The Continent of

Termain

The Songund Isles

THE STORY SO FAR...

What follows is a brief recap of the events of *The Blackguard's Bond*.

THE LOREMASTER

After being granted the title of LOREMASTER, Royne and his steward, Connor, fled Titanis for the Guardian-occupied Republic of Grantis in search of a Blackguard by the name of Salasco the WALL. During their search, they are captured by renegade soldiers of the Grantisi Fifth Legion and taken to the defeated army's camp. There, Royne is forced to use the miraculous abilities of the Guardians to heal the legion's dying leader, a famous general named Cornelius Navarro. Overtime, Royne befriends the general, serving as an advisor in the Legion's attempt to drive the Andochan invaders from their homeland. After a particularly disastrous battle--a battle that Royne advised against--the legion encounters a refugee camp led by none other than Salasco the Wall. Convinced that the conflict in Grantis is but a minor skirmish in a larger continental war, Royne convinces General Navarro to travel to Baronbrock to assist the folk of Galadin against the Guardian-King. Despite his intentions to travel with them and reunite with his best friend Lughus, Royne decides to delay the journey in favor of seeking greater knowledge at the University, the walled compound that is home to the Alchemists of the mysterious Sign of Four.

THE THREE

After traveling to Baronbrock, Brigid the BLADE, Geoffrey the VANGUARD, and Geoffrey's family make their home in the city of Galadin. Denied entry to the ailing baron's castle, the Houndstooth, they spend months awaiting an audience. While Geoffrey seeks work to support his family, Brigid haunts the city at night, hoping to find a way to infiltrate the castle and contact the baron. After a chance encounter with a pair of Andochan kingsmen and an enormous, golden hound, it is revealed that the Guardian constable Willum Harlow, known as the HAMMER, has also made his way to Galadin. When he sets his sights on arresting Brigid and Geoffrey, the small family makes a desperate attempt to flee only to be saved by the great hound, Fergus, and the new baron of Galadin, Lughus, bearer of the title of the MARSHAL. Together, they drive the Hammer and his allies from the city.

Since his return to Galadin, Lughus has remained within the confines of the Houndstooth attending to his ailing grandfather, Arcis. While it is expected that Lughus will assume the title of baron upon his grandfather's death, his long absence and status as a Blackguard require that his ascension must be approved by the Assembly of Barons of the Brock. While the Lord-Baron, Perin Glendaro supports

Lughus's claim, Arcis fear his perennial rival (and Lughus's paternal grandfather), Roland Marthaine, will object.

Following Arcis's death and the subsequent appearance of Brigid and Geoffrey, Lughus prepares for the assembly. Brigid's courtly acumen makes her an invaluable ally and the two young Blackguards grow steadily closer.

Lughus, Brigid, and the Galadin guard depart for Highboard, the capital of the Brock, to attend the Assembly and defend Lughus's claim. Before he can speak, however, Willum Harlow appears with the ambassador from Andoch. He denounces Lughus and Brigid as heretics and threatens war if the remaining barons do not release the two Blackguards into Guardian custody. To the surprise of all, Baron Roland Marthaine issues a biting rebuke of the Hammer and the Guardians while simultaneously reaffirming the sovereignty of the Brock. The Assembly comes to an abrupt end with the barons of both Galadin and Marthaine departing, side by side, to raise their armies in mutual defense.

Meanwhile, back in Galadin, Geoffrey of Pyle, with the unlikely aid of the crime lord, Adolfo the Madder, repels a Guardian surprise attack, earning himself the love of the people and revealing his strengths as a leader of men.

With war between Andoch and the Brock now inevitable, Lughus, Brigid, Geoffrey, and the other barons make ready. Roland Marthaine, moved by the sudden reappearance of a grandson he believed long-dead, visits Galadin in an attempt to lay the age-old rivalry to rest once and for all. At the same time, Lughus and Brigid continue to grow closer, eventually declaring their love for one another. No sooner do they declare their bond, however, when word reaches Galadin that the Guardians have invaded and lay siege to the monastery of St. Golan the Ram.

The army of Galadin, though hastily assembled and outnumbered, rushes to the relief of their friends at the monastery. They succeed at driving off the Andochan advance force and prepare to meet the main force of the Guardian army and their general, the CHOUGH. The Galadins mount a heroic defense and with the surprising and unexpected arrival of additional forces from the baronies of Nordren and Marthaine—as well as the famed infantry of the Grantisi Fifth Legion—the Guardian army is soundly defeated.

THE REAVER

As the Wrathorn Blackguard Magnus Bloodbeard, the REAVER, continues to scour the Sorgund Isles in hopes of tracking down his treacherous shipmates, Thom follows along, recording the great warrior's deeds. With the Andochan blockade of Grantis finally lifted, the unusual pair secure a ship and travel the coast in pursuit of Magnus's enemies. As they continue the search, Magnus reveals to Thom that he and his former crew mates had been hired by the Keepers of the Castone to recover a Guardian relic, the Key of Salvation, in exchange for an enormous reward. When Magnus refused to turn over the key to the Keepers, the rest of the crew rebelled and sold him out to the kingsmen in Galdoran.

The quest for vengeance eventually leads Thom and Magnus to the Lighthouse of Castone. There, Magnus finds the last of his former friends and the lost relic. With the Key of Salvation in hand, the leader of the Keepers, Grand Keeper Riggilo Huskarn, attempts to persuade Magnus to join him by promising the favor of the dark god, Dibhor.

Magnus refuses. Violently. To Thom's horror, the Keepers summon an army of undead warriors straight out of ancient myth to defend themselves. Thom and Magnus are forced to flee, but not before Thom steals the Key of Salvation. Once they escape, Magnus passes his title and his axe on to Thom, leaving him to fend for himself alone on the unfamiliar shores of Montevale.

THE TOWER

After surrendering to his brother Dermont in exchange for the lives of King Marius and Princess Marina of Gasparn, Beledain Tremont, the TOWER, returns to his childhood home to face confinement with his pregnant lover, Lilia. After Lilia dies giving birth to their son, Marcus, Bel revolts against his captors and escapes with his son, his ailing father, Marius, Marina, and a small group of loyal retainers. Before long, many of Bel's former friends, former comrades, and the great stallion, Tempest, seek him out. Together they raise an army in rebellion against Dermont's tyranny. With the help of another Blackguard, a forester by the name of the SHACKLE, they take the city of Pridel and establish it as the seat of power for a new monarch, Queen Marina. Furious at the rebels attempts to usurp his power, Dermont, the Plague King, sends his seneschal, Kurlan Malacco against the rebels while simultaneously ordering the assassination of Bel's infant son and the rebel queen. With the help of his loyal band of followers, Beledain defeats the enemy army and foils the assassins, firmly establishing the rebellion as a legitimate force in the fight against tyranny and oppression.

And thus, the story continues...

TABLE OF CONTENTS

PROLOGUE.. 1

CHAPTER 1: THE WRATH OF THE REAVER............................. 8

CHAPTER 2: THE BATTLE OF CRAGBARROW......................... 19

CHAPTER 3: THE UNIVERSITY....................................... 36

CHAPTER 4: NORDREN HARBOR...................................... 43

CHAPTER 5: THE GOLDEN GARRON 50

CHAPTER 6: THE BANE OF THE BLADE............................. 66

CHAPTER 7: THE REAVER & THE TOWER............................ 80

CHAPTER 8: EXORDIUM 92

CHAPTER 9: THE VOYAGE OF THE VANGUARD 104

CHAPTER 10: UNINVITED GUESTS................................. 113

CHAPTER 11: SUBSTANTIAL ALCHEMY 123

CHAPTER 12: ENVOYS & ALLIANCES 132

CHAPTER 13: MUCK & MIRE....................................... 150

CHAPTER 14: AN UNEXPECTED ALLY.............................. 159

CHAPTER 15: THE YOUNG TALON.................................. 167

CHAPTER 16: TENDERNESS.. 180

CHAPTER 17: ENEMY AT THE GATES.............................. 195

CHAPTER 18: THE KEEPER 205

CHAPTER 19: HARRIER'S KEEP.................................... 219

CHAPTER 20: THE COURT OF THE PLAGUE KING 229

CHAPTER 21: THE FEAST OF THE FATHER........................ 239

CHAPTER 22: A HEARTLESS FOE 251

CHAPTER 23: METAPHYSICAL ALCHEMY........................... 260

CHAPTER 24: THE SIEGE OF STONEBRIDGE 269

CHAPTER 25: THE IRON FIST 282

CHAPTER 26: THE VICEROY'S DECREE 293

CHAPTER 27: HOUNDSTOOTH IN WINTER 299

CHAPTER 28: THE VANGUARD'S RIDE 316

CHAPTER 29: BALANCE & DISCORD 336

CHAPTER 30: A GREAT HONOR 342

CHAPTER 31: TWIN SHADOWS 354

CHAPTER 32: RETRIBUTION 366

CHAPTER 33: THE SIGN OF FOUR 381

CHAPTER 34: PRELUDE TO BATTLE 391

CHAPTER 35: BETRAYAL 409

CHAPTER 36: TO THE NORTH 423

CHAPTER 37: THE WALLS OF GALADIN 431

CHAPTER 38: THE DECISIVE BATTLE 442

CHAPTER 39: THE BATTLE OF WHITEMANE 453

CHAPTER 40: THE ARMY OF THE DEAD 464

CHAPTER 41: LOCK & KEY 477

CHAPTER 42: THE LAST STAND 494

CHAPTER 43: CODA 514

DRAMATIS PERSONAE 521

ACKNOWLEDGEMENTS 525

ABOUT THE AUTHOR 527

PROLOGUE

From his quarters high atop the Tower of the Loremaster, Natharis Tainne sat before the open windows gazing out into the blackness of the night. A light breeze passed through the room, causing the sconces to flicker, hinting at the autumnal months that would follow this Harvestide. Behind him, three of his acolytes—young Keepers all, none of those ignorant fools of the Order—were just finishing their duties, seeing to the removal of the body of the young peasant woman and cleansing his private chamber of any traces of her existence.

Tainne sighed. He had hoped that in indulging himself, he would find a sense of tranquility—of peace—before the meeting with his fellows. Instead, he felt as if his agitation had increased, despite the fact that the girl had been both a bleeder and a screamer—qualities that he usually found to be exhilarating. Yet, even as he cut her and watched her body writhe against the restraints, even as he listened to the music of her sobs and saw the primal light of fear glistening in the bottomless pools of her eyes, and even at the very end—at the height of his excitement—when he finally opened her throat and watched the torrent of hot blood spurt forth, he felt no pleasure. Only emptiness and annoyance.

Tainne poured himself a goblet of wine from the decanter on the small table beside his chair, and took a sip, pursing his lips with discontent. A moment later, the acolytes concluded their business, bowing their heads in silent deference before withdrawing, carrying with them the gruesome burdens they had packaged for disposal. Tainne hurried them onward with a petulant wave of his hand. The time of the meeting drew near, and while he appreciated his acolytes' efforts, they seemed to take much longer tonight than he liked.

Surrounded by the self-righteous members of the Order, it was necessary to be thorough, however, even if the disappearance of one anonymous peasant was unlikely to cause a stir. Of course, it had long since gone beyond simply *one* anonymous peasant to a number that he could no longer quite recall.

Still, peasants were peasants. It was part of his preference for such types. They were just so...expendable, so meaningless. Furthermore, there was something about their poverty that he found so irresistible, so delightfully enticing. They were just so...filthy, so sub-humanly crass. At the same time, for one with the breeding, lineage, and learning as himself, there was something so deific about indulging in them. It evoked a type of ecstasy that made him feel, for lack of a better word, blessed, and to work his will upon them brought with it a type of rapture that made him feel that he truly were doing the divine work of his Lord Dibhor.

He sighed. It could not be long now, he told himself. Despite the recent setbacks, all was still going according to plan, or rather, to prophesy. Before long, his lord would return and a truly golden era would begin. The corrupt would be cleansed or purged accordingly, and the faithful would be elevated as princes of a new and more pure world. The false gods of the Kinship would be recognized as the corrupting forces that they were, and the one true god would reign eternal and supreme. Order would be restored.

Soon.

With that thought, Tainne emptied his goblet and refilled it from the decanter, this time stirring in a dose of powdered nightshade from the vial kept hidden within his robes. In the Tower of the Hierophant, the bells sounded to mark the hour. The time had come. With a whispered prayer to Dibhor, Tainne idly gave the goblet a swirl and downed it in one go. At once, he sensed the familiar bitterness of the toxin on his tongue. A normal man would not survive such poison; however, over the long years of his training, his body had learned to tolerate its effects. His heart slowed, his breath staggered, and a cold numbness crept from his fingers and toes up his arms and legs. Moments later, his vision grew clouded, his gaze narrowed, and all the world went black.

When at last his eyes opened again, he found himself beneath the deeper darkness of a moonless night. No longer was he surrounded by the opulent luxury with which he had furnished the Loremaster's quarters. Rather, he stood instead in a mist-shrouded clearing. A faint light emanated from somewhere, its source lost in the fog, but it was enough to discern a dozen or so cowled figures standing before him in deep purple robes. Tainne instantly recognized the tallest of the two as Riggilo Huskarn, the Grand Keeper, and to his right was Jeden Loris, another Keeper of the first degree. The remaining men, in their silence, were indiscernible beneath the shadow of their hoods.

"Good of you to finally join us, Natharis," Huskarn intoned.

"My apologies, Grand Keeper," Tainne said, "I had a matter to attend to, but I dealt with it swiftly and submitted to the nightshade as soon as I heard the bell strike the hour."

"Yes, I am sure," the Grand Keeper said belligerently, "Though I suppose late is better than never."

Tainne ignored the slight, though inwardly, he bristled. It was the Grand Keeper himself who lost the bloody Key. Tainne may not have succeeded yet in discovering the location of "the Lock" that kept their divine lord bound; however, he had made incredible strides, setting himself up as the most powerful man in Andoch. Even the self-serving oaf of a King had essentially become little more than Tainne's puppet.

Meanwhile from the safety of the Lighthouse, all Riggilo Huskarn had ever succeeded at was losing Callah's Key to some fucking Wrathorn Blackguard and the last of Rastis's wretched apprentices.

That had been quite the revelation—that the fat little bastard had somehow made his way to the very tip of the continent, to the very seat of the Keeper's knowledge and power. Well, the Grand Keeper could now know firsthand the trouble Rastis's whelps could cause in the company of a bloody Blackguard.

"In any case," Huskarn said, "What new information can you provide? Tell me that you have made at least some progress in your search for the Lock or in capturing the heir of St. Aiden."

Natharis Tainne pressed the tips of his fingers together and raised his head to meet the Grand Keeper's pallid gaze. His irises, like Tainne's own and those of every other Keeper, had faded in color to an unnaturally light shade of blue, nearly to the point of being completely white, a stark contrast to the deeper darkness of the narrow serpentine pupils.

"As we speak," Tainne began, "The Guardians control nearly the entirety of the Termainian continent. With my guidance, King Kredor has made vassals of both Dwerin in the west and Montevale in the east. In the south, he had conquered the Republic of Grantis, and in the northern wilds, he has secured the loyalty of the three largest Wrathorn Clans, effectively assuming control of those lands as well. Castone's diminutive size and traditional neutrality, coupled with our lack of any...*conventional* military, has placed the Lighthouse under Kredor's dominion too. In each instance, those in positions of power have already signed statements attesting to their support for the Protectorate, with King Kredor named as the supreme commander of Termain." He paused. "Thus, only the Brock stands between the Guardians and complete control of the continent, and when it falls—as it must against such overwhelming odds—the first part of the Bard's Heresy will come to pass, preparing the way for our lord's return."

"So long as we are able to secure the saint's heir" the Grand Keeper said, "and discover the location of the Lock."

"And recover the Lady's Key, of course," Tainne smiled. "For, what good is a lock without a key?"

"Indeed," Huskarn said shortly. "It is to that end that Keeper Loris has joined us."

Loris nodded. "Following the incident at the Lighthouse," he said, "we commissioned a search of the shore westward and south along the coast. As we understood it, the marauders were not aboard a ship, but rather a small rowboat. We discovered it just over the border into Montevale. There, we also found what appears to be the grave of the Wrathorn, Magnus Bloodbeard."

"And the apprentice?" Tainne asked.

"Gone," Loris said, "but we believe that tracking him down should not take too much effort."

"He was but a blubbering child," the Grand Keeper said. "In all likelihood you'll find his bloated corpse half-eaten by carrion creatures before long."

Tainne's lips twisted into a sardonic grin. "I would not be so sure of that," he said. "These apprentices are fools, but they've also got the blind luck of fools. Perhaps more importantly, they've been treading a path prepared for them by Rastis Glendaro, and the old Loremaster was certainly no fool."

"No," Huskarn conceded. "He was not."

"Then we shall be cautious," Loris said, "and leave no stone unturned."

Huskarn nodded. "And as far as the Lock and the Galadin boy are concerned?" the Grand Keeper asked.

Tainne sighed. "The Galadin boy is somewhat more problematic now that he is not only a baron but also anointed—as the famous Marshal, no less. I have convinced the King and the Chancellor to commit nearly every anointed constable in the realm to his capture. However, with the Blade and the Vanguard alongside him, it may be that we are forced to wait until the Brock falls before he is in our power." He paused. "As for the Lock, we have completed a thorough search of the Keystone and Castle Testament in its entirety and as far as we can tell, there is nothing here. This leads me to believe that the Lock is not to be found in Andoch."

"Then where else would it be?" Loris asked.

"Yes, it's a shame we do not have *The Book of Histories* to help us in this matter," Huskarn said.

Again, Tainne ignored the overt slight. "Even without the book," he began, "there are other means of recalling history, particularly where the Guardians are concerned. Part of the process of the anointing appears to involve a certain transfer of spirit, and with it, certain memories. My role as King Kredor's adviser and confidant has allowed me to learn a great deal about not only this process, which like so many things, the Guardians keep secret. It has also taught me about the true origins of the Order. Much of this is irrelevant to us now. However, as some have widely suspected, Halford Drude and Aiden Galadin were not the brothers-in-arms that history would have us believe, and following the fall of the Kalius Wrogan, while Drude chose to remain behind in Andoch to build the city that was to become Titanis, Galadin's men returned home with his body to see him entombed in his family lands. As such, while Drude kept Callah's Key as the symbol and scepter of the realm, whatever it opened, I believe, made the journey home with Galadin that he and his heirs might ensure its protection."

The Grand Keeper's expression fell. "So you believe that the Lock is in Galadin?"

"Yes," Tainne said, "entombed with the remains of Aiden himself."

"Yet another fine coincidence. Interesting, Natharis, that everything we've sent you to secure somehow slips through your fingers only to end up in Galadin," Huskarn said coldly. "Who knows? Perhaps we shall find *The Book of Histories* in Galadin as well?"

Tainne's gaze narrowed and his blood turned to fire. He had finally had enough. He would not leave this slight un-redressed, particularly when it came from such a lesser man as Huskarn. Like far too many of the Keepers, he was low-born, the jumped-up son of a craftsman or a courtier who believed that his education could wash away the impurities of ignoble blood.

That, Tainne believed, had been at the heart of the Dibhorites' failures 1,300 years ago, for Kalius Wrogan—the Warlock—had been a commoner too. He might have succeeded in overthrowing a corrupt, indolent emperor, but his reign could only last so long. Faithful as he might have been, Wrogan lacked real divinity. Truly, Lord Dibhor understood this, and it was Wrogan's own failings, his own love of a power of which he was not worthy, that led to his destruction at the hands of Aiden Galadin and the imprisonment of the Divine Beast. For the love of his lord, Tainne would not, could not, allow history to repeat itself.

"Perhaps," he seethed, drawing out the word with a sibilant hiss. "Though in fairness, they were never in my possession to begin with—unlike the Key. This loss I believe *you*, Grand Keeper, *you* bear sole responsibility. My apologies, Keeper Loris, that you seem to be the one to draw the short straw and must now wipe the doddering old man's ass!"

The remaining Keepers, who until now had remained but mute observers, began to murmur quietly at Tainne's direct challenge. The Grand Keeper's face contorted with anger. "How dare you!" he snapped, "Do not lash out at me to cover your own failures! The Key was stolen from the Lighthouse, but it will soon be returned! I can only hope that when it is, you will have something worthwhile to report!"

"We shall see!" Natharis Tainne growled, "But enough talk! I have a kingdom to manage, an army to raise, and a war to wage in the name of our lord—all from the very seat of our ancient enemy's power! Yet I will do as I have always done and I shall succeed! Perhaps I'll even clean up the mess you made and recover the accursed Key! When next we meet, we shall we learn very quickly who is the failure, and who truly has the favor of Dibhor!"

With that, he drew a black-bladed dagger from his robe and thrust it into his own heart. At once, the hallucinatory world brought on by the toxin faded away and he opened his eyes to find himself lying prone upon the floor of the Loremaster's chambers. A thin white vomit coated his lips. Small, foaming puddles marred the floor beside where he had fallen.

Dibhor curse Riggilo Huskarn! he thought. If only it were the Grand Keeper under his knife instead of the wretched folk of Andoch. Then he might really feel some relief. How freeing such an experience might be. Divine, transcendent, a glorious tribute to the Lord Dibhor. He would make it a point to have his attendants procure lanky old men with beards when next he felt the mood strike him. Perhaps a reasonable facsimile might offer at least some measure of balm to his distress.

Tainne released a sigh. Who was he kidding? The mood was still upon him, had not ceased to grip him, even after the final death rattle left the peasant girl's throat. The meeting with the Keepers had only made it stronger. He stood up from the floor and wiped the spittle from his mouth. The night was long and dark. There was still plenty of time to indulge himself, to free himself, before morning.

He crossed the room to retrieve the bell he used to summon servants. Yes, there was still time, and with Dibhor's blessing, all would be set to rights soon enough.

CHAPTER 1: THE WRATH OF THE REAVER

The sun was just sinking behind the jagged slopes of the far off Firriny Mountains when Thom reached the small crossroads village. His feet ached from the long march, but the prospect of a warm bed and a hot meal drove him onward with renewed vigor, calling to him like the siren's song of a Sorgund sea story. The air had grown steadily colder the further he trekked north, and his habit—filthy, bloodstained, and threadbare—after such long and hard use, offered little defense from the elements.

Still, Death offered some respite. For, with the great bearded axe he now carried strapped across his back, he could chop wood enough to build a fire, and to his surprise, his years of studying plants and herbs back at the Loremaster's Tower had allowed him to forage among the wilds. Additionally, he still had the rucksack with his journal, quills, and other accouterments, as well as a few other miscellaneous odds and ends that Magnus had either insisted that he carry or that Thom had seen fit to pack: flint and steel, a woolen blanket, a small work knife, a small pouch of coins, and an emergency ration of ship's biscuits.

Not that it was ever enough, and as the days turned into weeks since he had buried Magnus upon the shores, he knew that he was slowly beginning to starve. In truth, he found it somewhat remarkable that he had found the strength and endurance to carry onward, plagued as he was by hunger, cold, and a near constant weariness that resulted from sleep marred by perpetual nightmares. Some were dark dreams born from his own experience—visions of the Lighthouse and the horde of dead soldiers—while others appeared to have come from somewhere else. It was as if his mind had taken verses from "The Song of Magnus" and run with them, forcing him to relive the horrific ordeals the Wrathorn warrior had described himself. Regardless, it was impossible to say which visions were more frightening, and in either case, the result was the same. He woke up screaming.

Whatever it was that Magnus had done, whatever final words he had spoken (or not spoken) upon that stony shore, Thom knew that something had changed. Magnus's mad voyage, which seemed for all intents and purposes a cavalcade of absurd coincidences, Thom now believed to have been guided by providence, determined by the will of the gods themselves—be they Kinship or Wrathorn. Who else could have conspired to direct Magnus's fate in such an unlikely, but clearly purposeful manner? Who else could bring him in touch with a long lost Guardian hero like the Shield, expose the secret survival of the Dibhorites, and uncover the holiest of all relics, Callah's Key!

More than anything else, it was this—the Key—that kept Thom going, that strengthened his resolve in the darkest moments of the night. The gift of the Lady of Light herself, forged from a fallen star and granted to St. Aiden that he might seal away the darkness of Dibhor. The odds of such a thing were so unlikely, so bizarre, that only the will of some divine intelligence could possibly have allowed it to occur.

Strangest of all, however, was the fact that, if indeed it was the will of the gods that delivered the Key into Magnus's hands, it was the will of those same divine beings that had determined that he—Thom—should carry it too.

Of course, that thought was far too overwhelming for him to deal with just now, and so he pushed it away to the recesses of his mind and chose to instead focus on the faded signboard of the village inn. With a sigh of relief, Thom tromped up the dirt track from the roadway into the small, fenced courtyard of the inn, and with a curt nod to the stable hand, passed through the doorway inside.

The common room that greeted him was sparsely furnished with rough-hewn wooden tables and another long, low table that served as a bar. A large, iron crock of stew sat steaming over a central hearth, and here and there, peasant folk and wanderers sat in unfriendly silence picking at hard, brown bread and brooding over mugs of stale ale.

After the trials of the last few weeks, Thom could not have imagined a more welcome sight.

Behind the bar, a middle-aged peasant woman squared her shoulders and eyed him curiously. At first, Thom recognized the familiar skepticism he had always noticed, the sort of mild derisiveness with which people always seemed to treat him. However, as her eyes fell upon the haft of is axe, she seemed to pause for a second look, and with less gruffness than he was used to, she spoke.

"What'll it be, traveler?"

Thom took a deep breath, conscious suddenly of the strangest feeling, as if somehow Magnus were still standing at his side.

"Bread, stew, and a pint of ale," he told the woman.

The woman gave a nod, "You've got the coin?"

Thom produced a small pouch and, by way of reply, gave it a light jingle.

"Sit where you like then," she said, "Won't be but a minute."

"Thank you much," Thom said. He made his way to a small table in the corner, set Death down to rest against the wall beside him, and placed his pack beneath the table at his feet, conscious that within it, he carried Callah's Key.

What a funny fucking world we live in, eh? he could almost hear Magnus's merry voice observe. *What a great bollocking storm must be coming! I suppose I'm lucky that I won't be alive to see it!*

"You very well could have been," Thom muttered softly to the ether. "We could both be sitting here right now if it weren't for your bloody whims."

Nah, you were in a bad way. Worse than you realize. You never would have made it and I'd of been forced to kill you so as not to be carrying around the dead weight. Trust me, the Wrathorn's voice told him, *It's better this way.*

"If you say so. Though if I was already in such a bad way, I don't know why you needed to gut me with the axe..."

You don't? After everything? Really?

Thom thought to reply when the hostler returned with a tray laden with food. All thoughts of Magnus receded from the boy's mind.

"You're a godsend, woman!" Thom exclaimed as he dove into his stew, "My complements and my undying gratitude!"

The hostler eyed him curiously. "Alright, then," she said.

10

"And I'll be needing a room if you've got one available, but we can discuss that when I'm done here," Thom told her between mouthfuls. "Thank you much!"

The woman gave a skeptical nod before silently withdrawing to see to another table, and Thom was left to his meal.

From what he had gathered along the way, he was somewhere in the southern reaches of Montevale in the land that, during the War of the Horses, was known as Valendia. While adventuring with Magnus, he recalled hearing something about the war being over now, but he had no idea what relations were like between the new king of Montevale and the Guardian-King. He certainly hadn't noticed any kingsmen wandering about, though since Montevale was its own sovereign land, that wasn't much of a surprise.

In any case, as long as they were not openly hostile, perhaps his connection to the Order would grant him some manner of diplomatic status that would help to speed his return to Andoch. He had not decided yet how he would share the news of the Dibhorites return in Castone, let alone news of a second Army of the Dead. Surely, a tale such as that would only serve to cause others to question his sanity. Yet, Callah's Key was tangible proof of at least part of his story, and were he to show it to any member of the Order—particularly one of the Anointed—the Key might open a pathway directly to the Keystone and the Guardian-King himself.

Thom sighed. To return to Titanis after such a long time, to return to Rastis and Royne. Perhaps even Lughus—assuming that rogue Crodane didn't do for him. It would be just like old times.

You can't be that fucking stupid, Magnus's voice chortled. *You're on the path now, Crusher. There's no going home again. Believe me, I know.*

A sound from out in the yard stirred Thom from his musings, followed a moment later by the squeal of the inn door's hinges. Four men clad in leather and chain entered, gruffly muttering to one another over some prior joke. Thom eyed them from beneath his brows attempting to recall the insignia they wore upon their tabards—white with a black horse and a golden crown. Their muddy boots left big, streaky clumps upon the floor, but they paid them no mind as they sided up to the bar.

"Oi, darlin'!" the lead man shouted. A sergeant, Thom assumed, noticing the slight deference with which the others seemed to regard him. He hammered a mailed fist upon the bartop. "Bring us a round," he said, "and how about roasting a few of those chickens out in the yard?"

"Aye," one of the other men joined in. "By order of King Dermont!"

Dermont? Thom wondered. He suddenly wished he had paid a bit closer attention to the studies of noble houses.

From behind the bar, the hostler squared her shoulders and leaned toward the men. "And how does his majesty expect to be paying this time around, seeing as he seems to have forgotten to since the last time that you passed through?"

"I'd say he plans to settle it all the same," said the sergeant. "He is king after all."

"Aye," said another man, "and since we serve him, serving *us* is the same as serving *him*, and you wouldn't be expecting him to pay for that which is already his by right, eh?"

"He's the king of a united Montevale," said the last of the four. "The victor of a hundred years of war!"

"So run along now, darling," the sergeant said. "Do your duty and fetch us some ale."

The hostler pressed her lips together in a tight line, but remained silent. With an air of resigned indignation, she began filling tankards of ale from the hogshead behind the bar.

Meanwhile, the outriders made themselves at home, commandeering tables, kicking their feet up on chairs, and creating a general miasma of hostility that sent the majority of the local patrons tacitly heading for the door. For the most part, the king's raiders let them go, though not without a measure of boorish jeering or harassment.

Thom watched them with growing frustration. He recalled the bullies in The Kingfisher or how the kingsmen at the Sandstone had treated him so long ago. However, whereas in the past, scenes such as this often filled him with nervous anxiety or fear, he became acutely aware of a different sensation, a certain brash defiance. His jaw set and he began to feel once again as if Magnus were standing at his shoulder, just behind him, muttering in his ear.

What a bunch of fucking cowards! the Wrathorn said. *Another band of bully bastards hiding behind the bollocks of an unworthy king.*

Thom drained his tankard, hoping to cool the sudden fire kindling within him. He looked down at his empty dishes. Perhaps it would be better if he not stay. Perhaps it would be better if he were moving on. He shouldered his axe and his rucksack, gathered his dishes, and carried them to the bar top, setting them down with a clatter.

"Thank you," he said, depositing a pair of silver coins upon the bar. He was uncertain exactly how much the meal had cost, but two silver were certainly enough to cover it, probably the price of a room as well.

The hostler might have said as much, but just as she opened her mouth to speak, Thom sensed the outriders' approach, sauntering up beside him.

"Aw, do you hear that, Horgan?" the nearest said. He was a brute of a man, with watery, yellow eyes and a sour smell. "What a nice, polite young man we've got us here!"

Sergeant Horgan grunted a laugh. "Shove off, gelding," he said to Thom. "This inn is currently under the authority of King Dermont and those in the king's service. We've no time for the likes of you."

"Aye," another man scoffed. "We'll not have you souring the ale."

Thom took a deep breath, but remained silent, staring straight ahead with red-rimmed eyes. He felt...strange. Different. Again, he sighed and rubbed his hand wearily along his face and was surprised to find that all along his rounded chin and heavy jowls, patches of gingery fuzz had sprouted.

"Oi, fat ass!" another of the outriders snarled. He was a lanky fellow with brown teeth. "We told you to piss off so hop to it!" With a rough shove, Thom was thrown forward into the bar. In the scuffle, he lurched forward, knocking his clay bowl over and shattering it on the floor. The sound awakened something in him and as he whirled to face the men, he was surprised to find that by some odd instinct, his hand went to the haft of his axe.

The riders only laughed.

"What do you make of that, Elgin?" the yellow-eyed man said. "That ain't the weapon of a woodcutter."

"And I can't say as I see anything about the boy that says he's a warrior," the lanky man answered. "Probably just a thief. What do you reckon, sarge?"

The sergeant pursed his lips and Thom felt the man's skeptical eyes range over him. "Too fat for a thief," he said at last. "Too slow for a pickpocket, and looks too stupid to be anything else."

The other men guffawed with laughter. In a flash, Thom loosed Death and held the great, bearded axe tightly in his hands. His plump lips spread into a deep frown.

"*Don't* call me stupid," he said, the hard edge to his voice a surprise even to himself.

For a moment, the riders paused—whether out of confusion or disbelief—before erupting into torrents of ribald laughter. Yet rather than shrink or shrivel, Thom remained resolved.

You've had your brush with Death once already, Crusher. Magnus's voice said in his mind. *You stared him in the face. You looked him in the eye. You showed that bastard what you're worth. Now, matey, he stands at your side. Show him what you can do.*

Thom swallowed the lump in his throat, felt the surge of nervous energy tingling in his limbs. Part of him wanted to cry out in terror, flip over a table, and hide. Yet now there was another part, a part that, while long-buried, had been brought to life by whatever it was that Magnus had done upon that stony shore. This part of him was suddenly engulfed by a cold, black anger, a slowly simmering rage, and as the men continued to laugh at him, it threatened to boil over.

The sergeant was the first to collect himself.

"Listen here, boy," the man said, swaggering forward and puffing out his chest. "I'll call you as I like and you'll take it, you fat, sniveling tub o' guts! You great, stinking pile of horse shit! You stupid—"

The rest of the insult remained unsaid as the great axe struck out like a winter gale, cleaving through the sergeant's mail byrnie at the shoulder and sinking deep into his chest. All eyes went wide with stark disbelief as Thom wrenched the axe free from the man's body unleashing a great torrent of blood.

The other men stood by dumbfounded, for it wasn't that the attack had been particularly fast or skillful—far from it—but something about the manner in which the boy had raised his weapon and struck was so unexpected, so uninhibited, and so brash that the other outriders had barely noticed it had happened until their companion lay dying on the floor.

"Don't call me *stupid!*" Thom cried.

"Lady save us!" the hostler cried, diving for cover behind the bar. The few remaining patrons hunkered down behind their tables, or, if they were close

14

enough, fled through the door and out into the yard. In the shuffle, the three remaining outriders were able to collect themselves and regroup, drawing their swords.

Thom's grip tightened on his axe and he felt a surge of manic energy flood his veins. *Do you hear that, Crusher?* Magnus laughed merrily. *It's the Song of the Reaver! Your song and mine! It's the song that sings now in your blood! Tell me! Do you hear it?"*

"I hear it!" Thom cried.

Then sing, you glorious bastard! Sing! Sing! Sing!

With a cry, Thom threw himself at the nearest of the riders. It was the man with brown teeth. He raised his blade to parry the blow, but the force of Thom's attack was so great that a numbing tremor shook the man's arm and he was thrown back against another table. Before he could right himself, however, Thom had readied the axe again and struck, burying Death's head deep in the man's belly.

"You fucking bastard!" the yellow-eyed man shouted. Incensed by the sight of his fallen comrades, he roared and charged at Thom.

For a moment, Thom was caught off guard by the man's sudden madness, but by some uncanny reflex, he was able to parry the man's attack upon the haft of his axe, turning what might have been a mortal wound into a glancing blow. He winced momentarily, but gritting his teeth, lashed out, head-butting the yellow-eyed man squarely in the nose. It burst like an over-ripe tomato, and as the man staggered backward, Thom raised his axe high over his head and brought a final end to the man's pain.

With three of his comrades so suddenly slain, Thom turned his gaze upon the last of the outriders who stood now contemplating whether to fight or to flee. He was spared having to make the decision, however, when one of the few remaining patrons, a slight figure, hooded and cloaked, stepped forth from the shelter of an overturned table and drove a dagger to the hilt in his guts.

As the man lay breathing his last, two additional figures, similarly cloaked and cowled, stood up from behind the shelter of other tables throughout the room. Thom took a deep breath and tightened his grip on his axe, warily assessing the potential threat.

"Well, I'll be buggered!" said the largest of the three. He cast back his hood to reveal a shaven scalp and a pugnacious face with a thick, black mustache. "You never know what you'll find awaiting you at a crossroads."

Thom eyed him carefully, but held off his attack.

The slight figure with the dagger tossed back its hood to reveal a freckle-faced girl with tawny brown hair and a wicked grin. With casual ease, she wiped the blade clean upon the dead man's tabard and returned it to its sheath with a snap.

The third man, silent and stooped, set to work righting the nearest table and chairs, picking at the remains of a heel of bread.

Thom continued to watch them warily, uncertain whether their sudden appearance and casual nature marked them as possible allies or as an even greater threat. He kept Death at the ready.

The mustachioed man grinned at the sight. "Well, boy-o, I take it you're no friend of the Plague Prince," he said.

"I...I can't say as I know who that is," Thom replied, "though I'm no friend of any man who would call me stupid."

"No doubt." The big man laughed.

"You Wrathorn?" the freckled girl barked.

"No," Thom said, uncertain whether to take the question as an insult or a point of pride. "I'm not Wrathorn," he said, "but my friend was. He who gave me the axe."

The big man and the girl exchanged a glance.

"*You* Wrathorn?" Thom asked the man with the mustache. "You're about big enough for it."

The man chuckled. "Only by half," he said, "Horn Half-Wrathorn, they call me. The girl's called Sparrow and Donovan's the bloke cleaning up."

By now, the shock of the moment was beginning to pass and the cowering patrons that remained roused themselves and fled. Horn and Sparrow ignored their flight while Donovan moved to see to the hostler as she stood from her place of shelter and took in the carnage of the scene.

"I'm Thom," Thom told them, and without thinking, added, "Thom...Reaver."

"Well, Thom Reaver," Horn said. "We three ride for the Winter Rose and the Silent Prince, among those as stand against the Prince of Plague and this filth." He nudged the nearest corpse with his boot. "And while it seems you handle yourself well enough, the dead have a way of attracting flies, as they say. So..." he paused, exchanging another look with the girl. "If you've a mind to come along with us, we can at least show you to some place where the friends of these bastards won't find you."

Thom considered it, stooping to clean Death's edge upon the dead sergeant's cloak. He was beginning to feel like his old self again and his mind felt muddled at the magnitude of what he had just done. His stomach roiled with nerves and he feared he might be sick. *What is happening to me?* he wondered. *Magnus, what in the name of the gods have you done?*

He received no answer.

"I haven't got a horse," Thom said at last.

"There's four outside no one seems to be using." Sparrow smirked.

"Right," Thom took a deep breath, "But what if I told you I don't know how to ride?"

Horn and Sparrow erupted into laughter, though Thom could tell that it was not mockery, for he knew that sound all too well.

"Boy-o," Horn said, "you're in Montevale! There's no better place to learn."

Thom scratched at the patchy stubble on his chin. "I suppose that's true." He returned Death to the baldric across his back. "Alright, I'll ride with you."

Horn and Sparrow joined Donovan in conversation with the hostler, and Thom hurried to retrieve his pack, careful to avoid tripping over the bodies or slipping in the blood. When he finally joined the others, the big man clapped him on the shoulder and the four of them made their way out to the stable yard.

Horn and Donovan retrieved their own horses while Sparrow inspected those of the dead men. Finally, she selected a honey-colored mare. "This one looks good," she said, patting the horse on the rump. "Steady and strong."

Thom gave a slow nod. "Right then," he said, struggling to maintain a mask of unconcern. With an excess of movement, he clambered up onto the saddle. He knew that to a Montevalen, he must look the height of absurdity, but to the girl's credit, she refrained from any mocking jeer. When she did speak, however, her lilting question caught him off guard.

"So what do you got there?"

17

Thom followed her eye, and glancing behind him, noticed the flash of silver poking out from beneath the flap of his rucksack. At once, he reached behind him to adjust it, concealing it from view.

"It's nothing," he said quickly, and taking the reins of the mare, tried to change the subject. "Now, how exactly do I get this beast to turn around?".

Sparrow took the horse by the bridle and led it out into the yard where Horn and Donovan were already waiting for them. With a quick hop, the girl leapt lightly up to her own saddle, still gripping the reigns of Thom's mare.

"Just hold on for now," she said. "I'll guide you until you get the hang of it."

Thom swallowed, again struggling to maintain a facade of nonchalance. "Thank you," he said.

"Don't thank me yet." Sparrow grinned. "Your ass is going to be quite sore on the morrow."

Thom's cheeks went red. "My ass?" he repeated.

Horn gave a snort and Donovan shook his head. "Aright," the big man said. "Enough dallying. We ride for Pridel."

CHAPTER 2: THE BATTLE OF CRAGBARROW

Cragbarrow, the ancestral home of the baron of Agathis, had once stood as a mighty fortress guarding the mountain pass that allowed for travel and trade between the northern Andochan lands and the southern baronies of Baronbrock. For centuries, the city had maintained what was, for the most part, an open gate policy, encouraging easy transit between the perennially peaceful realms. Lughus had studied the city at one point or another during his time as an apprentice, and while he had never seen it in life, the sight of it now as a smoldering ruin filled him with disappointment.

And wrath.

Dorgan Agathis was not a man that Lughus had known well. In fact, in his relatively short time as baron, Agathis had refused to speak with him when he came to call, and later, allowed Andochan kingsmen safe passage through his lands, knowing full-well that their intent was to attack Lughus's own city of Galadin.

Yet, when the Brock came together to stand united against the unjust encroachment from the Guardian-King, though not a warrior himself, Agathis did his duty.

When the northern army of Andoch reached his city, where they had expected to find the gates wide open and welcoming, they found them barred by a defiant baron who refused to back down.

That unexpected resistance, though perhaps not epic or glorious enough to attract the attention of any bard, was enough to waylay the Guardian army long enough for word to reach Galadin and the other barons, culminating in the Brock's great victory at the Monastery of St. Golan the Ram.

In the days following the battle, though the enemy army was defeated and put to rout, there remained survivors—marauders intent on sowing chaos and destruction as they made their slow withdrawal. The largest group, reportedly led by the Anointed Guardians known as the Willow and the Jay, headed west, while a smaller group that included the Guardian artillerist, the Cockerel, headed east toward Nordren and the coastal road. Lughus and Brigid would make for the mountains, while Geoffrey, who had already encountered the Cockerel once, would accompany Theo Nordren back to his home.

From the beginning of the long, stone causeway that led to the main gates of the ruined city, Lughus eyed the scorch marks that remained as evidence of St. Aiden's fire, the thick, oily incendiary substance that the Guardians would have used to destroy St. Golan's as well, were it not for the clandestine actions of Sir Adolfo the Madder and Sir Geoffrey of Pyle.

Beyond the bridge, the walled city spread out into a series of concentric districts with the castle of the baron in the center and a second stone causeway leading up into the mountain paths on the far side. It had been an ingenious design and a mighty fortress, and were it not for the use of St. Aiden's fire, even a less martially inclined baron like Dorgan Agathis could have withstood a prolonged assault so long as he kept the causeways secure.

A horse's whinny brought Lughus's attention back around from the ruin and he glanced up to see the Grantisi General Cornelius Navarro—the famous Gray Wolf—at his side.

"I will have my men form a shield wall as we cross the bridge. Once we pass the gates, they will fan out into smaller squads and flush the streets toward the mountains on the far side. Your archers can provide support from behind the phalanx. You say there is a second bridge?"

"As I understand it, the city is roughly symmetrical," Lughus said. "Of course, with the rubble from the ruined castle, I can't speak to what it may look like now. I expect the Andochans may have set up barricades as well." His brow creased in thought. "I will lead my men in as an advance party to try to draw out the Jay and the Willow, then your men can provide the final sweep."

Navarro agreed. "I'll have my elite guard join you. The Andochans may attempt to dig in here so as to maintain a staging point through which they might return more easily. We will not let them have it." He called back to the brash captain—Deneron Velius, Lughus remembered—and began issuing orders.

Lughus turned to where Brigid and Fergus stood among the soldiers of the Galadin guard. "We on the hunt then, Marshal?" Brigid smiled at him.

Lughus gave a nod. "Fergus, Brigid, and I will take the lead. Pike and Tonkin in the middle, Kender and Sedge on the flanks. You others, fill in between. Sir Balric—" he called to the mounted knight behind them, "You have command of the archers. Have them form squads to support the legionnaires."

A chorus of "Aye!" sounded from the Galadin men and as they broke to ready themselves, Brigid stepped forward to join him.

"What do you know about the Jay and the Willow?" she asked.

Lughus chewed his lip and rested his hands upon his pommel. "Both are scouts from what I recall," he said. "The Willow is an archer with a horn bow. I think the Jay was a quartermaster or the like. He managed supplies and protected the stores. Perhaps not the most heroic role on the surface, but certainly important for any campaign."

Brigid smiled and gave him a quick kiss on the cheek.

"What was that for?" He smirked.

"Does a girl need a reason to kiss her betrothed?"

"No," he said, "I just wondered what brought on the urge. That way I know how to repeat it."

Her eyes sparkled and she laughed aloud, resting her hands upon her hilts. "If you must know," she said, "I find it cute when your apprentice starts showing."

"What?" He grinned.

"Your face gets very serious and your voice drops like you're reciting passages from a book by memory."

"Sometimes I am."

"I know." She laughed and gave him another quick kiss.

In the aftermath of the battle, the young couple decided that—with the destruction and the wounded—they would postpone the immediacy of the wedding in favor of the safety of the realm. Yet, while the situation may not have allowed for a ceremony befitting a baron of such a storied family, the morning after the battle, Lughus's grandfather, Roland Marthaine, suggested Abbot Woode officiate a formal betrothal beneath the eaves of the abbey they fought so hard to preserve. Such things were important for the morale of the people, he had said, particularly when the betrothal was to unite two great heroes of the realm. The public nature of the ceremony was not something Lughus would have chosen, but Brigid mollified his concerns, conceding that it was often just how these things were done.

Fergus sat back on his haunches and gave a loud sniff, drawing the young Marshal's attention back to the present. He paused to check the straps of the leather harness that the great hound now wore. A gift from the general, it had once belonged to an old war mastiff. Boiled leather barding now provided at least some defense to the dog's previously unprotected flanks while a spiked collar guarded his neck.

"It's better than nothing, brother," Lughus told the hound, "We'll get it fitted properly for you when we get back home."

General Navarro returned with Captain Velius and his warriors in their bright, segmented plate armor and plumed helmets in tow. "Ready to advance when you are, Baron Galadin," the Gray Wolf said.

Lughus gave a nod and the Galadin guard fell in beside him. "Follow at a distance," Lughus said. "We'll send word if there's any trouble."

"Good hunting," Navarro said.

Together, the two squads began a parallel assent across the causeway. Lughus readied Sentinel and behind him, he heard Brigid draw Whisper and Shade. The men of the Galadin guard carried embossed heater shields emblazoned with the mark of the golden hound, while across the way, the legionaries under Captain Velius readied tall, rectangular shields and short swords.

As they marched, Velius offered Lughus a sardonic smirk. "So you're the boy baron who's friends with the fox-faced Loremaster, eh?"

"I am," Lughus said, "and you're Captain Velius, the general's right hand. Royne mentioned you in his letter."

Velius smirked. "So my reputation precedes me. I assume he mentioned something about me being a boorish, black-hearted bastard with the sense of a donkey and the mouth of a seaside trollop?"

"Something like that," Lughus said. "Though he also said you were loyal, and that you liked to fight."

"Lady's teat! Such kindness!" Velius laughed. "I'm like to tear up."

Lughus motioned toward the barbican. "It's certain they know we're coming for them. When we enter the gates of the city, you and your men take the right hand path and we'll take the left. If you get cornered or need help, do you have a way to call?"

"Each man among us carries a whistle," Velius said. "You?"

"You'll hear the hound."

The captain knocked his pommel against his shield. "Right then. Let's move."

As a group, the two squads cautiously approached the ruined barbican, mindful of any enemy watchmen. Fergus loped along slightly ahead, nose to the ground. Though the city had fallen over a week ago, the smell of burning still hung heavy upon the air. Thick, wooden beams emerged crookedly from piles of rubble with the desperation of drowning men. Bodies, some burnt, others simply rotting in the open air. Just beyond the twisted remains of the broken portcullis, the path split. A pike bearing the banner of Andoch—the white key on a field of red—stood like a wax seal on a formal proclamation. With casual disregard, Captain Velius brashly kicked it to the ground.

"See you on the other side," the captain said.

The young baron raised Sentinel in a quick salute.

Together, the legionnaires began their slow march along the right-hand path like a great snapping turtle encased within a steel shell.

"They're like to draw the Guardians right to them for all the noise they make," Brigid observed.

"Let's hope it grants us the element of surprise then," Lughus said.

From the barbican, the Galadin warriors followed the main route left through the outer most of the circular city wards. Warehouses and stockyards gave way to flophouses and lower-class tenements. Here, the damage and destruction that marked the path seemed more like pillaging and looting than organized warfare. The bodies that littered the streets were less commonly soldiers and more often peasants and poor folk. In one section, an area of closely packed homes had gone up in flames. Skeletal remains formed small heaps where families huddled together in their last, futile moments. Ice water spread through Lughus's veins and beside him, he could sense Brigid's palpable lust for vengeance, yet they continued onward without pause, for they had all seen enough battle not to be distracted by the horrors that followed in its wake.

At what must have been a small marketplace or square, the cobblestoned street divided into two other pathways. With a silent wave and a nod to Fergus, Lughus led the group along the pathway that turned inward toward the next concentric ward. For some reason, he felt drawn to the center of the city, as if in the ruins of the baron's castle, they would find the encampment of the marauders. Fergus was about to bound on ahead when Brigid checked him with a call of "Hold!" and the entire group froze.

With the nimble footfalls of a forest creature, the Blade stepped forth along the path. With the tip of one of her daggers, she gently lifted a thin, braided rope from among the scattered rubble. With effortless care, she followed it to where it connected to several pitons that held enormous stone boulders precariously positioned to crush the unaware. With a swipe of her blade, she cut the tripwire and after a pause to ensure there was no secondary trigger, she motioned for the group to proceed.

"After you." She grinned.

Lughus returned her smile and suppressed a warm flood of affection. Fergus trotted on ahead, less swiftly, but more alert, and the group followed through the ruined archway on into the next ward where finer shops and townhouses had once stood. The fire had destroyed the majority of the buildings and it appeared that once the walls were breached, this is where the fighting had been heaviest. Carrion birds poked at the decaying corpses of the Agathis soldiery, though here and there they spied the odd kingsmen or Andochan man-at-arms.

"They didn't even bother to see to their own dead," Tonkin muttered. They entered a small square where a ruined fountain stood beside the husk of a large wattle and daub inn. Red-cloaked kingsmen corpses littered the area, outnumbering even the Agathis guards. All of a sudden Fergus growled and his lips curled in a viscous snarl.

"Because they're not dead!" Lughus shouted and raised his sword. All around them, the feigning kingsmen scrambled to rise. A pair of crossbow bolts flew through the air at Brigid, but she ducked adeptly and stepped to one side.

"For the Brock!"

As a pair of kingsmen ran to engage him, Lughus lunged forward in a wide arc, knocking aside their swords. In a flash, he whirled Sentinel around into a high guard and brought the blade down through an attacker's shoulder. Blood and bits of chain burst forth as he withdrew the blade, parried a counterattack from the remaining enemy, and with another quick turn of his wrist, ran the man through.

Behind him, the Galadin guardsmen raised their shields and split into groups of two or three to engage the attacking kingsmen. Each man among them had been trained by Sir Owain Rook, and while fewer in number, they were more than a match for their counterparts in the Andochan standing army.

Yet perhaps more importantly, morale was high—as was the confidence they had in their leaders. They were emboldened by their recent victory, and if Lughus had learned anything from his studies of military history, it was that this manner of faith—this belief—could move mountains. St. Golan's had helped to confirm that.

Another bolt whistled through the air—wildly—followed by a loud snarl and a cry of terror as Fergus brought the marksman down. From atop a broken stone wall, Brigid whirled about in circles with Whisper and Shade. A kingsman with a great axe raised his weapon, ready to split her in two, but the steel struck only stone. Through the resulting burst of sparks, Brigid leapt over his head, turned, and drove her daggers to the hilt beneath his arms.

Lughus dashed to join her, and in an instant, they were back to back, fighting in tandem as another wave of kingsmen rushed at them. With uncanny precision, the Marshal parried or struck out from the points of the five guards while the Blade opportunistically leapt in to strike like a viper whenever he countered. It was an elaborate and deadly dance, and together they were perfect partners.

One by one the red-cloaked soldiers returned to their former places among the fallen, though this time, they had no need to feign death. When the final kingsman turned to flee—only to be brought down by the slavering hound—a full score lie dead or dying. Of the Galadin guard, only Kender suffered any harm when the flailing blade of a falling kingsman caught the young man across the brow. While it bled something fierce, it was hardly a mortal wound and the group quickly prepared to continue onward, deeper into the heart of the destroyed city.

As they crept forward, Lughus considered the General's comments. If the Guardians were able to hold Agathis, it would certainly make Andoch's continued assault upon the Brock easier, ensuring an easy point of entry for the troops stationed at Stonebridge Castle in the north of Andoch. Otherwise, the invaders would be limited to the coastal road toward Nordren or else sail around the continent to the northernmost baronies of Denholm and Brabant. The Nivanus Pass provided another entry point, but not only did the topography create a natural choke point, it was also heavily guarded by the barons of Helmsted, Edgeforth, and Glendaro.

As such, Lughus knew that the fighting would become increasingly bloody and desperate with every street he secured, and while it was true that the general and his men followed after them with Sir Balric and the archers of the Brock, if he and Brigid could succeed in eliminating the Guardian leaders, the remaining troops were all the more likely to turn tail and run.

From the place of the skirmish, they crept forward through the ruins, passing on from the part of the city belonging to the burghers and the guildsmen to the larger tower houses belonging to the wealthiest of merchants and minor nobility who maintained homes in the streets just outside of the castle. The worst of the destruction wrought by the trebuchets seemed to have occurred here as the errant projectiles wreaked havoc on the aristocratic estates. Most of the corpses were little more than charred skeletons, though on occasion they came across a body only half-burnt, but contorted in agony.

While the sight of a dead body was never pleasant, there was a difference between the sight of a dead soldier versus the sight of a dead civilian. A warrior understood the risks that could occur as a natural consequence of battle, but the non-combatants—the elderly, the servants, the majority of women, and the children—were simply victims of the horrific conflict. It was the sight of such cruelties that led Brigid to take action at St. Golan's, using the Gift of the Guardians to heal the wounds of what innocent she could. Yet, as he unwillingly recognized the various sizes of the burnt corpses, Lughus knew that even the miraculous power of Gift was of no use to the dead. All he could do now was hold to his oath and fight to ensure such tragedies were never repeated.

Rise now, the Marshal, and drive the Dark away!

Still, unlike like many fighting men, his heart was not made of stone. He knew that such horrific sights would haunt him, just as they would haunt Brigid, and he was grateful that in their shared experiences they could rely on each other to help find a way through the darkness of man's depravity and return to the light.

But that was later. For now, Lughus knew that he needed to cling to that part of himself that was cold and unfeeling, that part that would allow him to carry on and lead.

"Keep a sharp eye," he called softly to his men. "Watch for any sudden flashes of light or the flight of carrion birds."

"And remember the Willow is an archer," Brigid whispered. "So try to keep cover as we proceed."

The men nodded or grunted in assent, and together they continued onward through a wide area that had once been a garden, and past the burnt-out shell of a small shrine. Lughus's eyes darted about cautiously, yet he still failed to hear Brigid's footfalls as she drew near.

"What are you thinking?" she asked him quietly.

"I don't know," he replied. "I expected to find much more in the way of resistance than what we've met so far. Maybe when they spied Navarro and the legion approaching, they knew they were outmatched and fled?"

"You're no slouch either," she teased.

"Or you," Lughus replied, allowing a small smile to escape him. "I suppose the defenders could also be concentrating on Velius. You haven't heard any whistles have you?"

"No, and a sound like that would never escape Fergus's notice."

Lughus nodded. "Well, we're nearly to the castle now, or what remains of it," he said. "If we meet no resistance, we can rejoin the captain and wait for the general to catch up before continuing on."

"Agreed. Perhaps I can—" She suddenly fell silent. "Hold on. Look up ahead. Just past the broken statue."

"I see it," Lughus said. He called Fergus to his side and held up a hand to halt the rest of the guard.

"Is that a man?" Tonkin asked.

"Looks like," said Grimes.

"Quiet now," Sergeant Pike whispered harshly. "Quiet and be ready."

Ahead where Brigid indicated, an armored figure stood in defiance and raised a heavy mace high above his head. "Death to the enemies of the Protectorate!" he shouted.

At once there was a resounding clatter as a double-file column of knights on horseback charged from behind the enemy officer. To Lughus's great surprise, however, it was not the crimson and white of the Order that they wore, but golden tabards emblazoned with the black anvil of Dwerin.

"Iron and Steel!" the riders cried, whooping and hollering as they charged.

Lughus cast a quick glance at Brigid, but the revelation of the attackers' origin did nothing to betray her focus. Instead, she stood poised in anticipation of the charge.

"Holy Brethren!" one of the Galadin guardsmen cried.

"Find cover in the rubble," Lughus commanded. "They can't charge through stone."

Barely had he finished speaking than the first rank of knights was upon them and the Galadins were scattered, leaping to the side or backing away behind their shields. Lughus twisted to avoid the first two riders, planted his foot, and whirled around to unhorse the third, forcing the men who followed to rein in their mounts. At once, Sergeant Pike, Kender, and Grimes rushed to join the fray beside him, and across the path, he heard Fergus's snarl and the shrill whinny of a terrified horse. He could not see Brigid in the chaos, but knew that she was at her deadliest when she was out of sight.

Lughus parried an attack from another horseman, then, while the man was unbalanced in the saddle, grabbed hold of the knight's vambrace with his free hand and pulled him down to the cobbles. Kender was quick to plunge his sword through the man's gorget before being knocked aside by the rider-less horse. Lughus stepped back to survey the melee and readjust his footing when a sudden flash and a low grunt gave him pause.

It was Grimes, pierced through the chest by a goose-feathered arrow. The guardsman fell to his knees before falling prone upon his side.

"Warlock's Balls!" Pike cursed as together they leapt for cover, pulling the wounded man after them.

Following now upon the tail of the Dwerin horsemen, the red-cloaked kingsmen rushed to join the fray. Commanding them was the lone figure with the mace, though two others—both archers—had joined him. One was tall and lean in leather lamellar and a burgundy cloak with a cowl. The other was a young man bearing the arms of Dwerin on his tabard. His mail gleamed in the light and onyx stones shone from his mail skirt.

With the uncanny premonitions of the Marshal, Lughus had the strong sense that the lanky man was the Willow. However, the other—the leader carrying the mace—was not the Jay. Rather, he was someone different, a Guardian for certain, and one of the Anointed, but not someone Lughus or Crodane or Wolfram of Parth seemed to know. *The Miller?* he wondered, recalling one of Adolfo's past reports. *And his weapon is...the Millstone. Yes, that's it. He was sent to Stonebridge to support a force of Dwerin Knights commanded by...*

A cold fire burned suddenly within him and his knuckles went white grasping Sentinel's hilt.

"Grimes?" he asked Pike.

The sergeant's face fell. "Dead, sir."

Lughus's jaw set and he clenched his teeth. "Then in his memory, let's make them pay."

Pike and Tonkin readied their weapons and rattled their shields as the Marshal led them back into the thickening fray.

With a deft swipe, Lughus unseated another horseman, whirled the blade around, and plunged it through the fallen knight's mail. A squad of kingsman rushed forth to engage him, and Tonkin and Pike hurried to join him shoulder to shoulder. With a deft strike he knocked aside a kingsman's shield and quickly turned his wrists to thrust up beneath the man's arm. Pike used his own shield to bash at the next man in the line, but as the kingsman braced himself against the sergeant, Lughus quickly dispatched him with another swift thrust. Tonkin traded blows with a third enemy soldier, hacking and blocking, back and forth. Pike hurried to assist him, while Lughus advanced in pursuit of the Guardian leaders.

Two more kingsmen fell to Sentinel's deadly song before Lughus finally reached them. The Miller shouted commands to his men while the archers at his sides shot into the fray. A bark that was more akin to a roar alerted him that Fergus was near, and moments later he watched as the great hound ripped another horseman from the saddle and pounced, pinning the man to the cobbles. In a flash, Brigid followed, sliding one of her blades between the seam in the knight's armor. Another pair of arrows flew past her head, and while both failed to hit their mark, one passed close enough to knick a thin like across the top of her cheek.

With a cry of fury, Lughus charged. In the chaos and confusion of the battle, the suddenness and ferocity of his assault caught the Guardian leaders off guard. Only by luck and instinct did the Miller parry the Marshal's blade, while the Willow dropped the arrow he held ready and raised his bow defensively. At once, the young archer from Dwerin made to flee, but in his panic, tripped on rubble, and fell hard to the stones with a high pitched squeal. Lughus offered him a swift kick to the abdomen, before pivoting to block the Miller's awestruck counter.

With another roar, Fergus joined the fray, catching the Willow's bow between his jaws. Like a wild beast, he whipped his head back and forth in an attempt to pry it from the archer's grasp. Seeing an opportunity, Brigid quickly wiped the blood from her cheek with the back of her hand, and with a forward roll to gain momentum, leapt through the air at the Willow's exposed back. Both daggers bit deep just above the shoulder blades, slipping through the seams in the lamellar. With a wail of pain and anguish, the Willow cried out, toppled to the ground, and fell still.

"Dibhor take you, Blackguards!" the Miller hissed at his comrade's fall. He lashed out with his mace in a series of heavy blows. Lughus stepped lightly away, parried, and counterattacked, scoring a hit to the Guardian's upper arm. With a grunt, the Miller reset his footing and began another succession of swings, each one powerful enough to crush the skull of a boar. Again, Lughus lightly circled back in a wide arc and swung Sentinel just as the Miller recovered his footing. The blade failed to reach any vital spot, but echoed like a blacksmith's hammer upon the Guardian's steel helm, knocking it to the ground. At once the man leapt back in panic, his curly, dark hair matted with sweat against his brow. He glared at Lughus with wild-eyed hatred and zealous hysteria.

"How dare you take arms against the Order that raised you, you traitorous, black-hearted dog!" He snarled. "To defy the will of the Guardian-King is a sacrilege—a sacrilege that shames your holy ancestor!"

"Your men burned my lands and murdered my people—to say nothing of what you did here!" Lughus said coldly, leaping forth to take the offensive. "The Galadins will not stand by idly while Kredor bullies his way to an empire—nor will any of the Brock!"

"Then you will die—you and all Broken bastards!" the Miller screamed. "Alan, now!"

Lughus spun on his heel just in time to see the Dwerin archer had reclaimed his feet and let loose an arrow from his bow. At such close range, and with Lughus engaged with the Miller, the young man probably thought he couldn't miss. But, in keeping with everything Brigid had ever told him about her cousin, Lughus knew that overconfidence was hardly the least of Alan Beinn's weaknesses.

With a swift shifting of his feet, Lughus crouched and the arrow went wide. In a flash, he parried the Miller's follow-up blow, knocked him back, and with a swift turn of his blade, separated the Guardian's head from his neck.

The fall of their commander instantly spilled the wind from the sails of the remaining kingsmen and Dwerin knights. The arrival of Velius and his men down one of the dilapidated side alleys shattered their courage completely. Now, they fought only to escape, to carve whatever path would most conveniently allow them to flee.

At the sight of the Guardian's fall, Lughus paused for the briefest of moments. Until today, he had never actually seen a Guardian die in battle. Even the Chough, the commander of the Andochan army attacking St. Golan's—once beaten, surrounded, and abandoned by his fleeing forces— had surrendered. To watch one die—and the accumulated knowledge of generations of bearers of the title die with them—was a strange sensation. To be the direct instrument of such a demise brought an odd guilt, as if in ending the man's life, he had not only taken a life, but set an entire shelf of illuminated manuscripts on fire. For one raised to hold knowledge in such high esteem, it was deeply troubling.

But isn't every man's life the same? Aren't we all but single volumes in the vast and endless library of human existence?

While lasting only an instant, in his moment of reflection, Lughus had forgotten Alan Beinn. The Miller's assistant was quick to seize the moment and fit another arrow to his bow. A wide leer spread across his lips that Lughus knew was not out of any sense of comradely vengeance for his fallen superior, but rather the blunt urge to inflict suffering and pain.

Of course, in his zeal to commit cruelty, Alan too left himself unguarded. There was a sudden flash of steel and Alan's bowstring snapped. The sudden release of tension caused the wood to violently lurch back and Alan squealed as the willowy shaft slipped from his grip. In a panic, he bent to recover it, but a swift kick to the rear sent him sprawling.

"Hello, cousin."

Alan hurried to right himself. "Brigid!"

Lughus paced forth to stand beside her, and they were joined at once by Fergus. With a light touch, Lughus patted the hound on the top of the head as the golden hound raised his hackles and uttered a low, menacing growl.

"I imagine this is the last place you expected to find me," Brigid said, "Particularly how our last meeting ended."

"You mean when that coward Blackguard refused to fight me?" Alan smirked. "Actually, we'd all heard you survived. That you found refuge with the heretic barons in the Brock." He gave a derisive chuckle. "What is it they say now? That you're fucking some baron or other?" His eyes shot to Lughus. "Is that him? I suppose it's true that opening your legs opens plenty of doors!"

Lughus's grip tightened on Sentinel and he made to rush forward ready to split the wretched bastard on his blade. He'd envisioned it a thousand times since the day Brigid first told him of her life at Blackstone. Now was his chance.

"You craven bastard—" he seethed. "Slaying you would be like lancing a boil from the bloody continent!"

"Lughus, no," Brigid said, calming the storms in his eyes with the softness of her sapphire gaze. "His blood would only tarnish your blade." She turned back to face Alan. "Besides, he's absolutely terrified right now, and like any cornered vermin, spitting poison is his only defense."

Alan's face twisted into a sneer, but Lughus could see now that she was right. Alan *was* terrified—and helpless—but that did not make him any less capable of sowing evil.

"Darling, please."

With a sigh, he relented and sheathed his sword. Alan was Brigid's kin. For the moment, he would leave it to her.

"Glad to know you've not completely taken leave of your senses," Alan said with what bravado he could muster. "So what are you going to do to me? Kill me like you killed our uncles?"

Brigid gave a weary sigh. "Actually," she said, "I'm going to let you go."

"What?" Lughus asked, nearly in unison with Alan.

"We both know that it was not I who killed our uncles," she said, "and the last thing I want is to have anything in common with the man who did."

"To be fair, I believe it was actually a joint venture," Alan said. "A betrothal gift, you know? Out with the old blood and in with the new? I suppose they just took it somewhat too literally."

"We will see to Dwerin's troubles in due time," Brigid said. She sheathed her daggers. "Now be gone with you. Slink back to whatever hole you crawled out of and nurse your bruised ego with delusions of divinity. The Brock is closed to those who would abuse its people in the name of the Guardian-King."

"Funny that you still think you can return to Dwerin," her cousin said, "or that you think anyone would even notice your return. Apart from the rumors of you killing our uncles, few enough—commoner or noble—even know who you are—or were, rather. Lady Josephine has been quite adept at erasing your very existence. The special teas the whores drink aren't half as effective."

At this, Lughus had finally had enough. He grabbed Alan by the tabard and lifted him to his feet. Brigid may have found a way to tolerate Alan's continued existence, and out of respect to her, Lughus promised not to end Alan's wicked life.

But he could still beat him.

And so he did, driving his fist hard into the Young Sheriff's vulgar mouth.

In his fury, he nearly mistook the sound of Fergus's growling for his own.

"I would feed you to the hound," Lughus said, "But you would only make him sick."

For once, the Young Sheriff had no nasty retort and with a hard shove, Lughus threw him backwards, sending him sprawling. For a fleeting moment Alan's facade broke and he shriveled like a worm in the high summer sun.

With the arrival of Captain Velius and his legionnaires, the remaining enemies had already broken and fled. Now, not far off, a bevy of war horns announced the impending arrival of General Navarro, Sir Balric, and the rest of the Fighting Fifth.

"Run for your life," Lughus seethed.

With as much dignity as he could muster, Alan collected himself and slowly backed away.

Yet, like all weak men, Alan could not depart without making some show of viciousness masquerading as strength.

"Tell me, Baron," Alan said with feigned nonchalance, "when you fuck Lady Frigid does she just lie there like a dead fish, or does she cry out to wake the dead like her mother?"

Lughus's hand tightened on Sentinel, but as before he felt Brigid's hand on his shoulder.

"My money's on the former, but you never know. Sometimes it's the quiet ones who turn out to be the biggest whores."

Sentinel's blade flashed out and Fergus readied to leap.

"Ignore him!" Brigid insisted. "Lughus, he is *nothing*."

Again, the general sounded his horns and Alan paced back another few steps. "You'll find the Baroness and her daughters in the ruins of the castle further in," the Young Sheriff said. "I told the stupid Miller we should rape them—make them Broken Brockan—but he looked at me like I was a mad man. I guess not everyone has my martial acumen." He laughed. "Well, fuck him anyhow. He's dead."

Lughus took a deep, bracing breath. "Alan?" he called.

"Yes, Baron Doggy?"

The storm clouds in Lughus's eyes flashed. "Brigid's mercy has spared your life today," he said, "but the next time we meet will be the last."

Again, Alan's facade broke briefly until once again, he conjured his smug grin. "I look forward to it!" He offered a final arrogant chuckle, then spun on his heel, and fled.

Lughus watched him go. Beside him, Brigid breathed a heavy sigh and hugged his arm. "I know what you're thinking."

"That the world would be better off if he were dead?"

She nodded. "I don't doubt it," she said, "but to simply murder him..." She shrugged. "I don't want that on your conscience."

Lughus sighed. "But by letting him go, have we allowed him the chance to sow greater evil?"

"His actions are not ours."

"I suppose." His jaw tightened and for a long moment, he was silent. "I don't like how he spoke about you."

"Oh Lughus, let him spew his nonsense." She gave his arm one final squeeze. "I believe that in the end, Alan's own wickedness will return to him tenfold," she said, "and who knows? Perhaps it will be by your hand? Only, let it be in the heat of battle and not when he is already lying defeated and helpless. Else, we become like him, if only by the tiniest of measures."

At length, Lughus gave a nod and kissed the crown of her head. "Let's see if there is any truth to what he said about Lady Agathis. Then, once General Navarro reaches us, we can set about securing the mountain pass."

CHAPTER 3: THE UNIVERSITY

There were very few occasions in which Royne considered himself to be stupid, for even when his actions might *objectively* considered so, it was extremely rare that he would be willing to admit such a failure himself. Thus when he did choose to characterize himself as such, it was not a matter of behaving a bit foolishly or of unintentionally committing a regrettably thoughtless blunder. No, when Royne deigned to the level of self-loathing required in order to acknowledge his own stupidity, it meant that he had committed an act so heinously ridiculous that it could only result in an absolute and indefensible disaster of truly epic proportions.

Choosing to remain behind in Grantis while the Fifth Legion sailed north to support the people of Baronbrock against the might of the Guardians of Andoch was, by his own assessment, perhaps the stupidest decision Royne had ever made in his entire life.

Of course, he hadn't intended it to be this way (a thought he maintained *anytime* he made a mistake). He had made the decision based upon what he believed at the time to be wisdom and in service to the ideals of the greater good. Royne knew very well that he was no warrior, and as he understood it, the Brock was at war. Thus, while General Navarro and the "Fighting Fifth" would be welcome aid to the work at hand, Royne was uncertain that his presence would be useful. Thus, he decided it was better to continue the fight in a manner more suitable to his skill set—by learning whatever he could about the Guardian-King's mad attempt to name himself emperor and Natharis Tainne's inane search for the mythical Lock and Key. They were notions that at one time he would have relegated to the realm of nonsense, but he now understood them as parts of the larger mystery known as the Bard's Heresy.

The Bard's Heresy, the last gift (or perhaps curse) imparted to the Order by Amarthia the Bard as she escaped from the clutches of a corrupt King. Royne had read it over and over and over again these last few weeks in *The Book of Histories*. While he himself refused to believe in such things, the fact that so many others did, including his mentor Rastis and nemesis Tainne, provided at least insight into their thoughts and motivations.

When all the lands of Calendral are bound by Callah's Key,
The Bard shall sing a doleful dirge for Wisdom's unheard plea,
For the Testament unto the Light will seek to snuff the Flame,
When the slumbering Beast of Dibhor wakes, who shall bear the blame?
The Armies of the Dead shall march whilst all the Children weep,
And the Scions of the Brother Dark shall rise from their long sleep,
If the last of Aiden's Blood is spilled to profane the Lady's Grace,
Will any man be left alive to rise up in his place?
So heed the words of Wisdom and mark well the strains of Song,
The Pariah whose heart remains still pure will be welcome erelong,
For all that Guard must take up arms to hold the night at bay,
Else who will rise to bring the Dawn and drive the Dark away?

The first part, he believed, had long ago been correctly interpreted by the generations of Blackguards. Callah's Key was the scepter of the King and the symbol of Andoch. Calendral was the former empire that spanned the entire continent. Thus, should the King, bearer of the Key, overtake Andoch, the first part of the prophesy would be completed.

Wisdom's unheard plea...

As members of the Council of Five, the Loremasters represented the Holy Virtue of Wisdom, and considering the Loremaster's generational skepticism and watchfulness (one might even say "distrust") of the Kings, from Sabrun to Rastis to Royne, Wisdom's unheard plea made a great deal of sense. Royne himself was present for one such instance, long ago as Rastis's steward. He remembered the old man's final stand decrying the Protectorate, a stand where only one man, the Warlord Dandon Rood, stood at his side.

"The Testament unto the Light" also made sense, for Testament was not only the name of the Castle in Titanis and the home of the Guardian-King, but the name of the King's heirloom sword. But "the Flame"? St. Aiden Galadin was often associated with the righteous fire of the Lady of Light and wielder of the magic sword, Luminaire. Could the "Flame" be the Galadin line? The poem goes on to mention "the last of Aiden's blood." Could that mean Lughus?

Then again, the poem also mentioned an Army of the Dead and the Beast of Dibhor and Scions of the Brother Dark so, who knew? Either way, the whole thing spelled doom and gloom and all manner of other delightful apocalyptic scenarios—as one might expect from a person who was so ill-treated as poor Amarthia.

Poor woman. Royne couldn't help but wonder if her son ever learned the truth of his birth, or if any of the other Kings ever knew. He could not imagine that the monstrous King ever told him. Rather, the child would have been raised to believe whatever lies his royal father told him.

In any case, that left the so-called pure pariahs, which for generations, the more noble of the Blackguards—those that refused to swear an Oath to a King they saw as nefarious—saw as themselves. According to Salasco, there were plenty of these men living in secret across the continent. Some, it's true, were villains, but many others were those like himself and the fabled Three, men who chose conscience and a duty to the people of Termain as priority over duty to any King. Considering the republic's separation from the monarchy of Andoch and relative religious freedom, many of them found shelter and anonymity in Grantis. Salasco hoped that he might be able to contact a few and recruit them as allies to stand with the Brock against King Kredor.

Meanwhile, whether due to his objective thirst for knowledge or his role as the Loremaster, Royne hoped to gain admittance to the walled complex within the city of Commonwealth known by the locals as "the University." It was here that the immigrants from Kord on the southern continent had been granted leave by the Grantisi senate to settle and where they practiced the strange philosophy known as the Sign of Four. If that were not on its own intriguing, it was also the only place in the city—perhaps in all of Grantis—that the Guardians had failed to breach. For, according to the locals, any kingsman to set a hand to the gates soon found himself the recipient of a swift and painful death.

Considering how easily the famous legions of Grantis had been swept aside, Royne hoped to find out what mysterious power or skill had allowed the university to succeed where the might of the legionnaires had failed. Whatever it was, perhaps it was something he might emulate so as to make up for his own lack of martial skill. Perhaps it was a way that he might help support Lughus against Kredor the royal thug, or rescue Thom Fatty from the consequences of his own foolishness. Perhaps it might allow him the power to do...*something*.

But upon returning to Commonwealth after General Navarro set sail, Royne quickly began to realize the folly of his decision, for not only were the gates of the walled complex shut tight, but there were also no sentries, porters, or gatekeepers of any kind to whom he might appeal for access.

He considered, momentarily, knocking on the gates or rattling the iron portcullis; however, he recalled rumors he had heard about kingsmen burned alive for trying. Some unnatural force or (more likely) clever contraption barred the way and spelled death to any attempting to force entry. Other stories told of a substance like snow that rained down in light flurries upon the encroaching kingsmen and burning their skin like fire.

In either case, Royne had no desire to draw down the ire of the University's inhabitants so, in the end, he simply stood before the gates with his arms folded across his chest, peering up past the unguarded battlements at the large, domed roof of the temple-like structure that rose from within. For if, indeed, these were men of learning, they would not respond to the clamor of impatience anymore than they would to warlike force.

How will you hear the song of wisdom without first knowing how to listen? Royne reminded himself. Thus, he would simply have to wait.

And wait...

And wait...to the point that he began to wonder if perhaps he was no longer learning how to listen, but had somehow gone deaf. For, it had been weeks now and to no avail.

Every morning, Royne would arrive at dawn to begin what had become a type of daily vigil. Occasionally, he might remember to bring a bit of bread with him, or, were he not busy assisting Salasco, Conor might come by to bring him something to eat or drink, but otherwise, he fasted, sitting and thinking to himself, and when the sun had risen high enough, he read.

He was nearing now the end of *The Book of Histories*—or rather, he was nearing now the present when it would finally be his turn to write. Yet for this very reason, he found his attention often wandering, for he knew that soon he would reach the time of his predecessor, the man who had been not only a mentor, but like a father to him. To see the old man's spindly hand upon the page and to hear his voice in Royne's own mind was a grief that he was uncertain he was prepared for.

The uncertainty surrounding Rastis's fate and his physical state when they parted in the Tower of the Judge was something Royne desperately tried to avoid thinking about. He was such a novice when it came to understanding emotions that it was simply easier to suppress the memory and bury it. Of course, he knew objectively that this avoidance was self-destructive and should he reunite again with Lughus or Thom, he would make certain to unburden himself then, but for now he would focus on his mission, and in doing so, ignore the terrifying prospect of loss and pain.

Still, in his more desperate or volatile moments, he had called out to the emptiness, if only to hear the echo of his own voice. It appeared that even the Grantisi burghers avoided the University, as did the soldier who seemed to have abandoned their attempts at entry, preferring instead to leave well enough alone. So, apart from the occasional rat or alley cat, Royne was somewhat alarmed to realize that he was mostly alone in the silence of a city that was beginning to feel like a ruin.

But what else was there?

To admit failure was not his way.

And so, Royne sat upon the ground before the sealed gate and allowed his head to droop forward. It would be another long day of sitting, waiting, wasting. But he had made his choice.

"What a bloody idiot I've been," he said aloud to the emptiness. "A great bloody fool."

To his surprise, the emptiness spoke back.

"Only when a man can recognize his own ignorance is he finally ready to learn."

Royne started at the unfamiliar voice and nearly jumped out of his skin. He whirled around to find a tall, brown-skinned man in a linen tunic standing before him with his hands clasped thoughtfully behind his back.

"Um...Yes," he finally said. "I suppose that's very true."

With a thoughtful sigh, the man began to pace slowly in a circle around Royne, scratching thoughtfully at his beard. Around his neck, he wore a small pendent shaped like a rhombus made of brass. A uniform pattern of lines and strange symbols has been etched into its surface, though otherwise it was unadorned.

"Tell me," the man mused. He paused in his pacing to look the young Loremaster in the eye. "What is it that you believe *you* must learn?"

Royne considered the question. He knew at once that it was a test, but after a month of frustrated waiting, self-loathing, and regret, his mind—now put on the spot—was drawing a complete blank. Yet here was this man, waiting expectantly for him to speak.

"I..." He stammered foolishly, mouth suddenly gone dry. "I...I suppose I don't even know anymore."

The man's brow creased. "You don't?"

Royne exhaled deeply and seemed to deflate. "I fight a war against an enemy that I do not understand on a battlefield that may not even be real. I seek answers without being able to speak the questions, and I feel compelled to sing a song to which I do not know the words." He paused, annoyed and embarrassed at the nonsense spewing forth from within him, but still he continued, unable to stop. "Yet most of all, I wish to make the world better, though I cannot say exactly how."

As soon as he finished speaking, his brow knitted in consternation, for what he had said was true—he felt as much—but he was a little surprised to hear it.

For a long moment, the man stood silent. He folded his arms across his chest and scratched again at his beard.

"Well, you're either a very great liar or a very great fool," he said. "Either way, I suppose you had better come inside." He raised a hand toward the complex and a moment later, the portcullis began to rise while the heavy doors beyond it slowly opened.

Royne's eyes widened in disbelief and he hurried to follow the man's brisk pace. "Um...sir?" he began.

"Udo."

"Udo?"

"Yes, Udo. And you are?"

"Royne."

"Royne?" the man paused. "That sounds like an ailment of the bum."

"Um...okay," Royne blushed. "I'm...sorry?"

"Do not be offended. Udo sounds like the sound one makes when one has indigestion."

"I...suppose."

"It's fine. Names are essentially just guttural utterances to which we have applied meaning—like all words. Some just happen to sound more pleasing to the ear than others."

"That makes sense."

"Does it?"

As soon as they passed the threshold of the gates, the doors slammed shut and the portcullis dropped with a clang. Royne jumped at the sound, but Udo appeared unphased. Regardless, it spared the young Loremaster having to answer.

"Enough, Royne of the ailing bum," Udo continued. "I do not believe you have been sitting here these past weeks because you wish to discuss linguistics—as fascinating a subject as it might be. Welcome to the University. Now, let us see if there is any truth about you."

CHAPTER 4: NORDREN HARBOR

Sir Geoffrey of Pyle at the end of the pier gazing out across the water. In the light of the rising sun, he could only just make out the broad sails of the fleeing cog. He was utterly exhausted, but relieved, for while the Cockerel and over a score of kingsmen had escaped, more than twice that number fell in the attempt and the damage to Nordren harbor from the fire they had set had been minimal. The lighthouse that overlooked the entrance to the harbor and the long battlement that stretched from it all the way to the baron's castle were still intact and undamaged. The townsfolk were spared what might otherwise have been considerable suffering, and in all likelihood the fishermen would be back on the water when the sun rose the next day.

Of course, this was due largely to Geoffrey's own efforts and those of Sir Adolfo and their men.

The Madder himself stood nearby, his crossbow slung over his shoulder. He took a heavy swig from his wineskin and silently held it out to the Vanguard.

"I think I've had enough fire for a while," Geoffrey observed, accepting the skin.

Sir Adolfo wiped a smear of soot from his bald head with a handkerchief. "You may regret those words when winter sets in, my southern friend."

"Maybe," Geoffrey said, "But I'll stand by them for now."

The staccato patter of footsteps put an end to further musing as Theo Nordren ran the length of the pier. "Mermaid's cunny!" he cursed, pointing at the far off cog, "Is that them?"

Geoffrey nodded. "Those that still breathe."

Theo looked stricken. "Then what are we doing here? We can still catch them!"

Adolfo shook his head. "They're too far away," he said, "By the time we could get underway, they'll have already reached the Andochan blockade."

"The Andochan blockade was scattered when the Legion landed!" Theo said.

"They've regrouped," the Madder said. "You can make out the lanterns atop the mastheads far off in the distance. It would be folly to chase them now."

"So you just let them go?" Theo said, aghast. "They burned four of my ships! With the one they stole, may as well make it five!"

Geoffrey glanced out over the harbor at the sunken hulks, their masts all now that was visible above the line of the water. "It was save the ships of save the town," Geoffrey said, "Besides, all that remains on that ship with the Cockerel are the survivors. There's forty men and more killed in the skirmish or floating in the sea."

Theo rubbed his eyes. "Those were *my* ships!" he said, "Five ships of *my* merchant fleet!"

"Your father approved it," Adolfo said, "And besides, the sacrifice of those five saved the rest of the harbor, the town, and perhaps even the keep."

"My father?" Theo's fair complexion reddened to match his hair. "What right does my father have to sacrifice my ships? How will I ever recover from this?"

"The loss of five cogs is nothing to a savvy merchant," Adolfo told him, "It's also but a fraction of the value of what we saved—most of which you stand to inherit someday. Besides, you have others, including *The Swordfish*, and as I recall General Navarro was more than willing to sell you the stolen galleys from Dwerin for a song—"

"Just...just don't," Theo interrupted, shaking his head in frustration. He rested his hands on his hips. "Where is my father anyway?"

"At the keep," Geoffrey said. "He was waiting for your return."

Theo sighed. "We should have known they would head for the harbor instead of taking the coastal road," he said, "My men and I could have been here saving my ships and instead I was riding south on a fool's errand."

"Yours was the more likely path for the kingsmen to take," Adolfo said. "Perhaps that is why they chose the harbor?"

"Matters little now," Theo said. Without another word, he turned and departed back the way he had come.

Adolfo accepted the wineskin back from Geoffrey. "And that is what sets Galadin apart from the majority of the other baronies."

"What do you mean?" Geoffrey asked.

"To most, the Guardian attack on St. Golan's would have been seen as a fortunate error on the part of the enemy commander. For while they wasted time attacking the monastery, we could have been stockpiling supplies and fortifying the Houndstooth to endure a siege. Instead, our baron rallied his men and rode out to meet them with whatever forces he had on hand. Do you know why?"

Geoffrey nodded. "Because the Andochans were slaughtering common folk, and because Abbot Woode is our friend."

"True," Adolfo said, "But more importantly, he did it because it was *right*. Even if it cost him his life, the baron would not sit idly by while others suffered in his name."

Geoffrey nodded and took another drink from the wineskin. "True."

"The world is filled with shit and horror, Geoffrey of Pyle, as I'm sure that you well know," Adolfo said. "The man who is willing to stand against it—to stand for others who lack the ability to stand for themselves—is a rare thing. Yet for whatever reason, it's something the Galadins and their close friends have done and continue to do. It's why I am willing to take risks on their behalf—for Baron Lughus, and for Lady Brigid, and it's why I value my friendship with you too."

Geoffrey breathed a heavy sigh. "I am glad to call you friend as well, Sir Adolfo," the Vanguard finally said. "In spite of what people say, you're a good man."

Adolfo pursed his lips. "I'm not," he said. "But, like my brother, and the man who raised us, I chose the path of darkness so that men like the Galadins, and men like you, could be free to bring the light."

Slowly, Geoffrey stood, stretched, and secured Oakheart to his belt and Acorn to his back. "Well, I suppose we should be getting on then. Sir Gosbert had the men setting up camp outside the city walls. We can rest there for the night and set out for Houndstooth at dawn."

"My mercenaries are there as well," Adolfo said, "though there is another matter I would discuss with you as we walk, if you'll permit me."

"I'm a man after my father, Adolfo," Geoffrey said. "Speaking to me costs nothing but your own time. You can decide afterwards if it was worth it."

Adolfo nodded as they began to walk past the line of fishing boats and merchant flutes to the town proper. Here and there, men of the Nordren guard stood watch while sailors and dockworkers set to rights any damaged cargo or other debris. "What do you know of Montevale?" he asked.

Geoffrey shrugged. "Land of the warring horses," he said, recalling fragments from the recesses of his mind and the little snippets that belonged to the Vanguard. "There was the black horse in the south and the white horse in the north, but now they're supposed to be at peace. First time in a hundred years, so they say, and the new king has pledged himself to the Guardian-King."

Adolfo scoffed. "Peace is an illusion when you're led by a man known as the Plague King." He pursed his lips. "No, the war never ended. They just fooled themselves and the rest of the continent into thinking it did. Regardless, it's back on in earnest, which is why we have yet to face down a cavalry charge from Montevale." He paused. "I intend to keep it that way, or at the very least, match the Guardian-King's new horse with one of our own."

Geoffrey's brow furrowed. "What do you mean 'one of our own'?"

"The rebellion against King Dermont is led by Queen Marina, daughter of Marius, the defeated king of Gasparn. By all accounts she is an intelligent and savvy woman, and the people—at least the common people—love her. Furthermore, her lord-general happens to be Beledain, former prince of Valendia and Dermont's own brother. That alone would be interesting, but what makes it even more so is that this Beledain is also a recently anointed Guardian turned Blackguard. They call him 'the Tower.'"

A pair of mercenaries loitering outside of a tavern nodded to them with respect. Geoffrey returned the gesture and continued on. "So you're hoping to forge some manner of alliance?" he asked. "Between the Brock and the rebel queen?"

"In a sense," Adolfo said. "I'm hoping *you* can forge an alliance between the Brock and the rebel queen."

"Ah!" Geoffrey said. "So *that* was the motivation behind the kind words earlier."

"I can see why you might draw that conclusion," he said. "And to be fair, the two are not unrelated, for it is *because* of my assessment of your character that I believe you to be the best suited for this task."

Geoffrey shook his head and walked on.

The Madder sighed. "You, of course, have every right to refuse," he continued, unperturbed, "but I ask that you will at least consider my reasoning."

"Which is?"

"First, for the purposes of forming any alliance, an individual with some manner of authority must be present. The Lord-Baron, while a decent enough man, is not a warrior, which is why in these current martial troubles, he has, more or less, ceded his authority to Baron Galadin and Baron Marthaine. In either case, with the politics of the Brock as they are, both must stand united, leading their forces together against the common threat of Andoch."

"Now," Adolfo continued, "You might suggest that we send another baron, to which I would refer you to our brief conversation with the young Nordren, and while I fully intend to force the father to impress the son into providing the necessary transport, I do not trust him or any other like him with any true authority—nor do I believe he would be well received by our potential allies."

"I considered asking Lady Brigid to make the journey, but with the absurd scandal surrounding the deaths of her uncles, a discerning mind would still greet her with skepticism. I do not intend that as any type of criticism of her character. I merely mean that with rumor and hearsay as they are, in the name of caution, she may have a more challenging time winning allies. Besides," he said, "I doubt that there is much in this world that could rip her from the young baron's side, or he from hers."

Geoffrey's gaze narrowed. They had nearly reached the main gates to Nordren town and the army encampment. Most of the chaos from the battle had already been cleared away and now folk hurried about finishing whatever final chores were necessary to end the day. Not for the first time, Geoffrey's thoughts went to Annabel and his children, happy that they were safe and secure back at the Houndstooth. At least he could count on that. Wherever in the world he may find himself, whatever dire situation he might face, in that mighty fortress, they were safe. He turned back to Adolfo.

"You have all the ideas," he said, "and you know so much about them. Why don't you go?"

Adolfo made a face. "From its very inception, an alliance must be built upon trust, and as we both know, I am hardly an individual who invokes trust," he said. "Further, with Sir Owain so grievously wounded, someone will need to see to the defense of Galadin in his stead, and while I am certain that you could see to it—as the old knight would prefer—there are certain elements that I manage who might attempt to take advantage of my absence and create new problems that would be quite inconvenient in a time of war."

"Certain elements? You mean criminal elements?"

"Yes."

Geoffrey sighed. "I still don't see why you think I'm so suited for this. Until very recently, I was a only a farmer."

"Because, Geoffrey, whatever else you are or are not, I know that you are a good and honest man, and while in politics that often does more harm than good, I believe that in this particular instance, with this particular queen— and with this particular prince—you are exactly what we need."

Geoffrey fell silent.

"You would not go alone," Adolfo added. "Not completely. You'd have a small command of archers, perhaps a sergeant or two, and I could see to it that your family could accompany you as well, if you like."

"I don't know," Geoffrey said, "I'll have to think on it, and I'll certainly have to talk it over with Annabel."

"Of course," the Madder said. "I would expect nothing less."

Yet, it was not long after Geoffrey's return to Houndstooth, while he was still considering the situation himself, that he discovered Annabel had not only been made privy to Adolfo's plans, but that she had already been discussing new clothing with Jergan and Willa to keep them warm though the autumn and, if need be, into the winter.

"With any luck, it won't be that long," Annabel said, "But it's always better to be prepared."

"So you were planning on coming too?" Geoffrey asked.

Annabel nodded. "What Adolfo says makes much sense," she told him. "And if it helps the Brock, then I say we do it. In the short time we've been here, look at how we've prospered! We went from living a life of struggle at the mercy of the powerful only to become powerful ourselves. A thing like that demands a certain service—not to the lords and barons, but to the everyday people. Imagine for even just a minute if we'd a man like you watching over Pyle. Imagine just how different things might have been."

"It takes more than just one man to carry the weight of the world," Geoffrey said, trying to ignore a stab of guilt at the mention of Pyle.

"That may be," Annabel said, "but sometimes all it takes is one man to show the others the way. Think on this city. Think on its namesake. What is that I hear you muttering to yourself all the time? 'St. Aiden was a farmer'?"

Geoffrey bit his lip. Even now he could hear his father's sardonic chuckling. "Fine," he said at last. "I'll tell Adolfo and speak to Lughus about it all. You can be the one to tell Brigid."

49

CHAPTER 5: THE GOLDEN GARRON

In the storeroom of the Dolebrook village inn, Inen Vilnois, Warden of Whitemane, sat upon a barrel with his wrists bound behind his back. His armor bore the marks of the recent battle, but his sigil, the Golden Garron shone majestically against the snowy white field of his tabard. As Beledain and the Shackle entered, he greeted them with an arrogant sneer.

"Ah, there he is!" Vilnois grinned. "The Silent Prince! It's been some time, Bel. How's your bastard these days? It must be hard raising him all alone without that common whore."

Bel's face remained impassive, though his green eyes smoldered. He had learned that, like his brother, Dermont's friends ran their mouths as a means of feeling powerful. It was a typical tactic among bullies, a diversion to hide their lack of backbone.

"Inen Vilnois," Bel said, "You and your men attacked the refugee train heading westward out of Bricehollow—"

Vilnois chuckled and his lip curled with maliciousness. "Aye, Bel, we certainly did!"

"You murdered innocent men, women, and children, slaughtered their livestock, and robbed them of what little they carried. People of Whitemane. People of Montevale. People you were sworn to protect."

"We also had quite a bit for fun with them as well," Vilnois said. "Especially the women. Warlock's Balls! I had this one girl—may not have even been old enough to bleed. Let's just say I blessed her with my nobility before she died—"

Bel's hand shot out, grabbed the nobleman by the throat, and slammed his head back against the storeroom wall.

"Woo! Woo! Look at you!" the Golden Garron managed to choke out with a smile. "So it's true! I'd heard you'd developed something of a temper! So much for being the good boy, eh? The beloved of the common people?"

Bel relaxed his grip and with one final shove, released the ignoble nobleman.

Vilnois snorted with laughter. "Even when we pushed you to finally act like you had a pair, it was always short lived. You haven't got the stomach for any real violence. It's why your brother put you in command of the rabble skirmishers. He let you feel important without having to risk your weakness bringing shame upon him."

"This one really likes to talk shit," the Shackle observed. "No wonder his breath stinks."

"Oh, it speaks!" Vilnois smirked. "Good for you. Many simpletons don't."

"He always has," Bel told the Shackle, "even more than the others."

"Oh the others? You mean Wilmar and Kurlan?" He laughed. "You know, I don't believe for an instant that you killed them." He paused. "Okay, perhaps Wilmar. He could have been drunk. In that case, yes. Maybe. But Kurlan? Never. My guess is he fell from his horse and bashed his head on a stone. It's far more likely than you cutting him down."

Bel breathed a sigh. "Do you remember the Tournament of the Sires in the year that Dermont came of age?"

"Vaguely."

"There was that boy from Ebon Keep. What was his name? Erkwald? Erkwright? When they called him to the lists to speak and swear his allegiance to my father, it turned out that he suffered from a terrible stutter. He only spoke but a few words, but it didn't matter. You all heckled him relentlessly throughout the entire tournament, mocking him, imitating his speech, and so on. Yet in spite of it all, the boy remained silent, for what could he say to a prince and a prince's companions? "

"Can't say I recall him specifically," Vilnois said offhandedly. "Though it certainly sounds like something we would have done. To be fair, I have a hard time remembering so much from that time. When you're plowing the servant girls two at a time little else seems to matter. Besides, whatever might be the case, I expect you remember it all well enough for whatever point you hope to make here."

"I do," Bel said, "I do remember it because on the final day of the Tournament, I watched this boy—Erkwald, I remember now—beat all five of you. One by one."

"Did he?" Vilnois said. "Imagine that!"

"He did." Bel leveled his gaze, and held it so intently that Vilnois seemed unable to look away. "When they called him forth to receive the prize of the golden horseshoe, my father asked him what had driven him to become so skilled. Erkwald looked down, and, in spite of his stuttering, told my father that since words were his weakness, he had learned to let his actions speak for him."

Vilnois gave a derisive chuckle. "Of course he did."

"My father was furious with all of you—not or losing—but for your behavior."

"Oh, King Cedric was always fuming—at least until he lost his mind," Vilnois said. "Condolences, by the way. I hear he passed alongside Marius. Sure enough, the life of a rebel only hastened his demise."

Bel ignored Vilnois's false sympathy and carried on, staring the prisoner in the face like a hangman before the gallows. "I saw the aftermath of what happened outside of Bricehollow. You killed those people. You raped those poor women. You rode the children down as they attempted to flee."

"You're fucking right I did," Vilnois said. "They sought to hide behind the skirts of your cunt rebel queen!"

The stinging backhand from Bel's gauntlet drew blood from the Golden Garron's lip, and for a split second, Vilnois seemed genuinely shocked by Bel's strength. The Shackle's scarred face twisted into a horrifying smirk.

"Your men—the mercenaries you hire with the scutage and the promise of spoils and looting—will all be hanged." Bel paused. "You, however—for your crimes—you will be disarmed and sent back as a message to my brother."

"I'm already disarmed, you fucking twit," Vilnois sneered. "The only reason I surrendered is because that bastard's chain snapped my sword."

"Oh?" the Shackle grinned. "He don't mean that weapon."

Vilnois's face was a mask of horrified shock.

"When you're finished," Bel added, "break both of his hands as well."

The Shackle nodded. "My pleasure."

Bel turned to leave and with sudden candor, Vilnois called after him. "Beledain? Beledain, please!" he pleaded. "You can't be serious. We grew up together. I was only joking! I mean, you *know* me!"

"I do," Bel said coldly. "All too well."

The Golden Garron screamed in horror. "Beledain! Beledain, no! Please!"

"Don't worry," the Shackle said. Bel turned to depart, and the Blackguard drew his chain sickle from around his waist. "I've done this plenty of times with horses, though working with something so small might present a bit of a challenge. I'll do my best to keep a steady hand..."

"No! *No!*"

Outside of the storeroom, Briden—Sir Briden—sat waiting atop his mare, Maggie, beside Tempest, the great searoan. When Bel appeared, the young knight tossed him Spire, the heirloom spear, and he climbed up into Tempest's saddle. It was a clear autumn day and the countryside beyond the village was pleasantly pastoral. A flock of sheep wandered about grazing, carefully watched over by a pair of dogs, while the young woman assigned to oversee them looked on. As Bel and Briden led their mounts out along the edge of the village to where their men awaited them, the young woman raised her hand. Sir Briden returned it, blushing beneath his arming cap.

Bel suppressed a smile. "She's pretty," he said mildly.

"Yes," the young knight agreed.

"Do you know her?"

"Only to see her," Briden said. "Horn and I came through this village once or twice before joining you at Sir Norton's."

"And you met her then."

"She offered us water."

Their horses trotted on. Ahead of them, the main force of Bel's men-at-arms stood tending to their horses and gear. Others stood watch over another dozen men dressed in an assortment of leather, mail, and plate. No single insignia united them, and some bore no mark or arms at all. Two of them men were large Wrathorn brutes, identifiable by their furs and skins, though the rest appeared to be wanderers, thugs, and bullies who had either been tough enough or cruel enough to make a living in service to the Golden Garron putting poor folk to the sword. They had sacked two villages and the refugee train before setting their sights on Dolebrook. Fortunately for the villagers, it was then that Bel and a detachment of his men finally caught up to them. These dozen were all that remained of the two score riders that followed Vilnois at the start of the battle.

But they will meet the same fate, Bel thought, eying a large sycamore not far from the edge of the village. "We'll do it there," he said aloud.

"Aye, sir," Briden said. "I'll fetch a rope."

Bel gave a nod and the young knight rode off, leaving him to his thoughts.

The Battle of Pridel, while a great victory for the rebellion, had not come without cost. King Marius and Sir Emory had both been killed when Dermont's spymaster, Canton, had attacked the castle in an attempt to murder Bel's infant son and kidnap the queen. Luckily, the Shackle and Bel's father, Old King Cedric, had been able to delay their assault long enough for Bel himself to return to foil the plot. Sadly, the strain of the battle appeared to be too much for the aged Cedric, who fell into a swoon shortly thereafter and never recovered.

Thus, three fresh burial mounds now stood upon the fields outside of Pridel, two for men who may have lived their lives as enemies, but in the end, died as friends. The third, while not of the Tremont bloodline, became no less than family to either king.

With both kings and their shared seneschal gone, the time had come for Bel and Marina to fully accept the mantle of leadership and declare themselves as the true defenders of a united land. Since then, Bel and his captains ceaselessly patrolled their domain, driving off Dermont's raiders and securing the trade routes from town to town and village to village and pressing their territory little by little and league by league. Now, the majority of Southeast Montevale and various islands of land throughout the west and northeast pledged their loyalty to the queen.

With Vilnois's defeat, Bel's men were hoping to soon secure the region known as Whitemane, essentially doubling the size of the queen's domain. Meanwhile, Marina, the Winter Rose herself, had devoted all of her efforts to the political side of the endeavor, keeping the peace between the nobles and ensuring that the common folk's needs were being met. It had not been easy, but together the one-time scions of warring houses had finally found success.

When the noose had been tied and secured over the thick bough of the sycamore, Bel ordered the prisoners brought before him and assembled into a line.

"You men are accused of crimes against the people of Montevale," he said, glaring at them from the back of the great searoan. "You have murdered, pillaged, and raped. You have stolen from folk who have little enough as it is, and made sport of the suffering of women and children." He could feel his blood beginning to grow hot. His latent temper flared. "For that," he said coldly, "you are sentenced to death."

The mercenaries' eyes widened in surprise and sudden terror. They began to mutter and protest. One man even tried to make a break for it and run, but was quickly clubbed down and returned to the line by Bel's men.

At length, one of the men called out louder than the others. "You can't do this!" he cried, "We acted under orders from the king himself!"

Bel glared at the man. "What manner of king makes war on his own people?"

The man looked around uneasily. "We don't ask questions," he said belligerently. "We follow the Golden Garron."

"Golden Gelding, more like," said the Shackle, ambling up to join them.

Bel's green eyes blazed with fury. "Any man who would prey upon his own people is not a lord, is not a king, but a blight, a boil to be lanced lest he festers his vile poison spreads!"

The men fell silent as Bel stared them down.

"Montevale has no king," he said at last. "Long live the *queen*!"

"Long live the queen!" Briden echoed.

"Long live the queen!" the rest of Bel's men cried out in agreement.

The prisoners bowed their heads in horror and despair.

Bel held his face impassive. "Carry on."

When the task was done, two men were assigned to transport Vilnois on a stretcher to the nearest castle sworn to the Plague King. Bel, Briden, the Shackle, and the rest of the riders readied their horses and prepared for the long ride back to Pridel.

Bel was weary. He was not a man naturally predisposed toward violence, but in the face of the horrors committed by Dermont and his friends, he had learned to be, and he would continue to be so long as it was necessary. Still, it wore on him. He feared that his hands had become too bloodstained, too tainted, to hold his infant son. Fortunately, in the wake of the Battle of Pridel and the sorrow of the threefold death, he had discovered a balm to ease his wounds and lighten the weight of his heavy soul.

The sun had only just touched the horizon when the riders returned. As soon as the sentries atop the barbican spied the queen's standard, dancing like a flame in the waning light, they sent word to the castle. At once, Sir Armel, the queen's seneschal, hurriedly rode down to meet them.

"How did it go?" he asked Bel, his mustache bristling.

"We sent a message," Bel said. "How are things here?"

"They're both safe and well," the knight said knowingly. "Norton and the Malets have returned too. Once you and the rest of the captains have returned, she wants to meet to discuss strategy for the coming winter. She's also hoping to hold a feast."

Bel nodded. Feasts at Pridel were not nearly as ostentatious as one would expect for a royal court. They often lacked the pageantry or the decorum one might expect. More often they were simply an excuse to gather with friends and loyal retainers as opposed to opportunities for political maneuvering and grandstanding. Perhaps this was why Bel could actually admit that he enjoyed them. "Has Horn returned yet?"

"No, but a few of the other riders have. By all accounts, Dermont's forces and their Guardian allies still make camp at the Nivanus Pass and their numbers grow daily. Thousands of men, including peasant levies, all sitting idle when they should be out seeing to their fields and farms."

Bel's brow creased. While he knew that the women of Montevale were just as capable as men, the reduction in the size of the workforce would result in greater hardship and a smaller yield. It would be hard times for the common folk of those lands still loyal to Dermont when the snows came.

The nobles, of course, would not suffer. In spite of their aristocratic obligation to protect the common folk beneath them, most would simply take what they wanted with fire and sword and leave the peasantry to starve.

"I thought your brother was supposed to be clever," Armel said as they rode slowly up the thoroughfare toward the castle. "But he treats the common folk little better than slaves. It's madness."

"Dermont's intellect is more of a wicked sort of cunning," Bel said. "He is like a rat that eats its young—it gains an extra meal while saving its stores for itself."

Armel shook his head. "Sick bastard."

Bel nodded. When they reached the gates of the castle ward, he paused momentarily to release his men and send them on their way. Most would make their way back to the castle town and their families while others would find a meal in one of the newly opened public houses. The captains—Briden and the Shackle included—would make their way to the hall. There, they could always get a crock of the aptly named "perpetual stew," a hunk of bread, and a tankard of ale.

Bel and Armel continued on in silence to the grander section of the stables and dismounted. While a groom saw to Armel's horse, Bel himself took care of Tempest. There was no real need to paddock a creature as intelligent as the great searoan, but the stallion enjoyed a good brushing and patting down.

As Bel worked, Armel hung around, assisting at times, but primarily out of a sense of companionship. While steadfast and stoic in the execution of his duties, Bel knew the elder knight to be a sentimentalist deep down. Armel had lost plenty of friends over the course of a lifetime of war, and learned to make the most out of whatever time was given. Further, while Armel was loyal to Bel, he had recently learned that his daughter's husband, while by all accounts a decent man hailing from the northeastern reaches of Gasparn, had pledged to Dermont, and though this had ensured the safety of Armel's daughter and his wife, it resulted in a painful separation for the father.

That last thought in particular brought a resonant ache to Bel's chest and as he and Armel made their way inside the castle, he was glad when Sir Welmsey, intercepted them.

"Lord Tower, welcome back!" Welmsey said with a grin, his long golden locks illumined in the light of the braziers of the hall.

"Welmsey," Bel nodded, gripping his friend's arm. While foppish on the surface and given to flights of terrible poetry, Welmsey was a good man and a stout fighter. He had styled himself after the warrior poets out of the romances of yore, and while he and Armel could not appear any more different, Bel knew that they were the best of friends.

"It is my great pleasure to inform you that in their infinite generosity, the Malets have brought a cask of Grantisi wine taken in their last skirmish near Ebon Keep. It belonged to the enemy captain, a Lord Something-or-other, but they were able to liberate it when he fled the field."

"To the victor go the spoils," Armel remarked.

"Indeed," Welmsey said, "and in celebration of such good fortune, they seek to share it with us tonight. Her majesty has already given leave to use the great hall."

Armel smiled beneath his mustache. "If the queen approves, then who am I to disagree?"

"Excellent!" Welmsey said. He counted on his fingers. "So far we have the Malets, Sir Norton, Sir Briden, the Shackle—though he'll probably limit himself to that mash he and his foresters make—and we three?"

Bel gave a reticent shrug.

"He still has to make his report to the queen," Armel said, clapping Bel on the shoulder.

"Ah yes," Welmsey said knowingly. "Well, if the opportunity presents, you will know where to find us."

"I'll see my son and then make my report," Bel said, "but I will keep it in mind."

"Yes, my lord," Welmsey said.

"Aye, you go on," Armel said. "I won't delay you any further."

Without another word, he hurried off to the staircase that took him to his own quarters. Guardsmen on duty saluted as he passed, and while he was quick to return the gesture, his longing increased by tenfold with every moment. When at last he finally arrived at his own apartments, a broad anticipatory smile spread across his face.

"Where's my little colt?" he said merrily, bursting through the door.

"Lady save us!"

"Sires' Hooves!"

At once, Bel's face reddened as the pair of young nurses gasped in shock and alarm. "I'm so sorry!" he said, holding out his hands as if to calm a startled horse. "Forgive my foolishness!"

They were a pair of young women from the town, Hilda and Eloise. Eloise, the taller and younger of the two, had been in the process of cleaning up what appeared to be the remnants of Marcus's smashed peas, while Hilda, the elder and broader sat gently rocked the sleeping boy in her arms.

"It's quite fine, my lord," Hilda said. "He only just went down, but I believe he's still out. I can wake him if you like though."

As unusual as it might have seemed to most men, Bel made it his custom to put Marcus to bed himself whenever he happened to be in the city. It was a practice that he had heard his own father had kept, and while other men might have scoffed, Bel believed that it was important. But not tonight apparently.

"No, no," Bel said. "Let him sleep." He could not escape a stab of disappointment, though in fairness he had yet to even doff his armor, and as much as he wanted to hug the little boy, to hold him close and feel his warmth, the cold hardness of his metal skin and the triple odor of oil, horse, and blood were realities he hoped to spare the infant boy for as long as he might. Instead, he took off his gauntlet, ran a finger gently across the boys forehead, and kissed him lightly on the chubby cheek.

"Thank you," he said earnestly. "Thank you both for always looking after him."

"Of course, my lord," they said together.

"Her majesty as well," Eloise said.

"Yes," Hilda agreed. "She sees to him as if he were her own."

Bel nodded silently. "I will be sure to thank her as well," he finally said. "and speaking of her majesty, I still have to give her my report." He cast his son one final, fond glance. "Goodnight."

The women nodded and went back to their duties as Bel stepped out into the hall and shut the door behind him. No sooner than he turned around, however, when he heard a stifled cry and his hand instinctively went to the dagger on his hip. In the light of the iron wall sconces, his eyes widened like a cornered animal, wildly searching for the threat. His muscles tensed and he readied himself for violence.

The sight of a slender figure half-shrouded in darkness stayed his hand, for no matter the lighting, there could be no mistaking her hair.

"Marina?" Bel whispered. "Is that you?"

"Bel!" she replied sheepishly. "I'm sorry! I didn't mean to startle you! I didn't want to wake Marcus."

Bel's cheeks flushed with embarrassment. Ever since the day of the battle—when he had literally fought and killed men in this very keep—he had developed a certain impulse, an almost primeval reaction to even the slightest surprise. He motioned toward the door to his chambers and followed Marina inside. To his surprise, the lamps had already been lit, a merry fire danced in the small hearth, and a plate of food awaited him.

59

"I'm so sorry," Marina said again. "I didn't want to impose on you and Marcus."

"You are a queen and this is your castle," Bel told her. "You may go wherever you please."

"But your time with Marcus is important," she said. "I don't want to interrupt that."

Bel gave an appreciative nod, but remained silent. He could feel the tension rising with his body temperature. She looked beautiful—as always—in a dark green gown over an ivory chemise. Her scarlet hair fell loose around her shoulders beneath a thin golden circlet set with a single emerald—the closest thing she would wear to a crown. There was a lightness to her and in contrast, his armor suddenly felt heavy and oppressive. At once, he paced forward, unconsciously loosening the straps of his pauldrons and vambraces. Marina stepped closer to help him.

"Here. Let me," she said. "So did you end up finding them?"

"We did," Bel told her, ignoring the flush he felt as her hands nimbly helped with the various buckles and belts. "You really don't have to do this," he said.

"Nonsense. I used to help my father and my brother from time to time so it's nothing new. It's much more difficult to do it yourself, and I know you haven't chosen a new standard-bearer since knighting Briden, so..." She shrugged and bent down to loosen the bindings of his greaves.

Bel glanced around the room, ignoring the sudden quickening of his heart. "Thank you for all of this," he said. "The fire. The food."

"I've also had water prepared for a bath," she said. "I thought you would need it after the battle and the long ride."

He gave a slow nod. "Again, thank you."

With Marina's help, Bel removed the various pieces of his armor and set them upon the table at the side of the room. He would oil and polish them himself later. As she said, he had not taken on anyone else since elevating Briden, but he would have to do so soon. Not just for the work that they could assist with. There was a symbolism about the role and so it would need to be filled eventually.

But not yet. Not right now.

When he was finally down to his gambeson, he rolled his shoulders and breathed a sigh of relief, though the tension had not eased from within him.

If anything, as the queen stood before him, her green eyes glimmering in the light of the fire, he realized that it had grown.

"Better?" she asked.

"Yes. Thank you."

She smiled and all of a sudden her eyes grew wide. "What is that?"

"What is what?" he asked.

"There," she said tentatively. "What is that?"

Bel remained silent. He knew perfectly well what it was she meant, but was uncertain how to explain.

Finally, with a timid hand, she reached forward and tugged at a piece of cloth that had been stuffed between the chest straps of his gambeson. As it came free, it was revealed to be a white handkerchief embroidered with a pattern of red roses. Marina recognized it instantly.

"You still have this?" she asked, her voice breathy with disbelief.

"Some time after we escaped from Tremontane Castle, I found it in among all of the gear Emory and my father had gathered in our flight," he said. "I've carried it with me ever since."

There was a heavy silence. It was not uncomfortable or disquieting, but full. Bel became exceedingly aware of the beating of his heart, and a warmth spread through him. He raised his eyes to Marina's, finally allowing himself to acknowledge the intensity of his affection.

With a sudden rush of movement, he reached out, took her in his arms, and pulled her close to him. At once, he felt her body fall limp against him, and as she held her head level to meet the intensity of his gaze, he lowered his head to taste her sweet, red lips. Quiet murmurs of delight escaped her, and her chest heaved with deepening passion at every quivering breath.

"I missed you," she whispered. "I always miss you."

Bel held her close to him and ran a hand through her hair. "As long as I live, I will always come back. My body may be elsewhere, but my heart is here with Marcus..." He paused to lift her chin so that he might meet her eyes. "And with *you*."

She smiled and swallowed a lump in her throat. "You are all I have," she whispered, "I don't know what I would do without you."

"You're a lot stronger than you give yourself credit for," he said. "Besides, I may fight, but so do many others. Meanwhile, you manage everything else—the people, the court, trade, and plenty of other things that I can't even begin to understand. The harvest! By the Stallion, if I were in charge of that, the whole bloody city would starve, yet you manage it like breathing."

"I'm sure you'd find a way."

"I am terrible at maths and figures and such. I have no idea what it takes to feed a village or a city, or how much to leave to the farmers and the workers so as to ensure they're taken care of for the winter," he said. "It's those things that really matter."

Marina gave a nod. "I suppose we all have our roles to play." She bent forward once more to kiss him deeply on the lips. "But come. I told you I had water drawn for a bath. I think you need it."

Bel's lips twisted into a smirk. "I smell of horse, don't I? I'm sorry. I—"

Marina shook her head and pressed a finger to his lips. "When did the Silent Prince become so chatty?" She grinned.

Bel shrugged. "It's a recent development," he said. "One of many."

Marina's eyes twinkled in the firelight. Then, taking him by the hand, led him through his chamber into the next room where a large washtub sat steaming. Various herbs floated upon the surface of the water and a pleasant aroma filled the air. In the corner near his bed, a large pot sat in the fireplace, heating additional water should he need it.

Bel breathed in the fragrant scent as Marina turned to him and smiled, her green eyes alight with anticipation and a hint of mischief. With another kiss, she drew out his handkerchief—her handkerchief—and placed it neatly on the small table beside his bed. Bel unfastened the leather straps of his gambeson and shrugged out of the heavy undercoat before pulling off his boots. Marina ran a hand through the water to test its temperature, and finding it satisfactory, returned to him.

"Let's get you in there," she said.

Once more, Bel's heart began to pound like a battering ram, but he did as she commanded and allowed her to pull off his shirt. Her finger traced softly along the muscles of his arms and his chest before gently coming to rest upon the thick, knotted scar that marked the place where Marcus Harding had struck him. The wound would have been fatal were it not for The Gift of the Guardians.

"I remember this one," she said quietly.

Bel gave a nod, then slipped his hand into hers and leaned in to her ear. "Join me, your majesty?"

Marina's emerald eyes shone. "I thought that was the idea."

Together, they shared a laugh, and as Marina stepped away to remove her circlet and set it beside his handkerchief, Bel stepped out of his breeches and braies, and into the washtub.

At once, the warm water began to work wonders for his tired and achy muscles, and he began to feel his tension washing away alongside the dust and dirt of horses and violence. He tilted his head back in the water to wet his hair, and, shutting his eyes, let his head sink below the surface to wash his face. When he opened them, his breath caught and his blood sang at the sight of Marina before him, gloriously naked, testing the water again and preparing to climb in.

"Is it warm enough?" she asked. "There's more hot water if you like."

Bel could tell by the rosy patches upon her ivory skin that she was attempting—and utterly failing—to keep from blushing at the way his eyes must have widened at the sight of her perfection.

Slender and supple as a statue, every line and curve of her body seemed carved out of alabaster by a master artist. Her thick, flowing hair trailed down in soft, scarlet tendrils framing her beautiful face—gleaming green eyes, delicate nose, and bright crimson lips—before continuing onward to half-conceal the tips of her pert breasts. It was not the first time he had seen her, but as always, it may as well have been, for it was never less thrilling. She truly was the winter rose.

As Marina approached the edge of the tub, Bel offered her his hand, and no sooner had she stepped lightly into the water, than he pulled her in to another close embrace. He marveled at the touch of her bare skin and when she turned and pressed her lips to his, the blood sang within his veins. His mouth began a slow march from her lips along the line of her jaw to the side of her neck. His hands played upon her with the adroit deftness of a troubadour, drawing forth a symphony of breathy mewling and soft moans. With every touch, with every kiss, Bel sensed in her a greater urgency, a more ardent need. Her body began to rock slowly against him with impatience, but he knew that—as it was upon the battlefield—the sweetest triumph was reserved for those who practiced patience, resisting the urge to be hasty in the name of the greater victory. As such, he steeled himself to ensure a prolonged campaign.

With a gentle firmness, he raised her hips and began to move with the slow, rolling force of an ocean wave. Like the rising of the tide his pace steadily quickened with deepening intensity. Marina's body shook with each staccato movement and her breath came only in short, airy gasps. Bel gripped her thighs and lifted her higher with mounting excitement as their pleasure peaked. Marina's legs shuddered like a newborn foal and her gasping cries became more desperate, but Bel's strong hands held her steady so as to prolong the moment. He could feel himself losing control, but willed himself to hold on until, at last, the damn within Marina broke. She stifled a deafening cry with the back of her arm and her body writhed as if she'd been struck by lightning. Only then did Bel let himself go, losing himself in one penultimate release.

Sometime later, lying exhausted together upon the bed, Marina turned her head from where it rested upon his chest to look him in the eye.

"I am not trying to pressure you," she began, "but I want you to know that if you were to ask me to marry you, I would. I love you, Bel. I love you with my whole heart, with all that I am and with every sense of my being."

Bel met her gaze unflinchingly. "I know," he said, "and believe me. I love you too. There is nothing in this world that would make me happier than to marry you."

"But?" she said, raising an eyebrow.

Bel's brow creased in consternation. "But you are my queen," he said. "And not only that, but you are the first reigning queen of Montevale in...well, perhaps ever. More importantly, you are exactly the monarch that the realm needs. You are kind, wise, compassionate, sympathetic to the poor. You are just. You are strong. You are willing to stand up for what is right and you have the people's love."

"I don't know about all of that," she said. "There are stronger women than I who fight alongside you in battle. Look at Sparrow or your cousin, Lady Valerie."

"There are many different types of strength," Bel said, "just as there are many different fronts upon which we wage war. I may be good at fighting or killing, but those are not qualities that make for happiness, that make for peace."

"But those are necessary qualities too."

"Yes," he said. "For now, but I would rather live in a world without such things. I only wish I knew how."

"Do you think I do?" Marina asked.

"You have a better mind for it than me," Bel said, "and though you may not know the way right now, I believe you are the only leader who can guide us there." He breathed a great sigh. "Now, I swear by all that I am that I will follow you every step of the way. I will protect you, defend you, and carry out your orders until our land and our people are truly at peace. However, until that day dawns I am unworthy to stand at your side."

CHAPTER 6: THE BANE OF THE BLADE

In the weeks that followed the Battle of St. Golan's and the skirmishes at Cragbarrow and Nordren Harbor, the war settled into a matter of course. Small border clashes or the occasional naval raid might occur, but by the end of the Month of the Falcon and the early days of Harvestide, there had yet to be any other major engagement. The barons continued to fortify their domain with a renewed sense of unity and pride. Banners bearing the symbol of the Brock, the great stone tower, could be seen flying from every precipice across the realm—more often even than the arms or devices of the local lord. Folk of every estate—from peasant to burger to landed gentry—felt their hearts swell with pride at the sight. For, just like the tower, they all understood that the Brock was the sum of its parts, with each individual stone placed precisely where it needed to be in order to create something stronger, something greater, something for all.

Of course, Brigid was not naive enough to believe that there was absolute truth to this. She knew well the ways of the gentry and that while the social classes were intended to serve one another in harmony, this was rarely the case. However, in Galadin as well as certain other places across the realm, the genuine effort was made to make this a reality, to ensure the safety and the opportunity for prosperity that one might expect from the blessed saint's birthplace.

More importantly, the effort was made because it was something that she believed was *right*, that Lughus too believed was *right*, and as she looked forward to their future together, she daydreamed about the kind of realm that she and Lughus could lead someday and how best to make that dream a reality.

She sighed, pacing about in the silence of the great cathedral of St. Aiden, appreciating the myriad colors that blazed like fire in the afternoon sunlight. Since the expulsion of Padeen Andresen, the provincial hierophant assigned to Galadin (anointed under the title of "the Breath"), the building had remained largely vacant. The cathedral and its relics were still cared for by the handmaids of the Lady, the nuns who lived in the nearby priory, but otherwise it remained largely empty. Thus, to Brigid, it had become a quiet place where she could clear her head and think.

In Blackstone, she had only very rarely visited any of the chapels or the cathedrals, and in truth, the Church of the Kinship had never been a real part of her life, as was the case for many in Dwerin. She had nothing against the faithful or the more devout followers of the Hierophants, but to her the stories had always seemed like guidelines, metaphors that were intended to provide a foundational moral philosophy to help support an individual in their search for truth. Lughus, apprentice as he was to the great Loremaster Rastis Glendaro, shared this view. It was one of the fundamental principles of the Loremaster's teachings and something that he and Rastis and his surrogate brothers, Thom and Royne, had spent years discussing and debating. Still, he warned her that there were many in the Order and across the continent who understood the Scrolls of the Hierophants not as symbolic, but as literal truth, and these folks were by far the most dangerous, for ironically, their zeal made them the most likely to commit atrocities in the name of their beliefs.

Of course, there were certain facts that seemed to go beyond the symbolic. The Gift of the Guardians, for example, and the whole business of the Anointed and their titles. It defied rational sense and seemed, if anything, more akin to what the fairy stories of her childhood described as magic. Yet, it *was* real. Absolutely real. She had the empirical evidence to prove it—not that this made it any easier to believe.

She paced along the aisle of the cathedral, and in a flash and a flurry of motion, she drew both of her blades and began to step and leap her way through an elaborate series of precise movements—thrusts, slashes, and parries. Each flowed together so naturally that she did not even need to think through them. She simply had to *act*. It always amazed her how easily it all came to her and how remarkably adaptive each motion was. It was as if she were following the steps for the most intricate dance imaginable set to music played by a bard who was constantly changing the tune. Now that she had the experience of true battle, she understood the genius of such a martial form. To be able to change, to adapt, to flow like water down a stony stream bed, was the only way to stay alive.

Her brow creased as she realized that this philosophy applied elsewhere beyond simply the arts of war. In fact, it was essentially how she had been living since she first met the Falcon in Blackstone. For, day by day and step by step, she had begun to dance, and while in the beginning, Gareth may have taken the lead, when he fell and passed the title of "the Blade" on to her, she had since proven herself time and again to be quite the virtuoso.

With a flick of her wrists, she spun Whisper and Shade around in her hands and returned them to their sheaths with a reassuring snap. Unconsciously, her hand touched the small of her back at the place where Alan had stabbed her. Unlike the other wounds she had suffered, either through battle or through her use of the Gift, this one still left a scar. A reminder, she assumed, of the oath she had sworn to uphold the duties of the Blade. It no longer caused her any physical pain, though it did bring with it feelings of sorrow and grief.

Alan Beinn. Never did she imagine she would ever have the discourtesy of meeting him in an actual battle. He had always been such a sniveling coward. Like so many noblemen, he was a spineless bully, content to abuse the servants and the poor from the safety of privilege and ignorance. He was cruel and sadistic, and in truth, the world would be far better off without him.

Lughus knew this, for her love knew a monster when he saw one. It was his prerogative as the Marshal to be able to, just as it was hers as the Blade. And yet, when the opportunity presented itself—to end Alan's evil once and for all—she had stayed his hand.

In truth, Brigid knew that it was not an act of mercy by which Alan Beinn still drew breath. It was an act of fear. In spite of everything she had done, everything that she had experienced, Alan's sudden appearance had made her afraid.

It was not that she was at all afraid of Alain himself. She was not, for she knew him for what he was and he was not in any way a match for her in a straight fight. Rather, she was afraid of what his presence might invoke in her, or more importantly, in Lughus. Alan was a perpetrator of evil, but even worse, he was a sower of evil.

She could still feel the nearly palpable fury that radiated from Lughus as he lifted Alan by the tabard to stare him down. She had to admit that in that moment, to see such contrasting figures—Alan, twisted, malicious, and wretched beside Lughus's stoic, deadly mettle—had been a different form of thrill.

He had fought for her before, and she for him, many times over by now. However, there was still something...exciting about it. In a world so barren and void of heroes, she knew that she could always count on him. Beyond that, though, there was...more. She blushed absurdly, recalling some of the lewd things Alan had said to needle Lughus.

Dibhor take you, Alan Beinn!

With a sigh, she sat down in one of the pews near the rear of the cathedral and buried her head in her hands. While her love for Lughus had come about beneath the guise of simple friendship—a comradely partnership born of a shared status as Blackguards—she would be lying to herself if she refused to admit that there was more. Annabel had teased her about it, and while she tried to feign ignorance and a type of detached objectivity as a means of maintaining some shred of dignity, she knew that it was there. She found him handsome, exceedingly handsome, from the first moment she saw him appear at the grotto to face down the Hammer. In the weeks that followed, her attraction only grew as she came to know him for not only who he was, but who he desired to be. They became inseparable, walking the city together, playing chess, sparring in the yard—talking all the while about their pasts, their thoughts, their troubles. She had never known anyone like him, never shared herself so openly with any other, never wanted to. In retrospect, their betrothal seemed almost inevitable.

She loved him—with every fiber of her being. He had become her heart, just as she had become his. And yet, in spite of that—no, *because* of that, she increasingly felt a compulsion to...express that further.

69

With a grimace, Brigid threw back her head and slouched in the pew. Again, she could feel her blush irrationally deepening. Her breath quickened and her stomach twisted into knots. At the same time, a swarm of butterflies fluttered about wildly within her chest and a wide smile spread across her tingling lips. Lady's Grace, how she loved it when he kissed her, when he wrapped his arms around her in that tight embrace. Never had she felt so safe before. Never had she felt so alive, gazing into the flashing storm clouds in his eyes, resting her cheek against the solid muscles of his shoulder or his chest. It stirred something warm within her, a warmth, an urgency, a need.

She sighed, savoring the memory of his mouth, his smile, his scent. Lately, when he practiced swordplay at the pell, he would roll his sleeves back, exposing his strong forearms and muscular hands. The sight was enough to set her blood ablaze, and she had to fight to keep from swooning. Afterwards, at night when she lie in bed, she would imagine him beside her, those arms gently embracing her, his lips tracing kisses down her neck. She wondered if he shared similar thoughts, similar impulses. His kisses certainly suggested so. However, in spite of all of their long talks about anything from their families to philosophy to ancient myths, the subject of intimacy had just never come up.

And now, here was Alan to appear out of nowhere to muck that up. Alan, for whom intimacy meant a bottle of wine and a crying servant girl, or one of the Drove sent to appease him and prevent the Sheriff from seizing her father's lands. Alan just had to make his comments, to shine an awkward light on the one part of their relationship that they had yet to figure out together.

I would certainly not lie there like a dead fish, thank you very much, Alan!

With everything that she had been forced to listen to as a member of the court at Blackstone, between her mother's soliloquies on love and Alan and his friends' boorish accounts of their conquests, there were few mysteries left in regards to what went on behind closed doors. Brigid had never embraced the chaotic frivolity of the Dwerin noble court, where the ultimate aim in life was to engage in base self-indulgence without regard for anything beyond one's own pleasure. To her, life had meaning, a person's actions had meaning, thoughts had meaning, and while she did not know if any objective meaning existed outside of an individual's own understanding, the meaning she created and the principles that she had chosen to live by prevented her from such an ignoble path. This, she believed, was what separated her from the darkness that she stood against, the exploitive nobility, and the ruthless marauders and killers—the monsters—that she fought.

Principled consciousness, Lughus had called it when she described it to him in one of their long, meandering walks. It was a phrase he said that Loremaster Rastis often used. Well, whatever it was, it was how she felt. A stark contrast between her and her mother. A rift that could never be crossed.

The sound of a door opening brought her out of her spiraling digressions and she felt a sudden flash of alarm. At once, she leapt to her feet to see Lughus walking toward her with Fergus, the faithful hound. He was dressed in the simple, everyday clothing he preferred, clothing that, to the average person, would have marked him as a common woodsman or itinerant wanderer. Certainly not a great lord and baron.

She smiled at the sight of him, ignoring the flush of heat she felt at his strong forearms.

"Found you," he said when he reached her, gently lifting her chin to kiss her.

"I wasn't hiding," she said, taking his hand in hers. "At least not from you."

His lips twisted into his little half-smile. "Is everything alright?"

She nodded spritely and hugged his arm. "How did things go with the Chough?"

His face turned grim. "He's going to pass on the title," Lughus said.

Brigid's face fell. When the Andochan commander surrendered after the Battle of St. Golan's, they were suddenly faced with the strange dilemma of what to do with him. As an anointed Guardian, he was far too powerful to be ransomed and released, but at the same time, simply executing him when he had surrendered seemed wrong, particularly as they sought to erase the stigma associated with Blackguards as bloodthirsty villains and murderers. Furthermore, both Lughus and Brigid knew that for the Chough to die without passing on his title, would mean the end of a lineage, a living history. It would be like setting fire to a library.

"I suppose that's the best possible scenario," Brigid said at last.

"There's an Andochan page dying at the priory hospital, a younger son of a minor noble. Keldorn is the family name. So long as he yet lives and swears to uphold the oath of the Chough, he'll be free to return to Andoch with Sir

Brennan's remains. We can see him as far as the coastal road when we go to see Geoffrey off in Nordren."

Brigid nodded. Geoffrey's departure was yet another surprise, though one that certainly made sense. The Brock was strong, but it could be stronger still with allies—as General Navarro and the Fighting Fifth had proven.

Geoffrey was a good man, one of the best, and he was wise, thoughtful, honest, and brave. He may not know the finer points of trade and such, but if the goal was to form a bond based on more than a common enemy and the flow of gold, she could think of no one better.

Still, she would miss Geoffrey, Annabel, and the children, even if it were only for a short while. They had become more family to her than she had ever known and she had no wish to be parted from them. With any luck, they would only be gone for a few weeks and would return by winter—long before the wedding was to take place sometime in the spring.

She released a sigh and realized with a start how long she had been silent. "I'm so sorry," she said with a laugh. "I lost myself in thought."

"It happens," he said, kissing her gently on the brow. "Places like this are designed for it."

"Yes," she said. "I suppose that's true. There is certainly plenty to look at—the carvings, the stained glass, the frescos."

Lughus gave a nod. "I spent hours researching this place back in Titanis," he said. "When I left, it was under the impression that I'd be spending the next year or so studying the artifacts and the relics. Funny that now, as the baron, this is only the third or fourth time I've actually been inside."

With a shock, she suddenly realized that the vast majority of the carvings were tombs, tombs that contained his entire line of St. Aiden. *Perindal's Sword! Baron Arcis is here, as is the mother he never knew!* At once, she felt like a trespasser, an invader, who out of ignorance committed a horrible taboo.

With an awkward reticence, she stepped away and turned to face him. "Lughus, I'm so sorry," she said. "I shouldn't have come here. It was thoughtless of me."

He gave a confused smile. "Why is that?"

"Because of...the tombs," she said hesitantly. "I'm sorry. I meant no disrespect."

All of a sudden he shook his head and gave a quiet laugh. "Brigid, they're my ghosts. They're not yours."

"But they will be. And soon."

His hand found hers again and she felt a surge of reassurance at its strength. "Fair enough," he said, "But if that's so, you should know that they do not haunt me. Not anymore. So don't let them haunt you either." He smiled. "Besides, Arcis and my mother and all the rest of the Galadins are down in the catacombs below. Only Aiden, Elisa, and Caleb are in the cathedral proper."

"I still can't help but find it strange to think that right over there lie the bones of the great saint," Brigid said, "It's like finding the legendary hero out of a storybook has suddenly come to life."

Lughus smiled kindly and gave her hand a squeeze. "Brigid," he said, "*You* are a legendary hero suddenly come to life."

For a long moment, she was silent as the magnitude of his words settled in. *He's right*, she thought, remembering *The Siege of Three*.

"Come on, Lady Blade," he said after a moment, "Let's have a closer look."

Together they made their way through the aisles toward he great stone sepulcher where the bones of Saint Aiden were entombed. Its surface was carved with the likeness of a man lying in repose, while along its sides, relief carvings depicted events from the man's life—battles against warriors with skeletal faces, a duel with an evil cleric and his acolytes, and finally, the warrior's final stand against a great beast that in some sense resembled a dragon and in others resembled a man.

Brigid gazed up at the carved likeness of St. Aiden, noticing how in the depiction he was not armed or armored, but like his descendent, clad in simple clothing that could be worn by any man. Upon his chest, his hands gripped not a sword or a shield, as one might expect of a famous warrior. Rather, he held a round, circular sphere very much like an egg or some manner of orb.

"What's that he's holding?" she asked.

"A globe, I think. You see it sometimes in depictions of nobles from the past—even in books. They were especially common in depictions of the emperors of Old Calendral. It's supposedly symbolic of the bearer's influence, that one way or another, their life somehow impacted the entire world. It's always seemed rather odd to me that Aiden should carry one. By all accounts, he was a simple man who had no designs on power. Clearly, once the legend took hold, the hierophants must have taken some liberties with the opulence of the saint's final resting place."

Brigid nodded. As she examined the orb more closely, however, her bright blue eyes noticed another strange detail—a small, oddly-shaped hole, situated directly in the center of the sphere. It did not look like the result of any damage or chipping, but as if it had always been there. She was about to investigate further when Fergus gave a loud yawn and huffed impatiently from where he lay upon the floor.

Lughus shot the hound a look. "I'm sorry," he said. "I sometimes babble on when it comes to things like this."

"Really?" Brigid smirked. "Surely I did not know that the one time you become chatty is when talking about ancient heroes and dusty old books." She hugged his arm. "Surely that is not something that I love about you."

"I know. I know." Lughus grinned. "So anyhow, do you want to head back to the castle?" he asked. "Have something to eat?"

"Yes to both," she said. "Maybe we can sit atop the keep. Play some chess?"

"As you wish." He made a clicking sound with his tongue and Fergus leapt to his feet to follow.

Outside of the cathedral, the afternoon sun shone brightly upon the Saint's Quarter. The cobblestone streets were quiet, though here and there, the occasional gardener tended to the flowers surrounding the various statues and topiary. Most were elderly peasants or wounded veterans no longer able to work a trade or push a plow. They bowed their heads as Lughus and Brigid passed, and the more bold even offered their hands to Fergus to sniff. Many of them, Brigid noticed with approval, Lughus knew by name. Unasked for, she recalled a man named Hodges back in Blackstone, a guardsman that was kind to her once, but that Alan—for no other reason than his own amusement—sought to shame.

Wretched bastard, she thought, *Why must you haunt me?*

They crossed through the archway in the Trade Quarter. Vendors sold wares of every assorted kind, from woolen clothing and blankets to fresh baked breads and pastries to various bulrush baskets and clay pottery. The sonorous clang of blacksmiths' hammers rang out across the city, while tanners worked at leather, and fletchers fashioned bundle after bundle of goose-feathered arrows. Half the work appeared to be related to the war effort: repairs to arms and armor or the creation of new pieces. However, life still carried on as always and the necessities of daily life could not be abandoned.

As in the Saint's Quarter, the burghers called out their greetings and well-wishes. Brigid responded appropriately, returning the smiles of the children or the fishwives and weavers. Yet, her mind was a fog. The insidiousness of her family was proving too much to endure and she felt, again, the terror that her past was beginning to threaten her future. Part of her wanted to run, part of her wanted to hide, and part of her felt the urge to kill something. It was maddening.

A gentle squeeze to her hand, brought her attention back to the present, and when she raised her bright blue eyes, she found Lughus's gray tempests.

"What is it?" he whispered. They were nearing the archway that passed into the Golden Quarter and the Houndstooth. "What is it that's bothering you?"

"Why do you think something's bothering me?" she asked, raising an eyebrow.

"I know something is bothering you because you get this little crease just there between your eyebrows." He flashed her a half-smile. "But it doesn't matter if I know. You need to admit it to yourself."

"Fine," she said. "There is something bothering me. I've admitted it."

"And this thing that is bothering you..." He smirked. "Does it have a name?"

Fergus sniffed the ground in a wide circle and paused to lift his leg beside the stone curtain wall. Brigid felt her jaw tense. "Yes, it has a name."

Lughus raised an implicit eyebrow. "And that name is?"

She slipped her hand free from his and folded her arms across her chest. "You know its blasted name."

"I do."

"Then why must I say it?"

"Because to know the true name of a thing is the first step on the path to understanding it."

"Rastis?"

Lughus nodded.

"Well, I know its name and the very sound of it is hateful to my ears."

"Brigid..."

"Lughus..."

He caught her hand and she halted, sighed, and turned toward him. "Fine! For the love of the bloody Brethren!" she said. "It's Alan! The wretched, bloody whoreson Alan Beinn!"

"There," Lughus smirked. They began to walk again and Fergus, having finished his business, loped after them.

"Do you feel any better?"

"Of course I don't feel better, you ass. Especially given the fact that it was I who let him go. Who knows what evil he's out there sowing as we speak?"

"Well, I did offer to kill him."

She folded her arms again. "Thanks."

Lughus breathed a sigh and took her hand. "In all seriousness," he said. "I understand. My personal hatred for him aside, to kill him in that moment— unarmed and defeated—would have been...well, something I expect he would do, and the last thing I ever want is to be anything like him."

"I don't think that's possible," Brigid said.

Lughus shrugged. "We all have bloody thoughts," he said, "as you well know."

Brigid gave a nod. They walked on a bit further in silence and she marveled at the strength of his hand, the calluses, the little scars. As she glanced down, she noticed an ink spot and wondered if he had been writing dispatches, calculating figures, or simply indulging in a bit of illumination as he sometimes still did. It made her smile and suddenly she felt not only moved by him, her future husband, but also emboldened.

"If you must know," she said, in spite of the sudden flutter in her chest, "there's something else Alan said that has been...well, that I have been thinking about. A lot recently."

"What is that?" Lughus asked. She watched as his eyes followed the flight of a small songbird—a troubadour or "trub," as they were popularly known.

She took a deep breath and fought the urge to blush. "Do...do you like kissing me?" she asked.

His eyes widened and he turned toward her. A splash of red across his cheeks. "Do I like kissing you?" he repeated.

She nodded.

"Um..." His eyes flashed. "I believe I can tell you in full faith that it is one of my favorite things in all this world."

Brigid felt her heartbeat quicken and now, in spite of any effort, she could not keep from blushing. He must have noticed because at once he began to apologize. "I'm sorry," he told her. "I...I'm sorry if that's boorish or base. I just—"

"I really like kissing you too," she interrupted. She took another deep breath. "In fact..." she tried to smile, but was certain that it must have presented more of a bashful grimace. "In fact," she said again. "I...I often think about you...more."

Lughus nodded. "I have also had...similar thoughts."

"That's...I think that's good, right?" she said, "We are betrothed after all. I mean, that's part of it, correct?"

"Brigid," he said gently. "Is this...is this because of what Alan said?"

"Yes. I mean, no. Well, in part, but not because of..." Suddenly she was mortified. "Just—just forget that I said anything. Ignore me. I'm...I'm not thinking clearly."

"Brigid..." Lughus said, turning toward her.

"Oh blood and fire! Forget I said anything!" She made to scurry off, suddenly feeling like the Mouse of her past, but he held her fast.

"Brigid," he said, the storms of his eyes crackling with lightning, "Please listen to me."

She held still, frozen by the intensity of his gaze and the sincerity of his voice. Why was she so nervous? This was Lughus, her Lughus. He was no scoundrel like Alan, or Reid, or a multitude of others—and she knew that, had known that for a long time.

Without another word, he led her along to a small patch of green where a dogwood tree stood next to a stone bench. With a wave of his hand, he invited her to sit down while he stood, leaning upon the bench beside her. Fergus trotted after them along the edge of the street.

"Now," he said, "I want to speak plainly and before I do, I just want to tell you that I love you, and if anything I say hurts your feelings or makes you uncomfortable, don't hesitate to interrupt me and tell me so." He sighed. "I'm...uncertain of any of this as well. Off the edge of the map, you might say. I have very little experience with any of this either so I want to do my best to be honest."

Brigid gave a nod and fought to keep her fingers from fidgeting.

"First..." He paused to take a breath, "Yes, I think of you and I feel...compelled toward you. Of course, I do, and if you feel that as well, I don't think that it's wrong. I know little of these things, as I said, but I am...looking forward to learning, learning *with* you, *together*."

"However," he continued. "I do not wish to push you or make you feel uncomfortable or coerced. I am not Alan or Reid." At the mention of the last name, his voice was more like a growl. "And I certainly do not want you to feel pressured by the poison that craven cousin of yours might have spat. Whatever he might say is no reflection upon you, but only highlights the loathsomeness of his own character." He rested his hands upon the pommel of his sword, took a final deep breath, and stared her full in the face.

"Do you hear me?"

In answer, she stood and overcome with feeling, wrapped her arms around him. Little by little, she felt the tension begin to leave her, as if the dark miasma Alan had cast was finally beginning to dissipate. Lughus kissed the crown of her head, and her throat thickened at the swell of love she felt for him.

"You should never fear to tell me what's on your mind," he whispered, "because—sorry to say—when I find myself lost, I fully intend to seek guidance from you." He laughed. "I already have."

Brigid gave a nod. "I know," she sighed, and ignoring the fluttering of her heart, spoke softly to him. "What do you think if some night—perhaps tonight even—what if I were to...find my way to your room? I'm not saying that we'll...that I'm quite ready for...anything." She took a deep breath. "But I would like to...start by lying with you. Side by side. If you don't mind, that is."

She could sense his smile without seeing his face. "Of course I don't mind," he said.

"You don't?"

"Of course not," he said. "As long as...as long as you feel comfortable."

She gave a nod and smiled inwardly, feeling her heart glow.

"Besides," Lughus added, "it'll certainly make things simpler for Fergus."

"For Fergus?" she asked, "What do you mean for Fergus?"

"Well, he'll no longer have to decide whose bed to lie beside."

Brigid stifled a laugh and craned her neck to kiss his lips. "Well," she said, "then I suppose for Fergus's sake, we shall have to try our best."

CHAPTER 7: THE REAVER & THE TOWER

The castle at Pridel was not nearly as grand as any of the other great citadels that Thom had seen in his short life. It lacked the classical beauty of the Grantisi cities he had seen sailing along the coast with their columns and pillars and open-aired villas. Nor could it be said that it possessed the elemental charm of Galdoran with its port and waterways, its great cathedral and its Alluvial Castle. And of course in no way could it possibly compare to the overwhelming majesty of Titanis, the great capital of Andoch and the home city of the Order of the Guardians.

However, after spending well over a year drifting about from port to port and shantytown to shantytown with Magnus, to say nothing of the last two weeks he wandering the rolling hills and wilds of Montevale, Pridel might well have been a faerie castle out of a Bard's Tale.

As Thom and his newfound companions approached the city from the south, he could make out a stout, square keep surrounded by curtain walls, squat round towers, and a small castle town that spilled out beyond its walls into the surrounding farms and peasant villages.

Additionally, just beyond it, Thom spied what amounted to a whole second town build from brightly colored pavilions and tents. While he had never seen the like before, he somehow knew it to be an army camp, and before long, everywhere he looked, men scurried about at all manner of tasks like ants upon a hill. In some ways, it reminded him of activity aboard ship, for the actions of the soldiers were marked by that selfsame sense of purpose. Yet, in spite of the obvious differences that separated the fighting men of land and sea, there was one thing that struck Thom as wholly unique in both the army camp and the castle town—the horses.

Never in his life had he seen so many! Great, towering chargers and graceful, prancing palfreys. Some were outfitted in shining steel plate while others roamed about saddle-free and wild. There were horses of all colors— from russet brown to midnight black to snowy white and every shade and combination in between. Truly, they were everywhere, and just as folk of other lands might keep dogs, so it was with the Montevalens and their horses.

For Thom, who had always been an animal lover, it was all very fascinating and it filled him with the strong desire to spend some time getting to know more about this bond, beginning with the mare that he taken at the inn.

In the half-day's ride since, he was surprised at how easily he had taken to her, for he had never been the most agile or coordinated. He could easily imagine Lughus to be a consummate rider—his obsession with his heroes would demand it—yet even Royne, as gangly as he was and as much as he hated animals (filthy creatures, he would say), Thom imagined the lanky apprentice more than capable of enforcing his will upon one if only out of stubborn rancor. So, to find that he was, by all accounts, a natural, he could not help but be surprised and even a bit proud.

True, the brown mare was not the finest of creatures, but she was sturdy and forgiving of his inexperience. He had not yet come up with a name for her, but he expected that as they knew each other better, he would figure it out. That was the way of it, the girl, Sparrow, had told him. In Montevale, a name was a thing that was earned.

At the gates of the city, they were met by a man wearing a kettle helm and a brown tabard. By all accounts he seemed little more than a sergeant, but when the other riders greeted him, Thom heard them address him as Sir Norton. It struck Thom how easy and casual the outriders were with a member of the gentry, cracking jokes and cursing, even making idle barbs at the other's expense.

Thom watched all of this with an inward sense of wonder, recalling the way the young aristocrats thumbed their noses at him and his fellows back in Titanis.

Then again, the world was a strange place. Magnus had certainly taught him that.

At length, the conversation turned to Thom.

"So they tell me you're called Thom Reaver," the knight said, "and that you're a fair hand with that chopper."

"I suppose so," Thom said, "since I'm still breathing."

He had not intended it as a joke, but it drew a round of smiles from the others.

"So is he in?" Horn asked.

"Aye," Sir Norton said. "Came in last night before sun down. The Malets took a cask of wine in their last skirmish and a few of us gathered in the hall to see to it. Apparently, he was still giving his report to the queen and never made it down."

Horn gave a snort. "Surely, he wants to be thorough."

"Always important," Sir Norton agreed. "In any case, the queen is meeting with members of the victuallers' guild today so he ain't with her. That leaves only two other places he'd be."

"We'll try the yard then," Horn said. "I'd rather not disturb him if he's with the little one."

"As you like," Norton said. He gave a sharp whistle and a wave. Moments later, the iron portcullis began to rise. "We'll see you later then, eh?" the old knight called after.

"Aye, maybe there's still some of that wine?"

"Not likely, but Shackle's always good for the forester's mash."

"We'll find something." Horn nodded to Thom. "Come on, matey."

Once inside the outer ward, the riders made their way to a long row of stables and stalls. At once, a pair of grooms ran out to meet them, taking the horses by their bridles as the riders dismounted.

"You go on ahead," Sparrow told Thom. "I'll take care of your girl there."

His eyes widened. "My girl?"

"Your horse."

"Oh," he said. "Thank you."

"You can owe me," she said with a wink.

Thom bowed his head, but himself too tongue-tied to respond with anything clever. Instead, he gave a nod, shouldered his pack, and hurried after Horn.

From the outer ward, Thom followed Horn across the grounds to the inner ward and an area where various devices and contraptions were set up for the purposes of practicing horsemanship. He was certain that Lughus would have known the proper names for such things, but Thom just thought of them as "jumping bars" and "ring-thingies" or "the swivel thing that knocks you over." Finally, on the far side of the ward was an area where six straw dummies had been set up in a circle. Directly in the center of the straw men was a man bearing a long, white spear. A large, blue-gray stallion stood silently beside him watching.

Thom eyed the man carefully, unconsciously assessing him as a potential threat. He was tall and lean, but muscular, and from the way he wielded his weapon, it was clear that he was a man intimately familiar with warfare. His simple clothing was well-made, but spotted in places with the rusty brown stains common to one who often wears armor. His hair was dark and relatively short with a light beard.

As Thom and Horn approached, he seemed not to notice them, so focused was he on the execution of his martial form. He whirled the spear around him with great precision, striking or piercing each of the straw dummies with the force of a Sorgund monsoon.

Only when he finished did he finally turn toward them, nodding in comradely fashion to Horn before fixing Thom in his green-eyed gaze. The young Reaver met his eyes unflinchingly, and in that moment Thom sensed a weariness that went far beyond the spearman's years.

"Good to see you back safely, Horn," the man said.

"How do, Cap'n?" Horn replied, "I thought I'd show you the fish we caught. As you can see, he's quite the lunker!"

The man took a deep breath and paced over to where a dipper of water waited beside the great gray horse. It was a beautiful creature, more beautiful than any horse he had ever seen, for now that he saw it close up, he noticed its coat was more than simply gray. Rather, it shone in a way that put him in mind of the great southern sea.

At once, his eyes widened and his breath caught in his chest.

A searoan? In the flesh?

His heart began to race as he marveled at the legendary creature. So many mysteries. So many new surprises.

The man finished his drink and gently ran a had along the great stallion's nose. "If Horn vouches for you," he said, "then you are welcome. What do they call you?"

An unusual feeling took hold of him, something so uncanny that he could not quite define it. As his mind continued to search for it, he misspoke.

"Thom," he said, "Thom the Reaver."

For an instant, the man's eyes widened and, absurdly, it seemed as if he exchanged a significant glance with the horse. "Did you say '*the* Reaver?'" he asked.

"Yes, sir," he said. "I did."

The man chewed his lip thoughtfully. "Are you a Guardian?"

"I...I suppose," Thom said hesitantly. "Though as yet unsworn."

"So, that would make you...a Blackguard?"

Thom winced. "I...I reckon so."

Again, the man appeared to exchange a look with the horse. Were it any other creature, such an action might have seemed comical, but there was something different about this creature, from its regal bearing to the oddly intelligent luster in its eyes.

"He made short work of the Plague Prince's men with that axe of his," Horn interjected. "I can tell you that."

"I don't doubt it," the man said. He turned back to Thom. "My name is Beledain Tremont, but I am also called the Tower."

Thom's brow furrowed. "The Tower?" he repeated. "You can't be the Tower. I know the Tower. His name is Marcus Harding."

The man—Beledain—patted the horse's nose. "Unfortunately, Marcus Harding fell almost a year ago in an attempt to end the War of the Horses. He chose me to take his place." He eyed Thom intently. "How is it that you knew him?"

Thom took a moment to gather his wits, unsure of how much to share. *The Tower? Here? And Marcus Harding fallen? What are the chances?* Then again, considering what he carried with him in his pack, it seemed well-past time for him to be surprised by whatever strange providence appeared to be directing his fate.

At length, he spoke. "I was once an apprentice to Loremaster Rastis Glendaro of the Order of the Guardians in Titanis. Marcus Harding was a friend of my master and would often spend time studying whenever he was in the city. I did not know him well, but he seemed...kind. Wise. Not exactly what you'd expect from a great warrior. He would even train with one of my brother apprentices from time to time."

Beledain's gaze narrowed. "I thought you said you were a Blackguard?"

Thom's jaw tightened and he looked away. "I don't know what I am anymore."

The Tower leaned upon his spear, continuing to eye Thom as if attempting to gauge the truth of his words. Beside him, the stallion gave a snort, shook his head, and gently nudged the warrior's shoulder. Beledain gave a nod.

"Well," he said, "I suppose we can find out together." He called to Horn. "Have a place made up for him in the guardhouse and see that he gets some clean clothes."

"Aye, sir," Horn said.

"Get yourself some food as well, Horn," he said, "We can talk after."

"Aye, sir."

Thom gave a nod. "Thank you, my lord," he said. "However, if you don't mind me asking, why are you helping me? As the Tower, you should be sending me back to Titanis right away—to either swear an Oath of Fealty to the King, or to be executed as a bloody Blackguard."

The corners of Beledain's lips curled upwards into a forlorn smile. "I'm a soldier, Thom Reaver, and while I may issue commands upon the battlefield, it's not my habit—nor do I think it's my right—to tell other men what they can or cannot be. You write that story yourself every moment of every day. *My* duty is to ensure that you have the opportunity to make that choice in the first place."

Thom gave a sigh. "You really are the Tower," he said.

Beledain nodded. "Besides, why would I send a man to face the block for something I'm just as guilty of myself?"

"What do you mean?"

"I mean that I too am a bloody Blackguard."

Over the next few days, Thom settled in to life at Pridel. He learned the names of the chief retainers, learned how to get from place to place, and helped Sparrow wherever he could with her duties.

Strangely, as he adjusted to the culture and customs of Montevale, be began to realize that, without ever having the slightest intention of doing so, he had somehow become rather cosmopolitan. For on the whole, the horse-lords were a more rustic, earthy people than the fine nobles of Andoch and Titanis; however, at the same time, they lacked the brashness of the Wrathorn or the guile of the Sorgunders. There was a nobility and a pageantry to the Montevalens—that was certain—with their heraldry and their nicknames, but there was also a pragmatism to them that could only have been borne from a century of war.

Thom recalled once long ago he had asked Rastis if the old Loremaster ever missed his home back in Baronbrock. Without even the slightest hesitation, the old man replied, "Every day." He then went on to explain how, to the people of the Brock, the land itself was something with which they felt a deep, almost spiritual connection. Even among the nobles, the land itself was not something that they *owned*. Rather, the people of the Brock— from the loftiest baron to the lowliest peasant—belonged to the land. It was why, after his death, St. Aiden had requested that his bones be returned to his homeland, to his family, to the place where his heart resided.

There was something of that sentiment to the Montevalens as well, though—Thom could not help but sense—it was mingled with something else. A sorrow. A grief. As if the land had been wounded and now simply languished, awaiting a time when it would once again be made whole. When he looked into the eyes of the men—and women—of the rebel army, it was clear how desperately they sought to heal that wound.

As the days went by, word continued to circulate that the queen intended to hold a feast. Thom, who had somehow fallen in with Horn, Sparrow, and the other skirmishers of the light cavalry, would be permitted to attend.

It was a new experience for him, this belonging. Until now, he had only ever felt it while in the company of Lughus and Royne, or—to a certain extent—with Magnus. Sigruna's crew had never accepted him, nor had anyone else in his mad sojourn around the Sorgund Isles. Pryce and the cadets simply bullied him, and apart from Rastis and Hob, the elder men of the Loremaster's Tower seemed oblivious to his (or anyone else's) existence.

It was strange. When Sparrow and Donovan appeared beside him at his bunk as he was making notes in his journal, he looked up at them in uncertainty. When the young woman cocked her head to one side and said "Oi, let's go," he was even more confused, but stowed his pack alongside his axe, and followed along anyway. When they arrived at the hall and sat down across from Sir Norton, who promptly began pouring them tankards of ale, he was utterly perplexed.

They were all so easy with one another, and he was shocked that this easiness should be extended to include him. It made him curious about the man with the spear that he had met earlier, this new Tower, and curious about the queen that he served. He had hidden Callah's Key within the straw mattress of his bunk, but he longed to share it with someone else, someone strong and wise who could be trusted. Between what he knew about the Keepers and the Army of the Dead, he was just so confused. He longed for someone to give him a direction, to just tell him what to do—not because he wanted to shirk his responsibilities, but because he so desperately wanted to do the *right* thing. He had failed so many times before and he knew that whatever it was he was caught up in—the storm, as Magnus called it—was far too important for him to risk failing again.

Yet every time he imagined himself speaking aloud about what he had seen in the Lighthouse it sounded so ridiculous, so absurd, that he feared no one would believe him and that he would instead condemn the people he had thought to save.

Before long, the hall had filled to the extent that folk unable to find a seat were content to stand. A small band of musicians played jaunty tunes on pipes and fiddles, and in addition to the pitchers of ale, servants began serving from great casks of wine. Horn appeared with a blond knight named Sir Welmsey and an assortment of other folk of varying ranks and degrees. Thom did his best to remember names, but since so many of the men also had titles and nicknames, it soon became too overwhelming. Luckily, no one seemed to mind if he made a mistake.

A short while later, a cheer rang out announcing the arrival of the Tower. Beledain was dressed simply in austere shades of green and gray, and that his clothing was chosen entirely for its function over fashion. He gave a nod to acknowledge the cheering of the assembled folk, but beyond this humble show of appreciation, he was content to fade into the background. For some reason, Thom was suddenly reminded of Lughus. Not that they looked alike. They did not—Lughus with his mop of golden hair and gray eyes, while the Tower was dark and green-eyed—but something about the way they carried themselves, their bearing, was similar. A quiet confidence or mettle that told all who met them that when push came to shove, they would do what needed done.

The memory of Lenard's Crossing came flooding back, and Thom felt the urge to slip into a wistful melancholy—or would have, had the entire assembly not suddenly risen to their feet to pay their respects to the rebel queen.

Over the course of his journey with Magnus, Thom had encountered many women, most of whom had made physical beauty their stock and trade. They used pastes, powders, and pigments to augment their appearances, dressed (or were dressed) in the finest, most fashionable clothing they (or their employers) could afford. Despite all of their efforts, they could not even begin to compare to the natural beauty and grace of the Winter Rose.

So that's the queen, eh? he heard Magnus's voice say, *Looks like one of those fair maids you used to sing about to the Sorgund whores.*

"I suppose so," Thom muttered.

Too skinny for my liking.

"I never considered you to be all that discerning."

Oi! Fuck off! The odd specter of Magnus grunted somewhere in the back of Thom's mind. *Does this mean the Crusher finally fancies a lass, eh? Sure enough the bloody Reaver gave you more than just the Reaver's skill with the axe, eh?*

"It's not like that," Thom said. "She just...she has kind eyes. Most nobles I've ever known have eyes of stone."

Fair enough.

"Besides. It's clear as day she's smitten with the Tower—and he with her."

"Plain as the nose on their faces," Sir Norton said. "But it took near a year before either of them was willing to admit it."

Thom's eyes widened with alarm at the realization that he had spoken his last comment aloud. "I'm sorry," he said, "I meant no disrespect."

Donovan shook his head. "It's what you might call an open secret," he said. "They still think no one knows, but of course, we all do."

"Welcome it, in fact," Welmsey said. "But that's our Prince Bel."

"What do you mean?" Thom asked.

"Well," Horn said. "He fears he'll scandalize the queen or somehow call into question her rule."

"And he don't want to disrespect the memory of the mother to his son," Sparrow said.

"Though I'd say we're well past any mourning period," Norton said. "And besides, Marina loves at little one as if he were her own."

"It's not that simple to the prince, though." Horn said. "You know how he is."

Thom listened to their conversation, little by little piecing together the events of the last year—from the surprise Gasparan victory at the White Wood to Marcus Harding's death at Clearpoint, and finally the birth of the rebellion and the defeat of the Deathknell. Some events he had heard bits and pieces of in his travels with Magnus, though at the time, he paid them little mind. Never in his wildest imagination did he ever believe that he would find himself in the land of the horselords. Without intending to, he found his eyes drawn time and again to the high table with the Tower and the Queen, wondering once more if he should confide in them regarding the Key.

He continued to deliberate as the meal was served, though he found himself easily distracted by the folk, the food, and the abundant good cheer. In his former life as an apprentice, there were few things Thom had loved more than feasting. However, whether due to his experiences of life at sea, or the near-starvation he had been forced to endure before meeting Horn, Sparrow, and Donovan, he found that he just couldn't tuck it away as he once could. To his surprise, he realized that—at least to a degree—he appeared to have lost weight.

Of course, he was by no means lean—quite the opposite in fact—but he had lost much of the softness to his appearance. His rotund shape now had a certain firmness to it, like that of a bear or a wild boar. He was uncertain how to feel about this change.

So much is different, he thought inwardly. *So much has changed.*

I told you as much, Crusher, Magnus's voice said, *You'd best be ready.*

As if on cue, there was a commotion at the entry to the hall and a somewhat ghastly man entered dressed in the raggedy garb of a forester or a beggar. His arms were as thick as tree trunks and a great scar ran the length of his scalp. A long iron chain encircled his waist, ending in what seemed a farmer's sickle. At once, Thom knew him to be another of the Anointed. With dogged purpose, he stalked forward through the hall toward the dais and the high table, pausing only once to fix Thom with a penetrating stare. In spite of his newfound confidence, Thom could not avoid a sudden chill. It lasted only a moment before the man continued on, but it was more than enough to stoke his curiosity.

A murmur of concern passed through the folk seated near Thom, particularly as the forester reached the high table and began making his report directly to the Tower and the queen.

"This can't be good," Donovan muttered.

Sparrow breathed a sigh and drained what little remained in her tankard.

"Hush now," Sir Norton said. "The prince is about to speak."

Sure enough, after a brief discussion with the queen and another knight— a bald man with a thick mustache—the Tower stood from the table and raised his hand for quiet.

"Riders of the Plague Prince have been sighted north of the White Wood," he said simply. His green eyes gazed out over the assembled retainers. "I ride to meet them. Who will join me?"

A sudden cheer echoed throughout the hall and at once, men and women began rising to their feet, swearing oaths, and clapping each other on the back. Thom rose with them, marveling that the prospect of battle, from which some of them might not return, could fill them with such excitement. Even more surprising, however, was that he felt this fire kindling within his own breast as well.

"So you're to join us then, Thom Reaver?" Sparrow said, elbowing him in the arm as they made their way out of the hall. The sky was gray and overcast, though it did not look like rain.

"I suppose it's only right," he replied, "The queen and the Tower have been more than hospitable."

"Good," said a gruff voice. Thom turned to see the scarred forester standing just behind him and he felt the same shock of familiarity as when he met the Tower. "We can find out what there is to you," he mused.

Sparrow gave a nod. "Oi there, Shackle," she said, "It was you that spied the riders?"

The Shackle pursed his lips and spit. "Aye," he said, "Looks to be another raiding party. Not sure what lord, but they've got plenty of those red-cloaked bastards with them too."

"Kingsmen," Thom said.

"Aye," the Shackle told them, "And I've heard tell that there's a ship that's been hugging the coast looking for a landing as well. Might be that the Plague King is sending men by sea so as to try and catch us by surprise."

Thom's brow furrowed. "Could be Sorgunders too," he said. "Looking to trade…or worse."

"I'm sure we'll find out sooner or later," the forester said with a ghastly grin.

After retrieving his axe and ensuring the Key was safely stowed, Thom saddled his mare (with the help of his newfound comrades), and joined the massing column of horsemen. Before long, the small force had assembled behind the Tower and beside him, a young knight raised the banner of the Winter Rose.

"We ride!" Prince Beledain shouted. The searoan stallion reared and shook his glorious mane. The horsemen broke into a cheer and, as one, spurred their mounts to follow their lord.

Thom took a deep breath, patted his mare upon the flank, and joined them.

CHAPTER 8: EXORDIUM

Three days had passed since Royne had been admitted into the walled complex of the University. In that time, he had been fed, bathed, and given a fresh set of clothes. He was quartered in a small, sparsely furnished cell with a bed, a simple writing table, and a small basin for washing. A single window provided plenty of light, but was high enough on the wall that he could not see out of it. Occasionally, the sound of a horn or the chatter of birds would reach him, but for the most part, the only noise was the whisper for the wind.

He was surprised at just how weak and exhausted he had been. In his vigil at the gates, he had spent so much time in thoughtful contemplation that he had neglected the needs of his body. As such, he had yet to really explore his new surroundings or interact with any of the University's other inhabitants. He recognized that a few individuals had come by to look in on him or to bring him food, but otherwise it was all a hazy memory.

Only now did he finally feel like he had regained control of his faculties. He sat upon the edge of his bed, *The Book of Histories* upon his lap, staring bleary-eyed into the soft light of the morning. It was not particularly early, but it was also not nearly hot enough to be noon. He thought about leaving to go wander about the place, though eventually decided against it, considering not only his status as a guest, but also the University's reputation.

Regardless, he did not have long to wait before Udo, the man who had more or less facilitated his stay, appeared in his doorway.

"You have regained your balance," he observed.

"I believe so," Royne said. "Though, to be honest, I cannot remember falling ill." His brow narrowed. For whatever reason, those who were anointed with a Guardian title were said to be immune to pestilence and plague. It was why he was able to cure the Gray Wolf's infection. *Perhaps it is all just nonsense after all...*

Udo watched him thoughtfully, his face curious, but free of skepticism or judgment. "Would you like to see where it is you find yourself?" he asked. "Some of it you may recall—the kitchen, the baths, the hall—though you were so close to swooning, that you may not remember it."

Royne chewed his lip. He vaguely recalled certain flashes of memory, but it was like trying to remember the details of a book he had heard of but never read. "I would not mind a bit of a stretch," he said.

Udo nodded and clasped his hands behind his back.

Against the stiffness in his legs, Royne stood up from the bed, shouldered his satchel containing *The Book of Histories*, and followed the old man out of the room.

"This is the dormitory," Udo told him, waving an arm up and down the hallway. Six wooden doors stood evenly spaced on each side of the hall, with Royne's room being second from the last on the western-facing side.

"Are all of these rooms occupied?" Royne asked.

Udo shrugged. "Not all. Some of the elder philosophers have quarters closer to their work rooms."

"Exactly what kind of work is it that you do here?"

"We think, mostly," the older man said. "On some days, we learn." He led Royne down the stairs to the first floor and through another short hallway into a large, circular hall. Small, round tables, evenly spaced, occupied the center of the room beneath a high, vaulted ceiling. Light streamed in through large, glass windows, and a variety of people in similarly simple tunics—both men and women—sat about reading, writing, or conversing in low tones. Most appeared to be of Kordish descent, though there were certainly others as well—from native Grantisi to still others who, at least by way of appearance, hailed from lands far beyond Termain. A wide, stone staircase spiraled upwards to additional floors and as Royne took in the height and breadth of the space, he surmised that he must be standing in the large, bronze-topped building at the heart of the complex.

"Would you like something to eat?" Udo asked.

"Perhaps later," Royne said. As he peered up at the vaulted ceiling, he suddenly realized intricate patterns etched in the bronze. Inwardly, he was impressed—even fascinated—though outwardly, his face remained impassive. "The patterns of the stars," he observed. "Unfortunate that with their movements, it is only accurate for a specific part of the year."

"Oh, it shifts," Udo said casually, "The plates are made to slide and move as the heavens move." He motioned out across the floor. "This is our symposium," he said. "Functionally, it is the same as one of your great halls, though we do not differentiate by order and degree." He pointed to a series of doors along the rear wall. "Through there are the kitchens, that way leads to the baths—which you've already seen—and the passage over there will eventually lead you to the stables."

"And I take it that's the way we came in?" Royne said, nodding to the large foyer to his right.

"It is," Udo said.

Royne glanced back and forth. Slowly, he was beginning to recall certain pieces of his arrival. He remembered the baths—large, tiled basins, the thick clouds of steam, and the iron boilers that kept the water warm. There was a separate section for men and another for women, and in his stupor, he got turned around and nearly stumbled into the wrong one.

"If you're ready to continue..." Udo said.

Royne gave a nod and the older man led him up the great stone staircase to the second floor and on to the third. As they walked, they passed more and more people wandering here and there. Some eyed him with a degree of curiosity, though to most—lost in the worlds of their own private thoughts—he was a ghost.

"I suppose you wonder why it is I came here?" Royne asked. He glanced into the rooms along the perimeter of the great round building, noting that in one, two people were crushing herbs and boiling water in various glass apparatuses, while in another, a half dozen people seemed to be swaying and moving as if attempting to perform the world's slowest dance. In another, a man was copying a manuscript at a lectern, while in yet another, a young woman pruned small potted trees.

It was strange. In some ways, the atmosphere was reminiscent of the Loremaster's Tower back in Titanis—the quiet, the contemplation, the almost palpable sense of focus. There was even a vague sense of uniformity in their linen tunics, which appeared much more appropriate given the Grantisi climate. However, the University differed greatly in one very stark manner: there were few books—or at least, fewer.

"You told me some of your intentions when we met at the gate," Udo shrugged. He continued up the next staircase to the third floor and paused outside of a door. "But come." He gestured for Royne to enter. "We can talk here."

Inside, the room was well-lit by another series of large windows, and in the center of the room two tables were adorned with more glass apparatuses, the functions of which Royne could only guess at. A large set of shelves stood along one wall filled with an odd assortment of bottles, pots, and bowls. Beside it was a writing desk with a pair of wooden chairs, and beyond it, in the far corner of the room, a door opened into another small cell with a simple bed and a wooden trunk.

"Would you like to sit?" Udo asked.

Royne shrugged. "Sure." In truth, he did not care, but given the circumstances, he was trying to be less abrasive than usual, which only served to make him more awkward.

He set down his satchel with *The Book of Histories* beside one of the chairs and sat. Udo took the seat across from him and folded his arms across his chest.

"So..." Udo said.

"So," Royne repeated.

"To what end have you come to us?"

Royne's gaze narrowed. "To what end?"

"For weeks, you were observed waiting outside of our gates with no invitation, nor did you receive any indication that you would ever be admitted. Yet, every day after day after day, there you were." Udo shrugged. "Were I a man to meddle in the affairs of others, I suppose I would wonder—why?"

Royne breathed a sigh. "I seek your aid."

"And what leads you to believe that we have any aid to provide to you? You mentioned an enemy. I can tell you right now that my people and I are not warriors so we cannot aid you in that regard, nor would we, as we are a peaceful people who abhor violence."

"So do I," Royne said. "But though I may wage war against an enemy, my fight is not one of arms and armor, but of knowledge."

"And you think that knowledge is not as dangerous or as destructive as a sword?"

"Oh no," Royne said. "I believe it is far greater. However, when it comes to defending the meek and safeguarding the innocent, it is also stronger than the strongest of castle walls."

"And this enemy you face, you believe they threaten the meek and the innocent?"

"I do."

"And so you would have knowledge to fight back against them, thusly threatening the meek and the innocent of their lands as well?"

Royne shook his head. "No," he said. "Though I understand why you might think that, for this is generally the way of war. Strike and strike back. However, that is not my way, for like you, I am no warrior."

"Then what are you?" Udo asked.

Royne paused. There was no sense in being evasive. He took a deep breath. "I am the Loremaster."

"The Loremaster?" Udo asked. "You mean, of the Guardians?"

Royne nodded. "Yes," he said, "or at least, I was. Now I find myself...at odds with the Order, for I believe they have lost their purpose and now inflict greater harm than good. Worse still, I feel like they have become the puppets to an even greater threat, one that I suspect, but do not entirely know, and it is this threat that I hope to somehow eliminate for the sake of the people and the sake of the world."

Udo's brow furrowed and he stroked his chin in deep thought. At last, he spoke. "I am familiar with your Order," he said at last, "And with its philosophy and religion—both before and after the appearance of your great saint. Like all forms of thinking, it has its good points and its bad, its wise men and its zealots. I ascribe to a different set of beliefs. However, I too know what it is like to see one's principles corrupted for the sake of the powerful.

Unfortunately, I have no advice for you, nor do I have any answers. I'm afraid I have little to offer in terms of combating the tyranny of your King."

"But this place," Royne said, "In all the city, despite the all the best efforts of the kingsmen and the Order, this place remains safe. Surely there must be some secret, some defense."

"Of course," Udo said, "For when the world falls to discord, the only one strong enough to withstand it is the man who knows true balance in his mind and in his heart."

"What do you mean?" Royne asked, arching an eyebrow. "You say finding balance is what has protected you from invading soldiers."

"In one sense," Udo mused. "Though one might argue that finding balance is the only way to keep anything alive."

Royne narrowed his gaze and scratched his jaw. "As the Loremaster, it is my prerogative to seek out knowledge and to stand for wisdom in whatever ways I can so long as it leads to the creation of better world."

"And what does that mean?" Udo asked. "A 'better' world? I imagine from his perspective, the Guardian-King believes that by subjugating the continent, he is creating a 'better' world."

Royne nodded. "Man is but a single eye staring out at all the world," he said. "We view the world from a single perspective, and, as such, our understanding is always incomplete. Yet, if we seek out other ideas or new ways of thinking to supplement our own limited knowledge, may we not overcome our own limitations and find ourselves that much closer to truth?"

Udo pursed his lips. "A wise maxim," he said.

"So," Royne asked, his eyes ablaze with anticipation. "Will you teach me of the Sign of Four? Will you teach me what it is to be an alchemist?"

The older man sighed. "No," he said. "I cannot."

The young Loremaster's brow creased. "Why not?"

Udo was silent for a moment before answering. "Now," he began, "Please understand that I mean no offense to you personally. You seem to be quite passionate about your desire to create this better world. However, as we just discussed, the notion of 'better' is a concept that varies from individual to individual."

Royne's face fell. "I understand what you mean to say, but I assure you, my intentions are pure, especially compared to King Kredor—or worse—his advisor, Natharis Tainne."

"I want to believe you," Udo said. "But it is a risk that the world cannot afford to take. Alchemy is dangerous and in the wrong hands it can have devastating results. Thus, at this time, I must decline."

Royne raised an eyebrow. "At this time?"

Udo stood slowly from his chair. "Walk with me, Royne."

Clenching his jaw to suppress his frustration, Royne stood and began to follow Udo back the way they had come. "Do you know why we say the Sign of Four?" the older man asked.

Royne shook his head.

"It is because of this," he lifted his medallion before him and indicated the simple, four-sided figure etched into the bronze. "The four dynamic elements of nature—earth, fire, air, and water. Individually, they may exist, but when combined in various orders or degrees with one another, they create all manner of things. These things then make up the physical world we inhabit, the physical world of which we ourselves are a part."

"However," Udo continued, "Existence, creation, the world itself—as least in so far as we know it—can only be maintained so long as these primal elements are able to coexist in a manner that finds balance—harmony. Disrupt that balance by even the slightest degree, and the harmony gives way to the destructive power of discord."

"This is at the heart of alchemy, of the philosophy of the Sign of Four. For just as all things are created by the balance of the elements, all things are also subject to the effects of harmony and discord. Nature, society, the self. An alchemist is one who is dedicated to the pursuit of harmony, but also understanding the effects of discord. With knowledge of the relationships that exist between these elemental forces, we alchemists can affect great change—upon simple objects as well as the larger world."

Royne's eyebrows narrowed. "What do you mean that they can affect the larger world?"

"Consider this," Udo said, "A log in the fireplace exists in harmony, correct? It is a stable object. It sits there. It simply is. The distribution of elements within the object, the log, are in balance. They need not be the same—in a log, I believe, it is primarily earth, though with latent elements of water and perhaps some sense of air. Regardless. It exists. It is."

"However," he added, "If we upset the balance—we introduce heat, for example, exciting the dormant igneous content—we disrupt the harmony of the object. Discord reigns. The log ignites."

"Now, the same effects of harmony and discord on the log here, can be true for individuals and entire societies as well. A stable society or individual is one who lives in balance or in harmony. In that society or individual, all opposing forces are essentially countered by another. When they fall out of alignment, though, it creates instability, which can lead to discord and, ultimately, strife."

Royne shook his head. "But this does not explain how you have been able to prevent the kingsmen from besieging this place, or the fates of those men who have tried."

Udo pursed his lips. "When an alchemist is able to achieve perfect harmony within himself, he is able to affect the harmony of the world outside himself as well. Of course, the same can also be said for those who embrace discord and achieve a perfect strife. In either case, the individual achieves a certain degree of power that is beyond the reach of average people. While that power can be used to improve the world, far too often, it is used for something much, much worse, and I would not see such strife inflicted ever again."

"Thus," Udo said at last, "While I invite you to stay with us, to learn with us, and to discuss your ideas with us, I cannot teach you alchemy until I know for certain that you will do no harm."

Royne breathed a sigh. Without realizing it, he had followed Udo, back down the great staircase to the symposium. "If you will not teach me," he asked, "then what am I to do?"

Udo shrugged. "As I said, you are welcome to stay here as long as you like so long as you do not create discord. Who knows? Demonstrate to us that you seek only harmony, and perhaps we will teach you," he said. "Of course, if that does not appeal to you, you are also free to leave. Just know that if you do, for the safety of my people, you will not be allowed to return."

Royne gave a nod and pinched the bridge of his nose. *Damn it, Salasco,* he thought. *This was a bloody waste of time.*

"Now, if you'll excuse me," Udo said, "I have some other matters to attend to."

"Thank you," Royne muttered, bowing his head. Udo returned the gesture and then departed back up the stairs the way they had come. For a long moment, Royne simply stood, uncertain of what to do. He simply stood upon the edge of the symposium, staring into the middle distance, his mind all a blur. Alchemists both young and old passed by on innumerable private errands.

Finally, he came to discern a nearby conversation between a small crowd of younger alchemists gathered around one of the tables. They appeared to be near enough his own age, perhaps a year or two older. He did not know exactly what it was that they were talking about, but as their voices carried so clearly, they soon had his full attention.

"I still say that it cannot be done. Not without direct contact," a young man said. In appearance and speech, he was typical of the Grantisi populace—olive complexion, dark hair, and dark eyes. If Royne had to guess, he seemed a standard representative of the successful middle-class citizen, the son of a merchant or a minor official. "You cannot do it, Amara," he continued. "Your mind will break."

"If that is true, then why do you refuse to bet?" said a young Kordishwoman. She smiled at the man in a way that seemed pleasant, menacing, and mischievous all at once.

Beside her, another young man, tapped his chin in thought. He was lean and muscular, though not quite so lean as the woman nor as muscular as the Grantisi man. His complexion had a warm, amber tone and his hair was dark and smooth. Like the others, he spoke the common tongue of Termain, though with the slightest hint of an accent Royne could not place, for it was neither Kordish nor Tulondis, but marked by a type of musical inflection.

"The masters are not fond of competition like this," he said softly. "Particularly with the dangers involved."

"Ha!" Amara said, "The masters are too busy examining their own navels to care." She leered at the Grantisi youth, "So what will it be, Fabius?"

"You should listen to Haruki," Fabius said coldly. "But, seeing as you will not, I will take the bet—so long as I get to choose the element."

"Let me choose the wager, and I will let you choose the element."

"Do you take me for a fool?"

"No, I take you for someone who hates shoveling shit beneath the ox mill," she said. "I take you for someone who might be willing to bet..." Her brow wrinkled in thought. "Three months of shit duty?"

Fabius raised his eyebrows. "So you're saying that if I win the bet, you'll take my shifts at the mill?"

'And if I win, you'll take mine."

"For three months?"

"Three months."

Fabius's lips twisted into a satisfied sneer. "Deal," he said, "And as for the element, I choose..." He paused. "I choose fire."

"Fire. Fine," Amara said, "Haruki?"

Haruki produced a lacquered box and from within it, he drew out a small wooden dowel no longer than a finger. He was about to hand it to Fabius when suddenly his eyes fell upon Royne and he froze.

"I am not so sure we should be doing this," he said quietly. "The outsider is watching."

At once, Royne felt extremely exposed as the eyes of the others fell upon him.

Amara gave a snort. "I do not think we need to worry about him," she said, turning back to the group. "He does not look very wise. With that pinched face of his, he looks more like a fox or a...polecat."

Royne instantly bristled, but he was suddenly so flustered by the young woman's brazenness that he could not think of a clever enough retort.

Fabius grimaced. "What if he says something? I have no wish to upset the masters."

"So then you forfeit?"

"I didn't say that."

Amara sighed and turned to address Royne. "Polecat!" she called. "Hey! Polecat! Come here!"

Not knowing what else to say or to do, Royne approached the table. His mind had suddenly turned to wood and he found he could not find his tongue to speak. Amara nodded to Haruki. "Give him the dowel," she said.

For a moment, it seemed Haruki was about to protest, but instead, he stood and walked over to Royne. "Here," he said, handing him the small piece of wood. "Hold it up away from your face."

The young Loremaster did as he was instructed.

"Now," Amara said, "Without touching..." She extended her hand, palm side out, and shut her eyes in concentration. The rest of the group fell completely silent and Royne, still not quite certain of what strange contest he had been roped into, continued to hold out the dowel, watching.

Little by little, he could see the strain and intensity steadily increasing upon Amara's face. Her eyes shut even tighter and the veins at her temples and in her arm began to stand out. A bead of sweat appeared on her brow, followed by another, and then another. Fabius's eyes narrowed, watching the dowel intently, and shifting his weight from side to side. Haruki shook his head slightly, a look of mild disapproval on his face. "If your vision begins to fade, you must stop," he said.

"And if you pass out, you still lose," Fabius added.

Amara continued to strain and her breathing grew heavier and more labored, as if she were running up a mountain. Finally, grinding her teeth, she curled her hand and pointed with a single finger at the tip of the dowel.

What in the black abyss is going on here? Royne wondered.

As if in answer, there was a brilliant flash, the smell of burning, and all of a dancing flame sparked to life upon the top of the dowel. He was so surprised by what he had seen that he nearly dropped it and threw up his hands in shock. At once, Fabius and a few of the other young people let out frustrated groans, while the rest clapped their hands and cheered.

The task accomplished, Amara laughed and fixed Fabius with a mischievous grin. "You can check the schedule for my mill duties," she told him, "And know that with every scoop of shit, I appreciate it."

Fabius's mouth twisted into an irritated leer. "I should have known better than to accept your challenge," he muttered. "But I'll honor it."

He walked off with his companions in tow and shortly thereafter the rest of the small crowd began to dissipate leaving Royne alone with only Haruki and Amara.

"Well, what do you think, Polecat?" Amara asked.

Royne fought to keep his face impassive as he continued to stare at the small flame. "Remarkable," he whispered aloud.

"I bet you've never seen anything like that before outside of these walls?" the girl said with an arrogant leer.

Royne shook his head and rubbed his eyes. "Was that..." he began, "That wasn't—?"

"That was Alchemy," Haruki said. "True alchemy."

"Or as the fools outside these walls will call it..."

Amara bent to blow out the small flame still smoldering upon the tip of the dowel in Royne's hand.

"Magic!"

CHAPTER 9: THE VOYAGE OF THE VANGUARD

By the midpoint of Harvestide, Geoffrey, his family, and two score of archers—volunteers from the Galadin peasant levees—had set sail aboard Theo Nordren's personal flagship, the *Swordfish*.

The *Swordfish* was a large three-masted carrack and the pride of the Nordren fleet. While the majority of the trading vessels employed by the barony consisted of galleys, caravels, flutes, and cogs, the *Swordfish* was a class of its own. Heavier, sturdier, and capable of carrying considerably more cargo or men, it was as fine a vessel as could be found anywhere across the continent. Theo Nordren, heir to the Nordren barony, commanded the ship personally, though on a day-to-day basis, the vessel was captained by an old mariner named Roderick Dawes.

A lifelong sailor of the Nordren merchant fleet, Captain Dawes knew his ship and his crew well, and with the captain himself at the helm, the *Swordfish* was able to slip through the Andochan blockade and head east along the southern coastline.

Due to Montevale's proximity to the Brock, Geoffrey expected the journey to take no more than a few days. However, as Theo explained, the city where the rebel queen held court was closer to the realm's interior. As a result, they would sail eastward around the far end of the continent before turning north and west to drop anchor along the coast. From there, it would be a few days' march inland to Pridel.

"Call me superstitious," Theo said, "but it may be an extra day or two going around the horn as well. For I intend to give Castone and the Lighthouse an extra wide berth."

"Why is that?" Geoffrey asked. "I thought sailors welcomed a lighthouse."

"Not this one."

"But why?"

Theo gave a shrug. "I can't say really. It's just a place all sailors shun. Bad luck or some such."

Geoffrey gave a nod. The mention of the Lighthouse seemed to trigger something in the back of his mind, the part that appeared to be occupied by the Vanguard. It was a vague feeling of disquiet, unease, and he knew at once that Castone's reputation was not merely built upon superstition.

"Whatever you believe is best, Cap'n," Geoffrey told the young Nordren.

"It won't extend the trip by too much longer," Theo said. "Not many proper ports in Montevale either. We'll have to ferry the men in with the launch and make our way best we can. If you like, your family can wait aboard the ship with Dawes and the crew until we send for them."

"Thanks to you and to Captain Dawes," Geoffrey said, "but we're a family of farmers, and I think I can speak for all of us when I say that farmers can only go so long without the feeling of solid ground beneath their feet."

"As you wish, Sir Geoffrey," the young Nordren said.

When all was said and done, a full ten days passed between when the *Swordfish* first set sail and when they came ashore, for a sudden squall delayed the ship as they passed around the tip of the continent, despite their extra efforts to avoid Castone.

At one point, during a particularly violent point in the storm, Geoffrey peered through the rain and the waves only to spy an eerie white pinpoint of light shining out from the rocky shore. It was only for an instant, but in that moment he could not escape an intense feeling of terror mingled with despair, as if all of his efforts, all of his life was fated to end in ruin. Only when he returned below decks and beheld the faces of his wife and children was he able to shake off the dark malaise.

They put to shore near a small fishing village along the northeastern coast of Montevale. The land here was not like the coastal plains of Grantis or the Spade, but was marked by rockier soil and uneven terrain as they began the slow march westward into the interior of the realm. Geoffrey marched at the head of the column accompanied by Annabel, Freddy, and Greta, with Theo and a half-dozen Nordren men-at-arms on horseback. The two score of archers were led by a pair of sergeants, Lachlan and Bryce, and supported by a supply wagon drawn by a pair of oxen. Each man as equipped with his war bow, quiver, and either a handaxe or some other manner of improvised melee weapon. Of course, with any luck, they would reach Pridel without running afoul of King Dermont's men.

Geoffrey still had little idea what to say or do. Adolfo and Lughus had provided him with various dispatches and documents, and the Madder had spent as much time as he could instructing Geoffrey on the finer points of diplomacy. Yet, Geoffrey could not help but feel woefully out of his element. Trade relations, numbers, and other such figures were not his area of expertise, and though he said as much on numerous occasions, Adolfo seemed to pay it no mind. He simply nodded, folded his hands, and said, "Geoffrey, you will do fine," before launching once more into an analysis of the price of wool or grain.

Yet, regardless of these misgivings, Geoffrey could do little else but shrug and carry on. He no longer allowed himself to be crippled by doubt or fear, but would simply do his best. Even back in Pyle, this had always been his way. For in a life so full of struggle and hardship, what else could a man do but try?

They were three days inland from the coast when the column came upon the eaves of a forest consisting entirely of tall, white birch trees. Since their arrival at the fishing village, they had made little contact with the Montevalen locals. Every so often they might pass a small collection of peasant hovels and one night they made camp beside an old stone sheepfold. With the realm at war with itself, Geoffrey was reluctant to approach any larger settlements or estates, uncertain as to which side of the conflict the master of the castle might belong.

"According to the fisherfolk, Pridel lies on the far side of the forest," Theo said. He motioned toward the pallid trees. "But Hound's Bollocks! The place has an ill-favored look."

Geoffrey chewed his lip and cast a discerning glance upon the wood. The wisps of mist common to the vale did indeed grant it a certain ghostly appearance. "Do you see a path through?" he asked.

"No," Theo said, "and I'd rather not make one. I say we go around."

Geoffrey gave a nod. "We'll follow it along the northern edge. That way, if we spy any trouble on the plain, we can use the trees for cover."

"And if the threat lies within?"

"Then we shall just have to keep a sharp eye."

Theo bobbed his head in agreement and rode back to his men.

Geoffrey watched him go. Truth be told, he was becoming increasingly frustrated with the young nobleman. Theo was a friendly enough sort, but he was clearly a different manner of noble than Lughus or Brigid or even Roland Marthaine. He was the type who was used to being dressed rather than dressing himself. That did not make him a bad person, of course. However, it seemed to suggest a certain level of expectation in regard to how he received and was received by others.

Theo's choice to join the journey inland was somewhat surprising as well, particularly when he could have simply stayed aboard his ship. Inwardly, Geoffrey suspected that the nobleman saw it as an opportunity to distinguish himself in a more heroic light rather than simply remain his father's heir.

In any case, Geoffrey led the column along the eaves of the forest, vigilantly watching for any sign of friend or foe. The air was crisp and the midday sun struggled to peer through the clouds. For a while, Freddy walked along beside him. His buckler and his naked dagger at the ready as he kept pace with his father. While a great part of Geoffrey wished that his family had remained back in Galadin, safe within the walls of the Houndstooth, it was moments like these, seeing the pride and excitement on their faces that made him glad to have them with him. They had covered a great deal of ground together for such humble beginnings as they had in Pyle, and where once the limitations of the world had been merely a few swathes of farmland in the Spade, their reality had expanded to include nearly two thirds of the continent.

Of course, the pleasure of their company quickly turned to regret when all of a sudden, the hammer of hooves echoed across the plain followed by a burst of war cries and the clamor of steel upon steel. At once, the supply cart turned for the shelter of the white birches and Geoffrey's family hurried along with it. The archers formed two ranks and readied their war bows while Theo and his men-at-arms rode up to meet Geoffrey.

"What is it?" the young Nordren asked.

Geoffrey peered out into the plain ahead. Dozens of men were embroiled in an intense and bloody melee. From the backs of heavier destriers and light coursers, they hacked and slashed away at one another with all manner of weapon and in all manner of armor—leather brigandines, chainmail byrnies, and heavy steel plate.

"Looks like a battle," the Vanguard said. He scanned the combatants for any manner of insignia that might identify who was who, but in the chaos of battle it proved impossible.

"What a mess!" Theo said. "How do we tell the rebels from the forces of the Plague King? I don't know Montevalen heraldry."

"Neither do I," Geoffrey said, "but I do know a red-cloaked kingsmen when I see one."

He tightened his grip on Oakheart and Acorn. A sudden twinge struck him, not unlike when Brigid approached him at the docks so many months ago. *There are Guardians out there...or perhaps, Blackguards!*

"Archers! Ho!"

Lachlan, Bryce, and the rest of the Galadin yeomen sounded a rallying cry.

"Sir Adolfo told me a first impression can last a thousand years!" Geoffrey shouted. "Well, let's make this one memorable! Aim for the red-cloaks! We may not yet know these Montevalen folks, but we certainly know an old enemy when we see one! Am I right?"

"Aye!"

"And what should my men and I do?" Theo asked quietly.

"Guard the wagon," Geoffrey said, "And keep a sharp eye for any who break off and come for us."

Theo chewed his lip and nodded. Geoffrey sensed the young nobleman's discontent, but he did not have time to ease his wounded pride. "Alright!" he called to the yeomen. "Let's show them that marksmanship that's made the Brock famous. Release the Hounds!"

"Release the Hounds!"

"Let fly!"

Forty arrows flew as one from the magnificent war bows of the Galadin archers. So focused were they on the mounted melee that the red-cloaked kingsmen were caught completely unaware. They fell like tall grass before a scythe.

All across the plain, men paused, if only for an instant, to judge the new threat. Geoffrey was quick to take advantage of the confusion.

"Again!" he shouted. "Loose!"

Another volley flew through the air, piercing metal breastplates and knocking more red-cloaks from their saddles.

At last, a small cluster of kingsmen and their allies were able to rally and separate from the main fray so as to attack the archers. Geoffrey waved his arms and pointed with his cudgel to Theo Nordren before calling back to the archers. "At your leisure, boys! For the Brock!"

"For the Brock!" came the echoing cry as Geoffrey charged the oncoming riders with the Nordren mounted men-at-arms at his side.

"For Pyle!" Geoffrey cried and leapt to strike at a mounted kingsman. The man's shield crumpled at the force of Geoffrey's blow and he fell from the saddle to the ground. With a whirl of his arm and a flick of the wrist, Geoffrey ensured the kingsman would not rise again.

A second horseman reined in his mount and attempted to cut Geoffrey down in passing. With a quick pivot, Geoffrey turned aside the blow with the Acorn, but was unable to land his counterblow. The rider whirled around to renew his assault, but before he could do so, the Galadin yeoman were upon him like a swarm of bees. Together, they pulled him from the saddle and he all but disappeared beneath the crushing onslaught of their hand axes and clubs.

Geoffrey turned back to the battle, hurrying forth to engage more of the Andochan men-at-arms. Again, he felt that odd twinge of familiarity, and peering forth, spied a pair of men fighting on foot. One was young—perhaps of an age with Lughus and Brigid. In his hands, he carried a great two-handed axe, heaving it about with an almost reckless abandon. The other was older, nearer to Geoffrey's own age. He was dressed as a rustic and fought with a long chain-like weapon, whirling it in wide arcs and scattering all who came close to him. Neither wore the crimson cloak of the Order.

Another kingsman reared his horse and made to strike at Geoffrey, only to be knocked from the saddle by a Galadin arrow. Oakheart ended the man's agony, caving in his great helm like an eggshell.

Before long, the remaining kingsmen and their allies saw that with the arrival of Geoffrey and his archers, their chances of victory were dwindling. Survival became their sole concern. At the sound of a war horn, they began to disengage, rein in their mounts, and withdraw across the field.

Geoffrey eyed the horsemen who remained, who didn't flee with the remaining kingsmen. They were a motley crew comprised of men who, on the one hand, appeared to be drawn from the highest circles of nobility, and on the other, looked like little more than vagabonds and horse thieves. Even more surprising was the fact that there were women among them—soldiers, armed and armored. They had fought toe-to-toe with the kingsmen, demonstrating that they were at least the equal of any man.

When the sound of a second horn recalled the riders from their pursuit, Geoffrey watched, spellbound, as the rebel band expertly maneuvered their horses around together to reform ranks as they assessed the late arrivals.

While they did so, Geoffrey called Lachlan and Bryce to report the state of the archers and restore their lines. Luckily, they had suffered no losses in the skirmish beyond a few minor bumps and bruises resulting from the melee scuffle. The same was true for the Nordren men-at-arms, though there was one man who took a minor wound to the shoulder from a kingsman's lance. The force of the blow pierced through chainmail, but was mostly stopped by the quilted gambeson beneath. It was certain to bruise something fierce, but so long as it was cleaned, it was not at any risk of being fatal.

Barely had they finished this hurried accounting than the remaining mass of Montevalen horsemen began a cautious approach, stretching out in a pair of ranks to effectively pin Geoffrey and his group against the forest. Again, Geoffrey felt the odd sensation of familiarity grip him as he focused his keen eyes upon the leader.

Clad within the steel casing of his plate and chain, he was an imposing figure, made all the more so by the sheer size and strength of the great stallion upon which he rode. In his right hand he carried a long white spear with a broad, leaf-shaped head at the top. His face was concealed beneath the visor of his helm, but his white tabard and heater shield bore the same insignia of a single, crimson rosette.

As a show of peace, Geoffrey removed his kettle helm, and bowed his head. He took it as a positive sign when the man returned it, raised his visor, and spoke.

"It seems my fate is tied to this weird forest, for whether by fate or chance, anytime I come near it, my life takes a turn."

Geoffrey gave a quiet chuckle. "I too know what it's like to be Fortune's fool—and favored."

A somewhat forlorn expression colored the man's features. His green eyes scanned over Geoffrey and his men with a maturity that defied his age. "Who are you?" he asked.

"My name is Sir Geoffrey of Pyle," he told him. "Though by my title, I am called the Vanguard."

"The Vanguard?" the knight repeated, "and as you fought with us against the kingsmen, I take it you are a Blackguard?"

"So I am," Geoffrey continued. "My men and I have come in good faith on behalf of Baron Lughus Galadin of the Brock to extend a hand in friendship to the rebel queen that we might support each other in the fight against our mutual enemies. With me also is my family, and Theobold, heir to the barony of Nordren."

For a long moment, the knight was silent, mulling over Geoffrey's words. Behind him, his riders sat atop their horses patiently awaiting their leader's command. Geoffrey sensed his archers were similarly expectant, and in his peripheral vision, he saw Theo Nordren impatiently nudge his horse closer to where the Vanguard stood.

"Well, Sir Geoffrey of Pyle," the knight commander said. "I suppose then you had better come with us. My name is Beledain Tremont, though I too bear a title—that of the Tower—and there are others here of our kind besides. Follow us to Pridel and I shall introduce you to our queen."

"As you wish, my lord," Geoffrey said.

The Tower nodded and turned back to issue orders to his men. At Theo's questioning glance, Geoffrey gave a silent shrug, then set to preparing his own men to march. While the Galadin archers formed their column, he paused by the ox cart to check in on Annabel and his children.

"All's well, then?" Annabel asked.

Geoffrey leaned in close. "They're going to lead us to the castle of the queen," he said quietly. "Then the real work begins."

"All will be well, Geoffrey. Mark my words," Annabel said.

Beside her, Freddy and Greta buzzed with repressed excitement. "What's got you two?" he asked. "Not scared from the battle?"

"Did you see it, dad? Did you see it?" Freddy asked, his eyes alight with wonder.

"See what?" Geoffrey asked.

Greta's voice was laden with reverence. "The searoan!"

"The what?"

"The man you spoke with," Freddy said. "His horse was one of the searoans of Galdorn!"

"A searoan?"

"They're said to be smart. Like Fergus," Greta said, "only instead of dogs, they're horses."

"A searoan," Geoffrey said again. "Huh."

"I reckon he's a good one if he rides a searoan. It wouldn't let him otherwise," Freddy said. "They can sense things like that."

Geoffrey gave a nod. "Maybe," he said.

The sound of hooves brought Geoffrey's attention back around, though in place of the mythical searoan, it was Theo Nordren.

"Geoffrey," Theo said, "they're ready to march."

Geoffrey gave a nod. "Aye," he said, "and we shall follow."

CHAPTER 10: UNINVITED GUESTS

Lughus woke early for the watch, that brief period in the dead of night the learned folks of Termain often reserved for reading or quiet reflection. It was his custom to do so, built over the years of his adolescence at the Loremaster's Tower. It was often in these moments when he found himself most focused and when he did his best reading, writing, or thinking. Yet even when he did not have any particular task set forth by the old Loremaster, he would often use this time to simply let his mind wander where it would. He might mentally pace through footwork exercises or martial guards from swordsmanship manuals, dreamily envision famous battles from the vantage point of a bird, or else let his imagination run wild with an array of hopes and dreams for the future.

Later, after his journey with Crodane and his arrival at Houndstooth, his observance of the watch became less and less common. For his sleep was so troubled by the visions and nightmares of the previous Marshals' experiences that he would often lie awake in bed, skipping the watch entirely in desperate hope that he might find some measure of rest.

Then, on those few occasions where he did wake (or simply gave up on sleep entirely), he would sit and converse with Arcis. For his grandfather's illness cared little for the hour and day or night Lughus feared that each breath or cough would be the old man's last. To make matters worse, when Lughus began to speculate that he might use the Gift of the Guardians to somehow alleviate or even cure the old man's affliction, Arcis would have none of it. He refused to risk any harm coming to his long-absent grandson and threatened to end their nightly chats entirely. As such, Lughus gave up on the plan in order to enjoy what little time the old man had. Of course, the old man's inevitable death did little to improve his sleep either.

And then, Brigid arrived, and as her presence in the castle and in his life grew and grew, he once more found a certain comfort in the dark hours of the watch. He would wake and walk to the top of the keep with Fergus and gaze out over the city, the lake—and on clear nights—at the endless expanse of twinkling stars. Little by little, he began to feel his vision clear, as if Brigid's presence alone had reawakened his youthful hopes and dreams, opened his eyes once more to a beauty that he had long believed in out of hope, but had steadily begun to doubt.

Yet rather than simply restore his faith in the world, she also helped temper it, to understand it, to shed his earlier naiveté. By sharing and reflecting on the reality of their experiences he began to recognize the world and all that was in it for what it truly was. Honor and dishonor. Hope and Despair. Darkness and Light. There was a certain beauty to be had in that truth—a truth that was somehow a deeply ingrained part of him, and a truth that seemed now to have become synonymous with her.

In the pleasant darkness of his bedchamber, he breathed a contented sigh. and with a gentle strain, pulled her slight form closer to him. Almost instinctively, she released a contented whimper, nestling her head against his bare shoulder. Her raven hair spilled out upon the pillow like silken shadows, and he took comfort in the warmth radiating through the gossamer layer of her thin shift.

It still shocked him sometimes—the immensity of his own feelings for her and the sense of wholeness he felt whenever he held her in his arms. By some strange antithesis, it made him entirely cognizant of himself as an individual—separate even from the Marshal—yet simultaneously so deeply bonded with Brigid that she was as much a part of him as his swordarm. Perhaps even more so.

He loved her, madly, desperately, fully, and somehow he knew without question that she felt the same for him.

And yet, he felt all of this while they had yet to move beyond simply sleeping *beside* one another.

This was not to say that there was any lack of desire on either part, nor had the past few nights been without moments of tension that very easily could have boiled over into indulging an increasingly needful passion.

Just, not yet.

A sudden upwelling of feeling stirred within him and once more, he tightened his arms around her and kissed the crown of her head. Again, she released a soft murmur, and, drawing her head back to face him, opened her eyes. Even in the near total darkness of the night, they caught whatever low light was to be found and shone like stars. At once, Lughus felt his heart begin to pound like a battering ram against the walls of his chest.

"I'm sorry," he whispered. 'I didn't mean to wake you."

Brigid shook her head, casting aside his apology, while her lips spread into a tightlipped smile. His breath deepened as he held her and his body came to life.

"Do you want to go back to sleep?" he asked her.

Her eyes seemed to glimmer with mischief and her body grew taut as a bowstring ready to loose. She bit her bottom lip somewhat nervously and, again, shook her head.

"Well, Lady Blade..." he began, his eyes traveling from her eyes to her soft, glistening lips. She threaded her arms around his neck and he could sense the quickening of her breath from the sudden rise and fall of her chest against him. A smile tugged at the corners of his lips. "What would you like to do?"

With a demure smile, Brigid shut her eyes and raised her chin to press her lips beseechingly to his. Lughus was more than happy to receive her, reveling in the sweetness of her mouth and the softness of her tongue. Her body radiated a tremulous excitement, and with every ardent gasp that escaped her, he felt his own passion intensify. He found himself involuntarily holding her closer and closer, enveloping her in his tight embrace. His fingertips traced along the contours of her body, her thin shift an increasingly bothersome annoyance as he longed to feel the smoothness of the flawless skin beneath.

Brigid too seemed intoxicated by her need to hold him and be held, kiss him and be kissed. When they paused momentarily to breathe, she was the first to recover, renewing her exploration of his body by tracing her lips along the side of his neck and the line of his jaw. He marveled at the notion that her desire for him could match his for her. An upwelling of love and affection swelled within him, and when next she halted to catch her breath, he guided her along with him as he sat up in the bed and taking her in his arms again, pulled her into his lap.

A great shuddering breath took her, and for a moment, he hesitated, wondering if he had done something wrong. He raised a callused hand to her soft cheek and his throat tightened at the sight of tears pooling in her eyes.

"What's wrong?" he whispered. A flash of panic gripped him. "Brigid, I'm sorry. Did I do—"

Before he could finish, she pressed a finger to his lips and shook her head. "No, no," she said, "I just..." She turned her head and looked away as a tear traced down her cheek. "I feel...I feel so much, so...strongly for you that I..." She sighed. "I love you so much that it's almost more than I know how to feel," she finally managed, "and I guess it just...overwhelmed me." Another pair of tears raced down the side of her face and she shook her head, smiling in spite of herself. "Ugh," she grunted, "I'm sorry."

With an affectionate sigh, Lughus cradled her in his arms and pressed a kiss to her brow. "I know exactly what it is you feel," he said quietly.

"I'm sorry," she said. "It's foolish."

"It's not," Lughus told her. He kissed her forehead again and brushed away a thick tendril of hair from her face.

Brigid sighed, but he felt her body relax in his arms.

"I suppose..." she began. "I suppose I've...ruined things, haven't I?"

Lughus shifted her in his arms and held her gaze. "Have you?" he asked, smoothing away another strand of raven hair.

Brigid's eyes widened and he felt her tremble in his arms. "I don't know."

Lughus lowered his head to hers, still holding her eye. "Brigid," he said, "I love you. You never have to hide your feelings from me."

"And you either," she replied.

"Agreed," Lughus said, and lifting her chin, bent to kiss her once more. At once, she raised her head to receive him and he felt her delicate fingertips trace along the muscles of his forearm. Again, as they kissed, he felt her body came to life like a tongue of flame, and when his hand slipped just beneath the hem of her shift to light upon the smooth skin of her leg, she did not push it away, but rather placed her hand on top of his.

And then, a sudden slam and a fanfare of barking once again, brought their excitement to a halt. In the small sitting room connected to the baron's bedchamber something heavy slammed against the door. "Perindal's Bloody Sword," Brigid cursed "Fergus!"

Lughus sighed. "I had no idea he was out and about."

Brigid shook her head and slipped from his grasp to lie beside him. "He was pawing at the door after you fell asleep and I figured he must need to go to the yard," she told him, "I completely forgot about it. I'll go let him in. I'm sure he'll just want to lie down."

Lughus shook his head. "I'll go," he said, kissing her again on the brow. "Are you hungry? Thirsty?"

"Not for any food," she told him as he stood up from the bed. Even in the low light, he could sense the splash of color that spread across her cheeks and at the time of her nose.

Lughus offered her a playful grin and gently ran a hand along the line of her jaw. With a sigh, she took it softly in her hand and kissed his palm. "I'll be right back," he told her.

In the adjacent sitting room, the fire in the hearth had been reduced to but a few glowing embers. Standing now in nothing more than his braies, he felt the sting of the autumn chill and paused to quickly poke the fire. Again, Fergus howled and pounded like a ram against the door.

"I'm coming, Fergus. I'm coming," Lughus called. "I'm just stoking the hearth for you, mate." When the flames had resumed their merry dance, illuminating the room in a warm glow, he added another log, and made for the door to admit the hound.

Yet just as he was about to set his hand to the door, a thin steel blade emerged from behind a tapestry, followed by a small man clad entirely in black but for a crimson sash.

"Hold, Blackguard!" the man sneered from beneath the brim of his hat. He leveled his sword menacingly. "Hold in the name of the Chancellor and the Guardian-King!"

Lughus remained stoic, though inwardly he raged at the intrusion. "You're a long way from Andoch, Guardian," he said coldly. Out of the corner of his eye, he spied a subtle movement in the bedroom, but kept his gaze steady so as not to alert his foe.

Lughus knew at once that Fergus had sensed the threat and come to warn them. The sound of the intruder's voice, which the hound most certainly heard in spite of the thick oaken door, sent him into a frenzy. He doubled his efforts, pounding against the door like a battering ram, barking and howling and snarling and snapping.

"I take it you work for the Hammer," the young baron finally said. "So what is it they call you? The Nail?"

"Don't play dumb, boy. You know as well as I do that the Nail fell in the battle with the Warlock thirteen hundred years ago." The man sneered. "I am the Needle."

"Adrien Lenoit," Lughus remembered. "Constable of the Chancellery and hunter of fugitives. Your progenitor was a tailor from a village in what is now...Brabant, is it? But he chose not to return to the Brock after Wrogan's defeat."

The man inclined his head. "He remained behind to help reestablish order in the wake of the Warlock's chaos," he said. "It seems your time with the Loremaster was not wasted after all, Lughus Galadin, Blackguard and traitor to the King."

"This is the Brock," Lughus said. "We have no kings."

"Marshal!"

At Brigid's shout, the Needle turned to face her and Lughus leapt back just as she tossed him his scabbard. Fergus snarled and hammered the door again while somewhere further off in the castle, someone had finally raised the alarm.

"This is your only chance at mercy," Lughus said. He drew Sentinel and raised it before him.

Whisper and Shade were already in Brigid's hands and she stood beautiful and terrible in the firelight.

"It was foolish to come here alone."

The Needle grinned. "Poor, Broken pup," he replied. "Whatever gave you that idea?"

From the window of the bedchamber, another figure—lean and lanky—crept like a shadow over the sill. He was dressed in a manner after the Needle, though in place of a hat, his face was concealed by a black leather mask. In each of his hands, he wielded what looked like farmer's sickles, and while he was utterly silent, there was no mistaking his animosity.

"We're not so foolish as to expect a fair fight from Blackguards," the Needle hissed.

"But you're foolish enough to think we're evenly matched," Brigid leered.

"We shall see."

For a long moment, the four of them stood together as if frozen, each one watchful, waiting to counter whomever it would be to make the first move. Fergus continued to pound and howl at the door while the fire in the hearth flared even brighter, casting dark specters of the combatants upon the walls.

The Needle was the first to act, breaking the fierce tableau. In a trice, he drew a small dagger from his baldric and threw it at Brigid. With an adroit step and a flick of her wrist, she deflected the blade toward the wall. Sparks flew where it struck the stone. As she recovered her stance, the man with the sickles whirled at her, but Lughus lunged forth to parry his strike and press him backwards. For a split second, the pair of curved blades caught around Sentinel and Lughus sensed the man's intent to disarm him. He might have succeeded had Brigid not slipped in beneath them and sliced the assassin's arm through his bracer, allowing Lughus to slide the sword free just as the Needle lunged.

With the Guardian off balance from his failed thrust, Lughus planted his feet and met the Needle shoulder to shoulder, knocking him back. Then, turning his wrists over, he struck upwards from the Guard of the Dragon, carving a deep scar in the Needle's chest guard.

With a flash of panic, the constable retreated against the wall and leveled his thin sword. "You black-hearted bastard!" he snarled, "Stand down! Have you no sense of honor!"

"Ha!" Lughus cried. "You slither like a viper into my bedchamber and yet you talk of honor?"

"Come now," the Needle leered, "It's not all lost for you, you know? The King wants you taken alive. Stand down. Give us the Blackstone whore and we'll let bygones be bygones. From the looks of it, you've already had your fun with her anyhow."

Lughus's gray eyes flashed and his blood turned to fire, but he swore no brash oaths or boorish curses. He simply fixed the Guardian with a vicious gaze, feeling the man's resolve begin to wither.

"Truly, the Order has fallen," he said, and raising his blade, renewed his attack.

Behind them, Brigid and the masked Guardian continued to match blades as dagger parried and countered sickle. Like dancers, they whirled about one another in an elaborate flurry of deadly steel. With the masked man's superior reach, Brigid was forced to move in close to take away his advantage. She crouched low beneath the broad branches of his willowy arms, tucked into a forward roll, and came up behind him, slicing the tendons behind his left knee. The man released an inarticulate scream before whirling around wildly in a tornado of bladed rage. Again, Brigid rolled across the floor and leapt back to her feet, just out of reach of the deadly sickles, but close enough to step in and strike. A slash from Whisper exposed the man's throat, and a thrust from Shade sent him to the grave.

As his comrade choked out his last breaths, the Needle made a desperate, final assault. Madness consumed him and he flew at Lughus, thrusting and counter-striking with frenzied speed. The Marshal turned aside each blow with precision, deftly countering with a swift riposte, but apart from a few minor scratches, he was unable to score a mortal stroke against the Guardian.

With the masked man dead, Brigid was free to run for the door. Barely had she finished drawing back the bolt when the great golden hound, lips drawn back over slavering jaws, burst into the room and charged. Engaged as he was with Lughus, the Needle barely had time to register the new threat before Fergus pounced and dragged the screaming Guardian to the ground.

There was a brief moment of struggle, a horrifying wrench, and the great hound tore out the intruder's throat.

Lughus turned from the carnage and found Brigid at his side. She took his hand and he pulled her into an embrace. "You're not hurt, are you?"

She shook her head. "You?"

"Not a scratch."

Fergus raised his red maw and trotted over to them with an air of benign self-satisfaction.

"Good boy," Brigid said, ruffling his ears.

Lughus patted the dog's head. "Brother, I owe you an entire roasted lamb."

Fergus panted happily and nudged the young baron with his great bulk, rocking him back on his heels.

Hurried footsteps echoed from the hallway followed by a clipped voice issuing commands. Brigid withdrew to the bedroom for her robe and tossed

Lughus his linen undertunic. He threw it over his shoulders just as Sergeant Pike appeared in the doorway.

"Baron Lughus!" he cried. Behind him, other members of the Galadin guard stood at attention. "Pardon my intrusion, my lord, but when we heard the hound going wild in the yard, I ordered a search of the grounds. I had no idea he'd tracked the bast—the intruders here, my lord. I'm so sorry."

"All's well, Pike," Lughus said. "As you can see, we took care of them."

"Oh! Lady Brigid! Excuse us!" Pike said, removing his helmet and casting his eyes down to the floor. "You're not harmed, are you?"

"Quite alright, sergeant," Brigid said. "I heard the commotion from down the hall and came running."

"Then the two of you made short work of them, I'm sure."

Fergus gave a low bark.

"You three!" Pike grinned. "Apologies." His smile faded. "Though they should never have made it this far, my lord. We should have had them and we failed."

Lughus shook his head. "They were Guardians, Pike," he said. "Anointed. The Needle and...the Mask, it looks like?"

"I just can't imagine how they could have gotten in, sir."

"There are much more difficult things than picking a lock," Brigid said. "Especially for a rogue like the Needle. "

"And the Mask," Lughus told them, "climbed the wall of the keep itself, which would explain why you didn't see him in the dead of night."

"But he couldn't escape Ol' Fergus's nose, could he?"" Brigid smiled.

The hound gave a happy bark, his red maw still glistening with gore.

"We'll do another search just to make sure," Pike said. "I'm so dreadfully sorry, my lord—and to you, my lady."

"Thank you, Sergeant," Lughus said. "I would appreciate it if you could send word to Sir Adolfo as well."

"Already done, my lord," Pike said. "I sent a man to Horus and to Sir Owain as well, though he's still convalescing."

Lughus suppressed a grimace. He would have rather not bothered Owain. The old knight was likely to reopen his wounds dressing himself for battle.

"Let Owain know the threat has been dealt with and that I'll be by to see him directly," he said.

"Aye, sir," Pike nodded. "I'll have men get these bodies out of here as well."

As the guardsmen set to work removing the dead men, Lughus recovered his baldric and sheathed his blade. Brigid gave Fergus a fond pat on the head and wiped Whisper and Shade clean on a piece of torn cloth.

"I'll meet with Adolfo while you talk to Owain," she said softly. "To be honest, I won't be able to sleep until I've had a chance to make my own search of the grounds myself."

Lughus nodded. "Fergus and I will do the same," he said. "Part of me thinks we should hunt together, but then again, if there really are any more of them, it might be better if we split up. They might see me coming, they'll never spot you."

"You do make rather handsome bait." Brigid smiled.

Lughus raised an eyebrow. "Do I need to ask you to be careful?"

"No," she said with a smirk. "But I love that you will anyway."

He reached out to give her hand a squeeze. "Please be careful."

"Always." She gave him one last, hurried kiss and scurried out to the hallway past the guards.

Lughus sighed and scratched Fergus's head. His eyes fell upon the Needle's thin-bladed sword, lying idly where it had fallen. With the battle over, his calm, collected persona—so necessary in the heat of combat—began to dissolve, only to be replaced by a seething, white-hot anger. He knew that the Guardians could not sit idly by after their disastrous defeat at St. Golan's, but he had not expected them to stoop so low as to send assassins.

Then again, in their eyes, a Blackguard was little more than a criminal, and few enough saw any point in behaving with honor against an enemy who they believed had none.

Regardless, they would keep coming. Be it on the battlefield or in the shadows, the Guardians were certain to return. Again and again and again until the Brock was broken and Kredor could finally name himself tyrant-emperor of Termain.

He would not allow it. By the blood of his ancestors and his duty to his people, something would need to be done.

CHAPTER 11: SUBSTANTIAL ALCHEMY

For the remainder of the day, Royne sat on the edge of his bed in his cell, struggling to comprehend what it was that he had witnessed. He still held the dowel in his hand, its charred end blackened with soot and ash. There must have been some trick to it, some manner of misdirection or legerdemain. Fire could not simply be drawn out of thin air. It was a basic elemental principal! It needed a source of heat, air to breathe, and material to burn. The symposium was full of air, the dowel could burn, but the what was the source of the combustion? What was it that ignited the spark? It was madness! A simple truth that had been understood since the days of the ancient philosophers of Old Calendral. The notion that fire might simply be... spontaneously *willed* into being was utterly preposterous! Shear Madness. Impossible.

As impossible as when he had miraculously healed the general...

Or read words from a book he had never written...

Royne pressed his fingertips to the sides of his head and leaned forward onto his knees. None of it made any sense.

With a sigh, he reached for *The Book of Histories* and set it upon his lap. Perhaps that was what he needed. To escape. To lose himself in the annals of the past that led through direct causation all the way to the present. He would deal with the alchemists in due course. One bloody conundrum at a time.

He flipped through the blank pages to find where he had left off, once more ignoring the absurdity implicit in such an action, for if the book was blank, wouldn't any page do?

At long last, he had progressed far enough to recognize the fine, spindly handwriting of his predecessor, Rastis Glendaro. With any luck, Rastis's records would offer insight into what was really going on.

Rastis's rise to his role was not direct or easy. He had begun his time with the Order as apprentice to a scholar at the court of Arcis Galadin's grandfather, Malcolm. Before long, his naturally astute intellect and diplomatic acumen distinguished him in the eyes of his masters and he was quickly identified as a potential successor to the previous Loremaster, Wilfred of Thistlevale. As the years went on, he continued his studies, traveling from time to time and rising through the ranks of the Loremaster's Tower, until he was eventually granted the rank of sage for his work examining the history of relations between Andoch and the Brock and the founding of the Order. As a man with strong ties to both realms, he was able to aid in the relations between the two nations and improve the overall stability of the continent.

Of course, since such matters were usually considered the responsibility of the Chancellor and his officials, Rastis made many political enemies among their ranks for advocating decisions that put the needs of the people— particularly the common folk—before matters of trade. Meanwhile, his devotion to history and truth had long since ruffled the feathers of the Hierophants, whose devotees often insisted on a romanticized or modified view of the past that they might use to reinforce or justify dogma.

Regardless, when old Loremaster Wilfred had finally reached his end and the time came for him to pass on his title, Rastis was still the obvious choice.

Royne thumbed his page and sat back, smiling inwardly at the old man's account of his youth. He couldn't help but feel warmed by the fact that his surrogate father had risen through the ranks as a perennial pain in the ass. It added yet another level of understanding to Rastis's choice of Royne as his successor. They might differ in height, appearance, and lineage, but in all other ways—or at least, in the ways that mattered—they were birds of feather.

Again, Royne breathed. sigh and his lips twisted into a sardonic smirk. A sudden urge took hold of him. He returned *The Book of Histories* to its satchel and stood up. He was here for a reason, for a purpose. It was time to get to work. He slung his satchel over his shoulder and left his room.

The symposium was rather full when Royne arrived. Platters of food sat out in the center of each table where anyone who wished might help themselves. The food was simple—thin flatbread, bowls of olives, a mixture of greens and tomatoes with some manner of oil, and a yellowish paste that smelled enticing, but did not at all look it.

Ignoring the food, Royne looked out over the round tables until he spied the group of young people from earlier. Haruki, Amara, and an assortment of others. Fabius, he noted, was not with them, but sat with a group of young men across the symposium.

With a deep breath, Royne strode up to the first group and ignoring the stares, sat down in the open seat beside Amara.

"I would like you to tell me what it is that you did earlier," he said to her.

The rest of the table remained silent, but looked on with a mix of anticipation, amusement, and mild discomfort.

Amara took a bite of food, chewed, swallowed, and took a sip of from her cup. "Go away, Polecat," she said.

Royne ignored her dismissal. "The philosopher Argomenos stated nearly two thousand years ago that combustion can only occur when three factors are present—heat, breathable air, and a material susceptible to burning. Air was all around us. The dowel was made of wood, which, of course, burns. However, I could not—and cannot still—identify any heat source."

Amara continued to eat, ignoring him. The others at the table watched in silence, growing increasingly uncomfortable. Royne was vaguely aware of all of this, but paid it no mind and continued to think aloud, prodding the young woman with statements that implied questions. At the end of his rambling soliloquy, he paused and folded his hands upon the tabletop.

"So?" he finally said.

Amara's jaw tightened. "So?" she repeated.

"Are you going to tell me?"

"Tell you what?"

Royne's brow furrowed with impatience. "The heat source. What was the heat source?"

She remained silent.

"Was it a ring?" he asked. "Or perhaps a pair of rings?"

"A ring?"

"Amara..." Haruki said quietly. "He is an outsider and only just arrived."

"A ring," Royne continued. "Perhaps one ring of steel on your finger, and then another made of flint, or with a piece of flint in place of some other precious stone? Put it on your thumb and rub it like so..."

The girl shook her head and fixed him with a stare. "That is without a doubt, the most idiotic thing that I have ever heard."

The young Loremaster's eyes widened in disbelief. "Idiotic?" he stammered. "Did you...did you just call me idiotic?"

"I called your idea idiotic." She turned back to her food. "Though if one's ideas are consistently idiotic, well, Polecat, then I would imagine..." She left the rest of the sentence unsaid.

Royne felt a cold fury burn in his chest. His brow creased with rage and he struggled to string together a coherent thought. When he finally managed to choke down enough of his anger to speak, all he could manage was an absurd, "Polecat? Why do you keep calling me Polecat?"

"Sabrun's razor."

"Sabrun? The Loremaster?"

Amara gave an exaggerated sigh. "The philosopher," she said, "But yes. I believe he was also called the Loremaster."

"Well, what in the bloody Abyss has he got to do with it?" Royne snapped, though inwardly he was more annoyed that she had exposed a gap in his knowledge that he felt should not exist, particularly given his own status as Sabrun's spiritual successor.

"The explanation that requires the fewest assumptions is most often the correct one."

Royne chewed his lip for a moment. "So what you're saying is you call me Polecat because...you think I'm some sort of weasel? I'm...untrustworthy?"

She rolled her eyes. "Why would I think that? I don't even know you."

Royne scrunched up his face. "So then you call me Polecat because..." he paused, "because you think that I...look like one?"

"Congratulations," she said. "You have just learned the principle of Sabrun's razor. Now leave."

Royne took a deep breath, trying to ignore the smirks and amused sniggering of the others at the table. Who were these people to laugh at him? He was the bloody Loremaster! How dare they! Once more, he ground his teeth, forcing his voice to be calm. "Look," he said. "All I want to know is how you did what you did earlier. Tell me and we don't have to ever speak to each other again."

"I already told you," she said. She turned toward him again and her eyes flashed. "Alchemy."

"I don't know what that means!" he snapped.

With an exasperated sigh, Amara reached out suddenly, grabbed him by the shoulder, and turned his head toward the far side of the room. "Do you see that man there?" she asked. "The bloated old man with the bristly white beard?"

"Y-Yes," Royne stammered. "I see him. What do you call him? The badger?"

"No. I call him the blowfish," she said. "His name is Kabir. He gives lectures every morning on the fundamental principles of alchemy. You want to learn something? Go to a lecture. I've wasted more time on you than I care to, time that I will never get back. Now go away, Polecat. Leave me in peace."

At length, Royne took a deep breath and stood up from the table, then, uncertain of what else to do, he grabbed a bit of food from a nearby table and returned quietly to the quiet solitude of his room. While he was also no stranger to bullying, he had never been so ill-treated by someone so educated and intelligent before. It was one thing to be insulted by the likes of Pryce or Captain Velius, but to be cast aside by these people, these other folk who had such a high reputation for learning and study stung worse than a thousand boorish insults? That, he simply could not abide.

The following morning, he woke early, dressed, shouldered his satchel, and made his way once more to the symposium. There, he sat for a time in silence, watching the alchemists come and go. Eventually, he spied the man Amara had pointed out the previous night—Master Kabir—and silently followed at a distance as the old man made his way to one of the many rooms off of the grand stairway from the symposium. A group of children no older than twelve sat awaiting Kabir's arrival and Royne flushed with anger as he realized that he had fallen for the wretched girl's prank.

Bloody howler! I'll show her who the bloody child is!

He was about to storm out in anger when Kabir's eyes fell upon him and the alchemist nodded and motioned invitingly to an open chair. Suppressing a sigh, Royne offered the lecturer a civil nod and took the vacant seat.

I guess there's no harm in hearing what he has to say...

Master Kabir assumed the position behind a lectern and began organizing a thick bundle of notes. Then, when he was ready, he folded his hands across his vast belly and began to speak.

"What is the world?" he asked. He waited, casting his glance around the room. When no one bothered to reply, he asked the question a second time. "What is the world?"

Royne kept his face impassive, but inwardly he sighed. Such a banal question. He understood the point of the man's pedagogy and his manufactured sense of drama—his purpose was, after all—to educate, but Royne had little time for such things.

Just tell me what I need to know, he thought. *Tell me how it is you draw fire from the ether! Prove to me that it is possible and—most importantly—explain how!*

The lecture continued with a slightly more in-depth explanation of the basic alchemical concepts that Udo had described to Royne during his tour. The four elemental forces. Harmony and discord. Kabir even used the same example of a log in the fireplace. Just when Royne's frustration was beginning to rise again, the lecturer paused.

"Now," he began, "Much of this is quite rudimentary, and I would not be surprised if much of it you already know. But it is easy to think of the forces of a single object, or of how the balance of a single object can exist in harmony. Matters become far more complicated when we introduce—for example—an iron brazier to hold the log, or a tapestry placed too near the fire. When we consider why one burns while the other does not, or when we substitute the burning log for the collective discontent of a village, or when we consider the larger amalgamation of what we call reality, matters become far more interesting. We begin to wonder just how far we can influence the elemental forces, and in turn, just how far we can instill harmony or create discord."

"As alchemists, we study the interaction—the balance and the discord—that may exist between these elemental forces. Firstly, we understand the interaction between various substances and how the elemental force of one may impact the elemental balance of another. This practice, we call substantial alchemy. Secondly, we learn how by sheer will and will alone, we may come to manifest—to influence, to create, and to destroy—the elemental balance or discord of other independent entities. This, we refer to as metaphysical alchemy."

"I can instruct you in the rudimentary processes of substantial alchemy—to set you on a path of study, if you will. It will take hard work, dedication, and a certain resignation that—at times—you are certain to fail. Yet, if you succeed, your contributions to the larger world will be of incredible significance. You will cure the sick, forge the finest metals, and build the greatest structures..."

He paused. "Unfortunately, however, to practice metaphysical alchemy, one may study an entire lifetime and never attain even a basic level of mastery. Much of it is intuitive and innate, and the practitioners of such arts often face persecution under such base misnomers as 'sorcerer' or 'wizard.' Still, while metaphysical alchemy is capable of sowing great discord through the manipulation of elemental forces, when used to create or restore balance, they are capable of the greatest good. They make the impossible possible."

Royne's brow narrowed in thought. *Substantial alchemy and metaphysical alchemy...* He stroked his chin. *Interesting...*

He'd had some rudimentary study of physic, though to be honest, he did not care much for it. For to devote himself to an intensive study of the varied consistencies and colorations of urine, pus, and other bodily excretions to be a waste of his time. The same could be said of the brewing of various teas and decoctions. Such things were necessary, he supposed, but they were more the prerogative of rustic herbalists or village crones. Certainly not worth the time of a serious and dedicated scholar such as himself.

Still, from what he gathered, the healing arts were merely one possible application of alchemical study. He recalled accounts of such substances as St. Aiden's Fire or the various powders said to create noxious odors when burned. There were stories of whole armies being forced to their knees when such stinking clouds were wafted across the battlefield.

Perhaps this manner of pursuit by the substantial alchemists is what allowed the University to remain secure in the face of the Andochan invasion. He would have to pursue the matter further.

However, it was the second manner of alchemy, the metaphysical alchemy, that truly interested him, and he had no doubt that this was what the girl had performed.

Instantly, it gripped him with the desire to know more. For it irked him that something so fascinating should leave him so utterly perplexed, irked him in the same manner as did all of the strange and unexplainable phenomena that he had experienced since becoming the Loremaster—reading from the book, healing the general, the insights and visions into matters he had not experienced firsthand. Perhaps it was all related somehow. Perhaps it might lead to some reasonable explanation.

Bloody Magic!

The remainder of Master Kebir's lecture passed. Royne listened quietly, observed as Kebir drew various diagrams to illustrate the structures of various objects, and described a number of preliminary alchemical experiments. It was nice to be back in an academic environment, though at the same time, he could not escape a certain longing for the past, particularly when, memories of Lughus, Thom, and Rastis appeared unasked for before his mind's eye. It immediately led him down a spiral of conjecture as he wondered how they all fared.

Thus, by the time Kebir finished, promising to continue in two days' time, Royne found himself under the shadow of melancholy and in no mood to suffer fools.

So it was with a particularly vile sense of rancor that he approached the girl, Amara, when he spied her sitting in the symposium eating her breakfast all alone.

"Do I look like a child to you?" he snapped.

"No, you look like a polecat," she replied, "as we have previously established."

Royne frowned. She was eating some manner of scone, not even bothering to look up at him. "I am not a fool," he told her.

"Good for you," she said.

Royne continued to stand awkwardly beside her, but could not quite figure out why. He felt so strange, so confused. What was he doing here? He had seen battle, had worked side-by-side with Cornelius Navarro, hero of Grantis. He was one of the most learned people on the continent, perhaps even in the entire world.

So why was it that he felt like such a bloody fool whenever he was around this girl? And why had it become so important to him that she acknowledge his intellect?

Perhaps I'm losing my mind?

He felt so very weary.

"Goodbye then," he said at last.

For the first time, the girl looked up at him somewhat quizzically. "Goodbye," she said.

Without another word, Royne turned and departed from the symposium, for the sanctity of his cell, and the familiar solace of *The Book of Histories*.

CHAPTER 12: ENVOYS & ALLIANCES

Night had fallen by the time Bel and his riders returned to Pridel from their battle with the Plague King's raiders. Sir Briden volunteered to see to the contingent of men from Baronbrock, ensuring that the archers were provided with a space outside the city walls to make camp, separated but not far from the main encampment of the queen's army. The young lord with the fish insignia—Nordren—would be installed with his men in one of the inns, while the acorn knight—Sir Geoffrey—would be lodged with his family in the castle.

Even before the man had introduced himself, Bel knew him to be a Blackguard. He could sense it in the same way that he had somehow recognized the Shackle or the new lad, Thom Reaver. By some uncanny sense of familiarity, he simply knew it to be so.

Yet, unlike the previous two Blackguards, Sir Geoffrey carried with him the authority of a recognized realm: Baronbrock, and not just the Brock, but Galadin in particular. It was the birthplace of the Guardians, the land of the Blessed Saint. He had heard rumors, of course, that the Brock and the Order had parted ways, severing the longstanding bond that had existed for thirteen hundred years. However, in light of Montevale's bloody generational war, the affairs of the realms that lie beyond the Nivanus Mountains were not his direct concern. Indeed, Marcus Harding's assignment to act as Marius's Lord-General was so surprising because—unlike the typical mercenary—he represented the active involvement of the other realms in what, up to that point, had remained an internal affair. He was a legitimate representative of a foreign power, not merely some hired sword. That, in many ways, had been what had raised so many Valendian eyebrows, for like all Montevalens, they had little use for the other realms, busy as they were fighting among themselves.

And now, here was this man, Sir Geoffrey of Pyle (wherever that was), here with men—skilled men with war bows—who without hesitation leapt into the fray, fighting alongside the queen's men.

Marcus was asleep upon Bel's return, but he crept in anyway to press a soft kiss to the little boy's brow. It amazed him how fast the boy had grown, and he could not escape a visceral flash of grief for the mother the boy would never know. As he left the nursery and withdrew to his own quarters to doff his armor, he allowed himself a moment to give in to the litany of trauma that he had witnessed, suffered, and endured. It was a burden he needed to carry if he was to ever fulfill the debt he owed the fallen, if he was ever to heal the divisions that plagued this land and end the war once and for all.

When the moment had passed and the bitterness and the grief had returned to lie dormant in the far recesses of his soul, Bel slipped silently from his quarters and down the hallway to the queen's chambers. Marina met him with hollow eyes, her body trembling with the aftershocks of relief, and as they lie together in the darkness, united in their shared struggles, their hearts were one and they knew peace. He knew that in some ways, while his body might be strong, inside he was broken, and it was only in these private moments with Marina, with his son, or riding alone across the plain with Tempest that he was able to find any sense of solace or stability.

The following morning, Bel offered his queen a full report of the battle and a detailed account of the meeting with the envoy from the Brock. She was, of course, intrigued, for while the Brock was Montevale's closest neighbor and the only neighboring realm accessible by land, relations between the two lands, while not hostile, had been limited, even distant. As such, Sir Geoffrey of Pyle was greeted with great interest and every courtesy was to be extended, including, first and foremost, a formal audience with the queen.

The meeting took place in the hall. Marina sat upon her high seat. Bel stood at her right hand and Sir Armel at her left. The remaining knights, captains, and retainers stood alongside the perimeter, eager to hear the emissary speak. Sir Welmsey, Sir Norton, the Malets, Horn, Sparrow, and the Shackle sat nearest the raised dais and the throne. The new lad, Thom, was also with them, and Bel couldn't help but find it a bit surprising. Then again, the boy certainly proved himself in the skirmish, and while his fighting style looked a bit strange—hurling his heavy great axe about like a drunken woodcutter—he racked up quite the butcher's bill.

I shall have to find a better use for him...

Sir Geoffrey himself was attended by a single squire, a boy who looked to be his son or at least some relation. Beside him, glancing around somewhat uncomfortably, was the other nobleman, Theobold Nordren. They were dressed in what amounted to their courtly finery, though in the case of the Vanguard and his son, their clothing lacked the ostentatious embellishment characteristic of the lordling. This austere pragmatism did not escape Bel's notice either.

Sir Armel stepped forward and called the hall to order. In truth, he did so purely as a formality, for the collective interest in the visitors had already discouraged any rowdy good cheer.

When the seneschal had returned to his place opposite Bel at the queen's side, Marina smiled benignly at him and spoke across the assembly.

"We welcome you, visitors from afar," she said, "and we appreciate your assistance in driving off the Plague King's raiders from our lands."

Bel watched closely as the men reacted to the queen's words of gratitude. The young lord of Nordren nodded proudly and stood straighter with his hands clasped behind his back. Sir Geoffrey bowed his head, his eyes staring vacantly at the flagstones.

Marina continued. "While we welcome your aid, it has not escaped our knowing—even here on the far side of the Nivanus—that the Brock has its own battles to fight and its own war to wage. As such, you can understand how your presence invites our curiosity."

Bel suppressed a fond smile at her. She may privately question her aptitude as queen, but there was no question in his mind that she was the one the realm needed, the only ruler who could lead the realm through the dream of lasting peace. Not only did she look the part of the benevolent queen—

resplendent today in forest green and ivory, her scarlet hair luminous in the light of the morning sun—but she knew how to speak pointedly and politely, to invite explanation while encouraging brevity. She had a way with words that was beyond his stoic silence.

Sir Geoffrey took a deep breath and cleared his throat. Before he could speak, however, Theobold Nordren stepped forward.

"It is an honor, your majesty, to stand before you." He grinned. "And may I also say that while stories of your great beauty have spread far and wide across the continent, they do you no justice. My ship is anchored three days from here, but I would ride twice that just to bask in your glory, for you are radiant."

Bel felt a tightening in his jaw. Marina nodded, but remained silent.

"In any case," Nordren said. "The Brock is currently at war with the Guardian-King of Andoch and his allies, but recently, we won a great victory on the plain outside of the Monastery of St. Golan the Ram. Such as it was, when news of your recent victory reached us as well, we thought that together we might achieve more still. The enemy of an enemy is often a friend, as they say."

"Well," Marina smiled, "I'm glad to know that Montevale is spoken of for more than my appearance. The bloody sacrifices of our fighting men and women certainly outshine my vanity."

Nordren's smile widened. "One is a testament to the other, I'd say."

For the briefest of moments, Bel caught Sir Armel's eye. He could sense the seneschal's palpable displeasure rising from his bald head like steam. It joined the growing miasma of annoyance collectively blanketing the hall. Bel too might have felt a flush of jealous resentment, but he had no doubt that Marina knew a fool when she met one. For when it came to social niceties, the queen was more than capable of taking care of herself.

"At any rate," Nordren continued, "Sir Geoffrey has the details. I simply wanted to offer my compliments and bask in the glory of the Winter Rose for myself." He smiled, offered a slight bow, and stepped backward alongside his comrade.

Sir Armel caught Bel's eye. "Did your father ever say anything about first impressions?" he whispered.

"He did," Bel said quietly, "But I'd like to hear this man anyway."

"Fair enough," Armel said.

As Sir Geoffrey of Pyle approached the throne, he pursed his lips and took a deep breath. It was clear that he was nervous, made all the more so from his comrade's awkward preamble. As he stepped forward, he gave his son a nod, inviting him to stand alongside him.

"Hello," he said.

"Hello," the queen replied.

Geoffrey took a deep breath. Seeing the man now, free of his armor, Bel was struck by the breadth of the man's shoulders and the strength of his arms. He was at least Bel's own height, perhaps even as tall as Horn, yet he was the Shackle's equal in brawn. For all of his size, however, he carried himself with an air of quiet humility.

"Please forgive me, your majesty," he said lowly. "My son and I have never...stood before royalty before and we're not certain of your customs. Should we kneel? The last thing we wish to do is to offend."

Marina paused and for a fleeting moment, she caught Bel's eye. "You have no need to worry," she said at last, "and no need to kneel, Good Sir."

Sir Geoffrey nodded. "Thank you." He paused, cleared his throat, and with a quick glance at his son, began to speak.

"My name," he began, "is Geoffrey of Pyle. I was born in a land far to the south and west of here called the Spade. Most of my life, I spent as a simple farmer, like my father before me, working the land alongside my fellows in hopes of keeping our families fed and safe."

"Almost two years ago, I was on my way home from market when bandits set upon our caravan. They intended to slaughter everyone, and in truth, were it not for a man named Regnar, I too would not have survived. I was shot by an arrow in the side just here, and quite frankly, I should have died."

"As it turned out, though, Regnar was known by others under the title of 'the Vanguard,' and though in the end it cost him his own life, he saved mine. He healed me—instantly—by what I imagine some might say was a miracle. In exchange, I swore to him that I would do as he had done. I would stand against the darkness and fight always for what is right."

"Since that time, I've fought in my share of battles. I've seen the great heights men might climb when they stand together, and the horrors that they unleash upon their fellow men when they stand divided. I left my home, but found another. I..." He paused. "I lost a son, but gained a daughter. I left friends I'd known my entire life, and forged ties with new ones stronger than blood."

"Your majesty," Geoffrey said, "I say these things not out of pride or the like. I say them because, in such a short time, I feel like I've learned...well, a lot. As a farmer in Pyle, I had little use for the larger world, and had you asked me then, I'd assumed I'd be buried a short walk away from the house where I was born."

"Yet, it was not to be. And now here I am caught up in a fight that, for whatever reason, I can't help but feel the fate of the whole continent depends upon, and that opposing the Guardian-King is only the beginning."

"Back in Pyle, as my old dad was fond of reminding us, no matter what trials and hardships we might suffer, that the only way to make it through was to hold together with our neighbors, side-by-side..."

Sir Geoffrey's eyes seemed momentarily to lose focus, staring into the annals of memory.

"As your majesty mentioned, the Brock and Montevale are neighbors, with only the Nivanus Mountains standing in between. We face a common enemy—and by that I don't just mean Andoch and its King."

"We fight against injustice and fear. We fight against evil and cruelty. We fight so that all people can have a chance at a good life where they can feel safe and secure, to prosper and raise their families."

Geoffrey took a deep breath. "I stand before you, good people of Montevale, with an offer of friendship and a pledge of aid. On behalf of Baron Lughus of Galadin, called 'the Marshal,' Lady Brigid Beinn of Dwerin, called 'the Blade,' and on behalf of all good folk of the continent whoever and wherever they may be, that we all might stand together against the darkness and greet the dawn of a new and brighter day."

With that, Sir Geoffrey finished and an intense silence fell over the assembled court. Many among them seemed to nod without thinking, or found that their hands had tightened around their hilts. Even Marina's green eyes blazed with passion and Bel felt his own blood stir.

"Well-spoken, sir," Marina said at last, "Woe be to the man who underestimates the 'simple farmer.'"

"St. Aiden was a farmer," the acorn knight said quietly.

"Indeed," the queen replied. She glanced at Bel momentarily and he offered her a silent nod of agreement.

"And you say that this...Baron Galadin—Lughus—and the Lady Brigid..." Marina's brow creased as she eyed the envoy intently. "You speak on their behalf?"

"I have formal documents and papers of all kinds," Geoffrey said. "I will have them sent to you for your perusal so that you might look at them more closely, but in the end, the result is the same."

"Alliance," Marina declared.

"Aye," Geoffrey said, adding, "your majesty."

The queen nodded her head thoughtfully. "This is something we shall certainly have to consider, but I swear to you that I will discuss this with my advisors at the first opportunity."

"Of course," Geoffrey said.

"This Baron Lughus is not well-known to us and there are other rumors that our enemies spread about this Brigid Beinn," Marina said. "Though, I will admit my skepticism regarding their validity, for I too know the lengths that men of power will go to discredit a women willing to stand for her people and her land."

"Indeed, your majesty," Sir Geoffrey agreed.

There was a shuffling to one side and Bel was surprised to see the new lad, Thom Reaver, cross the floor of the hall to stand beside Sir Geoffrey. His face was flushed and his eyes shone brightly, as if he had just suffered the shock of a lifetime.

"Pardon my intrusion, your majesty," he said, breathing heavily, "but I can speak to the character of Baron Lughus! I know him well!"

Sir Geoffrey eyed the younger man curiously. "You know Baron Lughus?" he asked.

"I do," Thom said. "I mean, I did, and if your majesty wishes it, I am more than happy to explain in greater detail. Suffice it to say for now, however, that I would pledge my life on the word of Baron Lughus above any other."

"And why is that?" the queen asked. "I do not doubt you, Thom Reaver. I simply wish to understand."

"Well, your majesty," Thom said, "The long and the short of it is that I have known him my entire life. He was like a brother to me, and—believe me—if he swears to stand beside you, not even the Beast of Dibhor could make him turn his back." The big boy's face fell. "You could never find a more loyal ally," he added wistfully.

Marina chewed her lip. "Clearly we have much to think on," she said. She cast Bel meaningful glance and a subtle nod. Even without words, he understood her command.

At once, quiet murmurings erupted all throughout the hall as folk remarked upon the strange visitors and their words. At a nod from the queen, Sir Armel brought the audience to a close. The assembly paused as the queen rose from her high seat, but no sooner had she departed before the hall erupted into the excited chatter of gossip.

"Interesting day," Armel said quietly to Bel, "and just when I thought we'd had our fill of surprises."

Bel gave a nod of agreement and patted the seneschal on the shoulder. "Invite Sir Geoffrey to the queen's solar, preferably without the other nobleman," he said. "Ask Horn and the Shackle to bring Thom Reaver as well."

Armel nodded. "Anyone else?"

"If Sir Geoffrey requests it, let him bring along his son," Bel said. "I'd like to meet this man free of the pageantry of the great hall."

Armel's mustache bristled and his eyes widened. "You don't trust him?"

"That's the thing," Bel said. "I do. "

Within the hour, Bel, Marina, Sir Armel, Horn, the Shackle, Sir Geoffrey, and Thom Reaver sat around the table in the queen's solar. Briden and Welmsey stood sentinel at the door beside Sir Geoffrey's wide-eyed son. Unfortunately, Armel had been unable to extricate Sir Geoffrey from his countryman, so Theobold Nordren was also in attendance.

In fairness, it was not that Nordren had been overly boorish. He had, in most ways, acted in accordance with the standards and expectations of his class. However, these customs and attitudes, while not uncommon, were hallmarks of the gentry of Montevale's past. They were the ways of Lord Harren and Giles Pronet, the knights of the court and the parlor who preferred the luxuries of the great hall to the battlefield. This was not to say that Nordren was a coward or lacked skill in the arts of war, but that his interest lie in his own advancement rather than the good of the realm. In a rebellion built upon establishing a new land built upon principle and conscience, though, it marked him as an outsider.

When all were seated and wine was poured, Marina began.

"You are a powerful speaker, Sir Geoffrey," she said. "As I cast my eye around the hall, it seemed there was not a soul who remained unmoved."

Geoffrey gave a reticent shrug. "I'm not a man for whom words come easy, your majesty," he said. "So I simply told the truth."

"Yes," Marina agreed. "But such is the claim of many powerful speakers to mask their true intentions—and yet, I find that I am not inclined in any way to doubt you. For there is nothing in your manner to suggest deceit and your words seem born of compassion rather than cunning. Such qualities are rare." She gave a soft smile. "Though not unheard of."

Bel ignored the subtle glances cast in his direction. As such, he was actually somewhat grateful when Theobold Nordren refilled his goblet and boisterously cried out.

"That's our Sir Geoffrey! A hero three times over, he is!" He paused to take a swig. "He saved the city of Galadin from a surprise attack, singlehandedly burned the enemy siege camp at the Battle of St. Golan's, and drove the surviving Guardian raiders back into the sea! Of course, I lost a few ships in the battle, but overall, the city was saved."

Bel could sense and sympathize with Sir Geoffrey's discomfort at being so publicly lauded. Even in his tenure as caption of Dermont's light cavalry, he was often reluctant to accept the accolades that came with his martial successes. While he might win a battle or prevent a raid, he knew that his victories were derived from his proficiency at killing. Unlike many warriors, Bel did not enjoy violence, but simply understood it as part of his duty. Sir Marcus Harding held similar beliefs, and unless he misjudged him completely, Sir Geoffrey did as well.

"These documents you mentioned..." Bel interjected, sparing the acorn knight further distress. "Do you have them?"

"Yes, sir," Geoffrey said. He motioned to his squire. "Freddy?"

With a smart salute, the boy hurried forth and set a thick leather scroll case on the table. Sir Geoffrey opened it and drew forth a roll of documents penned in a neat and narrow hand. Carefully he laid them out upon the tabletop and passed them along via Sir Armel to the queen. "These documents outline various trade agreements and other such potential benefits of a prospective alliance. They were compiled by Sir Adolfo of the Brock's

Guild of Weavers, though you will see that they all bear the official seal of Galadin as well as Baron Lughus's signature."

At this, Bel watched Thom Reaver's eyes peer over at the documents from afar. "That's Lughus's hand, alright," he said. "You can tell by the swirl of the 'L' and the loop of the 'G.' Old Hob used to tell him he signed his name like it was writ with the point of a sword."

Sir Geoffrey paused and eyed the big boy pensively. "Now, how is it exactly that you claim to know the baron?" he asked. "Who are you, if you don't mind my asking?"

Bel eyed Thom intently. He knew part of the young man's story, but was just as curious as Sir Geoffrey to hear more.

"My name is Thom Reaver, though when last I saw Lughus, I was simply Thom." He took a deep breath. "I was once an apprentice to Loremaster Rastis Glendaro, uncle to the Lord-Baron of the Brock and member of the Council of Five. Lughus and I and another apprentice—Royne—grew up together. It was the three of us, and Rastis's Steward, a Wrathorn of Clan Brindlebairne by the name of Hob."

"Anyhow, a week or so after King Kredor's coronation, Rastis sent Lughus and I on a journey to finish our studies. We were to go to Baronbrock together. Lughus was to..."

Thom's eyes widened like one who has suddenly reached a great epiphany.

"Lughus was to go to Galadin to the court of the Baron, while I was to journey onward to Wrathorn so as to record the history of Hob's people." He breathed a heavy sigh. "Our guide was another Blackguard, a man named Crodane."

Geoffrey's gaze narrowed. "You're *that* Thom?"

Thom nodded.

"Why would the Loremaster traffic with Blackguards?" Marina asked. "Doesn't the Council of Five lead the Order?"

"They do," Geoffrey said. "Though it appears that in an effort to undermine King Kredor's using Lughus as a hostage force the Brock to its knees, he sent him away in secret to inherit the throne of his grandfather, Arcis Galadin. " He turned toward Thom, "The man called Crodane, or 'the Marshal' as he was also known, gave his life to save Baron Lughus, passing on the title to him. They say Rastis was arrested on a charge of high treason, but beyond that no one is certain what happened to him."

Thom's face flushed, torn between great sorrow and great rage. Tears gathered in his eyes and in a tremulous voice, he asked in a voice that was little more than a whisper. "What about a third apprentice? He stayed behind with Rastis. Is there any word of his fate?"

"Oh I can answer that," Theobold said. "Apparently, your friend—Master Royne, is it? He escaped to Grantis and fell in with a general by the name of Navarro. Together, they rallied the scattered survivors of the defeated legions and commandeered a small fleet of Dwerin ships before sailing north to join us in the Brock."

"So Royne is in the Brock as well?"

"Well, no." Theo refilled his goblet. "I believe he was going to, but decided instead to stay behind with a man named Salasco the Wall. From what the general said, they're looking to rally more Blackguards to help in the fight."

"And no one has heard of him since?"

"No," the young lord said, "Though, speaking of Loremasters, when we first met the general, there was a bit of confusion. You see, the lord-baron, Perin Glendaro, is the nephew of the old Loremaster, but the general said he was sent by the Loremaster *Royne* Glendaro and Perin had never heard of him."

Bel watched the color drain from the big lad's face. "But Lughus?" he said. "You're telling me that at least Lughus is safe?"

"Aye, of course he is," Theo said. "He's the bloody Marshal. Ain't no finer hand with a sword than him. Plus, he's got Brigid the Blade to watch his back. Beautiful as she is deadly. Head over heels for each other, they are—and betrothed." Theo chuckled. "Lucky bas—bloke. At any rate, you've got nothing to fear about your friend."

Sir Geoffrey nodded. "What he says is true."

Bel's brow furrowed. Something about these titles—the Marshal, the Blade, the Wall. Each one struck some chord deep within the recesses of his mind. It was that same, vague sense of familiarity despite the certainty that he had never actually met them.

The Tower, however...

Sir Armel cleared his throat. "Perhaps we should return to the task at hand."

"My apologies, your majesty," Thom Reaver said, bowing his head.

"It's quite alright," Marina said, "and and your insight is appreciated." She turned to Sir Geoffrey. "But as for this alliance, what—specifically—does your baron propose?"

"As I understand it," Geoffrey began, "your enemies are massing along the Nivanus Pass, which leads directly to the eastern baronies of the Brock. Now, as it is right now, the barons already fight a war on two fronts—Andoch along the southern border, and there's talk of hired Wrathorn tribes given King Kredor's leave to raid along the north. We've no wish to have to face a third. If we can somehow…manage to drive off or defeat the army at the Nivanus, our forces could perhaps band together at the border and—in a sense—fight back to back."

Marina eyed Bel. "Lord-General," she said. She knew he cared little for the title, but in an official situation such as this, such honorariums could not be avoided. "You have been customarily silent. What do you think?"

Bel's brow creased pensively. "The Nivanus Army has long been a hornets' nest just waiting to burst, and while we've survived thus far by simply leaving it be, it might be time to knock it down, particularly if we don't have to do it alone."

"That being said…" he continued. "I'm not quite sure that we're ready for against such odds. We need more men, and if the Brock is already facing enemies to the north and south, it's unlikely that they realistically provide more." He turned to face the acorn knight. "Don't misunderstand me, Sir Geoffrey. I welcome this alliance. However, I do not yet know what either of us can do in a practical sense to help the other with what needs to be done."

"Surely four Blackguards is a formidable force," Nordren said. "There were but three on our side at St. Golan's.

"True," Bel said, "But the Guardians have yet to fully commit to battle— at least here in Montevale. We have fought Kingsmen, but none of them were men with titles, and as I understand it, that is where the true power of the Guardians lies."

"And let's not forget what happened in Grantis," Geoffrey said.

"True," Bel mused. "And while we've defeated a fair number of the Plague King's greatest generals, Dermont may be forced to cede some of these vacant commands to men of the Order—anointed men to match our own."

"There's still much and more I don't understand about the Order and the titles and such," Sir Armel said.

"You're not the only one," Theobold said.

"Regardless," Bel continued. "If we are to save this realm—and assist the Brock—we need to begin taking the offensive, and to do that, we need to rally more support."

"You have suggestions?" Marina asked.

Bel nodded. "There are many men who would support us against Dermont, particularly after our victory against the Death Knell. With Inen Vilnois defeated as well, the lords of Whitemane might also be inclined to stand with us."

"Agreed," the queen said.

"The Talondaire lands fall within the reaches of Whitemane," Welmsey said. "The very heart of Whitemane, one might say..."

"Indeed," Bel said, "and with his support, the other lords of the region might be convinced to stand with us. "

Sir Armel nodded. "A sound plan," he said, "But was not Lord Talondaire *also* forced to remain at court? After Clearpoint, I was under the impression that he too would be one that the Plague King wanted to keep close—like your cousin Lady Valerie or Marius's kinsman, Lord Guillon."

Marina shook her head. "I have not spoken to him," she said, "but word reached us some time ago that he had sworn his loyalty to the Plague King in order to maintain rights to his lands."

"And you think a man like that's worth chasing after?" the Shackle asked. "Considering the way those noble bastards fled the field after the Death Knell's offer of clemency, I'd be hesitant to trust any of that lot."

"You make a fair point," Marina said, "And though Tally is my cousin, his family has maintained the castle at Dunwald for generations. When my father and I agreed to submit to exile in Castle Tremontane, he felt obligated to see to the safety and security of his people. If doing so required that he bow before the Plague King, I expect he would have done it, in spite of his inner feelings."

"Still, if he were to join us—and with him the rest of Whitemane," Sir Norton said, "would we actually have a force sizable enough to take the Nivanus?"

"Perhaps," Bel mused, "but before we decide on any course of action, I would know what our potential allies think. How dire is the need? If we do not ride for the Nivanus now, will the Brock fall?" He eyed Sir Geoffrey intently. "Did your Baron indicate his thoughts in that regard?"

The acorn knight scratched at his beard. "He did not, though I believe his immediate intentions were to secure his southern border and prepare his people for the winter," he said. "After our victory at St. Golan's the Andochans were in such disarray that it might well take until the spring before they're able to field another army in the north."

Theo Nordren nodded in agreement. "And once the snow starts falling, the Brock closes up tighter than a—" He paused. "Tighter than a clam until the spring thaw. Quite frankly, I've never known how you folk do it— fighting onward through the snow and ice. Then again, after a hundred years, I suppose you get used to it."

Bel remained stoic, but he was aware within himself and his fellows of a subtle sense of indignity. The War of the Horses was an internal conflict, a family matter, more or less, and like any family conflict, it was not something they liked to discuss with outsiders. For it shined a bright light on the entire realm's great shame.

Indeed, while Sir Geoffrey seemed an honorable man, the young lord of Nordren—despite his lineage—seemed somewhat lacking in character.

In the midst of the awkward silence, Bel noticed Thom Reaver shifting uncomfortably in his seat down the table. A spastic grimace flashed across the big lad's face.

He knows something, Bel thought. *Something he's afraid to say...*

"Thom?" he began, breaking the stillness, "You have something else to add?"

Thom's face drained of color and it seemed to Bel that the boy was not so much looking at him, but past him at the wall. A quick glance told Bel that there was nothing there, but the boy's eyes continued to shift like one lost in the madness of a fever.

"Thom?" he asked again, his voice somewhat gentler, kinder. "What is it?"

At length, the big boy's shoulders slumped and his eyes fell to the tabletop. "As I said earlier," he began, "Lughus and I were to reach the Brock by way of a ship out of the Andochan city of Galdoran. It was there, though, that we were separated. Lughus followed Crodane northward by land to the Brock, whereas I..." He paused. "I ended up in the company of a Wrathorn Blackguard, a great warrior by the name of Magnus Bloodbeard, the Reaver."

Sir Geoffrey's brow creased with interest, but he remained silent.

"For many months, we wandered about the Sorgund Isles trying to find some of Magnus's old crew mates. It was them that betrayed him to the kingsmen in Galdoran and he wanted to…settle matters."

"I'm sure that was an experience," Nordren said. "Bloody pirates."

"Yes, well. There's much more to the story, but the long and short of it is that we ended up following the last of them eastward to the Lighthouse of Castone." Thom paused. "Castone is…well, let's just say it's an…unnatural place."

Geoffrey of Pyle pursed his lips. "It gave me an ill feeling as well."

Thom gave a nod. "As one of the Anointed, I'm not surprised," he said. "The Keepers of the Lighthouse have existed since the old empire of Calendral—before the Order of the Guardians came to be. They…" he paused. "How do I say this? They're followers of the Warlock."

"The Warlock?" Horn asked.

"Kalius Wrogan," the Shackle finished. "The one St. Aiden and the Guardians fought against. Ain't you ever been to church?"

"Nope," Horn replied.

"In fairness, nor have I." The Shackle smirked. "Least not since I was a lad."

"So, you're saying," Bel broke in, "that the Keepers…"

"They worship the Dark Brother," Thom said. "They worship Dibhor."

Theobold Nordren raised an eyebrow. "Now this might sound mad coming from a sailor, given our reputation for superstitions, but really? Are you sure, and if so, is that really a crime? I mean, the Keepers are rather well respected among the nobility across Termain. Plenty of noble houses have employed tutors from among those at the Lighthouse, particularly in a case where the Order lacked the men to send a scribe or a scholar." He shrugged. "I feel like if they were really a threat, we'd have heard about it. Castone barely has any settlements as it is, let alone an army."

"No," Thom said, his voice just above a whisper. "They have an army."

The others waited for him to continue, but he said no more, prompting Bel to speak.

"What do you mean, Thom?"

The big boy looked stricken. "An army of the dead."

Bel felt Marina's eyes upon him, torn between fear, concern, and disbelief. Bel offered her a silent shrug. Around the table, men made utterances of various pitch and tone, expressions of fear, shock, and disbelief.

Thom examined the tabletop. "I know how it sounds," he said. "Believe me, I know. But...it's what I saw, or at least, what I *think* I saw." He paused and breathed a heavy sigh. "I don't know. Maybe I'm wrong. There was a lot happening. Maybe they were just men, but...it didn't seem like it. They..." He paused. "They didn't bleed. Every time Magnus cut one down—arm off, leg cut away, head lopped off—there was no blood. No blood at all."

Beneath the shadow of his brow, Bel glanced subtly around the table in an attempt to gauge the others' reactions. Marina's face remained thoughtfully impassive so as to betray no judgment. Theo Nordren was clearly skeptical, while Sir Geoffrey remained deep in thought. Horn shrugged at the Shackle, and Armel's expression remained customarily stern.

Bel remembered the field outside of Clearpoint, the sting of the spear in his side, and the sudden, unnatural flood of vitality rush through him at the simultaneous moment of Marcus Harding's sacrifice.

"We've all seen our share of things we can't explain," Bel said at last, "and whether we speak of men or...something else, we cannot turn a blind eye to whatever may be happening at the Lighthouse."

"Rallying allies, liberating more lands, and defending ourselves from outside threats..." Horn shook his head. "It spreads our people out pretty thin."

Sir Geoffrey breathed a sigh. "If it helps the alliance," he said, "my people and I are prepared to stay through the winter, so long as you don't mind the extra mouths to feed."

"I'm certain we can find a place for forty of the famous archers of the Brock," Sir Armel said, "with their Blackguard captain to boot!"

"Of course, your family is welcome to continue to lodge here in the castle," Marina added, "as our personal guests."

"Thank you, your majesty," Geoffrey said, bowing his head, "You do us too much honor."

"Perhaps while you're here, your boy there can learn to ride." Armel said kindly. "Your daughter as well."

"Oh they'd like that," the acorn knight said, turning to smile at his son.

The Shackle picked his teeth for a moment and gave a grunt. "Anyways, while I don't doubt the Reaver, the Lighthouse is but a ghost story for the time being. Seeing as we've an abundance of Blackguards, why don't I do a bit of scouting and have a look-see, eh?"

Theobold Nordren gave a nod. "If we're agreed on the subject of the alliance, I can take you with me on my return. We can put you to shore just north of the Lighthouse and save you having to cross the mountains twice."

The Shackle nodded. "It'll certainly save some time," he said.

"If you're willing, I won't stop you," Bel said. "But I know you're not one to stray too far from Feyhold."

The Shackle shrugged. "I lived as a ghost myself for years. Who better to hunt for a ghost story? Just make sure the place is still standing for when I return."

Thom Reaver eyed him intently. "The town seems deserted, but I think the enemy simply lies in wait, hiding indoors until summoned," he said. "Whatever you do, do *not* climb the Lighthouse and if you hear the sound of a war horn, *run*. Run away as fast as you can."

"Yes," Marina agreed. "Please be careful."

The Shackle gave a nod. "I only aim to have a look," he said. "Nothing more...your majesty."

Once more, Thom Reaver breathed a heavy sigh and wrung his hands. "If you're headed back to the Brock, Lord Nordren, can I ask that you deliver something to Lughus for me?"

"Aye," Nordren shrugged, "Though if you like, I could take you there with me as well? Seeing as you're old mates."

Thom shook his head. "No, no," he said quickly, "I...I'm not quite ready to join him yet." He glanced around nervously. "I...feel it only right that after everything, I do what I can to help all of you here in Montevale."

Bel nodded, though he suspected there was more to Thom's reluctance than he chose to share.

"In any case," Thom continued, "I'd like you to take him this."

With a careful movement, the big lad carefully withdrew something from the belt of his tunic, concealed beneath his half-cloak. It was a large key fashioned from what appeared to be silver, though here and there it bore the marks of age. In appearance, it was relatively simple, though the end of its handle had been fashioned into a five-sided figure, the same as appeared upon the banners of Andoch and the tabards of the kingsmen.

At once, Bel felt a strange sensation, and as he glanced across the table, he saw that Sir Geoffrey and the Shackle appeared to be similarly affected. An intense fervor gripped his chest, and his eyes widened with wonder.

"Callah's Key," he declared.

Thom gave a nod. "Yes," he said. "The real one. Lost for centuries, but recovered once again."

"By the Brethren!" Sir Geoffrey whispered.

Bel turned toward the others at the table. "This is the scepter of the Guardian-King," he said.

"Forged by the Lady of Light herself to help St. Aiden bind the darkness of Dibhor." Geoffrey added. "To seal away the Beast."

The Shackle smirked at Thom. "Blood and fire, aren't you just full of surprises?"

Thom's face reddened. "It was won by the might of Magnus Bloodbeard atop the Lighthouse of Castone. It's how I came to know about the...the dead." He turned to Theo Nordren. "Will you take it to him?" he asked. "To Lughus, I mean? As a Galadin, I feel it's only right that he should guard it."

Nordren nodded sagely. "Absolutely," he said. "It would be my honor. I'll take it to him with compliments and—if I may be so bold—good news about the alliance?"

Marina nodded. "We shall still need a bit of time to go over the details," she said, exchanging a glance with Bel, "but yes. I believe we may safely name one another friends."

Theo grinned and raised his goblet. "Huzzah!"

CHAPTER 13: MUCK & MIRE

While Galadin had long held a reputation as a good and relatively safe place (as would befit the birthplace of the blessed saint), it was still a city—a den of humanity—and wheresoever one found an abundance of people, there one was certain too to find its seedier houses of crime and ill repute.

True, much of the this action had been significantly curtailed, reined in following the young Baron Galadin's elevation of the infamous Adolfo the Madder. And while it could never be eliminated entirely, with responsibility for its management placed in Sir Adolfo's crimson hands, it could at least be controlled.

The Bodkin was a large tavern along the shores of Lake Bartund and the seat of Adolfo's power. Damaged in the kingsmen's surprise assault during the summer assembly of barons, the Madder purchased the building, as well as the surrounding warehouses, only to renovate and expand the dilapidated structure. Now, it served as the seat of Sir Adolfo's unofficial fief from where he directed his scrupulously unscrupulous activities.

The acrid odor of pipe smoke mingled with the lingering fragrance of spilled ale greeted Brigid as she entered the tavern and passed into the large common room. In one corner, a bard strummed a lute to the accompaniment of a hand drummer. Opposite them, a brutish old man with a red nose stood behind the bar, scowling as he wiped out a tankard with a dirty rag. Ruffians and hooligans of all types sat here and there drinking, smoking, and playing dice while serving women bounced from table to table refilling clay tankards and drinking horns.

Brigid spied Sir Adolfo seated at his table upon the dais across the room. Throwing back her hood, she hurried through the common room only to find her path suddenly inhibited. A brawny sailor barred her way. His swirling tattoos ranged up and down his arms in an imitation of the Wrathorn fashion. He grinned, resting his hands on his hips and puffed out his chest.

"Hello, darling."

With a weary sigh, Brigid looked past him and raised an eyebrow at Adolfo.

From his seat, the Madder shrugged apologetically and waved his hand. "Bursa, if you please?"

Without hesitation, Bursa, the Madder's ogre of a bodyguard, strode over, grabbed the sailor by the throat, and drove his face into the nearest tabletop. Ale spilled as a pair of tankards overturned in the scuffle, and the men sitting there—a trio of bargemen fresh from the dock—leapt to their feet to avoid the sudden flood.

"Lady's teats! What the fuck?" the sailor gasped as Bursa began dragging him to the door like a sack of potatoes.

Brigid eyed Adolfo. "Don't kill him," she said testily.

Adolfo sighed. "Bursa?"

"Aye, boss. I heared her," the bodyguard said, hoisting the man to his feet. "I'll just frow him in the gutta."

Brigid rolled her eyes and slipped into the chair opposite Adolfo. Ledgers, scroll cases, and stacks of parchment were piled high around him along with ink pots, quills, and sticks of sealing wax. "So..." she said, taking pains not to disturb the organized chaos, "what did you find out?"

Adolfo paused to retrieve a decanter from a neighboring table. Carefully, he refilled the glass goblet in front of him and waved a hand implicitly at a second. When Brigid shook her head, he returned the decanter to its place and idly lifted the goblet to his nose.

"The baron is right. The Guardians you slew at the Houndstooth were not alone. There was at least one more anointed Guardian among them, as well as a number of their attending chancellery courtiers. However, from what I can tell, only the Needle and the Mask were able to find their way into the castle."

Brigid nodded. "The Houndstooth itself may be secure, but even surrounded by walls, a city is a sieve—particularly a city with a dockyard. Unless we order the guard to stop and thoroughly search every wagon, raft, or keelboat to arrive—unless we interrogate every man, woman, and child to enter through the gates—there is always the possibility of someone slipping through."

"In any case," the Madder continued. "When the Needle and the Mask failed to return from their assassination attempt, the courtiers split into pairs and fled the city while the third constable remained behind, hoping to succeed where the others failed."

Brigid sighed. A zealot. Like the Hammer. To such a man, slaying a Blackguard would be seen as a sacred duty—and a profitable one. Perhaps not in gold, but in prestige. The constable to defeat *any* of the famous Three would be to immortalized forever in the annals of the Order's greatest heroes. "And where is he now?" she asked.

"Where do all rats hide?" Adolfo mused.

"Among the garbage and filth, I would assume," Brigid said.

"Correct."

"So I'm to search every gutter and garderobe in the city?"

"Fortunately, no." Adolfo said. "You see, along the edge of the lake near the spillway is Galadin's very own shitbrook where the poor folk and the dung collectors deposit their refuse. It runs downhill to empty into a boggy moor so as to not cause problems for the town proper."

"Yes, I remember from the days we lived in Hounton," Brigid said. "And you believe this is where the last Guardian has built a little...nest?"

"I do," the Madder said. "It's the only place in the city where the baron's hound would be unable to sniff him out. Too many...confounding scents."

Brigid chewed her lip. "Can you take me there now?" she asked.

Adolfo pressed the tips of his gloved fingers together. "I can," he said, "unless you would rather wait for the light of day?"

"I don't mind the dark, and I imagine it won't smell any different after sunup," she said. "We should go now."

"If the Lady Blade insists, who am I to refuse," Adolfo said. He grabbed his crossbow from where it sat—loaded—upon a nearby chair. "I'll warn you in advance," he drawled, "it is a truly unpleasant odor."

"It's a shitbrook." She smirked. "It would be quite foolish to expect anything less."

In the streets outside of the Bodkin, the night was dark and crisp. Brigid pulled her cloak tighter and drew down her hood while Adolfo donned a woolen half-cape of his own and a fur-lined bycocket hat to protect his scalp. Few folk wandered the lakeside streets and alleys at this time of night, though braziers blazed at regular intervals, patrolled intermittently by members of the Galadin guard. From time to time the men might call out or hail the pair of nightwalkers as they passed, but both Brigid and Adolfo were known to them and they did not impede their progress.

There was a certain comfort Brigid felt beneath the shadow of darkness, as well as a certain thrill. It reminded her of her earliest days in Galadin when she would slip away from the small house she shared with Geoffrey's family in order to scout out the city, desperately hoping to find a way in to the Houndstooth. Even now, when their duties didn't keep them otherwise occupied, she would sometimes lead Lughus on moonlit strolls around the castle ward or along the paths of St. Elisa's Grotto where they had first met.

She sighed, feeling a touch of longing at his absence. Yet, while few folk could match the Marshal for stealth when ranging in the wilds, stalking prey through the forests and dales, in the streets of a city—particularly a city where he was so recognizable as their beloved baron—he and his faithful hound would stick out like a sore thumb. No, the streets and alleys were the hunting ground of the Blade.

"It's just up here, right?" she whispered to Adolfo.

"Yes," he said. "The gate will be closed, but there's a small postern that will allow us passage through."

Brigid followed Adolfo along the small pathway that led from the main road toward the wall. In the relative solitude of the night, she cleared her throat. "So," she asked the Madder, "was that Grantisi wine you were enjoying when I arrived?"

"I *only* drink Grantisi wine, Lady Brigid."

"Yes, but was this one accompanied by a friendly note from a friendly new ally?"

Adolfo stiffened. "It might have been," he said coldly.

Brigid gave a smirk. "Good for you."

They reached the postern and Adolfo paused as he withdrew the key from within his cloak. "I'll remind you, Lady Brigid, that while your title grants you certain...*knowledge* of me—about my life, about my past, things that only my brother knew—in certain circles, that knowledge could cause trouble."

"Adolfo," Brigid said, narrowing her gaze. "I know this, and you know well that I know." Her smirk returned. "I only mean to say that I am happy for you."

Adolfo unlocked the door and returned the key to wherever he had held it concealed.

"Well, yes," he said quietly, "Thank you."

He stepped back and Brigid carefully stepped forward to try the door. With some difficulty, it swung open to reveal an overgrown pathway alongside a muddy creek. Even now, she could sense a horrible stench wafting on the breeze. At once, she drew a handkerchief from one of the inside pockets Jergan had sewn into her cloak and tied it around her face.

"So..." Adolfo began, pausing to do the same. "Is the baron also aware of my history, of the story that brought Gareth and I under the wardship of Grendel the Butcher and former Blade?"

"He does," Brigid said idly, passing through the postern. "Much like his grandfather, he could not care less. He considers you a loyal man of Galadin, and—if you'll allow it—a friend."

Adolfo remained silent, and leaving the postern slightly ajar, followed after her. Together, they walked along the muddy creek toward the ever-strengthening odor. Brigid's stomach churned as she began to discern great piles of waste and leavings illuminated in the darkness by the dim light of the stars. Broken pottery, discarded food, rotting mounds of offal, human waste—all in various stages of decay. Thankfully, as she glanced back at the postern, a slight shift in the shadows told her that she would not have to endure the place for very long.

With an almost imperceptible click of her tongue, Brigid notified Adolfo and together they continued to creep along the creek bed, feigning interest in this or that false clue or imagined footprint. Adolfo stepped past her to investigate the base of an alder tree, carefully fingering the stock of his crossbow. Beneath the cover of her cloak, Brigid's hands curled around the hilts of Whisper and Shade.

Whoever it was, he was doing an excellent job of keeping to the shadows without even the slightest superfluous movement. In fact, were it not for the fact that she had somehow sensed the vague presence of a Guardian back at The Bodkin, he might have actually been able to get the jump on her after all.

As Adolfo proclaimed back at the Bodkin—in a voice loud enough to be detected by a discerning ear—they had tracked the movements of the Andochan intruders back to the shitbrook. Just as they also knew that the remaining Guardian was frequenting the Bodkin as a means of monitoring Adolfo. Yet Brigid knew that if they were to attempt to confront the man in the open, he would simply remain hidden or disappear. So she determined that in order to trap a predator, she would play the part of prey, drawing him out by feigning ignorance and walking blindly into what he falsely believed to be his domain.

But she was the Blade, the one who stood upon the shadow's edge. The darkness was her hunting ground and there she walked unafraid.

With an overt sigh, Brigid paused and knelt down to give the appearance of interest in the muddy ground. As she did so, she began to focus on her breathing, calming her nerves and preparing herself for the fight she knew was soon to come. It was an exercise that she had picked up from Lughus and he from Crodane. A way to center herself and clear her mind so as to be wholly present in the moment of combat. Beneath the cover of her cloak, she slipped Whisper and Shade from their sheaths. Adolfo was no longer discernible in the darkness in front of her, but he knew vaguely that he was still there.

The Guardian drew ever-nearer. Time seemed to slow. A light breeze toyed with a loose strand of her hair, before suddenly, riding upon the current of air, there came a low whirling sound that ended in a resounding *crack!*

Brigid anticipated the attack. She sprang forward, narrowly avoiding the vicious sting of a long leather lash. As she recovered her footing, Adolfo loosed his crossbow. The bolt went wide of its mark, but whistled near enough to throw the Guardian off balance.

Justin D. Bello

Mindful of the whip's return stroke, Brigid lunged forward and struck out with both blades. Whisper found only air, but Shade found flesh—not much, but enough to draw a grunt of pain. In the darkness, Adolfo cursed aloud and hurriedly began resetting his winch.

Brigid leapt back out of reach and turned to face her opponent. Only now could she discern him against the darkness. He was one of the bargemen from the Bodkin, one of the men whose ale had spilled in Bursa's scuffle with the boorish ruffian. She had felt his presence somewhere in the tavern, but could not quite hone in on exactly where. Now he stood before her leering and brandishing a long, leather bullwhip.

"I can think of no place better for a Blackguard to meet their end than a river of piss and shit!" he snapped.

Brigid ducked beneath another whirling strike from the lash and shifted her weight from one foot to the other. The Guardian was clearly skilled and the extensive reach and maneuverability of his weapon presented a challenge for her daggers. When he struck out again, forcing her to leap back into the revolting muck along the creek bed, she considered throwing one of her blades, but thought better of it. Given the darkness and the whip's protective lashing, she saw little chance of hitting her mark and to lose a blade would only put her at further disadvantage.

Again and again, the whip snapped like a frenzied viper. Brigid hopped from side to side to avoid each attack, but before long, she realized the intention of his relentless assault. With every strike, he was slowly driving her backward in order to position himself between her and Adolfo. For doing so would eliminate the threat of the crossbow by increasing the chance that a stray shot might hit her instead.

But Adolfo too must have sensed this strategy. He paced quickly in the opposite direction and let loose a quick shot. As before, it flew wide of the Guardian, but the distraction provided exactly the chance Brigid needed to dart in and score a slash along the man's left side. The wound wasn't lethal, but it bled fiercely.

Before she could jump to safety, however, the whip's stinging return stroke bit into her calf. For a fleeting moment, the intensity of the pain dropped her to one knee and she felt the squidge of cold filth as it soaked into the material of her trouser leg. but she ground her teeth and recovered her footing mere moments before the Guardian renewed his attack.

156

Adolfo made to reload his crossbow, but before he could do so, the Guardian turned and drove him back with another flurry of lashings. The Madder nimbly stepped back out of harm's way, but his boot landed in a particularly thick pile of slippery filth. His feet went out from under him and he hit the muddy ground with such force that his breath was forced out of him with a terrible *whoosh!*

With Adolfo down, Brigid knew that she needed to act quickly. Ignoring the stinging whip, she lunged at her enemy again and again weaving from side to side. Each time, the Guardian stepped backward, hoping to hold her at a distance like a circus performer baiting a bear. Brigid let him. She wanted him to feel in control.

Finally when the full length of the whip stretched between them, she raised her left arm, feigning an attack with Whisper. At once, the Guardian countered and the braided lash coiled around her left wrist and held her fast. She cried out at the searing pain. The Guardian smiled wickedly and with a rough tug pulled her toward him as he drew a wicked-looking stiletto from his hip.

"You're mine!" he said. With an arrogant chuckle he began to reel her in like a fish. Beneath her cloak, she readied Shade in her free hand, and as soon as she was near enough, parried his stiletto and slipped her dagger between his ribs.

At once, the man's smug triumph transformed into horror as he began to sputter and choke. Beneath the shadows of the moonlight, darkness stained his lips and trickled out of the corners of his mouth. He fell to the ground and Brigid felt the lash around her wrist slacken.

"Bloody Blackguard," the Guardian sputtered.

Brigid ignored the taunt and glanced past him to discern Adolfo slowly regaining his feet.

The Guardian winced and cried out in agony. "You've killed me, you Brokan whore!"

Brigid fixed the Guardian with an icy stare. "*You* were the fool who tried to match daggers with the Blade," she said. "But while you may fall here, you can die knowing that—unlike you—*I* will ensure a proper burial for your remains."

The man spit a great glob of blood. "It matters little," he grimaced. "Yet I will die happy knowing that I will be avenged. For there are many and more of us, and only three of you."

Brigid's gaze narrowed. "Yes, with men like Andresen the Breath or Lemb the Thrush, I fear I may never sleep again."

"Not them," the Guardian sputtered. "The Hammer...his need for vengeance knows no bounds..."

Brigid watched as the man's eyes glazed and the last rattle echoed in his throat. Adolfo joined her as she stood over the body, limping slightly, but otherwise unhurt.

"It seems your trap worked, Lady Blade," the Madder said. "Well-played."

Brigid nodded though her thoughts were elsewhere, weighing the dead man's final threats. In the aftermath of the attack on Houndstooth, Lughus had had been increasingly restless, and at night she had caught him lying awake, unable to sleep for the weight of the decisions he carried around with him. When at last she prevailed upon him to confide in her, he admitted the details of his potential plans: escalation. To move from simply defending the Brock, to attacking Andoch. For while they may have driven the Guardians back across the border, if those remnants remained garrisoned at Stonebridge Castle were not dealt with, they were bound to return with the spring thaws.

"I've known my fair share of bullies," Lughus had said. "You can drive them off, but soon enough their pride will send them back, and more often than not, they'll bring friends."

Brigid tugged the handkerchief from her face and sighed. It was late. She was very tired and her wrist burned like the fires of the Abyss. She needed a bath. She needed to lie down. She needed Lughus.

"Lady's Grace, this place stinks like shit."

"And so do we, I'm afraid." The Madder frowned. "But come. I'll have men retrieve the body of our friend."

CHAPTER 14: AN UNEXPECTED ALLY

It has been nearly a year now since my arrival in Andoch and my unexpected elevation to the rank of Loremaster. While at times I am aware of a vague miasma of resentment emanating from a few of those under my jurisdiction, most appear to have accepted the reality of my position.

Of course, I am not without empathy for those who balk at my leadership. As a true son of the Brock, I have often found myself at odds with the strict adherence to order and authority that is so much a part of the Andochan identity. Furthermore, to be suddenly elevated to the very pinnacle of leadership within the ranks of the Order—and at such a young age—was certain to ruffle the feathers of the more conservative, established sages and scholars.

Yet, I believe that in my brief tenure, I have found acceptance through my belief that knowledge and freedom are inexorably linked, and that the academic pursuits of the men of my tower are their own —so long as their endeavors are conducted with an eye to benevolence and the betterment of all people—regardless of realm, wealth, or lot in life. Is this not the mandate of the Order entire?

Unfortunately, if one were to survey my fellow counselors, it would appear not to be so. An attitude of insular superiority pervades the council chamber, though considering I am the junior of the Chancellor—my nearest colleague in age by over two decades—I suppose it should be somewhat expected.

Thus, I find my voice often falls upon deaf ears, and my topics for discussion and reform often ignored. I, in accordance with my perhaps regrettable nature, insist upon forcing various issues, and were I not responsible for the official council minutes, my motions would almost certainly be stricken from official records.

Yet, I refuse to become a complacent old stone gathering moss and hoarfrost while the poor suffer and the wealthy rejoice in abundance.

Luckily, I appear to have found an ally in the crown prince. In many ways, Valder appears to share many or my beliefs, and while he may disagree with others, I find that he is at least willing to consider them and to engage in civil discourse regarding the points of conflict. These debates give me hope for a brighter future despite the unfortunate stagnation that characterizes court politics now...

Royne looked up from *The Book of Histories* to consider the ceramic crucible beside him where he had been slowly attempting to emulate one of the alchemical experiments Master Kebir had described in his most recent lecture. The minerals had melted, yet rather than blend together smoothly, they had very clearly formed into their own separate puddles—as when adding a few drops of oil into a basin of water.

With a sigh of frustration, Royne rubbed his eyes and massaged his temples. Whether from the tension at his own struggles or the odors emanating from the burning minerals, he was beginning to feel the throb of another headache. Bloody alchemy! Why was it proving so—dare he admit it—difficult? In a fit of frustration, he blew out the flame heating the crucible only to burn his hand as he attempted to dispose of the molten materials in a pail of sand.

"Red Death and Black Abyss!" he shouted as the thick, ceramic dish clattered to the floor. In a matter of moments, the materials cooled, hardening into their distinct, solid states.

Damn it all Salasco, would that we could have swapped places! he thought. Surely turning fugitives to friends would have been easier than this bloody nonsense. What was the bloody point anyhow? Mixing things and melting things and distilling various decoctions. Most of the time, the resulting byproducts weren't even used for anything! They were simply discarded, which of course made anyone with even half a grain of pragmatic sensibility wonder why he even bothered in the first place. Was it simply an esoteric exercise of knowledge for knowledge's sake?

"Blood and fire!" he cried aloud. His voice echoed along the forgotten parapet that had become his private refuge away from the Symposium and the dormitory. A trio of pigeons, disturbed by his ranting, took wing and fluttered off across the rooftops. Royne watched them go, muttering curses under his breath and rubbing his wounded hand. So embroiled was he in his own bitterness that he failed to notice that he was no longer alone.

"Ah! Now I understand," said a voice. "It makes perfect sense now."

Royne whirled around to face the intruder and was not at all surprised to find Amara.

"Oh," he said, his voice edgy with disdain. "It's you."

Amara folded her arms across her chest and gave a smug smile. "Some of the children were spreading rumors that a cursing gargoyle had come to roost in the parapet overlooking the forum," she said. "But it's only the ignorant polecat."

Royne ground his teeth and fought to appear unbothered. "Can you just go away?" he asked. "I don't have time for your nonsense."

Amara sighed and rested her hands on her hips. "I would," she said, "but because of the red-cloaked soldiers, we are forbidden from walking the walls at this time of day, which means you will have to come inside as well."

Royne shrugged. "This is the first I'm hearing of it," he said, "and I've been coming out here for days. Over a week, I should think. It's quiet and it helps to avoid having to suffer the meddling of nosy fools."

Amara's gaze narrowed, though a smile spread across her lips. "It's quiet because it is forbidden. You could be seen."

"Unlikely," Royne said dismissively. "Besides, while you all might be content to shut yourselves away from the problems of the world, I have a responsibility to the people in it. I need to know what is going on so as to better defend against the cruelty of our enemies."

"Our?" she snorted. "Your enemies. We have no enemies."

"Yet you fear being seen." He gave a derisive snort. "Now who's ignorant?"

"Judging by that ruined crucible, I would still say you." She shook her head. "You're very lucky that you didn't poison yourself by overheating that much lead. The fumes could have killed you."

"Well then, it's a good thing I did it out here in the open air, isn't it?"

Amara rolled her eyes.

A fanfare from the forum below brought Royne's attention back around. Over the last day or so, the kingsmen had been quite busy with the construction of a large platform, almost like a stage. Now, as Royne peered over the parapet, he could tell that the show—whatever that might be—was about to start. Carefully, he peered over the crenellated wall and watched as an honor guard of heavily armored kingsmen marched into the forum and stood at attention before the stage. Their purpose, no doubt, was to serve as a line of defense separating the performers from the heavy throngs of Grantisi commonfolk who—whether by choice or coercion—had been packed tightly into the square.

An uneasy feeling settled into the pit of Royne's stomach and he forgot all about alchemy, crucibles, and annoying young woman. A pair of ancients bearing the bloody red standard of the Guardian-King marched up onto the stage to the beat of a drummer. They took up positions at either end of the platform, perfectly framing the Andochan officials who now made their appearance.

The first man, outfitted in fine, silver plate mail, bore a crimson tabard emblazoned with the white key of the Order of the Guardians. He was not someone Royne recognized, though due to the horned great helm carried by the squire at his side, he felt it safe to assume that the man might well have been the justiciar known as the Stone—one of three generals tasked by the Warlord to lead the armies of Andoch against the Grantisi legions.

Following the Stone and his squire, a second pair of men filed out onto the grandstand with the self-assured posture of political authority. Their clothing shone brightly in the sun, though in place of the vibrant red and white of the Order, their fine surcoats shone with a quartered pattern of violet and gold emblazoned with a swan.

Royne's brow creased with disdain, for he recognized the device at once. It was the arms of the Andochan viceroy, the arms of his perennial nemesis. His lips twisted into an involuntary sneer.

Curse you, Pryce!

While the Guardian general and his squire were content to stand, a trio of richly clad servants hurried to secure a pair of canvas chairs for the viceroy and his son. The captain of the armored guards shouted something and his men seemed to somehow inflate as the crowds drew back in a mixture of fear, interest, and resentment.

With the viceroy and his son secure in their seats, another man appeared, a courtier by the look of him, a man of the Chancellor's tower assigned as secretary to the great Lord Pryce. With an abundance of pomp, he made his way to the forefront of the stage and unfurled a long scroll of vellum. Again, Royne could not quite make out whatever it was he was saying, but the sinking feeling in the pit of his stomach told him there was no need.

Oh no...

It was at that moment that he remembered Amara. She must have sensed his sudden change in demeanor and with an air of reluctant interest, stepped up beside him to peer over the parapet.

"So what is it that we are staring at?" she asked.

For a moment, Royne remained silent. For reasons he himself did not know—perhaps it was due to the fact that her question was not laden with insults—he felt compelled to answer. He cleared his throat and pointed below.

"On the stage down there," he said, "Do you see the two men clad in purple and gold?"

"Yes, I see him."

Royne glanced over and felt a flash of discomfort at her close proximity. She was standing near enough that they bumped elbows; however, he fought to suppress his anxiety and refused to move away.

"The elder of the two is the Andochan viceroy, Marcel Pryce," he told her after a moment. "Beside him is his son."

Amara remained silent though her brow narrowed with interest.

"While not a Guardian himself, Pryce is one for the most influential members of the nobility in all of Andoch and sits upon the private council of the King." Royne frowned. "I'm actually quite surprised to find him here in person. I had heard that his role was solely nominal and that he left the day to day operations to the Warlord's justiciars. Perhaps recent events have required that he oversee the King's tyranny personally."

As the courtier continued to read from the scroll, a new procession of men came into view led by another squad of kingsmen. As they were herded into a tight rank upon the stage, Royne could see that their wrists were bound with rope and their bodies bore the telltale signs of hunger.

Little doubt remained as to the purpose of the assembly and his eyes darted quickly to the girl beside him to gauge whether or not she had drawn the same conclusion. For better or for worse, her face remained stoic, but he could sense a palpable anxiety radiating from her. Under normal circumstances, he would find it amusing to see such distress in such an adversary; however, with what he expected was about to unfold in the square, he could not rouse even a shred of sardonic joy.

As if on cue, two other men appeared and joined the congregation upon the stage. Between them, they carried a large wooden block with a scalloped depression carved into the top edge. Even if Royne had not already known the function of such a device, the man who came next in the procession—or rather, the large, two-handed axe the man carried—left little doubt to its function.

With a steady deliberateness, the executioner and his assistants finished their preparations, and the courtier called the first of the condemned men to the block.

Royne turned away and leaned against the parapet. Amara, however, seemed mesmerized, frozen in place with horrified anticipation. She continued to stare down into the forum, though her placid face remained unchanged.

Royne watched her, knew the abject terror and disgust that simmered behind her impassive mask. Inwardly, he was moved to sympathy, but he would not insult her pride by acting upon it. Instead, he frowned and folded his arms across his chest.

"Those men..." Royne began only to pause at the heavy *thwack!* that told him the executioner had began his bloody work. Amara flinched, but he made no note of it. He could tell that she was attempting to remain logical and unmoved—just as he might have done. "*Those* men," he said again, "are my enemies, and it is to prevent further atrocities such as *this* that I have come here hoping to learn alchemy."

"So you would use alchemy to meet violence with more violence?" she asked without turning.

Royne shook his head. "No," he said. "Rather, it is in my intention that in learning alchemy—in broadening my knowledge—I shall widen my eyes and extend the limitations of my vision in hopes that I might see another way."

Another *thwack!* resounded across the forum followed by a cheer. It would not be the locals celebrating the demise of their countrymen, Royne knew, but the kingsmen, encouraged by their superior officers to reassure their lord. Royne sighed.

"So excuse me if I seem impatient. I have little time to waste on bickering with those who would horde their knowledge, locking it away from the world behind stone walls and iron bars," he said coldly. "For, as you can see—" another *thwack!*—"these are dark times where the common man bleeds and the tyrant rejoices."

"And you would see it done differently?"

"I would see to the safety and the security of the people—all people—so as to free them from the block and ensure a brighter future."

The girl gave a derisive sniff. "Perhaps you should set your aim to something simpler like bottling the lightning and commanding the thunder?"

"Would that I were a wiser man, I might," Royne said with a sneer, "but alas! Popular opinion seems to hold that I am not."

A flash of anger burned within him as he cast a quick glance over the parapet. For a fleeting second he almost felt as if—even at such an absurd distance—his eyes met those of the younger Pryce, his childhood bully turned symbolic foe. A renewed sense of purpose flared within the center of his breast in that hollow place said to contain his bastard heart. He an unshakable compulsion to think, to plan, to plot, and-most of all—to read.

With an audible grunt, he gathered his alchemical materials, his notes, and the Loremaster's ancient book. "Enjoy the rest of the lesson," he muttered to Amara. "Good day!"

He turned to depart when, following another *thwack!* she called to him, checking his pace.

"Polecat?"

"Yes?"

"I will help you with your studies."

Royne's brow narrowed. "I did not ask for your help."

"No," she said, "but a fool seldom knows the extent of his own foolishness."

His jaw tensed reflexively, but when he whirled upon her, ready to lash her with his wicked tongue, something about her expression gave him pause. There was nothing combative about her demeanor, nothing openly demeaning about her tone. At length, he swallowed his resentment and offered her a slight nod.

"Thank you," he said quietly. "I accept."

CHAPTER 15: THE YOUNG TALON

Thom dismounted and handed the bridle of his mare to the boy beside him. "Thank you," he said.

"Welcome," the boy answered.

"You're welcome to ride her if you wish," Thom told him.

The boy's eyes went to his father. "Maybe just hang back and walk alongside for now," Sir Geoffrey said. "We don't want any of the enemy mistaking you for a skirmisher. First sign that this goes sour, though, you mount up and ride hard."

"Yes, Da." The boy lingered. "Good luck," he added.

Sir Geoffrey gave the boy a one-armed hug and kissed him on the crown. "Be safe," he said. "I love you."

"You too."

Thom leaned upon his axe and looked away, not wanting to impose upon the moment. Across the valley, the Tower and a contingent of knights rode forward in a tight formation, ready to meet the enemy lines. According to Sir Welmsey, it was a tactic they had learned from the last bearer of the title, Marcus Harding, though he sadly never got to see it action.

Meanwhile, to the east, Horn and the light cavalry waited on the edge of the treeline, ready to corral any enemy footmen or riders who might try to break away or attack their flank, and Thom stood with Geoffrey and the Galadin archers behind a reserve force of Montevalen men-at-arms led by Sir Norton Wherling.

The boy, Freddy, withdrew with the horse, and a moment later the Vanguard stepped up to stand beside Thom, resting his cudgel upon his shoulder. "So, you know anything about this Lord Talon?" he asked.

Thom shook his head. "I don't," he said. " I'm afraid I've never been much for names really. I have a hard enough time keeping them all straight as it is."

"You and me both," Geoffrey said. He sighed and adjusted his kettle helm. "So you grew up with Baron Lughus, eh?" he asked after a moment. "I imagine that means you're a deft hand with that chopper?"

"What?" Thom asked, "Brethren, no! That was all Lughus. The biggest blade I ever handled in those days was a little knife to sharpen a quill." He sighed. "No, no. Swords and battles and stories of heroes? That was all Goldimop's area of expertise."

Geoffrey's lips twisted into a smirk. "Goldimop?"

"Aye, on account of..." he motioned toward his head. "You know?"

Geoffrey smiled. "I'll have to remember that," he said. "I imagine his betrothed will have a quite a lark with that one."

Thom smiled. "It's not *that* original," he said. "Just something we used to call him." He paused as his mind suddenly caught up. "Hang on. Did you just say betrothed?"

"Aye, betrothed. Like I said at the meeting."

"As in, Lughus is *betrothed* to marry this girl?"

Geoffrey smiled and raised an eyebrow. "That is what it means, as I understand it."

Thom's brow furrowed as he struggled to comprehend the unusual twists and turns of life. Lughus was not only a baron, but set to be wed? He could only imagine what Royne had been up to as well. No doubt he'd authored several books criticizing the elder sages as well. So much had happened while he was at sea with Magnus. True, he'd had his own fair share of adventures, and it would be foolish to assume the rest of the world just stood still and remained the same, but the stark truth of it all—the sheer extent of the change—took him back.

"So..." he said to Sir Geoffrey. "Is she nice?"

Geoffrey glanced back from the battlefield. "Who?"

"Lughus's betrothed. Is she nice?"

"Oh!" Geoffrey smiled. "Aye," he said, "she is."

"Well, good," Thom said.

Geoffrey nodded. "Aye, they make a fine pair."

Thom returned his gaze to the field. To the northeast, the large stone tower house of Castle Dunwald rose above a small town. A thick curtain wall encircled both, but clusters of peasant cottages spilled out beyond the walls into the surrounding plain. To the west and south, he could see signs of other farming villages—folk who no doubt belonged to the lands defended by the tower house, but whose work required that they live further afield.

Thom sighed. "Nice enough place," he remarked, "Quaint."

Geoffrey nodded. "Lots of activity up at the castle," he observed.

"Yes. Strange that none of them have joined the battle."

"Perhaps they prepare for a siege?" Geoffrey shrugged.

"I suppose we'll find out eventually," Thom said.

In the fields below the city, a large contingent of mounted men-at-arms clad in the myriad shades of the noble houses loyal to King Dermont formed into a pair of ranks. A contingent of red-cloaked kingsmen formed the core of their formation and even Thom knew that these would provide the main threat, for as professional soldiers in the standing army of the Guardian-King, they were certain to have at least some real training at arms. The Andochan officer leading them rode the length of the line, rattling his blade against the outstretched lances of his men. Two riders followed in his wake, one to carry each of the enemy banners: the white key of the Order and the Crowned Horse of the plague king. Thom wondered, fleetingly, if the man was anointed, only to realize that the enemy charge was imminent.

"Oh, wait. I think..." Thom said, "Yes, I think we're getting on with it now. There they go, and there goes the Tower out to meet them."

Geoffrey nodded and called out to his sergeants. "Oi!, Lachlan! Bryce! Let's be ready, eh?"

The men responded with shouts of "Yes, sir!" and down the line, Sir Wherling rallied his reserves.

Thom breathed a sigh. "I hate this waiting." He tapped the haft of his axe and was humming an old sea chanty to himself when suddenly something caught his eye. It was another cadre of mounted kingsmen, and from the looks of it, they were riding toward the heart of the fighting, hoping to catch the Tower and his riders on the flank.

"Um, hey! Sir Geoffrey?" He pointed. "Do you see that? More kingsmen!"

Geoffrey grunted. "Aye, I see them."

"Wasn't Horn over that way with the light riders? Should we send some type of warning?"

"They're already engaged," Geoffrey said. "Look."

Sure enough, before the second force of kingsmen could reach the main melee in the field, Horn and the light cavalry had rode out to intercept them, checking their progress with a volley from their short bows before riding on to meet them blade to blade.

Yet the threat was not yet over, for a third force of riders appeared as well, ready to charge in on the opposite flank as the second group in a pincer maneuver. Thom's brow furrowed. He vaguely recalled Lughus describing this tactic once as they plotted ways to defeat Royne in chess. It was called something like "the trident" or "the trefoil." In any case, it didn't matter now. He turned again to the acorn knight.

"Do you see that?"

"Aye, I see it," Sir Geoffrey said. He shouted to his men. "Alright, boy-os! There's work to be done!"

"Release the Hounds!" the archers cried.

Thom followed along, axe at the ready, as Geoffrey led the archers down the slope of the vale to bring the riders within range. The baying and battle cries of the Galadin men attracted the attention of the riders at once, and with a swift turn, they wheeled their horses around to face them. Sir Norton hastily ordered his men into a tight rank to defend the archers, but without pole arms, there was only so much they could do against a charging destrier.

"We'll do our best should any get near," the old knight said hurriedly. "But we'd be quite grateful if you men of the Brock could show them exactly what it is you're famous for!"

"Hear that, men?" Geoffrey called. "Sir Norton asked to see the power of the war bow. How about you show them, eh?"

A cheer went up from the archers in answer, but as Thom stood beside Geoffrey he felt the thunder of the enemy hoofs through the ground. "They're almost upon us," he said, leveling his axe.

Geoffrey gave a nod and raised his cudgel high in signal. "Ready men?" he cried. "Let fly!"

"Let fly!" the sergeants repeated, and as one the archers loosed their volley.

From beside Sir Geoffrey, Thom watched as the front rank of horsemen crumpled, brought down by the deadly darts of Galadin. At such close range, the force of the war bow was easily enough penetrate armor, or at the very least, unhorse a man.

Thom and Geoffrey join Sir Norton and his men, ready to engage whatever men survived the deadly barrage while Lachlan and Bryce continued to call the command to loose. After this second volley, however, few enough remained of the enemy riders that Sir Geoffrey gave the order for each man to let fly at will. Before long, what few red-cloaks remained turned tail to flee.

"Well," Sir Norton said with a laugh, "I'd call that the most boring skirmish I've ever been a part of."

Sir Geoffrey gave a gracious nod. "Sorry to get you dressed for nothing."

"At my age, I'll take it," Norton said.

"Well, it might not be over yet," Thom said as a sudden fanfare drew his attention back to the castle town. As the main gates opened, another full complement of mounted men-at-arms appeared from behind the portcullis and began a slow and steady march out into the field. From the looks of things, the other skirmishes had also been resolved and now the Tower's combined forces were assembling into a long, formal column so as to receive the new arrivals. Geoffrey shouted orders to his men, and together with Sir Norton's small contingent, marched to join them.

As they approached, Thom noticed the prince and a small honor guard of riders were trotting out ahead of the column to parley with the contingent from the castle.

"Do you think we should join them?" Thom asked.

Geoffrey chewed his lip. "Looks like we're soon to find out," he said as a rider hurried over to greet them. Thom recognized him as Sir Briden, the prince's old standard bearer who was now a knight himself.

"Sir Geoffrey! Thom Reaver!" he said. "Prince Beledain asks that you join him as soon as you are able."

"We'll be along right now," Geoffrey said. As Briden rode off, Geoffrey quickly issued orders to his sergeants, and together, he and Thom made their way on foot across the field.

"Can't say I've ever gotten used to this part," Geoffrey muttered as they walked. "These chats with the great and powerful. Sometimes I wish that I could go back to my old life."

"You do?" Thom asked.

Geoffrey paused. "Well, actually no. I suppose I don't." He chuckled. "Funny to actually admit it though."

Thom shared his smile. "You know," he said with genuine surprise, "I think I know what you mean."

Geoffrey sighed. "There is one thing I'd change, though."

"Oh yeah?"

"I'd have my boy—my eldest. I'd trade anything to have him back with us," the Vanguard said sadly. "But apart from that, this life is a wonder."

When they reached the riders, Thom saw that alongside Prince Beledain were Sir Welmsey and Horn. Across from them, three armored knights mounted upon great white destriers stood to meet them. The foremost of the men removed his helmet to reveal a handsome man in his twenties with long dark hair and a haughty, aristocratic expression.

The handsome man raised his hand in greeting. "My Lord Tower," he drawled, "of would you prefer Prince Beledain?"

"I'm no longer considered a prince," Beledain said, "but I will answer to either."

Talondaire nodded. "Regardless of your name you have certainly been busy these last months and more." He paused. "I trust my cousin is well?"

Bel nodded. "She is," he said. "She said to tell you that she mourns your absence but that she wishes you well."

The young lord nodded and for a moment it appeared to Thom that his air of cultivated detachment appeared to weaken.

"I am..." He paused and cleared his throat. "Please convey my apologies for our strained correspondence," he said. "It was not by my choosing that it should be this way."

"As it is the case, though," Beledain began, "she asked us to visit in order to formally request your aid now." The Tower paused. "Of course, if you prefer we might discuss the specifics of such an arrangement somewhere more fitting to diplomacy than a battlefield."

"I'm afraid that will not be possible."

The Tower's brow furrowed. "You have yet to even hear what it is that I have to say."

"I know, but I..."

Talondaire fell silent. After a moment, he turned to the men at his side. "Return to the castle and dismiss the men to their regular posts," he said. "I will be along shortly."

The two men saluted and together rode off to carry out their orders. The Young Talon remained behind alone and Thom could not help but find it very strange. In his experience, any noble of high birth never went anywhere without some manner of entourage.

Except for the Tower, of course.

When the men were safely out of earshot and the forces of Dunwald began their slow procession back to the castle, Lord Talondaire ran a hand through his hair and breathed a heavy sigh.

"I know why it is you've come," he said, "and while it grieves me to disappoint Marina, I must refuse."

The Tower's head fell. "King Marius is dead, slain by Dermont's assassins," he said, "yet you would still turn your back on your cousin and queen?"

Talondaire shook his head in annoyance. "Do you not think that I would have ridden out to join you at the first call to arms?" he asked, "Even before your escape and the subsequent rebellion, Linton had been keeping me apprised of his activities for months. He wanted me to find some manner of pretense to visit you at Tremontane, but as I told him then, I will tell you now. I cannot join you."

"But why?" Beledain asked. "You are no coward and you have no love for the Plague King. I understand your duty to your lands and to your people, but were you to join us, you may rest assured, that we will fight to protect both. Our numbers have grown considerably since the Battle of Pridel."

"Your army could be three times the size that it is now and still I could not join you," the young lord said. "For not all of my people reside within my lands."

"What do you mean?" Beledain asked.

"My mother..." Talondaire said at last. "And my sister. Your brother holds them hostage at his court. Were I to do anything to challenge him in any manner, he will not hesitate to kill them both."

Beside him, Geoffrey grunted with disgust and shook his head from side to side. Thom sighed sympathetically. He knew from his studies that hostage-taking was an age-old practice often meant to ensure the loyalty of a newly sworn lord; however, there was a difference between reading about it happening in the past and witnessing the effects of it in the present.

"Do you know where they are being held?" Beledain asked. "Perhaps we could free them?"

"Reginal," the young lord said in despair. "They are part of the royal court in Reginal, the seat of your brother's power.

Beledain's expression darkened. "I'm sorry," he said. "My cousin Valerie is held hostage there as well. We've been trying to figure out a way to free her for weeks, but with the steady flow of reinforcements from Andoch, it seems a hard nut to crack."

"It is no nut but a solid stone." Talondaire said. "Reginal was built to be able to withstand a siege and the terrain inhibits the use of cavalry."

"But is there nothing we can do?" Beledain asked.

"You know your brother better than I," Talondaire said. "If he is willing to hold his own cousin hostage, he would certainly not hesitate to inflict suffering on my mother and sister. Do you remember Sir Trenton?"

"His emblem was the lilies?" the Tower said.

Talondaire nodded. "Believe it or not, he thought to join you only he was betrayed by Gurney."

"The cock," Welmsey muttered.

Horn stifled a laugh.

"It was the mark upon his arms." Welmsey smirked.

Talondaire continued. "When King Dermont found out, he and Inen Vilnois paid a visit to Trenton—and his sister. Your brother demanded Trenton renew his oaths while in the next room, they listened to Vilnois have his way with the man's poor sister."

"Lady's Mercy!" Geoffrey said, shaking his head in disgust.

"In the end, the Plague King stripped them of their lands anyway, but he allowed them to keep their lives," Talondaire said, "or what's left of them."

All fell silent as the lord finished and they hung their heads in sorrow and disgust at their adversary's monstrous actions. Slowly, a harsh grinding noise could be discerned among the stillness, steadily rising to the low growl of a wild beast. To Thom's surprise, the source of the sound was him. His fingers turned white as he gripped the haft of his axe and from somewhere deep within him, he spoke in a voice that was his and not his.

"There's only one way to deal with bastards like these."

Beledain nodded and Thom could see that his face, too, darkened with fury and grim resolve. "Vilnois has already been dealt with," he said, "but I wish to see to Dermont as well."

"So I had heard," Talondaire said, "but while my heart, and my loyalty, lies with my cousin the queen, I..." His voice broke. "I cannot help you. The risk is...far too extreme."

The Tower stood silent for a long moment, but at length, he nodded. "I understand," he finally said, "but I am sorry for it."

"So am I," Talondaire said.

Beledain sighed. "While it may not ease the pain of their captivity, I want you to know that I will do everything that I can to free your mother and sister, as well as any others that my brother holds captive."

"And should you succeed, Lord Tower, know that you will find my blade drawn and ready to fight at your side."

"Farewell, my friend." The Tower nudged the great searoan forward. "May the Kinship keep your family safe."

"And yours...save one."

Beledain nodded and turned to his men. "Return to the column," he said, "It's time enough that we should head for home."

The rebel captains nodded and offered affirmative grunts in response. All but Thom. For all of a sudden, he felt himself stirred to action like never before. Without even stopping to think, he stepped forward and raised a hand.

"Now hang on just a minute!" he grumbled. He paced forward after Lord Talondaire and called out. "You say this Plague King has your mother and sister?" he shouted. "You say he holds them captive at his court?"

Talondaire wheeled his mount around. "So he does."

Thom watched as Beledain and Sir Geoffrey exchanged a glance before turning their eyes upon him. To his surprise, however, they did not eye him with mockery or derision, but genuine interest.

"You have an idea, Thom?" Beledain asked.

Talondaire's brow furrowed. "Beledain," he said coldly, "excuse me, but who is this?"

Thom smiled wickedly. "Who am I?" he asked. "Why! I'm nobody."

Sir Geoffrey's lips curled into a small smile.

The young lord was not amused. He eyed Beledain with terse confusion. "Is this some manner of joke?" he asked.

Beledain patiently rested his hands upon the pommel of his saddle. "Lord Talondaire," he said, "allow me to introduce Thom Reaver, a Guardian—or rather—a Blackguard."

"A Blackguard?"

"A man with a Guardian title not sworn to the Guardian-King, like myself and Sir Geoffrey of Pyle who has come to us from Baronbrock."

Geoffrey raised a hand in greeting.

"What is it that you have to say, Thom?" Beledain asked.

Thom took a deep breath. "Well, you see, you men lead great armies, and of course, there are many great things about that—particularly when you're fighting against another army," he said. "But, an army, well, is an army, and if an army comes calling, you usually know for quite some time. If you were to lead this army northward to this Reginal place, there'd be plenty of time for the Plague King to prepare for a siege or rally his allies to face you."

"True," Beledain said.

"But—" Thom paused for emphasis, "a single man, a *single* man is no army..."

"You wish to attack Reginal by yourself?" Talondaire asked. "Beledain, I have heard that you drew men from all corners, but I did not expect you to indulge the whims of mad men."

Thom felt the Tower's green-eyed gaze upon him. "I would at least hear him out," Beledain said.

Thom continued. "What if you—Lord Talondaire—were to ride to Reginal? Claim that the queen's rebels have defeated the Plague King's troops and their Guardian allies, and while you and your men were eventually able to drive them off, you require reinforcements to stave off further assault. Maybe ask that he divert men from that great army at the Nivanus and send it here. You know?"

Talondaire sighed. "Why would I ever wish for more of the Plague King's men to be here?"

"Because while you play the part of the loyal retainer seeking aid, I can pose as a servant so as to find your mother and sister. I might even be able to find the Lady Valarie or that Lord Guillon fellow as well. Regardless, once I find…whomever, we can subtly find a way to sneak them out of the castle and flee back here to safety."

Sir Geoffrey nodded. "Then you'll finally be free to join the Tower and the queen."

Lord Talondaire shook his head. "You actually believe you can find your way into Reginal's court and escape with three noble hostages?"

"Four, if we count Lord Guillon." Thom smiled.

"Four, then," the young lord drawled. "But while there are plenty of tales of you Guardians accomplishing the extraordinary, forgive me when I admit that you do not exactly inspire confidence."

Thom folded his arms across his chest and rubbed at his chin like a man stroking his beard. "To be fair, I've had my fair share of…unusual situations this last year and more. I reckon this is basically more of the same."

"You *reckon?*" Talondaire repeated.

Horn gave a shrug. "He's a good hand with that chopper, I can tell you that—*and* he can read."

"He was an apprentice to the Loremaster as well," Welmsey said, "which might also work in our favor. Instead of a servant, perhaps he can play the part of a scribe or a clerk attached to Talondaire's court. We just need to find a habit or the like."

Sir Geoffrey pursed his lips. "Aye, it could work."

Lord Talondaire shook his head. "You wish me to put the lives of my mother and my sister in the hands of this boy?" he asked. "Impossible."

"Well, what have you got to lose?" Thom asked, strangely emboldened by the possibility of the venture. "If they catch me, you simply deny knowing anything. If they don't, your ladies are free." He gave a shrug and for a fleeting instant, envisioned Magnus wandering idly among the horses, a proud smile beaming from the tangled mass of his beard. It filled him with an uncharacteristic sense of vigor and daring. To his surprise, Thom discovered he actually liked it.

At length, Lord Talondaire gave a heavy sigh and looked to the Tower.

Beledain turned from the nobleman's questioning glance and eyed Thom meaningfully. "Thom," he began, "do you truly believe that you can do this? Understand that I do not ask because I doubt you. I ask because I have no wish to send you to your death."

"Well," Thom said, "to be completely honest with you, I don't know." He rested his hands upon the haft of his axe. "But you have all been very kind to me so…well, I figure I may as well give it a try."

At Thom's words, Beledain's brow creased and his eyes took on a strange light "In a world such as this one," he said, "so full of darkness and despair, what else can a man do but try?"

"I suppose that's right," Thom said.

"Then I will support you," Beledain said. "For months now we've been trying to find a way to free Val from Dermont and in all that time we haven't come up with anything better. However, Lord Talondaire must agree as well. He is, after all, your way into the court and the plot concerns his family too."

Lord Talondaire sat pensively atop his horse, his brow furrowed in thought. At last, he breathed a heavy sigh and shrugged. "I suppose it is as you say," he said. "I have no better idea and, as you put it, what have I really got to lose?"

"Splendid!" Thom said quietly, clapping his hands.

"We won't send you completely alone either," Beledain added. "Sparrow can go with you in the guise of a maid."

"And me!" Horn added. "If you're looking to spring Val, I'd be happy to help as well."

"Horn Half-Wrathorn?" Talondaire said. "Your size alone would betray us."

"I have to agree, Horn," Beledain said. "You've lots of skills, but blending in is not one of them."

"I'd offer to go too," Geoffrey said, "but I expect you get few enough with Kordish blood this far north either."

"Not so many," Welmsey said, "especially as the weather gets colder. It's a rare sight to find even a merchant cog from Grantis at this time of year, let alone Kord."

Thom chewed his lip. "So, we're in agreement?" he asked.

The Tower nodded. "In the meantime, I will continue to push onward throughout Whitemane to give credence to your request for aid. Granting it would require him to divert forces from the Nivanus, which will result in two smaller armies rather than one enormous horde."

"Can't say I'd mind those odds," Sir Geoffrey said.

"Then it's decided." Beledain said.

Lord Talondaire nodded. "I suppose it is. " He fixed Thom with a cold stare. "A lot is riding on you, Reaver," he said. "If all goes well, you will have gained—in me—a great and powerful ally."

"And if it does not?" Thom said, a hint of levity in his voice to mask his latent fear. "What then?"

"If it does not," the Talon said, "then regrettably, you will have earned a deadly and tenacious foe."

CHAPTER 16: TENDERNESS

"He was known as 'The Lash'" Lughus said. "When the Dibhorites rebelled against the Calendral emperor, the Lash was part of a slave uprising in the south. Once Wrogan's oppression became more and more pronounced, however, he rebelled again, claiming the Warlock's tyranny was no worse than slavery under the emperor. He joined with St. Aiden and Halford Drude shortly thereafter."

"Quite the collection," Sir Owain said, eying the weapon rack with a wistful smile. "The Lash's whip, the Willow's bow, the Miller's mace, and more—I only wish I could have been there."

Lughus eyed the old knight with sympathy. "Well," he said, "you were able to reach the solar. That's a start."

Owain gave a dismissive grunt and leaned heavily upon his crutch. "I just feel so damned useless," he said, sitting down heavily at the table. "I don't belong in bed. I belong on the battlefield."

"And you'll be back there," Brigid said, "but only after your wounds have had time to properly heal."

The old knight gave another grunt and Lughus felt Brigid's implicit gaze.

"Actually, Owain," the young baron began, "if you're willing and you feel able, we have need of you for something of the utmost importance. It's a task that, quite frankly, there is no one better suited."

"What is that?" He raised his crutch. "Poking holes so to plant seeds for next harvest?"

Horus sighed. "Oh come now, Owain," the old steward said. "You've never been one for self-pity."

Owain's gaze softened. "Apologies," he muttered. "What is it you'll be needing? Even as you see me, I'm ever-willing and ready to serve Galadin, as you know."

"There's never been any doubt about that, Owain," Lughus said.

From beside the fireplace, Fergus stood up, stretched, and sauntered over to sit at his side. Lughus offered him a quick scratch behind the ears to hide a vague feeling of discomfort. Guilt even. From the moment of Lughus's arrival at Houndstooth on that fateful day that now seemed so long ago, the old seneschal had always been such a large, benignly charismatic presence. Then later, once Arcis passed on and Lughus assumed the mantle of leadership, Owain's role evolved even further from that of loyal seneschal to a type of beloved uncle.

Yet, after the Battle of St. Golan's, where Owain sustained numerous deadly and nearly fatal wounds, the old knight appeared to fall under the shadow of a peculiar sense of gloom. Horus, who had known the old knight longer than anyone, said it was simply Owain finally coming to terms with his own mortality, a reckoning for which the old knight was long overdue. It would pass eventually, the steward said; however, Lughus remained concerned.

Hence, the current request.

Lughus cleared his throat and exchanged a quick glance with Brigid. "Given the recent Guardian attacks," the young baron began again, "I've been trying to determine the best way forward. I've held council with our knights, consulted the other barons, and kept up a regular correspondence with General Navarro." He paused. "As such, I think it's time that we strike back, that we cross the border into Andoch. Now. Before the winter and they have time to rest and lick their wounds—and we hit them hard enough to make them think twice about renewing their attack in the spring." Lughus paused and turned his gaze upon the old seneschal. "What do you think?"

"What do I think?" Owain asked, his brow furrowed with concern.

"You have more experience than any of us," Brigid said. "What say you?"

"That's just a kind way of saying I'm old," the seneschal said. Though despite his words, a light shone now in the depths of his eyes and he was once again the old veteran, void of melancholy. "The army's still encamped outside our walls, correct? And the Fifth has taken up the defense of Agathis?"

Lughus nodded. "We sent the peasant levies home for the harvest as soon as we returned from Cragbarrow, but Adolfo and the weaver knights have had no trouble hiring scores of yeomen archers to help defend the city—to say nothing of the volunteers. Every day it seems more and more men show up at the guardhouse asking to join our ranks."

"Of course they have! This is Galadin!" Owain said with a reassuring nod. "So tell me more about this attack. Have you chosen a target yet?"

Lughus nodded to Brigid.

"Stonebridge Castle," she said. "It was from there that the Chough's forces mustered to attack Agathis and it's Andoch's nearest fortress to the mountain passes."

"Good. If we command the mountains, the only route left to them by foot will be the coastal road that runs through Nordren," he said.

"Aye," Lughus said, "Otherwise, they're left trying to hike the highlands and the moors. Having done it, I can tell you. It wasn't easy, even with Crodane and Fergus to guide me. Leading a whole army that way—with supply wagons, siege weapons, and a whole bloody baggage train—would be impossible."

Owain nodded his approval only to pause. "Have you run it past Roland yet?" he asked somewhat hesitantly.

"We haven't discussed it in detail, but he agrees with the idea of it." Lughus said. "Brigid, Fergus, and I are to visit Harrier's Keep for the Feast of the Father while Sir Deryk leads our men to the legion camp outside of Cragbarrow. After the holiday, we'll join them with Roland and the Marthaine forces."

"So it's you three against Stonebridge?" Owain mused.

"The Lord-Baron and many of the others are already either supporting Helmstead in manning the border forts at the Nivanus Pass or helping Nordren keep watch at the port and along the coastal road. Luckily, while the Andochan blockade has been a nuisance, it does not appear that the

Andochans have the strength to attempt any type of landing yet, especially since the Fifth Legion defeated the Dwerin fleet meant to provide them with reinforcements."

"Aye, a stroke of luck that was," Owain said.

Lughus smiled inwardly imagining Royne's reaction to hearing his efforts attributed to mere luck.

"We're also hoping to hear word from Geoffrey soon about the alliance with the Montevalen rebels," Brigid added.

Lughus nodded. "If he succeeds, we can plan to capture the Nivanus together come the spring and—so long as we succeed—divert men elsewhere." He shrugged. "The northern baronies have reported a few Wrathorn raiding parties, but nothing truly organized yet. By all accounts, the Guardians did not expect to us to meet them with such resistance, but having learned their lesson, they're taking their time to muster forces for a major campaign this spring."

"Well, that buys us some time," Owain said, "and taking Stonebridge now will certainly make things a bit easier in the future. Besides, come spring I should be back on—" He suddenly stopped. "Did you say you're heading to Harrier's Keep for Harvestide?"

Lughus exchanged a look with Brigid.

Here it is…

"I did," Lughus said.

Owain's mustache bristled. "Now, I concede the point that Roland helped us through that spot of bother at St. Golan's, and I don't regret shaking the man's hand…" he grumbled. "But the rest of that brood—can we really trust them?"

"Owain," Brigid said, "I do not think that Lord Roland would allow any harm to come to Lughus any more than you would."

"Nor do I! nor do I!" the old knight said quickly. "But like I said, *the others?* Can they be trusted? What if some minor knight gets it into his head to make a name for himself by killing the last of the Galadins? What then, eh?" He began fiddling with his crutch. "You know, maybe I am well enough to accompany you. It's only just across the lake, after all." He made to rise, but Lughus, Brigid, and Horus all pressed him back to his seat.

"Please, Owain," Lughus said. "We need you here. With Brigid and I gone, who else would command the city?"

The old knight gave a shrug. "Why not Horus?"

The old steward shook his head. "I am not a military man, and you know it," he said, "and Sir Adolfo has his hands full managing...whatever it is he manages."

Owain gave a snort. "So the Madder's in on this too, is he?"

"I am," Adolfo said from the doorway. "Though if you prefer, I can just as easily perform my work from the shadows as the solar."

At length, Owain gave an exaggerated sigh. "No," he finally said. "And...accept my apologies. You're a much better sort than they say."

Horus smirked. "An apology? Why! You'd best write that down somewhere, Adolfo."

"Har, har!" Owain said. "In any case...fine. I will stay, but don't expect me to stop worrying for you three."

"We'll only be in Harrier's Keep for a couple of days," Brigid said. "After that, it's back to battling the Guardians and laying siege to Stonebridge." She grinned. "You know, the usual."

Owain gave a forlorn smile. "Fine," he said. "And I know you two can certainly handle yourselves. I don't mean to be so...maudlin these days. I simply feel..." He paused. "I just can't help but feel somewhat weighed down by the immensity of the times. I've seen my share of friends fall and—while I do not like to talk about it—I feel...weighed down by the memories of those lost. Arcis, Wolfram, Crodane, Gareth, Regnar, your mother. The list goes on and on and on." He sighed. "And while I have no wish to see it grow, the sad reality is that the longer you live, the longer the list of sorrows is guaranteed to grow."

Horus gave a sympathetic nod. "I understand, old friend, yet at the same time, take joy in the fact that—by surviving this long—you have been offered a glimpse at the future and, at least in my estimation, a promise of hope."

"I suppose you're right," Owain said. He eyed Lughus and Brigid intently. "Just look after each other. Can you at least promise me that?"

Lughus felt the warmth of Brigid's gaze as her eyes met his. "Always," she said. He nodded in agreement and took her hand, feeling at once both incredibly vulnerable and utterly invincible.

Together, they finalized the plans for the journey across the lake and the mustering of the Galadin forces marching to join the general outside of Cragbarrow. Unbeknownst to Lughus, Houndstooth owned several keelboats for the purposes of travel around the lake; however, they had seen little use since Lughus's grandmother passed away years earlier. Arcis used them only rarely, and with his illness these last few years, not at all. Adolfo volunteered to see to their refitting as well as to the hiring of a crew.

In other affairs of state, Galadin continued to thrive. The treasury was full, the harvest was bountiful, and the people were happy. They were proud of their heritage and their Golden Hound.

There was, of course, a small contingent of folks who had been loyal to the old provincial, Padeen Andresen, and who considered the new baron a heretic and a villain. However, Adolfo kept them under observation and claimed that—at least for now—they were no threat. "A small amount of dissent is healthy—and fair," the Madder said. "If we were we to find none at all, *then* I would be concerned."

The final point of discussion was a predominantly pleasant one: promotion and reward for those who had distinguished themselves in the recent battles. Sir Deryk of Lomedan, Sergeant Pike, and several others—a herder named Alban who turned out to be a crack shot with a war bow, a pair of brothers who led a band of men from Hounton, and a cooper's son who captured the enemy standard. Each was rewarded generously in accordance with their station: gold for the city folk, land or livestock for the farmers, and a few extra odds and ends (a fine blade for Pike, a steel breastplate for Sir Deryk). An enormous sum was also set aside to be distributed to the families of the fallen or maimed. Horus and his assistants would see to the distribution of coin, assisted, if necessary, by Sir Adolfo.

With these matters settled, the meeting concluded. Horus helped Owain to his feet and, bickering like an old married couple, the steward saw the seneschal safely to his quarters.

Not long after they had gone, Sir Adolfo too bowed graciously and prepared to depart.

Lughus's brow furrowed. He knew that what he had to say was long overdue. "Sir Adolfo," he began, "A moment, if you please." He could sense Brigid's eyes upon him in his periphery.

Adolfo paused, but his face remained impassive. Lughus met his gaze unwaveringly.

"I want to apologize. Formally," he said. "From the outset of our acquaintance, I feel that I have treated you discourteously. It was not right and for that I am sorry. You have proven yourself time and again to be not just a loyal man of Galadin, but—more importantly—a decent man." He held out his hand.

Adolfo stood very still and, for once, seemed uncertain of what to say or how to proceed. At last, the Madder bowed his head and spoke.

"The greatest courtesy a man may show to another, is to allow him the freedom to be himself," he said. "Though I cannot claim to have ever truly known him, your grandfather Arcis showed me that courtesy long ago and ensured that, so long as he was baron, no one would ever deny me—or anyone else—that same courtesy ever again. I told you that Galadin was precious to me, that there was no other place like it. Now you know something of why."

"As long as I am baron, Galadin will always be a place of honor and of courtesy," Lughus said. The storm clouds of his eyes flashed with lightning. "I swear it."

Adolfo remained stoic. "I do not doubt it," he said. "You truly have the blood of the Golden Hound, and as such, you have my pledge that I will always act with the best interests of the barony—with the best interests of the people of Galadin—at heart."

At last, he took Lughus's proffered hand, shook it, and departed without another word.

"Did I offend him?" Lughus asked Brigid. "It was not at all my intention."

Brigid smiled and shook her head. "Quite the opposite," she said.

When the Madder's footsteps no longer echoed down the hall, Brigid stood up from the table and took Lughus by the hand. "Let's go. I've had enough talk of politics and coin for today, and from the looks of it, so have you."

"What do you mean?" he said, following after her.

She smiled and patted his arm. "I can always tell when you're over-burdened by the world. Your brow gets so furrowed that it could sprout wheat and your eyes all but disappear beneath it."

Lughus gave a reticent smile. "I'm sorry," he said. "I've just had a lot on my mind."

She gave his arm a tug and led him out of the solar, past the guardsmen, and down the hallway. Fergus followed along idly, his claws clicking lightly upon the floor with every step.

"You worry that invading Andoch will escalate the war?"

"In part," he said. "It changes our role from mere defenders to aggressors. By invading Andoch, we can no longer argue that our intentions are solely peaceful and that we fight merely to protect our own sovereignty."

"Even though that's the truth?"

He shrugged. "The average Andochan is no more evil than the average Guardian," he said. "In their eyes, we are villains who threaten the rest of the continent in much the same manner as we see Kredor. They've been told by the powerful and the power-hungry that we mean to do them harm. I don't like killing men who have done nothing wrong, men who fight to defend their lands from a threat just as we defend ours. It's not right."

Lughus halted at the spiral staircase that led up to the roof of the keep. "At the same time," he continued, "I can't simply allow them to threaten the safety of our people, and I certainly won't let them threaten you—even if I know you can take care of yourself."

He turned to face her and took both of her hands in his. Her blue eyes shone as they met his gray, and as always, he felt his burdens begin to ease.

"The sword takes life, but may also give it," he mused, recalling Crodane. "I only hope that in the end, by will and by my choices, I can give more than I take."

Brigid held his gaze a moment longer. Then, with another gentle tug, she pulled him toward the stair. "Come on," she said gently.

Fergus darted past them in a golden blur, pausing halfway to bark at them impatiently before charging onward. Lughus and Brigid followed after, hand in hand. With every step, the young baron felt his heartbeat strengthen with his great affection. When finally she led him through the doorway out onto the rooftop, the dusky light of the setting sun ensconced her in a brilliant corona.

Yet for all its solar radiance, hers was the beauty of the moon and stars. Elegant. Ethereal. She was his light shining on in the darkness, leading him to greet the dawn.

"Do you know why I like being up here?" she asked, traipsing lightly to the battlement. Fergus loped after her, his tongue lolling out of the side of his mouth.

Lughus considered her question. The top of the keep was one of his favorite places as well. The height put him in mind of the view from the windows of the Loremaster's Tower while the relative quiet offered him a place to think. From this vantage point, he could see not only the hustle and bustle of the city below, but far out across the planes and the lake. It reminded him of his duty to his people and his lands, to protect them, to guide them, and to ensure a safe place where they might prosper and raise their children without fear. It reminded him of the oath he swore as he lay dying, the oath that passed the title of the Marshal to him from Crodane.

But those were *his* reasons. What were hers? She did not wait for him to answer.

"It's because when I come up here and I look out over the city, when I look down at wards, when I look out across the lake, or at the farmers' fields, or at the shepherds and their herds—when I look at you here standing beside me—I see hope. I see truth. I see a place of meaning and integrity where all folk, from its lowest peasant to its great baron, believe in the possibility of a better world. And not just for Galadin or the Brock, but *everywhere*. Dwerin. Andoch. Grantis. Everywhere."

She turned her gaze to the southwest and Lughus watched her blue eyes glisten at a sudden gust of wind. Her fair cheeks and the tip of her nose reddened.

"Perhaps it's silly or naive, but..." She shrugged. "It's important."

Lughus watched her for a moment longer, saw her shiver against the chill, and stepped closer to take her in his arms. Wisps of her raven hair tickled his cheek. "I love you," he whispered.

"I know." She grinned. "I love you too."

Lughus smiled and tightened his embrace. "I hope we can take Stonebridge before the winter."

"We will," she said, "and if we don't, we'll simply retreat, rethink, and try again in the spring."

"I suppose that's true."

The sun continued its slow descent below the western horizon and one by one the stars blinked to life. Lughus stood behind Brigid, losing himself in the infinity of the moment, the sensation of completeness he felt when she was close. *Do you know that you are my everything?* he wanted to ask her. *The breath in my lungs, the other half of my soul?* When she turned around within the gentle security of his embrace and gazed up into his eyes with those luminous orbs of hers, he knew that without a doubt she knew.

"I'll admit," she said softly, "I'm actually looking forward to the winter."

"It'll be cold," Lughus warned her. "The wind off of the river is bitter."

She smiled and rested her head against his shoulder. "Dwerin was cold," she said. "High up in the mountains. Believe me. I know cold." She pressed her lips against the side of his neck. "But this winter...with you. I think we can find plenty of ways to keep warm." Her blush deepened.

Lughus felt his pulse quicken and he kissed the top of her head. "As long as I breathe, I promise to keep you warm."

He felt her body stiffen and with a bracing intake of breath, she caught his eye. "You know," she told him, "I'm cold now."

"You are?"

"And it's getting dark."

"So it is."

"Perhaps...perhaps we should go inside."

His heart beat like a galley drum. "If...you're ready," he said.

She cast him a demure smile, bit her lip, and led him by the hand back to the stairwell.

The fire had already been lit for them when they reached the baron's chamber, and as Lughus pushed opened the door, Fergus brushed past him and curled up upon the warm stones in front of the hearth. They watched the hound fondly, amazed at how such a large creature could somehow make himself so small. and Lughus wondered if Fergus somehow understood that they would be wanting some time to themselves. He nearly commented as much, but realized how absurd such a comment would be at a moment like this. Instead, he held his tongue, noting how suddenly his senses seemed to sharpen and the steady rhythm of his heart beat still heavier in his chest.

At last, Brigid turned to him, her eyes shining in the firelight, and paced implicitly toward the bedroom. Lughus followed after her. She lit a small oil lamp on the bedside table next to what he had come to think of as her side of the bed. As he watched her, he tried to calm himself, realizing that for quite some time now, they had already been sharing a bed. He had seen her in her shift, felt her body close to his beneath the blankets, and, lying beside her, traced his fingertips along the smooth contours of her legs and hips. More importantly, she had become his best friend, his partner. There was nothing about himself that he feared to share with her, for she already knew his mind and his heart and every desire or fear that might hide deep within him. There was no reason to be nervous.

Unless there was. What if he hurt her, or frightened her? What if he was too rough or too weak? He could admit to himself, and to her, that he wanted her—of course he did, he loved her—but would that desire make her think less of him? Would that make him just another villain like the ones she had grown up with? He took a deep breath and rubbed his eyes. When he opened them suddenly she was before him.

"You're planting wheat," she whispered with a gentle smile. Her blue eyes danced in the lamplight as she ran a finger lightly across his brow.

He gave a soft smile. "I just want to make sure—"

"I know, Lughus." She pressed a trembling finger to his lips. "And yes. Before you ask again, yes. I am certain. I..." She reddened. "I want this. I want you."

Without another word, he smoothed back the long dark strands of hair that framed her face, lifted her chin, and pressed his lips to hers. She responded with equal fervor, matching his urgency as he savored the sweet taste of her mouth and traced the edge of her teeth with his tongue.

Despite the countless times he had kissed her, something about this moment made it feel somehow new. It was as if the world had somehow halted, paused, and that this moment existed outside of natural time. All of his cares and worries dissipated and the entirety of his focus was her.

When they were forced to separate for lack of air, Lughus slipped his arms around the small of her back and pulled her closer to him. Her eyes shone brightly and her lips were flushed from kissing. She breathed in heavily, and then, chewing her bottom lip, began to loosen the lacings of his tunic. He watched her clever fingers work, and as her head dipped closer, he kissed her crown. When at last, she pulled the thick garment free of his belt and over his head, her blush deepened as she ran her finger up the muscles of his arm and down his shoulder to his chest.

"The great baron of Galadin," she teased. "My hero."

Lughus smiled, wholly cognizant of how his body reacted to her touch. An immense rush of heat surged through him and he felt an intense urgency to touch her, to hold her, to worship her. Yet in spite of the impulses of instinct, he willed himself to maintain control. He would not be another base beast or boor. She'd known plenty of those bastards at Blackstone...

"Lughus?"

Her voice called him back from the darkness of his vengeful thoughts, calmed the violent storm clouds in his eyes.

"You know that I meant it?" she whispered softly. "You *are* my hero."

Lughus breathed a great sigh. "No," he said. "You're mine. I have no idea where I would be, *what* I would be without you."

Brigid bit her lip and her eyes shone again with emotion. For a moment, he feared that he had ruined things, that his sentiment had put her off. She reached up and tentatively touched his arm, then unfastened her baldric with Whisper and Shade and hung it upon the bedpost. Her smock fell long and loose around her as, with meek reserve, she slipped out of her boots, breeches, and braies.

Lughus watched her in silence, uncertain of what to say or do. An intense rush of heat surged through him, strengthening the rhythm of his heart. When at last she approached him, he was overcome at once by a mingling triad of desire, reverence, and affection.

He had always known her to be slender and fair, but he was unprepared for the sight of her before him. As a student of aesthetics and the great romances, her beauty was absolutely arresting. Her skin was as flawless and smooth as the petals of a lily, and her form, while willowy-thin, was still supple and strong as a young sapling in spring. He saw only perfection in each line and curve.

A crimson blush colored her cheeks, half-concealed behind the curtain of her luxuriant hair—a habit, he well knew, that betrayed her apprehension. "Well," she said softly, her eyes alight with sapphire brilliance. "Here I am."

A great lump formed in his throat and in his stupor, he struggled to swallow it. He was speechless. Undone.

Brigid looked up at him and quickly looked away, returning to the concealment of her raven shroud. "I'm...skinny. I know." she stammered. "And pale. My mother always said I look like a corpse."

Like the hero of a bard's tale ensnared by fairy magic, Lughus dared to step closer to her. Then, with gentle slowness, he moved aside the dark veil of hair and pressed his hand softly to the side of her cheek. "Brigid," he whispered, finally finding his voice, "never in all my life have I ever imagined anything as lovely or as breathtakingly beautiful as you. From the moment I met you, to this moment now, and for all the moments we share for all eternity, I devote all I am and all I ever will be to you." He leaned forward to kiss her on the brow and images flashed before his mind's eye of their time together, of all the ways she inspired him to be a better man. "I am...not worthy of you."

Brigid reached up to take his hand from her cheek and pressed it to her lips. "Lughus," she whispered, "You *are* worthy because I love you. You *are* worthy because in you I have found the perfect partner to my soul."

In silence, he wrapped his arms around her and delighted at the touch of her skin against his own. Brigid pressed into him, as if inviting him to hold her even closer, but when his fingertips found the thin scar just above her waist, he paused. For he knew at once that it was the place where she had received what for the Gift of the Guardians would have been a mortal wound. The thought of her lying upon the brink of death was nearly too much.

"This is..."

"Yes."

Her delicate fingers touched his own scar, the remnant of his own sacred wound. He knew she'd seen it these past nights together, but she had never mentioned it.

"Yours."

"Yes."

Again, she raised her chin in invitation and he kissed her deeply, savoring the taste that was her. Her body arched within the enclosure of his embrace and she motioned tentatively at his baldric. In answer, he let slip the belt and scabbard, resting them beside the bed, before returning to her desperate lips. Airy gasps escaped her beneath the shower of his kisses. Once more, their eyes found each other in the lamplight and together they shared a tender laugh.

Together they memorized the form and contours of each other's body, learned what it was to touch and be touched, and when finally the moment arrived for them to join together as one, it was with a bold tenderness, a perfect kindness that would forever be the hallmark of their love.

And they found it sweet.

Long into the night, they lie together, skin to skin and heart to heart. With Brigid's head nestled upon his shoulder, Lughus dozed in and out of consciousness, his dreams marked by a sensation of utter serenity and a joy unlike any he had ever known.

And each time, upon waking, he would find her gazing at him, guarding him, with an expression so overflowing with ardent love, that he understood, intuitively the truth he had always sought in his scholarship.

Twice more they professed their love before the first faint streaks of dawn lightened the eastern sky, peeking modestly over the horizon as if reluctant to disturb the lovers in their united bliss. Yet it would not be until the sun had full risen before, together, Lughus and Brigid finally stirred. With a kiss that very nearly returned them to the bed, Brigid gathered her blades, and returned to her own room to bathe and prepare for the day.

Lughus stood for a time, his heart and mind at ease, and gazed through the window overlooking the city—his city—and beyond to the far reaches of the surrounding fields and farms. Fergus quietly joined him, announcing his presence by nudging the baron with his great furry head.

"I'm sorry to banish you from the bedroom last night," Lughus said, scratching the hound behind the ears. "I'll ask Horus later today if he can send up an old mattress or the like. We can set it up with some blankets beside the fire."

Fergus gave a loud sniff of approval and gently closed his teeth around the Lughus's hand. The young baron smiled at him, took a deep breath, and ran a hand through his unruly mop of hair.

"I suppose we had better get moving," Lughus said. He retrieved Sentinel from where he had placed it and paused to draw the blade a little ways from the scabbard. The subtle rippling pattern of the folded steel was a thing of impeccable artistry, an ancient river of time recording the journey of one Marshal to another.

Yet it was not just the Marshals who swam those waters immemorial, but others as well. And while they left no physical marks upon Sentinel's deadly edge, every life taken and every life saved was borne upon the ebb and flow of those steel waves, carried upon the conscience of the swordsman from the moment he swore his oath to the moment he succumbed to the grave.

As he traced his finger now along the gleaming shoal, he was gripped by a renewed sense of purpose, of determination. In his mind's eye, he saw Brigid, and behind her Geoffrey, Annabelle, and their children. Owain, Horus, and Adolfo. Rastis, Royne, and Thom. And more, many more—all of the people of Galadin, of the Brock, of every land, far and wide across Termain.

He resolved that when his final tally was counted, the lives he preserved would far outnumber those he cut short. And from the depths of memory, he heard a voice intone:

Though many flee and many falter, this one will never stray.
Rise now the Marshal, and drive the dark away!

With regal bearing, Fergus sat up and raised his head. The morning sunlight dancing upon his thick, golden fur.

"We have work to do, Brother," Lughus told the hound, and with a *snap!* returned the blade to its sheath.

CHAPTER 17: ENEMY AT THE GATES

Under Amara's tutelage, Royne's mastery of basic alchemical principles, at least those belonging to the discipline of "substantial alchemy," grew and grew. At first, much of the learning was theoretical, but as time went by and his understanding grew, she guided him through certain practical experiments related to the creation of various metals and decoctions as well as others that applied these products to disciplines such as smithing and healing. By manipulating the forces of the elements that—at least according to the alchemists—comprised all material things, he could purify, corrupt, melt, transform, and utterly destroy a multitude of substances, and while he did not necessarily ascribe to the philosophy of the Sign of Four, he had at least begun to understand its meaning and intention.

Still, his progress was slow and he was frustrated by his own limitations; his reach exceeded his grasp. For while he found the principles of alchemy to be very interesting in and of themselves, his goal was application, innovation, to use this new knowledge in the fight against tyranny, against Kredor, Tainne, and the rest of the blasted oppressors. In short, he wanted more.

According to Amara, however, it was necessary to learn these principles before progressing to the more complex study of metaphysical alchemy, a practice that even the most experienced alchemist may spend a lifetime researching without ever gaining any true understanding, let alone functional ability.

"Then how is it that you seem to have mastered it?" Royne asked as they met together in one of the workshops above the symposium. "We seem to be of an age. Unless you've been able to discover some fantastic elixir of youth, what makes you so special?"

Her eyebrows narrowed and she fixed him with a terse stare. "You claim to be the Loremaster, but aren't most Guardians either old men or brawny warriors?"

"Not all of them," Royne said, "but I catch your meaning."

"Good." She huffed dismissively. "Now, I want you try this experiment again, but this time, keep the heat low. Fire is an impatient element so those who entreat it must emulate the patience of the Stone that does not burn. If you do not, if you allow the fire to run rampant, the shift in the elemental balance will occur too abruptly and the remaining elements will fall into discord."

"I will try my best," he said quickly.

"Then I will prepare myself for a very long day."

Royne frowned, but remained silent. There had been many long days in the month and more that had passed since his admittance to the University when he had effectively cut himself off from the outside world. He had received no word from either Salasco or Connor, though he did not find himself particularly worried. Salasco had already proven himself to be a rather evasive old rascal, and while Royne's continued observations of the forum suggested that the new Viceroy was tightening his grip over Grantis and its people, the young Loremaster expected that the Wall would see to it that neither he nor the boy would come to any harm.

Besides, as soon as Royne mastered alchemy, or at least learned enough to satisfy his own purposes, he would join them. The alchemists could have their absurd isolation and esoteric asceticism; as the Loremaster, he had a duty to fulfill and a tyrant to depose.

Already, he had begun making notes for various applications of alchemy that might assist in the defense of the common people: various substances that might be used in war, improvements to the arms and armor already put into use, salves and decoctions that might assist in healing. He imagined great new devices for sieges, as well as incendiaries and other projectiles that could turn even the weakest of men into a match for any seasoned warrior. His designs were largely theoretical, but he had faith in them, or at least, in their potential.

And for that, he hated himself.

Even before becoming the Loremaster, Royne had always dedicated himself to the belief that knowledge was meant to serve humanity in a benevolent and positive manner, to alleviate suffering, and support the commonweal. Yet, in his designs, he saw only the potential to unleash greater horror, greater suffering upon the world. For they were weapons and what was the most basic purpose of a weapon but to cause harm? He tried to delude himself, to justify his ideas by convincing himself that his end goal was benevolent, but he knew better. He was crossing lines and opening doors from which there was no return—not just for his own line of inquiry, but for any who might study his work in the future and seek to take it even further. Would his scholarship, his legacy, amount only to a host of terrifying progeny fated to bring about greater suffering upon the world? In his quest to defeat one evil, would he give birth to even more?

In all of this, *The Book of Histories* was equally a source of comfort and guilt, for in reading the words of his mentor, Rastis, he simultaneously felt a welcoming familiarity as well as a fear that he was somehow letting the old man down.

According to Rastis's log, after ascending the throne, King Valder, Kredor's father, had been a deeply troubled man torn between the demands of his role as King and his personal desire to renounce the Order to live the quiet life of an ascetic. From what Royne could tell, this impulse was not shared by Valder's wife (and Kredor's mother), Queen Ordana, and remained one of many points of contention that resulted from an artfully maneuvered political match brokered without love.

As a result, the King was often unhappy and in spite of his position as the most powerful monarch on the continent his life was marked by little in the way of joy. As his friend, Rastis did his best to counsel the King, but he often sensed within Valder a deeper darkness, an internal struggle to resist the shadow's call. It was at this time that the old Loremaster would wonder just how much the line of Kings recalled about their corrupted legacy, of the sad story of Amarthia the Bard and the dread prophesy that spoke of the Order's end. It was his suspicion that this knowledge was indeed the source of the King's troubles, a generational guilt resulting from his ancestor's sin.

However, the King never spoke of it in specifics, not did Rastis directly bring it up. How could he? No records of the events existed outside of the blank pages of the Loremaster's tome. Even in the old books of genealogy, the official records that traced the lines of the Andochan nobility, no record of Amarthia existed. Next to King Erolan's name, in the place where Amarthia should have been, there was listed another woman's name, a Queen Narania, who was listed as having died in the same year as her only son's birth. Yet, despite all of Rastis's efforts to discover more about her, there seemed to be no evidence of her having existed either. Perhaps she was simply a fabrication, a lie concocted by the Chancellor or the Hierophant to cover the greater sin. Regardless, the line of Drudish Kings continued unbroken, and, to the best of Rastis's knowledge, whether they knew or remained themselves completely ignorant, Erolan's dark secret never saw the light of day.

Does Kredor know? Royne wondered, *or has the strength of the title dwindled to the point where only fragments remain of the memories and experiences of the previous Kings? And what of the Bard's Heresy? Does he know of it? Do any of them know of it? Or will their ignorance be our doom?*

"Oi! Polecat!" Amara snapped. "Pay attention!"

Royne gave a start as the contents of the small crucible in which he had been working began to smolder and blacken, releasing a foul-smelling odor that soon had both him and Amara sputtering and coughing.

"Fire and Blood!" Royne cursed, fanning the dark tendrils of smoke toward the open window. As he glanced outside, however, he saw red.

Amara was too busy dealing with the mess to notice his sudden distress and when he touched her arm, she drew back in alarm.

"What are you doing, Polecat!"

"We're about to be under attack!" he cried.

"What?"

"Look!" He pointed through the window. "The kingsmen are at the gates!"

With a grimace, she brushed past him to peer out of the window. "Oh," she said with only mild interest before returning to the ruined experiment. "Not to worry."

Royne's mind reeled. "What? We need to raise the alarm!" he cried, "Where can we find Master Udo?"

Amara shook her head. "Why would you bother my father with this?"

"What? Your father?" Royne shook his head, returning to the task at hand. "Come! We need to let people know. You saw the executions! You know what they are capable of!"

Amara frowned at the memory. "I do," she said, "but that was out there. We are safe here."

"Yes, yes, so I've heard, but how can you be so sure?" he asked. "Look! They've brought a battering ram!"

Amara sighed impatiently and glanced out of the window again. "They tried this very thing six months ago. Though I suppose the ram *is* a bit bigger this time." She shook her head. "Such fools."

Royne was flabbergasted. "So we do nothing?" He asked.

Amara sighed. "The people who need to know already know," she said. "Go back to your studies, Polecat, or if you must, keep staring. The University can always use another gargoyle."

Royne ignored the barb. With all the rumors he had heard regarding the strange and wondrous defenses of the alchemists' compound he was curious to see them in action.

Apparently, he was not the only one either. Viceroy Pryce must have heard something about them as well, for he stood well away from the gates, far behind his men with a full honor guard of warriors in plate mail to protect him.

Like father, like son... Royne thought, *A bully and a coward.*

At this distance, it was impossible to make out any voices, but he could tell from their body language that an order had been issued and passed along from the viceroy down through an officer to a sergeant and finally to one of the red-cloaked enlisted men who made up the brunt of the Andochan standing army.

With a reticent salute, the kingsman readied a long spear and approached the gates. Behind him, his comrades watched in silence, though Royne could sense the tension that hung over them like a dense fog.

When at last the kingsman reached the iron gates, he stopped and stood before them like a man condemned. Again the sergeant shouted a command and with visible reluctance, the kingsman lowered the point of his weapon. As the iron spear tip touched the wrought metal of the gate, there was a brilliant flash of light and a luminous, arcing tendril leapt from the iron bars of the gate to the tip of the spear. At once, the kingsman dropped the spear and jumped back two or three paces in fear. To his great relief, he was unharmed.

"Interesting," Royne mused aloud. "So the gate only reacts when it comes into contact with metal?"

"Yes," Amara said without looking up.

Royne rubbed his brow, recalling all that he had read regarding the elements and natural philosophy. "So am I to understand that you, or rather, your people, have discovered a means by which to create and control lightning?"

"My father realized that the animal mills that we use to grind grain might also serve a secondary purpose," Amara said. "He created a device that uses lodestones and copper to produce an effect rather similar to the lightning."

"Do you know how it works?"

"I do not. It is a secret known only by my father and a few of the highest ranking masters."

Royne frowned. "I thought your father abhorred violence."

"He does," Amara replied. "But he is still responsible for the safety of his people."

Outside, the dozen kingsmen carrying the battering ram began to advance. Royne's frown deepened. "They're trying the ram now," he said. "Look."

Together the kingsmen drew back the ram, and—as one—struck the iron bars of the gate. A hollow thud echoed throughout the city. For the first time, Amara made a slight show of interest, joining Royne at the window to gaze outside.

"Ah! They left the iron cap off of the ram this time," she said. "They're learning.

Royne gave a snort. "You seem pleased."

"Not pleased," she said, "but I can appreciate the fact that they are not repeating the same mistakes."

"Will you still feel the same way if they breech the compound?"

"Oh, they won't," she said. "Just watch."

Again, the men drew back the ram and prepared to strike, but before they had the chance, a small barrel dropped from the battlement above the gates.

As soon as it touched the ground, it burst. A flurry of glittering white particles filled the air, expanding into a dense cloud of sparkling stars. For a brief moment, as it expanded to envelop the ram, the dozen men, and their sergeant, Royne found it oddly beautiful.

And then the screaming began.

Within the billowing fog, bright flashes of light burst to life punctuated by inhuman cries of agony. It was the stuff of nightmares, a cacophony of suffering the likes of which Royne had never experienced nor could have conceived. At once, the remaining kingsmen and the viceroy, as far back as they already were, began a panicked retreat to the forum fearing that they too would be consumed by the incendiary cloud. No sooner had they gone, however, before the cloud had burned itself out leaving only charred bone, smoldering ash, and armor melted into slag.

As Royne stared, spellbound by the carnage of the scene, he could not help but find it all fascinating—horrifying, monstrous, and utterly cruel—but fascinating all the same.

"It is clear now why the kingsmen were unable to take this place," he said without emotion.

Amara eyed him and looked away. "And that was mere substantial alchemy. It is bound by materials and ratios. It is tangible and predictable. It functions as mathematically defined," she said. "Yet its power is nothing in comparison to metaphysical alchemy—when such power can simply manifest in the palm of your hand."

Royne ignored the sickness he felt in the pit of his stomach, the growing sense of disgust. "So what exactly was that?" he asked. "St. Aiden's Fire is a liquid incendiary that burns on contact. At first glance that seemed to be a vapor or a gas, but I suspect it was actually some manner of finely ground powder?"

"We call it the Star Dust," she said. "It ignites as soon as it is exposed to the open air and burns anything it touches.

"Star Dust?" he mused. "A strangely pretty name for something so utterly devastating."

"It *is* horrible," she said. "But as I understand it, the horror is intended as a deterrent."

"You know, for a man who abhors violence, your father seems to have devised some rather efficient means of killing," Royne remarked. "And to think, you seemed so utterly disturbed by the execution. I suppose it's much eerier when the suffering is hidden away from direct view—be it behind the veil of a cloud or the stone walls of this complex."

"What did you say, *Polecat?*"

He turned away from the window to find her standing directly behind him, posture rigid, sinewy muscles as tense as iron. Hard eyes bored into him, alight with the fires of indignation.

But still he persisted.

"You have seen with your own eyes the tyranny of Andoch and the injustice inflicted upon the people," he began. "Yet when I asked your father for assistance in combating the Guardians, in standing against Kredor and his nefarious advisor, Natharis Tainne, he refused. Instead he offered me a lecture, soliloquizing upon the misuse of alchemy and the suffering that could result from such discord. How interesting to discover that—in spite of his warnings—he is more than willing to misuse that same knowledge so long as it suits his purpose."

For a long moment, Amara held him steadily in her gaze and her large brown eyes shone with the light of myriad emotions. Royne said nothing, intending his silence as an invitation to speak.

At length, the girl gave a frustrated sigh. "You judge my father too harshly," she said, "for if anyone knows the full consequences of discord, it is him."

"How so?" Royne asked.

Amara paced slowly across the room. "Did you know that this building, this University, was once a temple?"

"So I had surmised from the architecture," Royne said. "Most likely built in the waning days of Old Calendral."

"Yes," she said, "but when my father and the first of the alchemists came here, it was little more than a ruin. Yet, over the course of time, they restored it so that it is now as it stands today. It was my father's intention that where once it was a place in which man might beseech the gods for salvation, as the university, it would become a place where man might learn to save himself."

"A noble endeavor," Royne said, "but hardly to the point."

Amara ignored him and continued. "You see, the first alchemists did not arrive in this city as missionaries hoping to spread the Sign of Four—as many of your people believe. They came here as refugees, fleeing the warlike demands of the Kordish empire in hopes that they might pursue the quest for knowledge in the name of peace."

She paused. "My father carries on his conscience the victims of a hundred battles in a hundred wars. Through his forced service to the Kordish emperor, he was—at one time—a great champion of discord, for while his knowledge of substantial alchemy is extensive, his mastery of metaphysical alchemy is unmatched. He can call down lightning from a cloudless sky, cleave open the ground to swallow entire villages, and freeze the very blood in a man's veins. All this and more he did under the edict of the Kordish emperor. All this and more he did against his will. So when he and his fellows finally made their escape, they swore that never again would they use their knowledge for such nefarious purposes."

"Yet, my father knew that the warlords of Kord would not simply allow their greatest weapons to disappear, and as the leader of the refugees, he would need to ensure their protection. So, he built this compound and designed its defenses, for if there is one factor that is sadly universal, it is man's unquenchable thirst for power."

Royne narrowed his gaze and rubbed his chin in thought. "Some decades ago there was talk of another war with Kord and the possibility of another Protectorate for the united defense of Termain. However, almost overnight, the hostilities ceased and the Kordish invasion simply…collapsed. Might these two events be linked in some way?"

Amara shook her head. "Perhaps. I don't know. My father doesn't like to speak of those days." She sighed. "In any case, do not misjudge him. He is, like I said, a man of peace, though sadly that has not spared him from the ambitions of men of war."

"Fine," Royne said at last, "but if I am to suspend my judgment, I would expect to receive the selfsame courtesy. I may be an outsider, and— admittedly—I possess certain…defects of personality, but my intentions are the same as your father. I want to save my people and to bring about a peaceful world. Will you at least grant me the opportunity to prove it?"

"Do you think I would be helping you if that were not the case?" She raised an eyebrow. "You have stated your intent as peaceful, that you wish to expand your knowledge to safeguard the world. For whatever reason, I have chosen to believe you."

Royne bowed his head. "Thank you," he said. "And I am...sorry if I insulted you or your father."

"Accepted," Amara said. "Yet, while I agreed to help you, I will also warn you. If you do choose the path of destruction or your ambitions turn from balance to discord, I will do whatever I can to stop you. No matter what."

Royne pursed his lips. "Accepted," he said.

CHAPTER 18: THE KEEPER

Since the battle on the field of Dunwald, Geoffrey and his men seemed constantly on the move. In an effort to not only liberate more lands in the name of the Winter Rose, but also lend credence to Lord Talondaire's request for aid from Reginal, the Tower continued to press on throughout Whitemane, harassing Dermont's loyal retainers and driving out the Andochan kingsmen wherever he could.

At the same time, with winter's arrival imminent, it was essential that the peasant folk across Montevale be protected while they finished the long and arduous process of harvesting, threshing, ploughing, and sowing so as to bring one year's farming to an end while already beginning the new.

Of the forces that remained encamped at Pridel, nearly all were professional soldiers or retainers sworn to serve the queen or one of her minor lords. The common levies and volunteers had all been released to return to their farms, and while they could be roused to supplement the queen's forces at a moment's notice, their true import in the functioning of the domain was not to fight, but to work the land. Geoffrey found this of particular interest, for not only did Beledain defend the folk of lands loyal to Queen Marina, but also the peasantry of lands loyal to the Plague King as well.

"Why should these folk starve because King Dirt-mouth is an asshole?" Horn had said when Geoffrey remarked upon it. "Just because one of his bastards lives in the castle, doesn't mean they're our enemies. It's all one Montevale, so says the queen."

Of course, this sentiment was not shared by her rival king, whose mercenaries, men-at-arms, and kingsmen seemed to have no problem slaughtering peasants of any land and stealing their stores of supplies. As such, in the name of the queen and for the sake of the people, it was the Tower's prerogative to stop them. Knowing firsthand the horrors of a raid, Geoffrey was more than happy to assist in the regular patrols against the marauding raiders.

Indeed, the court of the Winter Rose was an interesting place. To hear Freddy and Greta describe it, Montevale was like something out of a faerie story, where knights in shining armor fought in service of a wise and benevolent queen. Yet for all of the pageantry, the heraldry, and the brave and noble steeds, Geoffrey also recognized a certain rustic quality to the people of the realm, an earthiness—particularly among the skirmishers of the light cavalry— hat made him feel somewhat at home.

The fact that there was such equality among the genders was something that Geoffrey found rather interesting as well. While it was true that in Pyle there were some jobs often reserved for men and others for women, both worked the fields side by side, and the basic hardships of life often demanded a certain level of respect and equality simply for survival. There were certainly men who balked at such attitudes and made it their prerogative to run their households with harsh words and iron fists, but the majority of couples seemed to rule jointly, understanding that, to put it bluntly, two heads were better than one.

Yet such was not the case elsewhere, as Geoffrey well knew. In many places, men reigned supreme as sad little kings upon sad little hills. On the rare occasions where Brigid spoke of the court at Dwerin, she painted a picture of a life where where women existed as mere playthings for the wealthy and the powerful, *encouraged* by the archduchess.

The Brock, or rather, Galadin, was much more open and much more equal as well, due in part to Lughus's late mother and grandmother. Both had been beloved by the people and through their intercession women could both own property and manage their own businesses without the oversight of some absurd male guardian. Still, while Arcis and his forebears were known for their forward-thinking attitudes towards life and people, it was still rare for the women of the Brock to take up arms and fight. Not that they were denied the right, rather, it was simply not the done thing. However, as stories of the future baroness continued to spread, Geoffrey could not help but wonder how quickly that might change.

In Montevale a generation or more saw men and women standing shoulder to shoulder in the shield-wall or riding to battle in the light cavalry. It was interesting and certainly inspiring.

Not that Geoffrey wanted women like Annabel or his daughter Greta to fight. He absolutely did not, though no more than he wanted Freddy to fight. In fact, he himself did not *want* to fight either. At least, not really. Yet the fact that fighting existed as an option represented something bigger, something more. It represented a freedom of choice that would otherwise have been denied. At the end of the day, if a woman wanted to fight, well, let her. If she did not, that was fine too. What mattered—in the case of anyone—was that the individual had options, regardless of wealth or gender or native land.

In any case, the longer he spent among the folk of Montevale, the more he came to like them. They were good people. Kind, compassionate, friendly. They cared about each other and understood that while a man might be powerful on his own, he was nothing without his fellows.

Perhaps it was simply a lesson learned the hard way, that after a hundred years of bloody war, those with any sense awakened to realize how pointless it was to be selfish and cruel. How stupid.

Not all learned this lesson though. There were always those who refused to see beyond their own desires and ambitions, those who would see the whole world burn because they felt the slightest chill. This King Dermont seemed to be one of them—a man who would unleash plague and disease upon his enemies regardless of the innocent lives lost along the way.

Pyle had endured its share of illness over the four decades of Geoffrey's life. He had seen the suffering firsthand, had lost friends to various afflictions in his youth. Only an evil man would unleash such horrors willingly and Geoffrey was long past the point of tolerance when it came to evil men. Too much had happened. He was the Vanguard. It was his prerogative in life to hunt the evil where it slept and to crush it beneath his cudgel.

But, thankfully, he had other duties, and far more pleasant ones at that. Duties to his wife, to his children. Duties where blood was not spilled, but celebrated. As such, he was overjoyed when the Tower finally ordered his forces to return to Pridel for a few days of well-deserved respite.

So it was that Geoffrey found himself standing upon the gabled terrace of The Gilded Rosette, the large inn that sat outside of Pridel's main gate. He watched, grinning fondly, as Sir Armel led Greta around the yard on the back of a sprightly little pony. So enraptured was he, that he failed to notice the queen's approach.

"She sits a horse well." Marina observed.

"Thank you, your majesty," Geoffrey said, bowing his head. Behind where he stood, Annabelle chatted with the pair of nursemaids and fawned over the Tower's infant son.

Marina smiled and leaned against the wooden rail that surrounded the perimeter of the terrace. Despite her status as queen, Geoffrey found it interesting that she did not look out of place in the rustic confines of the inn. She was dressed in a dark green kirtle embroidered with a pattern of red roses, and while the air had grown colder in the recent weeks, she wore only a light mantle lined with fur. A fine contrast to Geoffrey's quilted arming coat, stained as it was from battle.

"I believe I was about her age when I first learned to ride," Marina said. "My father and my brother taught me." She smiled wistfully. "Unfortunately, the war claimed them both."

Geoffrey nodded. "I'm sorry, your majesty," he said. "I know the...pain of such loss."

"Ah yes," she said. "I recall your speech. You lost a son?"

"Yes," Geoffrey said. "His name was Karl."

"My father was Marius," Marina said, "and my brother was Gislain."

"Kin keep them both," the Vanguard said.

"And your Karl as well." She breathed a sigh. "Such a shame that so many should share in the sorrow and the grief of violence and war. A shame that grief should remain the lone quality to unite the people of Termain."

"So it is," Geoffrey said, "but perhaps it allows those of us with open eyes and wounded hearts to recognize that in our shared sorrow, we may also find a shared purpose."

"Which is?"

"Ensuring that none other should have to know such grief," Geoffrey said, "or that we should have to suffer such pains ourselves ever again."

"Indeed." Marina's green eyes regarded him curiously. "You know," she said, "despite your claims, you don't speak like a simple farmer."

"I assure you, your majesty—"

"Don't misunderstand me," Marina said quickly. "I am not doubting your story or your past." She paused. "What I meant is that while you might present yourself as a rustic, there is clearly much more to you."

Geoffrey shrugged. "A farmer's day begins before sunrise and ends after sunset. It affords us a great deal of time to think. Too much even." His lips spread into a forlorn smile. "Or so my father used to say."

Marina's eyes widened at his words and he suddenly remembered that only moments ago they had spoken of her own father's passing. Yet it was not the shadow of grief that so illumined her eyes. Rather it was curiosity.

"At any rate," he said, "I am grateful for your hospitality, your majesty, and for the kindness that you have shown to my family."

"Think nothing of it, Sir Geoffrey," she said, "And if your friends in the Brock are even half the folk that you and your family are, I imagine that we will soon become the best of friends." She smiled, watching as Greta reined in the little pony and gave it a scratch behind the ears. "Truly, it has been a pleasure to have you all with us. Your family is absolutely delightful."

Geoffrey smiled. "They take after Annabelle," he said, smiling at her as she sat with the nursemaids. She cast him a kindly glance and he felt his heart warm. "I often find myself wondering how I could be so lucky."

Marina smiled. "Annabel is a wonderful woman, if I may be so bold to say," she said, "and your children are a credit to you both."

"Thank you, your majesty," Geoffrey said, "and might I say that Marcus is a lovely boy and no less a credit to you and the Tower as well."

The queen's eyes widened with apprehension and once more Geoffrey feared he had given offense. Perhaps the comment, though kindly intended, was too invasive or too forward. As he was about to apologize, however, the she spoke.

"While I love the child dearly," she said, "he is…not mine to claim."

Geoffrey's face fell and while he was uncertain of her exact meaning, he understood the greater part. "I meant no offense, your majesty" he said, "My apologies."

Marina shook her head. "You misunderstand me." She paused to think before continuing. "The boy's mother died in childbirth shortly before we took up arms against the Plague King. Her death was, you might say, the spark that lit the fire of our rebellion." She smiled placidly. "For my part, I have simply helped see to the child's care since then. I have no intention to replace the Lady Lilia, and yet I...will do what I can to ensure he is safe and secure, particularly while his father fights to ensure the safety and security of us all."

"Well," Geoffrey said, "as a boy who lost a mother at a relatively young age, I'd say he is quite a lucky one to have someone like you in his life." He chewed his lip and his eyes fell fondly upon Annabelle. "And please pardon my assumption about you and the prince. I just—the way you two get on with one another—it just struck me as...familiar."

Marina sighed. "You are not wrong," she said, "and once more you prove my earlier point."

Geoffrey remained silent.

"Since you see so clearly then, Sir. Geoffrey, I will confide in you. I fear for him," she said. "I fear for him because I love him."

Geoffrey gave a thoughtful nod. "If it's any consolation, your majesty," he began, "I have seen him fight. Not only is he unmatched with the spear, but he has the loyalty of his men and the support of that great searoan as well."

"Oh I do not fear for him in battle—at least not beyond the normal range of concern—and what you say about Tempest and the rest of the men is also true."

"Yet," she continued, "I fear for his spirit, for his soul. In spite of his martial prowess, I do not think he was a man made for war. He was born to it, had it thrust upon him, and—as much as he hopes to end it—I fear he cannot imagine himself living without it."

Geoffrey sighed. "To be fair, your majesty, I believe no good men were ever actually *made* for war. Rather, good men choose to fight because they have no other options and because they will do anything and everything to keep what they love kept safe. As for your other point..." he said. "It is hard to see a life outside of the one you know. I can say that from experience. But that does not mean that when given the opportunity, we cannot change—one way or another."

The queen nodded slowly and her eyes stared off into the distance across the plain. "I sincerely hope that you are right," she said, "But look! They return."

Across the plain three riders came into view. The foremost figure, and the smallest, pressed on ahead of the other two, increasing his speed and leaping over a fallen standing stone. Geoffrey smiled. Even at this distance, he could sense the boy's pride at the display.

Moments later, the riders—Freddy, Beledain, and Sir Briden—trotted up along the main thoroughfare to the yard of the inn.

"Well done!" Geoffrey cried, walking out to meet them. He held Freddy's horse by the bridle as the boy agilely slipped from the saddle to the ground.

"He's a natural rider, my lord," Sir Briden said kindly. "He'll make a fine horseman."

Geoffrey grinned and patted his boy on the shoulder. "Thank you, sir!"

The Tower stepped down from Tempest's saddle and patted the searoan on the nose. Queen Marina paced over to join them and offered both horse and rider an endearing smile. In an instant, the intensity of the prince's features softened and Tempest trod forth to nuzzle the queen's shoulder.

"You've a good lad there, Sir Geoffrey," Beledain remarked, "though I doubt I have to tell you that."

Geoffrey smiled. "No, but I appreciate hearing it. Makes me feel like maybe I'm doing something right," he said. "You've a lovely boy as well. I believe my wife's just about fallen in love with him."

Beledain gave a somber nod. "He's not had the easiest of beginnings. I just hope I haven't done enough wrong that he'll have to pay for my mistakes later in life."

"I don't know about that, my lord," Geoffrey said kindly, detecting the subtle concern in the queen's eyes. "At the end of the day, what matters most is that a child knows it's loved. Sometimes it's hard for us to see that, but when I think about my own father, I realize now that everything he did, he did out of that sentiment."

Bel nodded. "Mine as well."

"And mine," the queen added.

"Then count us all as blessed," Geoffrey said, "for there are far, far too many who cannot say as much."

Marina smiled kindly and Geoffrey noticed that for the briefest of moments, her fingers lightly touched the Tower's hand. "I've already sent word to the castle to begin preparing a meal for our return," she said. "But there's no rush if you'd like to sit a minute, Lord Tower."

Beledain was about to reply when from close by they heard Sir Armel's gruff voice ask, "Now what do you make of this?"

Geoffrey's gaze followed the seneschal's eye to where a large wagon was slowly trundling along the thoroughfare toward the inn. The driver was a thinly-built figure clad in a luxuriant purple robe, not at all the type of garment one would expect for someone traveling a war-torn land alone.

At once, Tempest gave a snort 1and Beledain exchanged a glance with Armel and Briden. Without a word being spoken, the two knights gently ushered Geoffrey's children over to where Annabelle sat with Marcus and the nursemaids. Marina followed them as well, but cast the Tower a significant look that Geoffrey knew meant that she would expect to be kept informed.

The Tower slid his spear from its brace upon Tempest's saddle. "Walk with me, Sir Geoffrey?"

"I am with you, my lord," Geoffrey said quietly.

Together the pair of Blackguards paced down from the yard toward where a beaten tack veered off from the road to the city to reach the inn. The prince leaned idly upon the haft of his spear and Geoffrey sat down beside him upon the end of a low stone wall. The great stallion appeared to have wandered idly after them as well, though the Vanguard suspected that the dumb manner in which the horse grazed at the sparse grasses along the thoroughfare was merely for show. For Geoffrey had long sensed that in terms of intellect, Tempest was at least the equal of the great hound, Fergus.

The robed man brought the wagon to a halt a good ten yards away. "Is this the city of Pridel?" he called out. Beneath the shadow of his cowl, a pair of strange, pallid eyes gazed out with an expression of aloof intensity. It instantly put Geoffrey off and he felt a feeling of creeping dread deep within his breast.

"It is," Beledain said. His voice was not overly friendly, but neither was it hostile. "What is it that brings you to the city, traveler?"

"I am looking for someone," he said, and after a pause, added, "Would you say that you know this city and its inhabitants well?"

For a moment, Geoffrey was taken aback, though he realized that there was nothing about Beledain's appearance that would suggest he was anything beyond a common guard. He wore but a dark green tunic, a shirt of mail, trousers, and leather boots. In fact, Geoffrey's white surcoat with its embroidered acorn suggested a higher social status than that of the Tower.

Beledain kept his eyes level. "I do," he said. "Is there someone in particular that you seek?

Silence hung upon the air like distant smoke from a burning village. At last, the man spoke. "I hunt a thief," he said.

"A thief?" the Tower repeated.

"Yes," the man said. "A relic of great importance was stolen from my homeland and I seek to return it to my people."

"A relic?" Geoffrey folded his arms across his chest. "To be sure, I feel we would have heard of something about that! What manner of relic was it, if you don't mind my asking?"

The man fixed Geoffrey with his strange gaze. A vague disquiet set his skin prickling. "It is an object of no consequence."

"Hardly seems worthy of being called a relic then," Beledain said.

"To you perhaps," the man told them. "To my people, it holds certain...religious significance."

Geoffrey feigned indifference and sucked at his teeth.

"I'm not sure I can help you," the Tower mused. "Perhaps if we knew more about the thief. Can you describe him?"

"Describe him?"

"Aye, was he tall or short? Old or young? Thin or fat?"

The man breathed a sigh. "He was a young man. Short and extremely fat. He might have been clad in the guise of a monk or a country cousin. I have heard rumors that he was involved with the murders at an inn to the south of here some weeks ago."

"A thief and a murderer to boot!" Geoffrey said. "Lady save us!"

Beledain gave a nod of agreement. "Sadly, with the ongoing war these are dangerous times. Queen Marina does her best to keep these lands safe, but there are always men willing to take advantage of the strife."

"Indeed," the traveler said.

"Yet, I can't help but wonder," Geoffrey observed, "in spite of such dangers, you travel all alone—with a full load and no less." He eyed the back of the wagon. An oiled tarp lie covering what, from the shape of them, appeared to be long, wooden boxes or crates. "What is it that you carry here?" he asked with a smile. "Coffins?"

Geoffrey had intended it as a joke, but the man's pale eyes flashed.

"Is this the hospitality of Pridel?" he snapped. "A traveler seeks aid hunting a thief and a murderer only to be met with an interrogation?"

"We both know that you're no mere traveler, Keeper," Beledain said. "Just as you know that we're no simple sentries."

An intense silence spread like a thick fog on a gray morning. Geoffrey leveled his gaze at the cowled man and his muscles tensed like a wild cat ready to spring. On the periphery of his vision, he could sense Beledain slowly shift his weight from one foot to the other, and behind him, he heard the heavy breathing of the great searoan as it tramped nearer. A light breeze fluttered past, toying with the edges of the wagon's oiled tarp. In the infinity of the moment, Geoffrey felt the familiar flood of sensation as his own mind drew upon the instinctive prowess of the Vanguard, the intense calm that preceded the violent storm,

The Keeper was the first to act. From within his robes, he drew a strange sword with a crooked blade and cried out in a tongue Geoffrey did not know. The harsh, guttural words sent an involuntary shiver down the Vanguard's spine and for the first time ever, he flinched. Beside him, however, Beledain was unphased. He whirled his spear around and slashed the Keeper's shoulder, tearing through the purple broadcloth and flesh.

At the scent of the blood, the pair of draught horses pulling the wagon began to stomp and snort like wild boars driven half-mad by pursuing hounds. Geoffrey stepped back, drawing Oakheart and Acorn, just in time to turn aside a flailing hoof from the nearest of the horses. Only then could he discern that beneath the creature's blinders a vivid crimson iris whirled about in madness and pulsated with a subtle glow.

What devilry is this? Geoffrey thought fleetingly.

The second of the horses reared up onto its back legs and lashed out with a strength that would have caved in Beledain's skull. But the prince was far too wise in the ways of horses. With a deft sidestep, he whirled the haft of his spear before him to ward off the frenzied animal and drove it back down to all fours.

Heedless of the wound to his shoulder, the Keeper leapt up to stand upon the driver's seat and once more called out in the unknown tongue. With a flourish, he whipped the tarp from the back of the wagon to reveal three long, wooden boxes lying side-by-side. Within each, a hulking Wrathorn warrior—fully armored and ready for battle—began to rise with the slow, halting movements of one who has just awakened from a long sleep. The Keeper uttered another sibilant command and the Wrathorn raised their heads, their hollow eyes ablaze with an intense scarlet hue.

The Dead! Geoffrey's heart hammered in his chest and his eyes widened in horror. *Thom was right! The Dead rise to make war against the living!*

"Beledain!" he cried.

"I see it!" the Tower cried. He set his spear against his boot and with a sickening sound, the red-eyed beast reared and impaled itself upon Spire's shaft. Yet, in spite of the gravity of the wound, the beast continued to buck and lash out while the prince struggled to free his weapon from the horse's fetid entrails. Geoffrey hurried to his side and with a mighty blow from Oakheart hammered the side of creature's skull. Almost at once, the red light dimmed in its eyes and it collapsed in a heap upon the ground.

"Lady save us!" Geoffrey exclaimed, staring at the corpse. Any further comment remained unsaid as Beledain withdrew his weapon and whirled the haft of his spear to turn aside the sudden onslaught of the three Wrathorn. The remaining draft horse, anchored by its dead companion, fought to reach Geoffrey with its sharp hooves, but a shrill whinny announced Tempest's charge as he joined the fray and engaged the flailing creature.

With the extra weight of the dead beast and the wild rearing of the second, the Keeper leapt from the driver's seat and sliced through the leather straps of the harnesses, freeing the wagon from the bucking madness. At once, Geoffrey rushed at him, leading with the Acorn, and sent the man sprawling into the roadside undergrowth.

Before he could follow through with Oakheart, however, Geoffrey turned to see Beledain hard-pressed by the Wrathorn warriors. Heedless as they seemed of any flesh wound, the Tower was struggling to hold them at bay alone and Geoffrey was forced to give up pursuit of the Keeper to come to his comrade's aid. Striking with his shield, he knocked the nearest warrior off balance, and with a crushing blow from the cudgel, crumpled the dead man's helm. The red light of his eyes faded like the embers of a dying campfire.

Heedless of their comrade's fall, the remaining Wrathorn continued their violent onslaught. Beledain whirled his spear before him, knocking aside their blades, and with a quick turn of his wrist, swept the legs out from under one of the dead men. As the warrior toppled over, the prince flipped his weapon around a second time and drove the spearpoint through the Wrathorn's left eye. By the time he pulled it free, the man's body lay still and the red light had gone out.

In a flurry of snorts and grunts, Tempest continued his duel with the odd draft horse, rearing and lashing out with his powerful hooves or viciously biting his opponent along the neck and shoulder. Like the Wrathorn, the strange horse appeared to feel no pain, even when the great searoan was able to turn and strike with both hind legs, knocking it off balance and breaking one of its forelegs.

With one Wrathorn warrior remaining, Geoffrey stood shoulder to shoulder at the Tower's side. As the dead man advanced in a reckless charge, Beledain thrust his spear into the warrior's abdomen, lodging its point within. The dead man struggled against the holy oak haft, impaling itself deeper in relentless pursuit of its enemy. In response, the prince traced a wide arc with his feet and maneuvered his weapon to force the Wrathorn to his knees, allowing Geoffrey the opening he needed to rush in and shatter the red-eyed skull with a resounding *thwack!*

Barely had the light gone out of its eyes before Beledain once again ripped his spear free and joined Tempest in bringing down the draft horse. With another thrust from the spear, he skewered the creature's neck and with all of his strength forced its head downward, low enough for Tempest to deliver a sharp kick that knocked it to the ground. A swift strike from Geoffrey finished it once and for all.

As soon as the horse lay still, the two Blackguards turned back to the roadside and peered out across the plain for any sign of the Keeper. Despite the man's brightly colored robes, however, they saw nothing. He was gone.

"What in the name of Lady was that?" Geoffrey asked.

Beledain gently took Tempest by the bridle and checked the stallion for wounds. Finding none, he turned toward one of the fallen Wrathorn and, using the tip of his spear, pried about in the dead man 's pallid flesh. "It's just like Thom said," he observed. "No blood flows forth."

"Nor do I see any upon the ground," Geoffrey added.

"It's as if it's...stopped. Become like...mud or tar."

Geoffrey eyed the body of one of the fallen draft horses. As it lay on its side and its harness fell askew, he noticed a strange wound in its chest. It appeared to be some manner of cavity the edges of which were marked by burnt flesh and blackened fur. An unnatural sensation gripped him and he could not escape a tremor of fear. Unconsciously, he glanced up at the inn and felt an irrational stab of panic as if at feared at any moment the building might burst into flames.

Geoffrey eyed the derelict wagon with its empty wooden caskets. "Perhaps they really were corpses," he said lowly.

Beledain's green eyes smoldered and he gazed eastward away from the city. "We have trouble enough in Montevale without having to worry about the risen dead," he said. "Perhaps when the Shackle returns..." He trailed off.

Geoffrey felt a weight settle in his chest. *If he returns...* He thought to himself, but did not say. "We should have a better look at these corpses," he finally said. "But...quietly so as to not cause a panic. Tell the queen, but no one else. Not yet."

"Agreed." Beledain gave a nod and patted Tempest on the nose. "I'll have men search the area for any sign of the Keeper, but we'll keep the details of his...companions between ourselves until we have a chance to think. Any idea where he ran off to?"

"No, I'm afraid." Geoffrey shook his head. "Something tells me he's not likely to be found either."

Beledain's gaze narrowed as he scanned the horizon. "None of this makes any sense."

"Perhaps," Geoffrey said, " Or perhaps it does and we just don't want to believe it."

"Lord-General!"

Geoffrey and Beledain turned back toward the inn to see Sir Briden riding towards them. "Are you well, my lord?" he asked, sword drawn and ready. "The queen sent me to help. Were you attacked, my lord?"

Beledain exchanged a glance with Geoffrey. "We're fine," he said. "Nothing Sir Geoffrey and I couldn't handle."

"Aye, sir," Briden said. "Can I do anything to help you?"

Beledain considered it. "Nothing at the moment, my friend," he said. "Let the queen know we'll be along directly and we can all return to the castle."

Briden nodded. "Would you like me to fetch some men to clear the path here?" he asked.

"Thank you, but no," Beledain said. "Sir Geoffrey and I will see to it."

CHAPTER 19: HARRIER'S KEEP

With his extensive network of contacts, it did not take long for Adolfo to settle the matter of refitting one of the baronial keelboats and selected a crew from among those captains, fishermen, and bargemen he knew to be permanent residents of the Galadin wharf. Horus prepared a bevy of gifts for their hosts, Jergan arranged an appropriate wardrobe for each of them, and Lughus met with Owain to draft final, formal orders for the knights of the Galadin fiefs. Meanwhile, Ada took care of preparing anything a young noblewoman might need, and so Brigid was left to wander at will.

When at last, the day of their departure arrived, Brigid stood leaning on the rail of the wharf, overlooking the dock where the keelboat was moored. Fergus sauntered about beside her, idly sniffing at the barrels of fresh fish or pawing lightly at the odd crayfish or eel trap. She watched as a ship's cat crept carefully past him with the discarded tail of some manner of perch in its mouth, nearly as intimidated by the great hound's presence as the local dockside thugs who stood beneath the eaves of the numerous taverns. The small chest of clothing and personal items Ada had packed had already been loaded alongside Lughus's, and once the baron himself arrived they would be off.

She had to admit, she was looking forward to the journey. Even though they would only be staying in Marthaine for two or three days en route to another battle, she was looking forward to seeing Lord Roland and Lady Morgana. She knew very little of her own grandparents, and the open affection with which the Marthaines had entreated both Lughus and herself had solidly endeared them to her. In fact, for fear of causing a scandal among the Marthaine gentry, she'd even decided to forgo her usual leggings and don a modest kirtle of baronial blue—at least for the duration of the stay at Baron Roland's court.

And of course, while the purpose of their journey was to finalize battle plans for the assault on Stonebridge Castle, there were certain to be moments of celebration. With the suddenness of their departure to relieve the besieged monastery at St. Golan's, Lady Morgana was openly disappointed at not being able to celebrate the announcement of the betrothal, let alone the fact that the reunion with her long-lost grandson was to be cut short. Then, from the occasional comments Lord Roland made throughout the campaign, Brigid got the sense that the baroness did not share her husband's austere disregard for frivolity.

Let her fuss! she thought, smiling to herself. *After so much strife, let a grandmother have her due.*

Fergus returned to her side and she idly scratched behind his ears. *Golden Hounds and Silver Eagles. What a remarkable thing life is!* In a rare moment of self-indulgence, she imagined herself outfitted in a gown that included the trappings of both house shields. Blue had always been her color. Perhaps she might commission a circlet crafted of braided silver and gold?

Perhaps. There were, of course, plenty of other, more practical uses for that amount of coin. It was still fun to imagine it, though.

She sighed and shook her head, wondering how foolish she must look. She just found it nearly impossible to keep from grinning like a bloody fool these days. In spite of everything—the war, the danger, the assassins—she was happy, so happy. It was as if an entire flight of butterflies had taken wing inside her chest and carried her a good six inches above the ground. Each intake of breath brought with it an exhilarating rush, and her heart shone with the brilliance of a thousand stars.

Oh Lughus...

Again, she smiled and scarlet roses blossomed upon her cheeks and at the tip of her nose. A heady warmth and a dull ache spread throughout her body as she conjured up the memory of their morning together and the strength of his arms he when held her close. Lady's Grace! Their bodies fit together so perfectly! Like statues carved from the same stone, or a pair of perfectly balanced blades.

It was utterly intoxicating.

Her blush deepened with her breathing and she fought to maintain an impassive facade. She felt a tight pressure building in her abdomen. From the looks of it, the keelboat had a cabin. Perhaps, once they were underway they might find a quiet moment of privacy to share.

With a sudden grimace of self-consciousness, Brigid shook her head and rubbed her eyes. As easily as she could lose herself in pleasant memories and blissful anticipation, she had no wish to appear unseemly in full view of the whole bloody city.

Still, it was a glorious thing to be so in love, to be united not only in heart and mind, but of body too. How absurd that men like Padeen Andresen would equate such beauty with sin. The mind and the heart were part of the body. What nonsense to imagine that they could be separate.

However, no less tragic, she thought, were her mother's views. For she recalled the countless hours she had been forced to sit and listen to Josephine's self-absorbed lectures espousing her views on the nature of love.

To the archduchess, love was born only of the self and belonged only to the self. It was the sensory equivalent of looking into a mirror. Of course, this was not surprising, for Brigid's mother lacked the capacity to feel for anything beyond her own desires. Sympathy, empathy, compassion—these were all things unknown to her. How could she possibly know true love?

As Brigid considered this, she could not help but feel a certain pity for her mother. Pity that Josephine should deny herself what seemed such an integral part of being human. However, when she recalled the years of instruction and training that the archduchess oversaw in her wardship of the Drove—instilling her views into the bevy of young girls—her pity turned instead to anger and regret.

She was grooming them, Brigid realized, *Raising them to be mounted like prized horses, willing sacrifices to powerful men...*

Her stomach churned.

A short bark of greeting brought her attention back from the mountains of Dwerin to the bustling docks of Galadin, and she looked up to see Lughus, Adolfo, and a squad of Galadin guardsmen making their way toward her. For a moment she wondered at the steward's absence, but she realized that Horus would have stayed behind with Owain to assuage the old seneschal's belief that it would be his duty to see them off.

As soon as he saw her, Lughus's lips curled into his benign half-smile and she hurried to join him at the wharf.

"Baron Galadin," she smirked.

"Lady Blade." He offered her his hand and she gave him a quick peck on the cheek.

Adolfo cast her a bemused glance, raising one eyebrow imperceptibly to anyone other than her. "Good day, Lady Brigid," he said.

"Sir Adolfo," she said. "I hope all is well with you."

"Not half so well as it is with you, my lady," he said politely.

"I trust all is well with our allies in Agathis?" she barbed. "General Navarro and Captain...Velius is it? "

"All is progressing," Adolfo said shortly.

"Good," Brigid said. "Perhaps if all is well here and Owain is improved, you might join our men as they march west. Contact the legion and renew...diplomatic relations."

"I had considered as much myself," the Madder said. "Alas, he is not. Such as it is, safe journeys and I look forward to your return." He offered the young couple a polite nod and stepped past them to direct the newly appointed captain of the ship.

"Don't tease him," Lughus whispered to her.

Brigid flashed him a grin. "He's teasing me," she said. "It's only fair."

Lughus shook his head fondly and called out to the sergeant. "Take care, Pike," he said, offering his hand. "We'll meet you in Agathis."

"Will do, sir," Sergeant Pike said. "Though are you sure you won't be needing *any* of us? Even for *ceremonial* purposes?"

Lughus gave a half-smile and patted the guardsman on the shoulder. "Appreciated," he said, "but if my grandfather was willing to put himself at our mercy, I feel it only fair that we do the same."

"Aye, sir. And I suppose they'd have to be pretty damn clever to get the jump on both the Marshal and the Blade," Pike laughed, "Let alone Ol' Fergus."

The great hound gave a bark.

"Do be careful though, sir."

"I will, Pike," Lughus said. "You too."

Moments later, Adolfo returned with the captain, a man named Jorik. Brief introductions were made, assurances given, and the keelboat was on its way.

According to the captain, the journey across Lake Bartund usually took about half a day so, barring any unforeseen circumstances, they could expect to dock in Marthaine by midafternoon. Thus, in spite of her earlier ideas about creative ways to pass the time, Brigid decided to forgo such adventures for now. Besides, the cabin was much smaller than she had expected and was already overflowing with spare cables, cargo, and various other items necessary to the maintenance of a vessel. Fortunately the view from the deck was so breathtaking, so majestic, that as she stood with Lughus gazed out over the placid waters, enjoying the feel of the strong wind in her hair and the warmth of his arms around her, she could not say she was disappointed.

So it was that the journey passed pleasantly and without incident, and the Marshal, the Blade, and the great golden hound arrived at the docks in the city of Marthaine to be greeted by the baron and baroness.

Two dozen Marthaine men-at-arms stood to receive them followed by a four mounted knights in gleaming plate mail with a bevy of household officials. As the Galadin sailors ran out the gangplank from the keelboat to the dock, the guardsmen snapped smartly to attention and the silver eagles enameled upon their heater shields blazed in the sun.

Brigid took Lughus's arm and together they stood waiting for the invitation to come ashore. For a fleeting moment she felt a flash of anxiety, but was unsure if it was her own nerves at the auspicious nature of the meeting or perhaps some lingering sensation that harkened back to the legendary Siege of Three. Whatever the source, it was quickly forgotten at the sight of Baron Roland's craggy face positively beaming at the sight of them.

"Baron Galadin! Lady Brigid!" he shouted. "Welcome to Harrier's Keep!"

"Thank you—" Lughus began, only to be cut short when Lady Morgana hurried forth widening her arms to enclose both Brigid and the young baron in a warm embrace.

"By the Brethren! Every time I see you my heart leaps with some new joy!" she exclaimed. "You're like to kill an old woman!"

Baron Roland suppressed a grin. "My dear..."

"Oh shut it, Roland. You ignore propriety enough for the both of us. Allow me this." She stepped back and took the young couple by the hand. "Congratulations to both of you—for the betrothal and for St. Golan's! From what Roland tells me it was a victory worthy of song!"

"We fought hard," Lughus said, raising his voice loud enough for the entire retinue to hear, "But without the arrival of the silver eagles, I do not know if we would have lived to be here today."

"Indeed," said a man from behind Roland, "but we appreciate your acceptance of that simple truth."

Brigid eyed the speaker. He was perhaps thirty years of age, dark-haired, and handsome, and while his eyes lacked the lightning strikes characteristic of Lughus and Lord Roland, they were unmistakably gray. Over his noble garb he wore the standard tabard of baronial blue emblazoned with the silver eagle, though unlike the others of Roland's household, this man's eagle bore two heads as opposed to the single-headed symbol of the baron.

Guy Marthaine, she remembered, Lughus's cousin and Roland's eldest nephew. It was he who led the Marthaine horsemen across the lake to reinforce the Galadins at St. Golan's, and it was he, she remembered, who had stood beside Roland and his grim seneschal, Sir Ulfric Gond, at the assembly of barons in Highboard. She had never spoken to him directly, though he was present for the peace talks following the battle when the Chough formally surrendered.

"You remember Guy," Roland said to Lughus.

Lughus offered Guy his hand. "Good to see you, cousin," he said.

Guy's lips spread into a thin smile. "Be welcome," he said before shaking. He turned toward Brigid. "We've never been formally introduced," he said. "I am Guy Marthaine, Lord of Silverdale and nephew to Baron Roland."

Roland waved his hand. "This is Lady Brigid Beinn," he said, "daughter of the late Archduke of Dwerin, and soon-to-be Baroness of Galadin."

"So I gathered," Guy said. "Congratulations—to both of you."

Lughus nodded graciously, and Brigid watched him rest his hands casually upon Sentinel's pommel. To anyone else, the gesture would have gone unnoticed, but Brigid had long understood it as one of Lughus's tells. He was wary, on guard, and despite his joy at their arrival, she sensed that Roland too was slightly on edge.

Sure enough the old baron's affection and his happiness were genuine, as they were with the baroness, but Brigid also sensed a certain undercurrent of frustration, even annoyance. She wondered now if perhaps there was credence to Owain's concerns and that the peace between the rival baronies was not as widely accepted as believed.

"Come," Roland said to them, "You can take some time to rest and eat. Afterwards, we can take you on a tour of the castle and the town." He paused. "I have to say, I'm surprised. I know he's not one for the water, but did you really leave Fergus behind?"

At the mention of his name, the great hound appeared at the gangplank and with a happy bark, loped down and leapt up on his hind legs to greet the old baron. Roland laughed and grumbled good-naturedly as Fergus licked his face; however, the remaining folk of the Marthaine court cried out and either dove for cover or scrambled to draw their arms. Brigid's hands reflexively went to her hilts and Lughus had Sentinel half-drawn before the Baroness scoffed and called out to her people in a voice of stern command.

"What foolishness!" she scolded, shaking her head. "Come now, he's only a dog!"

"In fairness, this dog may have cut down more men at St. Golan's than I did. " Roland laughed and ruffled the hound's ears. "But you're right, my dear. Fergus is a friend. Be at peace, men, and stand down."

Brigid suppressed a smile. *Let that be a warning though.*

Lughus let his blade sink back into its sheath. "We've brought gifts," he said, hoping to dispel the lingering tension. He raised his hand to motion to Captain Jorik and at once, the crew hurried to unload them.

Roland smiled as he watched a pair of sailors roll a large barrel down from the deck of the ship to the wharf. "Perindal's Sword, you've brought the Ram's Reward!"

"In Galadin, they say it isn't Harvestide without it," Lughus said.

"And I'd say that's one tradition we'll definitely be adopting here." Roland grinned. "Have your men unload anything you need and I'll have mine carry it the rest of the way."

Lughus gave a nod and went off to give final instructions to Jorik and the crew of the Keelboat while Lady Morgana joined Baron Roland in playfully fawning over Fergus. Brigid watched, amused that for a creature so large and intelligent, the great golden hound could be as needy and puerile as a puppy less than a quarter of his size.

"Never a dull moment when the Galadins come to visit," Guy Marthaine observed, suddenly standing beside her. "Even less so the Marshal and the Blade."

Brigid sensed the challenge implicit in the comment, but feigned ignorance. "Yes," she said with a benign smile, "it seems that wherever we go there is no shortage of fools willing to make trouble." She allowed a pause to linger before adding, "We certainly taught the Guardians what happens when they threaten the Brock, did we not?"

Guy's lips pressed into a tight line and she knew at once that her comment had hit its mark. Before he could reply, however, Baron Roland called to his seneschal, and Sir Ulfric Gond barked the order to return to the castle.

As the soldiers assembled their column, Roland strode over to Brigid and offered his arm. "I believe your betrothed has already been commandeered by his grandmother," the old baron said, "but if you'll allow me, I would count it a great honor to have my future granddaughter walk at my side."

She glanced over to catch Lughus's eye and smiled at him, casting aside his unspoken apology. "Of course," she said, taking the old baron's arm.

From the docks, the procession passed through a large stone archway into the town. The city of Marthaine consisted of a series of concentric rings, each of which marked a greater height above the surface of the lake and the greater social status of those who called that district home. At the pinnacle of the city, looming over all, stood the great castle of Harrier's Keep surrounded by its thick curtain wall and three storied gates.

Walking alongside Baron Roland, thought back on what she had read in *The Siege of Three* and she wondered if being here would invoke any memories of the Blade. To this point, she had experienced nothing specific; however, she continued to sense a certain generalized disquiet, and while she did everything that she could to appear courteous and poised, she remained on guard.

"This absurd feuding has deep roots," the Argent Eagle muttered as they made their way through the city beneath, "and as much as we may wish for it to be over, I'm afraid old habits die hard. In any case, I'm sorry for it."

Brigid was somewhat surprised at the old baron's intuition. "I don't mean to be suspicious," she said, "and—as I hope you well know—I do not doubt you or the baroness. I just can't help but feel as if I must—"

"Watch his back," Roland finished, "And your own."

"Yes," Brigid said. "I mean no offense."

The old baron shook his head. "Of course not," he said, "and I would expect nothing less. You're both fine warriors and you fight for what you believe is right and good. It's inevitable that you'll make enemies. I just hope you believe me when I swear that I will never be one of them."

"Of course!"

"As for the others..." He shrugged. "Give it time. A thousand years of hostility is hard to erase in a few months, but I believe things will change. Eventually. The more they fight side-by-side, the less they'll wish to fight each other."

Brigid nodded. There was a truth to that. Even Sir Owain, who had spent his life fighting against the Marthaines, had admitted a begrudging respect and a reluctant camaraderie for the old baron. One might even say it bordered on friendliness.

At last, they reached the southernmost of the three castle gates. Another two dozen men of the Marthaine guard stood at attention to formally welcome them, ushering them in with full martial pomp and fanfare into the outer ward. Once more, Brigid found herself smiling inwardly. As Lady Morgana had mentioned, Roland Marthaine was well-known to dislike unnecessary displays of grandeur so the fact that he was making such an effort for his grandson was endearing.

At the gate to the inner ward, Sir Ulfric shouted another command and at long last the knights and retainers of the court began to disperse. The castle steward, a small, hairless man by the name of Gilbert, met them at the great doors to the hall and greeted them with a low bow. He exchanged a few private words with Baron Roland, and enlisted two of his assistants to show Lughus and Brigid to where they would be staying. Gilbert was quite the professional, Brigid thought, noting how well the old man masked his discontent when Baron Roland informed him that Fergus would remain in the keep and not the kennels.

"I think I'd feel more comfortable if he stayed with you," Lughus told her after the stewards showed them to their apartments—separate, as she expected, but adjacent. Each had its own bedroom, sitting room, and a small room to the side for a bathtub and adjoining garderobe. Small plates of bread, cheese, apples, and grapes had been left out for them, but rather than dine alone, they shared the meal together in Brigid's quarters.

"I'm not sure how well I'll be able to sleep," Brigid said quietly. "I've become so accustomed to having you beside me."

Lughus shrugged and took a bite of an apple. "Slipping next door shouldn't be too difficult for the Blade." He smiled. "Though if you'd prefer, I can always come to you."

Brigid blushed. "As long as we don't...scandalize your grandparents. Your grandfather seems to be somewhat preoccupied at the moment, though he tries hard not to show it."

"You sensed that too?" Lughus murmured.

Brigid nodded. "That and...something else," she said. "It's clear that not everyone is as open to ending the feud as Baron Roland."

"Yes," Lughus agreed. "And to them, little enough of my Marthaine blood counts against the Galadin." He shook his head and set the core of the apple aside in mild frustration. "I'd hoped that after St. Golan's we were past all of this. The Guardians are far too dangerous and enemy for this type of division."

Brigid gave a shrug and sat down on Lughus's lap. "Well, I can tell you this much at least..." She rested her head against his shoulder and felt his arms encircle her waist. "Whatever happens, we'll face it together—as always," she told him. "Come what may."

"As always," he repeated, kissing her softly on the cheek. "Come what may."

CHAPTER 20: THE COURT OF THE PLAGUE KING

"So," Sparrow said, "you're telling me that you spent the majority of the last two years at sea gallivanting about with Sorgund pirates?"

Beside her on the driver's seat of the wagon, Thom slipped his hands into the wide sleeves of his new scribe's habit. He had no idea how Lord Talondaire had been able to procure it, but there was something oddly comforting about being back in the burgundy uniform of his youth.

"Believe it or not," he said, "Yes."

Clad in the plain woolen garb of a maid, Sparrow gave a snort. She arched her eyebrows in surprise. "Well, fuck me."

Thom's cheeks blazed with color. "I'm sorry?"

"What a mad fucking life you've lived."

"Ah. Well, yes," Thom said, " I suppose that's true." He inhaled deeply and released a great puff of cold air. It lingered in the ether like some forlorn specter before fading into nothingness. A few yards ahead, Lord Talondaire, his seneschal, Sir Lloyd, and two chosen men of his personal guard (Dagny and Anton) ambled along conversing among themselves while far off in the distance, through the veil of wafting snow flurries, Thom could just make out the vague outline of a great stone city built into the terraced, highland outcropping. It was Reginal, the Plague King's capital and the journey's end.

"Oi, Thommy, you better take these," Sparrow said, handing over the reins. "Would look out of sorts for a maid to be driving a wagon."

"Perhaps that's true," Thom said, though he knew no scholars who doubled as wagoners either. His knuckles turned white as he gripped the leather thong, fighting against the flash of anxiety that he perennially felt at being forced to experience something new. While Ol' Thom Fatty might have balked at such a thing, he had determined that Thom Reaver would not live a life enslaved by fear.

Of course, the veritable flood of new experiences since inheriting Magnus's title was nothing if not overwhelming. From barroom brawls to pitched battles, riding horses and holding council with a queen, it was all so much. And although he had observed plenty of strange and wondrous things in his journey with the great Wrathorn, Thom's had been a benignly comical supporting role. Now, he was the hero of the story, the subject of the next verse of the song, but while it left him feeling like a fish out of water, he was determined to sprout legs and learn to run.

He did not expect, however, that the source of his greatest discomfort would come from the close proximity he shared with a young woman.

"Warlock's Balls!" Sparrow grunted. "I hate bloody corsets. Feels like my tits are going to pop out every time we hit a rut in the road."

Thom made a noise of acknowledgement, but kept his gaze leveled straight ahead.

Sparrow gave a smirk. "And don't be taking that as an invitation to hit them on purpose now."

Thom looked stricken. "I won't!" he said. "I wouldn't!"

The girl erupted into a fit of giggling. "Hush! I'm only teasing," she said. "Aren't you an easy one? And here I thought all pirates were wanton brutes who spent their days bouncing back and forth from the bottle to the brothel."

"That's…not inaccurate," Thom said, "though I wouldn't exactly consider myself a pirate. I was more…along for the ride."

"That so?" Sparrow pursed her lips and took another swig from the wineskin. "You chop heads easy enough," she said. "I'd have figured you for quite the daring rogue."

"No, no, no," Thom said dismissively. Somewhere in the back of his mind, he heard Magnus give a heavy sigh.

Idiot.

"So there's no great gaggle of strumpets staring earnestly out to sea?" she asked, her great brown eyes alight with mischief. "No lady love anxiously awaiting your return?"

Thom shook his head. She had a slight chip in one of her front teeth that for some reason he found rather endearing. So much so that he sometimes caught himself staring. "There is not," he said.

"Well, that's a relief," Sparrow said, playfully punching his arm. "It'd be a shame to find out now that you caught the pox from some seaside strumpet."

"The what?" he cried as the color drained from his face, but he received no answer beyond her raucous giggling.

In the midst of the commotion and the subsequent hot and cold flashes he felt at the young woman's rapturous mirth, he failed to notice Lord Talondaire had trotted back to pace alongside them.

"What is this nonsense?" he asked.

Sparrow arched her eyebrows and stifled her giggling, through she could not keep the smile from her lips.

"It's nothing," Thom said.

"Nothing?" Talondaire asked.

"Yes, nothing," she repeated, struggling to regain her composure.

Lord Talondaire released a sigh. "We're nearly to Reginal," he said. "While there's no accounting for the moods of the Plague King, my lineage warrants the hospitality of the castle. If such is the case, my men will be installed in the barracks, while you two should be quartered among the servants. This should hopefully allow you access to those who we seek to free. With the exception of his personal guard, the Plague King does not allow anyone to go about armed within the walls of the castle and passage in and out is restricted."

Thom gave a nod. He still had no real idea how he was going to accomplish any of this, but he had to try.

Besides, he thought, *Magnus never had a plan for anything and look at all he was able to accomplish—from tracking his shipmates to attacking the Lighthouse to recovering Callah's Key!*

Traffic on the road became more and more congested as they neared the gates of the castle town. Carts laden with sacks of oats and grain trundled along the road pulled by draught horses and the occasional ox. As Lord Talondaire and his men approached, the common folk stood aside to allow them passage, bowing their heads in deferential silence; however, Thom could sense an undercurrent of resentment. Clearly the common folk were not happy with their new king, but they had been made to accept the relative powerlessness of their social position in the face of the martial strength of their social betters. The armored guards—clad not in the traditional arms of Montevale, but the crowned sable stallion of the Plague King—did little to assuage the peasantry's discontent. Even Thom could not resist a sudden flash of seething anger as he spied a pair of guards turn out a woodcutter's wagon, strewing its contents all about on the ground.

"Fucking bastards," Sparrow muttered. "Surely with himself up there they wouldn't dare to be searching us."

"Let's hope." Thom said. He turned his gaze away from the city so as to avoid even an unconscious glance toward the place beneath the bed of the wagon where his great bearded axe was concealed. Amidst the curtain of snow flurries, he could make out what seemed an entire village of crimson tents.

"The kingsmen camp is there to the west," he muttered, "though I expect any anointed Guardians they have among them will be at the castle as well, or at least lodged at an inn in town."

The thought gave him pause. With such great numbers of kingsmen sent to support the Plague King, it was certain that they would be commanded by anointed men of the Warlord's Tower. He couldn't help but wonder now, which ones. And while it was true that Thom had never known them as Lughus, he had no wish to be recognized.

Nothing can be done about that now...

Luckily, it was as Sparrow said, and with a great lord at the head of their little caravan, they passed through the gates with ease and began the slow procession through the city wards to the castle of the Plague King.

Reginal was a significantly larger city than Pridel, and though it too lacked the aesthetic grandeur of the Andochan fortresses; however, the more time he spent in Montevale, the more he was coming to prefer the simple beauty sturdy walls, blocky battlements, and broad archways. The design, clearly built to accommodate the passage of horses and carts, created a sense of openness that defied the claustrophobic oppressiveness often characteristic of such architecture.

Yet whatever beauty might characterize the city was marred by the palpable hostility that marked many of its people. Never before had Thom seen such disparity between the wealthy—be they merchants, guildsmen, or burghers—and the peasant classes—servants, laborers, and the like. Even a cursory glance revealed a gaudy opulence among the folk of the former, and a destitute squalor among the latter. When he recalled that this was the city where Queen Marina had been born and raised, and where her father had so recently reigned as king of Gasparn. He knew that she would weep to see what had become of it, and the thought of such a thing filled him with a simmering rage.

At length, they reached the great barbican that guarded the entry into the castle proper only to be met by heavily armored men of the royal guard. Lord Talondaire strode forth to meet them, and at once a runner was sent to announce their arrival to the king. While they waited, the Plague King's men brashly swaggered up and down the length of the wagon, puffing out their chests and shamelessly eying Sparrow with their lewd stares.

For a third time now, Thom felt the anger course through him and now wondered if it was part of Magnus's legacy. While in some ways this new-found rage of the Reaver frightened him, what frightened him even more was the fact that the more often he felt it, the more he was beginning to like it.

In any case, before long the runner returned. Lord Talondaire and his men surrendered their arms, and the iron portcullis slowly rose to admit them. As they passed through, another squad of armored guards met them and led the contingent onward to the castle's inner ward. Thom urged the wagon onward, though watched over his shoulder as the portcullis slammed shut behind them.

"We're in it now," Sparrow observed. "Trapped."

Thom nodded in agreement, but otherwise remained silent, focused as he was on directing the wagon toward the stables. His eyes were wide with the preternatural awareness of the hunted beast. The Song of the Reaver resounded within him, thrumming through his veins with the beating of his heart. Yet, he could not embrace the chaos just yet. Despite the fey compulsion to simply ready his axe and call his enemies to him in a great, teeming horde, he knew that such a thing would be folly, for he had work to do first.

After securing the wagon and horses in the stables, a steward and two of his assistants appeared to direct the party to their quarters. As Lord Talondaire had expected, Sir Lloyd, Dagny, and Anton would be housed in the barracks with the rest of the castle guard. Sparrow would quarter with the other maids, and Thom would bunk with the assistant stewards. Barely had they any time to stow their belongings before the meal was announced in the great hall. Thom followed along after the other young stewards, pleased that once they had deemed him their social equal, they were content to leave him alone.

The Royal Hall at Reginal was a fine and lofty space. A large, blazing hearth ran the length of the floor, stretching from the king's high table to the carved oaken doors that separated the hall from the vestibule. Additional lighting came in the form of great, wrought-iron chandeliers and at least a dozen large braziers. The Plague King's banners hung limply from the walls, interrupted at regular intervals with the searoan banner of pre-war Montevale the crimson banner of the Guardian Order. Folk sat by rank and order, with Lord Talondaire in a place of honor at the head of the table known as the reward. Sir Lloyd, Dagny, and Anton sat among the general household men-at-arms, while as a maid, Sparrow had been enlisted to assist with the service of the meal.

Thom took a seat at the end of one of the side tables in the place of least importance among the stewards. He had no wish to draw attention to himself by disrupting the established order, for he knew very well that when it came to such matters, scholars, stewards, and clerks could be just as snooty or self-important as the gentry. Plus, his overall mission was, in part, dependent upon his anonymity. He needed to be able to fade into the background, to move about unnoticed right under the Plague King's nose.

Once the lower tables of the hall were mostly full, the cheerful ringing of a bell announced the arrival of the king and those companions deemed worthy enough to sit at his side. Thom watched them enter, men and women in equal measure, clad in the finery as would befit a royal court. All were unknown to him, though he could not deny a certain familiarity with the manner in which they carried themselves. He had seen such attitudes among the members of the nobility who made their home in Titanis. An obscene, almost unspeakable arrogance. An entitlement that rattled the Brethren themselves.

In no personage was this more on display than in the Plague King himself. Dermont Tremont, King of Montevale, victor of The War of the Horses entered the hall with the deific majesty of the ignorant and the cruel, a man who considered it his highest duty to honor himself and to see to it that all others followed his example. He was clad from head to toe entirely in black with embellishments of soft sable fur, onyx, and gold. A gilded longsword encrusted with gemstone glittered from his golden belt of plates, perfectly complementing the golden crown upon his brow.

The entire assemblage of the hall rose to their feet as he made his way to his seat at the high table. His cold, green eyes surveyed them critically, privately weighing each man's loyalty, or at least, submissiveness. When at last he was satisfied, he offered a careless wave of his hand, indicating that all should be seated. Only then did he deign to smile and the steward gave the order for the meal to begin.

Thom returned to his seat and was surprised to find his jaw aching. Apparently, without realizing it, he had been clenching his teeth. Fortunately, no one else seemed to notice. The stewards nearest to him were already lost in their own argument over whose turn it was to oversee the servants cleaning the garderobes. Thus, Thom stared, unnoticed and uninhibited, at the Plague King and his chosen fellows at the high table.

"You know that's his brother, right?"

Thom's eyes widened as he glanced up to see Sparrow standing beside him carrying a pitcher of ale. As she leaned forward to fill his tankard, he couldn't help but notice that she had been right about the effects of the corset.

"What now?" he muttered. He casually averted his eyes and fought the urge to blush.

Sparrow gave a smirk and paused to fill another drink. "The King,' she remarked with casual indifference. "He's brother to the Tower."

"Oh that's right," Thom said. "I nearly forgot." Once more, he fixed his gaze upon the Plague King, this time with a mind to comparison.

There was, he supposed, a family resemblance. They had the same dark hair, the same fair complexion and green eyes. Yet while in appearance the Brothers Tremont might share these physical similarities, the spirits that gave life to their features could not be more different, and though Thom had not known Prince Beledain for very long, the qualities that defined him, that drew folk to him and made him a great leader of men—integrity, humility, and fellowship—seemed wholly absent in his elder sibling.

"Have you seen anyone else?" Thom whispered.

"The elder knight across from Lord Tally is Lord Guillon, kinsman to the queen and former general. The redhead two seats down is King Dermont's cousin, the Lady Val."

Thom took a deep swig from his goblet and Sparrow paused to refill it.

"Lord Talondaire's sister is the dark-haired beauty at the high table. Beside her is the king's new seneschal, Vaston Delon, called the Boiling Sea." She paused. "Haven't seen his mother yet, but—hold on. There she is. Making her entrance on the arm of that old lord."

Thom glanced over and instantly felt a chill run down his spine, for it was no mere nobleman who gently saw the dowager Talondaire to her seat at the king's table. He was a brawny old knight, past his prime but obviously still quite capable. His hair was cropped close to his scalp and he wore a fine embroidered surcoat emblazoned with the mark of the silver key declaring for one and all that he was a member of the Order of the Guardians. "Lady save us!" Thom gasped. "It's the bloody Warlord."

"Who?" Sparrow asked.

Thom rubbed his eyes. "Dandon Rood, the Warlord himself," he told her. "Commander of the Guardians' elite warriors and member of the Council of Five."

Sparrow gave a smirk. "I take it that means he's important."

"Very," Thom said. "Strange that he should be here, though. His duties usually keep him in Titanis."

Sparrow nodded. "I've lingered here too long," she said, topping off Thom's tankard one last time. "Ain't no one gossips like servants, and we wouldn't want to cause a scandal."

"What do you mean?

"A scribe and a lord's maid talking in hushed tones? Why, folks are bound to think I fancy you."

Thom reddened. All thought of the warlord, the Plague King, and the sudden, eminent danger departed from his mind. "Yes," he said at last, "I suppose we wouldn't want to give anyone the wrong idea."

"Who says it's the wrong idea?" She flashed him a quick grin before turning away to serve the neighboring table.

Thom watched her go, a strange, slightly confused smile playing upon his lips.

About fucking time, Crusher.

"Shut up, Magnus." He muttered under his breath. He took a swig from his tankard and wiped his mouth on the sleeve. He needed to think, to strategize.

Unfortunately, this had never been his strong suit.

Whereas Lughus and Royne could spend hours over the chessboard locked in a strategic battle of wits, Thom often found himself checkmated within a half dozen moves.

Yet now he found himself locked in the chess match of his life, one that used not carven pieces on a board, but real people and real lives. How was he ever going to manage that?

You know what I say? Magnus's voice mused. *Flip the board and loose the axe.*

"You would use a great sword to sew a handkerchief."

What need would I have for a fucking handkerchief?

"I was just making a point."

Aye, well, shut up.

The Warlord was a complication that Thom had not anticipated, though when he took the time to consider it, he did not necessarily believe the old knight was altogether someone to fear. Dandon Rood was a famous warrior and a master when it came to leading men, but he was also known for his great sense of honor. Espionage and the like were more the domain of the Chancellor and his constables. In all likelihood, Rood was sent to oversee the companies of kingsmen the Plague King requested as part of the Andoch-Montevale alliance.

Still, while Thom did not know Dandon Rood as Lughus had, Rood had been friendly with Rastis, and there was always the chance—albeit small—that the Warlord might recognize him. As such, he made up his mind to avoid the old warrior just in case.

Thom released a sigh and gazed into the depths of his ale, reflecting on the day. So far, so good. He had accomplished what amounted to the first step of his mission. He had gained entry to the Plague King's castle and identified the folks he was meant to rescue. Sure, there were...complications: speaking to them, convincing them to leave, and discovering a means by which to escape the castle. However, he was strangely confident that he would figure things out. There was a blind luck to fools, it was said, and if anything, Thom had always been foolish. Magnus too.

With a reassuring nod, he took a swig of his ale only to pause when he felt something soft and furry move between his legs. He glanced down just in time to see a lanky orange cat leap up onto the bench beside him.

"Well, hello there," he said aloud, watching as the creature hopped onto the table and began cleaning itself.

At once the stewards seated down the table began to gripe, grumble, and hiss at the little creature who regarded them with a weary indifference until, unperturbed, it leapt down from the table and padded off to a forgotten corner to continue to wash.

"Whatever you do, don't you dare start feeding that piece of shit," one of the stewards told Thom.

"Bloody thing got into our quarters once and pissed all over Treven's bed, ain't that right?" another said.

"Tore up one of the tapestries in the south passageway as well," said a third.

Thom arched his eyebrows in surprise. "Does it belong to someone?"

"It's a stray, as far as I know," said the first man.

"It slips in somehow from outside the walls. Drops mice and other dead vermin all over the ladies' hall."

"Aye, that's because the Lady Valerie keeps bloody feedin' it!"

"Not surprising to see a woman that muscular's got a fondness for puss-puss," another man said with a leer. "The color even matches."

The men shared a laugh and Thom took another drink from his tankard to avoid having to join them.

Before long, the conversation turned to other matters and Thom slipped back into comfortably anonymity. The cat remained nearby, and as Thom watched it out of the corner of his eye, he resolved to make it his friend, for if indeed the creature had found some covert way into the castle, perhaps it might also know a secret way out.

CHAPTER 21: THE FEAST OF THE FATHER

The celebration of the Feast of the Father took on added grandeur this year as Baroness Morgana took it as an opportunity to not only welcome her long-lost grandson to her home, but to celebrate his great victories as well. No expense was spared in any course of the meal.

As the guest of honor, Lughus could not help but feel overwhelmed. Never had he known such elaborate gestures of open endearment. As an apprentice, he had lived a relatively simple life with few opportunities for self-indulgence. Then, after he arrived in Galadin to take his place as Arcis's heir, the old man was so wracked by illness that there was little time to do much more than sit, talk, and try to learn what he could about running a barony. Even after Arcis's death, he continued to maintain a sense of frugality, figuring that in the face of war, any gold he saved could potentially outfit additional men-at-arms. The few expenditures he had allowed himself were limited to the rare occasion when a trader or merchant would show up with the odd book or manuscript for sale, and he could count on one hand the number of times that had happened.

So from the moment the festivities in the hall began—with performances by bards, recitations from poets, and platter after platter of fine food—he felt simultaneously appreciative at such effusive magnanimity and anxious concern over being the subject of such munificence.

Brigid must have sensed this, for he noticed that anytime he gripped his pommel or withdrew into himself, she would reach over and take his hand. She was, after all, no stranger to the elaborate displays common at a noble court, and more than that, she knew him for who he was. She understood that while few could match his mettle on the battlefield, the posturing and pageantry of courtly life was sometimes challenging for him who had been raised to value truth. At court, so much seemed a complex weaving of illusion and intrigue, and while he knew that his grandfather had a reputation for finding it similarly distasteful, he had no desire to embarrass his grandmother or appear ungrateful.

And so, he smiled and nodded, and danced when required. He bowed graciously, applauded the musicians, and joined in the toasts. When Brigid deemed it appropriate, they had a servant fetch the gifts Horus had prepared, as well as the more personal gifts that they had chosen themselves, and presented them to their hosts before the entire court.

Not to be outmatched, Gilbert, the Harrier's Keep steward, announced that the Dwerin armorsmith commissioned by Lord Roland to craft Lughus's armor had finished his work. One by one servants appeared in a grand procession to present the young baron with each shining piece. No sooner had they finished than Lady Morgana began begging Lughus to try it on so that she might see him in it. Lord Roland gave a half-hearted protest against making such a fuss, but it was clear that he too was curious. Even Brigid—with a mischievous twinkle in her eye—threw in her support for the baroness, echoed by more calls from throughout the hall, until at last, Lughus conceded. Roland summoned a pair of squires, and there, before the entire court Lughus donned the armor one piece at a time.

When at last he stood fully outfitted for battle, the firelight glimmering off of the polished metal, Lady Morgana clapped her hands and beamed proudly. "By the Brethren!" She exclaimed. "You look the very image of St. Aiden himself!"

Despite his discomfort at being the center of such lavish attention, Lughus too was quite pleased. The armor fit him like a second skin and as accustomed as he had become to the weight of chainmail, the design and fluidity of plate not only allowed for greater dexterity, but did not feel nearly as burdenso1me.

"Fine indeed," Baron Roland said simply. He took a sip from his tankard and said no more, though Lughus could tell from the gleam in his eye that the old baron was just as proud and pleased as his wife—if not more so. Yet, like Lughus, the Argent Eagle was not one to gush.

Lady Morgana shook her head. "Men!" she said with a roll of her eyes. "Brigid, my dear, what do you say?"

"Well, I'm not half so skilled with words as a former apprentice to the Loremaster…" Brigid teased, "but even if I were it would do me no good, for the very sight of him leaves me speechless."

Roland nodded. "The man was truly a master at his craft," he said, "and a credit to the storied smiths of Dwerin."

"Indeed," Brigid agreed.

Lughus glanced around him at the other folk of the Marthaine household—knights, courtly officials, and others. They were seated throughout the long hall as was befitting to their rank and favor, though since space had to be made for the honored guests, a few of the usual members of the high table were obliged to be seated now at the lower table known as the reward. He had tried to protest, not wanting to cause further disruption to the everyday conventions of the court, but his grandparents would have none of it.

Now, parading around in his gifted armor—expensive *full-plate* armor—seemed certain to ruffle some silver feathers.

But it did not cease there, for the presentation of gifts was not over. With a wave of her hand, the baroness again motioned to Steward Gilbert, who in turn called upon another pair of assistants, and the three of them quickly excused themselves from the hall.

"We have something for you as well," Morgana said to Brigid. "After all, you'll be part of the family soon enough and it's only right that we should properly welcome you!"

Brigid shifted uncomfortably in her seat. "Oh, Lady Marthaine, You really don't have to…"

Lughus offered her a smirk. *Have a taste of your own mischief then…*

The baroness gave a chuckle. "Oh Brigid dear, believe me. I never do anything I don't *want* to do," she said. "And as I understand it, that is a quality that you and I share."

Brigid blushed and Lughus could not but find her lovely. "That is not...inaccurate," she said.

"Good," Lady Morgana said. "A woman needs her talons, and speaking of which..."

With a smile, she waved the returning steward forward. Upon his arm, he wore a thick leather glove on which there perched a large bird of prey. Its feathers shone with a luminescent beauty that ranged from dark, bluish-gray to fine, luminescent silver.

"This..." Morgana began, "is Cassiadorra, or, if you prefer, 'Cass.' She's young, she's spirited, she's loyal, and once she sights her prey, there's none fiercer." The baroness raised an eyebrow. "Which is precisely how Roland described you."

Lughus smiled. "That is not...inaccurate," he said.

Again, Brigid reddened. "Lady Morgana," she said at last, "I...I don't know what to say. Thank you. She's...she's beautiful." She smiled sheepishly and turned to Baron Roland. "As I remember, Lord Roland, you mentioned falconry on the eve of St. Golan's. I shall certainly have to learn now."

"It's actually quite simple. The bird does all of the real work." Morgana said. "I suppose that explains why Roland is such a skilled falconer."

The old baron huffed a laugh and Brigid smiled.

"Besides," the baroness continued, "Lughus had got such a beautiful golden hound in Fergus, it seemed only fitting that you should have a silver eagle to match."

At the sound of his name, Fergus paused where he lay chewing on a large cattle bone and gave a snort. Morgana smiled and continued.

"You're a charming girl, Brigid, and Roland and I appreciate you. We've not had much joy in these halls these last fifteen years, but now..." She paused. "It was as if the Brock were under some dread enchantment, as if we were buried beneath the snows of sixteen winters, yet now—with you two—a new sun has finally risen, a new sun that was promised so very long ago. It brings with it new life and new hope."

"Thank you," Lughus interjected. "We—together—we shall try our best."

"That's all that can be asked of anyone," Roland said, "But come. Let's get that armor off of you and enjoy the rest of the evening." He raised his goblet and cast his gazed across the length of the hall. "To Harvestide!"

"To Harvestide!" came the answer.

With the servants' aid, Lughus doffed the armor and returned to his seat beside Brigid. As he passed her by, he ran a gentle finger along the back of her neck and she turned to offer him a closed-lipped smile of contentment.

"I'm sorry about parading you about in the armor." She grinned. "But I just couldn't wait to see you in it. Besides, it made your grandmother happy."

"It did," he conceded, "so I suppose it was worth a bit of discomfort."

"Well, Marshal, you cut quite the dashing figure," she said softly, her eyes all aglow. "As for the discomfort, I promise to make up for that later."

Lughus returned her smile, took her hand in his, and lifted it to his lips. An upwelling of affection surged within him, and for the moment at least, he was able to set aside the sense of disquiet that had sharpened his senses and furrowed his brow since their arrival.

With a contented sigh, he took a swig of his ale and watched as Lady Morgana and Gilbert the steward introduced Brigid to Cassiadorra. The look of sheer joy on her face as she donned the falconry glove and gently stroked the eagle's feathers smoothed his care-laden brow. A mellow sensation spread through him, and as he idly traced his finger along the rim of his tankard, he smiled. Beside him, his grandfather leaned in to refill his cup and, replacing the pitcher, gripped him by the shoulder.

"It's so good to have you here," Lord Roland observed, "though one of these days, we'll have to visit each other without having to march off straight away to battle."

"Here's hoping," Lughus agreed.

"So your men march as we speak?"

Lughus nodded. "They're to meet General Navarro and the rest of the Fifth in Agathis. Once we join them, we can all march south together to reach Stonebridge.

Roland nodded. "Good. Let's hope the sight of all of us together will be enough to force a quick surrender. We don't want to be caught in the mountains once the snows begin."

"Agreed," Lughus said.

243

Roland took a swig of his ale. "And Baron Nordren still defends the harbor and the coastal road? Alone?"

"Not entirely," Lughus said. "When Theo sailed eastward with Geoffrey to Montevale, the Lord-Baron sent his men to reinforce Nordren Port and Helmsted at the Nivanus. As I understand it, he's also sent crews of peasants from Glendaro lands to assist in the harvests of the baronies where their own farmers may have been marched off to war."

"Good," Roland said, nodding with approval. "Perin's no warrior, but he's a good leader and a good man. Like all Glendaros, he finds a way to pull his weight just the same no matter the circumstances." He paused to take a drink. "Thank you for this," he said, raising his tankard. "And for the others gifts. You needn't have done so, really."

Lughus shrugged. "Horus said it was tradition to exchange gifts at formal meetings among barons," he said. "He prepared most of them with the exception of the book. That was from Brigid and me."

"*The Kordish Rose*," Baron Roland recalled.

"I read it back at the Loremaster's Tower. I thought you might like it since you said you preferred poetry to tales of heroics."

"I do," Roland said. "I heard a bard recite part of it years ago, but I've always wanted to read it for myself."

A servant appeared bearing a falconry perch and set it down behind Brigid's chair. Carefully, Brigid allowed the raptor to step from the glove to the perch before returning to her seat.

Lord Roland smiled at her. "You should bring her with us when we march to Andoch," he said. "There's plenty of good hunting in the highlands. If you like, I can teach you. I'm sure she'll enjoy the freedom as well."

"I will certainly do so." Brigid smiled. "Thank you again, my lord," she said. "She is beautiful."

Roland's craggy face blossomed into an expression of benign satisfaction. "Lughus is my only grandson and you're soon to be my granddaughter by marriage," he said. "I'm afraid you're going to have to suffer a bit of doting for at least a little while."

Brigid cast Lughus an affectionate grin. "Fair enough," she said.

"I want you both to know..." Roland paused. "I want you both to know just how proud I am of you, and while I can't claim any responsibility for having a hand in your upbringing or education, I want you to know how honored I am to know you now and to stand beside you in defense of the Brock."

On the far end of the table between Baroness Morgana and Roland's gaunt seneschal, Sir Ulfric Gond, Guy Marthaine cleared his throat. "I must admit, Uncle, that I am still somewhat uncertain about our...current situation."

Roland turned slowly to face him. "What is it that you find confusing, Guy?" the Argent Eagle asked. "You were present in Highboard at the Assembly and led our men in the Battle of St. Golan's. What is it that you find unclear?"

"Much, I'm afraid," Guy said, raising his voice to carry across the hall. "To be perfectly honest, I am uncertain as to why we find ourselves so embroiled in conflict with the Guardians at all. For hundreds of years, Andoch and the Brock have been the staunchest of allies, yet in half a year, that longstanding friendship has devolved into war. Why? Because Arcis Galadin—your sworn nemesis—had a disagreement with the Guardian-King? Because these two, these Blackguards—and not just any Blackguards, but two of the *Three*—have taken a stand against him? The lives of our men seem a heavy price to pay for such tawdry squabbling."

Roland's jaw set like stone and his eyes flashed. Across the hall, the gathered folk of the household fell silent, and their faces, Lughus noticed, drained of all color. Where they stood on the issue was uncertain, though it was clear that not one of them was willing to get between the two great lions of the court.

"You know that the conflict goes far beyond this, Guy. Kredor seeks to name himself emperor in violation of the Brock's own sovereignty," Roland growled. "Besides, when have we in Marthaine ever cared a fig for the Guardians?"

"When have we in Marthaine ever cared a fig for the Galadins?"

"You forget yourself, Guy!"

"No, uncle, you forget yourself!" Guy seethed, "And as your recognized heir, it is my prerogative to remind you!"

Morgana's voice cracked like a whip. "This is unseemly!" she said, "And completely inappropriate for the Feast of the Father!"

Guy's gaze narrowed, but he bowed his head in deference to the baroness. "My apologies, Auntie," he said, "I only speak out of concern for the barony."

"Your concerns are noted," Roland said coldly.

***

A chill passed throughout the hall. From the high table to the reward and on to the tables of the periphery, the folk of Harrier's Keep sat stiffly, uncertain of how to behave in light of the awkward exchange. Gone was the merriment. Gone the lightheartedness. The diaphanous bubble of hope had burst, leaving behind a miasma of resentment and a lingering generational despair.

Brigid watched the assembly carefully, for she was quite familiar with courtly life, having spent so much time as its prisoner back at Blackstone, and while it was clear that there were fractious contingents within the Marthaine court (as there were fractious contingents among every court), Harrier's Keep, like Houndstooth, seemed void of the usual fawning sycophants and hangers-on. Like the rest of the Brock, the people here seemed honest, open, and relatively pragmatic.

The one exception, however, was Guy, and from their first official meeting at the docks, she had decided very quickly that she did not trust him. He was too much the traditional aristocrat. He might speak of his concerns over the Marthaine fallen, but she had a hard time believing it. Rather, she thought it far more likely that his frustrations with Lord Roland and resentment of Lughus was born out of a perceived threat—a threat to his status as Roland's heir apparent. He feared that he would lose that which he had long coveted, and under those conditions, many an inferior man was driven to commit uncounted acts of heinous cruelty, as the Beinn Brothers had shown.

"If I may..." she began. She glanced at the baron and baroness. "If I might address the court?"

"Of course, my dear," Lady Morgana said. In spite of his anger, Roland's eyes softened and he gave a nod.

Brigid smiled at Lughus and took his hand. "On behalf of Lughus and myself, I would like to thank all of you—Baron and Baroness, lords, ladies, knights, and retainers, and everyone else from the craftsmen and burghers to the farmers and peasantry of Marthaine..." She paused. "Thank you. Thank

246

you all for your hospitality, for your gallantry, and for your stalwart commitment to peace."

She stood. "In Blackstone, where I hail from, there is a great disconnect between the classes of people, a disconnect that—to me—has always been a black mark standing in the way of Dwerin's greatness. In Dwerin, the common folk work primarily as miners, harvesting the iron that our craftsmen need to create their famous work. Men, women, and even children are made to work in dangerous conditions, slaving away for a daily ration of what little we can trade for or what little our farmers can coax from the infertile mountain soil."

"Meanwhile," she continued, "the nobility live in luxury, believing themselves touched by the divine, and chosen to exercise a privilege over any and all." She sighed. "It always disgusted me."

Roland gave a thoughtful nod of agreement.

"However, from the moment I arrived in the Brock—from Galadin to Highboard to what little I have seen of Marthaine—it is different. Your people work together. Your people are united—within each barony and *together* as an entire realm. True, you may have your rivalries and disagreements, and it would be folly to assume that all members of the gentry treat those below them with the same courtesy as they deserve. However when you all stand together, you do so with one spirit and one heart, and in the face of such resolve, the enemies of the Brock cannot help but smash like waves upon a rocky shore."

She gazed out over the assembled folk of the hall. Her heart pounded like a war drum and her fingers felt like she had just thrust them into a nest of bees.

"Think on St. Golan's," Brigid said. "When the army of Northern Andoch arrived, led by the Chough, the men of Galadin were sorely outnumbered. Yet, we stood fast against the invaders and we triumphed. Galadin, Marthaine, Nordren—all of us together. And of course, who could forget the sacrifices of the good people of Agathis? From the common folk of Cragbarrow to Baron Dorgan himself. They fought like heroes so that the rest of us—the rest of the Brock—might have a chance. Even now, Baron Dorgan's widow and her daughters continue the fight, for while they host the Fighting Fifth, General Navarro has chosen to remain strictly a military ally. The day-to-day management of the barony remains with the baroness, and from the ruined castle at Cragbarrow, she remains vigilant, ever-watchful should our enemies return."

"As such," Brigid said, "I believe we owe it to her and to the memory of Baron Dorgan to strike back at the Guardians at Stonebridge Castle, to deny them a staging point from which to further threaten us, for—correct me if I'm wrong—but Agathis lies just south of Marthaine?"

"It does indeed," Roland said.

Brigid cast Lughus a meaningful glance and extended a slender hand. She knew that it was one thing for her to speak, but as the baron of Galadin, the lost heir, and the child that was supposed to mark the ending of the ancestral feud, he must say something. Yet, she knew that to confront the tragedy of his parents in such a public manner was something that—as fine and brave a warrior as he may be—filled him with shame and terror.

But the time had come, and he knew it. With a resolute nod, Lughus took her hand and rose to join her. "I know that, as baron of Galadin, many of you might see me as a threat, and while many of you might have many deep and personal reasons to view the people of my lands with distrust or even hatred, it is my goal to heal the wounds of a thousand years."

Brigid felt his hand give hers a gentle squeeze. "What Lady Brigid says is true. The Brock is strongest when we stand together. We've *already* proven that, and we will continue to prove that."

For a moment, he paused and Brigid sensed that he was steeling himself. "I..." he began, "I...never knew my father, or my mother. I suppose that, at least in some regard, I must have, though I have no real memory of either of them. However...I'm certain that there are many among you who did."

He took a deep breath. "And while their end was...as it was, for the good of the Brock, they at least attempted to adhere to the Lord-Baron's decree. Perhaps I am a result of that, the result of their duty to their lands and their commitment to peace. I don't know."

Baron Roland sighed heavily and Brigid felt a palpable sorrow that defied his stern impassivity.

"In any case," Lughus began again, "as a son of both Galadin *and* Marthaine, I believe strongly in *both* lands and strive to uphold the honor and legacy of *both* great houses, and I hope to earn your respect so that one day you too will find me worthy of not only the golden hound, but the silver eagle as well."

"This conflict with the Guardian-King goes far beyond either Brigid or myself, beyond Galadin or Marthaine," he continued. "It began long before I knew anything about my heritage and well before I was granted the title of the Marshal. No, for many years now, King Kredor has sought to extend his dominion beyond the borders of Andoch, to create a new Empire of Calendral and name himself as emperor. As it stands, the Brock remains the last realm to fall—the great blue jewel that he would see added to his imperial crown—and he must *not* get it. Galadin of Marthaine, Blackguard or Guardian, for the sake of the people—of this land and every land, we must not allow a tyrant to hold us under his boot. We must stand together or we will find death all alone."

With that, Lughus gave Brigid's hand a gentle squeeze and together they returned to their seats. Baron Roland offered them a fervent nod while the baroness offered them a wistful smile. Across the court, folk stared somberly into their ale, mulling over their private thoughts or else whispering softly to their neighbors.

At length, from the table known as the reward, an older nobleman stood and bowed his head. "Baron Roland," he said, and turning, added, "Baron Lughus. "

"Sir Varen," Roland said. "You wish to speak?"

The knight nodded. "To be sure, the baying of the Golden Hound still haunts many and more of us—particularly those who can recall the days before your parents' wedding…"

Low murmurings of agreement sounded throughout the hall.

"However," Sir Varen said, "it would be folly for us to believe that the cry of the Silver Eagle is any less terrifying to the folk of Galadin."

"Here, here!" someone muttered.

The older man continued. "But along those same lines, if those yellow-bellied dogs across the lake can put aside centuries of strife for the safety of the Brock, then I'll be damned if I can't do the same!" he said, And if a wretched boor like Sir Owain Rook can hold out a hand in friendship, why! I'll not give him the satisfaction of being the better man by rejecting him! No! I'll shake that bastard's hand and wipe the look of smug superiority right off his face!"

The other men of the court chuckled and gruffly sounded their agreement.

"So, my barons," Sir Varen said, "if it's peace or harmony or whatever bollocks you be after—by the Brethren—I say we spite those Galadin bastards by being the best damned allies they've ever seen!"

A general cheer rose up from the fighting men of the court and Baron Roland's stony face split into a sardonic grin.

"So you'll come with us to Stonebridge?" the Argent Eagle shouted.

"Aye!"

"To show those yellow dogs how it's done?"

"Aye!"

Brigid laughed at the absurdity of the rivalry and the ways of men. Still, she could sense that not all of those in attendance shared Sir Varen's enthusiasm. Lord Guy, she noted, was not particularly pleased with the rest of the assembly's zeal.

Regardless, the rest of the meal passed without incident. At times, there were members of the court who would approach and offer some measure of kindness or greeting to Lughus and Brigid. Men of a certain age or older would say, "I knew your father," or refer to Lughus as "the son of Gaston," and while he smiled or nodded through these comments, Brigid knew the tempest of emotion that they invoked.

However, it was clear that the men of Marthaine were ready and willing to follow their baron to war, to cross the border into Andoch, and to smash the stone fortress that stood as a threat to them and to the sovereignty of the Brock. At the end of the day, she knew that such commitment meant more to Lughus than avoiding the ghosts of his past.

Still, as she lie in bed later that night with his arms wrapped tightly around her, she could not shake a subtle feeling of foreboding, a sense that some unseen threat lie just upon the edge of her vision. She wondered to what degree he felt it too, for there had been a certain intensity, a fervor, in the way that he had kissed her—like a storm-tossed sailor holding fast in the midst of an autumn squall.

With a sigh, she shut her eyes and snuggled into his embrace. Her tension faded away, replaced by the gentle comfort of his warmth. She would keep a watchful eye, peering into the shadows to root out the darkness wherever it might try to hide. She was, after all, the Blade, and together with the Marshal, they would clear the way forward so to usher in the Dawn.

CHAPTER 22: A HEARTLESS FOE

Following the strange encounter with the Keeper and his Wrathorn guard, Bel found himself even more dour and grim than usual as he struggled to make sense of just what it was he had seen. Between Dermont's men and their Guardian allies, there were already plenty of enemies to be found among the living. If indeed it were true that the Keepers had somehow managed to raise the dead to fight a second time, the number of their foes had essentially doubled. Not only that, who was to say that even allies, friends and shield-brothers, could not be returned to fight once again, their sullied flesh corrupted to turn friend into foe.

If indeed...

Bel sighed. It was so far-fetched that even now he had a hard time admitting the reality of it all to himself. Were it not for Sir Geoffrey's presence at his side and Thom's earlier report about the Lighthouse, he might very well have denied the truth entirely. Added it to the growing list of evidence that he was slowly losing his mind.

But it was true. They were the risen dead.

There was no other way to explain it. From their antiquated armor to the dried, decrepit flesh that clung to their bones, it was clear that they were creatures whose time had long since passed.

They were soldiers of the dead, mindless abominations called forth to slaughter the living.

And if what Thom said about their numbers were true, the Shackle's prolonged absence took on an even more dire level of concern.

Bel sighed and rubbed his sleepless eyes. In the darkness of the bedchamber, shafts of moonlight illuminated the shape of Marina's slender form in the bed. She lay half-concealed beneath a pile of skins, a vision of loveliness--alabaster skin, radiant and flawless, crimson tendrils effortlessly cascading down the pillow as if placed there by an artist's brush. Bel sat opposite her atop his wooden armor chest, concealed in shadow. A revenant specter unable to rest for fear that with the discovery of yet another enemy, she might come to harm.

His eyes widened and his blood thrummed within him as he felt himself moved by his great desire for her, a desire born of deeper love. For in her, he realized, not only had he found another who's heart sang in perfect harmony with his own, but one in whom he discerned the live-giving powers of the very world itself. She was the future. The light to his darkness.

In short, he loved her not only for all that she was--mind, body, and soul-- but also as the personification of Montevale, the Montevale that—together— they fought to build. The world that his son and all the sons and daughters of their tragic, war-ravaged land deserved. She was his heart, she was his homeland, she was his queen.

The flicker of a cloud passing before the moon brought a sudden chill to Bel's amorous zeal, and from the recesses of his mind—the place that stood ever-watchful since he had fought within these very walls to save her from Dermont's rats—a new shadow emerged, one that even Dermont could not rival. He envisioned a pair of glowing, red eyes gazing out from the lifeless visage of a dead man, a husk of flesh made to rise with but one purpose.

Killing.

It was so maddening, so impossible to believe. Dead men? Dead warriors? And the Keeper, what of him? Vanishing—as it seemed—into thin air?

He could accept the vague thoughts that seemed of a mind that was at once his and the Tower. He could acknowledge that something utterly wondrous and unexplainable had occurred outside of Clearpoint when Marcus Harding traded his life for Bel's own. However, to find himself literally face to face with such dark and unnatural power (he was still working his way up to calling it "magic") was something that his already fractured mind was still struggling to rectify.

It was strange. When Thom Reaver mentioned it at the council meeting, he had not found it unbelievable, as far-fetched as it had sounded. It was as if, somehow, his mind had taken the notion of a Dead Army in stride. Even when he and Sir Geoffrey had confronted the Keeper and the dead men (and horses) revealed for what they were, he had still remained unaffected as the old battlefield calm, that self-preservational detachment that all veteran warriors seemed to develop, took hold of him. The dead men were simply adversaries, enemies to be vanquished so that he and his might yet live.

But now, hours later, alone with his thoughts beneath the pallid light of the moon. Now, they became something else. A reality. A truth. A threat that could not remain unresolved.

It was a new front, another Bloodline, and he would need to be ready for it. There were just so many of them now. So many enemies, so many fronts. Dead men to the east, Guardians to the west, his own brother to the north. Raiders, marauders, and the chevauchée slaughtering peasants as they struggled to bring in the harvest. Winter's cold. Starvation. Death. Enemies everywhere.

They were surrounded, hedged in, trapped. So many gone already. Larius. Lilia. Sir Emory. His father. All dead. Casualties of the violence, of the bloody war. His pulse quickened and his fist clenched. Marcus. Marina. They would not take them. He would not allow it. He would fight until his dying breath.

"Bel?"

His eyes flashed at the whispered sound of his own name. His muscles tensed and his senses sharpened. Like a wild creature, a wolf of the steppe, he gazed into the darkness seeking whatever dare threaten his home and his peace.

It was Marina. The softness of her emerald eyes met the harshness of his own, and as his tension eased, it was replaced by shame.

"Bel, what is it?"

Beledain took a deep breath and rubbed his eyes. "It's nothing," he said. "An unquiet mind. I'm sorry."

Marina slipped from beneath the cover of the furs and sat down in his lap.

"Do you want to talk about anything?"

Bel shook his head. "I don't know if I can yet."

Marina gave a nod. She lay her head against his shoulder and kissed the side of his neck. "Then come back to bed," she finally said. "Whatever troubles you will be easier to face in the light of day, but only so long as you *rest*."

Bel slipped his arms around her and held her close. "I'm trying," he whispered. "The weight of my thoughts makes it...difficult."

Marina smiled kindly and traced her lips along his collar. "Then come back to bed," she said, a warm light in her eyes, "and we shall endeavor to find another way to put you at ease."

Beledain's lips spread into a soft smile and as his eyes met hers, he once more felt a stirring in his blood. Marina stood and, taking his hand, led him back to bed.

"Lie down," she whispered and kissed him deeply on the lips. She pressed her hand to the center of his chest, gently urged him to the mattress. At once, his senses were consumed by her—the scent of her hair, the soft touch of her skin, her body gloriously luminous in the moonlight. His heart began to pound with the steady strength of a thousand horses. As the blood coursed through him with intensifying desire, Marina's lips spread into a satisfied smile and she slowly climbed on top of him.

"Lady's Grace..." she murmured, and with an effort, began to rock, shifting her weight in a steady roll. An involuntarily shudder ran through her and she bit her lip to keep from crying out. Overcome with the sight of her, Bel's hands tightened on her hips, and with a great, halting breath, he finally felt the tension behind his eyes ease.

With every movement, every rolling motion, Marina's breath deepened and he felt the irresistible compulsion to move with her, matching her accelerating pace. Her wild red mane streamed out behind her like a curtain of flame, and an overwhelming sensation of unbridled pleasure ignited within him, curling his toes and urging him to even greater passion. When at last he could stand it no longer, he caught her around the middle and whirled her down to the mattress. In one swift motion, their places were reversed while their bodies below continued the arcane dance that made them one.

Before long, the great bonfire of their passion could no longer be contained. Marina's back arched in ecstasy, and she threw back her head in a soundless cry that ignited the great explosion within him.

All sensation, all reality was defined by her and the limitless expansion of their bond. She was the light that guided him through the darkness, just as his son was the light that marked the dawn, and with the pair of them to lead him, he knew that no matter the magnitude of suffering that marked this life, he would endure it and remain strong.

When Bel rose the next morning, it was with a renewed sense of vigor and he marveled at the regenerative power of love. He kissed the sleeping queen's brow, dressed, and after a short visit with Marcus, made his way to the locked storeroom off of the stables where he and Geoffrey had secured the bodies of the dead Wrathorn.

The acorn knight himself was already waiting when Bel approached. Tempest wandered idly about the yard and ambled over to Bel's side, greeting him with a snort and a nudge.

"Sir Geoffrey," the Tower said, gently patting the stallion's nose.

"Prince Bel," Geoffrey replied. "I'd hoped to find you here."

"You wished another look at our friends?" Bel asked.

"I did indeed."

"So did I."

Geoffrey nodded and stood aside while Bel unlocked the door. "I don't like concealing matters from my people," Bel said, fiddling with the key, "but in this case, I felt it might be best if those…like us investigate the matter first—particularly with Thom and the Shackle still abroad."

"You mean those of us with titles," Geoffrey observed. "That may be wise. No need to cause a panic. At least, not yet."

Bel unlocked the door and nodded to Tempest. "Warn us if anyone draws near," he said.

The horse knackered and shook his mane. Bel opened the door and led Geoffrey inside, closing the door behind them.

"I suppose I must seem half-mad," Bel remarked, "talking to a horse as I do."

Geoffrey shrugged. "I was a farmer, my lord. Many a lengthy debate have I had with all manner of barnyard creature." He smiled. "They make for far better listeners than most men."

255

"Indeed," Bel smiled as he set about lighting a pair of small oil lamps. In the chilly confines of the storeroom their breath wafted about upon the air like a brigade of miniature ghosts.

"Besides," Geoffrey said, "if the stallion is a searoan of the Brother Galdorn, then he not only listens, but understands. Baron Lughus's hound Fergus is the same. A spirit hound of Perindal, he is."

Bel handed Geoffrey one of the lamps and the farmer took it with a gracious nod. "What days we live in where such legends walk among us," he remarked.

"Or in this case..." Geoffrey said, motioning to where the bodies of the dead Wrathorn had been placed atop a trio of wooden table, "where legends *lie* among us."

Bel gave a nod. "Let's have a look."

Together, the two men examined the bodies of their vanquished foes. While less than a day had passed since the skirmish outside of the inn, the evidence provided by their bodies gave every indication that they had been dead for much longer—long enough, at least, to have passed many of the more putrid stages of decay. The flesh that clung to their bones was dry and flaking, while the metal and leather that comprised their armor bore signs of rust and rot. The rigidity of death rendered their limbs as hard and immovable as iron, but Bel remembered well enough the strength and swiftness of their deadly assault.

"They look as if they crept right out of a tomb," Geoffrey observed.

Bel nodded. He continued to scan the body of the nearest man by the light of the lamp. It was the warrior Bel himself had dispatched with a spear thrust to the eye. As was typical of the Wrathorn, he was outfitted piecemeal in an assortment of light armor pieces—a single leather bracer, a single steel vambrace, a single spiked poleyn, and a leather harness with a single, fur-lined pauldron. He wore no breastplate or chest guard, nor even any tunic, revealing a multitude of ancient, puckered scars and distorted, shriveled tattoos. Most noteworthy of all, however, was the man's beard. While in death, the hair had lost its luxuriant grandeur, in life, it had clearly been a source of meticulous vanity. Enormous, braided, and bejeweled, it easily reached down to the man's waist.

All of a sudden, Bel paused in his inspection, for within the layers of thinning hair, something caught his eye. He drew the dagger from his baldric and with careful precision, moved aside the braids and beard rings to reveal a great gaping cavity rimmed by charred and blackened flesh in the very center of the man's chest.

"Lady save us!" Sir Geoffrey uttered.

Beledain nodded, but otherwise remained silent. Geoffrey sided over to him and took his lamp, holding both up to provide more light. The two men exchanged a resolute nod, and with a bracing inhale, Bel carefully slipped his blade into the wound and began to prod about the open space. To his surprise, most of the cavity was empty, void of any bone, muscle, or sinew. It was like a gourd that had been hollowed out.

Finally, however, his blade struck something, a dense lump that gave off a tinny ring when he tapped against it—like metal or stone.

"There are tongs just there," Bel said, pointing to the foot of another table.

With a nod, Geoffrey hurried to retrieve them and handed them to the prince. "What is it?" he asked.

"I'm not quite sure," Bel said, "but I doubt it's anything…natural." With a deep breath, he reached into the cavity with the tongs and carefully drew forth a hard, obsidian lump.

"What in the world is that?" Geoffrey asked. "Some manner of bezoar?"

Bel chewed his lip in thought, turning the odd mass over and over to examine it in the lamplight.

"It's a heart," he finally said.

"A heart?" Geoffrey repeated. "It looks more like a lump of coal than a heart. Are you sure?"

Bel gave a slow, thoughtful nod. "Burnt, blackened, and shriveled," he said, "but yes. I believe it was once the man's heart."

Geoffrey's jaw tensed and his brow furrowed in thought. "We should check the others."

"Agreed."

Sure enough, they found the same open wound and blackened mass in each of the other bodies as well. A sickly feeling took hold of Bel's innards.

"I'm willing to wager it was the same with the horses," Geoffrey observed.

"Me too," Bel said. He released a heavy sigh. "It appears we face a new enemy, my friend. One that is truly heartless."

"A new enemy," Geoffrey said, "or perhaps a very old one."

Bel sighed. "If only Thom were here. He seemed to know something of all of this. We're not as well-versed in the stories of the Kinship or the lives of the ancient saints here in Montevale."

Geoffrey gave a nod. "I know the stories of the faithful," he said, "but I'm no scholar."

"I'm certain that you know much more than I do," Bel told him. "So what can you tell me?"

Geoffrey paused, collecting his thoughts. "I know the old stories and the legends," he said. "Of St. Aiden, the Warlock, and the founding of the Order, but everybody knows those."

Bel bowed his head. "Assume that I know nothing of these things," he said, "or at least, assume I know little more than a child when it comes to the Kin."

"Alright, then," Geoffrey began. "Well, the way I learned it, back when the continent was united beneath the banner of the Calendral emperor, folk lived under the shadow of fear and slavery. Kalius Wrogan, the Grand Hierophant at the time, led a rebellion against the tyrant as punishment for his lack of devotion to the Church of the Kin. In the name of Dibhor, the Dark Brother, he raised an army of the dead and overthrew the emperor to set himself up as the new lord."

"So the Warlock saved the people from the tyranny of the emperor only to replace it with a tyranny of his own?" Bel asked.

"Aye. So they say. It was he that St. Aiden and the Guardians fought against." Sir Geoffrey shrugged. "Of course, like I said, I'm no scholar so I can't say much more than that. However, I'd say we've proven the whole army of the dead business is much more than just a story..."

"Aye, seems like," Bel said with a grim smile. He sighed. "I'll have men search for any books or scrolls related to the history of the Order and the Guardians." He held up the blackened stone that was once the Wrathorn warrior's heart. "But in the meantime, we should find that Keeper. If what Thom said about this dead army is true, he could be the harbinger of a much larger invasion, to say nothing of what other mischief such a man might make."

Geoffrey nodded. "Leave that to me," he said. "You've a whole bloody army to command and lands to secure here and in Whitemane. If you can't protect the farmers as they finish the harvest, the entire realm will starve."

Bel's brow narrowed. "I suppose that's true," he conceded, "but you've already done more than enough for Montevale as it is. Your duty is fulfilled, my friend."

"I am the Vanguard. My duty is to *all* good folk of the continent, regardless of land or realm." Geoffrey said with a shrug. "Consider my men at your disposal. I'll have an easier time tracking him by myself anyway."

Beledain's brow narrowed in thought. His impulse was to see to the Keeper personally; however, he knew that Sir Geoffrey was right. As the lord-general of Marina's armies and as the bearer of the title of the Tower, his own duty was to lead. As he understood it, the Vanguard was a warrior, a hunter. A man perfectly suited for such a quest.

"Very well," he said at last, "but title or no, I don't like the idea of sending you entirely alone, especially since we have yet to hear any word from the Shackle." He paused, ignoring the sudden flood of concern. "Let me at least find you some guides—men native to the area—and see you fitted with a horse."

"I prefer my own two feet," Geoffrey said, "but this is a wide country. I suppose it's best to ride."

CHAPTER 23: METAPHYSICAL ALCHEMY

This past week has been marked by great celebration, for at long last, and after so many years of sorrow, Valder finally has an heir. His name is Kredor. When he inherits the throne, he'll be the second of his name, the first having led the continent against the great invasion from Tulondis centuries ago.

Valder is thrilled. In fact, I might even go so far as to describe him as joyful. Gone is the dreadful melancholy that so often plagues him. He smiles. He laughs. He feasts. The queen too seems tolerably pleasant and there is a fondness between them that I have never before observed.

By the Lady's Grace, I hope it lasts.

Yet the birth of the prince was not the only exciting arrival to grace Titanis recently, but one of two, for this week was also marked by the sudden appearance and subsequent disappearance of one of the most auspicious figures of the Order's history: the Bard.

It was the day after the young prince's birth. As the sun was beginning to set, I was seated upon the stone bench outside of the tower smoking my pipe and enjoying the pleasantness of the warm summer air. I could hear faintly the sounds of rejoicing among those of my own sect as well as the more raucous members of the Warlord's men. Surely everyone felt the invigorating hope, the optimistic relief, that accompanied the birth of the new heir.

However, as I sat there, I was gripped suddenly by the strangest sensation. It was, in part, very familiar—the selfsame feeling that often accompanies the presence of another Guardian with whom one's title has, throughout the ages, been familiar. Yet this was…stranger, stronger. It was so strong in fact that I could not help but feel concerned.

I turned to look at the source only to see an unusual figure illuminated by the waning light. It was a man, lean and gaunt as an old wolf with long, white-blond hair that hung straight down past his shoulders. We carried with him no arms apart from a small dagger and he wore only a tunic and simple hose with no armor. Despite the pallid shade of his hair, he was not old, nor would I call him young, but perhaps near enough to my own age, give or take. At first, part of me wondered if he was a lost servant or laborer until he drew nearer and I discerned two very curious qualities. First, it was clear from the milky white shade of his eyes, that he was completely and utterly blind, and second, across his shoulders, slung upon a leather strap, was a beautifully crafted lute.

"Loremaster," he greeted me in a voice like the rippling song of a stream. "It has been a long time."

Without hesitation, he stepped closer and sat down upon the bench at my side. So certain and sure were his movements that—at first—I questioned whether he was truly blind.

"Do you know me?" I asked, uncertain of what else to say.

"I know the part of you that is more than you," he said.

"Forgive me then for asking. Who are you?"

"My name is Sigmund," he said, "the Bard."

While I did not in any way doubt the truth of his words, you can imagine my astonishment. For few enough had heard of the Bard since the departure of Amarthia centuries earlier. In fact, between the Hierophant and the Chancellor, a concerted effort had been made to relegate the figure solely to the realm of legend, casting doubt upon whether such a figure even existed.

Yet here he was. In the flesh.

"An auspicious occasion," the Bard observed. "He will be a child of great significance. One of several."

I knew from The Book of Histories that the Bard was long known to possess the gift of foresight so I was unsure whether this comment was made in passing as part of genial conversation, or if it carried greater weight. "I assume the birth of any royal heir caries a certain degree of importance," I replied.

"And this one more than most."

"You know this?"

"I know nothing," he said, "but I hear things."

I will admit that as an empiricist, such vague comments were quite frustrating and I found myself suddenly skeptical of this strange and mysterious figure. *"I see," I said at last, "and what is it that you hear?"*

The man turned toward me, fixed me with his unseeing eyes.

"Prophesy," he said, "and heresy."

When all the lands of Calendral are bound by Callah's Key,
The Bard shall sing a doleful dirge for Wisdom's unheard plea,
For the Testament unto the Light will seek to snuff the Flame,
When the slumbering Beast of Dibhor wakes, who shall bear the blame?
The Armies of the Dead shall march whilst all the Children weep,
And the Scions of the Brother Dark shall rise from their long sleep,
If the last of Aiden's Blood is spilled to profane the Lady's Grace,
Will any man be left alive to rise up in his place?
So heed the words of Wisdom and mark well the strains of Song,
The Pariah whose heart remains still pure will be welcome erelong,
For all that Guard must take up arms to hold the night at bay,
Else who will rise to bring the Dawn and drive the Dark away?

When he finished, I sat quietly for a long time, so moved was I by the song. Myriad emotions gripped me and I found myself arrested by such overwhelming feeling. *"I know this song," I finally managed to speak.*

"It is Amarthia's Lament," he said. "The Bard's Heresy, and with the birth of this child, the song begun so long ago shall soon strum its final refrain. For as we speak, the scions of the Dark Brother begin to make their play, spreading like an affliction from their coastal spire."

"Dark Brother?" I repeated. "You mean Dibhor?"

He nodded. "They walk among us beneath the light of a false flame," he said, "professing a knowledge intended not to illuminate, but to corrupt."

"A false flame?" Then it hit me. "The Keepers? The Keepers of the Lighthouse in Castone?"

"As you say."

"Then they must be dealt with at once."

"By whom?" he asked. "Their influence has grown in certain circles while ours has dwindled. Even among our own, the titles have lost their potency and the Anointed have forgotten the Old Ways."

"Then what hope have we?" I asked.

"Look to the pure pariahs."

"Pure pariahs?"

"The Vanguard, the Marshal, the Blade," he said, "and others yet like them."

"Those men are outlaws," I said, masking the truth I already knew. "They are villains and their lives are forfeit."

"Yet still they guard," he said. "From the coastal plains of Grantis to the fields of Montevale, the mountain peaks of Dwerin to the forests of Wrathorn far in the north, from the islands of the Sorgund Isles to the highlands of the Brock...."

I fell silent, for I knew well the secret of the Galadins, of their perennial harboring of the Blackguards known as the Three. Arcis Galadin and I have been friends since long before my anointing, and while it has never been explicitly stated, the fact that his seneschal, Sir Wolfram of Parth, bears the title of the Marshal is, of course, known to me.

"Dark days appear on the horizon," he said, "and we must be ever vigilant if we hope to bring them to light.

"This is quite a lot to take in," I finally said. "You have given me a great deal to think on."

"And think on it you must." He stood up from the bench. "For when the time is nigh, Loremaster, it must be you who is the first to sound the call to arms."

With that, he turned and departed, leaving me with my thoughts and my uncertainty. Even now I have little idea what he was talking about, but his words have haunted me ever since...

"Bollocks and shite!" Royne shouted.

In the small iron cauldron nestled in the brazier before him, a viscous green liquid began to bubble and hiss like a thousand snakes.

"Fuck-shit-cock-bollocks-nut-puddle!"

He tried to douse the flaming brazier with a cup of water, but while doing so appeared to put out the flame, it set the odd decoction fizzing and now it

263

spat out green globules in random directions. Whatever they touched instantly began to sizzle.

"Cock-roll-nugget-bastard-doodle-fuck!" He prattled on in a panic. "Bollocks and shite! Bollocks and shite! Bollocks and shite!"

His eyes continued to dart back and forth in madness, so uncertain was he as to what to do, when without pause, Amara strode in unhurried from behind him and placed the steel lid atop the cauldron. Moments later the snapping and sizzling ceased and the hissing became little more than a soft whisper.

Royne's brow narrowed and he gazed shamefacedly at the floor. "Thank you," he muttered.

Amara raised an eyebrow at him. "Apologies, Polecat, but I could not hear you."

He forced himself to take a deep breath. "I said thank you," he said again.

Amara's lips twisted into a wry grin. "No, Polecat," she said, "it is I who must thank you."

Royne pursed his lips. "Should I ask why?"

The girl could no longer keep her grin contained. "I knew that you fancied yourself a scholar," she said, "but I had no idea that you were also a poet."

"Hilarious," Royne said. He forced a frown and folded his arms across his chest. He was annoyed that the failed experiment interrupted his reading ,and he was annoyed that the experiment failed. He was embarrassed that he panicked, and even more embarrassed that Amara had not. Worst of all, he was furious that she should have the audacity to laugh at him, and even more furious at the strange and unwelcome feeling that the sight of her smile had begun to conjure in the center of his chest.

"How is it that you always seem to show up just in time to witness my mistakes?" he asked. "Do you lie in wait just to jump out and mock me?"

Her willowy body straightened and she folded her arms across her chest. "You asked me to help tutor you," she said. "So yes. I do."

"Perfection," he said. "Sometimes I wonder if I truly *have* lost my mind."

"Oh for certain," she said, "but regardless, you know as well as I do that failure is often the greatest teacher." She grinned at him once more and he suppressed the unusual sensation that spread through him as he watched the corners of her lips curl upward.

"Perhaps I do lie in wait," she said, "so that when you fall flat on your face, I can be there to help you back to your feet."

She fixed him with her gaze and while his impulse was to meet it, he forced himself to look away.

"So what went wrong this time?" she finally asked. "What can we learn from this mistake?"

"I was..." he sighed. He glanced at the ground and his eyes fell upon the smooth spindles of her legs. They lingered for but a moment before he ground his teeth and, again, looked away. "I was reading," he said sullenly. "I learned something very important and it distracted me. It won't happen again."

Amara shrugged and paced over to his side. "It will." She shrugged. "It is the scholar's lot. It happens to me all the time."

"It does?"

Her eyes flashed. "Have you ever wondered how it is that I can so easily discern the cause of your mistakes?"

Royne chewed his lip. "You have made them before," he said at last.

"Not *all* of them," she said, "But many of them—and others besides."

Royne nodded silently and began to clean up his most recent mistake. Amara joined him.

"So what is this book?" she asked. "It is the same one you carry with you at all times. I imagine it is very interesting to be so distracting. Either that, or it is very personal." She offered him another smirk. "A diary perhaps?"

"No, it's..." He paused and his brow creased. "You know, now that you mention it, I suppose it is a diary of a sort."

"Then I won't ask you to read it," she said. "It would be far too embarrassing to hear all of the poetic odes that I surely inspire in you. The testaments to my brilliance. The ballads to my beauty." She raised an arm in the dramatic gesticulation of a poet—only to press her arm against the side of the hot brazier. At once, the skin sizzled and she cried out in pain.

Royne hurried over to her side. "How about the arias to your arrogance and the songs to your stupidity?" he said, though not unkindly.

"Perhaps," she said through gritted teeth. An angry red line stood out upon the flesh. Already it was beginning to blister.

"I was joking," Royne said without looking at her. "You are clearly not stupid, which is why it was amusing. In any case, here. Give me your arm."

"It's fine," she said. "I will put some balm on it and it will heal."

"Don't be ridiculous," Royne told her. "Give me your arm. Believe it or not, I actually have some…skill with such things."

"Do you now?" she said skeptically.

"Trust me."

Perhaps it was something the tone with which he said it, but regardless, with a sigh, she offered him her arm. Not without a certain degree of tentativeness, he took it, turning it over and inspecting the wound. True enough, it wasn't terrible, but it was probably much more painful than she let on and would surely leave a scar.

"Close your eyes," he said at last.

"What are you on about, Polecat?"

"Please," he said.

With a skeptical sigh, she chewed her lip, and closed her eyes.

Now, he thought, *how in the name of the bloody Brethren did I do this again?* He checked to see that her eyes were closed only to find himself suddenly arrested with emotion, a feeling he knew of in vague terms, but for the most part, he had seen fit to push away. He found himself staring, infatuated, at the lines and curves of her face—her cheekbones, her furrowed brow, her lips. Her hair fanned out behind her and he suddenly discerned the scent of vanilla or perhaps citrus.

And then, out of nowhere, he felt a balmy coolness in the tips of his fingers and as he pressed them to her wounded arm, he felt an energy pass between the point of contact of their flesh. At first, it was pleasant, soothing, and he sensed her body unconsciously relax. Before his very eyes, he watched as the burn and blisters began to change, decreasing steadily in size and severity until moments later, they were gone—completely healed.

Only then did his own pain begin.

No sooner had the mark of the wound disappeared upon Amara's arm than his own began to seethe and burn. He ground his teeth so as to not cry out, though the intense pain was like nothing he had ever experienced before. Even when he healed General Navarro's infection, the fact that he had lost consciousness seemed to spare him the full shock of the transfer.

When at last, it was over and the intensity of the pain had settled into a dull ache, he cleared his throat to steady his voice. "Open your eyes."

Amara did as he said, opening one eye first and then the other. "What have you done, Polecat?" She glanced at her arm and gasped. "By the elements! It's gone!"

Royne remained silent. He crossed his arms behind the small of his back. "It is," he said.

Amara shook her head in shock and rubbed at the unmarred skin. "This was metaphysical alchemy!" she said. "You performed true metaphysical alchemy!"

"Call it what you like," Royne said, "as long as you do not call it 'magic.'"

"But wait…"

"What?"

Amara's gaze narrowed. "For balance to be maintained, the energy that created the burn must be redirected or reapplied somewhere else." She fixed him with a stare. "Show me your arm."

"What?"

"Show me your arm," she demanded.

"I don't know what you are talking about—hey!"

Without warning she reached out and grabbed at him. He had not expected her to be so strong. Before he even had time to react, she had turned over his arm and only to reveal the luminous, angry burn. Once again, her eyes grew wide with shock.

Royne pulled away and went back to straightening up the mess. "Look, I'm a fast healer," he told her. "Better me than you. It'll be gone by tomorrow or the next day at the latest."

Amara remained silent. It was clear from her expression that she was thinking, trying to wrap her head around it like she would an alchemical conundrum. "Fascinating," she said at last.

Royne hemmed and hawed. "I suppose."

"If you can do this, then…" she paused. "Perhaps there are other ways you might use this skill."

"What do you mean?" he asked, torn between interest and an uncharacteristic sense of meekness. "Like draw fire from the ether or soften solid stone?" His lips twisted into a sardonic grin. "Maybe I can freeze the rain or call down the thunder?

"Unlikely," she said. "It's hard enough to manifest one pair of diametrically opposed elemental affinities, let alone one such as yours."

"One such as mine?"

"Harmony," she said, "and Discord."

"What do you mean?" he asked. "I don't understand. Speak sense!"

"Earth, fire, air, water," she said, "the Sign of Four."

"Yes," Royne said. "The four elements."

"Yes," Amara said, "but remember, when in perfect balance, they create Harmony, and when unbalanced, they create perfect Discord." She paused, "Or to put it a different way, Harmony is elemental force of Life, whereas Discord is the force of Death. Your affinity lies between those two incredibly powerful forces."

"See," Royne smirked to mask his sudden uncertainty. "I told you I was incredible."

"You didn't," she said, "and for the record, I did not say so either."

Before they could discuss the matter any further, however, there was the sudden sound of hurried footsteps in the hallway outside of the room. Moments later, Haruki, the young man from across the sea, appeared in the doorway, his face stricken with concern.

"Something is happening," he said quickly. "The soldiers have assembled at the gates again, but this time it is different."

"What do you mean different?" Amara asked.

Haruki's face fell. "They have brought someone with them."

"Who?"

Haruki breathed a sigh. "Fabius."

Royne thought back to the bet he had observed between Amara and the other young alchemist so long ago. "What is Fabius doing with the soldiers?" he asked.

"I do not know," Haruki said, "but the masters have directed all of us to assemble in the courtyard outside."

Royne exchanged a look with Amara. All talk of the elements, alchemy, and magical ability was instantly forgotten. "Ready yourselves for blood," he said. "This is not going to end well."

CHAPTER 24: THE SIEGE OF STONEBRIDGE

"Again!" General Navarro shouted. As one, the legionnaires dug their heels into the stony ground and charged. The ram hammered against the ironbound doors of the castle with a resounding crash. Upon the walls, red-cloaked crossbowmen attempted to pick off the men manning the battering ram, but the archers of the Brock provided little chance for the defenders to line up a clean shot.

"Well done, Alban," Lughus said to the yeoman beside him after another kingsman collapsed upon the battlement, felled by a goose-feathered arrow.

"Thank you, my lord," the man replied. He was a rustic from one of the villages of Sir Deryk's fief and an expert hand with the war bow to be true. Already he had distinguished at St. Golan's and now Lughus made a mental note to set aside some manner of additional reward. Perhaps a horse or a dairy cow. Something beyond coin that the man and his family could actually use.

As Alban lined up another shot, Lughus watched, idly scratching Fergus behind the ears, while the men of the Fifth readied themselves for another charge.

"I'd say we've certainly got their attention," General Navarro observed, trotting up on his white steed.

"I'm sorry to use your men as decoys," Lughus told him. "I dislike playing games with men's lives."

The general waved it away with his hand. "My men are professional soldiers. They understand the ways of war," he said. "Besides, they've taken it as a challenge to see if they can breech the gates before the Lady Blade succeeds at securing the alternate route inside." He smiled. "Call it a wager."

"Well then, I'll bet a hogshead of the Ram's Reward on that," Lughus smirked.

"I've three bottles of Wolf's Blood that I can set against that," Navarro mused.

"Excellent," Lughus said, drawing Sentinel. "I'll collect them after the battle, so long as you agree to share a glass with me."

Navarro's eyebrows arched. "You're that confident in your fair lady, Marshal?"

"Always!" Lughus smirked. "But in this case, I also trust my eyes." He motioned toward the battlement where a new battle was suddenly raging. There, above the gate, Brigid whirled and slashed against the defending kingsmen, supported by Baron Roland and a contingent of men-at-arms bearing the silver eagle of Marthaine.

"Well, well," the Gray Wolf observed with a grin. "A shame the mountain paths were too treacherous for the elephants, else it might have been more of a challenge."

"Fair enough," Lughus said. "For now, though, we should make ready to join them."

"Agreed."

Lughus watched the battle with interest, and at his side, Fergus's hackles stood on end. While he did indeed have full faith in Brigid and her abilities, he could not numb himself completely to the deadly realities of combat, and he wished that he had been able to accompany her as she infiltrated the fortress. Nevertheless, his role as baron and as commander of the Galadin forces required that he maintain an overt presence, leading his men from the front. As Brigid reminded him, after nearly a month-long siege, it would do no good for the morale of the men to were their commander suddenly to disappear. They needed him there, visible, as a reminder that their service was appreciated and that when battle was finally met, he would be with them fighting shoulder to shoulder.

Of course, knowing this did not make it any easier to stand idly while he watched from a distance as she fought on. He chewed his lip anxiously, his hand tight around Sentinel's pommel. He longed to charge in and join her, but until the gates opened, such a thing would be impossible.

Thankfully, he did not have to wait long. As the legionaries once more drew back the ram and prepared another charge, the heavy doors began to open, and, just beyond them, the iron portcullis stiffly rose.

"It seems that you are victorious, my friend," General Navarro grinned, "but let's hope now that your victories extend beyond our little wager."

"What is the old adage?" Lughus asked. "Even the finest wine tastes sour in defeat?"

"As we say in Grantis," the Gray Wolf grinned. He nodded to his valet who in turn passed on word to the remaining legionaries to ready themselves to charge. Lughus turned to Sir Deryk and Sergeant Pike and did the same.

Fergus gave an impatient bark and Lughus nodded in agreement. "Steady, brother," he said. He turned to address his men. "Lady Blade thinks the Guardians have kept us out in the cold long enough," he shouted, "so she found us a way inside! What say we join her?"

A hearty cheer rang out among the men followed by cries of "Release the Hounds!" and "For the Brock!" Down the line of battle, Lughus could see Guy preparing to lead the Marthaine reserve forces into the fray. His cousin had been very quiet since openly challenging Roland during the banquet on the Feast of the Father, but while the aftermath of the incident may have humbled him into silence, Lughus suspected that Guy's renewed obedience was merely ostensible.

The legionnaires manning the battering ram dropped their heavy burden and at a shout from Captain Velius, readied their shields and short swords. Lughus, with Fergus at his heel, reached the Grantisi soldiers just as they began to flood through the gates into the courtyard. Without even needing to be issued a command, the legionaries packed together in a tight shield wall to defend the flanks of the onrushing attackers while Lughus, Pike, and the other Galadin men-at-arms funneled in between them.

Already in disarray due to the surprise attack, the kingsmen fought like cornered beasts, desperately hacking and slashing and the oncoming assault.

Lughus met a red-cloaked sergeant head on, knocking aside the man's furious blow before cutting him down with a swift counter. Fergus caught the next man's boot in his jaws and with a powerful jerk, ripped his feet out from under him. Lughus wasted no time, whirling his blade around and with a single downward thrust, sent the man to the grave.

By now, the fighting was thick and furious with the carnage of the melee closing in on all sides. Lughus focused his mind and his breathing, centering himself as a beacon of calm in the madness of battle. The kingsmen fought with increasing desperation before the gates, shoulder to shoulder, pressed in so tightly that there was barely enough space to swing a sword. At last, the rising tide of invaders proved too much for the Andochan defenders and they began to withdraw to the interior of the small keep, bracing the doors behind them.

Baron Roland, outfitted in his steel plate, met Lughus at the base of the stairs that led down from the battlement.

"I'd say that went off about as well as we could expect," he said. "There can't be more than a score or so left in the keep, but hopefully they'll see the wisdom in surrendering. I'd like to be safely back home before the snows."

Lughus gave a nod. "Did you meet any Anointed?"

"Not that I could tell, though you'll have to ask Brigid to be certain." He paused. "How's the new armor?"

"Like a second skin." Lughus said.

Roland gave a dour smile and patted his grandson on the pauldron. "Good."

The shrill note of a whistle called their attention back to the gates. Lughus watched as General Navarro began shouting orders and motioning with his arm at Captain Velius and the other legionnaires of his elite guard. At once, they hurried back to the forgotten ram and hoisted it anew to resume the attack on the keep.

"You have to admire their dedication," Baron Roland said, "though it's hard to imagine how an entire social class of soldiery occupies themselves in a time of peace." He glanced over his shoulder at a sudden movement among the crowd of men. "Ah," he said, "Here she is."

Brigid hurried up to them, the hood of her cloak drawn up over her head. Lughus held out a hand to her, and as he drew her near enough to quickly kiss her, she stayed him from getting any closer with a touch of her hand.

"You don't want to get any closer," he said. "I smell absolutely horrid."

Lughus's eyebrows arched momentarily in disbelief. It took a moment before the rank odor reached him. "Perindal's bloody sword," he coughed. "What happened?"

Brigid suppressed a grin. "I was able to slip in through the grating where they sweep out the stables," she said. "It's how I was able to slip in and unlock the postern."

Roland laughed. "Thatta girl," he said, "I'll bet they never saw it coming." He rested the haft of his mace upon his shoulder. "I'll go check in with the general and we can determine a plan for once the doors are open."

"I'll be along in a moment," Lughus said. He turned back to Brigid. "I won three bottles of wine from Navarro betting that you could beat the ram."

"Oh, so you were betting on me?" Brigid smirked.

Lughus grinned. "Always."

She smiled up at him from beneath her cowl, blue eyes shining like stars, and Lughus felt his heart flood with warmth.

"Did you meet any of the Anointed?" he asked.

Brigid shook her head. "No, but I have a feeling there are still some here."

"We never did catch up with the Jay after St. Golan's and Cragbarrow," Lughus said. "I suppose he could have remained here rather than return alone in disgrace."

Brigid nodded. "I suppose so, but I can't shake this sense of something...more. Something...sinister."

Lughus felt it too. A familiar anger. A familiar fear. Could it be the Hammer? By all accounts, Harlow had been recalled to Titanis after being driven out of Highboard. If that were true, could it be some other old enemy of the Three? He gazed at the keep, boring into it as if attempting to see right through the solid stone.

Beside him, Brigid wrinkled her nose. "Ugh, I stink," she said. "Granted, it's not as bad as when I fought the Lash by the Shitbrook, but still."

Lughus stirred from his own contemplation and offered her a half-smile. "It's not nearly as bad as you think," he said.

She pulled a face. "Doesn't change the fact that I need a bath," she said. "Maybe you can help me with that. Once we take the keep."

Lughus smiled and offered her another quick kiss. "Hang on. I'll knock those bloody doors down myself. Won't be but a minute."

Her lips spread into a wide smile. "Hurry," she called after him as he marched off to join the general and his grandfather.

"Are we all ready there?" Lughus asked the older men.

At the head of the ram, Captain Velius gave a sardonic smirk. "There's space in the line if you'd care to lend us a hand, baron," he said.

Roland and Navarro exchanged a look of amusement, but remained silent.

Lughus gave a shrug. "I don't see why not," he said.

"Well, well," the brash captain said with a smile. He nodded to a space along the side opposite where he stood.

As Lughus assumed his station, Pike and Tonkin hurried up to join him. "We're with you, my lord," the sergeant said.

Lughus nodded his thanks, and following the captain's lead, braced himself as together the men draw back the heavy ram.

"Alright, you whoresons," Velius shouted. "Let's break down this fucking door!"

The men loosed the ram and with a resounding thud it struck the doors like the hammer of some mythical titan. Fergus began to bark with anticipation, loping back and forth in circles around where Baron Marthaine and General Navarro stood at the head of the mass of men. Brigid joined them, calling out rallying cries and words of encouragement with the others.

Luckily, they did not need to wait long, for the doors of the castle's keep were not nearly as sturdy as those of the main gate. Before an hour had passed, the wood began to splinter under the blows of the ram's iron head.

In the center of the mass of soldiers, General Navarro's legionnaires formed a tight shield wall. Beside them, Lughus and Roland assembled the men of Galadin and Marthaine respectively, ready to storm the breach and subdue whatever defenders lie in wait within.

At last, with a resounding crack, the gates gave way. A volley of arrows and crossbow bolts sailed through the air, striking a few of the men at the ram who were too slow to seek cover behind their shields.

"For the Brock!" Roland Marthaine shouted.

Scattered cries of "Release the Hounds!" echoed through the yard accompanied by the wolf pack's lupine howls.

Together the warriors rushed the broken doors, pressing them back and flooding into the hall of the keep. Red-cloaked kingsmen rushed to meet them. Lughus drove his shoulder into one man then whirled his blade around from the Guard of the Dragon to open a second man's chest. With a sickening gush, he freed Sentinel's blade just in time to parry the first man's vengeful thrust and counter with a stroke of his own.

One after another after another, the kingsmen fought and fell, until finally, at last, they began to scatter and flee like rabbits from the wanton melee of the hall. Overcome by the madness of battle, the attackers loosed themselves upon their foes. Their frustrations at the prolonged siege quickly devolved into wanton slaughter.

As Lughus watched the man before him turn tail and flee, a golden flash from behind him brought the man down to his knees. It was Fergus, his maw red and glistening, ready to add another tally to the butcher's bill. Before he could sink his teeth into the soft flesh of the fallen kingsmen's throat, however, Lughus called him to heel, and with preternatural discipline, the great hound obeyed.

"Do you yield?" Lughus shouted as Fergus snapped and snarled at his side. "Tell me! Do you yield?"

"Yield? Yield! Blood and Fire! Yes, I yield! I yield!" the man replied. At once, Pike and Tonkin disarmed the man, and saw him taken into custody.

With victory all but assured, Lughus came to his senses. The red-cloaks were beaten. There was no need for slaughter and senseless executions. He clambered up onto one of the hall's tables and shouted across the roaring din.

"Show mercy!" he cried. "Any who lay down arms are to be taken prisoner and shown mercy!"

Whether anyone heard him was as uncertain as whether they would pay him any mind. From across the hall, Baron Roland offered him a forlorn grimace.

At last something inside of Lughus snapped. He understood the desire for vengeance. He understood the lust for battle. However, to give in to it, to allow oneself to be swept up in the violence of the moment, wantonly murdering the vanquished, was to become the very thing that he fought against.

"Stop!" he shouted in a voice both clear and cold. "Everyone, *stop!*"

At once the men of Galadin—from man-at-arms to yeoman archer—halted and stood at attention. Yet, to Lughus's surprise, so too did the men of Marthaine and the soldiers of the Fifth Legion.

"We have already *won!*" he declared. "The castle is ours and the battle is over. I know that it has been a long month—encamped in the hard stone of the mountain, living in tents, and sleeping on the stony ground—while all the while the wind grows colder and winter draws ever nearer. But it is *done!* We have won! I will *not* have this victory tarnished by the butchering of the vanquished or the mistreating of whatever servants cower within. This is not a sacking! This is a victory!" His eyes flashed in the dim light of the hall's dying hearth. "And so I say to you all—any enemy lays down arms, who begs mercy, is *not* to be harmed. Is that clear?"

A low chorus of affirmation sounded from the weary soldiers. At the far side of the hall, General Navarro had joined Baron Roland. The two older men stood watching with interest.

Lughus felt his temper flair. "I said, *is that clear?*"

"Aye!"

This time, the reply echoed throughout the chamber.

"Then secure the castle, and well done."

As the men dispersed to continue scouring the keep, Lughus stepped down and found Brigid. Roland, Navarro, and Captain Velius soon joined them.

"Well, well, Baron Galadin," said the brash captain, "I knew you had quite the viscous bite, but who'd have thought you could bark so loud?"

Brigid smiled. "Ignore him," she told Lughus. "Well-spoken."

Lughus gave a grim half-smile. "There *is* something wrong here," he said quietly.

"I know," Brigid said. "I'm still feel it as well."

As if on cue, a man wearing the arms of Sir Deryk appeared and bowed his head. "Baron Lughus," he said. "My lord, Sir Deryk sent me to summon you. We've found defenders holed up in the cellar. There are not many of them, but they appear to be what remains of the Guardian officers."

Baron Roland chewed his lip. "Go," he told his grandson. "I'll see to things here." He turned to the Gray Wolf. "General Navarro, perhaps you and your men might secure the gates and the grounds."

"Certainly, Baron Marthaine," the general said. He nodded silently to Velius and at once the captain began piping his whistle and shouting at his men.

Roland offered Lughus a meaningful look. "Be careful," he said. "We all know the dangers of a cornered beast."

Lughus nodded and motioned for Sir Deryk's man to lead the way, Brigid, Fergus, Pike, and Tonkin followed with him. For the most part, the fighting had ceased. Men tended to the wounded or ushered the odd prisoner back toward the hall. At the entrance to the cellars, an assortment of soldiers—Galadin, Marthaine, and Legion—stood vigilant. In the dim light of the wall sconces, the men's faces had resumed the impassive seriousness of battlefield resolve. A man in the brown habit of a cousin tended to the wounded while Sir Deryk of Lomedan looked on. As soon as he spied Lughus and the others approach, however, the knight stepped forward to report.

"I doubt there's more than a dozen down there, my lord," Sir Deryk said, "but they refuse to surrender and we've been unable force our way through. With the narrow space between barrels and the low ceiling, they seem to have the advantage."

Lughus sighed. "And there's no other way in?"

"Not that we've found."

Brigid chewed her lip. "It's a solidly defensive position," she mused. "Any attempt to storm them is going to lose men and with the single entry point, I doubt I'll be able to slip down without being seen."

"There's an arbalester as well, my lady," Sir Deryk said. He motioned toward a damaged heater shield. "Blasted thing nearly pierced right through."

Brigid shrugged. "I suppose we could smoke them out?"

Lughus nodded. "I'll offer them one last chance to surrender," he said, "and if they insist on a fight, we'll do as Brigid says and cut them down as they flee."

"Aye, my lord," Sir Deryk said. "I'll have men ready materials to burn."

Lughus approached the small stone staircase and peered into the dimly lit space beyond. While it was difficult to discern much, he could vaguely make out the placement of numerous barrels, crates, and other goods. "Men of Andoch!" he called into the gloom, overly conscious of the arbalest. "Can you hear me?"

He strained his ears and could only just make out the sibilant sounds of voices speaking heatedly in hushed conversation. At last, a voice replied.

"We hear you. Who calls?"

Lughus's brow furrowed. At his side, Brigid silently slipped her daggers from their sheaths.

"My name is Lughus, Baron of Galadin, and one of three high commanders of this army of the Brock." The disquieting sensation returned to him in full intensity, straining his muscles like a bow at full draw. "I am here to offer you one last chance to surrender, to lay down your arms and be treated with the dignity and respect afforded to fellow knights and warriors. What say you?"

At once the hushed voices resumed their chatter, growing in intensity and volume. He exchanged a glance with Brigid. It was clear that there was some disagreement between the vanquished defenders.

Finally, one voice rose above the others and called out to him.

"We shall accept your mercy, Baron Galadin, so long as you offer us your word that none of us are to be harmed."

"You have it," Lughus said, "But I would have you surrender the crossbow to us first."

In answer, a man in a chainmail byrnie and sallet paced out with the large crossbow held high over his head. As he stepped forth, Sir Deryk, Pike, and Tonkins rushed to confiscate the weapon and take the marksman prisoner.

Behind the arbalester, other men issued forth, their hands raised in appeasement. Like the arbalester, they wore chainmail and red-cloaks, though upon their tabards they did not wear the Guardian's key, but the crest of an Andochan noble house—three yellow caltrops upon a field of white."

"Lord Mongrath, I presume," Lughus said to the man who followed behind them. He was clad in plate armor, but his tabard bore the same mark of the yellow caltrops.

"Baron Galadin," the man said stiffly and with as much dignity as he could muster. "I expect that you understand the privilege of ransom afforded to members of the nobility."

"I do," Lughus said, "though I'll refrain from asking if you would extend such privileges to myself or to Lady Brigid should the tables be turned."

Two other men clad in heavier armor approached bearing the same arms and Lughus wondered if they were perhaps Mongrath's sons.

"I would prefer not to dwell on hypotheticals," the Mongrath said. "Let us instead focus on the situation as it is now."

"Agreed," Lughus said.

He ushered the lord and his sons onward followed by two other men bearing the arms of lesser houses, when a sudden tremor of rage came upon him. Before he knew it, Sentinel was in his hand, and a feeling of unbridled fury set his blood ablaze. Beside him, Brigid's slight shadow tensed to spring and Fergus snarled and snapped in barely subdued fury.

"Harlow."

"Well, Marshal," Willum Harlow said, sauntering forward to meet him. "I would lay down my arms, but your predecessor already saw to that."

Lughus's eyes flashed. "I should kill you right now."

Harlow laughed. "Do it," he said, "and prove yourself to be the cold-blooded villain I've always known you to be."

"Is it villainy to slay a monster?" Brigid seethed.

"Is it murder to slay a murderess?" said another voice.

Lughus ground his teeth. "Alan Beinn."

"You remember me," Alan leered. "Good dog."

Lughus grabbed Alan by the throat and threw him back against the wall. The Young Sheriff squealed with pain as his head struck the masonry, though he tried to pass it off as laughter.

"I told you what would happen if we met again," Lughus said.

Harlow made to join the fray, but Brigid checked him with her flashing blades. Fergus growled menacingly and the soldiers not tasked with guarding the other prisoners quickly gathered to support their baron.

"Just like a bloody Blackguard," the Hammers sneered.

Lughus tightened his grip on Alan's throat while the young sheriff continued to kick and squirm. Brigid's eyes shone with cold light, never leaving Harlow for fear that he would attempt to make a move.

"I should end you," Lughus said to Alan. "For the betterment of the world, you should be put down."

He readied himself to follow through with his threat when a smarmy drawl from behind him stayed his hand.

"So for all your self-righteous calls for mercy, it seems the great baron of Galadin is little more than a hypocrite."

Lughus quickly glanced over his shoulder to see Guy Marthaine saunter forward accompanied by a squad of his men.

"Perhaps that should be the motto of the Golden Hound," Guy continued, "Do as I say, not as I do."

Sergeant Pike audibly ground his teeth while Sir Deryk and his men put hand to hilt, ready to defend their lord. Only the legionaries remained unmoved, watching with great interest at their allies sudden feuding.

"What say you, Baron?" Guy leered.

Torn between fury and shame, Lughus loosened his hold on Alan and let the young sheriff slide, sputtering, to the floor.

Harlow smirked and bowed his head toward Guy. "Finally, a sensible man appears," he began, "My lord, I am Willum Harlow—"

"I know who you are, Chief Constable," Guy said, "and it grieves me to see enemy officers treated with such indignity."

"Guy, if you really knew these men, you would think me fawning," Lughus snapped. "You have no idea of the evil these two might sow when left unchecked.

"Perhaps not," Guy replied, "but I will not allow you to kill them in cold blood, particularly as it would be a violation of your own decree." He returned his attention to Harlow and Alan. "I will offer my personal guarantee of safety. No harm shall come to either of you so long as you swear to conduct yourselves with honor."

"Ha!" Brigid scoffed. "You could sooner expect a pig to shit gold."

Harlow ignored her. "It would be my absolute pleasure," he said, bowing to Guy.

Lughus had had enough of his cousin's attempts to undermine his authority. "You do not command here, Guy," he said, "and while I will spare their lives for the time being, these two will *not* go free." He turned to Sir Deryk. "Clap these men in irons and see them safely to the dungeon. Lord Mongrath will show you the way."

"Yes, sir," the Galadin knight said. At once he began issuing orders to his men and together they ushered the prisoners onward before them.

Guy stood watching, his eyebrows raised in an expression of arrogant disregard.

Lughus glared at him. "I have no interest in this absurd feuding," he said, once the prisoners had gone, "but I will not allow your insistence on being contrary place our men or the Brock itself at risk." He stepped forward to stare the other older man in the face and was surprised to find that they were of equal height. "I am not a threat to you," he said coldly.

Guy's face remained impassive. "You know," he said at last, "I knew your father. As a boy, I admired him, looked up to him. In many ways, you could say that he was my hero."

Lughus remained silent.

"He was a man who was willing to do whatever it took to ensure the success of his barony and his people," Guy continued. "I can only imagine the depth of his disgrace were he alive to see you championing his enemies and turning his own father over to their side."

Lughus's jaw set and his eyes smoldered. Behind him, Fergus began to growl low and menacingly. Brigid stood beside him, shushing him gently with one hand, while the other rested comfortably upon the hilt of her blade.

"My father's failure was his insular vision," Lughus said at last. "He failed to see beyond his own selfish lust for power and authority. Had he realized that the Brock is more than a single barony, perhaps he might not have fallen to evil or met such an ignoble end."

"You disgrace yourself when you speak ill of your father," Guy seethed.

"My father disgraced himself when he murdered the mother of his only son," Lughus replied, "and it's only through my grandfather that the honor of the Silver Eagle had been restored!"

"Roland is a sentimental fool," Guy said.

"Yet, he is the baron of Marthaine," Lughus said. "Not you."

"For now," Guy said, turning away with an arrogant smile. "For now."

Lughus breathed a sigh. Unasked for, he heard Royne's sardonic drawl sound in his head. "Guy, what are the odds that this conflict between you and I does not end in blood?" he asked.

Guy huffed derisively and checked his pace. "I put no stock in prophesy or mad attempts to divine the future," he said, "so in this, as in all matters, I suppose that only time will tell…"

CHAPTER 25: THE IRON FIST

Thom awoke at dawn with the other stewards on the morning after the feast in Reginal. While the other men groaned aloud and nursed their hangovers, in the dim light of the new day, Thom donned his habit, gathered his parchment and quills (props to reinforce the ruse), and set off to wander the halls of the castle in search of the orange tabby cat.

Under the watchful eyes of the Plague King's household guard, servants were already hard at work cleaning up the remnants of last night's feast. Thom did not envy them, for whether due to the early hour or perhaps some lingering effect of drink, the guards were ill-tempered to a man and seemed to have no hesitation in taking out these frustrations on the staff. While much of what he had seen since his arrival in Montevale provided a rustic contrast to the refined decorum of the Andochan capital of Titanis, here at least he found a familiar parallel. For in the relations between the classes, between the hierarchy of rank, humanity's inherent tendency to needlessly assert dominance was on full display.

It was bad enough that a grown man should be forced to his hands and knees to clean up a nasty pile of sick that resulted from a nobleman's overindulgence, but then to see the man made sport of for the amusement of the brutish guards kindled the ever-ready bonfire of resentment that had somehow made its home in the center of Thom's chest.

When one of the guards pretended to stumble so as to knock the servant into the malodorous puddle, Thom found his hand literally grasping at the air just above his right shoulder. Only then did he remember that he had left Death safely hidden beneath the bed of the wagon in the stables. Otherwise, he might have blown the whole mission right then and there.

Thom's assumed role as a scribe allowed him the relative freedom to explore many areas of the castle unimpeded. From the great hall to the kitchens to many of the storerooms, he made a cursory map of the fortress's layout, paying special attention to those rooms that exited out into the ward. His travels with Magnus had taught him that such knowledge was invaluable, for when the fighting began, as it so often did, it was important to have an escape route in the event that things went wrong.

Another lesson he had learned in his travels with the former Reaver was that if a person acted like they knew what they were doing, folks were only too willing to go along with that assumption. Thom knew for a fact that it was only on rare occasions that Magnus had even the slightest clue as to what he was doing, and yet because he carried himself with such irrational bravado, most people simply assumed that he did and were more than willing to stay out of his. Sure, his size and his overt aggression played a part as well, but for the most part, it was his confidence that was the real key.

Thom was not known for any charismatic swagger, but he did understand the social conventions of a castle, and thus, by feigning some important— even dire—purpose, it was with relative ease that he was able to make his way to the southwest wing where the noble guests were confined.

While the number of guards on duty was twice what was to be found in other sections of the castle, as Thom approached, they offered him little more than a cursory glance or an amused smirk. Such was the disarming symbolism of the habit, he thought, for whether scholar or monk, any man who went about dressed in such an unflattering garment was surely no threat.

From the brief conversation with the stewards in the hall last night, the cat appeared to be seen most often in this section of the castle, which made sense if it were indeed true that Lady Valerie had taken to feeding it. It was Thom's hope that in finding the cat, he could not only find the means by which it was infiltrating the castle, but also make contact with the Tower's cousin in a manner that would not arouse suspicion.

From what Horn and Sparrow had told him, Lady Valerie was as stout a fighter as any man, a skilled rider, and a brilliant tactician. Due to her lineage, however, no man would accept her into service for fear that should she come to harm, it would draw the ire of her father, Lord Leon, King Cedric's brother. When Prince Beledain was assigned the command of the light cavalry, however, she was finally granted the chance she more than deserved. Time and again, she distinguished herself, and in truth, her prowess and her fame soon rivaled that of her cousin.

It was for this reason more than any other—the perceived threat of having to face her in the field—that the Plague King insisted that she remain at his court in Reginal. Thus, while Lord Talondaire subtly sought to entice Lord Guillon to their little conspiracy, Thom and Sparrow would seek out Lady Val. Then, together, they could endeavor to extricate the Talon's mother and sister and ride for freedom at the court of the rebel queen.

Why don't you just grab the bloody axe and kill them all? Magnus asked from the recesses of Thom's mind. *Much less fuss.*

"Maybe for you," Thom said, "but I'm not you."

No, I suppose you're not.

A door opened and a maid appeared with an armful of soiled linens for washing. Thom quickly sidestepped out of her way and bowed his head in a mixture of apology and greeting. The woman nodded back, but otherwise remained silent until Thom called her back.

"Excuse me, ma'am," he said politely. He offered what he hoped was a pleasant grin. "Have you seen a rather large cat wandering about here? Orange in color."

The woman grunted and adjusted her arms around the bundle of linens. "Yes, I know the wee beastie," she said. "I saw it not long ago. Ran off down that way when one of the guards hissed at it."

"Would that be the southern hallway?" Thom asked, motioning to where the hallway diverged in two opposite directions. "There and to the left?"

"Aye, so it is."

Thom bowed his head again. "Thank you." As he moved to head off, however, the woman called him back.

"Oi, hold up," she said. "That's the ladies' quarters down there. You best be mindful of that if you're hunting that cat. Don't be sticking your nose where it don't belong."

"Ladies?" Thom asked, feigning ignorance. "Are there many ladies at the court?"

"Aye, many and more so you'd best watch yourself," she said. "I'd tell you not to head that way at all, but if you're to catch the cat, well..." She shrugged.. "Besides, it's clear you ain't one of them rakish courtiers. Least not dressed like that."

"No, ma'am," he said, though he was surprised by a sudden flash of indignation.

"Well, then, get on with you," she said. "I've this washing and more to see to as it is. Can't be wasting time with idle chatter."

Thom gave a nod. "Thank you again," he said.

He hurried off down the hall and turned the corner to the section dedicated to the ladies. At once, the scent of flowers and spices filled his nostrils from large basins of potpourri along the walls. Intricately woven tapestries depicting unicorns, searoans, and various other fanciful creatures added a splash of color to the otherwise cold stone, and behind the closed door of one of the rooms, he could make out the sound of a harp.

Reminds me of a brothel, Magnus's voice chimed in, *an expensive one, but a brothel still.*

"I don't think that's true," Thom returned.

Just then, a door opened suddenly beside him and a young nobleman exited, adjusting the buckle of his baldric. Thom averted his eyes deferentially and, without a word, the nobleman pursed his lips and went on his way.

Told you, Magnus grunted.

"Alright, fine." Thom sighed aloud. "Perhaps there are certain...similarities, but I still wouldn't call it a brothel."

"Fair enough," said a voice, "the girls in a brothel get paid."

Thom was about to disagree, noting how in most cases, it was the proprietor of the business who actually made all of the money, only to be struck dumb with mortification at his lack of discretion. He had yet to determine if his conversations with the Wrathorn warrior were real or perhaps a type of madness brought about by traumatic experience. However, he did not think such matters relevant right now.

"Um, yes, well..." He shuffled his armload of scrolls and turned to face the speaker. To his surprise, it was a woman. Tall, broad-shouldered, and strong. Her auburn hair had been tightly plaited and woven atop her head. He knew there was probably a name for the style, but whatever it was he did not know. Still, it looked functional enough to keep her hair out of her face and prevent an opponent from grabbing onto it in battle.

By the gods! Magnus's voice said. *Now that is a woman!*

"Quiet, you," Thom muttered.

"Excuse me?" the woman said.

Thom flushed scarlet. "Would...would you happen to be the Lady Valerie?" he stammered. "The Iron Fist?'

The woman sighed. "I am," she said.

"My name is Thom Reaver," he said. His voice dropped low. "I have been looking for you."

Val scoffed and turned away from him. She was clad in a simple, unadorned gown, that while certain to have been tailored specifically for her, seemed ill-fitting and uncomfortable. "I cannot imagine what cause my cousin would have to send a scribe to me," she said. "If he seeks to update the record of our genealogy, I fear he may not agree with my contributions."

"Actually..." Thom breathed a sigh and glanced quickly up and down the length of the hall. A pair of guards stood sentinel at the entrance while another two leaned against the wall at the opposite end; however, they seemed more interested in their own private conversations to bother with a bumbling scribbler from the Order.

"Actually," he began again, "I am here on behalf of your...*other* cousin."

Val's eyes widened. "Bel?"

Thom nodded.

Val glanced up and down the hall.

"Not here," she said. "Come."

Thom followed her through a nearby doorway into a large bedroom. A small table with two wooden stools sat along one wall. With a wave of her arm, Lady Valerie invited him to sit. Thom did as he was commanded, dumping his armful of scrolls and other accoutrements upon the tabletop.

"Now," Val said, closing the door. "Tell me. Who are you and what is your purpose in coming here? What news from Bel?"

Thom heaved a heavy sigh and paused to collect his thoughts. The lady eyed him impatiently, her green eyes alight with interest. "Like I said, my name is Thom, Thom Reaver," he began. "I have come with Lord Talondaire and a girl called Sparrow—"

"Sparrow is here as well?" Val broke in.

"Aye," Thom said. "She's here somewhere in the guise of a maid." He paused. "We've come here hoping to free you, Lord Guillon, and Lord Talondaire's mother and sister. The Talon had pledged that if we can free them, he will commit to joining Bel and Marina in their rebellion against the Plague King."

Val folded her arms across her chest. "Much easier said than done," she said.

"Isn't it always?" Thom smiled.

Val sat down at the table beside him. "The king..." she paused, "The king does not sit an easy throne. He is suspicious of one and all and is ever-watchful for any sign of treachery or deceit. I mean you no offense by this, but I wonder that Prince Beledain should have chosen you to lead this mission. You do not seem the type made for war."

"Oh I am not!" Thom grinned. "Though, I guess you could say, I'm learning."

Valerie bit her lip.

"That being said," Thom began again, "If I may say so, I am—surprisingly—a lot more capable than I present. Reaver is not actually my surname. It is my title. Like Prince Beledain, I too am what the Guardians would call 'anointed.' The Reaver is my title and my weapon—my axe—is stowed away in the stables for such time as we need it."

"Well, that's a start," Val said. "For apart from his guards, the king does not permit anyone to go about the castle armed. Even I have no sense of what has become of my arms and armor—to say nothing of my horse. They were confiscated upon my arrival, though that was not the word they used. I can only imagine Lord Guillon received similar treatment. Perhaps worse, considering he was on the other side of the Bloodline. Of course, I suppose he was lucky just to have kept his head."

Thom rubbed his jaw in thought. "What do you know of Lord Talondaire's mother and sister?" he asked. "You said something about a brothel. Is that..."

"Thankfully, no," Val said, "though it remains an unspoken threat to ensure many a nobleman or noblewoman's compliance."

Thom shook his head. "Despicable."

Val nodded. "I have the privilege of being close to the king in blood and am thus spared any such indignity," she said. "However, there are many young maids here who the king has taken on as wards. He intends to use them to broker alliances by marriage, strengthening his position among the nobility in both Montevale and abroad." Her gaze narrowed and her eyes grew hard. "In the meantime, they serve at the pleasure of the king and his boon companions, Vaston Delon and Inen Vilnois. There are others too, but they come and go as the war wages on. In fact, I have not seen Vilnois for some time now."

"Vilnois..." Thom mused. "Is he the one they call the Golden Garron?"

"The same."

Thom gave a nod. "Well, I doubt you'll be seeing around the young ladies anymore," he said. "According to Horn, Prince Beledain caught up with him some weeks back and brought him and his raider to justice. The story among the men is that Bel hung the soldiers, but relieved Vilnois of a certain...piece before sending him back to the Plague King."

"Shhh," Val said quickly. "You cannot call him that here! He hates it."

"Sorry! Sorry!" Thom said quickly, "I just—"

"He's seen men tortured for such a slip," Val said. "I would not let it become a habit."

Thom nodded. "It won't."

Val took a deep breath. "So," she began, "we should not linger here together overlong. I must be out and about so as to be seen and avoid arousing suspicion. However, now that we know each other, we can work together to plan the escape. I will see what I can do in contacting the Talondaire ladies myself, though if I can find Sparrow, I may try to work through her as well."

"Yes, ma'am," Thom said.

"Of course, all of this is somewhat moot if we cannot find a means by which to escape. It would be the absolute folly to believe that we can fight our way out, and the gates are heavily defended."

A sudden flash of orange drew Thom's eye to the far side of the room and he nearly leapt to his feet in surprise.

"Ah!" he cried. "There it is!"

Val suppressed a laugh. "Peace, peace." She called across the room. "Is that you, you little rascal? Come for your morning meal?"

Without a sound, the orange cat padded into the center of the room, fixed the two humans with a stare, and meowed. With a smile, Thom stood up from his stool, crossed the room, and knelt tentatively before the little creature. The cat regarded him with an imperious stare, decided he was worthy, and ran the length of its body along the bottom of the young man's habit.

"As luck would have it," Thom said, "I believe the solution to our problem might be found right here."

"What do you mean?" Val asked.

"Well, according to the other stewards, this little fellow is a stray," he said. "But somehow he—or she—has found a means by which to come and go as it pleases from the town. Perhaps if we can discover the means by which it enters and exits the castle grounds, we might find our own way out as well."

Val's lips curled with amusement. "Well," she said, "I already know the answer to that, though I'm not sure it will do us much good."

After his meeting with Lady Valerie, Thom withdrew from the women's section of the guest wing to seek out Lord Talondaire in the area reserved for the men. Curious, Thom thought, that the nobles should be divided by gender in such a manner; however, given what Val suggested about the Plague King's political intentions regarding the unattached young women, he was not surprised. From the sounds of it, King Dermont kept company with rascals and villains. Roosters who could not be allowed to roam freely in the hen house. In such a situation, restriction would be a requirement.

At least for the noble ladies. The servants were another story. As Sir Lloyd led Thom into the Talon's room, Sparrow was pacing back and forth in a rage.

"He lays a hand on my ass again, I'll fucking cut him! I swear it!" she seethed.

Immediately, Thom's heart began to pound and he saw red. "Who?"

"The fucking cock knight, that's who," she said.

From his velvet chair, Lord Talondaire sighed wearily. "His name is Sir Gurney," he said. "He too was a member of the Tower's Guard. However, in the wake of all that has happened, I am not surprised to see him in the court of the Plague King. His is an old house who survived much of the war through political maneuvering, though he is clearly not without some skill. He and Beledain were not what I would call friends."

"Well, the cock might adorn his bloody arms, but he touches me again, we'll see how he likes losing his," Sparrow said.

"Say the word and I'll see it done," Thom grunted, surprised to find his voice more reminiscent of his Wrathorn predecessor than his own. "I'll serve it to him on a golden platter."

"I'd rather he eat it off the floor," she added with a wicked leer.

The Talon held up a supplicating hand. "While I am not condoning Gurney's behavior, such rash action will leave us exposed," he said wearily. "I will speak to him, or—if you prefer it—you may tell him yourself that you belong to me. He will take that to mean what it does not, but all the same, he will stand down and leave you be."

"I think I'd prefer Thommy's option," she said.

"I'm sure you would," the lord said, "but an open threat will only encourage him to harass you more, particularly if what the gossipmonger say is true and that Gurney is in line to be elevated to a lordship—perhaps even a wardenship." He offered a sardonic leer. "It appears that our friend the Tower has been so efficient at eliminating the king's close friends and allies that he finds himself with a surplus of honors to distribute. In fact, if the rumors are true, then I stand to be offered the wardenship of Whitemane."

Thom rubbed his chin. "Could you not just accept it and then declare for the queen afterwards?" he asked.

"I could," the Talon said, "but it would not solve the problem of the hostages."

"Ah! Speaking of which," Thom said suddenly, "Lady Valerie is with us."

"You spoke with Val?" Sparrow said.

"I did," Thom told her. "When the time is right, she's going to try to approach Lord Talon's mother and sister. She said there's no sense in alarming them without a concrete plan."

"True," Talondaire said. "No need to place them in further risk either."

Thom folded his arms across his chest. "I believe we might have found a way out of the castle as well. One that circumvents the gates entirely and leads directly into the town."

"Then what are we waiting for?" Sparrow asked. "We could make our escape tonight."

Thom shrugged. "Not yet," he said, "for we've still got a few details to hammer out."

Talondaire eyed Thom questioningly. "Such as?"

"Horses," Thom said. "We can get outside of the walls, but in doing so, we would abandon the wagon and our horses."

"Then that's not much of an escape," Lord Talondaire said. "We can't possibly expect to get very far on foot."

"True," Thom agreed, "but why do we need to fight our way out at all? What if we arrange for the escape to coincide with when the king releases you to return home?"

"Explain," the Talon said.

"If it's offered, accept the wardenship of Whitemane and request leave to see to securing your defenses and the raising of new levees. With the rebels already in the vicinity, he's certain to grant you leave," Thom said. "Then, once we pass through the gates into the town proper, Lady Valerie, Lord Guillon, your mother, and your sister will slip out to the town wherein we can meet with them, load them into the wagon, and make our escape in secret. I can even stay behind to guide them and guard them personally."

"Or me," Sparrow said. "A maid might be less suspicious."

Thom shrugged. "We can decide that later." He eyed Lord Talondaire. "What say you, my lord?"

The lord sat in silence for a long moment, his fair face a mask of stone. Thom glanced behind him through the small window at the pallid afternoon sky. Wispy trails of cloud stretched across the horizon, punctuated by the silhouette of a large raptor wheeling about in great circles. It was like watching the needle of some divine hand daintily sewing together the great vaulted expanse. Only then did he realize that he was gazing in the direction of the Andochan camp and that the wheeling bird of prey was likely a Calendral kite, the swift-winged messenger birds of the Guardian-King. With a shudder, Thom pressed the tips of his fingers together, feeling the small scar he still bore from one of the ill-tempered birds.

What might they be up to? And what of the Warlord? What could have brought him so far from Titanis? Thom thought back to when he had seen the old warrior in the great hall. He looked…diminished. Weary. It was strange, for in spite of his size, there had always been a liveliness to Ol' Dandy, as Rastis had called him, and while Thom had not known him well, his great boisterous laughter echoed throughout the vastness of the Loremaster's Tower whenever the two councilors happened to meet.

At length, Lord Talondaire stirred from his contemplation and cleared his throat.

"It is as good a plan as any," he said. "And, unfortunately, it seems that is all we have."

"Splendid!" Thom said.

"Though I have one final question," the lord said. "This escape route? You never said. Where exactly is it?"

"Ah yes...well..." Thom said. "It's a place that few enough would expect."

"And that would be?"

"The garderobe."

CHAPTER 26: THE VICEROY'S DECREE

Together, Royne, Amara, and Haruki joined the teeming mass of students as they filed through the building to the symposium. No sooner had they arrived than Royne was able to discern the sound of a fanfare of horns. For the first time in recent memory, the doors of the symposium opened and the massive flood of people emptied out into the courtyard.

Beyond them, on the far side of the gates, Royne saw a similar scene to the one he had witnessed the other day. An honor guard of soldiers stood in silence, while between them Marcel Pryce the Elder stood beside his son. Fabius, the young Grantisi alchemist, knelt upon the flagstones between them.

Royne's stomach churned with bile as he followed behind Amara to stand at the front of the assembly beside Master Udo, Master Kebir, and a group of other senior alchemists. Apart from the occasional gasp or murmur of concern and disbelief, all were silent in anticipation of the viceroy's speech.

"At long last..." Marcel Pryce called out from the other side of the gates. "At long last, the University finally pays me the courtesy of a proper greeting."

Royne gave an inward huff. His eyes wandered to the younger man at the viceroy's side, his childhood bully, his tormentor, Pryce the Younger. His brow creased and he fixed his enemy with a vengeful stare knowing full well that he was too far away to be recognized.

"As I am sure you all know, Commonwealth and the realm that formerly comprised the Republic of Grantis surrendered to the protection of Andoch and the Guardian-King Kredor Drude II. As the King's representative, it is my mandate to maintain order across the region and to ensure the safety of its citizens."

Surely executing a dozen of them is a great way to ensure their safety... Royne thought bitterly.

"For nearly a year now, we have made entreaties to you, people of the University. Peaceful entreaties. And yet in every case, my representatives have found themselves at the very least repelled or—more often—murdered!"

Yes, and I'm certain no harm would have come to these folk had you been permitted to enter...

The viceroy glared through the iron gates at the silent alchemists and Royne could sense his temper flare. "Thus, I am afraid that you leave me no choice but to answer hostility with hostility. Violence with violence." He paused for effect. "And death with death."

The elder Pryce nodded to his son and Royne saw the flash of the younger Pryce's grin as he drew his bejeweled sword.

"This man wears the clothing that marks him as one of you and he was captured sowing insurrection among the poorest of the city, those whom already suffer greatly due to the senate's foolishness," the viceroy said. "Yet, he—like you—would have them suffer further still, confounding our efforts at peace, rejecting the succor we provide with rage and anger!"

"That's not true," Haruki whispered to those standing nearby. "Fabius's father was killed in one of the viceroy's public executions. He just wanted to find out if his mother and his brothers and sisters were safe. He was no rebel."

Royne frowned. "How did he sneak out?"

"There are secret ways. One passes through the sewers. Another opens into the street just beyond the gates," Amara whispered. "But they are kept locked and access is severely restricted."

Royne remembered how Udo seemed to appear out of nowhere when he first met him before the gates so long ago. "Why is it no one ever told me that?"

"You never asked. Besides, in your case, if you left, you might not be permitted to return."

Before the gates, the viceroy nodded to his son and raised his arm. "And so," he said, "if you will not unbar your gates in the name of friendship, then I have no choice but to judge you as enemies!"

With that, he lowered his arm and the younger Pryce brought down his sword. Royne forced himself to watch as the younger man's head was separated from his shoulders. It hit the ground like a wayward melon from a fruit stand followed shortly by the heavy thud of the torso.

The wicked leer that stretched across the visage of his old enemy filled Royne with a cold rage. Beside him, Amara was silent, but her expression was haunted, her eyes glazed with grief. Haruki wept openly.

Yet, otherwise, there was only silence. The remaining body of men and women, old and young, stood without expression. Royne could hardly believe it. Surely they had more Star Dust or some other alchemical substance that could put an end to the viceroy once and for all! Surely he had given them just cause and provocation! Yet, they did nothing. They simply stood in silence.

This is intolerable! How can they possibly endure this!

The viceroy addressed the assembly without remorse. "I expect these gates to open—without hostility—within one week! If they do not, I will return. Your rebellious associate here was captured in the company of a rather prodigious family. Should these gates not open in the allotted time, you shall all bear witness to the execution of another of his kin. But know this..."

Pryce the Elder raised his finger and pointed through the gates directly at the crowd.

"While ours might be the hand that wields the executioner's blade, it will be by your refusal to act that the next person dies. *You* shall bear the blame for any subsequent deaths just as *you* bear responsibility for the death of this man."

The young Pryce wiped his blade clean upon Fabius's tunic and returned the sword to its sheath.

"Think upon what I said," the viceroy shouted. "For rest assured, this defiance ends *now!*"

With that, the fanfare sounded again and the procession of soldiers turned and departed from the gates, leaving the decapitated corpse upon the ground where it lay.

The assembled alchemists watched in silence until at last the fanfare ceased and sound of marching footsteps receded. Only then did the gates open and a half dozen men scurry out to retrieve what was left of Fabius. Without a word, they carried his remains through the doors of the symposium. The rest of the community followed after them in observant silence.

Again, Royne cast his gaze around him and was shocked to find that, with the exception of Haruki, not a single person wept or sobbed. Rather, their faces all bore the same placid expression of stoic indifference.

Madness!

Once inside the great circular space of the symposium, the body was taken off to be prepared for whatever funerary rights were customary and the remaining members of the community began to silently disperse.

Royne felt gripped by a sense of righteous indignation, confused at the pervasive attitude of unconcern. He cast his critical gaze back and forth from student to student and master to master, furious at their lack of fury in the face of such boldface injustice.

"Wait, wait, wait..." he said aloud. He rubbed his temples against a sudden pain behind his eyes. "Wait!"

His shout echoed throughout the great vaulted chamber halting all movement. All eyes turned to him and beneath the myriad stares, he clambered up to stand upon a chair.

"What are you doing, Polecat?" Amara asked in a harsh whisper. "This is not the time to cause trouble."

"This is *exactly* the time to cause trouble," Royne replied.

Her brow creased and she bit her lip, but he could not tell if her expression was one of agreement or disapproval. There was little time to dwell upon it now though.

With a deep breath, he braced himself and called out over the symposium. "So the viceroy threatens!" he shouted. "How will the alchemists answer?"

All around him, her began to hear the murmurs of concerned whispers and the sound of muffled confusion. At last, a voice from somewhere in the crowd replied.

"We won't."

"Come on now!" Royne cried, shaking his head. "He *killed* one of your own! He's promised to kill more!"

"We will play no part in the Guardian-King's war!" came another reply.

"War?" Royne paused, scanning the crowd for the speaker but to no avail. It could just as easily have been anyone. He shook his head. "Haruki! Fabius's family? Who does he leave behind?"

At the sudden attention, Haruki instantly appeared uncomfortable. "A mother. Two young sisters and a young brother," he said at last. "I...I believe he has a grandmother that lives with them as well."

"So ordinary people? Children. Certainly not warriors."

"No," Haruki said quietly.

"And yet, the viceroy threatens to kill them." Royne said. He shook his head. "No. Not threatens. For that was no idle threat. He *will* kill them. If we do nothing, they *will* die!"

The crowd began to buzz and hum and Royne felt his heart race.

"Fabius broke the rules," someone shouted. It was Master Kebir. "He left the sanctity of the gates. By doing so, he not only put himself at risk, but all of us as well. He made a choice and the natural consequences of that choice have come to pass. There is nothing we can do."

"He left to see to his family!" Royne cried.

"And are they better off for his having done so?" Kebir asked.

Royne frowned as the crowd renewed its murmuring. His anger flared. "So for that you will see children murdered—*beheaded*? You will be complicit in this injustice, in this tyranny?"

At last, Master Udo breathed a heavy sigh and spoke.

"Are you suggesting, Master Royne, that we be held responsible for the actions of the viceroy?"

"If you have the power to stand against injustice—against evil—and choose instead to stand idly by and do nothing, then yes, I *do* believe that you are complicit. I *do* believe that you are responsible. I *do* believe that you too have done evil."

The crowd began to murmur and grumble. Again, Udo spoke.

"The choices of the viceroy or the Grantisi senate or the Guardian-King himself are not anyone else's choices but their own. It is they alone who bear the responsibility and they alone who bear the blame," he said. "Our actions are our own, Master Royne. They belong to each of us and to no other."

"As does our inaction," Royne seethed. "As does our shame!"

Udo gave an exasperated sigh. "So what would you have us do?" he asked. "Open the gates? Invite the enemy in? Surely, these Andochans have proven themselves to be such pleasant and polite guests!" The old man fixed Royne with his questioning gaze. "Please. Enlighten us. What would you have us do?"

Royne took a deep breath. For a brief moment, his eyes met those of Amara and he saw the weight of her thoughts as she grappled with the realities of the situation.

"I would have you fight," he said. "I have seen what your alchemy can do. I would have you use it to fight against this injustice and to help usher in a new day."

For a long moment there was only silence as all eyes seemed drawn to the lanky young Loremaster with the pinched face. Then, somewhere in the symposium, someone laughed. A brief, derisive chuckle. Moments later, it was echoed by someone else somewhere across the vast room. Soon, it was repeated elsewhere and elsewhere. Before long, the entire symposium had erupted into boisterous laughter and mirth.

Royne's blood ran cold, but in defiance of the sudden eruption of levity, of mockery, he remained unbowed. With what dignity he could muster, he stepped down from the chair, adjusted the strap of his satchel, and turned to go—only to find himself face to face with Amara. She, he noted, was not laughing. Far beyond her in the crowd, he could see that Master Udo was not laughing either.

"I'm sorry, Polecat," Amara said softly.

"I'm sorry too," he said."

She sighed. "Don't forget to put some healing balm on your arm."

Wisdom's unheard plea...

"It's fine," Royne said without turning. "The pain will serve to remind me that *I* at least am still alive."

CHAPTER 27: HOUNDSTOOTH IN WINTER

Less than a week after their return from the siege of Stonebridge castle, winter arrived abruptly and in full force. In less than half a day, the entire city surrounding the Houndstooth had been blanketed in a thick layer of fine, powdery snow.

Fergus was in his glory—romping through the wards in great circles at a breakneck pace. In spite of the chill wind and the biting cold, the great hound spent hours outside, his long pink tongue lolling out of the side of his mouth in a canine expression of utmost bliss.

As she watched him from atop the keep, Brigid too could not help but share in the hound's delight over the change in the season. With the challenges that the changing weather brought for the functional maintenance of an army, winter traditionally brought with it a temporary cessation of hostilities, promising a well-needed interval of rest before the fighting resumed in the spring. Thus, Brigid prepared herself for a quiet season of domestic comfort comprised of roaring fires, warm hippocras, and cozy blankets. Over the last few weeks, Adolfo's mercantile connections had led to the acquisition of a number of new books and she was filled with romantic daydreams full of long nights lying in bed beside Lughus while they took turns reading aloud to each other. She would rest her head on his shoulder and listen to the sonorous timbre of his voice as he traced along the lines of text with a callused finger.

Since the victory at Stonebridge, the threat of a Guardian invasion from the west was considerably lessened, and while Nordren Harbor remained under blockade, an invading force would have an incredibly difficult time making landfall. This left only the coastal road in the southeast, the Nivanus Pass, and the cold northern waters of the Bay of Brabant as viable routes for an enemy assault. With Galadin and Marthaine doing the majority of the heavy fighting thus far, the other barons had taken up the defense of these remaining routes, eager to demonstrate that they too were integral in the defense of the Brock. As Perin Glendaro's declared in a recent message, more than two stones made up the tower of the Brock. Galadin and Marthaine had carried the load for too long; it was time for the other baronies to do their part.

Brigid sighed and pulled the fur-lined cloak more tightly around her shoulders. A rest would indeed be welcome. In spite of the Andochan raids, the harvest had been fruitful so the peasantry were well-stocked in grain, stores, and mutton, and the improved connections with the weaver's guild meant that folk had a bit more coin in their purses than usual. For perhaps the first time, she sensed little of the doom and gloom that so often accompanied the changing of the seasons.

This subtle optimism was present among the castle folk as well. Sir Owain's wounds continued to heal, though it was still uncertain as to whether the old knight would be able to take the field ever again. He would certainly try, but with any luck he could be prevailed upon to accept a position in command as opposed to fighting on the front lines. In any case, he was moving around a lot better than before the siege, no doubt motivated by having been left behind, and had even gone so far as to spar with the new men recruited to the Galadin guard.

The interval of rest also allowed Horus to begin planning for the impending wedding ceremony in late spring. While Brigid already considered herself and Lughus to be bonded in mind, body, and spirit, she recognized the symbolic importance of the wedding...and, truth be told, she could not deny a certain feminine thrill at the pageantry surrounding the event—the feast, the frivolity, even the gown. At Blackstone, such things disgusted her, for they were further reminders of the toxic facade that masked the nobility's abuses of power. A fairy story to conceal a wretched reality. Yet in Galadin, to be surrounded by good people, true friends, and to marry a man not for politics but because he was the perfect partner to her own heart? Well, perhaps that was something to celebrate.

Gazing out over the yard, she felt her cheeks warm as she giggled at the memory of Jergan's euphoric exultation when it was *she* who breeched the subject of designing a new gown for the occasion. The poor man nearly fainted, so excited was he to share his craft.

Why not? She blushed at her uncharacteristic admission of self-indulgence. *It's my wedding day. Let it be a daydream come true.*

Of course, in spite of the winter break and the impending festivities, they could not afford to be idle either. They were still at war and the Guardians were legendary opponents—quite literally. Further, while the winter was an unlikely time for a pitched battle, there were always more subtle—if less honorable—methods to continue the fight, as the Chancellor's assassins had already proven. Adolfo's network of ne'er-do-wells (who, oddly enough, were little by little becoming *her* network of ne'er-do-wells) kept them fairly well informed, but the fact that they had already succeeded in infiltrating the Houndstooth once meant that Whisper and Shade were never far from her side.

Large white snowflakes began to fall in earnest, and as the wind picked up, Brigid watched as they whirled around the drab gray sky in an elaborate dance. She recalled other moments such as this from her past, stolen moments of beauty and peace in the eternity of ennui that defined her life in Blackstone. Her gaze narrowed as her thoughts turned to her mountainous homeland.

While she had fully embraced the Brock and to her role as the soon-to-be lady of Galadin, her duties as the Blade (her own conscience) would not allow her to simply abandon the common folk of Dwerin. From the miners to the servants to the folk like Geoffrey who worked the lands of the Spade, she felt an obligation to stand for them against the exploitive policies of her mother, her uncle, and all the generations that came before.

With the help of Adolfo's network of contacts, she had begun to make tacit inquiries, reaching out to individuals who had achieved a certain degree of standing in the eyes of their fellows. It would, of course, be some time before they could be carefully vetted and organized into a single, unified resistance, but it was her hope that by winter's end, she would have a means of undermining her enemies in a manner that did not require a pitched battle. Even now, while Adolfo's journey to Agathis was in part personal, he also planned to strengthen his network across the Firriny Mountains and gather more information about the Dwerin state of affairs.

A sudden fluttering stirred her from her private thoughts. It was Cass. The beautiful silver eagle perched erect and regal upon the battlement beside the dovecote, the corpse of a rabbit clutched tightly in her talons. Splashes of red stood out sharply against the white fur.

"Well, look at you," Brigid said with a smile. In spite of the cold, she'd brought the bird out for a chance to stretch her wings for a bit. She had no intentions of hunting, but whether the result of opportunity or instinct, it appeared that Cass had other ideas.

Carefully, Brigid donned the falconry glove and as she held it out to the silvery bird, Cass leapt to her wrist, the carcass still gripped tightly in one vicious claw.

"What a fine and deadly lady you are, my dear," Brigid said, gently stroking the bird's feathers with her free hand. She was mindful of the eagle's beak, but in their short time together, she had endeavored to build a rapport with the young raptor so as to gain her trust. As such, in her dealings with the bird, she was cautious, but confident in her movements, ever-mindful to show no fear. For now, it seemed to be working, and as Lughus and Fergus seemed to share a deep and unspoken bond, so too did she one day hope to find a similar connection with Cass.

As if on cue, Fergus's idle barking suddenly took on a new, more purposeful tone and Brigid peered over the battlement to see a rider making his way through the cobbled streets of the Golden Quarter toward the barbican of the Houndstooth. Even at this distance, she could make out the trappings of the tawny salmon emblazoned upon his tabard and the caparison of his horse.

Nordren. Perhaps Theo had finally returned with word from the horselords. With Lughus out meeting Faden about improvements to the Hounton quarter, someone would need to receive the messenger. Hopefully, he would have news of Geoffrey and Annabelle as well.

"Come," she said to the silver eagle perched upon her arm, "Let's go inside where it's warm so you can enjoy the spoils of your hunt in peace."

By the time the messenger had been fed and his horse quartered, Sir Owain was able to send a man to recall Lughus to the castle. When she met him in the solar, he was already seated at the table, his brow furrowed pensively as he doodled with a piece of charcoal. Brigid smiled inwardly and offered him a quick kiss on the cheek.

"What's that?" she asked.

"Just some vague thoughts for Hounton," he said as she took the seat beside him. "In the days of Old Calendral, they made use of improved sewage systems to manage waste and help minimize the spread of disease. Some cities like Commonwealth and Titanis still make use of them. As I was meeting with Faden today, it came to mind—as did your duel with the Lash out in Shitbrook. Perhaps when the war is over, we can dedicate more time to construction and sanitation..."

From where he lay in front of the fireplace, Fergus's great maw opened in a massive yawn and the young couple shared a quiet laugh.

"I look forward to those days," Brigid said, "as mundane as they might seem."

Lughus nodded. "Me too."

"Not me," Sir Owain said, hobbling into the solar. "Quite frankly I've had enough lying about. It's high time for some excitement!" Lughus moved to assist him, but the old knight waved him off and sat down heavily in the chair at the baron's left.

"It's good to have you back with us," Brigid said.

"I'll never forgive myself staying behind for the attack on Stonebridge—especially with that Hammer fellow turning up," the old knight said. "If it were up to me, we would have hanged the bastard from the battlements and left him as a winter feast for the carrion birds."

Brigid noted the subtle changes in Lughus's expression—the hardening of his jaw, the slight narrowing of his gaze, the sudden flash of lightning in his stormy eyes. She knew that he too regretted the fact that the Hammer—and Alan—still drew breath. However, with burgeoning power struggle between Lughus, Roland, and Guy, captivity seemed the least of the possible evils.

Let them rot in the dungeons at Harrier's Keep then, Brigid thought, though she could not help but wonder inwardly what manner of mischief they might still sow from the depths of an oubliette.

Pike's arrival with the Nordren messenger put the matter to rest for now. "Here we are, my lord," the sergeant said. "Catch of the day, you might say."

"Thank you, Pike," Lughus replied. He motioned for the messenger to sit and the man removed his nasal helm and bowed his head before taking the proffered seat. "What news from Nordren?"

The man drew forth a thick leather scroll case and passed it to the young baron. "My lord Theobold sends his regards," he said. "These documents, which have been copied for distribution to the Lord-Baron in Highboard and to each of the individual barons at their home courts, outline the details of the alliance my lord has managed to achieve between Queen Marina of Montevale and the Brock."

Lughus's eyes widened. "Alliance?" he repeated. "So the mission was a success?"

"Yes, my lord," the messenger replied.

"Why? Then where are Geoffrey and Annabelle?" Brigid asked.

"Aye," Owain nodded, "and the archers?"

"I'm afraid I do not know anything about that, my lady" the messenger said.

One by one Lughus began to scan the carefully penned missives before passing them to Brigid, who in turn passed them on to Owain.

Despite her noble heritage, Brigid realized she had little experience with these forms of legal documents, and while she might well understand courtly politics, the written form of such things was unfamiliar. She cast Lughus a questioning glance, hoping to silently ascertain his opinion, but was surprised to find him stricken with concern. All of a sudden, he began to flip quickly through the folios until he reached the end of the documents.

"What is it?" she finally asked.

Lughus's brow creased and for a long moment, he rubbed his jaw in consternation. "I know this hand," he said at last.

"What do you mean?" Brigid asked.

Lughus eyed the messenger. "Were you among the men who traveled with Theo?" he asked.

304

"I'm afraid not, sir," he said. "I am sworn to his father. Until being assigned duty as courier, I was on watch at Nordren Port."

Lughus exhaled in frustration. "Pike, see that a place is arranged for our friend here in the barracks." He eyed the messenger. "Thank you, sir. I will draft a response for your master and you may depart for home tomorrow morning. In the meantime, you have our hospitality."

"Thank you, baron," the messenger said.

"I'll see him settled, sir," Pike said with a nod, and with a friendly wave, ushered the man from the room.

"Lughus, what is it?" Brigid asked again when the sound of their footsteps could no longer be discerned. Sir Owain looked up with interest from the parchment he was reading, but remained silent.

"This handwriting," Lughus said at last. "I know it."

"You know it?"

"Yes, and here. On the final page. Just look." Brigid followed his finger. "Here is the signet for Queen Marina, and this one is for her general, Prince Beledain. Over here is the seal of Nordren, and there you can see Geoffrey's mark, but here..." He paused. "Here. Signed as witness."

"Thom Reaver," Brigid read aloud.

"Yes," Lughus said. "Thom."

Brigid chewed her lip. "You mean?"

"I can't imagine how," he said, "but yes. I'd know his handwriting as I'd know his voice—as with Royne, or Rastis, or Hob." He paused. "What are you doing in Montevale, Thom?" he mused aloud, "and why are you calling yourself Reaver?"

"I take it that's not his surname?" Brigid asked.

Lughus shook his head. "His father was a nobleman from the southwest reaches of Andoch, but the family name wasn't Reaver."

"His mother?"

"She was a servant in the lord's house and didn't have a surname." His brow furrowed. "Whatever it is you're up to, Thom, may the Kin keep you."

Brigid returned to the documents. "Do you see any word regarding Geoffrey?" she asked.

Lughus stirred and returned to the documents. "Yes," he said, "Yes here. It says that Geoffrey and the archers will winter in Montevale as a show of good faith and will rejoin with us in such time as our allied forces can secure control of the Nivanus Pass."

Owain nodded. "To be fair, that was to be expected," he said. "As I understand it, that was always part of the Madder's plans."

Brigid nodded though she could not mask her disappointment. "I just hope that they return before the spring. I know that it's selfish, but I'd like them here for the wedding."

"As would I," Lughus said.

"As would *they*, I'm certain," Owain said. "But never fear. Unlike the rest of us, the horselords fight on through the winter. They're quite like the Wrathorn in that regard."

"Then perhaps we should send more men to reinforce the pass from our side?" Lughus said. "Should Geoffrey and the rebels attack the Nivanus encampment, we would be in a more advantageous position to support them.

Owain shook his head. "Let Helmstead and the other barons of the eastern Brock see to defending the pass. We've got enough to concern ourselves with right now watching the southern border. Sacking Stonebridge bought us some breathing room, but there's still the coastal road in Nordren, let alone the miles of moor and highland directly south. They don't make for the easiest route for an invading army, but that don't mean it can't be done."

"Fair enough," Lughus said. "I just want to ensure that we do our part."

"My lord, by all accounts, it's been Galadin, Marthaine, and the Fighting Fifth who have done most of the heavy lifting so far. Like the Lord-Baron said, let the other baronies carry the burden for at least a little while," Owain continued. "We'll train more men, gather more arms, and when the thaw comes on—mark my words—we'll be ready to strike like the hammer of St. Golan!"

Lughus gave a nod, but Brigid could sense his restlessness. She knew that he saw his own role in the war as one of primary responsibility, that it was his duty to safeguard the Brock and stand against any that might threaten it, just as his famous ancestor had before him. Should it come to battle in the east, he would want to be there leading the charge to stand in solidarity with their new allies. The fact that Geoffrey and now possibly Thom might also be in harm's way only fanned the fires of his sense of obligation. The storm clouds in his eyes roiled with passionate zeal.

Brigid caught Sir Owain's eye and the old knight offered her a covert nod.

"Speaking of which," he began, "I'm due to inspect the guard and take stock of our needs. Pike tells me there's a few among the yeomen and the peasant levies who might serve to replace those we've lost and then some. I'll meet with them later today."

"Pike's a good man," Lughus said. "He's more worthy than a mere sergeant."

Owain nodded. "As it stands, we've been without a captain of the guard since the attack on the docks. Of course, we haven't had the need with Geoffrey and Adolfo, but with them both away..."

Lughus nodded. "See it done."

The seneschal carefully rose to his feet. "Aye, sir," he said, and with a final nod, departed from the solar. Brigid watched him go, warmed by the sense that the old knight's pride had been mollified. What creatures these men are, she thought, so ardently driven by the desire to be useful, the desire to serve. Were it not for the physical limitations of the body, would any of them ever bother to eat or sleep? *I suppose that's what makes them heroes...* she thought with a fond smile. Perhaps that was what made people consider *her* a hero too...

She breathed a contented sigh and turned back to Lughus, once again pouring over the finely penned pages of the Montevalen accord. His expression was at once that of a man who had just received remarkably good news mingled with the look of one who had just seen a ghost.

"Lughus?" she asked. "Is everything alright?"

Lughus stirred from his inward thoughts and glancing up a her with a look of disbelief. "This has to be Thom's hand. I'm sure of it," he said.

"I don't doubt you," Brigid told him.

"After we parted in Galdoran, I thought that he went back to Titanis. What could he possibly be doing in Montevale?"

"I'm sure that we'll learn," she said, "in time."

Lughus breathed a heavy sigh. "I am...not proud of the manner in which we parted."

Brigid reached out and gently took his hand. Her hand always looked so small in his, so delicate. It was but a small taste of what she felt whenever he took her in his arms. A sense of safety, security. He was her armor just as she was his hidden blade.

"Have you eaten?" she asked.

"Early this morning," he said, "but nothing since. Touring sewage channels and the like seems to keep the appetite at bay." He laughed. "Though I suppose I am hungry now. Have you?"

Brigid shook her head. "There's a perpetual stew going in the hall," she said, "but it's just so lofty and cold down there right now."

Lughus rubbed at his jaw. "Well," he said, "when I was with Faden today, I passed a tavern just outside of Hounton. It was a place called The Rampant Hound. It seemed a cheerful enough, and I realized that it's been quite some time since you and I have been able to walk to city like we used to..."

"The Rampant Hound?" Brigid repeated. While she had never been there herself, she knew of it—like she had come to know of most places in and around the city. "You want to go there?"

"The night before I left Titanis, Thom and Royne and I went to a place called The Book & the Barrel. It'd be nice to see a place like that here in Galadin." He tugged absently at his surcoat. "Of course, I'd rather we go as simply Lughus and Brigid than the baron and baroness."

An involuntary thrill ran through her. *The baron and baroness. Yes. That's us, isn't it?* A smile lit her features. "Yes. Let's go." She nearly leaping from her chair. "I'll just need a minute to change into something less...heraldic."

"Me too," Lughus said. "Of course, if Fergus tags along, they'll know us at once."

"I'm fairly sure your hair alone will broadcast to one and all who we are, with or without Fergus" she said, "but let them know. Better a leader who is known by his people than one who remains an anonymous oppressor."

"A lesson you taught me long ago."

She smiled. "Dispensing with the pageantry and noble raiment, however, will certainly help in putting the people at their ease."

"And it's far more comfortable." He grinned.

So it was that Brigid, Lughus, and Fergus made their way down from the hidden postern at the Houndstooth, through St. Elisa's Grotto and the Saint's Quarter to where the Rampant Hound stood beside the archway that marked the border of Hounton. It was a relatively middle-sized public house with a stone foundation and three stories constructed of wattle and daub. Faded blue and yellow paint decorated the shutters and the window frames, while the signboard bore the image of a yellow dog up on its hind legs—the very same as decorated the arms of Galadin. The muffled sounds of merriment welcomed their approach, accompanied by the occasional fragment of a fiddler's song. As they approached, Fergus ran about in circles leaving great paw prints in the dust of the new-fallen snow.

Outside of the tavern, a man sat on a bench smoking a pipe and watching the antics of the great hound with a mixture of apprehension and interest. As Brigid and Lughus made for the door, the young baron—clad in the woolen garb of a typical traveler or wanderer—offered the man a silent nod of greeting, and Brigid stifled a laugh when she noticed the man's eyes travel from the golden-headed youth to the great hound and back again.

"Evening," she greeted the man.

"Evening," the man repeated, bowing his head.

Inside, the smell of woodsmoke from the hearth mingled with the aroma of ale and stew. Folk laughed and grunted amidst half-heard conversations, and a small man in a woolen cap sawed away at a fiddle on the far side of the room. The din of conversation lulled only slightly as the young couple entered, but at the appearance of the great hound, it ceased altogether. Even the bard abruptly broke off his song.

Well, so much for not causing a stir... Brigid smirked.

"Holy Brethren!" uttered the man behind the bar, "it's the golden hound."

Lughus and Brigid remained silent under the scrutiny of their stares before making their way to barman. "Pint of ale for each of us," Lughus said, his voice carrying through the stillness, "and whatever you're serving in the way of food."

The old man shook his head as if waking himself from a long sleep. "We've mutton pies or fisherman's stew," he said.

"The pies," Lughus said. "Thank you."

"Aye, sir," the man said.

Brigid tugged at Lughus's arm and led him through the silent crowd to an empty table along the wall. Fergus followed, his tail wagging with amusement at the palpable apprehension his sheer size generated.

Once they were seated, the low hum of voices slowly returned and steadily grew. The barman hurried over at once with two pewter tankards, and with a respectful bow of his head set them down upon the tabletop with a reassuring *thud!*

"Pardon me, my lord," the man said lowly, "but I do recognize you both, though if you're not wanting it to be known, I'll say not a word."

"I think it might be a bit late for that," Brigid smiled.

"Aye," Lughus said. "I suppose it was rather foolish to assume we could avoid notice—not that we were attempting to remain hidden. Rather, we had no wish to cause a disruption or make others feel ill at ease."

"No disruption at all, my lord," the man said. "We welcome it."

Lughus gave a nod. "Thank you."

The old man bowed and casting a glance across the room to the fiddler, motioned for him to carry on with his song. "The food won't be but a moment," he said, and with another bow hurried off to make it so.

Brigid drew back her hood. "I'm sorry," she said. "I know this isn't perhaps what you had in mind."

"It's not so much that," he said. "I just wanted to spend time with you in some place outside of a castle or a bloody army camp. I wanted a chance to be out in the world as just ourselves."

Brigid reached across the table and took his hand. "I don't know if our lives will ever allow for it," she said, "but I appreciate you trying."

"Perhaps if we were to travel?" Lughus said. "Crodane, Gareth, Regnar— they went where they were needed, unknown and unwatched for, rooting out the darkness where it lie hidden." He suddenly reddened. "I must sound like such a child."

"No," Brigid said. "You sound like a dreamer. You sound like the man I love."

Lughus gave a wan smile. "I suppose I'm just tired."

Her blue eyes flashed and she gave his hand a squeeze. "Well," she began, leaning in closer to him across the table. "I hope you're not *too* tired."

He smiled. "Never," he said, raising her hand to his lips. "You, Lady Blade, are all that sustains me."

"I do a fair job of wearing you out as well," she said, reddening, "no less than you do me."

He barked a soft chuckle and she cast him a demure gaze.

"I love you," he said.

"I know," she said spritely. "I love you too."

The barman returned a moment later with their food, and once again, with a deferential bow, left them to their privacy. Unlike the dockside alehouse Adolfo owned, the food here was remarkably good—unexpectedly so, for meat was an uncommon commodity for the common man, even in a place where sheep were in such great abundance as the Brock.

Then again, Galadin had always been prosperous, its leaders priding themselves upon the quality of life it sustained for all social classes. It was something she thought to emulate in a future Dwerin, modified, of course, as would befit an economy built upon mineral wealth and manufacturing as opposed to agriculture.

Again, the thoughts of Dwerin filled her with a pervasive sensation of ambiguity. In marrying Lughus, in becoming the lady of Galadin, was she abandoning the place she called home? At that, could she truly even say that Dwerin *was* her home? It had certainly never felt like one, nor had it ever treated her as such. Yet, what of duty? What of the people? Did she not owe them something as well? Especially now that she was no mere waif ornamenting her mother's grandeur, but a force to be reckoned with, a veteran of many battles, and one of the most powerful women in all the world?

"What's that you say to me?" Lughus said, pausing to take a drink from his tankard. "Something about my thoughts digging great trenches in my brow?"

Brigid smiled. "Something like that."

"Well," he said, raising an eyebrow, "you're doing it now."

"I was thinking about Dwerin."

Lughus nodded. She knew that she did not need to elaborate further. He knew her thoughts just as he knew her. He reached across the table and took her hand, catching her eyes in his. She felt a flush of heat at the intensity of his gaze, the flash of lightning. It was these moments that she loved the most, when she felt so clearly that when their eyes met, so too did their hearts. It was the way he looked at her when they were about to go into battle together. It was the way he looked at her after they made love.

"We will see to it," he said.

Brigid gave a nod. "I know."

Lughus took a pull from his tankard. "There's something oddly familiar about this place," he said. "I felt it as soon as we walked in. Are you sure that we've never come here before? Not in any of our walks through the city before the war began?"

Brigid tried to remember. She had come to know the streets of Galadin so well now that she could easily traverse them blindfolded. However, she had never had much time to actually explore the majority of these locations either. She had to agree with him though. There *was* something genuinely familiar about the place. It made it hard to believe that she had never been there before—

And then it hit her. *She* had never been here before, but Gareth certainly had. Plenty of times. Often enough at least for her to recognize it from her dreams, her visions, the memories that were written upon the part of her mind that had become the Blade.

She traced a fingertip along the rim of her tankard and took a sip.

"You and I have never been here before," she said at last, "But the Marshal and the Blade might well have been regulars."

"Aye, my lady, so they were."

Brigid turned to address the speaker as her hands instinctively slipped to her hilts. It was a middle-aged woman, stalwart and homely, wiping the top of a nearby table with a rag.

"You knew Gareth and Crodane?" Brigid asked.

"Regnar too," she said, "and Ol' Fergus there, though he's pretending he don't know me—aye, that's right, you big golden oaf, I see you! Stole a whole roast lamb I had cooling on the hob last he was here—and that was *after* he turned over an entire stewpot so as to gorge himself upon the spillings." She eyed the great hound sternly. "Yes, I'm talking about you, you great bloody glutton."

Fergus's ears drew back contritely and he lie down, resting his great head upon his paws.

The woman made her way to the next table, walking with a gait that suggested some prior injury, and set to wiping it down. "I take it since you bear their titles and their blades, the old Three are no longer with us?" she said.

"They fell," Lughus said quietly.

"Pity. They were good men."

Lughus's expression was thoughtful. "So you knew they were Blackguards?" he asked.

The woman gave a snort. "I did, as did anyone else who knew them. You might say the Three were Galadin's 'open secret.' Of course, sworn as they were to Baron Arcis, they were afforded a certain degree of protection—at least within the confines of the barony. They might have to slink around the continent like hunted men anywhere else they went, but they was free enough to breathe here." She stood up straight and stretched her back with a grimace. "Time was where the line of the Blessed Saint carried as much weight as the Guardian-King. Shame that it no longer appears to be the case."

Lughus's eyes stormed. "A disparity that I hope to remedy," he said.

"And good luck to you in doing so, my lord," she told him. "You know, you've grown into a bloody great lord since last I saw you."

"You knew me?" he asked, stricken.

"'Twas my sister Mary and her husband Walter who saw you to Andoch," she said. "Crodane was the guide, but you can't trust a man on the open road to mind a babe. In return, Baron Arcis and Lord Rastis set them up with a place of their own in the city. They called it The Book & the—"

"—Barrel," Lughus finished.

Brigid eyed him. His face had gone pale and his brow furrowed with consternation. How often the ghosts of his past life, a life he never really knew, seemed to haunt him. She wondered if he would ever fill in the empty spaces of his own history. *No matter*, she thought, *for we shall write our future together.*

"What is your name?" Brigid asked.

"Molly," she said, "and that's Burt, me husband." The mutton-chopped old man behind the bar gave a nod and Brigid realized that the whole tavern had fallen silent again.

"I'm sorry it's taken so long to meet," Lughus said. "Clearly, I owe you and your family a debt."

Molly shook her head. "We've been rewarded fair enough for what little we've done indeed," she said. "You owe us nothing."

"It's not about debt," Lughus said. "It's about duty. As baron, my purpose is to serve my people."

Molly gave another snort. "Aiden's Flame, were it not for your eyes, I'd wonder if Crodane wasn't your true bloody father."

Lughus gave a forlorn smile.

313

"As such," Molly said, "do you mind me asking how it was they met their ends?"

Lughus exchanged a glance with Brigid. Brigid shrugged. "Regnar fell against a company of bandits far to the south. Sir Geoffrey of Pyle bears the title of the Vanguard now."

Molly nodded. "Regnar was always going on about minding the roads. Kin keep him now." She paused. "And the others?"

"Gareth fell helping me to escape Blackstone," Brigid said. "Without him, I'd be dead."

Molly sighed and shook her head. "Regnar used to tell him his love of the ladies would be the death of him," she said, "though I don't quite think you're what the graybeard had in mind. He was good one, though he might not have seemed it." She turned to Lughus. "And Crodane?"

Lughus bowed his head. "He died returning me to my grandfather. The Hammer ambushed us as we crossed the highlands on the southern border." He paused. "He died saving my life."

"Then he died the way he lived—in service of the House of Galadin," Molly said. "He wouldn't have asked for anything more."

Brigid watched Lughus stare into the depths of his tankard. "I suppose so," he said.

Molly sighed. "Well," she said, "they were good men all and they'll be missed, but at least from the sounds of it, they died well."

"As much as any man might," Brigid said. Lughus remained silent.

"Meal's on the house," she said, adding to Fergus, "and I suppose we're square as well, you mangy heathen. You all are welcome anytime."

"Thank you," Lughus called after her, "But we're happy to pay."

"I don't want you to," she said sternly. "Least not today. When I do, I'll ask it, and when I don't I'll tell you. This is my place." She paused to stoke the fire in the hearth. "My lord."

Beneath the tabletop, Brigid put a hand on Lughus's arm and she felt his tension fade. It was clear that Molly was not a woman to be trifled with, especially in her own domain. "It's a kindness well-intended," she whispered.

"I know, but—"

Brigid smiled. "Let it be."

Lughus's eyes met hers and his expression softened. It warmed her.

In the weeks that followed, throughout the remainder of Moontide, the snows became heavier, the nights longer, and Brigid was happier for it, for all she wished had come to pass and more. By day, she read, she trained, and she hunted with Cass, while her nights were spent playing chess by firelight or blissfully entwined in Lughus's arms. Truly, in spite of the weather, in spite of the war, the winter stood as a welcome respite in a world of darkness and fear.

At least, until the second day of the Month of the Wolf when the eagles arrived. A full dozen of the great birds, circling the sky above the Houndstooth and alighting upon the battlements of the keep. It was an ill omen, for many of the birds bore tethers and bells and other trappings associated with falconry, but had clearly lost their falconer.

"It's a signal," Sir Owain said after the birds had been gathered and settled in Houndstooth's mews. "It's a sign."

Lughus was grim. "Something is wrong at Harrier's Keep," he said. "My grandfather calls for aid."

"And we shall certainly answer," Brigid said, her mind racing with thoughts of Guy Marthaine, Alan, and the Hammer. "I only hope we are not too late."

CHAPTER 28: THE VANGUARD'S RIDE

The day after Geoffrey and Beledain examined the bodies of the dead Wrathorn, the Vanguard set out in pursuit. With him, the Tower had sent two brothers named Yorick and Durnhiem. Both were experienced hunters and trackers of the light cavalry and had known the heaths and moors north of Pridel from childhood. Geoffrey could not tell which of the two men was the elder, for their faces both bore the weary lines and silvery dust of middle age, but they were hale and hearty and used to rough life in the open air. According to Beledain, neither man cared much for superstition nor were they so grounded not to believe in the possibility of the uncanny. Rather, they possessed a certain practical sense of openness that would be necessary for such an unusual errand.

In addition to the two guides, the Tower had also provided Geoffrey with the gift of a horse—a piebald mare by the name of Constance. As her name implied, she was stolid and calm, and while she was not overly spirited, she was in no way sluggish or slow. Again, she seemed a perfect fit for the stalwart Vanguard, and Geoffrey marveled at Beledain's knack for matching horses and men.

While Annabelle was not particularly pleased with Geoffrey's wild hunt, she understood the significance and knew that Geoffrey would not have volunteered unless he knew that it must be done. Queen Marina offered her whole-hearted assurance that in Geoffrey's absence, his family would have her personal protection and want for nothing. This was certainly a comfort, as Geoffrey hated to be parted from them for very long, and he knew that just as Marina appreciated Annabelle, Annabelle too held the young queen in high regard. Greta positively idolized Marina, and while he would never say as much aloud, it was clear that Freddy was somewhat love-struck.

Perhaps it was due to this newfound sense of courtliness and a desire to prove himself that the boy so vehemently insisted that he be permitted to accompany his father on his quest. In spite of the boy's pleading, however, Geoffrey refused.

"This isn't a normal errand, son," Geoffrey told him, standing outside the stables on the morning of his departure. "It's not like hanging around the reserves in a battle. It's...well, it's not like anything I've known before. So much so that I can't even tell you what to expect."

"But Dad," Freddy pleaded. "I'm your squire! I need to go where you go!" He waved his arms in exasperation. "I promise I won't be a bother. I've even got my own horse!"

"Since when do you have your own horse?" Geoffrey asked.

"Queen Marina gave him to me. The one I rode with Sir Briden and the Tower," he said. "She said I sat him so well, he would never accept another rider. I call him Flash on account he's so fast."

"Freddy," Geoffrey sighed. "Son, I can't take you with me. Not this time. I need to make sure that you stay safe."

Freddy's eyes burned, but he held back his tears. "But who's going to make sure *you* stay safe? Lughus and Brigid aren't here. Neither is Adolfo. Who's going to make sure you come back?"

Geoffrey didn't have an answer. "Mind your mother and sister," he said at last. "I love you. Always." He kissed his son on the top of his head, climbed into Constance's saddle, and trotted off after his guides toward the gate.

They began the search a short ways north of Pridel at a small farming village called Fennel. Considering the Keeper was forced to flee on foot and leave both his wagon and his horses behind, Fennel would have been the nearest place wherein he may have been able to procure some other manner of transport.

Yet, while the people of the village were friendly and open enough to Geoffrey's inquiries—particularly after he showed them the notice he carried bearing the mark of both the Tower and the Winter Rose—it appeared that no one knew anything. No one had seen a man in purple robes, nor could anyone recall any horses having been stolen.

"And so there's been nothing out of sorts?" Geoffrey asked. He was addressing a small cluster of men gathered together in the public house that marked the village center. "Nothing strange or unusual going on?"

"Well, I'm not so sure about that," one of the men shrugged. "There's always plenty of unusual happenings in these parts. He took a slow draw on a long-stemmed pipe and allowed the smoke to slowly curl upwards out of his nostrils.

Yorick and Durnheim sighed impatiently, but Geoffrey simply waited. He knew the type. "What do you know, old timer?" he finally asked.

The old man frowned. "Well," he began, "just yesterday, my son—he keeps pigs, mind you—my son's old plow horse—a broken down old thing if there ever was one—just up and died."

"And you say that's unusual?" Geoffrey asked.

"Well, not so much," the old man said. "With the age of the beast, I suppose it was bound to happen sooner or later. Particularly with the times being what they are and all."

Yorick grunted. "We'd best be moving on."

"Hold on, then. Hold on a minute," the old man continued. "Like I said, my son keeps pigs. Times being what they are, well..." he shrugged. "Waste not, want not. He was going to feed the horse to the pigs."

"Better option that than hunting for acorns in the Whitewood," said another man.

"Aye, and risking the ghosts," said a third.

The first old man nodded and took another draw from his pipe. "As it happened, though," he continued, "as my son was going out to feed the pigs yesterday morn, what is it he should find? Well, not the horse, I can tell you that."

"You say the horse was gone? The *dead* horse?"

"So it was."

"Another mystery solved then," the second man laughed. "Old Cole the smithy was all up in arms yesterday claiming someone had been into his forge. Said they left it blazing with his tools all scattered about. Maybe your son's dead horse sought to shoe himself before taking to the road!" He guffawed.

Geoffrey sucked his teeth, remembering the blackened mass that was once the dead Wrathorn's heart. "Thank you," he said to the men, and with an implicit nod to his guides, returned to the hitch outside where they had left their horses.

"That's our friend," Geoffrey told the hunters. "Strange as it might sound." He untied Constance and led her a few paces away. "Seems we're looking for a lone rider. Probably heading north."

"Why north?" Durnheim asked.

"The Talondaire lands are north," he said. "The Keeper—the man we seek—asked after Thom Reaver, who we last left in the company of the young lord."

"Well," Yorick said, "I can't say as I understand much of any of this, but you're the boss.

Durnheim nodded in agreement.

"Let's check the grounds outside of the smithy," Geoffrey said. "Perhaps we may find some manner of trail."

"As you say, sir."

With Geoffrey in the lead, the three men rode the short way to the smith's home and, with his permission, set about examining the fog-shrouded grounds behind his forge. At once, Geoffrey spied the pig pen belonging to the old man's son thirty yards away across the heath. Even to Geoffrey's untrained eye (or perhaps, due to the preternatural senses of the Vanguard) it was clear that something large had been dragged across the ground and out into the center of the uncultivated field. Upon further inspection, Yorick and Durnheim found traces of dried blood and bits of flesh, like the carnage left behind after an animal attack though without the usual shards of bone and rotting carcass. Most curious of all, however, were the hoof prints. Still discernible in the muddy ground, they encircled the entire area.

"Looks like you were right, sir," Durnheim said. He motioned to where a clump of tall grass and reeds had been matted down or broken. "North."

"Can't say I quite understand how a dead horse should walk again, though," Yorick grunted. "But the path is clear enough."

Geoffrey gave a nod. "Well, that is the mystery, isn't it?" he said, gazing off to the horizon. "Either way, we've no choice but to follow."

Yorick held up a hand. "Hold, sir." He remained still, casually placing his hand upon the haft of the hand axe he carried in his belt. "There's someone coming."

Beside him, Durnheim slipped from his saddle and loosened the blade in his scabbard.

Seated atop Constance, Geoffrey stood at the ready. He was expecting it to be the blacksmith, or perhaps the pig farmer, but knew it was better to be cautious, particularly given the unnatural nature of their quarry. For a long moment, he counted his breaths, his hand upon Oakheart, the Acorn slung within easy reach upon his back.

"It's a rider," Yorick whispered.

Geoffrey peered into the mist. The vague outline of the rider was only just discernible. Durnheim drew a short bow from behind his saddle and nocked an arrow.

"Ho there!" Geoffrey called. "Who approaches?"

No reply came. Yorick drew his hand axe.

"I say, who draws near?" Geoffrey called again.

The rider's slight form began to materialize in the fog. Geoffrey drew Oakheart and readied Acorn. Between his legs, Constance gave a snort and whinnied.

At last, the approaching figure spoke.

"Dad?"

Geoffrey's eyes went wide. "What? Freddy?"

With a sheepish grin, Freddy urged his horse forward into the clearing. "Hi Dad," he said. "This is Flash."

"By the Brethren, Freddy! I told you to stay with your mother." Geoffrey and the two hunters stood down and put their weapons away. "Does she even know you rode out here?"

"I left her a note," Freddy said.

"Freddy!" Geoffrey said, "You know your mother doesn't know how to read."

"She's started learning," Freddy said. "Otherwise she'll have someone read it for her."

"That's not the point," Geoffrey said. He rubbed his eyes and felt his limbs twisting up with tension. "Lady's Grace, Freddy. We're on the hunt for a very dangerous person, a person who is already ahead of us. Now I have to waste more time taking you home."

"Or I could just go with you," Freddy said hopefully.

"No," Geoffrey said. "You're going home."

"But..."

"Whatever you decide, sir, we should be off soon," Yorick said. "Every moment we stand here is a moment more this Keeper fellow has to escape."

Geoffrey sighed. "Don't I know it." Freddy gazed up at him, wide-eyed and full of excitement. On the one hand, it filled the former farmer with pride, but on the other hand, he knew the very real pain of losing a child. It was a pain he could not survive a second time.

But if this Keeper is allowed to go about freely, raising the dead to threaten the living, how long before all the world is in danger?

With a great effort, Geoffrey took a deep breath. "Alright, fine," he said. "But at the first sign of fighting—the first *bloody* sign—you and this Flash here ride off in the opposite direction as fast as possible, you hear?"

Freddy's delight lit his features like a second sun, but he fought to contain his joy in the name of maturity. "Of course, Father," he said.

"I mean it," Geoffrey said again. "I tell you to ride, you *ride*."

"Yes, sir."

Geoffrey breathed a sigh and turned to Yorick and Durnheim. "Are these prints clear enough to follow?" he asked.

"Aye, sir." Durnheim said. "It's not been cold enough for the ground to freeze yet leaving the prints quite clear."

"Good. I just need to speak with the blacksmith and we'll be off."

It took only a few moments to engage the smith, paying him to engage a messenger to take word to Pridel that Freddy had indeed found his father. It was a slight delay; however, Geoffrey knew that, in spite of Freddy's note, Annabelle would be beside herself with worry over his disappearance. At least now she would have the peace of mind that they were together.

With that accomplished, the small party set out across the plain following the trail. Strangely (or perhaps *not* so strangely considering the unnatural nature of his steed), the Keeper kept clear of the beaten paths and roads, choosing instead to ride across the plains. With the ground made soft by the transitioning rain and snow, Yorick and Durnheim had a relatively easy time following the signs of their quarry's passage, pointing them out to Geoffrey and Freddy wherever they appeared.

As the sun was setting in the west, they came upon a small hollow along the steep side of a hillock. A leafless beech tree stood sentinel, beneath which they discovered the telltale signs of a campsite.

"Whoever this bloke is that we follow," Durnheim said, "he's no outdoorsman. Didn't even try to cover his fire. Left it here smoldering to burn itself out."

"Lucky he didn't light the tree," Yorick said. "Or worse, attract any of the Plague King's raiders. We're far enough north into Whitemane now that there's always the chance of that."

"Still," Durnheim added, "fair enough place to rest. We can pick up the chase at first light. If'n you're in agreement, sir?"

Geoffrey gave a nod. "I suppose it's no easy thing to follow a trail in the dark," he said. "I only wish there were a way of knowing if we've gained on him any."

"I'd say we have," Yorick mused. "Whatever that nag is he's riding, I don't think it's got much in the way of speed. With any luck, we'll catch up with him soon enough."

Together, the party made camp beneath the shelter of the hollow. They kept the fire burning low and made a meal of oatcakes and dried strips of venison. As they ate, Yorick and Durnheim regaled Freddy with tales of the War of the Horses, exploits of the light cavalry, and past deeds of the Tower."

"Of course," Yorick said, "that was back when he was just Prince Beledain, third son and forgotten heir to King Cedric, the Black Horse of Valendia."

"Aye," Durnheim added, "Back in the days of the Silent Prince."

"Sir Armel told me that in Montevale, all men earn their names," Freddy said. "What did the Tower do to be called that?"

Yorick pursed his lips. "Well, as I heard it, they started calling him that on account of him being so clever. So crafty was he that even with two hundred men, he could come up on the enemy unawares and take them by surprise. Many a band of raiders fell to such a tactic."

"That's true enough," Durnheim mused, "but I heard it different. I heard he's the Silent Prince on account he leads by actions, not by words. Always made sense to me. What other nobleman you ever see stand shoulder to shoulder with the common in the heat of battle, eh? None I ever seen, least not before him."

"Baron Lughus does," Freddy said, "and Brigid." He gave a proud nod. "My dad does too."

Geoffrey shrugged uncomfortably. "Aye, but I'm no nobleman," he said, "and I'm certainly no prince. I will say, though, that it takes a certain type of man to fight alongside his fellows when he just as easily don't have to. The Tower is a good man and I'm proud to have fought at his side."

The brothers nodded. "Here's to that," Yorick said. He took a swig from a small flask and passed it to Geoffrey.

"Aye, and what's this?"

"Forester's Mash," Durnheim said. "Shackle and the other men of Feyhold make it. Stiff stuff and strong. Warms you right quick too."

Geoffrey gave a quick swig and felt his face pucker. It wasn't bad, but it was a far cry from the ale that he was used to. Even Adolfo's wine was not nearly as strong. At once, a fiery warmth spread throughout his limbs. He blew a great breath out through his mouth and let his tongue wag back and forth. Yorick and Durnheim shared a comradely chuckle.

"Packs a punch, don't it?" Durnheim said.

"You weren't joking," Geoffrey grinned.

"Can I try, Dad," Freddy asked.

"No, no. None for you, boy-o," Geoffrey said. "But I believe your mother packed some elderberry cordial in my pack there. We'll share that." He paused, and grinned at the guides, "Just after I take one more nip of this stuff, if that's alright?"

"Of course," Yorick said.

Geoffrey took one final swig and passed the flask on to Durnheim before digging through his pack for the clay bottle. As soon as he found it, he pulled the stopper and passed it to his son. Freddy took it with a smile and together they returned to staring into the depths of the fire.

In spite of the wilderness and the cold and the danger, Geoffrey couldn't prevent a smile of his own. A great swell of affection filled his breast and he reached out to tussle his son's hair. As he watched the boy, a delighted trespasser in the world of grown men, Geoffrey became aware that without realizing it, he had once again fallen into one of those seemingly rare moments where he was not only happy, but that he actually recognized his own happiness and its source.

"Hey," he said to Freddy, "listen." The brothers' conversation devolved into some age-old, good-natured squabbling.

Freddy looked up at him, wide-eyed. "I'm sorry, Dad," the boy said. "I know that you told me not to come."

Geoffrey shrugged. "I'm...not displeased that you did," he said. "In fact..." He breathed a heavy sigh. "I'm...glad to have you along."

Freddy beamed. "You are?"

"Yes," he said. "But when your mother comes to kill you, I'll deny ever having said a word of it."

They shared a laugh. "I can't say this is the life I expected for us back in Pyle," Geoffrey told the boy, "the life I expected for you and your sister, but it is what it is, and it's all we've got. I'm only sorry if it's not as you would have it."

Freddy shrugged. "I don't mind, Dad."

"Do you ever miss it?"

"What?"

"Pyle."

The boy stared into the small fire. "Sometimes," he said. "Sometimes I miss Granddad, and...Karl."

Geoffrey felt his heart turn leaden.

"But most of the time, no," Freddy said. "More often, I'm glad we left, and when I think about Granddad or Karl, it's more I wish they were with us. I wonder if Karl would have become a knight, or if Granddad would like living so near the Cathedral."

Geoffrey gave a silent nod.

"I think Karl would have liked Galadin. Granddad too."

"So..." Geoffrey said after a long moment had passed. "Would you say that you're happy?"

Karl's brown eyes sparkled in the firelight. "Of course, I am. Greta too. And mum." He smiled. "We all are."

Geoffrey nodded.

"What about you?"

"Hmm?" Geoffrey asked.

"Are you happy, Dad?"

Geoffrey gazed up at the sky and out across the plane. "You know something," he pursed his lips. "Sitting here right now with you..." He smiled softly. "Yes," he said, "I am."

Before long, the fire died down, watches were set, and the small party went to sleep.

At sunrise the following morning, they saddled the horses and continued the pursuit. The day was brisk and overcast, but the trail easy enough to follow. As they rode further into Whitemane, they passed teams of farmers hard at work finishing the harvest or preparing their fields for the winter. Geoffrey paused at times to question them regarding the passage of a man in purple robes riding a strange horse, but while they could recall having seen him, few could say more beyond that he was headed north.

"Take care if you're headed that way though," one of the farmers told him. "A few of the towns up that way were hit by the Red Flux. It might still be catching."

Geoffrey's brow furrowed. He gazed at his son and the pair of guides. According to what Lughus said, the strength of the Vanguard would make him more resistant to illness and disease, but the same could not be said for Freddy and the brothers. He massaged his jaw.

"Any knowledge of how it is the plague spreads?" Geoffrey asked.

The farmers shook their heads.

Geoffrey sighed. "Listen here," he said, once they were on their way again. "Should we find a village such as they described, skirt around the outside. I'll ride through and see what remains to be seen."

"Ruined village wouldn't be a bad place for someone to hide out," Durnheim said.

"Aye," Yorick said, "but with plague about, I'm not sure I'd want to stay long. Nor at all, actually."

"And you won't have to," Geoffrey said. "You two simply mind the boy. I'll have a look."

"Aye, sir."

It was but a few hours' ride before the first of the abandoned settlements appeared in sight. With no more than four cottages, it could hardly even qualify as a village, but seemed more like a larger family homestead or multi-family farm. The thatched roofs were collapsed or sunken in multiple places, and the fences and paddocks were falling apart. Apart from the sound of the wind whistling through the open windows and doors, there was no sound. Even the crows and magpies seemed to shun the place.

Leaving Freddy and the brothers behind, Geoffrey rode into the ruin to have a look. He was not surprised to find the village deserted. However, whether it was the flux or something else, he could not tell, for there were no corpses. Not even the skeletal remains of the plague dead could be found inside the homesteads or piled in some mass conflagration.

Regardless, when they made camp that evening, they did so far off from the village, preferring the shadows and the undergrowth of the wilds to the eerie, abandoned village. Even then, Geoffrey slept restlessly. For every sound—from the wind rustling the branches of the trees to the hasty shuffling of a wild animal—set his heart racing. He would lurch upright, Oakheart gripped tightly in his hand, ready to fight to his last breath in defense of his young son.

They resumed the hunt the following morning with a heightened sense of caution. Whether due to lack of sleep, or the Vanguard's preternatural senses, Geoffrey felt even more driven to take care.

The next village they came upon was much the same as the last—empty, abandoned, but hardly a ruin. It was as if the people had simply left, walked off into the wilds, never to return.

The search continued. Over the next few days, they came upon other villages. Most appeared to have recovered in some measure following the touch of the bloody pestilence, though here and there they found the odd farmstead on the outskirts of the cluster of cottages that showed similar signs of abandonment.

After a full week had passed since their departure from Pridel, they emerged from the fields and farms to reach a large singular building situated at the crossroads of two earthen roads. According to Yorick, it was a livery stable that saw to the needs of horsemen traveling throughout the eastern reaches of Montevale. During the War of the Horses, it had survived by remaining neutral, seeing to the needs of both the Valendians and Gasparns. However, while it appeared to have avoided assault from either side, it could not avoid the fickle fortunes of plague. For it too had been abandoned—not only of man, but of horse as well.

As Geoffrey searched the vacant barn and yard, he discovered something else that filled him with concern. It was the faint odor of burning emanating from the farrier's forge. Upon further examination, he could sense a latent heat. At once, he wondered if the other villages had similar signs and if in his haste or caution he had been too careless to notice them. An uneasy feeling settled into his chest as he returned to where Freddy and the hunters awaited him upon a small hillock overlooking the crossroads.

"Abandoned?" Yorick asked.

Geoffrey gave a nod. "Are we at all near to Lord Talondaire's lands?"

"Aye, so we are," Durnheim said. "Dunwald lies but a short ways north. Were the weather any clearer, we might be able to see it."

Geoffrey sat atop his horse gazing at the vacant livery and gathering his thoughts. The Keeper could not be too far ahead of them now, particularly if he had been making stops along the way. Soon enough they would catch up to him. But then what? Capture him? Question him? The man had not seemed amenable to such things when last they met. Besides, what exactly did Geoffrey hope to learn? The man's purpose was clear enough. He wanted Thom. He wanted the Key.

Of course, the Key was long gone. For by now, Theo Nordren would have delivered it safely to Lughus, Brigid, and the other leaders of the Brock. What would the man do once he discovered that it was beyond his reach?

The warmth of the forge filled him with cold dread and he thought back to the relentless assault of the dead Wrathorn and the strange, red-eyed draught horses. If the man had already succeeded in raising a new horse, could he also raise more men, and if so, how many?

"The times we live in..." Geoffrey muttered aloud.

The others eyed him questioningly.

"Do you want to carry on to the Talon's lands then?" Durnheim asked.

Geoffrey thought about it. He had hoped to overtake the man in the wilds or on the trail where any confrontation might avoid drawing unwanted attention or causing harm to innocents. Unfortunately, it seemed that ship had also sailed.

"I suppose it's as good a course as any," he finally said. "Besides, I'm sure there's an inn. May as well have a hot meal while we can."

"Can't say no to that," Yorick grunted. "Let's go then."

It was late in the afternoon by the time they reached the gates of the castle town of Dunwald. As they approached, Geoffrey was reminded of the battle and his conversation with Thom Reaver. He smiled at the memory. Indeed, it was rather quaint. It was a testament to the young lord that—in spite of the many long years of war—he had been able to keep it that way.

A gate guard held up a mailed mitten, halting them at their approach.

"State your names and your business,"

Nearby, another guardsman sat on a wooden stool holding the leash for a stocky war hound. The dog wasn't anywhere near as large as Fergus, but he was heavier built with a shorter snout and smaller ears. It was the kind noblemen used for hunting wild boar, though Geoffrey imagined it could take down a man just as easily.

For all its size and toughness, however, the dog seemed unnerved, agitated. It let out a high-pitched whimper and wagged its stubby tail back and forth in agitation.

"Names and business?" the guard said again.

With the alliance between the Talon and the Tower still contingent upon the mission in Reginal, Geoffrey figured it best not to name himself as anything more than a simple traveler. He offered the man a polite smile.

"Geoffrey's my name," he said. "Those two are Yorick and Durnheim. Over there is my boy, Freddy. We're hunters by trade, but we'd come hoping to find work for the lord. Perhaps as scouts? We've some experience with the woodlands."

The guardsman eyed them carefully. "The lord is away," he said. "Though you might wish to speak with the master-at-arms. You can leave word with the sergeant at the tower house."

Geoffrey gave a nod. "There an inn here?"

"The Dandy Gander," the guard said, "though it may well be full up now. Unusual amount of visitors for this time of year."

"Really?" Geoffrey asked. "What's the occasion?"

The man shrugged. "Whole group of pilgrims just arrived to see the ruined chapel. Monks or the like, all hooded and cowled. Seemed to be those poverty types you hear about from time to time. No shoes or boots. Just bindings of leather and cloth." The man gave a chuckle. "It'll be the fullest the place has been since the old war began."

Geoffrey's stomach tightened and his eyes fell upon the whining hound. The beast wasn't so much agitated, he realized, but frightened.

"This group of pilgrims," he asked the guard, "did they have a leader?"

"Aye," the man said, "Part of the Order, he was. Said he was here to meet another of his type. More and more of them these days what with the alliance with the Guardian-King. Until the recent battle, we had whole scores of kingsmen patrolling the area between here and Pridel. I suppose it only natural the scribes and scholars should follow, so long as they spare us the hierophants..."

Geoffrey gave a nod. "Well, we'll try the Gander anyhow. If they're as you describe them, with any luck the pilgrims will request a stable in place of a room."

"Ha! You never know. The sorry old nags they had with them looked to be in better shape than the people. I just hope whatever they had wasn't catching. They say the flux hit some of the villages south of here."

"We'd heard that," Geoffrey said.

"Aye, well, you know country folk ain't always the most hygienic," the guard said, "though I suppose it ain't easy when you're sleeping beside cows and such, and we all have our own ways of dealing with the winter."

"True enough," Geoffrey said knowingly.

"Ah well. You carry on." The guard cried out and the gates swung open from the inside, allowing the four riders entry. Geoffrey led his small group down the main thoroughfare, past market stalls and store fronts where folk sold fresh bread, meatpies, pretzels, and other baked goods. Yet, in spite of it all, Geoffrey found he had suddenly lost his appetites.

As soon as they were out of earshot of the guards, he slowed to allow the others to catch up to him. "I've a feeling that these 'pilgrims' are not what they seem," he said.

"You think it's our quarry?" Yorick asked.

"And those who follow him," Geoffrey said.

Durnheim sucked his teeth. "And these followers are..."

"I know it's hard to believe, but yes."

The brothers exchanged a glance. "So what would you have us do?" Yorick asked.

"And what about the guard? Should we tell them?" his brother added.

Geoffrey scratched at his beard. "I don't know," he said. "They'll probably think us mad men. Besides, as it stands, the Talon is still an ally of the Plague King. Declaring ourselves openly might create...complications."

"So what do we do?"

Geoffrey's eyes fell upon his son. At length, he breathed a sigh. "You two mind the boy," he said. "If things go badly, get him out of here."

"What are you going to do?" Durnheim asked.

"I'm not exactly sure," Geoffrey told him, "but it falls me to try."

They led their horses the rest of the way to the inn at the sign of the Gander. Geoffrey hitched Constance to the post outside as a young man ran up from the stables to meet him.

"I can take her if ye be staying, sir," he said, rubbing his hands together to stay warm.

"Still deciding," Geoffrey aid. He held out a coin to the young man nonetheless. "Perhaps you can tell me. Has a man in purple robes come through here? He may have had a whole group of others with him. Pilgrims, I believe."

The lad slipped the coin into his pocket. "Aye, sir," the young man said. "Having seen the rest of his folk to the chapel ruin, he's inside having a crock of stew right now." He smiled. "Friend of yours?"

Geoffrey nodded. "Something like that." He offered Yorick and Durnheim one final, implicit nod before stepping past the groom toward the door to the inn.

Inside, Geoffrey found a quiet, dimly lit common room with a roaring hearth, a bar, and several long, rectangular tables. A lone bartender stood examining his stock while a stout woman stirred an iron kettle.

He also found the Keeper seated at the bar, hunched over a pint and a crock of stew.

"Help you?" the bartender said as Geoffrey paced into the room.

"Pint of ale?" he said quietly.

The Keeper did not turn, even when Geoffrey sat down upon a stool just over an arm's length away from him at the bar. A moment later, the bartender set down Geoffrey's pint and returned to his business.

Geoffrey took a swig of his ale. It was a decent brew, though he couldn't help feeling that he had been spoiled by The Ram's Reward. Out of the corner of his eye, he watched in silence as the Keeper finished his meal, still deciding on the best course of action.

At length, the strange man sat up and pushed the empty bowl away from him. "Mediocre at best," he declared. "You would be wise to avoid it, Blackguard."

Geoffrey took another sip of his ale. "So you remember me?"

The Keeper snorted. "I am no fool. I know you are here to kill me."

Geoffrey took a deep breath and stared straight ahead, the Keeper only just visible in his periphery. For the moment, his body appeared calm, but at the first sign of any threat, he would be ready to act. "Not necessarily," Geoffrey said. "I'm no murderer. I simply…wish to understand…"

The man's lips curled into a subtle smile. "Consider me a harbinger," he said. "A warning of what is to come."

"I'm not sure I catch your meaning," Geoffrey replied.

The Keeper folded his hands upon the bar top. "Where is the fat apprentice?" he asked pointedly. "Where is Callah's Key?"

Geoffrey sighed. "Can't say as I know."

"Can't say, or won't say?"

Geoffrey felt a flash of anger. It was the Vanguard. "Both." He slowly rested his hand on the haft of Oakheart. "Who are you people? You Keepers?" he asked. "What exactly is it that you hope to accomplish?"

By way of reply, the Keeper began to chant:

When all the lands of Calendral are bound by Callah's Key,
The Bard shall sing a doleful dirge for Wisdom's unheard plea,
For the Testament unto the Light will seek to snuff the Flame,
When the slumbering Beast of Dibhor wakes, who shall bear the blame?
The Armies of the Dead shall march whilst all the Children weep,
And the Scions of the Brother Dark shall rise from their long sleep,
If the last of Aiden's Blood is spilled to profane the Lady's Grace,
Will any man be left alive to rise up in his place?
So heed the words of Wisdom and mark well the strains of Song,
The Pariah whose heart remains still pure will be welcome erelong,
For all that Guard must take up arms to hold the night at bay,
Else who will rise to bring the Dawn and drive the Dark away?

"That's all very well and good," Geoffrey said, ignoring the odd sensation of familiarity, the notion that the words were already writ upon the annals of his own mind. "But that don't exactly tell me what I want to know."

"Fool!" the Keeper snarled. He leapt from his stool and squared on Geoffrey. "Bumpkin! You and all your ilk shall fall when the Lord of Darkness returns."

"The Lord of Darkness?"

There was a panicked shuffle in the street just outside of the door to the inn. All of a sudden, Freddy and the brothers burst in and slammed the door behind them. "What is happening?" Durnheim asked. Geoffrey's eyes widened at the sight of his son.

The Keeper screamed. "Where is the apprentice? Where is the Key?"

Geoffrey's jaw set. "You won't find it with Thom, I can tell you that."

"Then where is it?" the man growled. "Tell me! Now!"

"No."

"Then die!"

In the blink of an eye, several things happened at once.

The Keeper, his eyes blazing with madness, drew his strange, curved dagger from within his robes and lunged at Geoffrey, seeking to open his belly with one swift strike.

At exactly the same moment, Geoffrey rolled his shoulder to grasp the Acorn shield in his left hand while simultaneously drawing Oakheart with his right. With a hard shove, he used the targe to push the deranged Keeper backwards long enough to secure his footing and turn aside the man's dagger.

Meanwhile, heavy pounding echoed through the common room as if an angry mob were attacking the wooden door to the inn in a desperate attempt to enter. The innkeeper and the barmaid cowered behind the bar as Durnheim braced himself against the door. Yorick drew his hand axe and Freddy readied his dagger and buckler.

"Lady save us!" Geoffrey cried.

"That bitch can't help you now!" the Keeper snapped. Again, he lunged at Geoffrey, but again the Vanguard was too quick. He sidestepped the attack and raised the Acorn defensively.

Somewhere outside the inn, a woman shrieked in terror. Yorick waved at Freddy and together the two of them began sliding benches and stools over to Durnheim as a means of barricading the door. In answer, the window shutters began to flutter and shake until finally there was the sound of splintering and one of the windows finally burst. At once, a pair of wretched looking figures clad in hooded cloaks and rags began jostling one another to be the first to enter.

Wasting no time, Freddy hurried forth as they were grappling with one another and began stabbing at the dried, stringy flesh of the foremost creature's leg. It made no sound at the repeated entry of the blade nor did any blood flow in answer.

"Freddy! Get back!" Geoffrey cried as the wretched figure swatted at the boy with primal savagery.

He made to rush to his son's side, but the Keeper pressed his attack, swatting savagely with his curved blade. Geoffrey easily deflected the attack with his shield and countered with Oakheart. The sickening snap of shattering bone resounded through the chaotic din and the Keeper cried out in pain, clutching his wrist in pain and fury.

Geoffrey did not pause to celebrate. He hurried to Freddy's side. With a swift strike, he crushed the skull of the lead figure. As it fell to the ground, its hood drew back revealing—to his horror, if not his surprise—the fading red eyes of a dead man.

"Get back!" Geoffrey yelled again. Freddy followed his father's command without hesitation, freeing the farmer to return to his former opponent.

Nursing his broken wrist, the Keeper scurried behind the bar and with his good hand, grabbed hold of the cowering bartender's shoulder. With a horrific squeal, the man froze and Geoffrey turned just in time to see the bartender's face turn ashen. His pallor took on that of those afflicted with a terrible plague, his eyes rolled back into his head, and weeping sores appeared in patches upon his bare skin. A cry of great pain escaped him and he writhed in agony as his right arm—the same appendage that now hung uselessly at the Keeper's side—snapped audibly like a dry twig.

At the sight of Geoffrey's horror, the Keeper laughed aloud and released the limp body allowing it to flop lifelessly to the floor. As his cackling laughter raised in pitch and volume, he lifted his own broken limb before him. By some dark power, it had healed, returned in an instant to full vigor.

A second window splintered beneath the onslaught of the dead mob and at once, they too began to jostle for entry. Yorick cut the nearest down with his hand axe while Durnheim attempted to use an overturned table to hold back an additional three. Geoffrey felt his muscles surge with desperate energy as he readied to renew his battle with the Keeper.

"Come, Blackguard," the wretched man said, retrieving his blade from the floor. "I will send you as a sacrifice to my Lord Dibhor and then—*then*—I will see to the boy!"

"You will see to *nothing!*" Geoffrey shouted in a voice of cold command. "For I am the Vanguard, one of the Three, and by my blood and by my will, I will right what evil wrongs!"

He charged.

The Keeper nimbly sidestepped, swiping with the curved blade as Geoffrey passed, but the holy oak shield easily deflected the attack. Geoffrey pivoted on the ball of his foot to regain his stance, and with a whirl of his wrist, raised Oakheart. He brought the cudgel down with the force of an avalanche, but again the Keeper narrowly dodged.

"Dad! Behind you!" Freddy shouted.

Geoffrey whirled back around just in time to see two more dead lunge for him, their gnarled hands, twisted into blunt fists, found only empty air. Geoffrey stepped back, then leapt forward, knocking them back with the Acorn before crushing the nearest man's skull with his club. He was vaguely aware of Yorick and Durnheim fighting across the room, but in the frenzy of battle, he could not see them.

With a swift backhand, he crushed the skull of the second dead man, and turned back to the Keeper. The man's strange, pallid eyes glared at him with madness. The pupils constricted to tiny slivers in milky, white orbs. It was the face of evil.

Once more, Geoffrey charged, raining down blows with Oakheart again and again in a punishing onslaught. Like a viper, the Keeper darted back and forth with preternatural speed, smiling maddeningly, hissing and snapping like a wild beast. It was as if some strange change had come over him, that by stealing the poor bartender's life force, he had become somehow faster, stronger. More savage.

Too late Geoffrey realized that while his opponent continued to dodge and weave as if to avoid his attacks, the man was in fact leading him, maneuvering him around the room until Freddy was just beyond arm's reach. Geoffrey's heart froze in his chest and his blood turned to ice at the sudden realization. With a malicious grin, the Keeper made his move.

In an instant, Geoffrey's mind shattered with visions of Karl's funeral, the stone marker of his grave, and his cold, dead corpse. Despair and sorrow tore at him, a pain worse than any physical wound. He knew that he could not endure such a thing again, that his heart would break beyond repair, and with it, his soul. From the depths of his being, he cried out.

"No!"

Time slowed to crawl. The Keeper's blade lashed out, ready to tear into his son's soft flesh. Freddy's eyes went wide with sudden terror and he raised his arm defensively. The Keeper's wicked grin gleamed. Geoffrey's heart was in his throat.

Despite the din of the ongoing battle and the thundering of his own pulse, a single, solitary whisper resonated in Geoffrey's ears. It was the sound of metal on metal. It was the sound of the Keeper's blade turned aside by Freddy's buckler. It was a technique Geoffrey had seen him practice with Lughus a hundred times. Ever since the day he'd bought him the damn thing from the Dwerin armorer. The boy had practiced it until it had become reflex.

Time returned to normal. Freddy dove out of harm's away, and when the Keeper turned around in pursuit, Geoffrey fell upon him with the force of a falling oak. With all of his might, he drove the edge of the targe into the Keeper's face, shattering his teeth in an explosion of blood and bone. A gurgling sound escaped him, punctuated by grunts and groans, but Geoffrey was relentless, and as the Keeper's body reeled backwards, the Vanguard stuck out again and again and again with Oakheart.

Over and over and over, the cudgel landed blow after blow, shattering bone and sinew like so much kindling. Again and again, he hammered the Keeper, long past the point where the man's life had fled.

So blinded was he by righteous fury, so full of desperate rage at the prospect of losing another so, that he failed to notice the arrival of the town guard and their ensuing battle with the remaining dead.

When at long last the battle was over, Geoffrey stood above the pulpy remains of his red work and cried out. "Freddy? Freddy, where are you, son?"

"Just here, Dad," the boy said, appearing at his side.

With a great heaving breath, Geoffrey reached out and pulled the boy into a tight embrace. He wanted to speak, wanted to say something, but all words escaped him.

CHAPTER 29: BALANCE & DISCORD

Ill news has arrived in the form of a message from my brother. It seems that this most recent escalation of the conflict between the Galadins and the Marthaines has threatened to plunge the entire Brock into civil war. With the other realms across Termain consumed with the potential threat of attack from the Kordish Empire to the south, internal conflict among the barons could tear the heart out of any attempt to defend ourselves. The War of the Horses provides more than enough civil strife as it is. Surely, the continent could not survive any more.

Perhaps as a result, it is with great reluctance that my brother, the Lord-Baron, has determined to resolve the conflict once and for all through the marriage of Luinelen Galadin to Gaston Marthaine.

Needless to say, Arcis is not pleased. He absolutely doted upon Luinelen and, as I understand it, her maidenhood is the result of a father's gift of choice to his daughter. I cannot imagine Roland is very happy either, though from what little I know of his character, he is sure to welcome a new daughter with open arms—even one of the bloodline of his enemy. Despite the generations of hatred, both men hold fast to rare, if antiquated, codes of honor.

Gaston is perhaps the greatest mystery, for in an effort to spite his enemies, Roland did not employ a tutor from my tower, but chose instead a Keeper of Castone. Fortunately, the placement did not last long, but considering what Sigmund has suggested regarding the nature of the Lighthouse Keepers, I hold lingering concerns…

I find myself beset with many doubts and questions of late. The worsening hostilities between the Termainian realms and the Empire of Kord have sparked some debate over the necessity of establishing a Third Protectorate. While Valder is resistant to such calls, for now, the Hierophant and the Chancellor continue to encourage him…

I fear that to establish a single, autocratic leader is to invite the danger of The Bard's Heresy. I would be lying were I not to admit that the dread prophesy has been a constant subject of my thoughts these many weeks, and it has been far too long since I have last had any correspondence with Sigmund. As such, I have resolved to send him a message via the Wrathorn mercenary who delivered the message from my brother.

I only hope that Hobart proves as resourceful as he seems. It would not do for any to know the Loremaster consorts with Blackguards…

For two days, Royne confined himself to his cell, angry and bitter over the incident at the gates and the alchemists' subsequent and disappointing response.

He—at least—would fight. He was not certain as to how, but he knew that he could not sit idly by while the viceroy continued to murder innocent people for what seemed so tawdry a purpose.

Of course, *how* exactly he would fight remained a mystery, for it had been well established that he was no warrior, nor did he feel that had he learned enough alchemy to create substances or incendiaries that posed any true threat. About the only practical device he had been able to manufacture with any ease were smoke bombs, and those he only discovered by mistake when another experiment went awry. He knew of nothing that could serve any actual martial purpose, nor was he any closer to manifesting any form of metaphysical alchemy beyond the healing ability granted to him through the Gift. What he wouldn't give to be able to spit fire or call thunder or any other nonsense he didn't actually believe in.

And yet, he must fight. He must. It was his duty as the Loremaster, as a true Guardian, to stand against the darkness and to usher in the light.

But how?

He sat upon his bed, his head in his hands, contemplating scenario after scenario. He could not defeat the Guardians in the field—of course not, for he was certainly no Navarro. But the viceroy himself? Could he somehow confound Pryce's efforts to tyrannize the public? Put a stop to the executions? Or at the very least, prevail upon him to spare the children?

"Dibhor take the wretched fiend!" he shouted and rose suddenly to his feet. He grabbed a glass vial from where it lay idly upon his desk and chucked it at the back of the door, smashing it to pieces.

As he returned to the edge of the bed, breathing hard, his brow creased in impotent rage. A moment later, a light knock sounded upon the door, but before he could answer, Amara let herself in.

"So I sense that you are still upset," she said.

"I'm fine," he said sullenly. "I've just been thinking."

"Ah yes. Thinking." Amara looked away from the shattered bits of glass upon the floor and sat down beside him on the bed. "So, Polecat, in the two days that you have been in confinement here, what mysteries have you managed to unravel?"

Royne sighed. "Nothing of consequence."

"I see," she gave a slow nod. "Well, if you are interested, I have had several ideas, many of them involving you."

"Wonderful," he grimaced. "And I imagine they're perfectly designed to make me feel even more inadequate." He sighed. "I believe I will pass. I do a fine enough job of creating my own suffering. I do not need anyone afflicting me with more."

Amara eyed him impatiently, refusing to acknowledge his wretched self-loathing. "Actually," she said mildly, "I have been contemplating your abilities in an effort to understand what other feats you might be capable of. However, if you feel that such endeavors are a waste of time and would prefer to wallow in...whatever you call this...then I will leave you be."

She made to stand, but he called her back.

"Wait."

"Yes?"

"I'm...sorry," he said, an irrational flash of pleasure to be occupying so much of her mind. "I do not mean to be...rude." He tried to shake off his crust of annoyance. "I...thank you, I suppose."

She returned to her seat and turned to face him. "Would you like to hear my ideas?"

He nodded, though her close proximity set his skin prickling. "Please," he said at last, "tell me."

She waited while he shifted his weight to face her. "As you know, alchemy is understood through the relationships between the four elements—fire, water, earth, and air. However, between all of them—that is, when they are all four in either prefect balance or in fundamental discord—we may find life and also death. You, my friend, for whatever reason, seem to possess the ability to give life, though in doing so, you risk death."

"In the Order," Royne told her, "the ability to heal in this manner is known as the Gift of the Guardians, for in the old days of the Order, just after Wrogan's defeat, the Guardians existed as a form of...shall we call them knights-errant, who traveled about fighting injustice and defending the poor and weak."

He sighed. "Personally, I never put much faith in the old myths and legends. I figured they were just stories told to give the common folk false hope, encouraging the Order's dominion by perpetuating morality tales about its most heroic figures. Now..."

He shut his eyes as if bracing himself.

"Now...I am uncertain. I have seen things, *done* things that I cannot explain. I pride myself on my rationality, my search for truth through reason and reality. To suddenly admit to myself that there might be forces beyond my understanding, forces that appear to defy those truths I hold so dear, to have to accept the existence of bloody *magic*..." He shook his head. "I just don't think I can do it."

"Just because you have not yet found a rational explanation, a reasonable cause, does not mean that there is not one," Amara told him. "Perhaps it means exactly what it seems—you simply do not know it yet."

"But..." his brow furrowed. "I have a hard time believing that some things are beyond my understanding. I have always believed that with the right focus and with enough time, I can learn anything. I can *understand* anything."

"Perhaps a demonstration then," Amara said. She gave a determined nod and without warning, turned to him and kissed him softly on the lips.

Royne's mind froze and for a moment he wondered if his heart had stopped. A warmth unlike any he had ever known spread through him and he found himself arrested by the strange intermingling of what seemed simultaneously a physical, emotional, and even spiritual sensation. When at last, he could finally speak, he turned to Amara, noting the hint of a smile that played upon those indefinably soft lips.

"W-w-what was that?" he stammered, touching his fingertips to his own lips. In a fleeting moment of irrationality, he was suddenly terrified that in the absence of her lips, the memory of the sensation would forever fade away.

"What," he said again, "was that?"

Amara's gaze narrowed in a feline smirk. "Magic," she said.

"Magic?" Royne repeated. "*Magic?*"

She pursed her lips. "Or perhaps it's simply a suggestion of something that you do not yet understand."

"Perhaps..." he said softly. "Perhaps you are right."

She smiled. "Or perhaps further study is necessary?"

"I...I think perhaps you're right," Royne said, his voice just above a whisper. "If you'll permit me."

Amara chuckled and, taking his hand, pulled him closer and kissed him again.

The experiment was repeated three times more before, breathless yet alert, Royne took her hands in his.

"You must finish telling me your idea," he said.

Amara leapt from the edge of the bed and retrieved the box she had brought with her. Inside, there were indeed two small potted plants. Ferns of some kind by the look of them. Then, she retrieved a third pot. In this one, the poor plant had wilted and seemed so dry as to stand upon the brink of death.

"My thinking," she said, "is that your ability, your mastery, operates in accordance with a certain ebb and flow. You see, when you healed me, the burn was not eliminated, but transferred to you."

"So it was, though it's healed now," Royne said, revealing his unmarred arm, "but you're right. It did. That's how the Gift appears to work. The Guardian bears the suffering for those who might otherwise be destroyed by it—or so the legends say."

"But could the opposite also be true? For example, if you were wounded, could you push the wounds onto an enemy or somehow draw upon their energy to heal yourself? In another instance, say you were not wounded, could you still siphon the life force one thing to empower yourself only to release it in a different elemental form? Could you manifest the energy in a manner that distorts the physical nature of a thing, or perhaps enervates the mind of an opponent?"

Royne considered it. Having only recently been willing to even accept the notion of something so oddly miraculous, he had taken no time to bother to consider any of this himself. "I don't know," he said. "I suppose I could try. However, such things seem born from discord, and was it not you who cautioned me against such things? Was it not you who swore to do whatever you could to stop me should I find myself following that path?"

Amara sighed and she folded her arms across her chest. "That is what I said," she told him, looking away. "However, that was...before. Before I beheld the evidence of such injustice with my own eyes."

Royne grimaced. "While I would welcome your assistance," he said, "I do not wish you to compromise your principles."

"I...I still have concerns," she said. "But...I also understand the threat to the larger world." She looked away. "Since Grantis fell, it is as if the entire realm has been broken, wounded. Now, this viceroy appears like a boil, an infection, that threatens the wellbeing of the entire body." She paused. "I am beginning to understand that—perhaps to save the rest of the body—the boil must be lanced."

"I am not a warrior. I abhor violence and cruelty in every manner and to every degree," Amara continued. "But I remember that day upon the parapet when we saw those men executed, and I see...I see Fabius's death still in my dreams..." Her voice fell to a whisper. "It haunts me, and I have no wish to see any others suffer, especially this family who have already suffered so much."

"So what are you saying?" Royne asked.

For a long moment, she was silent until at last, she took a deep, bracing breath. "The viceroy cannot be allowed to harm innocent people beneath a facade of legitimacy," she said. "Such actions are evil, and while I do not wish to kill him, should he persists in this course of action, I will have no choice but to do what must be done."

CHAPTER 30: A GREAT HONOR

With each passing day, rumors of Lord Talondaire's anticipated elevation to wardenship grew and grew. Of course, as was the case with such things, the more widespread the rumor, the less it was acknowledged by the parties involved. So, while the young lord was to be found almost continuously at the king's side as part of his noble retinue, the promotion was never mentioned or discussed and the rumors were not even slightly acknowledged publically.

In the meantime, while Talondaire fulfilled his social obligations at the king's side, Thom and Sparrow were free to continue their clandestine endeavors, aided now by Lady Valerie.

Val was a formidable woman. Strong, determined, capable. By the time Thom had managed to casually run into her the next day, she had succeeded in making contact with Lord Talondaire's mother and sister while also managing to procure an entire wardrobe full of woven sheets and blankets. When spliced together, Val believed the bedding could form a strong enough rope to ease their descent down the garderobe's sloping chute.

It was also determined, based on Val's recommendation, that Sparrow be the one to remain behind to assist in the escape. Her status as a maid would be less scandalous were she to be discovered scurrying around the ladies' quarters than a young scribe like Thom.

To his own surprise, Thom found he was bothered by this. While he did not doubt Sparrow's capabilities, he was determined that the mission would be a success and he felt personally committed to seeing it through. Furthermore, he did not like the idea that Sparrow, Val, and the others should be at risk without his being there to defend them. Not because they were women, not at all. They were his comrades, and because they were his comrades, if something about the plan were to go wrong, he wanted to be there to stand with them in the ensuing fight.

It was a strange though not unwelcome realization. For it was a stark reminder that he was no longer the coward that he had been for most of his youth. He had seen battle. He had killed. In short, he had grown.

Almost a man now, Crusher! Magnus's laughter echoed in the recesses of his mind. *Now all you need is a beard, a bottle, and a willing woman! Ha!*

Thom reddened. "Shut it, Magnus," he muttered aloud, unconsciously rubbing at his gingery stubble. "A willing woman indeed! What nonsense!"

"What do you need a willing woman for?" Sparrow asked.

Thom's stomach clenched and his blush deepened. "Um, What?" he sputtered.

"You said you needed a willing woman?" A slight smirk played upon her lips. "What for?"

Thom's mind suddenly went blank. He was sitting in the great hall, minding his own business, awaiting such a time as he was called upon by Lord Talondaire. Before him on the tabletop was his old journal, an inkwell, and a quill. His thinking had been that in order to keep up appearances, he might as well play the part right. He watched as the castle folk came and went on one errand or another. For the most part, they paid him no mind, writing him off as "one of those bookish scribblers of the Order." He couldn't help but find it somewhat funny that he had actually become something more.

But then stupid Magnus with his blasted comments made him go and say something stupid and now here was Sparrow looking at him like he had gone insane.

"Um," he said foolishly. His eyes glanced around the hall in a desperate attempt to avoid hers. "Just...um. I was just thinking."

"Really?" she asked. "What about?"

Thom took a deep breath.

"Sometimes I talk to myself," he said at last.

Sparrow pursed her lips. "You shouldn't do that, you know?" she said. "People might think you've gone mad."

"Sometimes I think I might be," he said.

Sparrow gave a snort.

Thom's eyes fell to his journal. He suddenly felt very warm.

Sparrow smiled and held out a hand. "Come with me."

Thom began shuffling his things together. "Where are we going?" he asked, taking her hand.

Sparrow grinned, but said nothing, leading him away from the great hall to a narrow staircase and down to another long, dimly lit corridor. At the midway point, she paused at a small door, opened it, ushered Thom inside. It was a tiny storeroom no larger than a monk's cell. An empty wine barrel stood upright in one corner and a large wooden crate sat against the far wall. Otherwise, the room was empty.

"What are we doing here?" Thom asked.

"Quiet!" Sparrow whispered sharply. She took Thom's journal and ink from his hands and set them atop the wine barrel.

Thom felt his heart beat quicken. "Did you...did you need help moving something?"

The young woman smiled and shook her head. "Don't be so daft."

"I don't think I understand," he eyed her curiously. "What is happening?"

Sparrow ushered him backwards to lean against the wooden crate, then gently took his hands and pressed them to her chest. "I'm giving you your 'willing woman.'"

Thom's breath caught in his throat as his fingertips grazed the tender flesh beneath Sparrow's tunic. His heart hammered against the wall of his chest and he felt his entire body flood with warmth as Sparrow let out a breathy moan and pressed her lips to his.

For a moment he was nervous, not certain how to go about it, but whether through instinct or nature or something else entirely, his body already seemed to know.

"Fire and blood, I've wanted this," she said when they paused for air.

Thom was shocked. His lengthy sojourn with Magnus through the brothels and ale houses of the Sorgund Isles had left very little to Thom's imagination in regards to the activities that occurred behind closed doors. While he had never partaken in such things himself, he had unintentionally observed, or perhaps more accurately, been subjected to witness just about any act one could imagine.

Yet, now—here—he was surprised to find himself so compelled. Not only that, but he was even more surprised to find himself the object for compulsion for another. Short, fat, and forever fearful, he was more a target of ridicule than desire. He knew he must have grown somewhat over the past two years, and in the near-starvation he had experienced following Magnus's passing, perhaps he had thinned out somewhat. He was still big, but there was a solidness to him that decried his former flab. A layer of muscle that hit beneath the layer of padding. Perhaps he was a man grown after all.

And here was this young woman pressed against him, her breath coming in rasping gasps, speaking of want. Genuine want.

Not only that, but he wanted her too. Not simply for her body—Aiden's Flame! He'd seen naked women enough to last a lifetime in the Isles—but because she was his friend, his companion. They shared an intimacy and concern for each other that went beyond merely the base joining of flesh. Perhaps that, that was it. That was what drove him suddenly mad with excitement.

Sparrow bent and kissed him again, and this time, he noticed her hands, pulling at the hem of her skirt, lifting it up around her waist. He tentatively raised his hands up beneath it, resting them on her hips. She clambered up onto his lap and kissed him with renewed fervor while her other hand began to paw gently as his habit. She pulled her lips away from his to catch her breath, and when he opened his eyes, he saw her smiling. At once it filled him with anticipation and concern.

"Listen," he said, "I am...shall we say...ignorant of this."

"I know, Thommy," she smirked. "It's not hard to tell."

"Just thought you should know so as to...not disappoint."

She eyed him thoughtfully. "Just relax, mate, and let me."

Thom did as she told him, steadying his breathing while she assumed control. Half-formed thoughts and feelings swirled within his mind, cast out by the pure sensation of the moment. His entire body came alive with sensation and for sometime afterwards, he forgot all about Towers and Talons and missions. There was only bliss.

When at last, the moment passed and reality returned, they separated with a pleasant affection. Thom gathered his book and his quills, and they made their way back out to the dim corridor.

"I should find Lord Talondaire," Thom said at last, breaking the companionable silence. "Find out if he's had any word yet from the king."

"I think I saw him back in his quarters," Sparrow said as they began to pace slowly alongside one another, "just before I happened upon you." She gave a snort. "Happened upon you in the hall that is. "

Thom reddened. "That was...very nice," he said bashfully. "I...I would like...perhaps some time we might..."

Sparrow eyed him with amusement. "I think we can manage that," she said, punching his arm. "Now get on with you, Reaver. Go and find his lordship. I'm off to find Val."

As it turned out, Lord Talondaire was still in his quarters with Sir Lloyd and his men when Thom found him. The young lord was pacing back and forth in agitation. When his eyes fell on Thom, his gaze narrowed and his lip curled.

"Where in the bloody Abyss have you been?" he snapped. "I have need of you."

Thom felt a flash of resentment, but he choked it down. "What is it you require of me?" he asked.

"King Dermont requests our presence in the solar. He has called a meeting to formulate a plan to strike back as the Tower as he continues to ravage Whitemane."

"I see," Thom said.

"I would like you to attend in order to record the minutes of the meeting," Talondaire said.

"Of course, sir," Thom muttered.

"Then let us go now. If you think a lord grows easily impatient, wait until you meet a king."

With the young lord in the lead, Thom followed the members of Talondaire's retinue as they made their way to the solar. To his surprise, the hallway outside of the chamber was clogged with other soldiers. Armed men bore the devices of various lords he didn't recognize stood beside a squad of red-cloaked kingsmen sworn to the Warlord. For a brief moment, he felt a dagger of anxiety, convinced that somehow their deception had been revealed; however, when Talondaire continued to pace forward, unbothered, to the king's chamber, he realized the foolishness of such a worry and fought to keep himself calm.

At the threshold into the room, King Dermont called out to them from across the room at his seat at the head of the table. "Ah, there we are! Lord Tally!" he grinned. "Or perhaps we should call you Lord Tardy!"

"My apologies, your majesty," Lord Talondaire said. "My scribe needed a moment to prepare materials for recording the minutes."

King Dermont smiled, but Thom was aware of a subtle menace behind that smile. "No matter," he said. "You're here now and that is what counts— so long as you do not repeat the error on the battlefield."

"Never, my lord," Talondaire said, assuming the vacant seat opposite the king. Thom stood just behind him, his journal, ink, and quill at the ready. As he once again fell back into his role as the bumbling scribbler—a part he found easy to play—he glanced casually at the men seated around the table. King Dermont, of course, sat at the head opposite the Talon at the foot, with two other men seated along each side in between. Of these four, three were completely unknown to him, but the fourth man, seated at the Talon's right, was someone he could have recognized in his sleep. It was none other than the Warlord, Dandon Rood.

"I'll take you at your word then," King Dermont said. "For as the new Warden of Whitemane, I will tolerate nothing less."

The men seated at the table raised their eyebrows and the guards and valets standing behind them uttered soft remarks of congratulations. Lord Talondaire bowed his head graciously. "Truly, my king, you do me too much honor," he said.

"A fault of mine for certain." He grinned. "But one from which you may all benefit."

Polite applause again broke out and the king graciously inclined his head.

"Now," Dermont said, "let us speak of our unified purpose—the destruction of my brother and the whore he calls his queen."

Snap!

Thom fought to keep his face an impassive mask, but inwardly he was torn suddenly between great embarrassment and greater rage. All eyes were upon him and the nib of his broken quill.

"A thousand apologies, your majesty," he muttered sheepishly. "Old quill. Won't happen again."

King Dermont diverted his gaze from him as if he were nothing, and continued his remarks.

"While certainly an auspicious occasion, Lord Talondaire is here in Reginal not to accept his new title—in truth that was a surprise I graciously sprang upon him—rather, he has come seeking aid. For while it pains me to admit it, my brother was recently able to defeat the force of kingsmen stationed on Tally's lands leaving only Dunwald's small household guard to defend them. You see, it seems since the untimely defeat of our dear Vilnois, Beledain has ambitiously thought to add Whitemane to his dominion. It is my intention to resume control and restore legitimate rule."

King Dermont snapped his fingers. At once, a steward hurried over to the table and rolled out a large map. From his vantage point, Thom could clearly make out the regional names, major cities, and geographical features of Montevale.

"As you all know, the majority of our forces are encamped here at Reginal, to defend our seat of power, and here, just outside of the Nivanus Pass to assist King Kredor as he prepares for his assault upon the Brock." The king indicated the positions with his finger. "I have recently been informed that the day of reckoning is nearly at hand. However, in order to ensure that we can provide the King with our full support, we must first settle the matter of this foolish uprising. As such, here is what I propose."

He motioned to the pair of noblemen seated to Lord Talondaire's left. The first was a man in his early forties with a pasty complexion and a thin, black mustache. Upon his yellow surcoat, he bore the emblem of a brown tern. The second man was younger and bore the bearing of a man to whom social class had provided little in the way of adversity. A strutting rooster was emblazoned upon his tabard and while Thom had never seen him before, he immediately recognized him as Sir Gurney.

"Warlord Rood will lead the majority of the forces encamped here at Reginal southward. At the same time, Sir Gurney will lead one half of the forces encamped at the Nivanus Pass eastward toward Whitemane. Lord Talondaire, meanwhile, will return to his lands so as to rally his forces and those of the other lords of the region. Once the armies rendezvous, you will attempt to force my brother's army to take the field, or—should he flee—lay siege to the city of Pridel and force the queen to her knees." He paused. "Figuratively, of course. I shall have the honor of doing so literally."

Thom felt a fire burn in his belly, but, like Lord Talondaire, he kept his expression impassive. Warlord Rood gave an involuntarily frown of disapproval, but he held his tongue.

"The other half of the Nivanus forces will remain in reserve under the command of Lord Pronet to await King Kredor's orders. Then, once this rebellion nonsense is resolved Gurney and Warlord Rood will return to the Nivanus to rejoin the Guardian-King."

Dermont paused and held out a placating hand to the Talon. "While your new role as warden obviously grants you rights to Vilnois's castle at Whitemane, I would ask that you do not take possession until *after* this situation has been dealt with. Whitemane is a mighty fortress and Beledain will be too cowardly to attempt a siege. If we seek to draw him out, Dunwald is a much more tempting—and less risky—target." He shrugged. "However, defeat my brother and the castle is yours."

The Montevalen noblemen observed the plan in approving silence, particularly Sir Gurney who seemed quite excited by the prospect of such a major command. From what Thom had heard, Beledain had been rather successful at cutting off the heads of Dermont's hydra of sycophants. Perhaps Gurney recognized the opportunity for what it was—an invitation to join the king's inner circle.

Only the Warlord seemed hesitant. He leaned forward onto his fist and stared pensively at the map. Thom watched him out of the corner of his eye. He could sense deep within him a subtle familiarity that went beyond the reality of their past acquaintance (which was clearly not significant enough for the Warlord to recognize him now). It was the same sensation he had felt upon meeting both the Tower and Sir Geoffrey, though not quite as strong.

Regardless, he could not help but sense in the old warrior an undercurrent of...sadness? Shame?

At length, King Dermont brought the meeting to a close, releasing his captains to make their preparations. Together, the men stood, shook hands, and made encouraging remarks regarding the king's plan. Thom finished scribbling down the minutes and carefully removed the sheaf of parchment from his journal. Beside him, Rood's valet limped over to his side carrying the Warlord's mighty great sword. For the briefest of moments, Thom felt the

Warlord's eye upon him, a vague spark of recognition glimmered in the depths of his eyes, though not enough for him to comment.

Instead, the old warrior turned to the Talon. "I've had the opportunity to get to know your mother these past weeks," he said. "She is a fine woman. I regret never having had the opportunity to meet your father as well."

"Thank you, sir," the Talon said. "I only hope to follow in his footsteps."

The Warlord gave a nod. "I understand you were there when Sir Marcus Harding fell?"

Lord Talondaire cast his glance over at the king and the other noblemen as they shared a laugh at some private joke. "I was," he said quickly. "Sir Marcus was a man of great honor."

"And a man of great wisdom as well," Rood said, "which is why I wonder what it was that led him to pass on his title to this Silent Prince? I hear such conflicting reports regarding the man's character..."

Talondaire's face remained impassive. "You knew Sir Marcus better than I," he said quietly. "I imagine that reflecting upon the nature of one man may provide some insight into the nature of the other."

"I see," the Warlord said.

"Lord Tally," King Dermont called out. "Hold for a moment longer, if you would. There is another matter that I would like to discuss with you."

"Of course, your majesty." Talondaire bowed.

Warlord Rood shook the Talon's hand one final time and nodded to his valet. "Thank you, my lord," he said. "May we safely meet again when the battle is won."

"Yes, sir," Talondaire said.

Rood offered Thom one final, silent glance, and without another word, departed the solar with his valet in tow.

Giles Pronet too made his exit, though Sir Gurney and the other man (who Thom surmised to be the king's new seneschal, Vaston Delon) resumed their seats at the table. Understanding the action as a nonverbal cue, Lord Talondaire returned to his seat as well. Thom could already sense a great, buzzing anxiety emanating from the young nobleman, but it remained hidden beneath a shroud of aristocratic arrogance.

When Pronet, the Warlord, and their retinues had departed from the hall, King Dermont waved his hand and a steward indicated to Thom that he was to resume the minutes.

"It has been quite the auspicious day for you, my lord," King Dermont said, "in no small part, thanks to me."

"I am unworthy of such lavishness," Lord Talondaire said. "I only hope to return the honor with my service."

The king exchanged a meaningful glance with the men seated at his sides. "Funny that you should mention service," he said. "For there *is* actually a simple service that I require, and while—as king—I may simply demand it, I am no tyrant. Rather, I shall instead request it of you by way of courtesy."

"How might I better serve, your majesty?" the Talon asked.

At the king's right hand, Vaston Delon cleared his throat. "Since his majesty's great victory in the War of the Horses, we have been quite pleased to find that the majority of the noble houses of Gasparn have been extremely supportive. Some, like Lord Pronet for example, have been invaluable in their public support of King Dermont, encouraging others of their social rank to join with him. Then, there are those like yourself who has the potential to demonstrate their loyalty on the field of battle."

"Then," Delon continued, "there have been those like Sir Gurney here who has been extremely helpful in rooting out corruption and deceit— particularly since the murder of the late Lord Canton. It was Gurney, for example, who helped us to root out the traitorous members of the Tower's Guard when they sought to disturb the peace. Linton Travers, Cardolan, and others. As they approached him for aid, he did his duty and reported it."

Lord Talondaire's face remained stoic. "I see."

"Now," Delon said, "we seek to consolidate this loyalty by binding those who have done such great service to us beneath one banner."

"With your consent," King Dermont resumed, "I have decided to marry Gurney to your sister."

The Talon's eyes widened. "Cordelia?"

"Is that her name?" The king smiled. "Then yes. To Cordelia."

Thom scribbled idly upon the parchment, watching the Talon from beneath his brows.

Lord Talondaire folded his white hands upon the tabletop. "Cordelia has only just turned fourteen," he said. "I am not sure she's ready for marriage."

Vaston Delon grinned at King Dermont. "What was it Vilnois used to say? Old enough to bleed, old enough for seed?"

Gurney guffawed and the king's lips twisted with amusement. "I'm afraid
Inen's not saying much about such things these days." Dermont smirked.

"Fair, fair," Delon laughed alongside the king. He cleared his throat and
returned his attention to the Talon. "In any case," he said, "the point is that
by arranging the match, we ensure that two great families become even
greater."

Thom gazed at Lord Talondaire. There was no doubt in his mind that the
Talon was angry, livid, but to his credit or shame, there was no trace of it in
his face.

"What could I possibly say?" The Talon said at last.

"Well, to be fair," King Dermont said, "nothing. However, it's much
better for all of us if you simply acquiesce."

"Then there you have it," Lord Talondaire said.

"Splendid!" The king grinned.

"She'll be well taken care of, Tally," Sir Gurney said. "You have my word
on that."

"In more ways than one." Delon winked at the knight of the cock.

The other men shared an unsubtle chuckle and Thom saw the Talon's fist
clench beneath the table.

"If you'll permit me, your majesty," Talondaire said, "it will take some
time to rally the lords of Whitemane and to see them assembled in the field.
As one who has so recently been honored by your munificence, I admit that
my eagerness to prove myself has filled me with haste." He forced a benign
smile. "Do I have your leave to depart so that I might do my utmost to carry
out your will?"

King Dermont breathed a contented sigh and offered the young lord a
gracious nod. "I suppose you must," he said. "Very well. You have my leave
to return to your lands and rally the lords for battle. If all goes well, perhaps
we shall even celebrate the impending nuptials at Whitemane castle?"

Lord Talondaire rose from his chair and bowed. "I suppose it all depends
upon the outcome of the battle," he said.

"True enough," Dermont said.

Thom quickly finished recording his last note before offering the short
stack of pages to one of the attendant stewards. Lord Talondaire had already
withdrawn from the solar and began tramping off down the hallway with his
men in tow. Thom had to run to catch up to him.

"Find the maid and Lady Valerie," the young lord said in a harsh whisper. "I would have them get word to my mother and my sister. Old Lord Guillon as well."

"Aye, sir," Thom said. "What would you have me tell them?"

"We leave tonight!"

CHAPTER 31: TWIN SHADOWS

Lughus guided the small boat inland toward the shore, his gray eyes alert and watchful, searching the darkness for any threat. With a sound that was little more than a whisper, he dipped the paddle into the midnight waters and propelled the little vessel forward. It was cold, bitterly so, yet not enough to freeze the lake. A light flutter of snow flurries provided cover, concealing them from the watchful eyes of any enemies lurking in the darkness. Beneath the blackened vault of the heavens, made starless by the great sheets of winter clouds, he had the odd sensation that it was not Lake Bartund upon which he found himself, but the endless expanse of the Abyss itself.

Well, he thought, glancing at the figure kneeling at the bow, if granted the choice of anyone to stand beside him against the darkness, there could be no other but her.

With the grace of a black swan, Lughus guided the small boat—a currach, he noted—to the cover of a large willow that stood sentinel over the shallows. Without a word, Brigid leapt out onto the stony shore and stood watch as Lughus stowed the vessel away within the shelter of a large clump of reeds and set about covering it with fallen branches and boughs. He knew that before long the snow was sure to add an additional layer of concealment as well, and he was glad for it. Not that he expected many to be out and about at this hour, but given the surreptitious nature of their endeavor, he would not risk discovery for the sake of haste.

When the work was done, he joined Brigid where she stood eying the harbor and the keep that stood watch from above. A light mist was forming out upon the lake and Lughus was glad for it, for it would ensure that Captain Jorik and the keelboat would remain hidden from the eyes of any watchmen stationed upon the battlements. The city surrounding the keep was quiet, as one would expect after dark, though at the harbor, the occasional barge or keelboat still shone with the light of the odd lantern.

"Ready?" she whispered without turning.

"After you."

"Mind your footsteps and try to step where I step. Do you have the rope?"

"Right here," he replied.

Brigid turned, her blue eyes glimmering in the darkness, and he felt her hand gently upon his arm. "Just in case," she whispered, her breath warm beneath his cowl. "I love you."

Lughus nodded, pulled her close, and savored the taste of her lips. The moment would forever remain illuminated upon the vellum of his memory.

"I love you too."

She offered his arm one last squeeze.

"Let's go."

Together they stole from the cover of the willow and made their way to the shadows of the stone walls. A cold wind howled across the surface of the lake, jostling the keelboats at their piers. A bell rang gently, upset by swell of the lake, but otherwise there was no sound.

Like a pair of church mice, they scurried soundlessly along the base of the wall until they reached the outline of a small postern. An ironbound door barred the way, but drawing a small, twisted piece of wire from within the hem of her glove, Brigid made quick work of the lock. With a soft thump, the postern swung open and they were inside, gazing down a snow-covered lane that led to the town proper.

Lughus sniffed at the brisk air and pulled his cloak tighter around his shoulders. Brigid wrung her hands and flexed her fingers to keep them limber. With a silent nod, he drew her attention ahead to where the cobblestone road led upward through the ward toward the archway to the next district. The toothy edges of another portcullis were just visible below the apex of the arch and Lughus surmised that they must have been raised in advance of the snow and ice. Otherwise, the iron bars, chains, and winches could become frozen in place, effectively cutting off one district from another—one social class from another—leaving them stranded and vulnerable.

It was a stroke of luck. With the way clear, the young couple made their way through the concentric districts of the city as easily as they had at Harvestide, for no mere watchman, no matter how devoted, could hope to mark the passage of such legendary figures as the Marshal and the Blade.

Brigid took the lead, scouting swiftly ahead and beckoning to Lughus to follow when the way was clear. They kept to the shadows and tread lightly so as to leave as little trace as possible. The snow made this somewhat more difficult than usual, though the Marshal's perennial knowledge of hunting provided Lughus with plenty of tricks to obscure or misdirect their tracks.

So it was with little challenge that they passed through the city of Marthaine to return now to Harrier's Keep itself.

There was no doubt in Lughus's mind that the arrival of the silver eagles in Galadin was intended as a plea for aid and a call to arms. He would consider no other course of action but to answer; however, he knew at once that to rally his army in defense of his grandparents would only add credence to Guy's assertions about Galadin usurpers looking to reignite the feud.

As the Marshal and the Blade, he and Brigid could slip in quietly, free Roland, and—with any luck—aid the Argent Eagle as he put his house back in order.

As the story of *The Siege of Three* had so famously made known, entry to the castle's ward was guarded by three great gates—one to the south, one to the north, and one to the west. In their previous visit, Roland and his entourage had led Lughus and Brigid through the southernmost gate, which was marked by two lofty watch towers and commanded a view of the harbor. The north and west gates, meanwhile, boasted not only the reinforced doors commonly featured in such defensive structures, but a pair of portcullises arranged in a type of lock system within which invaders might be stalled and subjected to falling stones, arrows, or pots of boiling oil.

Regardless of the defensible advantages, unlike the district gates of the city below, each of the three castle gates was shut.

Unfortunate, but not unexpected.

"So what do you think?" Lughus whispered to Brigid as she stood contemplating this new barrier.

"I'm thinking it's a good thing we brought a rope," she replied. "But not here. There."

Together, they hurried along the edge of the wall that spanned the distance between the southern and western gates. At once, Lughus realized that it was from this direction that, with all factors considered, they could expect the longest shadows and the least resistance.

Still, there was something strange about the whole affair, for there was no sense of heightened tension, no pervasive worry hanging like a hood over the barony's capital. While the cold and the hour were certainly enough to confine the common folk to their homes, Lughus expected to find at least the standard complement of guardsmen on patrol, if not more. For in the aftermath of a hostile coup, it was absolutely vital to reestablish order and control. Had Guy indeed succeeded in overthrowing such an indomitable figure as Roland, he could not possibly hope to sustain his power and authority without a show of overwhelming force. It was curious. Very curious.

"Here," Brigid said, "Toss it here."

Lughus slipped the long coil of rope from his shoulder and readied the iron grappling hook. At Brigid's signal, he tossed the hook, waited for it to catch on the crenellated battlement, and tested it with a forceful tug.

"I'll go first and then pull you up," he said.

"Be careful," Brigid whispered.

Lughus loosened Sentinel in its sheath. "I will," he said, "though I can't help but get the feeling that this has all been—"

"Far too easy?" she finished.

He gave a nod.

"Well," she said, "if it's a trap, we'll find out soon enough." She gave him another quick kiss. "Go."

Lughus grabbed hold of the rope, pressed his boots against the stonewall, and slowly began to climb. While his hauberk—the very same he had inherited from Crodane—had long ago become as a second skin to him, he felt its weight now. Fortunately, due to the direction of the wind, the stones were not slick with frost and melting snow, and once more he marveled at the easy cunning of his future bride.

Once he reached the top of the wall, he rolled over the battlement and crouched low, warily scanning the walkway for any watchmen. Again, while he did not consider the men of Marthaine to be his enemies—he had fought alongside so many of them now—he knew that he had entered uninvited. At the very least, his discovery would be met with suspicion if not open hostility. Further, if Guy had indeed succeeded in wresting command from Roland, men who were once his allies might now be ordered to see him as an enemy.

A familiar flash of anger coursed through him. The part of his mind that belonged to the Marshal took hold of him and his jaw set with grim determination. It was all so meaningless, so wasteful. All for the selfish ambitions of a single man.

A blast of cold wind stirred him from his bloody reverie and he turned back to the grappling hook and the dangling rope. Peering over the side, he saw Brigid's vague outline. With wordless understanding, he waited for her signal, and when she tugged at the rope, he braced himself and quickly pulled her up.

As soon as she reached the top, Brigid leapt over the side, crouched low, and stood watch while Lughus coiled the rope and stowed it to one side. Her hands rested comfortably on her hilts and her blue eyes pierced the darkness of the inner ward below them.

"Six men have the watch," she said. "Two at the entrance of the keep, one at each gate, and then a sergeant who commands them. There could be another man stationed in one of the towers atop the south gate—perhaps even two—but I can't quite tell from here. In all likelihood, their attention will be on the lake anyhow."

Lughus crouched beside her and followed where she indicated. "Wait," he said suddenly, "Look at the emblem on their tabards."

"The silver eagle," Brigid said.

"But look closer."

Brigid gave a sharp intake of breath. "The eagle has two heads."

"Those aren't my grandfather's men."

"They're Guy's"

Lughus opened and closed his fists and once more shifted Sentinel in its scabbard. It was cold and growing colder, but the fire within him was growing hot with wrath. "And if Guy has taken control of the castle," he said, "there's a good chance that he's freed Alan and the Hammer."

Brigid's eyes shown with an icy hue. "We need to find your grandparents. Right away."

"Then lead on, Lady Blade," Lughus said.

Crouching low, they passed swiftly along the battlement towards the western gate to where a thatched overhang provided shelter for visitors' horses. Currently, the area was unoccupied but for an empty wooden cart, the horses having all been safely sheltered in the stables for the winter. As the snow began to fall in heavier curtains, they leapt from the wall and onto the roof before rolling down the thatching to the ward below. The man guarding the gate barely had time to register his surprise before Brigid was upon him. With a single swipe of her daggers, she opened his throat.

Lughus caught the body as it fell, dragged it behind the cart, and leaned it upright against a wheel to bleed out. By the time he had finished, Brigid had already slipped off to dispatch the guard stationed at the north gate. Lughus joined her just in time to hear the rattle in the man's throat and conceal his corpse within the shadow of the gate as well.

The sergeant and the southern gate guard were in the midst of a half-grunted conversation about the weather when Brigid sprang from the shadows to appear between them. In a sudden flash of steel, she drove Whisper's point up under the sergeant's chin, and plunged Shade deep into the gate guard's heart.

"You know," Lughus said, hurrying to catch up, "you don't have to do this all by yourself."

Brigid's lips twisted into a wicked grin and Lughus felt the burning desire to kiss her. "Well, Marshal," she said, "with the amount of time we've spent in the field since the start of this war, I'm fairly certain your count outnumbers mine by two to one." She wiped her blades clean upon the dead men's tabards. "So forgive me if I use this opportunity to catch up."

Lughus smiled. "I suppose the darkness is the domain of the Blade," he said, "and…to be honest there is a certain pleasure in watching you work."

Brigid's gaze narrowed and she offered him a flirty wink. "I know the feeling," she said, "but if it makes you feel better, we can take the final two together. They're standing too far apart for me to bring down in one go. You take the one on the left and I'll go for the one on the right."

When the final sentries had been eliminated, Lughus dragged their bodies out of sight while Brigid considered their surroundings. Again, Lughus felt the pricking of discomfort, the uncanny sensation that—in spite of the circumstances—all was not as it seemed. Without having to ask, he knew that Brigid felt it too.

"Perhaps we should have brought Fergus along after all," Brigid said. "We could use his nose."

"We would never have ever gotten him on the row boat." Lughus chuckled. "Poor boy hates the water. Remember how he whined when we brought him aboard the keel boat last time?"

Brigid smiled. "Fair enough," she smiled briefly and returned to the task at hand. "The south east tower of the keep—that one there—is the falconry tower," she said. "When the eagles arrived in Galadin, they did so as a group without any messages or the like attached to them. I've been thinking about that ever since. Why would your grandfather do that? He doted upon his birds. To simply release them into the cold like that is not something he would do..."

"Unless he was under duress," Lughus mused. "He may have barricaded himself inside once Guy made his move."

"Exactly," Brigid said. "What if they cornered him in the falconry tower and in an act of desperation, Roland released the birds all at once? The lake hasn't frozen yet so with the snow as it is, they might have thought it an easier source of food, which would have driven them further and further away from Harrier's Keep and—"

"Straight to Galadin."

Brigid nodded. "I think we should make the falconry tower our first objective."

Lughus slid Sentinel from its sheath. "Agreed."

With the sentries dead, the way into the keep was clear. Together, they pressed open the ironbound doors just enough to allow them to pass inside. A rush of wind howled through the stone entryway and into the great hall, stirring the hearth fire and the pair of iron braziers that remained ablaze throughout the night. By all accounts, however, none were awake to notice it.

Once more, Brigid took the lead, stepping silently across the flagstones and along the outskirts of the hall to where a staircase spiraling upward to the other floors of the keep.

Lughus found it all so strange. Since their recent visit, the layout of the keep was still quite fresh in his mind. Yet, the circumstances made him feel as if he were visiting for the very first time. Once more, though, he was emboldened by the presence of the Blade beside him, as temporal comrade-in-arms to the Marshal, but also as Brigid, his love and mate.

As the Marshal, his domain consisted of the forests, fields, and streams—the wild and open places of the world, standing against the darkness so as to create the conditions that would allow for a new and brighter day. As the Blade, however, Brigid was synonymous with the moon and the stars, shining like a light in the darkness, banishing the sinister servants of Dibhor wherever they sought to hide. As such, her domain was often the cities and towns, the castles and the courts—places where the corrupt and the wicked went about freely with vipers' smiles to mask the insidious souls beneath.

Onward, they continued, up the spiraling staircase all the way its lofty end. At the final landing, a corridor stretched out before them, dimly lit by a pair of sconces. As Lughus crouched low, just beneath the level of the final stair, he spied the glimmering reflection of candlelight on steel. Again, without having to speak, he knew that Brigid, crouched beside him, saw it too.

There were four of them. Men in chainmail, their surcoats bearing the mark of Guy's double-headed eagle. They stood outside the oaken door to the mews. Two of them passed a wineskin back and forth. Another dozed against the wall. The fourth paced back and forth in an effort to stay awake. For the moment, they seemed completely unaware that they were being observed, but their presence seemed to support Brigid's theory about Lughus's grandfather.

"How do you want to do this?" Brigid whispered, her breath cool upon his ear. "If you get the pacer, I can slip in and make sure the sleeper never wakes. Then we can both take the men with the wine."

Lughus nodded. "Whatever we do, we need to be quick and cut them down before they have a chance to call out. My grandparents' private rooms were on this floor, weren't they? If Guy has named himself the new baron, we may find him nearby as well."

"Or the Hammer," Brigid said, "though I have yet to feel sense his presence anywhere nearby."

"Nor have I."

361

Brigid took a deep breath. "So, shall we?"

"Now."

Casting back his cowl, Lughus charged the pacing sentry, striking from on high as he ran. The guard's face froze in horror as he was cut down before he even had the opportunity to cry out. No sooner had he withdrawn his blade from the man's corpse, than Brigid leapt past him like a bird of prey, talons gleaming in the low light. The dozing sentry would never open his eyes again.

At the sight of their comrades' deaths, the remaining pair threw the wineskin to the floor and drew their swords. They barely had time to raise them before Lughus and Brigid were upon them. With a swift tap to his opponent's blade, Lughus deflected the man's oncoming strike and countered, slicing him from his shoulder down through his chest. Brigid dodged a low thrust from the remaining guard, whirled her blades around, and thrust first one into the man's abdomen and the other to his throat.

Wasting no time, Lughus stepped over the bodies and pressed against the heavy door to the falconry tower. "Something is braced against it on the other side," he told Brigid. "But if we start calling out our pounding against it, we'll wake the whole castle."

"Hang on." Brigid said suddenly. With a quick swipe of her blades, she tore off a piece of a dead man's surcoat and slipped the Galadin signet ring from her finger. Carefully, she dipped the ring face into the widening pool of blood, and pressed it to the cloth.

"Very clever." Lughus grinned.

"Let's just hope there's enough light for whoever is in there to see it," she told him.

She allowed a moment for the blood to dry, then used one of her daggers to feed the cloth beneath the door.

An eternity seemed to pass as they waited for a response. Brigid knelt in the shadows while Lughus stood motionless against the wall with Sentinel naked upon his shoulder. All was silent but for the occasional crackle of flame in the sconces. As quickly as they had silenced the four guards, it was only a matter of time before someone discovered their presence.

Lughus sighed, trying not to think of the bodies of the men lying beside him or hidden in the yard. Had any of them fought with him at Stonebridge, he wondered? At St. Golan's? Had they hated him then? Had they even hated him at all, or were they just following the commands of their lord.

In his mind's eye, he saw Crodane beside him at Lenard's Crossing so long ago. *It gets easier*, he had said, standing over the bodies of the men they had killed. *It shouldn't, but it does.*

The sound of something heavy being shifted away from the door brought him back to the present. On reflex, he shifted his feet and readied his blade while Brigid, acting upon the same impulse, rolled forward onto the balls of her feet. In the off-chance that it was not an ally but an enemy who awaited them behind the barricaded door, they would be ready.

With a squeal, the oaken door drew back on its hinges and Lughus tightened his grip upon his sword. Within the chamber, what little moonlight broke through the clouds was multiplied by the falling snow outside the great aerie window. A shuffling figure appeared in the doorframe, dark against the light, but little by little, the sconces revealed the man's craggy features. Lughus breathed a great sigh of relief.

"Baron Roland?" Brigid whispered.

For the flicker of a moment, the old baron peered at them with the cautious eyes of a cornered beast. Then, as recognition settled in, his scarred face softened. He gripped Lughus tightly by the shoulder and pulled him in to a bone-shattering embrace. Brigid stood up from where she crouched and the baron eased his hold on Lughus long enough to wrap an arm around her too.

"I knew you'd come," he said when at last he released them. He waved them into the tower behind him and shut the door.

Lughus's eyes widened at the scene. Perches, cages, and a large cabinet stood just beside the door, the evidence of Roland's makeshift barricade. To one side, a bucket of water sat atop a wooden crate beside a wooden rack where strips of stringy meat had been hung to dry. A single, hooded eagle sat regally upon a gilded perch beside an area on the floor where a cloak had been lain out as a makeshift bed. A second bucket, its purpose clear, sat covered on the far side of the room, and beneath the great aerie window, a second cloak concealed the identity of another prone figure.

At once, Lughus's blood ran cold. "Who...?"

"Ulfric," Baron Roland said, his deep voice dry and gravelly. "He took a blade to the belly in the fight to secure the room."

While he grieved the Marthaine seneschal's passing, Lughus could not resist a certain sense of relief. "Where's Gran?"

"Guy has her," Roland said. "For now."

Lughus's eyes flashed. "Will he—?"

"I do not believe Guy will harm her," Roland said, cutting him off. "He will try to use her to legitimize himself."

"How long have you been trapped here?" Brigid asked. She remained beside the doorway to keep watch.

"Just under a week," Roland said. "Guy and his men arrived shortly before. He claimed he wanted to pay his respects and discuss strategy for the coming spring. Such a thing is not unusual, and in the past, his visits were common. Welcome even. This time, though, my gut told me not to trust him. I should have listened to it."

"We came as soon as the eagles arrived in Galadin," Lughus said. "We thought about bringing more men, but—"

"No, you were right not to," Roland said. "Guy is already trying to push the idea that I'm a puppet dangling upon Galadin strings." He sat down upon a stool. "But never mind that now. In the end, the matter will be decided when one of us lives and the other is dead. Just give me a minute to catch my bearings and we'll set things to right."

"Are you well enough to fight?" Brigid asked.

"Nothing too serious. A few scratches. Some bumps, and bruises, but I've certainly had worse." Roland's craggy face split into a smile. "Orlando there has been keeping me fed." He motioned to the perched raptor. "He's a wily old bastard, which is why I kept him behind with me when I released the rest. Brought me a pair of rabbits and a grouse, even with your bloody cousin trying to shoot him down."

"Alan's free?" Brigid asked.

"And the Hammer," Roland said.

Lughus and Brigid exchanged a glance.

"Don't worry. All will be settled," Roland said. "Now..." He stood and stretched his back. "It's time to take the castle back."

"Hold, hold," Brigid said suddenly. "With respect, Baron Roland, are you certain that you're well enough to fight?"

"Let Brigid and I see to it," Lughus said. "Just help us find Gran and then we'll take care of Guy."

Roland gave a snort. "Appreciated," he said, "but this is my house. My barony."

"Fair enough," Lughus said.

Brigid shot him another implicit glance.

"Well, at least let us heal you," Lughus said. He held out a hand, but Roland drew back quickly and swatted his arm away.

"No!" the old baron cried.

"But—"

"No!"

Brigid touched Lughus's arm and they drew back at the stricken expression on the old man's face.

"I'm sorry," Lughus said.

Roland breathed a sigh. "No," he said gently, "I'm sorry. I mean no offense and I appreciate your intention." He took a deep breath. "But I remember how Brigid suffered at St. Golan's and I'll not have either of you weakened on my account. You'll need your strength."

At length, Lughus nodded.

Roland removed the hood from the remaining eagle and untied the tether from its foot. "Thank you, old friend," he said. "We'll see each other again, I hope, but just in case, take care of yourself. If an enemy come for you, fly free and live well."

Brigid opened the door a sliver and peered out into the corridor. "I hear something," she said. "I fear we may have finally been discovered."

"Then let's waste no more time," Roland said. He strode past the young couple and retrieved a sword from one of the fallen guards. "*I* am the rightful baron of Marthaine!" he declared. "And I'll not suffer these two-faced bastards any longer!"

Lughus and Brigid joined him in the hall, the three of them terrible to behold in the flickering light of the sconces. "We are with you," Lughus said. "For Galadin, Marthaine, and the Brock!"

CHAPTER 32: RETRIBUTION

The staccato sound of running boots echoed through the stone hallways and stairwells of Harrier's Keep, punctuated here and there by shouts of alarm or command. Within moments of their emergence from the falconry tower, a squad of soldiers appeared. In the tight coronas of the wall sconces the two-headed eagles blazed brightly on their tabards. There were five of them, clad in mail and armed with swords and heater shields. At the sight of Roland and the two Blackguards, defiant and free, the men hesitated and drew back.

At length, the sergeant in command stepped forth.

"Baron Roland," he said, raising his sword, "Lord Guy orders you and your companions to surrender your arms and stand down. He will *not* offer you another chance."

Baron Roland's lip curled into a ghastly leer. "No," he said. "This is *your* last chance. You can continue to follow Guy into dishonor and death, or—" He paused and cast his steely eye upon each of the men in turn. "You can remember your duty and stand with us while we put this madness to rest."

Brigid stood tense and silent, alert and ready for the soldiers to make a move. The sergeant's face shone with haughty arrogance, but beneath the shadow of their nasal helms, the eyes of the other soldiers shone with conflict and fear.

"Make your choice," Roland snarled. "*Now!*"

The whip-crack of the old baron's voice echoed throughout the corridor, breaking the spell. The guardsmen flanking the sergeant glanced sheepishly from man to man, then lowered their arms, and knelt.

"What are you doing?" the sergeant snapped. "Take them!"

When the men remained unmoved, Lughus stepped forth, a smile playing upon his lips, and knocked the sword from the sergeant's hand.

"Bind him," Roland commanded the remaining soldiers, "and if you truly wish to regain your honor, follow me."

With the sergeant secure, Roland stormed off down the corridor with dread purpose. Brigid and Lughus walked just behind him with the Marthaine soldiers split into pairs to guard their flanks. As they turned the corner, another squad of men stood ready to oppose them at the end of the hall.

"At least Guy's ambitions were not so blind that he would cast an old woman out of her quarters," Roland sneered. "You men, stand aside! Now!"

The guards had mere moments to decide, not nearly enough time to rally any measure of organized defense. As one, they lay down their arms and held up their hands in surrender. Roland strode right past them accompanied by Lughus and Brigid.

The room they entered was a large sitting room, comfortably furnished with dark woods and upholstery of baronial blue. Along one side of the room a bookcase stood beside a small writing desk, and on the other, a pair of comfortable chairs sat before a fireplace. Embers still glowed softly in the gloom casting just enough light to make out a single doorway that opened into a second chamber just beyond.

"Morgana?" the old baron called.

"It's about time, Roland," the baroness called. She appeared in the far doorway illuminated by the light of a single candle. "This tantrum of Guy's has gone on for long enough. Oh!" She paused. "Lughus and Brigid are here! Hello, dears!"

Roland strode across the room to her, took her hand, and kissed her gently on the cheek. "Are you well, my dear?"

Morgana brushed off the concern. "I don't mind being confined," she said, "but they took my maids. The poor girls are probably scared to death."

Roland gave a terse sigh. "All will be answered," he said. "Ulfric is dead."

"Ulfric?" Morgana repeated. "Poor man. We will honor him as a hero when this is done."

"Indeed," Roland said. He disappeared momentarily into the darkened bedchamber past the baroness and appeared moments later with his heavy mace, Thunderclap, resting on his shoulder.

Morgana smiled at Lughus and Brigid. "It's so good of you to come," she said, "I only wish it were under better circumstances."

Brigid marveled at the Morgana's demeanor. She had always understood the Baroness of Marthaine to be a formidable woman; however, to show such mettle after a week of imprisonment was unlike any woman she had ever known.

With mace in hand, Roland renewed his command. "Darling, do you have any idea where we can find Guy?"

"The solar, I believe. He told me I had until you surrendered to gather up my belongings." She gave a chuckle. "I told him that at that rate, I would think about packing sometime next year."

"Too soon." Roland smirked. He called back through the doorway. "You there," he said. "Quinn!"

One of the men-at-arms appeared in the doorway. "You know my name, my lord?"

"Of course, I do," he grunted. "Your father served me when you were just a child."

"He did at that, my lord," the man said.

Roland eyed the man carefully. "I want you to stay here and guard the baroness," he said. "Choose another man to stand with you. Nalwin, perhaps."

"Yes, sir."

The baron offered the baroness a final kiss on the cheek. "Stay safe," he told her.

"You too," she replied. "All of you. Guy released the Andochan prisoners and they've been helping him."

Brigid and Lughus locked eyes.

"The Hammer," Lughus said.

"And Alan," Brigid added.

"Then there's not a moment to lose," Roland said. "Let's go."

Three of the men outside of Morgana's chamber had chosen to join with Roland, replacing the pair of men left behind as her guard. The remaining two would join the captured sergeant in the falconry tower.

Brigid stood aside with Lughus while Roland issued his commands and learned what he could from the guardsmen. Despite the circumstances, she could not resist a certain amusement at the similarities between grandfather and grandson. So strange that Lughus's father should have come to such an ignoble end with such parents as Roland and Morgana. Then again, like a blacksmith with a blade, sometimes it took the fires of tragedy to temper the heart into something stronger, something purer.

Whatever the past, there was no doubting Roland and Morgana now, and while they were Lughus's grandparents, she had come to love them as her own just as much as she knew they had come to love her.

As for her own blighted family tree, well, it seemed she had no choice left now but to do some pruning.

"Alright, men," Roland said at last, his jaw set and expression stern. "Let's take the castle back."

As one, they made their way down through the castle staircase and assembled in the corridor of the floor that led to the solar. By now Guy's guard had gathered to mount a concerted defense. A dozen or more, armed, armored, and ready for battle readied for the assault. Torches, sconces, and braziers sparked to life, scattering the shadows and bringing dark to light. As Roland approached, once more, he offered the soldiers of the guard the same opportunity to lay down arms that he had offered the guards upstairs. These men, however, refused.

"My men won't turn their backs on me as easily as yours did, Uncle," Guy called from behind his guardsmen's shieldwall. "In Silverdale, we know the true meaning of loyalty—as once did you."

Roland shook his head and sighed with great weariness. "You still refuse to understand," he said. "You still insist on holding on to pointless squabbles while the true enemy sharpens his knives at our very gates."

"Andoch is not our enemy, Uncle," Guy said, "The true enemy stands by you."

Brigid tightened her grip on her daggers. Beside her, she could hear Lughus grinding his teeth. "You're a fool, Guy," he said. "As foolish as this ancient feud."

"Ha!" Guy cried. "You are a disgrace to your father!"

"No," Roland snarled, "He is his redemption." He raised his mace and shouted, "Charge!"

The clash of arms and armor echoed through the hallways of the castle punctuated by the cries of battle and wounded men. Brigid fought in tandem with Lughus, as was their custom, carving a path through the enemy soldiers in an effort to reach Guy.

Yet with every passing minute, more men appeared, drawn to the sound of battle. Some joined with Roland while others joined Guy, though dressed as they were in uniform tabards and speckled with blood and gore, it soon became difficult to discern whether an eagle had one head or two.

Luckily, for Brigid and Lughus, this was not a problem. Recognizable as they were in their unadorned traveling garb, they could safely assume that any man who attacked them was an enemy and so they swiftly cut them down. One after another after another. All the while, Brigid's eyes peered ahead down the hallway to the door of the solar, hoping to spot their greatest foe.

"Strange not to feel Harlow close at hand," Brigid said to Lughus over the clash of arms.

"I don't sense him either," Lughus said.

"Perhaps he fled?"

"Not likely. I can't imagine he'd pass on a chance at both of us." Lughus parried an oncoming attack and knocked the man off balance. In a flash, Brigid stepped in to dispatch him.

"True, though I can't say I've seen Alan either." She dodged a blow from a morningstar, twirled to the side, and drove her daggers upward into her attackers' innards.

"We'll find them," Lughus said. "One step at a time." He raised his hilt in a warrior's salute and waved another pair of enemies on to engage him.

Supported by the Blackguards and uplifted by the old baron's visceral wrath, Roland's men began to surge. Guy's forces had dwindled to but a handful of men and as soon as an opening appeared, they withdrew to the confines of the solar. After knocking aside the baron's table to use as a barricade, the three remaining guardsmen stood with their shields before them. From their jerky movements and panicked expression, it was clear that at any moment they would begin begging for quarter. At their back, a man in heavy full-plate—Guy's seneschal—whirled a two-handed sword like the blade of a windmill. Guy himself stood at the very rear with his back against the wall. In one hand he carried an arming sword, while in the other he held a gilded buckler bearing his arms. Wherever Alan and the Hammer had gotten to, Brigid noticed, it clearly was not here.

Baron Roland, his mace bloodied and jaw set, stepped forward, unafraid, and addressed the traitors.

"Lay down your arms, and you three can leave with your lives," he said to the guardsmen. "You will be banished from my lands, but at the least, you will not hang."

The men barely had to pause to consider it before the weapons slipped free from their hands and they lowered their shields.

"Dibhor take you cowards!" Guy snarled as the men were escorted away.

"What was it you said?" the old baron mused. "About the true meaning of loyalty?"

Without warning, Guy's seneschal charged; however, limited by the size of the room and the upended furniture, he barely made it a single step before Lughus knocked aside the great sword and used his free hand to lock the big man's arm. Once again, Brigid leapt in like a shadow and slipped both of her blades between the seams in the armor under the seneschal's arms. He gave an anguished cry of pain, twitched in the throes of death, and collapsed like a brick wall upon the floor.

"It's over, Guy," Roland said. "Stand down.".

Guy remained defiant. His lip curled into an arrogant sneer. "Once again, you rely on outsiders—on *enemies*—to hold on to your power," he said.

Roland stepped forward and with little effort, wrested the sword from Guy's hand. It clattered to the floor as the old man stood eye to eye with his nephew, mere inches separating their faces.

"The Brock is more than a single barony. More than Galadin. More than Marthaine," the old baron said. "And while it's true that we enjoy our independence and the pride we feel for our own domain, and while it's true that we have our squabbles and skirmishes, our border wars and our feuds, at the end of the day, the Brock survives because it stands together, because it is a family—in more ways than one."

371

"A family? Ha!" Guy snorted. "You made peace with the people who murdered your only son!"

"And you would make peace with those who seek to murder his!" Roland growled. "Do not *dare* attempt to claim the moral high ground, you who would condemn me for seeking peace while you would stand for a King who seeks only dominion and war." Roland paused and took a deep breath. "And as for my—" He paused. "As for my son, you cannot even begin to comprehend the magnitude of grief I felt and still feel every waking moment of every day at his death. The Black Abyss would be a welcome reprieve from the suffering and the pain that I carry *constantly* at his loss, let alone for the manner in which he fell."

"He died for the sake of Marthaine!" Guy cried.

"He died for the sake of hated!" Roland replied. "He died for the sake of power! He died because I encouraged these qualities in him, because I was so consumed with the bloody feud that I raised him to scorn peace and lust for war. He died because in my pride, I refused to cultivate wisdom and compassion. He died because when he called upon me to be his father, I turned him over to his bloody tutor."

"At least that's something we can agree on," Guy said. "Master Huskarn was more of a father to him than you ever were."

"And I will bear that shame and that regret for all eternity," Roland said. "For in turning him away, I allowed Huskarn to poison his soul, and by the time I realized it and sent the bastard back to Castone, it was too late."

"He never forgave you for that," Guy said, "for banishing the only father he ever knew."

"I know," Roland said. "I have made more mistakes over the years than I can count, but I wholeheartedly believe that peace with Galadin is not one of them. For fifteen years, Arcis Galadin and I both paid the price of for the foolishness of our ancestors. We not only lost children, but our infant grandson had to be taken from us as well."

"Yet," the old man continued, "while we grieved and learned the errors of our ways, it was a Glendaro who raised him—and I could not be more proud of the man he has become." He cast Lughus a warm glance and breathed a heavy sigh. "The Brock stands together," he said, pausing to meet every pair of eyes around the room. "You must *all* understand that. When we support one another, we are strong. When we don't, or when we turn on each other, we crumble."

Guy gave a condescending sniff. "What nonsense," he said. "Who would have thought that the once-great Argent Eagle would become such a sentimental old fool?"

Roland nodded to two of his men. "Take Lord Guy and see him installed in the dungeon."

Brigid looked to Lughus. Throughout the entire exchange, he had stood in silence, eyes hard and brow furrowed. *How long must these ghosts haunt him?* she thought, and with a covert movement, slipped her hand into his. *Speaking of ghosts and hauntings...*

"Apologies, Baron Roland," she said, breaking the doleful silence with a renewed sense of urgency, "but where are Willum Harlow and Alan Beinn? I'm afraid that until they are accounted for, the danger has not yet passed."

"Guy?" the baron called, as the guardsmen bound the nobleman's wrists. "Where are they?"

"Oh Uncle, why would I ruin the surprise?" Guy snorted. "They will reveal themselves. In due time."

Brigid felt an uneasy feeling in the pit of her stomach. She exchanged a glance with Lughus. "We need to find them," he said.

Baron Roland nodded in agreement. "They've cannot have gotten far," he said. "Go. As soon as Guy is secured and the wounded are seen to, we'll join you." He reached out to grip Lughus by the shoulder. "Thank you. Both of you."

Brigid smiled. "Of course," she told him. "The Brock stands together, just as you said."

Roland's lips split into his ghastly grin. "Good hunting," he said.

From the solar, Brigid and Lughus took the corridor to the staircase and downward toward the great hall. With no clear lead from Guy as to the whereabouts of Alan or the Hammer, Brigid figured it was just as good a place as any to begin the search.

Lughus was silent as they walked, brow furrowed and jaw set. She knew that the argument about his father was enough to darken his thoughts and send him into a spiral of brooding, but with Alan and Harlow loose in Marthaine, she could ill afford to have Lughus distracted. She didn't care a fig what might happen to her, but she would never forgive herself for letting him go into battle thusly burdened.

And so, as they reached the landing that would lead to the great hall, Brigid tightened her grip on Lughus's hand, pulled him back into the stairwell, and stood on her toes to kiss him deeply on the lips. At once, his body seemed to relax, and when his arms closed around her, it was with the selfsame gentle firmness to which she had grown so accustomed.

When at last she pulled away to breathe, the light in his eyes told her that—as she hoped—she had succeeded in scattering the shadows of his mind.

"Ah!" she said. with satisfaction, "there we are!"

Lughus held her, an expression of delighted confusion plastered on his face. "There we are?" he repeated. "Did you lose something?"

"No," she smiled, "but I could tell that you were beginning to."

Lughus cheeks reddened. "I'm sor—"

Before he could finish, she pressed a finger to his lips. "No apologies," she said. "It's what we do, right? Whenever one of us is lost or confused, we can always count on the other to help find the way, right? Isn't that it? Come what may?"

Lughus gave a nod. "Come what may," he said.

Brigid eyed him meaningfully. "I know you. I know your mind," she said, "and if you believe that we're not going to talk about it, then you're a bloody great fool—which I know you're not." She smiled. "But right now, we need to focus."

"I know," Lughus said. "It was just...the mention of Castone."

Suddenly, she understood the level of his preoccupation. Castone. The Keepers. Was this Huskarn a Keeper? Was he too a Dibhorite? At once she realized the size of the door that had suddenly been opened.

Yet, it did not change the fact that—for the moment—it needed to remain closed.

"We will discuss it later. I promise." She smiled and pressed another kiss to his lips. "Come on, Marshal. It's time to bring the dawn."

"Any idea where to start?" Lughus asked.

Brigid paused to think. "I do not think we will find them together," she said. "Alan may have been able to weasel his way to Harlow's side at first, for while he may be a fool, he is not without a wicked sort of cunning. However, once Harlow realized how little my cousin is actually worth when it comes to the execution of a plan, he would have abandoned him at once." She shrugged. "Say what you will about the Hammer—and there is plenty to say—but he is, at the very least, a man of action. Alan is not."

Lughus nodded. "Harlow's ultimate aim is to destroy us. Even his duty to the Order and Guardian-King are secondary to him at this point," he said. "Blood and fire! If only Fergus were here, he could sniff them out."

Together, they began walking again and stopped as they reached the great hall. Apparently, minor skirmishes between guardsmen loyal to Roland and those loyal to Guy had broken out here as well, at least once word spread that the Argent Eagle was taking his castle back. A pair of men were busily dragging away the body of one of the men bearing the mark of the double-headed eagle, while a maid mopped up the blood.

"My grandmother said they took her maids," Lughus said. He eyed Brigid thoughtfully. "Do you remember from our last visit whether they were old matrons or were they pretty maidens?"

Brigid's stomach twisted into knots as instantly she recalled one of her cousin's favorite haunts at Blackstone. "I know where he is," she said.

They passed quickly from the great hall out into the ward, pulling their cloaks tighter around them against the cold. Snow flurries continued to fall intermittently, and in the east a slight lightening of the sky foreshadowed the coming dawn. Brigid led the way, no longer concerned with hiding their footprints, and together they passed like a pair of ravens across the ward.

As they approached the Marthaine stables, Brigid drew her daggers. "At Blackstone," she whispered, "I often wondered that Alan was no great horseman considering all the long hours he spent in the stables until well after dark. It wasn't until later that I realized how these nights would often precede mornings when so many of the young maids winced or gasped as they went about their work."

Lughus remained silent, but his eyes blazed with vengeful wrath.

The air was thick with the smell of hay and horses as they passed through the doors to the interior. Stalls lined both sides of a wide central passageway within which the Marthaine chargers, palfreys, and destriers stood singly or in pairs to keep warm. Beyond them, at the far side of the building, a doorway led to another room where, Brigid imagined, the stablehands and farriers kept their stores of supplies and gear. Lamplight shone through the gap in the doorframe and from inside came gasping cries and whimpers punctuated by cursing and laughter. Brigid could feel the anger radiating from Lughus like iron from a blacksmith's forge, but rather than charge off, he kept his head and followed behind her.

However, the sight of what lay beyond the door, nearly sent them both flying into a rage.

In the center of the storeroom, a space like an arena had been cleared. Within were four of the maids. Two crawled about on all fours like beasts of burden while the remaining two rode upon them wielding wooden sparring weapons. In spite of the cold, all four were utterly naked and their breath hung upon the air in visible puffs as they exerted themselves in an approximation of gladiatorial combat. Vivid red lashes stood out upon their backs and rear ends, many of which were fresh and bleeding, and their eyes shone with numb horror.

Presiding over all of this, was Alan Beinn. He reclined upon a stack of wooden crates that had been arranged to resemble a throne. An arming sword leaned against one side of his absurd high seat next to a pair of loaded crossbows. He too was utterly naked and it was clear that the suffering of the serving girls excited him. He held a goblet of wine in one hand and a horsewhip in the other, which he waved about idly in circled urging the reluctant combatants on.

"Come on now! Put some effort into it!" he cried. "Lady's teats! This is pathetic! Hit each other!"

With an arbitrary swing, one of the women happened by chance to strike the other a glancing blow, unseating her and knocking her to the floor with a grunt of pain. The remaining women shrieked in terror while Alan laughed merrily and took a deep swig.

"That's more like it!" he said. "At last!" He stood up and raised his arms triumphantly. "Now, my darling, to the victor goes the spoils! Come over here and be the first to pay your tribute!"

In utter silence, Brigid and Lughus burst into the room. In the lamplight, cloaked and cowled, they appeared as shades escaped from the Black Abyss itself. At once, the women screamed and scurried for cover behind the crates and barrels while Alan shrieked and stood at the foot of his absurd throne.

With his longer legs, Lughus easily outpaced her, and Brigid watched as— with one hand—the young baron caught Alan by the throat and slammed him down into his seat. The Young Sheriff kicked his legs in a frenzy, struggling against Lughus's iron grip to breathe. The lightning flashed in Lughus's eyes again and he raised Alan's head just enough to slam it back down against the wooden crates. Alan continued to sputter and writhe, his normally sallow pallor turning red as a beet.

Brigid knew that she would be lying to herself is she did not admit a certain satisfaction at the sight of her betrothed unleashing his righteous fury upon her nefarious cousin. As such, she allowed another minute longer before, at last, she sheathed her blades. "Release him. We need him to speak."

Lughus smashed Alan back into the base of the crates one last time before letting him go. At once, the Young Sheriff began gasping and sputtering as he fought to regain his air.

"B-Brigid!" his eyes widened in horror as they darted back and forth between his cousin and her betrothed. "What-what are you doing here?"

"We'd heard a rumor that Harrier's Keep had been overrun with vermin," Brigid said wickedly, "so we thought we'd help Baron Roland clear them out."

Alan pushed himself up to a sitting position and sat as far back in his seat as he dared. Lughus's eyes never left him and his swordarm shook with desperate restraint.

"You were fools to come here then," Alan said, attempting to raise some manner of arrogant exterior to mask his fear. "Roland is dead. Lord Guy reigns now in Marthaine."

Brigid smiled and shook her head. "Guy has already been dealt with," she said. She gathered a large pile of discarded clothes from the floor beside Alan's chair and gently set the bundle down near the cowering maids. "Lughus and I are merely...tying up loose ends."

As red as it so recently was, Alan's face went suddenly drained of all color and turned ghostly pale. "I—" he froze. "I have done nothing! I merely did whatever Guy asked me—"

"You have done plenty," Lughus snarled. He raised his hand again and Alan cowered in terror.

"Darling, wait," she said to Lughus. "We need him to tell us what has become of the Hammer."

"The Hammer?" Alan repeated.

"Willum Harlow," Lughus said. "Your sniveling master."

"Harlow is not my master, dog—" he paused, perhaps thinking better of antagonizing the Marshal further.

"Then tell us where he is!"

"I don't know!" Alan squirmed. "He left yesterday after the bloody red bird came back."

"Red bird?" Brigid repeated.

"A Calendral kite," Lughus said. "A Guardian messenger bird."

"Roland would have seen it," Brigid said, "He was locked in the falconry tower."

"In the wild, kites and eagles are competitors. They would have fought if they came any nearer to each other." Lughus paused. "That's why you have the crossbows. Not only to shoot down any birds my grandfather sent for help, but to clear the path for the kite's return."

"But where did Guy even find a kite?" Brigid asked.

"We had a pair of them at Stonebridge," Alan said. "After the battle, Guy had his men smuggle them to Silverlake while he followed Roland to see us imprisoned here. Harlow taught him the cipher on the march and he's been corresponding with the Chancellor ever since."

Brigid exchanged a look of concern with Lughus. "And you say the kite returned yesterday?" she asked.

"Landed on the roof by the dovecote yesterday afternoon," Alan said. "I almost shot the bloody thing. They had me—*me*—stationed up there in the cold. Said it was my fault the bloody flock of eagles got away." His face twisted with irritation. "Of course, they ignore the fact that it was *my* idea to kill all the bloody doves so as to draw the kite to the roof and away from the falconry tower. No one acknowledges that! Bloody things love carrion!"

"Save us your self-pity," Lughus said, "and tell us where we can find the Hammer."

"For fuck's sake!" Alan whimpered. "After trapping the old man, Harlow told Guy to assemble his army and they would rendezvous across the lake. Then he took off on horseback south and eastward. He wanted me to come with him to serve as his blasted servant but I told him he could fucking sod off in this cold."

Brigid's eyes flashed. "Across the lake?"

"They mean to attack Galadin," Lughus said.

"How can they?" Brigid asked. "Stonebridge is gone and we've men guarding the whole of the border—from the legion in Agathis to the Nordrens at the port. We'd know well in advance if an attack was imminent."

"Perhaps not all your friends are as friendly as you think," Alan said wickedly. "Perhaps they've realized that principle matters little against practicality. How do you think we took this place so easily? The old man was so caught up in his beliefs about honor and unity that he was blind to the treachery right before his eyes. Just like you, Baron Doggie."

He turned his wicked gaze upon Lughus and Brigid could sense that, just like old times, the more Alan drawled on, the more confident he became. Nothing could embolden him more than the sound of his own voice.

"You believe that the Brock stands with you, that you can defy the will of the Guardian-King, but you can't! The entire continent backs Kredor—from Montevale to Grantis, Dwerin to Castone. All kneel before the King!"

Brigid eyed Lughus. "We need to return home," she said. "And we need to send word to Perin and the other barons about the possibility of an attack."

"Oh, I'm sure some of them are already well aware." Alan laughed.

Lughus's eyes smoldered and Brigid knew that at this moment he wanted nothing more in all the world than to separate Alan's vile head from his neck. However, in moments of such grave import, he would not allow wrath to overtake reason. Rastis Glendaro had seen to that.

But Alan was a blight, a poison that spread throughout the land inflicting harm and trauma on all who encountered him. He was a disease, a boil that—for the good of the world—must be lanced. While she was determined not to become a kinslayer, she knew that she could no longer allow mercy to overtake reason.

At what point does my mercy make me complicit to his crimes?

She breathed a heavy sigh and turned to Lughus, ready to offer him her just consent.

Yet, to her surprise, Lughus sheathed Sentinel.

"I can think of few who deserve death more than you," he told Alan. "For while the Hammer is my enemy, I know that in his own twisted way, he believes that what he does is right, that what he does is right and just." He paused to collect Alan's bevy of weapons: the horsewhip, the arming sword, the pair of crossbows, even the blunt blades the poor women used when forced to fight. "You, however, *you* sow chaos for your amusement. You harm others simply for your own delight. You take joy in the suffering and pain you inflict to justify your sheer and unutterable pride. For that reason, Alan Beinn, you—*you*—are truly evil."

Brigid bowed her head. "Lughus..." she said softly. "Do as you will."

Lughus's gray eyes met her blue and to her surprise, she found them not so much wrathful as resigned. He paced over to her and kissed her crown. "I realize now that it's not my place," he said.

"What do you mean?" she asked.

He crossed the room to where the four maids cowered behind the crates and barrels and set Alan's assortment of weapons down upon the floor. "It's not my place to deal out death and judgment upon such a vile and wretched creature," he said. "It's theirs."

"What?" Alan cried.

"Goodbye, Alan," Lughus said. He offered Brigid his arm and as she took it, she glanced back to see Alan's dawning horror as the women exchanged keen glances and pawed at the pile of arms.

"You can't be serious!" Alan sneered, desperate to maintain his defiant facade. "Is this meant to frighten me?"

Brigid turned away. "Farewell, Cousin," she called as Lughus led her to the storeroom door. "May you die as you lived."

"Brigid!" Alan cried after her as the maids began to advance upon him. "Brigid! No! You can't! Brigid, please! No! No!"

The first rays of the sun were cresting the horizon when Lughus and Brigid passed out of the stables into the chill of the inner ward. In the cold stillness of the early morn, the muffled sounds of Alan Beinn's screaming could only just be heard.

CHAPTER 33: THE SIGN OF FOUR

When I committed myself to the Order so many years ago, I knew that—at least in some sense—I was sacrificing many of the aspects of life that so many see as an important, if not integral, components of the human experience. When I accepted the title of the Loremaster, this denial appeared to become all the more certain—that in choosing wisdom and service, I was giving up many personal joys for the sake of creating a better world.

Imagine my surprise, then, that as old age begins to claim me, I find myself the primary caretaker for not just one child, but three!

Lughus, Thom, and Royne.

Each child is little more than a year old and already they begin to show signs of uniqueness and independent character. It is fascinating, though as one to whom children and the ways of children are somewhat foreign, perhaps it is normal. I do not know.

Regardless, it is an interesting thing after a life of relative solitude to be suddenly so directly responsible for the well-being of other people.

We make a strange family, I imagine. While I still do not quite know how to define my role to the boys—teacher, caretaker, father, even grandfather—I suppose my position as Loremaster makes me the default head of household.

Then there is Hob. In truth, Hobart is still adjusting to life among the Order, having been anointed with the title of the Ox while delivering my last message to Sigmund. When he returned as a foundling, it was assumed that—as a fighting man—he would join the Tower of the Warlord. However, the regimented life of a cavalier or justiciar would in no way align with the *carefree spirit of the Wrathorn. As such, I accepted him into my ranks and offered him the position as my steward. Many of the scholars and sages balk at his size and his manner, but he is a good man with a good heart and in my experience, that is all that truly matters. Furthermore, as one of a brood of ten children and more, he has experience that I have found invaluable.*

Of course, he makes for an amusing nursemaid.

Regardless, where once I believed that I was entering my twilight years, I see now that I am instead greeting a new and glorious dawn. I do not know if I will be an adequate caretaker, but I swear by my title to give it my all. For if what Sigmund says is true, the world will demand much of these boys and more...

When the viceroy's procession arrived on the morning of the fated day, one week after the execution of the young alchemist called Fabius, not a single member of the insular community was there to greet him. Even after his trumpeters sounded their fanfare until they were blue in the face, not a single person appeared.

The viceroy was furious. To be ignored in such an offhanded way was, to him, more insulting than if the mob were to raise their voices in rebellion or in anger. And so, he intended to make a great show out of the suffering of this prisoner, Fabius's nine-year-old brother.

"Lady's Teats!" he cursed aloud as the honor guard moved into a semicircular position that was at once defensive and intimidating. The young boy knelt with his hands bound in their midst, sobbing in a mixture of confusion and shock. It was clear that he had little idea what exactly was happening, but no one—from the kingsmen to the viceroy—saw fit to tell him either.

"What do you want to do, father?" the younger Pryce asked. "Do we just kill him and leave him here for the birds?"

"We may just have to," the viceroy said, "though I had hoped to make a show of it all first. Diminish their morale. I did not expect them to surrender just yet, but after witnessing two or three executions, fear and guilt would force them to stand down."

From the darkness of the hidden passage, Royne watched and listened to the Pryces' conversation, peering through a tiny crack between the stones of the wall. Amara stood alongside him, her body leaning so close to his that he could smell the lovely scent of her hair and skin. He had tried to prevent her from joining him, tried to have her remain behind in the safety of the symposium. She refused.

Royne knew that it was very likely that he was going to die, that in this absurd, rather haphazard assassination attempt, the chances that he would be successful were incomparable to the likelihood that he would simply be cut down. It was all so stupid, so foolish. He was no assassin! What was he thinking? And now he'd somehow enlisted Amara in this nonsense too! What was he doing?

His heart began to pound in his chest and his breathing became deeper and more urgent.

"I really wish you would return to the symposium," he whispered, pausing to check the edge of the small knife he carried in his belt. Normally, he used it for cutting ingredients to mix in his decoctions. Today it would serve a much darker purpose.

"And I really wish you would stop saying that," Amara replied.

"We're too intelligent for the both of us to die so foolishly."

"Then don't die."

Royne sighed. "What if the masters release the white cloud—the Stardust or whatever you call it? Would we not be burned alive as well?"

"They will not do such a thing with the boy there," Amara said. "As an innocent, they will not do anything that would risk directly causing him harm."

Royne's brow furrowed. "So, last time, with the ram. If the kingsmen had brought an innocent with them, they very likely could have broken through the gates?"

"Yes."

"Interesting."

Amara peered through the crack beside him. "They're getting ready now," she said. Over her shoulder, she carried a cloth satchel and from within it, she retrieved a handful of bulb-like vials. "It will take them a moment to realize it is not the real thing," she said, handing him a pair of the bulbs. "So we will need to act quickly."

"You save the child," he told her. "Grab him and pull him back in here as fast as you can. Then shut the door and bar it. Leave the viceroy to me."

Amara frowned. "I am not going to just—"

"Quiet!" Royne hushed her. "It's starting!"

Just beyond the door to the hidden passage, the viceroy cued the trumpeters to sound another fanfare, then raised his voice toward the empty courtyard outside of the symposium.

"Alchemists of the University, I have returned as I said I would!" he shouted. "And as I promised, I have brought with me another of your former student's treacherous family." He waved his arm in the direction of the sobbing boy. "Yet still I find the gate is closed to me, and thus it is that you have sealed this boy's fate!"

He nodded to his son and with a smirk, the younger Pryce drew his sword. The boy's sobs grew louder as he came to realize that no one was coming to save him, that in a matter of moments, the sword would fall and his life would be done.

Royne breathed a heavy sigh and pushed open the concealed entrance to the tunnel. Then for one so thoughtful and rational, he gave himself over to reckless abandon and embraced discord.

At the sound of shattering glass, the red-cloaked kingsmen of the viceroy's honor guard stood rigid in alarm. Suddenly from four separate locations, thick white smoke began to waft throughout the courtyard. With the vivid memory of their former comrades' deaths still fresh upon their minds, the soldiers threw down their weapons and ran, desperate to escape the slow expansion of the deadly fog.

Viceroy Pryce and his son also made to flee; however, before they could escape, two figures emerged from out of nowhere and charged them. Both father and son cowered in fear allowing one of the figures to run right past them. The second figure paused and from its belt, drew a small blade.

"Death to tyrants and murderers!" Royne cried. He swung the blade at the viceroy and missed, but he was at least grateful that his voice had not cracked as he shouted his war cry. Ahead of him, he vaguely discerned that Amara had reached Fabius's brother and was now hurriedly helping him to his feet. The momentary distraction, however, had left him open to a counterattack and in a moment of reflexive panic, the viceroy lashed out and pushed him backward in his effort to escape. Royne toppled head over heels, bashing his head against the ground.

"Damn it!" He grunted, righting himself. The fog continued to expand, but as it did so, visibility improved. The initial shock upon which the entire ruse depended was quickly fading.

"You Kordish devil!" the younger Pryce cried, leaping to defend his father. "I'll kill you!" He turned on Royne and suddenly paused. At once, recognition illuminated his features. "You!"

"Me!" Royne snarled.

"Surely, the Brethren favor me!" Pryce laughed, raising his sword. With all his might, he attempted to hew the young Loremaster in half. Royne didn't even attempt to parry with his absurd knife. Rather, he leapt back, only narrowly avoiding the blade.

"So this is where you've been since they cast you out of the Order," Young Pryce sneered. "A white lamb among a flock of dark-skinned Kords? Fitting place for the former black sheep of the Order. I nearly didn't recognize you without your dress!" He attacked again and Royne leapt to the side, once again narrowly avoiding the bejeweled sword.

The young Loremaster knew that he could not continue playing cat and mouse indefinitely, but with the constant threat of Pryce's sword, he could not focus enough to think of a way out. It was clear that his haphazard attempt at assassination had failed, though at least it seemed Amara had managed to save the boy.

"I was never cast out," Royne told him, hoping to bait Pryce into providing some unknown opportunity. "I was never cast out," he said again, "but I believe that the Order has lost its way and it had fallen to me to correct its course!"

"Ha! You?" Pryce scoffed. "You think by murdering its soldiers, you correct its course?"

"No," Royne said, fixing his nemesis with a cold, hard stare, "by destroying the true evil-doers."

"Ha! What bloody drivel!" Pryce laughed uproariously. "You sound like that bastard, Goldimop!"

"You mean the Baron of Galadin?" Royne smirked. "Does it sting less that he beat you, knowing now his true worth?"

Pryce attacked and once more, Royne narrowly scurried out of harm's way.

"It matters little what he calls himself. He's soon to be dead—like you!"

With a deep lunge, Young Pryce thrust forward to skewer the young Loremaster upon his shining blade. Royne sought to dodge again, but in his clumsiness, his feet tangled up and he began to fall. With an uncanny calm, he watched as the tip of the sword came for him. He waited for the pain of the plunge, the sensation of the sharpened steel impaling his innards. He shut his eyes.

But no pain came. In its place, he heard only a muffled grunt and a staggered breath.

"What?" he heard Pryce sneer. "Who the fuck are you?"

Royne opened his eyes. In the space between him and Pryce stood Amara. Her eyes were half-closed and her mouth hung slack. Bright crimson blood shone upon her lips and spilled over down her chin.

"No!" Royne cried in anguish and rage. "No!" He cast his glance to her abdomen and saw where Pryce's blade thrust into her and out again through her back.

"No!" Royne shouted again. "No! *No!*"

For a moment, even Pryce seemed taken aback by the shock of her sudden appearance as she intercepted his thrust. Then, seeing the pain and the anguish upon Royne's face, his surprise become a satisfied—even elated—leer.

"Who's this, Royne?" he asked, withdrawing his blade. "Finally find yourself a whore?"

Royne's fists clenched and from the depths of his being, came the sound of ultimate suffering. It was the cry of one who for so long denied his own humanity, and having finally begun to accept it, finds it ripped from him and crushed into dust.

Amara turned as best she was able and her eyes met Royne's. She tried to speak, but no sound came. Her legs went out from under her and heedless of the blood, Royne hurried to catch her in his arms.

"Amara, no!" he managed, choking on the words. "Amara, I'm so, so sorry!"

With what seemed a final effort, Amara's hand alighted softly upon his cheek. Her eyes glossed over and her lips were wet with crimson.

"Polecat..." she whispered gently.

Royne's eyes burned with bitter sorrow and a great chasm opened deep within his chest. It was unlike anything he had ever before experienced. A profound emptiness. An eternal abyss.

Pryce laughed arrogantly. "Aw, poor Royne," he jeered. "Never fear, you'll join her soon. We'll just wait until the light goes out of the eyes. That's how you can tell—hey!"

With a speed that defied the eye, Royne's arm lashed out and grabbed Pryce by the wrist. His long, thin fingers clenched like an iron vice. Pryce struggled to free himself, to slip his hand away, but Royne refused to release him. From deep within his soul, he felt a cold, seething anger, a blind, unbridled rage. The air around him seemed to grow colder and with every exhale, a tiny specter was born only to be scattered upon the rising breeze.

With every fiber of his being, every piece of his conscious mind, he concentrated on the forces of nature, the balance of the elements, the ebb and flow of life and death. Before his mind's eye, he saw flashes of the cosmos, ten-thousand stars expanding forever and ever into the darkness of the void.

Ebb and Flow. Balance and Discord. Life and Death. Everything and Nothing. It was all one. It was all eternal. Two sides of the same coin.

Cradling Amara in one arm, he felt the dwindling of her being, the fading embers of the fire within her. The skin of his neck tingled with each puff of her waning breath. At the same time, so close at hand, he felt the vibrant pulse of life in Pryce, the raging flame of defiance, the exultant tide of humors at the suffering of a vanquished foe. In the angle of his vision, he saw, simultaneously, the setting of one sun—bright, beautiful, and warm—and the rising of a second—frigid, wan, and red as blood.

"No," Royne whispered harshly, his voice little more than a low growl. "I will not allow it," he said—to himself, to Pryce, to the cosmos. "This is *not* the way!"

All of a sudden, Pryce gave a sharp cry and the air was forced brusquely from his lungs. His eyes widened with horror and upon the abdomen of his surcoat, there appeared a tiny crimson stain.

"What are you doing?" the bully shouted as the spot steadily began to grow. Pryce's voice became halting, breathy. He tore at Royne's grip. "You bastard! Let me go!"

Royne's brow furrowed and he fixed the viceroy's son with a steel-eyed gaze. Again, he focused his mind, his entire being, on the inexorable dichotomy of nature. Balance and discord, life and death. "No!" he said.

Pryce dropped to one knee, the red spot upon his surcoat was now a great crimson stain. Blood began to drip from the hem of it, collecting on the ground beneath his feet.

"Royne!" he shouted. "Royne! Let me go!"

Royne stared into the eyes of his enemy, taxing every least, last bit of his iron will. "Never fear," he said. "It'll be over soon. Just wait until the light goes out of the eyes. That's how you tell…"

With one final shriek of terror, Pryce writhed like an anchored vessel on a storm-tossed sea. An ocean of blood poured forth from his middle and pooled at the ground beneath his feet. Only then did Royne ease his grip upon his enemy's wrist and the lifeless body collapsed in a heap.

At almost the same moment, Royne heard a sharp intake of breath, and in his arms, Amara stirred, her eyes fluttered opened, and with an effort, she tried to speak.

"Polecat?" she whispered.

"You live!" Royne gasped. He pressed his lips to her forehead and held her closely in both arms. "Fire and Blood! You live!"

Amara's lips spread into a weak smile.

By now, the white powder, the false Stardust, had mostly dissipated and the path before the gates had largely cleared. The heavy tread of boots and the clink of armor echoed through the area as the viceroy and his soldiers returned.

"What! My son!" the viceroy shouted in fury and anguish. "My son! You murdered my son!" He drew his sword and advanced, rallying his soldiers to follow him. Royne raised his arms defensively to shield himself and Amara. He knew that his energy was entirely spent and that there was nothing that he could do. Like so many of his actions of late, it had all been for nothing.

Still, he thought, holding Amara gently in his arms, despite the absurd chaos of existence, there were certainly some things that were meaningful and worthwhile. If this was the end, he would face it with dignity and honor. He bowed his head, awaiting the final blow.

But it never came.

For all of a sudden, he was knocked prone by a great blast of force and a terrible, earsplitting roar.

From the direction of the secret door, a thick torrent of fire burst forth, engulfing the viceroy and the nearest kingsmen, melting flesh and blade and armor in a great, fiery inferno.

It was Udo. With a slow, precise movement, he swung his arms, planted his feet, and pushed the air in the empty space before him. A great gale erupted from his open palms forcing the remaining kingsmen backwards and snuffing the flames upon the burning corpses.

"Be gone!" he shouted at the surviving soldiers. He stomped his foot and a tremor shook the ground at their feet. "The University is closed to you. We only wish to live in peace."

The soldiers eyed each other in a mixture of confusion, fear, and disbelief.

Once more, Udo shouted. "Be gone!" He clapped his hands and a sound like thunder echoed through the street. At once, the soldiers took flight, scattering throughout the alleyways of the city.

As soon as they were out of sight, Royne and Amara shuffled to their feet.

"Thank you," Royne said, "I did not—"

Udo cut him off with a wave of his hand.

"You!" he shouted. "You are to leave at once!"

Amara held up a hand. "Wait, father," she said. "He saved my life—"

"Saved it?" Udo growled. "He may have saved your life, but he also put you in harm's way. He put *all of us* in harm's way!"

"They would have killed the child!" Royne shouted.

"Killers kill! It is what they do!"

"And so we do nothing? We simply let them?"

"Killing is killing, regardless of purpose," Udo said. "And now—thanks to you—I too have been made a killer." He shook his head. "After all this time, after all these years, you forced me to kill again."

Royne sighed. "I am sorry," he said, "but I cannot sit by and allow such open injustice, such cruelty. They were going to behead that boy! Amara and I stopped it and given the chance, I would do it all over again."

"I am certain you would," Udo said, "and that is why you must go." He sighed. "You are no longer welcome in the University. You must gather your things and leave at once."

Amara shook her head. "Father!" she said again. "Did you not see what he did? He saved my life!" She felt along her torso where once the blade had been. The skin was smooth and unmarked. "He healed me! He brought me back from the brink of death!"

"He misused alchemy. His actions were a crime against the natural order." He winced and cast his gaze upon the charred bodies. "As were mine."

Amara's face twisted with anger. "So you would rather I be dead?"

"I would rather you were never here in the first place," Udo said. He turned again to Royne. "You are banished, unwelcome, expelled from the University." He took Amara's hand and pulled her along after him to the door of the concealed passage. "Within the hour," he said one final time, "you are to be gone."

CHAPTER 34: PRELUDE TO BATTLE

With the Shackle, the Reaver, and the Vanguard on missions of their own, the Tower stood now as a lone Blackguard before the main gates of Pridel. Clad in polished plate and glimmering mail, a red rosette shone resplendently upon the alabaster purity of his tabard. Beneath one arm, he held his great helm, and in his other hand, he held the mighty Spire. Ahead of him upon the snowy plain, the army of the Winter Rose had gathered, awaiting the order to march.

According to the messenger sent by Sir Allard, one of the knights of Whitemane recently persuaded to the rebel cause, the Guardians encamped at Reginal had begun to march south toward Lord Talondaire's lands. At the same time, Bel's own scouts had reported that a large contingent of the Plague King's forces from the Nivanus encampment had begun marching eastward as well. This sudden show of reinforcements suggested that Talondaire's false pretenses for journeying to Reginal may have worked a little too well—that, or it failed and in order to safeguard his mother and sister, the Talon had been forced to remain the Plague King's friend.

Beledain was reluctant to believe the latter. However, he had received no word either way regarding Thom's plan nor had received any word yet from the Talon himself.

Sir Geoffrey's fate also remained a mystery, to say nothing of the Shackle. However, he held more hope for the Vanguard. With his son having joined him, Bel doubted that Geoffrey would take unnecessary risks in his pursuit of the missing Keeper. The Shackle, though, had been gone for so long now that it was becoming more and more difficult to believe that he would ever be seen again.

In any case, the duel reports of their enemy's movements could not be ignored. Whether his anointed comrades were successful or not, Bel could not allow Dermont's forces to march unimpeded.

And so, it became his turn to act, his turn to stand against the darkness and hold back the tide of this increasingly mad war.

With a sigh, he pressed his hand to his breastplate, beneath which he carried the queen's handkerchief. It was joined now by a second item, a folded piece of parchment that bore Marcus's inky footprint. It was a final gift from Marina as they said their goodbyes. As he placed Marcus in her arms after one final cuddle, she offered it to him with tears in her eyes and a promise that she would do whatever she could to keep the boy safe.

A tightness gripped the center of his chest, as if his heart were caught in an iron vice. *No harm will come to them,* he swore. *Even if I have to fight Dibhor himself.*

With an impatient grunt, Tempest nudged Bel's shoulder as if to scatter the sudden gloom. Bel gave a forlorn half-smile and gently patted the great stallion's nose just as another rider approached.

"The column stands ready, my lord," Sir Briden said, gently reining in his horse.

Bel gave a silent nod and climbed up into his saddle. "Then we should be underway."

Together, they trotted down from the barbican to the roadway and halted. On the left stood the inn called The Gilded Rosette, and on the right, the assembled column stood ready and awaiting him. At the head of the army, the banner of the Winter Rose billowed in the chill breeze and Bel wondered who it was that now carried the pennant.

Bel grinned as they turned to follow the road toward the column. "So you finally found a suitable replacement to carry the standard, eh?"

"Aye, sir," Briden said. "I know it seems a simple thing, but I just wanted to make sure it was the right person." He paused. "I'm sorry it took so long."

Beledain waved the apology away. "I left the task to you because I trust your judgment," he said. "I imagine whoever it is will do us proud."

"Aye, sir. I hope so, sir."

Before long, they reached the end of the column, and with a slow, steady pace, rode along rank after rank of men and women, from peasant levy to mounted soldier. Shouts and cheers followed in their wake as the soldiers acknowledged the passage of their commander and Bel received the greetings with nods of acknowledgement or encouraging tips of his great spear.

At long last, they reached the head of the column and took their places beneath the standard. Horn was there, and Welmsey, Sir Norton Wherling, Malet the Elder, Malet the Younger, and several other knights, retainers, and squires as well as the new standard bearer.

Bel eyed Briden's successor carefully. It was a noble youth, as he had expected, clad in a mail shirt with an iron helm and seated atop a dappled mare. However, he was mildly surprised upon closer inspection, to find that it was not a boy, but a girl.

As Bel took his place at the head of the front rank, the girl dug her heels and urged her horse to join him opposite Briden. She avoided his eye as she did so, but while it was clear that she was nervous, Bel noted the manner in which she mastered her fear.

"What is your name, rider?" he asked.

"Marguerite of Roanshead," she replied, hurrying to add, "my lord."

"How old are you?"

"Fourteen, my lord, as of the fourth of Moontide."

Bel pressed his lips together. Moontide had only just given way to the Month of the Wolf. She was young. Perhaps too young. "And what brings you to us, Marguerite of Roanshead?" he asked.

"I..." the girl paused. "My uncle sought to marry me to a man I did not wish to be wed to."

"So you thought you would join us to escape him," Bel said without judgment.

"No, my lord, it wasn't that," Marguerite said.

"It wasn't?"

"No—I mean—it helped, yes," she said. "But, it wasn't the real reason, my lord." She took a deep breath. "I didn't come here to escape being forced into a marriage I found unwanted. I came here to fight for Queen Marina so that no girl should ever have to."

Bel gave a silent nod and cast Briden an approving glance. The young knight suppressed a smile.

"You will do well, Marguerite of Roanshead."

"Thank you, my lord."

Bel turned to Briden and the rest of his assembled retainers. Beyond them, he could see the cold exhalation of men and horses and hear the stamping of feet against the cold.

"Gentlemen," he shouted, "we march!"

The weather remained clear, if cold, as the army made its way through the snow-covered fields and rolling hills of the Montevalen interior. Like a great frost wyrm out of a Wrathorn folktale, it slithered northward, growing in strength and length with every mile as more and more minor knights, yeomen, and peasant farmers rallied to the banner of the Winter Rose.

It was an impressive sight and Bel was pleased, for it was a clear measure of the success of the rebellion, the culmination of skirmish after skirmish and battle after battle, from the moment he and the others broke free from Tremontane Castle, through the Battle of Pridel, and on to now. His breast swelled with pride—not for himself and his own efforts, but on behalf of his land and his people. In the face of tyranny and injustice, these were the folk who stood up, who stared their enemies in the face, and said as one, "I do not consent, I will not consent, and I will not allow the darkness to poison my heart and to claim those I love and those who stand beside me."

At times, as he rode the length of the column, he could not help but recognize the grim determination that blazed like a bonfire from their eyes. It nearly moved him to tears, and he believed himself so privileged to have such men and women at his side.

The journey offered him plenty of time to become accustomed to Marguerite of Roanshead as well. Since knighting Briden on the battlefield, he had been without a standard bearer, who, in the Montevalen tradition, doubled as the commanding officer's squire or valet. While Bel was more than capable of seeing to his own needs, he realized that the importance of the position was not so much about himself as it was about the symbolism and the optics. Briden had been at Bel's side through thick and thin, a trusted lieutenant, and—as a scion of a minor noble house—he served as an example that it was not wealth or prestige that earned great honor, but merit, loyalty, and courage. The man to succeed him, Bel and Briden knew, would do the same.

It just so happened that the successor was a young woman.

Yet in this choice too, Bel realized the maturity and the wisdom of his former standard-bearer. For a land led by a queen that purported to regard equality as tantamount, the armies needed heroes of all types, yet at the same time, the appointment could not merely be symbolic or else risk the life of all involved. When the army halted at the end of the long first day of the march, Bel took it as an opportunity to evaluate the new standard-bearer's martial skills. As she would be expected to follow him in battle, and his own skill and responsibilities required that he place himself wherever the fighting was thickest, he needed to ensure that he was not simply setting her up to be slaughtered.

Fortunately, while Marguerite may have lacked the strength and experience of some of the other young recruits, Bel could safely admit that he rarely seen a better rider. Truly, she rode like one trained to dance, leading her mare through a pattern of agile steps and leaps in a manner that Bel had never seen before, and while she fared rather poorly at the ring joust, Bel knew that her role would not be to run her enemies through with the standard, but rather to hold it high and evade attack so as to aid the men in support of the leader.

"You'll do well," Bel told her again. She removed her helmet, wiped the sweat from her brow, and tucked loose strands of mousy brown hair behind her ears.

"I should have done better, my lord," she said.

"No doubt you will," Bel said, "in time. For now, though, you are as you should be and that is all we can hope to ask of anyone."

"Yes, lord," she said.

Bel smiled. "Go, pat down your horse and get something to eat," he said. "I can see to Tempest and my own needs. You've had a long first day. Rest."

She began to protest, but paused, took a deep breath, and said, "As you wish, my lord."

"And Marguerite," Bel said as she wheeled her horse around to head off to the main camp, "well done."

"Where did you find her?" Bel asked Briden after she had gone.

"Her father was friends with mine," he said. "He was a good man, but he died at the Battle of Stonehoof about ten years ago. Her mother's brother took her and her mother in, but..." He shrugged. "He's a man who pays the scutage, if you catch my meaning, sir."

Bel nodded. "Well, she's one of us now."

"Aye. sir." Briden agreed. Nothing further needed to be said.

At first light the following day, the army resumed the long march northward. A light snow fell as the serpentine column continued its slow passage toward Whitemane and the lands of the Talon. By nightfall, the air hard grown colder, but the snow had ceased, numbing fingers and toes. Still, the army's numbers continued to grow as more and more folk rallied to the banner of the Winter Rose. As a result, Beledain increased the pace, not only to warm the soldiers' blood against the deepening chill, but because he knew that—while right now they might be caught up in a moment of martial zeal—over time, hardship and cold could freeze such sentiment faster than a mountain gale. And so it was that they crossed into Whitemane and set up camp upon a hilltop just in sight of the Talondaire estate at Dunwald.

They were not alone, however, for two additional encampments had sprung up upon the edges of the demesne as well. The larger one, to the north, was a sea of brightly colored pavilions, the majority of which shone bright scarlet or else striped black and white, clearly identifying it as the main encampment of Guardian kingsmen sent from the Plague King's capital in Reginal.

The second, smaller and more diverse in the coloration of its pennants and pavilions, seemed to consist of the lesser knights and nobles of the surrounding area. In other words, those lords of Whitemane who had not already committed to Marina, but had offered their fealty to the Talon. It was a sizable force, and as Bel and his men set to raising their camp, speculations abounded regarding the allegiance of this second camp and the young lord. When the battle came, who would they support? And on a more personal note, what did this mean for Val, Sparrow, and Thom Reaver?

After nightfall, if it did not come to battle before then, he would send a messenger to the lord's estate to learn the truth. In the meantime, it was imperative that his men and horses be fed and ready to fight. It was a long march, and a cold one. With the numbers as they were, it was almost guaranteed that when the battle was met, some of those who had followed him, would not be returning home. The least he could offer them in recompense was a hot meal and a bit of warmth.

But then, just as the cook fires had been kindled, another large force appeared from the west to join with the already massive force from the Reginal. This group, he knew, was the contingent from the Nivanus, though from the look of it, it was not merely a portion of the border forces, as had been reported, but the entire bloody army.

"Dibhor's Cock!" Horn swore as the captains stood together outside of Bel's tent, warming themselves around a large campfire. An iron cauldron of pottage steamed between them though it remained mostly untouched.

"There are indeed quite a lot of them," Welmsey observed.

"But not so many as at Pridel," Briden said. "Man to man, we were far more outnumbered there than here."

"And if the Talon joins us—" the younger Malet began.

"Aye, but he hasn't, has he?" Horn broke in. He broke a twig in threw it into the fire.

Bel gazed into the embers in deep thought. He understood Horn's frustrations, understood his unvoiced fears. "I don't think there's a man among us who marched all this way thinking to avoid a fight," Bel said. "The battle will happen. It's simply a matter of when." He turned his gaze to the gray sky above and watched the passage of a singular snow flurry settle upon his arm.

"Marguerite?" he said suddenly.

"Yes, my lord!" the girl called.

"Ready Tempest and your own horse." He glanced at Briden. "Do we still carry the old flag of Montevale?"

"We do," Briden said. He turned to Marguerite. "I'll show you where."

"What do you mean to do?" Horn asked.

"You wish to speak with them?" Welmsey asked.

Bel nodded. "We can stand here and speculate, or I can simply find out."

"Alright," Sir Norton said, "we'll join you."

Bel shook his head. "I need you all to see to the camp and the men," he said. "Sundown is not far off and while I doubt we we'll see battle before dawn, I'd have us ready to take the field at first light."

Bel finished issuing orders and with nods, salutes, and grunts of assent, the men dispersed to see to their duties.

By the time he had finished, Marguerite had saddled Tempest and her own horse and replaced the queen's standard with the Montevalen flag of truce. Tempest whinnied at Bel's approach. Bel gave the stallion a pat on the flank and noticed with satisfaction the shine of his chamfron. In particular, the spiraling horn in the center of his brow shone like a beacon in the winter light.

"Thank you, Marguerite," Bel said, climbing up into the saddle. He reached for the standard. "I'll see to it from here."

To his surprise, the girl was reluctant to relinquish the flag. "Pardon me, my lord," she said, "but I believe the first duty of a standard bearer is to, well, carry the standard."

Bel eyed her curiously, suddenly noticing that she had done her best to hastily outfit herself and her horse for battle as well. "I see," he said at last. "Then I suppose you had better follow me."

Hastily, the young girl mounted her horse, and with the standard held high, followed as he rode out onto the frosted plain toward the enemy encampment.

The sun sank lower in the western sky as Bel stood like a statue awaiting a response from the enemy camp. It was clear that they had been spotted. It was only a matter of time now before the opposing commanders rode out to meet them. Marguerite stood beside him, the banner of Old Montevale flapping wildly in the cold. Bel could sense her anxiety and he wondered if she had anticipated that accepting the position as his standard-bearer would be such an immediate ordeal. It wasn't fair that it should come to pass this way, but then again, when it came to war, little ever was.

"What is your horse's name?" he asked, his eyes leveled upon the enemy camp where a squad of grooms was readying horses.

"Luna, my lord," the girl said.

"She seems sure-footed," he said.

"She is, my lord."

At the enemy camp, a half dozen men were mounting horses and from somewhere within the camp, another pair of riders joined them.

Eight men, Bel thought. Quite the diplomatic party. His hand felt along the shaft of Spire, checking the loosely tied lashings that kept it in place alongside his saddle. On his other hip, in place of a sword or a battle axe, he carried a horseman's pick, and slung across his back, he carried a heater shield marked with Marina's red flower. Marguerite likewise carried a shield across her shoulders as well as a thin-bladed saber.

While the flag of truce should guarantee that any verbal barbs not devolve into physical blows, Bel knew Dermont far too well to completely let his guard down. Still, it was unlikely that his brother would take the field himself, preferring to leave the matter to one of his cronies while he sat safe and secure in Reginal.

With Bel's handiwork this past year, Dermont was running out of boon companions, and unless he were able to suddenly woo new followers with promises of power and gold (an area, admittedly, in which he was not without skill or resources), he might find himself forced to appear in person.

He was considering all of this, when a preternatural shudder gripped him and he gazed across the field to see that the enemy riders had begun their approach. While he could plainly make out the emblems upon the tabards of the men flying the colors of the new king of Montevale, Bel's mind ignored them, so focused it was upon the veritable juggernaut that accompanied them.

He was a mountain of a man, encased in shining silver plate mail that in the waning light was like a second sun. His scarlet tabard matched the finely embellished caparisons of his great white stallion and across his shoulders he carried what was perhaps the largest great sword that Bel had ever seen.

Yet it was not fear that so gripped Bel's breast at the sight of such a mountain of an opponent. It was *familiarity*. He *knew* this man—like a captain or a brother.

And so once again it slowly dawned on him that it was not *he* that knew this man. It was the part of his mind that was the Tower.

So affected was he by this sudden sense of recognition that he failed to mark a third contingent of riders who appeared now to join the parley. A trio of men had approached from the castle town: an older knight in mail, a standard-bearer, and finally, the Lord Talondaire himself, fully outfitted in his heavy plate, stoic and silent beneath his great helm.

A hundred questions leapt into Bel's mind as he marked the lord's slow approach, but he held his tongue, for he had no wish to discuss such private matters within the hearing of the enemy commanders. Instead, he sat erect in his saddle and when the other men had closed to within twenty feet of his position, he removed his helm and held up a gauntleted hand in greeting.

"I am Beledain Tremont, called the Tower, commander of the armies of Queen Marina the Winter Rose."

"We know who you are," a snide voice said from within the confines of a great helm. Bel recognized it at once as Sir Gurney, a suspicion confirmed by the emblem emblazoned upon his tabard. "What is it that you want?"

"I would hope it is to surrender," the man beside Sir Gurney said, his whining drawl echoing within the hollow of his helm. It was Giles Pronet, Bel recalled, although they had only met once before. Yet, he had heard that Pronet commanded the armies of the Nivanus. Did this mean, then, that they had *fully* abandoned the pass? Was the way now clear between Montevale and the Brock? He wondered that Dermont would take such a foolish risk.

Bel shook his head. "I am not here to surrender," he said.

"Then I ask you again. What is it that you want?" Gurney asked. "What price would you have for the safe return of my bride and Lord Talondaire's sister?"

Bel's brow creased with consternation. "Lord Talondaire's sister?" Bel repeated. "Your bride?"

"Enough with the deception," Gurney said. "We caught the bloody maid. We know she was one of your bloody wild women masquerading as a servant."

Bel fought to remain impassive, but inwardly he felt the invisible knife wounds of pain and loss. No wonder Talondaire stood so silent. Something had gone wrong in Reginal.

"Unfortunately," Bel said at last, willing his voice to remain steady. "I cannot return what I do not possess, but I am heartily sorry that the young lady is not where she *belongs*."

"Yes, well, perhaps when you are dead, I will take a different bride," Sir Gurney said.

With an impatient sigh, the Guardian in the polished armor removed his helmet. He was an older man, clean-shaven, with close-cropped hair and blue eyes that under different circumstances seemed made for laughter. Yet, he was not laughing now. In fact, from the looks of things, the man seemed careworn and profoundly weary. Again, Bel felt the flash of recognition beyond knowledge. This, he knew, was a man of honor forced to shame himself in the name of misplaced duty.

"We should get to the matter at hand," the man said shortly. He fixed Bel in his gaze. "I am Dandon Rood, Warlord and High Commander of the Order of the Guardians." He paused. "I know by your spear that you, sir, are the heir to Marcus Harding's title, the rebel prince Beledain Tremont. The Tower."

Beledain gave a courteous nod. "I am," he said. "Would that we had met under different circumstances."

"Indeed," the Warlord said. "I am sorry for it, heartily sorry for it. Sir Marcus was a good friend."

"He was," Bel agreed, "and a man of great honor."

"Yes, getting to the matter at hand..." Giles Pronet said.

The Warlord met Bel's eye and in an instant, an understanding passed between them that moved Bel to pity. He cleared his throat and, perhaps to spare the Warlord any further indignity, spoke.

"I have come to request that your army withdraw from the field and return to those lands still loyal to my brother, your king. Since Inen Vilnois's ignoble defeat, the lords of Whitemane have chosen to declare for Queen Marina. As such, I would like to request that you cease any further hostilities and depart."

"The lords of Whitemane?" Giles Pronet scoffed. "Like who? Lord Talondaire stands there before you. King Dermont has just named him the new Warden of Whitemane. Surely you realize that with that type of authority, those fools you may have been able to persuade to your side will most assuredly abandon you in the name of their true lord."

"If you don't believe us, ask him yourself," Sir Gurney said. "What say you, Lord Talon? Where does your loyalty fall?"

Bel eyed the Talon intensely, and through the visor of his helmet, Bel met the young lord's green-eyed stare.

But Tally has blue eyes... Bel thought.

The man in Talondaire's armor raised a gauntlet and with a sweeping gesture ran his hand through the air across his neck.

"There you have it," Giles Pronet said with an arrogant leer. "Now, Silent Prince—or whatever you call yourself these days—I suggest *you* surrender. Else know that we shall kill you all."

Bel gazed at the armored imposter in wonder, for there was something all too familiar about those eyes.

"You will have my answer at dawn," Bel said.

"Oh how dramatic!" Giles Pronet scoffed. He wheeled his horse around and raised a hand. "Come," he said to his attendants. "I would return to the warmth of my fire."

Sir Gurney eyed Bel. "Until Dawn, then."

"Until Dawn," Bel repeated.

Dandon Rood hesitated. "Would that this nonsense had never come to pass," he said at last. "Sir Marcus was not a man to make choices haphazardly. I would hear of his fall and his final moments."

"And I would tell you," Bel said. "Perhaps should we both survive the battle, the opportunity will present itself."

The Warlord nodded. "This is an unfortunate business," he said, "a most unfortunate business."

"It is," Beledain said, "but I would see an end to it, as Marcus Harding made me swear."

"Then may the Brethren be with you in your task," Dandon Rood said, "and may we both survive the morrow." He replaced his great helm and with a nod to his attendant, wheeled his horse around and returned to the enemy encampment leaving Bel alone now with the false Lord Talondaire.

"You look well, cousin," a feminine voice echoed from the Talon's helm. "The beard suits you."

"Val!" Bel's eyes shone and he fought to contain his joy and surprise while in sight of enemy eyes. "So the escape was a success?"

"In part," Val said, "though not without cost. Lord Talondaire was injured, though he will recover, but Sparrow..." She paused. "Sparrow was grievously wounded in the escape and hung back to buy the rest of us time. They may have captured her, as they said, but...but it was unlikely that she had to endure torture. The scribe—Thom—has taken it especially hard."

Bel's features darkened. "She will be avenged."

Val nodded. "I should not linger lest they become suspicious," she said. "Suffice it to say that in spite of appearances Whitemane is with us." She drew the mace from her belt and for the benefit of the onlookers waved it threateningly at Bel. Were he not weighed down by the news of Sparrow's death, he would have laughed at Val's dumb show.

"Kin keep you, cousin," Val said. "I should return. The Talon has placed me in command and we need to keep up appearances. We shall see you on the field."

"Until the dawn then," Bel said. He made to turn away and then paused and called her back. "You haven't met a man named Geoffrey of Pyle, have you? He carries a shield bearing the mark of a red acorn?"

"You should find him returned to your camp," Val said. "Farewell, cousin, and thank you."

"It was long overdue," Bel said. "Farewell."

When Bel returned to camp, he left Tempest with Marguerite and returned to his pavilion only to find Sir Geoffrey seated by his fire and surrounded by the other captains. To his right stood his son, Freddy, an arming sword hanging upon his baldric opposite his dagger, while on his left, morosely leaning upon the haft of his axe, Thom Reaver stared, pale-faced and red-eyed, into the flames. All around them, the other captains—save Horn—stood in silence, listening closely as Geoffrey explained the situation with Lord Talondaire and the lords of Whitemane. Bel knew well that the half-Wrathorn outrider would have withdrawn to be amongst others of the light cavalry—what few still remained—to solemnize Sparrow's passing. In all likelihood, he had invited Thom to join them, but the haunted look in the boy's eyes suggested that he was in no place for such a thing. Unlike the others, Bel could sense that, while no stranger to death, the fall of a comrade was something the Reaver had little experience with. He had not yet learned the necessity of honoring those lost as a means of finding a way forward without them.

At the sight of Beledain, the Vanguard lurched to his feet.

"Lord Tower," he said grimly.

Thom Reaver remained seated, staring into the middle distance.

"Sir Geoffrey," Bel returned. He drew closer and placed a hand solidly on the Reaver's shoulder. "Thom."

The boy gave a deep sigh.

"We should speak," Sir Geoffrey said implicitly. "I have news."

"As do I," Bel said. He paced to the flap of his pavilion and drew it back to allow Geoffrey and Freddy to enter. "Thom," he added when the Vanguard and his son had passed, "why don't you come too."

With a shudder, Thom stirred and silently followed them inside the pavilion.

"So," Bel said to Geoffrey, replacing the flap. He motioned toward a cluster of wooden stools and a canvas folding chair. "Were you able to find the Keeper?"

Geoffrey and Thom sat down upon the stools, leaving the chair for the Tower. "It took some time," Geoffrey said, "but we were able to catch up with him at the inn right here Dunwald—him and about a dozen or so other types. Peasant folk with burnt hearts and red eyes, just like the Wrathorn we slew outside of Pridel." Geoffrey paused. "By the way, whatever did you do with them?" he asked. "Are they still lying there in the storeroom?"

"I had them burned," Bel said.

"Good," the Vanguard said. "In any case, I'd have been back sooner, but the fight with the Keeper and his...what do we call them? Dead men? Followers? It caused a stir in the town, understandably, and the captain of the guard insisted we remain in custody until the Talon's return."

"You were imprisoned?" Bel said suddenly.

"Aye," Geoffrey said, "but not mistreated. In fairness, the guards took it rather well, all things considering. A mob of strange, dead-looking pilgrims show up in my town and get into a brawl with another group of unknown travelers? It's a lot for the mind to take. I think they were confused more than anything else."

"Perhaps you had better tell the whole tale then," Bel said.

"Aye," Geoffrey said. Carefully, he recounted the story of his journey from Pridel through the peasant villages and onward to the inn called The Gander. Bel listened in silence, and while in one sense, it sounded like absolute madness, the elaborate fiction of an eccentric bard, he somehow knew it all to be true.

"When the Talon returned, he was in no state to be receiving, but the urgency of the skirmish in town forced the sergeant of the guard to press upon Sir Lloyd, the seneschal. He mentioned it to his lordship and to Thom and they saw to our release. We'd have ridden for Pridel at once, but with things as they were, there was..." He paused. "There was too much going on and we knew you'd be headed this way soon enough."

Thom Reaver leaned upon the haft of his axe. "I told you," he said. "The Army of the Dead."

"We never doubted you, Thom," Bel said kindly. "We simply hoped such things would never come to pass."

"This Keeper..." Geoffrey said. "He was able to make more soldiers to replace the fallen Wrathorn that we cut down."

"It's some manner of ritual," Thom said. "They burn a man's heart black and then replace it in his chest. Don't ask me how, but they do it, but what rises is no longer a man, but a...a mute instrument of death. A corruption of the life that once inhabited the flesh, leaving behind an empty shell with only one goal in mind—killing."

"Aye, but destroy the head or the heart and they fall like autumn leaves," Geoffrey said.

Thom sighed. "Perhaps that is why death hungers so unjustly," he said, more to himself than to anyone else. "Finding his larder empty, he seeks to fill it with those in whom life flows so abundantly."

Bel bowed his head and for a long moment, the three men sat in heavy silence. In the dwindling light, the shadows lengthened and outside of the pavilion, lanterns and torches began to spark to life like fireflies. Hushed whispering sounded at the flap of the tent and a moment later, Bel spied Marguerite, Geoffrey's son beside her, standing just outside with an iron lantern. Quietly, Bel stood, retrieved it from them with a nod of thanks, and returned to his place beside his fellow Blackguards.

"I grieve with you, Thom," he said. "Sparrow was a hero of the rebellion, but more importantly, she was a good friend."

Geoffrey gave a sympathetic nod.

Thom took a great rasping breath, though his red eyes remained dry. "King Dermont had just named Talon the new Warden of Whitemane and announced that he was marrying his little sister to that Sir Gurney. Talon requested leave at once so as to raise the army of Whitemane in the Plague King's name. He gave it and we made a show of our departure so as to encourage the belief that the Talon was still their man. Meanwhile, Sparrow—still posing as a maid—was to help Lady Valerie, Lord Guillon, and the Talon's mother and sister make their escape."

He paused. "We found a way out through the garderobe. There's a long, sloping trough that channels the filth downward along the castle wall to feed into the sewage channels for the city of Reginal. They were to wait for nightfall, slide down the trough where we would meet them, then smuggle them back here in our wagon."

"A solid plan," Bel said. "Many a great fortress fell in a similar fashion."

Thom nodded. "So Lady Val told me."

"But I take it something went awry?"

"Gurney," he said. "With Talon riding out to raise his forces, Sir Gurney and the Warlord were ordered to follow the Talon's example. While the Warlord mustered the lords of Reginal and the Guardian kingsmen, Pronet and Gurney were to leave to return to the Nivanus on the morrow so as to divide their forces for the coming battle. Seeing as he was headed off to battle, Sir Gurney thought to spend his last night...with his newly betrothed."

Thom's jaw tightened. "When he found her chamber empty, his men began searching the neighboring rooms and discovered them just as they were slipping out of the garderobe." The Reaver's voice fell. "Sparrow and Lord Guillon held back to cover their escape and to buy them time. Guillon was able to slide down the chute, though he was sorely wounded and the filth caused his wounds to fester. He fell to fever shortly after we returned. Sparrow..." He took another deep breath. "Sparrow never made it out of the castle."

Thom shook his head. "Guillon said she was wounded, but she was still fighting on so we waited as long as we could. I even made to try to climb back up the chute, but there's a part where it drops off a ledge and I couldn't climb so slick was it with filth. Eventually, guardsmen reached us and we were forced to flee."

"Lord Talondaire took an arrow to the shoulder, but otherwise, we were able to get away unscathed. We were all dressed as common wanderers and we shouted curses to the Plague King and Lord Talondaire in equal parts so as to further fool the enemy, but though we were able to press escape through the city gates and lose any pursuit out along the northern plains, it is hard for me to consider the ordeal a victory."

Geoffrey breathed a heavy sigh. "The bitterness of loss makes it impossible to enjoy the taste of triumph."

"Well said," Bel agreed, "and sadly we've been served that bitter meal so often that I fear it shall always taint the sweetness of our successes."

"But still we keep on," Sir Geoffrey said, a zealous light shining from the depths of his eyes, "for I fear there are many worse things ahead, and I imagine only those like us have the strength to do anything about it."

"What do you mean?" Bel asked.

"The Keeper..." Geoffrey said. His brow furrowed and he wrung his hands together. "I'm afraid there's a bit more to the story than just raising the dead."

"Well," Bel said, "I'd say we're all well beyond doubt, considering what we've seen, what we've experienced."

"Fair enough," Geoffrey agreed. He took a deep breath. "So I told you I found the man and it came to fighting, but it wasn't like outside of the inn at Pridel. This time, he didn't just stand back and let the dead do his fighting for him. This time, he fought back."

Thom's eyes widened. "The men I saw at the lighthouse were all old or frail," he said. "Could this one have been a warrior?"

"Not by appearance, no," Bel said.

"But he was," Geoffrey said. "It's as if there was a...a change that overcame him. He became suddenly strong and fast as a serpent. It was wholly unnatural."

Bel gripped his chin in thought. "Is there any chance we might see the corpse? His and the dead who followed him?"

Geoffrey shook his head. "The guard burned the corpses after the battle for fear of plague. "Many had come from villages afflicted by the flux." He paused. "What's more, however, during the fight, I wounded the man. Broke his bloody arm, I know I did. Yet..." He sighed pensively. "If the Gift of the Guardians allows us to heal the wounds of others, what if...what if the Keeper's have a similar gift that does the opposite."

"What do you mean?"

"Well, during the fight, after I wounded him, he runs off to where the bartender and the maid were cowering. I thought he was going to try to hold them at his mercy, hoping to buy himself a means of escape. Instead, next thing I know, he grabs hold of the man, and before my very eyes, it was like the poor man's life was drawn right out of him—like an apple left to dry in the sun. Then, just as this is happening, I look at the Keeper and watch as his bone seemed to knit all by itself. It was as if simply touching him, he stole the poor man's life and used it to heal himself."

Bel remained silent. He thought back to that day upon the snow-covered field outside of Clearpoint Keep, the day when Marcus Harding traded his life for Bel's own. He recalled the sensation of lying upon death's doorstep, his vision fading, until with a touch and an oath, his and the Tower's roles were somehow reversed.

"If the Lady of Light grants the power to heal to those of us anointed under a Guardian title," he finally said, "I suppose those sworn to Dibhor could possess a certain affinity for staving off their own deaths. Do you think that is what happened?"

"Makes sense to me," Geoffrey said.

"The Gift of the Guardians," Thom grumbled, "and the Keeper's Curse."

Bel gave a slow nod. "Regardless," he said, "We should focus on the enemy before us, for there will be time enough to speculate after the battle—Kin willing we all make it through." He stood and raised his voice toward the front of the tent. "Marguerite?"

In an instant, the girl appeared. "Yes, my lord?"

"Pass word along to my captains," he said. "We meet our enemies at dawn."

CHAPTER 35: BETRAYAL

With Baron Roland safely back in command of Harrier's Keep, Lughus and Brigid paused only long enough to say their goodbyes before taking to the lake once again. Between Guy's vague implications and Alan's open threats, they were filled with consternation. What larger treachery had the Guardians sown? What was the betrayal that their enemies had alluded to?

From the prow of the keelboat, he stared into the distance across the lake, as if urging the vessel to greater haste by sheer force of will. His hands rested comfortable upon Sentinel's hilt, taking comfort in the feel of the leather wrappings, the broad quillons, and the solid pommel.

A sword is the man who wields it... He heard Crodane's voice resonate through his mind. *His will given substance, his heart given form, and his soul revealed to al the world...*

What was it that his enemies saw when he drew his blade? A hero? A villain? A baron? A Blackguard? Who was he and what had he become?

"Tilling your field again, I see."

Lughus turned just as Brigid stepped up alongside him and slipped her arm in his.

"Tilling my field?" he asked.

She gently pressed her finger to the crease between his brows. "Geoffrey told me that in Pyle, husbands and wives work their fields together," she said.

"They do the same in Galadin," Lughus said.

"Oh do they?" She smiled and rested her cheek against his shoulder. "Well, in that case, why not pass the spade and let me have a go?"

Lughus exhaled deeply. "I fear I've been a fool. I fear for our friends. I fear for the city. I fear we've been betrayed."

"So do I," Brigid said gently, "but you know what else?"

"What?"

"I fear for our enemies," she said with a grin.

The corners of his mouth curled upward and he kissed her on the crown. "We are stronger together," he said. "That much is true."

It was nearing sunset when the keelboat arrived back in Galadin. The creeping darkness and the biting wind off of the lake quickened their steps as they made their way through the cobblestone streets of the city to the great stone barbican of Houndstooth. The men on duty snapped to attention at the sight of them, and a man was sent running ahead to inform Sir Owain, Horus, and the rest of the castle folk of the baron's return. He might have saved himself the trouble, for Fergus's joyful barking was a clarion call that proclaimed it to all.

Within the hour, riders were sent to the knights of the seven fiefdoms calling upon them to rally their men. A pair of pigeons carried word to Abbot Woode at St. Golan's and a general alarm was sounded to call upon any able-bodied burgher, farmer, or shepherd who could draw a bow or carry a blade. The weaver knights began rounding up whatever unemployed mercenaries remained within the city, and Brigid sent word to Adolfo's lieutenants to prepare for an imminent threat.

Of course, the exact nature of the threat was unknown, but Lughus sensed the storm that was coming, could feel it deep within his soul, and he knew that with Willum Harlow free to sow mischief, it was absolutely necessary to be prepared.

At least, he did not have to wonder long. As the city continued its preparations for the expected assault, scouts returned with reports of a massive army marching northward along the coastal road. At the same time, the fleet of ships blockading Nordren harbor had doubled in size as it appeared more ships had sailed north from Grantis or from the far Dwerin ports. Unlike the army that attacked St. Golan's, however, or the men stationed at Stonebridge Castle, these forces consisted of not only the sworn retainers of the great Andochan lords, but the true might of the Order and were commanded by cavaliers and justiciars, anointed Guardians all.

"What I don't understand," Sir Owain said as they sat together in the solar to prepare for the arrival of the enemy, "is how they should reach our very doorstep without us ever receiving any word. I mean, a bloody great fleet of ships appears on the horizon—to say nothing of the forces marching by land—you'd think that would cause some concern. Why did Nordren not send a rider? Leoric has never hesitated to call for aid before."

Lughus's gaze narrowed. He had no wish to voice his inward concerns, but as he felt Brigid's gaze upon him, he knew that he did not have to.

"If the force is as large as the reports say," Lughus mused, "we can expect to be besieged. Taking the field against such overwhelming numbers would be little more than suicide. Besides, what happens to the common folk should the army crumble and flee? The kingsmen have already shown how little virtue weighs against spoils. We cannot abandon them."

"Houndstooth has withstood plenty in the past, my lord," Sir Owain said. "She's the rock of the Brock!"

Horus steepled his fingers. "Following the yields of this autumn's harvest, we are extremely well-provisioned. However, if we begin to take in folk from the countryside, we may find our resources limited. It may be wise to encourage our people to seek temporary shelter westward in Agathis."

"It'll be a hard journey in this cold," Sir Owain said.

"Fair enough," the steward said. "I suppose we might load them into keelboats to seek refuge in Marthaine?"

Owain shrugged. "Possibly," he said, "though to be fair, I'd say the safest bet it to have them flee for the hills and the highlands. Let them take shelter in the hidden places they already know. Some might also be more suited to take what supplies they can and withdraw to the tower houses and baileys of the seven fiefs. I expect Woode will likely offer shelter to many and more within the walls of St. Golan's as well."

"I'm not quite sure how that makes them any safer though," Horus said.

Sir Owain held out his hands. "Think of it this way," he said. "The Guardians have chosen to march northward in the middle of winter. In terms

411

of warfare—as I'm sure you already know—it's just not the done thing. As such, I don't believe our enemy seeks to engage in a prolonged and drawn out war. The cold and the snow simply won't allow it." He paused, his mustache bristling. "No, this is a targeted assault, an assassination of a different sort than we've dealt with before."

Horus remained silent. Lughus and Brigid exchanged a glance.

"Now, don't get me wrong," Owain continued. "I like Perin. He's a good man and in times of peace, there's no better man to lead the Brock. Roland too—though I can scarcely believe I'm admitting it. He's proven himself a stalwart friend that, frankly, makes me ashamed that peace between our baronies took so bloody long. However—" He raised a finger. "Perin is no warrior, and between his age and the recent troubles, Roland is nowhere near his full strength."

"No. Kredor's target is Galadin, and while the other barons stand with us, it is we who will incur the full force of his wrath. Galadin is the very mortar that holds the Brock together, and should Houndstooth fall, the realm will sunder and Marthaine, Glendaro, Helmstead, Brabant, Nordren, and all the rest are sure to follow."

"You truly think so?" Lughus asked. He knew what the old seneschal said was true, but so strong was his faith in the Brock, that he was reluctant to admit it. Furthermore, it was still nearly impossible for him to see his own worth as greater than that of any other baron—saint's blood or not. He was human, and while his position and his title had bestowed certain responsibilities upon him, he was nonetheless comprised of flesh and blood.

"Have any other barons had to fend off assassins sent from the Order?" Owain returned, "or been the sole pursuit of entire armies?"

Lughus remained silent.

"Galadin is the target," Owain said again. "Kredor couldn't give a fig about anywhere else."

Brigid took a slow, deep breath. "Owain is right," she said.

Lughus sighed. "Set criers to inform the people of the invading army, and send riders to spread word among the farms and villages across the countryside. They should at least know of the threat that exists. They can make the decision for themselves whether they wish to stay on their lands or seek shelter here or elsewhere. And though it may be a bit presumptive, remind them that St. Golan's is also willing to provide sanctuary as well."

"Yes, sir," Owain said, "and I will continue to see that the city is prepared to withstand the siege."

"Yes, they're likely to have trebuchets and St. Aiden's Fire so we should prepare the buildings for that eventuality."

"I'll see it done."

"I'd also like to send messages by bird and rider to the other barons—if we can spare them," Lughus said. "My grandfather said that he would send word, but with the winter and all, I would rather not leave it to chance. Horses can slip on ice and snow, and Alan Beinn slaughtered all of the Marthaine messenger pigeons. We need to ensure that our allies know of the coming threat."

Though if Guy is to be believed, some of them already do...

Horus inclined his head. "I will see to it at once, my lord."

With orders thusly given, preparations continued as the Houndstooth readied for war. Within days, the knights of the seven fiefs arrived with their retinues of mounted men-at-arms as well as contingents of yeomen archers gathered from across their holdings. Many of the men had already seen battle—whether at St. Golan's, Cragbarrow, or Stonebridge Castle—so in spite of the deepening chill and mounting snow, the men were in high spirits as they shared warm cups of broth with old comrades from atop the mighty stone battlements surrounding the city and its wards. For while they knew the cold to be a hardship, they also understood that however badly they felt it within the walls, their enemies were sure to face even greater suffering upon the long and hasty march. Why the king would order such an assault was unthinkable and their confidence grew and grew.

The arrival of messengers from both Agathis and Marthaine only added to their faith in victory. The "Fighting Fifth" was on the move, ready to lend their aid, and even though they could only march as fast as the great war elephants would allow them, men cheered to hear that they were on their way. It was, after all, the Month of the Wolf.

Baron Roland too had sent word that he would be arriving as soon as possible. Having finished setting his house in order, he wasted no time in calling his banners and readying the Silver Eagles for battle. The only problem was the procurement of enough boats to transport his men across the lake. Guy had certainly done what he could to raise a sizable fleet, but Roland's full force demanded many more, and so decisions were being made regarding whether to forget the marine transit and instead simply march around. Regardless, where once men cursed the name of the master of Harrier's Keep, they now looked forward to his arrival with great anticipation.

Yet, in spite of these commitments from such staunch and powerful allies, the other barons remained silent, and while Lughus did not doubt the support of the Lord Baron, he could not, with absolute certainty, say the same for the others. And he certainly could not count on their arrival to snatch victory from the jaws of defeat like at St. Golan's. Surely, lightning could not strike twice.

But Houndstooth was a mighty fortress and the walls of Galadin were high and thick. For centuries they had stood strong, repelling enemies and protecting those within. His ancestors had built it, defended it, and so too would he, for he knew that in some strange sense, they were watching him, from the somber interior of the cathedral and its catacombs. This was their city and these were their people—from the lowliest beggar to Brigid, his betrothed. This was their home. He would not see it fall.

Of course, this grim determination, this ardent resolve, could not but waver, ever so slightly, when the great army of the Guardian Order finally arrived.

It was from the east that they came, appearing on the horizon like a morning fog. Delicate, silent, like ghosts lightly drifting in with the snow. At once, the men on watch sounded the alarm. Lughus and Fergus had been touring the massive stockpiles of arrows and recognizing the skill of the city's numerous bowyers and fletchers who had worked so tirelessly these many months to ensure that the army of the Golden Hound would remain well-armed. Without warning, Fergus's ears perked and the thick fur on his shoulders stood on end as a low growl sounded from the depths of his throat. Lughus knew at once what it meant and he was already on his way to the main gates of the city by the time the bells of the cathedral started ringing. When he reached them, Brigid was already waiting.

"They're here," she said.

Lughus gave a nod and leaving Fergus to wait alongside the men of the watch, the pair climbed the ladder into the gatehouse to view the approaching army from the highest point atop the battlement.

"Blood and fire," Brigid uttered.

Lughus's gray-eyed gaze peered into the distance. The line of kingsmen marching forth from the hazy concealment of the fog stretched across the entire plain. Rank after rank after rank, they emerged, their polished helmets shining with the tips of their spears. Red cloaks and tabards swayed with their steady footfalls like lapping waves upon the shore of a great sea of blood. They numbered in the thousands. Perhaps tens of thousands.

Yet it was not infantry alone that comprised the might of the Guardians. Following behind them, their deep exhales rising in a thick shroud, came the great muscled destriers of the heavy cavalry. Heavily armored knights and men-at-arms encased in ring mail and plate, secure within their steel skin and anonymous behind the masks and visors of their great helms. The land itself seemed to shudder beneath the steady footfalls of the horses, so great were their number, and Lughus knew that should they spur to charge, it would be with the force of an avalanche and the sound of thunder.

If this were not enough to stir a sense of terror and impending doom, the massive horde of peasant levies, the wagon trains of siege engines, and the smaller hosts of individual knights and nobles from across both Andoch and Dwerin that followed in the wake of the main force was enough to challenge even the bravest man's nerve.

But before it all, leading the impressive array of martial superiority was something the likes of which few, if any, could claim to have ever faced before and lived.

Flanked by a dozen horsemen bearing standards emblazoned with the crimson banners of the Guardians, another squad of armored men marched in formation holding aloft as one an enormous silver reliquary fashioned in the shape of a giant key.

"What is that?" Brigid asked.

Lughus's eyes flashed and he felt his heart beat quicken. "It's the Key to the Kingdom," he said. "It's said that an army that carries the Key cannot be defeated." He paused and he peered into the distance at the gloriously adorned contingent of men that rode alongside it. "It also means that the army is personally led by the Guardian-King."

By the time the grand army had made its way across the plain to stand before the Galadin gates, the defenders had assembled, taking up their positions upon the walls. Sir Owain Rook, though much recovered from his wounds, limped down from the Houndstooth with Sergeant Pike and the rest of the baron's guard. The majority of the weaver knights and the knights of the seven fiefdoms had already assembled.

"Is it true?" Owain asked, hobbling to where Lughus and Brigid stood with Fergus before the gates. "Has Kredor himself come forth?"

Lughus gave a nod.

"It looks as if they mean to parley," said Sir Gosbert of Clomanse. "There are riders approaching."

Sir Burnel of Wrendale peered below. "Is that..." He paused. "Is that Theo Nordren?"

Brigid caught Lughus's eye, but remained silent. "It is," she said.

"Blighted bastard!" Owain cursed.

Lughus's jaw tensed, but he remained impassive. Theo had always been ambitious, and in retrospect, Lughus could recognize now a certain hint of resentment. While a great barony in its own right, Nordren's influence failed to extend beyond the fact that the Nordren estate commanded the Brock's southern port, which, Lughus remembered, lacked the prestige of Houndstooth or Harrier's Keep. Cessation of trade with Andoch and Grantis as a result of the recent hostilities must have caused significant strain. Still, the sting of the betrayal—both personally, and to the Brock—was unforgivable. Theo knew what was at stake, had been privy to all private plans.

Yet, Lughus knew he could ill afford to lose his head and allow his passions, his rage, to control him. There was far too much at stake. What happened today, or in the coming days, could very easily mean the end of the war.

"I will go to meet them," Lughus said.

"I'll go with you," Brigid said.

Lughus gave a nod. He glanced around the assembled knights and other leaders and sorely felt the absence of Geoffrey and Sir Adolfo. The Madder, at least, was on his way, riding with the Fighting Fifth, but Geoffrey...

A sudden flash of anger contorted his otherwise placid features. What did the Nordren betrayal mean regarding the fate of the Vanguard? Was any of the news Theo's messenger brought to Houndstooth those many weeks ago actually true? The storm clouds in his eyes flashed with latent wrath.

Owain gave a nod. "I'll call for an honor guard." He turned to Sergeant Pike. "Call the men and have our three finest horses sent—"

"No," Lughus interrupted. "We'll meet them alone and on foot. The rest of you ready for battle. See that the poles are ready to repel ladders and double-check that the ballista are stocked with a plenty of ammunition."

"Are you sure, baron?" Sir Balric of Parth grunted. "Excuse me if I am not inclined to trust that men such as these will respect the customs of a parley."

"I understand your caution," Lughus said, "but at such close distance, they'll be well within bowshot. If they try anything, let fly." He turned to Brigid and they exchanged a silent nod. "We'll return shortly."

Leaving the main gates secure, Lughus and Brigid passed through a small postern in the gatehouse out onto the field. Fergus, unwilling to be left behind again, loped after them. A light breeze blew, its chill fingers stark as a razor against Lughus's cheeks. Beside him, Brigid's raven hair, long and loose, danced along with it. She would tie it up later when the fighting started, but for now it hung majestically. It was a mark, he knew, of her femininity, an overt sign that not only a woman, but a woman Guardian stood against them unafraid. His heart swelled with pride and, for neither the first nor the last time, his blood warmed with affection for her.

They had barely spoken a word since the last meeting in the solar. They had not needed to, for somehow he knew her mind just as easily as she knew his, so united were they in mind and heart. Regardless of what might happen today or any day hence, they were together. One. It made them powerful, the sum of their individual natures stronger than either on their own.

Together, they paced slowly to where the enemy leaders awaited them. Apart from the sound of their footfalls, the idle pawing of the horses, and the ebb and flow of the breeze, the world was utterly silent—until it was broken by the voice of the Guardian-King.

"So you're the Galadin boy, I take it."

Lughus raised his head proudly and fixed the enemy horsemen with his piercing gaze. There were over a dozen of them, most of whom were clad in the colors of the Order. Legendary men of the Warlord's Tower, men whose stories he had studied from the time he had first learned to read. The Shell, the Finch, the Motte, the Bear, the Bell—and the Brethren only knew how many others stood among the massive horde that lie beyond. As a boy at the Loremaster's Tower, he had seen them often enough from afar, and like the Chough, he would be forced to face them as they sought to wash their legendary weapons in his and his allies' blood. These men, these heroes, were

417

easily recognizable by the glorious, gilded embellishments of their plate armor and the polished barding and embroidered caparisons of their white steeds, and though their faces were concealed by their helmets and visors, Lughus knew them all the same.

In addition to these men and their accompanying squires, standard-bearers, and attendants, rode a small grouping of great Andochan lords—Fowler, Cordetta, Delucion—families with estates in the Golden Quarter of Titanis, some of whom could claim lineage derived from ancient men of title or who, through political maneuvering had, at times, been able to inherit additional Guardian titles of their own. Again, they were men Lughus knew of, but to whom he was unknown.

The final four riders were men that Lughus knew.

The first, was Theo Nordren.

Theo had come dressed for war, though in his chainmail and baronial blue surcoat with its tawny salmon, he looked like a child playing at war beside the armored guardians in their crimson and plate. He was doing his best to look dignified and defiant, though Lughus could sense his latent discomfort. Perhaps he was realizing that once a man commits himself to such profound treachery, he rarely finds himself a welcome friend anywhere.

Beside him came Willum Harlow. For who but one so single-minded in the pursuit of treachery would be better suited to monitor a new and questionable ally?

Harlow had been outfitted with a fresh set of clothing, the formal dark garb of the Chancellors' constables, complete with a bright scarlet sash and a black chaperon hat. Upon his hip, he carried a light mace and the wooden fist that he wore as a replacement for his missing hand had been fitted with a lethal spike. Harlow's face was stern, but satisfied. It was the expression of a man who stood upon the brink of seeing his life's ambitions finally realized.

The last two were men that needed no introduction and while Lughus had never before spoken to them, there was no doubt as to who they were.

The first, in armor bedecked with intricate enameling and gilded scrollwork, was Kredor Drude II, Guardian-King of Andoch and Master of the Order of the Guardians. Truly, he was resplendent in his fine armor, the storied blade known as Testament fitted to a baldric across his back. His horse was an enormous white destrier, and in its gilded barding, it was a veritable juggernaut. The King's visor was up to reveal a handsome face marred by a type of sardonic smile. It was a disquieting visage and one that Lughus found not altogether unfamiliar. It was the face of a man of privilege, a man confident in the belief that he was fundamentally superior to any and all other human beings.

And at his side, in his illustrious purple robes, pallid hair, and alabaster skin was the man Lughus had never met, but had been warned of—Natharis Tainne. If Royne were correct, Tainne was the true threat, for in less than two years, he had been able to corrupt an Order that had stood as a beacon of hope for nearly thirteen hundred years.

Lughus fixed the King's advisor with his gray-eyed gaze, eagle eyes locked with pale serpent's stare. It was he who sought to had sought to usurp the Loremaster. It was he who engineered Rastis's imprisonment and downfall. It was he who would see the entirety of Termain brought to thrall.

The young baron's hand tightened around Sentinel's handle and his knuckles turned as white as the snow.

At length, Kredor gave an impatient sniff. "Well, say something, boy," the King said. "Don't tell me we've another deaf mute like that Prince Whatever-his-name-is in Montevale."

"He speaks, your majesty," Harlow said humbly. "Though in my experience it amounts to little more than bravado."

Fergus released a low, threatening growl. Lughus took a slow breath to calm himself and when he had mastered his anger, fixed the King with his eyes and spoke in a voice that was clear and strong.

"I am Lughus, Baron of Galadin, and this is Lady Brigid Beinn of Dwerin," he said at last, "though by our anointed titles, we are the Marshal and the Blade."

Brigid and Fergus stood defiantly on either side of him and he felt once more the strength of their friendship and resolve. The anointed men flinched at the admission—spoken as it was without a hint of shame. Even Kredor's sardonic grin twisted into a sneer.

"Then I shall greet you as a Galadin," the King said. "For let us focus on the part of you that maintains a shred of honor, rather than that part which reeks of shame."

"They are one and the same," Lughus said coldly.

Kredor's face flushed, but he held his temper. "Very well," he finally said. "Then in the spirit of our families' long and storied history, and out of respect for the many centuries of friendship that have united our realms, we have come to you with a final offer of peace. Stand down, swear an Oath of Fealty, and we shall celebrate our renewed peace with a celebratory mass in the cathedral of your legendary namesake. Bygones shall be bygones and order shall be restored to all Termain."

"Your army certainly offers credence to such an accord," Lughus said. "Surely your intentions can only be peaceful."

Kredor pursed his lips. "Alternatively, we could simply kill you all and raze the city to the ground."

"Yes, destroy the city of the Blessed Saint," Lughus replied. "The history books are certain to sing your praises for all the ages."

"I could not give a runny shit about the books." Kredor smirked. "Few enough people can read as it is, and those that write the books will record what we tell them. It's one of the great privileges awarded the victorious." He gave a snort. "Well, that and not being dead."

Lughus felt his bile rise, but he fought to maintain his control. "I suppose it's too much to expect wisdom from a man who would reject the Loremaster and sell his soul to Dibhor."

Natharis Tainne's eyes flashed, though King Kredor simply grinned.

"Jealous hearsay and baseless slander!" He laughed. "So typical of the Loremaster. Tell me. How wise can a man truly be when he so brazenly chooses to stand against his King?"

Lughus's hand tightened again around Sentinel's hilt, so angry was he that he found himself unable to speak. He didn't have to.

"Swine."

Kredor's eyes widened at the insult and his lips twisted into an angry sneer. The word, spoken so casually, so dispassionately, cut like a sharp blade straight to the bone.

"Excuse me?" The King growled.

Brigid released an impatient sigh. "No."

Kredor tightened his hands upon the reigns of his steed and as the great destrier stamped and snorted, Lughus reflexively loosened Sentinel's blade. "How dare you speak to me as such," the King seethed. "Shame I didn't take your mother's offer else you would have been taught to know respect."

Fergus snarled and Lughus would have drawn had Brigid not stayed him with her hand. "I've always found my mother's taste in men to be rather lacking," she said. "Fortunately, I discovered I have a mind of my own. Sad that so few other women have the chance to realize the same. Of course, I suppose that if they did, few enough of you would have ever been born." She smiled wickedly.

Kredor snarled and, sensing the rider's ire, his horse continued to grow restless. Hand on hilt, Lughus positioned himself between Brigid and the King, ready to draw and strike at the first indication of a charge. Even in the unlikely event that he should miss or the King should parry, Fergus was certain to leap and drag him down before Kredor had time to counter.

True, the remaining horsemen would be upon them at once, but the King would be dead and his title lost with him.

In spite of his anger and boorishness, Kredor seemed to sense this and it gave him pause. He settled his mount and contented himself with a nasty sneer. "If you will not listen to reason, then let it all be settled by the sword!" he snapped. "This was your last chance to surrender!"

"No, this is *your* last chance," Lughus said. "Cease this false call for the Protectorate. Return to Andoch before your absurd greed and lust for power bring greater ruin down upon us all!"

For a long moment, silence reigned as the mounted warriors stood awaiting the Guardian-King's answer. Before them, defiant, stood Lughus and Brigid, bodies tense and ready, beside the great golden hound.

At last, the Guardian-King gave a maddened chuckle, breaking the intense tableau. "Enough," he said, wheeling his horse around. "I grow tired of the mad jabbering of fools. Farewell, Heir of Galadin. When next we meet, I shall bathe in your holy blood."

Lughus leveled his gaze, but remained silent, his hand resting comfortably upon Sentinel's hilt. As the cold wind strengthened, howling like a lone wolf across the plain, he watched as the King and his procession turned their backs upon him and rode slowly back to their camp. Beyond them, under the overcast vault of the winter sky, the Key to the Kingdom shone brilliantly. It reminded him of the only other time he beheld the Guardian-King with his own eyes—that coronation day so long ago when the old Loremaster administered his final test before setting them each upon their path. He recalled Royne's sardonic drawl as he casually called out the scepter as a fraud. Were the circumstances not so dire, the memory might have brought a smile and a placid sensation of nostalgia.

But not today, for while the royal scepter encased within the giant reliquary might not be the true Key forged by the Lady of Light so many centuries ago, the power of the symbol and the impressive sheen of the enormous reliquary was enough to fill him with a sense of dread and embolden his enemies to unimaginable heroics.

Beside him, Brigid stood with her arms folded across her chest, defiantly calm, but with her daggers in easy reach.

"He was lying, you know? His whole offer of a mass and all of that?"

"I know," he said.

"That is not a man who knows the meaning of peace."

Lughus breathed a heavy sigh and released his hilt to offer her his hand. With a forlorn smile, she accepted it and together they began to pace slowly back to Galadin, to home. "This is going to get bloody," he observed.

"Probably," Brigid said, "but whatever happens, we'll see it through together. Come what may."

"Always," he told her. "Come what may."

CHAPTER 36: TO THE NORTH

Valder has fallen ill. Unusual for a Guardian, though not completely unheard of, particularly from a title passed on solely by blood rather than sacrifice. Clearly there is truth to the conjecture that such an anointing dilutes the potency of the title and I can only wonder at what the Order must have been like in its earlier days. I want to believe that, at least for a time, it truly was the shining beacon of hope guiding the good folk of the continent to a brighter day.

But no more.

While it pains me to admit it, the Order has fallen. Power, dominion, and wealth have become the guiding force behind nearly all of the Order's actions. Titles are offered now to courtiers and nobles in exchange for political favors and coin. The Chancellor deems a man's worth by the weight of his purse while to the Hierophant the selfsame arithmetic determines the value of a man's soul. The warriors of the Warlord have become thugs and bullies, proving honorable men like Dandy and Marcus Harding to be the exception rather than the rule. Even among my own tower, scholarship has become trivial as men choose to horde their knowledge like a dragon hordes treasure, locking it away in great impotent piles when it should instead spur them to action, leading them to create a better world.

In short, the Guardians no longer guard.

Now, I do not state this out of a self-indulgent sense of pity, for to do so would be to fall victim to the selfsame criticism that I so recently espoused, and there is more than enough hypocrisy plaguing the Order these days.

Rather, I intend it, perhaps, as a type of justification. A justification and, perhaps, an apology.

For generations, the Bard's Heresy has loomed upon the edge of darkness as a secret threat to the Order. Only the Loremasters—perhaps due to the uncanny phenomenon of The Book of Histories—seem willing to not only acknowledge the danger but actively prepare to stand against it. At the same time, the Order's willful ignorance regarding the true nature of the Keepers of Castone coupled with the continued persecution of the so-called Blackguards leaves all of Termain vulnerable.

Thus, it fall upon me to act.

As Sigmund has long foreseen, the time of the prophesy is at hand. With Valder on his deathbed, Kredor—his only son and heir—will become the next Guardian-King. Kredor is ambitious, brutish, and selfish. In spite of Valder's efforts, his long association with his mother's kinsmen, particularly those of the House of Tainne, has cultivated many of the qualities that Valder sought to prune. Furthermore, the Tainnes' long history of friendship with the Keepers of Castone are an ill omen and the current scion of the family, Natharis Tainne, is a recognized Keeper in his own right.

Driven by ambition and encouraged by Tainne, Kredor even went so far as to corner Marcus Harding to ask him for information regarding the history of the Protectorate and the legal stipulations surrounding its enactment. The prince's disdain kept him from approaching me directly and he sought to exploit Harding's scholarship and familiarity with the archives of the Loremaster's Tower. Marcus, ignorant of this, approached me for assistance, and together, we were able to satisfy the prince's curiosity. Sir Marcus is a good man, and while his status demands that he follow the prince's orders, he knows that his ultimate duty is to the safety and security of all Termain.

Regardless, the incident forced me to act, for when Valder passes on the title and Kredor claims his crown, I fear the time of the heresy will be upon us. If my plea is indeed to go unheard, then I must ensure that there are still those willing to stand for what is right. The wandering Guardians. The pure pariahs.

The Blackguards.

The Shield, the Cup, the Wall, and of course, the Marshal, the Vanguard, and the Blade. Those of us who were there at the beginning. Those of us who—in some sense—knew Amarthia the Bard.

Thus, it is a conspiracy, and as with all conspiracies, some of us are sure to be discovered and some of us are sure to fall.

I only hope that in damning myself, I do not damn the boys as well.

Lughus, Thom, and Royne.

Never in all my life have I known anything to be more important or more worthwhile than to be their guardian. I love them as if they were my own, and if I have one hope, one wish, in this future of uncertainty and darkness, it is that they will be spared the sorrows and the pain and may come to stand together to greet the new dawn...

Royne's departure from the University was marked by even less ceremony than his arrival. After gathering what few belongs he had—his original set of clothes, a few quills and pieces of parchment, and, of course, *The Book of Histories*—he was met by Haruki in the Symposium.

Neither Udo nor Amara were anywhere to be seen. Judging by their behavior, it seemed that few enough, if any, of the other alchemists had bothered to pay the viceroy's arrival, ultimatum, and untimely death any real mind. Master Kebir was busy arguing good-naturedly with a respectable-looking old woman with wiry gray hair while about a dozen or so students watched on. Servants and maids set tables, cleaned up discarded dishes, and swept floors. For all intents and purposes it was just another regular day.

Royne sighed. "It's kind of you to see me to the gate," he said to Haruki. "I regret that we did not have the opportunity to know one another better. I would have loved to hear of your homeland.

Haruki gave a sheepish grin. "Actually, I was asked by Master Udo to see you out through one of our other secret paths," he said. "The red-cloaked soldiers are gathered at the main gate to retrieve their fallen lord and the general who leads them is one of the more clever ones we have observed. I believe they call him the Stone. After the fall of the senate, it was he who commanded the soldiers until the viceroy arrived. With any luck, he will do as he did in the past and simply leave us in peace."

Royne gave a sniff. "Here's hoping," he said. "For your sake."

Haruki bowed. "Now, if you will follow me, I will lead you out through a safer path."

From the symposium, Royne followed the young alchemist past the kitchens and through a series of long hallways to a winding staircase that opened into a large, underground canal, dimly lit by a pair of hooded lanterns. Haruki lifted one from where it hung upon an iron hook, and motioned for Royne to follow.

"This way," he said.

Royne glanced wistfully back the way they came. He had not really expected Amara to see him off, but he had hoped that he might at least have an opportunity to say goodbye. Funny. He had never really cared about such sentimentalism in the past—even when he parted ways with Lughus and Thom so long ago. However, with Amara...

He breathed a sigh. "Lead on," he said to Haruki.

By the light of the lantern, they followed the canal in the direction of the flow of the water. Royne had little sense of direction at the best of times, but underground and absent of the sun, he might as well have been blindfolded and spun around.

Fortunately, it was not long before Haruki turned a corner to reveal a light at the far end of the tunnel. The smell of brine and fish grew stronger as the light grew brighter and Royne could discern bits of flotsam and jetsam in the waters of the canal. Somewhere close by a ship's bell sounded and the laughter of gulls echoed over the lapping of waves.

"This will see you out to the waterfront," Haruki told him.

"Thank you," Royne muttered in reply.

The young alchemist bowed. "I'm to tell you that if you should not attempt to return by way of this path," he said. "For it is guarded by many different forms of mechanical and alchemical defense."

Royne gave a nod. "Don't worry," he said. "I won't."

Haruki bowed. "While we at the University do not approve of your methods, we are at least grateful for the life of Fabius's brother," he said stoically. "I only hope that with the viceroy gone, the rest of his family does not become subject to any further retribution."

"I will look in on them," Royne said. "For I know that no one else will."

Haruki ignored the implied slight, and in fairness, he was not really the intended target.

"Well," Royne said at last, "Goodbye."

Haruki nodded and held out his hand. Royne moved to take it only to see that the young man's palm was not extended in farewell, but in offering.

"What's this?" Royne asked.

"I do not know," Haruki said, "and as long as I do not know, I cannot lie should anyone ask about it."

It appeared to be a single piece of vellum folded into a square. A flood of conflicting emotions tightened Royne's chest as he speculated at its contents. At length, he took it and thrust it into his satchel with *The Book of Histories*.

"Thank you," he said.

"Balance be with you," Haruki said.

The young Loremaster suppressed a derisive chuckle. "And you," he said instead. "Farewell."

Without another word, Royne turned his back on the young alchemist and passed out of the tunnel into the bright light of the afternoon upon the shore.

For a while, he wandered aimlessly through the city, heedless of the danger and cognizant of the growing sense of anxiety that hung like a shroud over the citizens and seemed to ignite a spark of fear beneath the boots of the kingsmen. He heard cries of shock and surprise as word of the viceroy's death at the hands of the alchemists spread, but while a normal man might feel a certain sense of satisfaction at the public interest at his exploits, Royne felt only a mild sense of frustration that bordered on dread.

Eventually, he found himself standing alone at the center of the forum. Despite the relatively early hour, many of the merchants were already packing up for the day while the number of red-cloaked kingsmen seemed double what he had come to know as normal. *What had been the point of any of it?* he wondered. *Had it all just been a colossal waste of time?*

He gazed up at the University, at the far-off parapet from which he and Amara had watched a full dozen men beheaded as a testament to the authority of the viceroy.

"I am a sower of discord," he said aloud. Beside him, a pair of pigeons pecking at a discarded crumb eyed him with dumb uncertainty and took flight. Royne watched them for a moment, then with a sigh, recalled the folded vellum that Haruki had given him.

With one final glance at the pigeons, he retrieved the note, and unfolded it to reveal the image of a slender hand with the fingers splayed wide. However, it was not ink that defined the image upon the calfskin. Rather, the slender outline had been delicately singed into the vellum. Just enough to avoid compromising the integrity of the material and set it ablaze. Beneath the image, in a fine, scrolling hand had been written a single word:

Magic!

Royne breathed a heavy sigh and gazed up one final time at the distant parapet. Then, sliding the vellum inside the cover of *The Book of Histories*, he turned his back upon the University and headed for the city slums.

Nothing much had changed in his absence. Rats scurried about in broad daylight feasting upon the wretched refuse and filth that marred the pathways of the ancient city. A youth in rags ran past, half a loaf of stolen bread clutched against his breast. An old woman with less teeth than Royne had fingers sat upon a bucket plucking the feathers from a scrawny pigeon. The odor of rot and decay flourished under the oppressive humidity.

At last, he arrived at the ramshackle quarters marked by the scrawled insignia of the Wall. Beyond the threadbare curtain that served as a door, Royne could hear the muffled sound of unknown voices, though beneath them all, he was able to discern a single, familiar tenor.

He cast aside the curtain to reveal a trio of men seated on stools around a rough, wooden table. At once, conversation ceased.

"Salasco," Royne said quietly. He glanced to the far corner of the room and spied a young boy seated upon a barrel. He had grown taller since Royne had last seen him and more tanned. "Connor."

"Hello, sir!" the boy said cheerfully. "We missed you!"

Salasco grinned and stood. "Master Royne! We were just talking about you. So good to have you back!"

Royne nodded. Salasco was just as bandaged as he had been when Royne had last seen him, though the bandages appeared to be in different places than before. Consequences of the older man's use of the Gift, no doubt. He eyed the other two men at the table as they slowly got to their feet to greet him. One was extremely tall and gaunt with hollow cheeks and a heavy brow. His flesh was extremely pale and fine, tufts of flaxen hair sprouted in patches from his crown. The other was a broad, thick-shouldered man with a wiry black beard and leathery, weather-beaten skin. He wore a sleeveless tunic and sailcloth pants and stood noticeably bowlegged.

"Gentlemen," Salasco said to them, motioning toward Royne. "Allow me to introduce the Loremaster."

The two men grunted greetings. "The Stave and the Helmsman," Salasco told Royne.

"Blackguards?" Royne asked.

The men nodded.

"Both have agreed to join us," Salasco said. He motioned to the empty stool at his side and together the four men sat down.

"We've secured a ship that should be able to get us to the Brock," Salasco said. "She's nothing special, but with the Helmsman to guide us through the old smuggler routes, we should be able circumvent the blockade."

Royne nodded without understanding, but he trusted Salasco enough to know that it was positive.

"How did things go at the University?" Salasco asked.

Royne paused to consider how to answer. "Well..." he began.

"Well..." a new voice interrupted cheerfully, "for the viceroy and his son, I'd say they went rather poorly."

Royne glanced at the curtain to see another pair of men. The speaker was a short man wearing a forester's tunic with a hooded half-cape. Both were dyed a drab shade of green and he carried a short bow and quiver upon one shoulder. He had a long, thin nose, mischievous eyes, and a somewhat unnerving grin that put Royne in mind of some dread trickster from a faerie story.

The second man was tall and muscular with darker features suggestive of a native Grantisi or Kordish heritage. His head and face were cleanly shaved, and in place of a tunic he wore a leather harness bearing a pair of hand axes across his back.

"The Fox and the Thresher," Salasco told Royne.

"And I take it you're the Loremaster then?" the Fox said. "The famous Master Royne?"

"I'm not sure about famous," Royne grumbled.

"Perhaps 'Slayer of Tyrants' would be more suitable," the Fox leered.

Royne's gaze narrowed as the eyes of the others fell upon him. "Word travels fast," he said, "but not faster than a falsehood."

"So Viceroy Pryce did not fall by your hand," the Fox asked with a skeptical grin.

"He did not," Royne said. "But...to be fair...I killed his son, though it was in defense of another."

"Ah, so I see."

"It was one of the masters at the University that killed the viceroy."

The Stave scratched his chin thoughtfully. "If what you say is true, by nightfall the whole city will be swarming with guards."

"It already is," said the Fox. "With the Viceroy dead, command has fallen to the justiciar called the Stone. He lacks the men to place the city under full martial law, but they say he's recalling patrols from the countryside. For now, they seem limited to closing off the area surrounding the University, but are reluctant to draw too near."

"Well," Salasco said, "since Master Royne has returned, there is nothing else to keep us here." He turned toward the Helmsman. "How much time would you need before we can make sail?"

"We can leave now," the Helmsman grunted. "So long as the tide allows it."

"There's a family I'd like to see to before we depart," Royne said, "so long as there's time."

"I'm sure we can manage," Salasco said with a nod.

Royne breathed a heavy sigh and rubbed at his eyes. "Onward to Galadin, then," he finally said. "It's time to join the fight."

CHAPTER 37: THE WALLS OF GALADIN

It was after nightfall when the Guardian siege weapons began their merciless barrage upon the city of Galadin. Stone after stone from mangonel and trebuchet hammered the walls relentlessly while infantry men in covered rams charged the main gates of the city in an effort to smash the iron portcullis and shatter the ironbound doors. The city's defenders did their best to withstand the assault of the rams, forever bracing the doors from within while dropping cauldrons of boiling oil from above. Meanwhile, a deadly duel was playing out between the Andochan crossbowmen before the walls and the peerless Galadin bowmen above.

As Brigid ran about the city, helping to support the defenders wherever they might need, she was thankful—at least—that the Guardian engineers had not brought Aiden's Fire with them. Perhaps the surprise attack that Geoffrey and Adolfo had inflicted upon them at St. Golan's had encouraged them to take no chances and leave the volatile substance at home. Either that, or they simply lacked the time and resources to create more.

Regardless, the siege weapons were doing plenty of damage already and while they had yet to breach the city's outer walls, the general feeling among the men suggested that it would not be long. Lughus had even ordered squads of men-at-arms to go door-to-door to usher what few common folk remained to the Houndstooth to take shelter. From a distance, Brigid recognized the folk from The Rampant Hound among them. Molly, the owner, had even sent one of the men-at-arms to her with a gift of a wineskin. Something to keep the Lady Blade warm through the long night, the woman had said.

Of course, Brigid could think of plenty of other ways that she'd rather keep warm—a pot of tea, a crock of soup, a warm fire, and Lughus's arms wrapped around her.

But alas, the King had come to call, and as she had long ago learned at Blackstone, the loftier the title, the larger the pain in the ass.

In any case, dawn would break soon enough, and with its arrival, so too would begin a new phase of the war. In the waning light of dusk, she had witnessed men constructing other structures, tall frames built upon what appeared to be repurposed wagons. While she had never seen one in life, the part of her mind that was the Blade understood them to be great ladders and siege towers.

Well, she thought, at least then she might finally feel useful in this fight. It was certainly preferable to waiting around only to be smashed by a giant stone.

She found Lughus atop the battlements with Fergus, Pike, and a peasant archer named Alban. Alban, she recalled, was one of the peasant men, a herder, who had distinguished himself at St. Golan's. Carefully, Lughus peered over the crenellations, directing Alban's shots, while Pike provided cover with his shield. The work must have been going well, for as she watched them, Lughus craned his neck quickly, pointed, and in a flash, Alban stood up with Pike and fired before dropping back down to cover. Lughus peered over the side, and with a sturdy nod, clapped the archer heartily on the shoulder.

"Crack shot," the young baron said with a grin. "Well done."

The archer tipped his bycocket. "Thank you, my lord."

Pike pulled a flask from where it hung on his baldric and passed it to his lord. Lughus nodded his thanks, took a quick swig, and passed it on to Alban just as Fergus announced her approach with a happy bark.

"My lady," the archer said humbly. He was a rustic sort, perhaps somewhere around Geoffrey's age with a manner somewhat reminiscent of the Vanguard.

"Lady Brigid." Pike saluted. Alban returned the bottle to the sergeant and somewhat sheepishly he offered it to her.

Brigid took it with a smile, downed a quick swig—some manner of weak mead—and passed it back. "Dawn approaches," she said. "Should we expect guests?"

"It seems likely," Lughus agreed. "They've not made much progress with the ram, but I thought I saw the shadow of a siege tower or two among the enemy camp."

"I counted ten," Brigid said. "There was a group of men trying to mine the curtain wall to the south, but Sir Deryk's archers were able to clear them." She gave a forlorn sigh. "We seem to be holding for now, though those trebuchets have wreaked havoc with the parts Hounton. The house where Geoffrey's family and I used to live is nothing but rubble."

Lughus's face turned grave. "Are there many wounded?"

"Not as many as there could be. Luckily most folk chose to heed the order to evacuate. They either fled for the safety of the highlands and St. Golan's, or have taken refuge with Owain and Horus at Houndstooth."

"Thank the Brethren for that."

"Aye, but they'll need much help rebuilding. The damage is...extensive."

"Worse than Cragbarrow?"

"Not *as* bad. I mean, we lack the bodies, but...in some places, yes." She paused. "Granted, I saw it all by lantern light, which makes it a bit harder to truly tell, but still..."

Lughus's eyes flashed. "This cannot go on." He breathed a heavy sigh. "You can tell me this is madness," he said, "but I've been thinking of opening the main gate."

Brigid's eyes scanned the area below them. It was a large, cobblestone square lined with warehouses, storerooms, a livery, and a few cheap alehouses. Some of the buildings had already been damaged from the siege engines, but for the most part, they remained intact, clustering together into what would become Hounton. Beyond it, she could see the gateways through to the other area of the city—the Trade Quarter the Golden Quarter, the Saint's Quarter, the docks along Lake Bartund, and the pathway that led up to the great barbican of Houndstooth. Slowly she began to understand.

"You want to herd them like sheep," she said.

Lughus gave a nod. "More like fish in a barrel."

Brigid smiled. "Fine," she said, "but you'll have to rig the gate so they think they broke through it on their own."

"Agreed," Lughus said, "and for that reason, I think we'll need to withstand at least the first assault against the walls. Otherwise, it will appear too obvious and they'll see right through the deception. They need to think they've softened us up first so that when they break through the gate, it's through their own actions."

Brigid nodded. "Then let's ready ourselves for a long day."

Soon enough, the sky began to lighten and the men of both armies prepared for the bloodshed that all knew would mark the dawn. Outside of the city, indeed, the Guardians had constructed a plethora of siege towers while teams of kingsmen stood by with tall ladders. The knights, for the most part, held back in reserve, ready to be called upon should the kingsmen and the peasant levies require help. The latter of the two, it was known, would likely be cut down first, little more than fodder to weaken the defenders enough for the professional soldiers to push through.

Within the walls, the defenders prepared as well, restocking quivers, distributing pikes and long poles to dislodge ladders, and replacing any shields too battered or broken to be useful. A hasty breakfast of thick porridge was distributed among the men, and Brigid could not avoid the sorrowful thought that for many, it would serve as a last meal.

Finally, at long last, when the great golden orb lifted clear of the far eastern horizon, trumpets rang out from among the battle lines of the Guardian-King's camp, and with a cacophony of raucous shouts and war cries, the grand army of Andoch began to advance.

Brigid stood beside Lughus upon the battlement of the gatehouse. "So it begins," he said, reaching out to squeeze her hand. In the rosy light of the winter dawn, his golden armor shone like a second sun.

Her heart gave a flutter at the sight of him—her love, her partner, her soul— and for a moment, she felt as if she might swoon.

Please, Lady of Light, protect him, she silently prayed. *Let no harm come to him.* She squeezed his hand and then hurriedly leaned closer, ignoring the cold touch of his armor, to plant a kiss upon his warm lips. "I love you," she said.

"I love you too," he replied, and smiling, added, "come what may."

"Come what may," she repeated.

Together they drew their weapons and Lughus raised Sentinel high above his head. A great cheer rose from the men of Galadin and Fergus let loose a resounding howl.

"Release the Hounds!"

"Release the Hounds!"

"Galadin! Galadin! Go!"

Together the ranks of archers gathered atop the walls loosed a volley into the charging Andochan horde. The front rank of men collapsed beneath the onslaught, but still the men behind them pressed on, leading with their shields. However, they offered little defense against the skilled marksmanship of the Brock. Man after man fell to the deadly bodkins of the Galadin archers, yet in spite of such devastation, the Andochans pressed on in a great swarm, flooding the base of the walls in frantic attempts to secure the ladders. Before long, there were too many men, too many targets for the archers to handle and the ladders began to rise like timbered logs in reverse. Atop the walls, Galadin men-at-arms with long poles, pikes, and halberds pressed back against the wooden scaffolding, tipping them over only to see them return.

Brigid watched the action unfold. These men, these climbers, were largely drawn from the peasant levies. Most of them were unarmored and pressed into service before being marched northward to a foreign land. Like Lughus, she disliked killing them, but she knew that in their desperation, they would certainly not hesitate to kill her. She watched as the Galadin men-at-arms cut them down, pitching their bodies over the battlements to collect in great heaps below, until at last enough of them had been cut down for the kingsmen to finally have their turn.

"Ready?" she asked Lughus.

"After you," he replied, and together they climbed down from the top of the gatehouse to join the men fighting upon the walls. Fergus followed at their heels, his great size—made slightly more bulky with the addition of his spiked collar and barding—occupying the entirety of the narrow staircase.

Their emergence into the fray brought forth cheers from the defenders and cries of anger from the kingsmen. Together they rushed to the site of the nearest ladder where the Galadin men-at-arms, in need of a pause after repelling the peasant levies, were suddenly hard-pressed by the eager kingsmen. Lughus whirled Sentinel before him, driving the red-cloaks back onto their heels. With the swiftness of a shadow, Brigid darted in and dispatched the foremost soldiers with a pair of strikes from Whisper and Shade. Before their bodies fell, Lughus had recovered his stance, and with a strike from above, cut a third man down, sending him toppling from the wall to crash upon the flagstones of the courtyard below.

Rallying behind their leaders, the Galadin men-at-arms beat back the remaining kingsmen, tossing their corpses over the side while Brigid's flashing blades kept the next man atop the siege ladder at bay.

"Polearms!" Lughus shouted. "Here!"

At once the men-at-arms took up the long repelling pikes and at the young baron's command, pushed the ladder backwards, toppling it back over to the plain. The red-cloaked climbers near the bottom scrambled to escape the fall, while others—those closer to the top—clung on in mad desperation, hoping in vain that doing so might somehow soften the impact of the hard ground. It did not.

"Well done," Lughus told the heaving Galadin men-at-arms.

"Aye, sir!" they replied. "For Galadin!"

"Lughus!" Brigid called. She motioned with one of her blades to where the siege towers had begun a slow advance toward the walls. At the top of the towers, teams of crossbowmen fired into the ranks of defenders already hard at work repelling the swarming ladders.

"I see them," Lughus said. He saluted the men-at-arms once more and followed Brigid to the next of the ladders. "Sir Deryk is at the corner tower ahead," Lughus said, as together they joined the defenders and dispatched another pair of kingsmen before hurrying on.

In response, those Andochans lucky enough to top the battlement drew back and attempted to form a shieldwall. However, before they could fully find their feet, Fergus charged, scattering them aside like chickens in a barnyard. In the chaos of the great hound's passage, the Galadin men-at-arms easily leapt upon the invaders and repelled another ladder back down to the plain.

Onward Brigid and Lughus hurried toward Sir Deryk and the corner tower, nearly running now as they followed in the wake of the great golden hound. To their enemies, Fergus was truly a thing of terror, a living symbol of the city of the Blessed Saint. His slavering jaws were a thing born of nightmare. Divine retribution made manifest. The kingsmen cowered at his passage, hid behind their shields, leapt or were knocked aside against the stone crenellations fearful of being cast over the side altogether. And at every turn, the Galadin defenders were quick to fall upon them.

When at last Fergus halted, he turned about, tail wagging, and Brigid could have sworn she detected a cheerful light of self-satisfied amusement twinkling in the great hound's green eyes. She couldn't help but smile as offered him a quick scruff beneath his chin.

"Good boy, Fergus," she said.

"Well, that's one way to clear a wall," Lughus remarked, catching up. "Can't say I've read about that in any of the old military manuals at the Loremaster's Tower."

"Then you'll need to write it yourself once all of this is over." Brigid grinned. She cast her glance out over the plain. The siege towers had rolled steadily closer, almost within range of lowering their gangways to allow easy passage to the battlement. Her smile disappeared. "Where's Sir Deryk?"

Lughus cast his gaze around the men-at-arms and yeomen stationed at the tower. "Where is Sir Deryk?"

"He took a quarrel to the side, my lord," one of the guardsmen said. "He insisted on staying as long as he could, but when he fell to swoon, some of the lads took him to the priory."

Lughus's face darkened. Sir Deryk was a stout fighter and a hero of St. Golan's.

"May I be of service, my lord?"

Brigid turned and at once her lips spread into a wicked grin. "Sir Adolfo," she said. "You're late."

She had intended it as a joke, but the Madder looked stricken. "My apologies, my lady," he said. "This is my city and I should never have left it."

"How did you get inside the walls?" Lughus asked.

Brigid eyed the Madder with concern. "The postern by Shitbrook?"

Adolfo nodded. "I ran into Sergeant Pike on my way here. He is currently having men see to its reinforcement."

Lughus gave a nod. "I'm glad to have you with us," he said. "Is the legion close?"

"No," Adolfo said, though Brigid noticed a subtle tick in the Madder's expression. "The snow and ice have caused no shortage of delays, but still they march and will relive us when they can. General Navarro asked that I give you his personal pledge. The wolf and the hound hunt together, he said."

"I never doubted them," he said, though his face was grim.

"But come," Adolfo said. He unslung his crossbow from his shoulder. "The towers approach."

"Yes," Lughus said. He called to a group of yeoman, "Ready fire arrows," he said, "and hurry."

At once, the men spurred to action and took up positions upon the battlement and atop the corner tower. As Lughus took command, Fergus following at his heel, Brigid took up a position under the cover of the battlement beside Adolfo.

"Is everything well?" she asked him.

"I should have been here," Adolfo said. His gaze narrowed as he readied his crossbow, searching among the ammunition in his quiver. "Galadin is important to me. It will not happen again."

Brigid rolled her eyes. "You know, you deserve happiness just as much as the next person," she said. "And don't make me angry by arguing any differently."

Adolfo remained silent. All around them, the archers began to ignite their arrows and line up their shots.

"Well, I hope you at least allowed yourself some respite," Brigid said.

The Madder paused to ignite the tip of his bolt in the flame of a nearby brazier. "I did."

"Good," Brigid said. Along the wall, the men atop the siege towers were preparing to lower the gangplanks.

"Alright, lads!" Lughus raised Sentinel high. "On my sword, let fly!"

Brigid watched the first of the gangplanks fall, saw the red-cloaked kingsmen readying to charge across to the wall. Her heart began to pound and her fingers tightened around Whisper and Shade.

"Let fly!" Lughus shouted.

"Galadin! Galadin!" Men echoed. "Let fly! Let fly!"

At once the volley of fire arrows shot forth, a multitude of shooting stars across the early morning sky. With a rhythmic series of thumps, they struck the sides of the siege towers, igniting the stretched skin and wooden panels meant to protect the soldiers within. Before long, the three nearest towers were ablaze and men stationed in the other corners towers around the city, having spied the blazes, were beginning to adopt similar tactics.

Still, the time it took for the fires to catch was enough for several squads of kingsmen to pass along the gangplanks over to the battlements. The chaos and confusion that ensued also allowed some of the Andochan soldiers below a second chance to secure the overturned ladders as well.

Brigid, Lughus, and Fergus, joined now by Adolfo and the Galadin knights, yeomen, and men-at-arms, rallied to turn them back. Before long, the stone parapets were slick with blood and frost, and the air was filled with the crackle of flames, the clanging of arms, and the cries of wounded men.

For what seemed like hours, they fought rank after rank of enemy soldier. Eight of the ten siege towers had collapsed into heaps of charred kindling, but still the kingsmen fought to raise the ladders only for the Galadin defenders to knock them down. Over and over again in an endless cycle of bloody violence.

Brigid fought on and on, side-by-side with Lughus, the pair of them cutting down kingsman after kingsman in tandem. Her arms were soaked with gore to the elbows. Lughus had discarded his baronial blue tabard, so soaked was it with the blood of his enemies as to weigh him down. Fergus's golden fur had turned several shades of crimson, from his rending maw to the scarlet tip of his tale. In the biting chill of the winter cold, muscles ached and bones stiffened, but still the battle carried on.

Sometime after midday, it began to snow again, soft flurries drifting lazily down from on high. A hazy sun shone vacantly through the clouds, and with weariness weighing upon the defenders, the anointed officers of the Order finally came forth.

They were not the heavily armored men who stood beside the King at the farce of a parley—Brigid was certain of that, for she had marked each one mentally by relative size and armament. Those were, as Lughus had told her, cavaliers—officers and field commanders of the Warlord's Tower. No, the men who climbed the walls with the kingsmen now were different. They wore the black and scarlet garb of the constabulary. They were killers.

She did not know their names anymore than their titles, but by the preternatural senses of the Blade, she knew that they were anointed, a fact confirmed as soon as they entered the fray.

The constables were first, flipping over the siege ladders near the main gates, and onto the battlement in the wake of a teeming mob of kingsmen. As Lughus and Brigid made to join the Galadin men-at-arms in repelling the assault, the constables were upon them, the first two slicing through the air at them with broad-bladed short swords while the third attempted to smash them with a flanged, iron mace. Lughus parried both blades in lightning fast succession, then dodged the blow from the mace by leaping backwards to the edge of the battlement. Brigid swept in while the man with the mace was off balance and scored a deep wound to his upper arm, the black leather pauldron peeled free like wood shavings beneath her blade. Before she could finish him, however, a broad blade of one of the other men turned aside her second strike and she was forced to leap away to safety.

Or so she thought. Behind them, two other Guardians had appeared, two other anointed. They must have somehow climbed one of the other siege ladders on the far side of the main gate and fought their way through to the fray. These men were not constables, but warriors clad in chain hauberks after the fashion Lughus generally preferred, the fashion of Crodane.

Fergus was the first to act, leaping to protect her. His teeth caught the leather bracer of one of the new arrivals and wrenched the wrist to the side, forcing him to drop his battle axe. At once, Lughus charged and thrust. A shower of steel rings burst from the man's mail at the entry wound, followed by a great torrent of blood as he withdrew Sentinel's blade. The second warrior cursed and sought to avenge his comrade by striking at Lughus as he recovered his footing. He raised his blade, but before he could follow through, Brigid was upon him, plunging Whisper to the hilt below the man's arm before following through with Shade at his throat.

They had forgotten the trio of constables, and just as the pair of warriors fell, one of the men lashed out and notched Fergus's ear with his short sword. The great hound snarled with rage and reared up onto his hind legs. In horror, Brigid saw the second constable step in and raise his blade, ready to plunge it deep into the unprotected belly of the great golden hound.

"No!" she cried, and with a precision she did not know she possessed, she hurled Whisper through the air. She was aiming for the man's eye, but the blade came in slightly low, catching the constable just above the cheekbone. Still, between the suddenness of the attack and the great splash of blood, the man was thrown off kilter. The moment's delay was enough to save the great hound's life as Lughus burst forth, driving his shoulder into the bleeding man and knocking him to the floor. A swift, downward thrust from Sentinel ensured that the man would never rise again.

In response, the constable with the mace rushed at Brigid, hoping to take advantage of her single blade. Gripping his weapon with both hands, he swung at her with enough strength to shatter the skull of an ox.

Yet she was far too quick, and even with one blade, she was a force to be reckoned with. With an easy step, she dodged the mace, and on the follow-through, twirled around behind her attacker, tugged aside the collar of his leather armor, and slipped Shade downward along his spine. At once, he collapsed in a font of red gore and she had to step carefully so as not to slip in the crimson lake that marked the triumph of the two Blackguards.

Still one constable remained. Incensed beyond measure at the implausibility of his comrades' fall, his eyes widened with madness and he readied himself to spring in one final desperate struggle.

He never got the chance.

Thirty feet down the wall, Adolfo stood leaning upon the crenellated battlement, lined up his crossbow, and fired a quarrel into the base of the man's skull.

Lughus raised his blade in thanks and salute, and the Madder nodded in return before turning away to reload.

Brigid's eyes blazed with battle fury and her chest heaved as she struggled to catch her breath. "They're falling back," she observed, as Lughus retrieved Whisper for her and wiped it clean upon the surcoat of one of the enemy dead.

Sure enough, the siege ladders that remained were receding from the walls, and from the enemy camp, the Andochan trumpets sounded the call to return.

Lughus breathed a heavy sigh, handed her dagger back to her, and returned Sentinel to his sheath. "Are you hurt?" he asked, his weary, gray eyes shining with concern.

She shook her head. "You?"

He wound an arm around her waist, pulled her close, and kissed the top of her head. "We've weathered the storm," he said. "Now we spring a trap."

CHAPTER 38: THE DECISIVE BATTLE

Lughus was tired, weary. The battle to defend the walls of Galadin had certainly taken its toll, and while it was clear from the bodies of the honored dead that the Golden Hounds had fared far better than the red-cloaked kingsmen of Andoch, the crimson horde encamped outside of the city was still a formidable force. Furthermore, even with the five anointed Guardians that Lughus and Brigid had dispatched, the King, the Hammer, and the generals remained—to say nothing of any others who lacked the rank to attend the parley.

Sure enough, the battle was far from over, and while the odds may not have seemed in the defenders' favor, hope yet remained. General Navarro was on his way, as was Lughus's grandfather, Roland Marthaine. True, the winter weather had been a hindrance, slowing the legion's march from Agathis and—they recently discovered—making travel by keelboat from Marthaine impossible by freezing the surface of the lake; but still, it was emboldening to know that relief was on its way. If they could just hold out long enough for it to arrive.

And so, as he had learned so long ago under the tutelage of the Loremaster, Lughus turned to the past as a means of understanding the present, and thereby ensuring that his people had a future.

"Tell me I've not gone mad," he said to Brigid. They sat together by the light of a brazier sharing a quick meal and going over his plan. The winter sun was setting, yet the siege weapons of the enemy had not yet resumed their barrage, leading the young baron to wonder if the Guardians had run low on ammunition. Regardless, it was a welcome reprieve.

"I realize it's a sacrifice, but it may allow us an advantage, despite being vastly outnumbered." His brow furrowed. "What do you think?"

"It's a risk," Brigid said with a shrug, "but so is everything."

"But do you think it's worth it?"

Brigid smiled wearily and reached out to take his hand. "I know that you value my opinion, darling," she said, "and—believe me—I love you for that. But *you* are the Marshal. *You* are the baron. And just as you place your faith and your trust in me, so too do I place my faith and trust in you."

"Fair enough," Lughus replied, "but it's a foolish man who refuses wise counsel."

"True," Brigid said. "However, this is your area of expertise, is it not? It's what Rastis prepared you for from the time you first learned to read?"

"It is," he said.

"Then in this," she said, "*you* are the master. You know best. If you believe this plan to be our best chance, then I will stand by you just as I know that were the tables turned, you would stand by me."

At length, Lughus gave a nod and kissed her upon the brow. "Thank you," he said.

"For what?"

"For the reminder," he said. "For the perspective." He kissed her again. "For your love."

"You never have to thank me for that," she grinned.

"Aye, but I will anyway." Lughus smiled and called out to Sergeant Pike as he stood nearby ruffling Fergus's fur. The notched ear was not nearly as bad as they had feared and with the great hound's unnatural nature, it had already begun to heal. "Pike, pass along word to Adolfo and the other knights and tell them to meet Owain, Brigid, and me at the great hall."

"Aye, sir," Pike said. "Anything else?"

Lughus thought for a moment. "Yes. Ask Adolfo to gather a team of carpenters. You can tell him I trust his judgment in the selection."

"At once, sir."

Pike ran off and Fergus bounded over to nuzzle Lughus's side, though he found the steel plate of the young baron's armor less comfortable than the usual hose and woolen surcoat.

You and me both, Brother. Lughus grinned. *You and me both.*

Night had fully fallen by the time Lughus and his retainers broke from the great hall to prepare for the next Guardian assault. While the Andochan trebuchets remained silent, the mangonels had resumed their attack and the iron-capped battering ram had once more been put to work against the main gates of the city barbican. Sir Burnel and Sir Gosbert took command of the yeoman archers on watch, confounding the artillery teams and attempting as best they were able to cut down the kingsmen working the ram. Alban in particular continued to be especially deadly and once again Lughus made a mental note to reward the man with a generous parcel of land.

Kin willing that we all survive...

And so a second night passed as both armies readied for another day of fighting while simultaneously licking their wounds from the previous battle. Lughus did his best to rest when he was able, but while he had prevailed upon Brigid to take Fergus and return to their bedchamber to get some measure of respite, the young baron himself found that sleep was hard to come by—especially when pitted against the duty he felt to his home and his people.

Your enemies will not hold on account of rain, he heard Crodane's words echo from the depths of his memory, *Nor will they pause for weariness, nor illness, nor grief; if anything, these will be the very moments when they choose to attack. Therefore, you must learn to defend yourself even under the worst conditions and at the worst of times.*

Well, he thought, standing upon the roof of the great keep and gazing out at the twinkling watch fires of the Andochan army below, it was fair to say that their current situation was not what one would call the best of conditions or the best of times.

"This was your grandfather's favorite place to think as well," said a familiar voice. Lughus turned to find Owain leaning upon his cane in the doorway that led down into the keep's interior. "And by grandfather, you know I mean Arcis," he said. "Sure enough, Roland wasn't the only brooder. It seems you come by it naturally on both sides."

Lughus gave a half-smile. "When lofty thoughts weigh you down, sometimes it helps to climb to a lofty height and think."

"Well said," Owain told him. He joined Lughus in leaning upon the cold stone crenellations, peering down at the city and the enemy camp.

"I can't take credit," Lughus told him. "That one comes from Rastis."

"Ah," Owain said. "Another great brooder. Though he had less of the dourness to him than either of your grandfathers, as I remember it. Always quick with a smile and a clever remark, he was. Or so I remember it."

"Brooders all of us, it seems," Lughus said.

Owain gave a shrug. "That's the Brock for you," he laughed. "We all do it. Save maybe your mum. All of the cleverness and wit, but none of the grim. Then again, Crodane carried more than enough of it for the both of them."

Lughus gave a forlorn smile.

"She'd be proud of you, you know?" the old seneschal said. "Arcis too, and Crodane. All of them. You're a fine baron, maybe even finer than Arcis."

"So long as I don't lose the city," Lughus said.

Owain pursed his lips. "You've a solid plan. Least, it sounds solid to me." He breathed a sigh. "I'm sorry I'm not there to fight beside you."

"You've nothing to be sorry for," Lughus said. "And we need someone to command the castle and protect the folk who remained behind."

"Fair enough," he said. "But if I may, my lord, I would ask that you at least try to rest. There'll be few enough chances for it after daybreak and with the state of things, standing about keeping watch is one duty that I can still carry out."

Lughus breathed another sigh and gazed out one final time at the enemy camp. Even in the low light, he could make out the shine of the enormous reliquary, the Key to the Kingdom. At one time, the sight of it would have roused in him a veritable geyser of adventurous glee. Now it filled him with only dread. And perhaps rage. For no longer was it a symbol of justice and freedom, but of tyranny, of domination, of captivity.

"I suppose rest would be wise," he said at last. "I sense that tomorrow will be a long day."

"One for the history books," Owain said, "so long as you're here to record it."

"Indeed."

An hour before sunrise, Lughus awoke and readied himself. In place of his fine, golden armor, he donned his old hauberk, preferring the ease and comfort of the tried and true familiarity over the golden skin. He would be forever grateful to Baron Roland for the impressive plate, and he would certainly continue to make good use of it in the open field; however, if all went according to his plans, today would be a different sort of fight, a fight full of grit and dirt and mud and blood. There would be no regal cavalry charges or pristine pageantry. This would be a street fight, a gutter fight, and for that, he needed to be clad accordingly.

As he tightened the baldric around his waist, he sensed Brigid stir in the bed. Her blue eyes caught the dwindling light of the fire's embers, her face half-hidden behind the cascade of her raven hair. She was watching him, momentarily untroubled, free for just a moment of the troubles that defined their world. Without a word, he drew close to her, lifted her chin with his finger, and kissed her deeply on the lips. His heart swelled with love and memories of the bliss they had shared when he had descended from his rooftop vigil to join her in bed. It had not been his intention, for he was certain both of them were weary from the day's fighting, but beneath the warmth of the skins and blankets, their bodies were drawn together seeking solace and respite.

"Are you ready?" Brigid asked him, her voice little more an a whisper.

"I am," he said.

She gave a nod and slipped a spindly arm from beneath the blankets to gently take hold of his hand. "Go," she whispered. "Take Fergus. I'll find you soon."

Lughus pressed her hand to his lips. "I love you."

"And I you," she said.

From his place on the floor, Fergus stood, stretched, and gave a great yawn. Someone must have attempted a cursory wash, but rusty stains still flecked the fur around his mouth. Lughus quickly buckled the great hound's harness and spiked collar into place, and together they made their way through the keep to where men gathered in and just outside the great hall. Horus had ensured that great cauldrons of gruel had been prepared, a hearty meal to fill the belly and warm the blood. Jars of honey and assorted berries sat out to sweeten the bland oatmeal.

Owain was leaning against a long table scraping the last bites of gruel from a wooden bowl. Beside him, Adolfo the Madder stood stoically with his arms resting upon the butt of his crossbow. As soon as they spied the young baron and the hound, they stood straighter and nodded to him in greeting.

"Sir Owain," Lughus said. "Sir Adolfo."

"Were you able to get some rest, my lord?" Owain asked.

Lughus gave a nod. "Yes," he said, "Thank you."

Adolfo cleared his throat. "The carpenters have finished their work." If the kingsmen continue at their present rate, the ram should break through the main gate at dawn."

"When they do, they'll attempt to hold their position long enough for the rest of the army to rally and storm the gates," Lughus said. "We'll need to ensure that the men are in position and well-supplied for what comes next."

"Aye, my lord."

Lughus sighed. "Any word on the wounded? Sir Deryk?"

"The handmaids have him and he's resting with the other wounded. I suppose he's in the hands of the Lady now."

Lughus nodded. Deryk was a solid fighter. He owed it to him to visit him personally. He made a mental note to do so soon.

"That being said, we've actually fared rather well so far, all things considered," Owain continued, "and if the legion gets through or the bloody ice melts, we'll be in even better shape. Still outnumbered, mind you, but not by nearly as much."

Lughus gave a nod and after a pause, held out his arm to each of the men in turn. "Well," he said, "we've done all we could to prepare. Let's hope now that it was enough."

Orders were disseminated and final preparations were made. The knights of the fiefs and the Weavers' Guild, save Sir Deryk, were placed in command of various contingents of men-at-arms at their assigned positions while companies of yeoman archers and peasant volunteers readied their bows and reloaded quivers from the great stockpiles. Nearly a third of the arrows had been spent in the previous day's fighting and Lughus expected that today would see even more spent. For a land so dependent upon its archers, forcing the decisive battle to occur sooner rather than later was of even greater importance lest they run out of ammunition.

When all was sorted, Lughus gathered Sergeant Pike and a select squad of others of the Galadin household guard to join him upon the barbican. Alban the archer was among them, clad now in a boiled leather breastplate that Lughus had gifted him for his services on the first day of fighting.

True to Adolfo's conjecture, the main gates of the city had buckled and splintered under the continued assault of the ram, aided, unbeknownst to them, by the careful sabotage of the Galadin carpenters. Of course, the archers on watch continued to fire upon the teams of kingsmen as they relentlessly battered the gates, but while Alban might occasionally take a man down with a shot to the thigh or the ankle, the shots were often wide on purpose, serving merely to keep up appearances rather than mount a serious defense. For it was absolutely necessary that the Guardians believe that it was by their own strength and tenacity, their own overwhelming martial prowess, and the iron will of their headstrong King that the mighty gates of Galadin fall.

It would not be long, Lughus thought, leaning upon the battlement and gazing down at the Andochan camp below. In the widening light, he could make out the Guardian horde as it assembled, rank upon rank of kingsman, cavalryman, and noble house guard. They loosened weapons, stamped their feet, and beat their breasts against the cold. Many laughed or called out cheers, anything they could to get the blood flowing in anticipation of the coming battle. For a sacking was different than a standard victory in the field where a fortunate man might grow rich by looting the bodies or ransoming noble prisoners. No, in a sacking, a man barged into the home of his enemies and took what he pleased however he pleased, filling his pockets and glutting his passions upon whatever he could grab hold of. In short, for the common fighting man, the common thug, it would be a festival of wanton delights.

And the darkest of days for the conquered.

It was strange. There was a time when Lughus believed the Guardians to be above such things, that with their storied honor and legendary virtue they would not stoop to such base evils. He had since learned better.

Well, he thought, idly scratching Fergus behind the ears, as baron and as Marshal, he would see to it that Galadin was not sacked, that his people remained safe, and that peace and prosperity would be theirs once again—even if it took his dying breath.

Of course, he thought as Brigid appeared, armed and ready for battle, *Let's hope it doesn't come to that...*

The men of the guard saluted and bowed as she approached, and Fergus turned about in a circle out of excitement to see her. Her eyes shone with anticipation and a nervous smile tugged at her lips.

"Ready?" she asked him. "I passed Adolfo below and he said that it's a matter of minutes."

Lughus gave a nod. "Let's just hope they fall for it."

"They will," she said. "If that parley taught me anything, it was that Kredor is a brash fool."

"Aye, but Tainne is not," Lughus said. "Even Royne admitted as such, and Royne believes *all* men are fools."

"Fair enough," Brigid said with a shrug, "but conquering Galadin is the final step in their grand stratagem. With victory so close, their impatience is bound to get the better of them."

A resounding crack echoed throughout the area followed at once by the dull thud of the ram bashing open the gates and splintering heavy timber. At once, the Guardians let out a raucous cheer that echoed through the crisp morning air like the sounding of a thousand war horns. In the enemy camp, the great horde began to undulate like a stormy sea and the great silver reliquary caught the light of the rising sun and seemed to blaze with the dazzling light of the gods themselves.

"Well," Lughus said to Brigid, kissing her quickly upon the brow, "I suppose we shall find out." He tuned to the men of the guard gathered around them. "Now we come to it," he said. "Stand strong together and remember our quarry is the King himself."

The men answered with a rallying cry of their own. Lughus clapped Alban on the back and gripped Pike by the shoulder. "I don't know what the day will bring," he said, "but in case the worst should come to pass for any of us, I want you all to know how proud I am to call myself your baron and to name you all as friends."

A great fanfare exploded now from the Andochan camp and sure enough, the ranks of kingsmen and the mounted knights began to charge, flooding towards the broken gates and smashing them back with the force of an avalanche. In the blink of an eye, they had forced the Galadin defenders away from the gates, filling the courtyard with a veritable horde of red-cloaked warriors. Rank after rank, horse after horse, man after man. All of them flooding inside, hungry for blood and plunder, secure in their invincible blessing of the Key to the Kingdom and the near divinity of the Guardian-King.

Before long, they stood shoulder to shoulder, overflowing now into Hounton's cobblestone streets. Yet still more passed through the gates, encouraged now as the Galadin defenders continued to fall back or else climb higher for the safety of the walls and battlements.

Lughus drew Sentinel as Brigid and Fergus stepped up alongside him. When at last he was satisfied with the teeming flood of humanity crammed into the restricted confines of the wall below, he whirled his storied blade in a great flashing arc, signaling Adolfo and the other knights and warriors, peasants and yeoman archers.

"Release the Hounds!"

At the command, the defenders paused in the retreat, turned from their new positions—upon every wall and every rooftop, nocked their arrows, drew, and let fly.

It was bloody mayhem. Packed in as they were, the Andochan forces froze, for they had nowhere to run, nowhere to hide. They fell uncounted at the first volley. And the second. Only by the loosing of the third did they finally begin to react, scrambling behind one another, cowering behind shields, or attempting to drive deeper into the city. Anything they might do to avoid the deadly bodkins of the Galadin archers.

"Fish in a barrel," Brigid said with a smirk. "You were right."

Lughus watched as a bevy of kingsmen attempted to turn around and flee from the gates back out into the plain, but as they did so, they ran into their comrades further down the column, unaware of the deadly trap yet equally as eager to sack the city as the first ranks were to escape it. In the general standstill that resulted, the defenders found them easy targets for cauldrons of boiling pitch and oil.

Still the arrows continued to rain from the walls and rooftops and the air was filled with the cacophony of cries—men dying, horses squealing, futile threats and oaths. At last, however, the heavily armored knights of the cavalry—those most securely protected in their steel skin and plate barding—decided to spur their mounts and break through. From his vantage point upon the barbican, Lughus could sense the Warlord's generals among them. Ignoring their own infantrymen, the horsemen charged, over and through their own soldiers and deeper into the streets of Hounton.

Further down the walls and across the courtyard, Lughus caught sight of Sir Beric and Sir Gosbert and waved his blade. At once the two men, bowed their heads in a salute and set out with contingents of pikemen and archers to waylay them. The young baron's mouth became a grim line. He had told all of his knights and captains not to engage the anointed Guardians directly, or at least, not in melee. They were to content themselves with harassing them from the rooftops and alleyways with arrows and caltrops and the like. However, he could not help but feel that he was sending a pack of terriers to face a pride of lions. He ground his teeth and scanned the mob once more. If only he could find Kredor, he could face him directly and force an end to this madness once and for all.

And then, he felt it—the familiar twinge of recognition, of vengeful wrath. His eyes met Brigid's. "Harlow," he said.

Brigid peered out over the battlement. "There." She pointed.

Lughus followed her arm. Sure enough, there was the Hammer, slinking along the edge of the wall like a rat in the basement of a tavern. Behind him followed a small squad of men. Two carried large rectangular tower shields. The third was a small man, barely the height of a child. He leapt along nimbly in red and white motley clutching a bundle wrapped in bright white cloth beneath his arm.

The final two men, easily identifiable, though hidden beneath dark cowls and black cloaks, were none other than Natharis Tainne and the Guardian-King.

"Kredor," Lughus whispered as he spied them slip from the arrow storm of the yard into an alleyway that led along the edge of Hounton in the direction of the Saint's Quarter.

Brigid's brow furrowed. "Harlow knows about the secret path from the grotto, remember?"

"You think they seek to face us directly?" Lughus asked.

"They know as well as we do that this can only end with one of our deaths," she said, "and since you're not wearing your gold armor, they might not have noticed you from here on the barbican."

Lughus chewed his lip. "Even Harlow?" he asked. "If we can sense him, sure enough, he has to be able to sense us."

"I don't know," she said. "But either way, whatever the Hammer might be up to, I can promise you that it can't be anything good."

"True." Lughus turned to his chosen guard. "Kender, run to Adolfo and tell him he has command. The rest of you, on me." The storm clouds flashed within the depths of his eyes and he felt a great flood of vigor in his breast. "It's time to end this."

CHAPTER 39: THE BATTLE OF WHITEMANE

Geoffrey of Pyle, the Vanguard, awoke shortly before dawn with the scent of green fields and fertile soil heavy in his nose. It was a phantom smell, he knew, a memory born of a lifetime of working the Spade, but from time to time when it happened upon a morn, he always took it as a good omen.

And with the prospect of fighting for his life in yet another major battle, Geoffrey could use a good omen.

He allowed himself another moment of peace to enjoy the warmth of his blankets and the quiet of his pavilion, then rose, woke Freddy, and together they readied themselves for battle.

As Freddy helped Geoffrey with his armor, the Vanguard breathed a sigh. "Once the battle begins..." he began. "You know..."

"I know, Dad," Freddy said. "I know."

"I just...these things..."

"I know, Dad."

"I just want you to be safe."

Freddy looked up at him. "I now, Dad," he said without resentment. "I want you to be safe too."

Geoffrey breathed a heavy sigh and reached out to ruffle the hair on Freddy's head.

The rest of the camp was mustering when Geoffrey and Freddy emerged from their pavilion. Men and women readied their equipment and their horses for battle, stood in groups chatting quietly, or sat around fires doing their best to enjoy what, for some, would be their last meal. Geoffrey recognized various knights and officers hurrying here and there, issuing commands, organizing ranks, and doing their best to raise morale. Chief among them, at the very head of the evolving line of battle stood the Tower seated upon the great searoan stallion, Tempest. The sight of the pair of them, silent and stalwart, ready to lead the charge and stand shoulder to shoulder with the folk of their command was a beacon of hope in the dim light of dawn. Geoffrey wondered that there were such folk who could instill such confidence simply with their presence. Lughus and Brigid had it too. And Captain Barrow, Geoffrey's old soldier friend from the Spade.

He was wondering vaguely after the well-being of his old friend when he noticed Thom Reaver sitting cross-legged beside a small fire, scraping the last bit of porridge from a wooden bowl. Lachlan and Bryce, the sergeants in charge of the Galadin archers, stood nearby.

"I'll see to Flash and Connie," Freddy said. "Make sure they're safe among the baggage train."

"Make sure you eat something too," Geoffrey said.

"I will."

"The men are ready," Bryce said, once the boy had gone. "They'll be happy to see you safe and sound, sir."

Geoffrey nodded. "I'm sorry that I had to be away," he told them. "Not befitting of a commander, I'm sure, but it could not be helped."

"Can't say we've minded," Lachlan told him. "The Montevalens have been more than hospitable, though that forester's mash ain't nothing compared to the ales we have in the Brock."

Geoffrey smiled. "Can't say I've ever tasted anything quite like the Ram's Reward."

"The Brethren's own brew." Bryce grinned.

Geoffrey gave a nod. "When the men have eaten, have them form ranks behind Sir Norton's pikemen. I'll be along to join you shortly."

"Aye, sir."

When the sergeants had Geoffrey sat down beside Thom Reaver and helped himself to some of the tasteless porridge bubbling in the pot over the campfire. "How is it?" Geoffrey asked.

"I've had much worse," Thom said, "Though I've had much better as well."

Geoffrey tried a bite. "Aye, that's about right," he said.

Thom gave a silent nod and stared thoughtfully into the flames. Geoffrey focused on his meal, but as the silence grew heavier, he took a swig of water from his skin and cleared his throat.

"You alright?" he asked mildly.

The Reaver gave a sigh and setting his bowl aside, heaved upon the haft of his great axe. "I'm angry," he said, "and...sad."

Geoffrey nodded. He recalled the story of the fall of the girl called Sparrow, had noticed the heavy grief that had hung like a millstone over the young warrior ever since the Talon's return from Reginal. Even while they awaited the arrival of the Tower's army, he had chosen not to press the issue, despite his concern and growing fondness for the young man. For Geoffrey was no stranger to grief and he knew that all folk dealt with it differently. The best he could do was to remain present and receptive should Thom ever find himself ready to unburden himself.

Thom sighed. "So much has changed," he said. "So much has happened since I left home."

Geoffrey nodded. "So it has," he said.

Thom gave a grunt. "I never expected my life to turn out this way," he said. "I miss Lughus and Royne. I miss Rastis. And Hob. And Magnus, though I suppose I still see him from time to time." He shook his head. "I'm just tired of being alone and...I thought that...perhaps...I had actually made a friend." He fell silent, and for a long moment, Geoffrey joined him in staring into the flames.

"Well," the Vanguard said at last, "I'm sorry for your loss—heartily sorry. However, I can tell you one thing at least."

Thom's eyes widened with interest.

"While there's no replacing those we've lost—nor should there be," Geoffrey said, "You can count me as your friend. The Tower too, I reckon. And Horn. And all the others—Lady Valerie, Welmsey, Armel, even the queen."

Thom offered Geoffrey a forlorn smile. "I suppose that's true."

"It is," Geoffrey said.

Thom stood up and hefted his axe over his shoulder. "Well," he said, patting the Vanguard on the shoulder, "if the worst should come to pass today and Death should finally come to claim us, at least it will be among friends."

By the time the sun had fully risen, the opposing armies had assembled in the field. The forces of the Winter Rose consisted of two large contingents of heavy cavalry, a force of light cavalry skirmishers, Sir Norton's pikemen, two large masses of peasant conscripts, and the archers of the Brock. Across the field, the nobles of Western Montevale, under the command of Pronet and Gurney, consisted of four large blocks of heavy horsemen, two ranks of armored footmen, and an enormous mob of peasant levees pressed into service. Lord Talondaire and his fellow lords of Whitemane stood alongside them though nearer to the town, adopting a defensive posture that Geoffrey knew was intended to hide the fact that they secretly stood for the Winter Rose.

The Guardian forces, led by the Warlord, had been relegated to the rear, effectively functioning as the enemy reserve. Geoffrey wondered if this was indeed by design, or if this had been the choice of the Warlord himself. Regardless, it remained a sizable force consisting of kingsmen both mounted and on foot, and while it was not nearly as large as the force commanded by Pronet and Gurney, each man among them was a professional soldier who made his living by the strength of his sword arm.

With the armies assembled, Geoffrey walked among his men with Freddy and Thom. The light snow that had begun earlier had continued and a thin sheen of white frost coated the field. Such a thing was certain to be a hazard for the horses on both sides, but the added caution required of the riders might be a benefit to men who fought on foot like himself and his archers.

Still, for a surefooted steed like Tempest, a little snow would prove no problem, as the great stallion demonstrated when he appeared suddenly at Geoffrey's side.

"Sir Geoffrey," Beledain greeted him. "Thom."

Geoffrey gave a nod and Freddy offered a silent wave to the young standard-bearer following in the Tower's wake. The girl waved back. Thom Reaver leaned upon the haft of his axe.

"They sent a rider not long ago just to remind us that they offer no terms," Bel said, "But they renewed the invitation for any Blackguards in our ranks to surrender in exchange for a quick death."

"Well, that's kind of them," Geoffrey said, "but I'm afraid that I must refuse."

"So I assumed." The Tower grinned, and then turned serious. "You know, there are men like us among the enemy ranks? Anointed or the like. Guardians."

Geoffrey nodded. "I assumed as much."

Thom peered off into the distance at the enemy forces. "Let's not forget the Warlord either," he said. "He's old, but he's quite formidable."

Beledain nodded. "So he seemed," he said, "though unlike the others, he seemed a man of honor."

"He is," Thom said.

"Well," Bel said, "that's something." He sighed and wheeled Tempest around. "Be well—all of you."

"And you," Geoffrey echoed.

Moments later, the trumpets sounded across the field and the enemy drummers began to play in time. Geoffrey called out to his men and the archers sounded a defiant cry. Soon, it was echoed by Sir Norton's pikemen, and then by the light cavalrymen under Horn. Before long, the entire army was roaring with battle lust and enthusiasm, shouting challenges and curses across the snowy plain, hungry for honor and blood.

And moments later, the battle had begun.

Where exactly the first strokes came, Geoffrey could not say. However, within moments, the ground itself shook like an earthquake and before he knew it, the roar of horses' hooves echoed like a thunderstorm.

The Tower himself led the charge, with his standard-bearer and the young Sir Briden behind him. Like a tidal wave of steel and horseflesh, they met the oncoming charge from the enemy riders like an avalanche. The pounding of hooves, the clang of steel, the screams of dying horses and men rose in a great and terrible symphony of battle. In the midst of it all, Geoffrey spied the flashing spear of the Tower—Spire—whirling in great arcs knocking men from the saddle to be trampled upon the snowy ground. It was a thing of beauty and horror, and as Geoffrey watched, he could feel himself growing restless. Thom Reaver ran his thumb upon the edge of his axe and the archers strummed their bowstrings in anticipation.

"Freddy..." Geoffrey said at last.

"I know, Dad."

Geoffrey fixed him with his gaze. "I love you, son."

"I know, Dad," Freddy said. "I love you too."

Thom hefted his axe. "They're sending another rank of knights this way."

Geoffrey heard Sir Norton call his men to order. At once, they packed together into tight ranks with their pikes held before them. Geoffrey ordered his men to take up positions behind them and ready their great war bows. With practiced efficiency, the archers pressed their arrows into the cold ground before them like little palisade fences so that they would be in easy reach.

As the enemy riders drew nearer, Geoffrey raised Oakheart. "On my order," he shouted, watching as the knights closed in. With mounting tension, he waited as long as he dare for the moment he could hear the riders began to shout.

"Let fly!"

As one, the archers of the Brock loosed their arrows, decimating the front rank of enemies. Men and horses, felled by the precise bodkins, tumbled in heaps along the frozen plain. Other riders following too closely tumbled after them, and those that miraculously made it through faced the vicious spikes of the pikemen. It was a tactic both the men of the Brock and the soldiers of the Winter Rose had employed to deadly effect in recent months. For the cavalry charge depended upon the infantry line breaking, upon intimidation, upon fear.

Yet if the line did not break, if the men kept their resolve, well...

"For the Winter Rose!"

"For the Brock!"

"Huzzah!"

With a terrible roar, Geoffrey and Thom charged into the stymied mob of horsemen, followed at once by Sir Norton and his pikemen and any archers forced into melee range.

With a heavy bash with the Acorn, Geoffrey knocked a man from the saddle like he was swatting a fly. The armored knight hit the ground and fell prone only to find his head separated from his shoulders by Thom Reaver's axe.

No sooner had Thom struck, however, than another rider advanced, slower, but at a pace to run the Reaver down. As the knight raised his mace, Geoffrey stepped ahead to meet him, but a stone thrown through the air knocked the knight's helmet and caused him to flinch. Seizing the chance, Geoffrey dodged the whirling mace and crushed the rider's breastplate like so much tin.

"Freddy, stay close!" Geoffrey shouted when the man lie dead.

A knight on foot, sword raised high above his head, rushed them, but just as he was about to reach them, Thom Reaver stepped in, whirling his great axe crosswise and the man collapsed in a bloody heap.

"More on the way!" the Reaver yelled, his eyes alight with an almost manic glee.

To Geoffrey's right, Sergeant Bryce loosed an arrow, point-blank, into the chest of another horseman. The force of the impact knocked the rider from the saddle, but in the fall, the man's flailing blade scored the horse's flank sending it into a frenzy. As men scattered to avoid its thrashing hooves, Sir Norton and a pair of pikemen rushed forward to put the poor beast down.

Before long, any horsemen who still stood turned their mounts around and withdrew, carefully navigating the field of dead to make for the enemy camp. Geoffrey's archers continued to fire the occasional shot in pursuit; however, few enough remained and in the end, Geoffrey ordered them to hold in the name of conserving ammunition.

Meanwhile, in the main fray, the Tower's men appeared to also carry the day—for now. As Geoffrey and Thom watched, the surviving forces of the initial charge had also taken to their heels and a great cheer sounded from the ranks of the Winter Rose.

Yet, the battle was hardly won, for not only did fully half of the Nivanus army still remain, but the entire Guardian reserve force.

And so, with shouts, calls, and a wave of the Tower's standard, Beledain's riders reformed just as Pronet and Gurney called the next wave of their army to order.

"It seems they call the Talon's forces too," Thom remarked, leaning on his axe at Geoffrey's side. "Won't that be a surprise!"

Geoffrey gave a nod. Sure enough, across the plain the remaining forces of the Nivanus army began to advance, calling on the forces of Whitemane to do the same. In answer, the Tower's infantry marched forth to join the horsemen and as Geoffrey watched on, it seemed clear that the decisive moment of the battle had begun.

"Alright, men!" Geoffrey roared. "After the clash, run like madmen to take advantage of the confusion!" He turned to his son. "You alright, Freddy?"

The boy gave a slow nod. "Fine."

Geoffrey took a deep breath. "You wouldn't mind staying out of this one, would you? Keeping an eye on Flash and Connie in the baggage train?"

Freddy took a deep breath. "If I do, can you promise me you'll come back alive?"

Geoffrey winced. "I'll do everything in my power to make it so."

"And I'll keep an eye on him too," Thom said. He offered Geoffrey a beneficent smile and shrugged. "That's what friends do, eh?"

At length, the boy nodded. "Okay, Dad."

The Vanguard released a great sigh of relief. "Thank you," he said, "Love you, son."

"Love you too, dad," the boy said.

"Good lad," Thom said when the boy had run off. "Reminds me a bit of Lughus when he was that age actually."

"Oh yes!" Geoffrey smiled. "Fairly sure the boy counts him as his greatest hero."

Thom shook his head. "Can't say as I agree with that," he said.

Geoffrey's brow creased. "What do you mean?"

The Reaver hefted his axe onto his shoulder. "It's you who is that boy's greatest hero," Thom said.

Geoffrey felt a warmth spread throughout his chest and his throat thickened as he ventured a glance back to watch his son running toward the baggage train. With a deep breath, he rubbed his eyes, and tuned back to Thom. "Let's get this done, eh?"

"Yes," the Reaver grinned. "Let's."

As the army of the Nivanus neared the army of the Winter Rose, a clarion call of horns erupted to sound the general charge. At once, men and horses shouted their battle cries and began to run, hungry for blood and battle. Confident in their overwhelming numbers and secure in their alliance with the forces of Whitemane, Pronet and Gurney committed every man and horse under their command, leaving only the Guardian reserves. Even the commanders themselves joined the charge, though from the relative safety of the rear.

And so, they were utterly devastated when Lord Talondaire, instead of joining their line, led the Whitemane cavalry directly into their unprotected flank mere moments before colliding with the forces of the Winter Rose.

Pandemonium reigned.

In the tumult of violence, blood, and steel, chaos reigned as men fought with blade and bow and tooth and nail. In the center of it all—at the eye of the storm—Geoffrey spied the Tower upon Tempest, carving great swathes through their foes in an effort to unite his forces and maintain some sense of order in the frenzied chaos.

It was into this maelstrom of violence that Geoffrey led his men. As his heart beat like the drum of a war galley, Geoffrey was a mad beast, turning aside blows with the Acorn, cracking skulls and sundering armor with Oakheart. Beside him, stalwart and dauntless, was Thom Reaver, felling enemy soldiers like a woodcutter felling trees.

The snow-covered plain had long since turned murky with the blending of mud and blood, and men slipped and fell in the spilled entrails of men and horses. Geoffrey's arms ached with the effort, and he had long ago lost count of his red tally. Yet, still, he fought on as the sun crept onward across the gray, winter sky. At some point in all the madness a weary fanfare sounded from across the plain followed soon after by the staccato cadence of a drum. Focused on the bloody work at hand, Geoffrey thought nothing of it until suddenly, in the midst of sodden red ground, he turned to face a rearing horseman, only to check himself at the last moment. For the horse was none other than Tempest, the great searoan, and the rider, was, of course, Prince Beledain.

"Sir Geoffrey!" the Tower roared, his voice hoarse from shouting orders. Beside him rode the young standard-bearer and the armored knight in the guise of Lord Talondaire who Geoffrey knew to be the Lady Valerie.

Geoffrey waved with his cudgel as Thom Reaver finished off a pair of men-at-arms, his great axe biting through chainmail like soft pine.

"Good to see you standing tall, Lord Tower," Geoffrey said.

"You two as well," Beledain said. Tempest trotted closer and Beledain leaned forward in his saddle to be heard. "Pronet and Gurney have fallen back to regroup with the Warlord. It seems they're readying their reserves for a final push."

"Let them come," Lady Valerie said. "Every enemy I cut down scrapes away a bit of rust from my mace."

"Here, here," Thom said with a grin.

Geoffrey marveled at the change in the young man. It was as if the longer the battle raged on, the higher Thom's spirits. There were even times in the midst of the fighting that he could have sworn he heard the young Reaver singing to himself.

Geoffrey gently patted Tempest's flank. "What do you want to do?" he asked the Tower.

"We've suffered losses, but they pale in comparison to our enemies. That being said, our men are weary whereas the Guardians will take the field fresh. Not only that..." Beledain paused. "My men have faced kingsmen often enough," he said, "But Guardians. Men like us. Anointed..."

Geoffrey nodded.

"I trust my people," Bel said, "But I would not see them slaughtered by an enemy that they cannot match."

"Then I guess it's up to us," Thom said.

"We'll be stronger together than we will be alone," the Vanguard said.

Bel nodded. "My hope is that we can force the Warlord to come to terms."

All of a sudden, Horn rode up to them, weaving and dodging through the waning melee. As soon as he reached them, he reined in his horse and Ol' Bastard reared up and released a piercing squeal.

"Lord Tower!" he cried.

"Horn?" Beledain said. "What is it?"

Horn's head snapped back and forth. "Val! Searoan's Bollocks! I'm glad to see you!"

Val nodded. "What is it, Horn?"

Horn turned back to Beledain. "Prince Bel," he said hurriedly. "There's wagons! Wagons from Pridel!"

"From Pridel?" Bel repeated.

"Aye!" Horn said. "Wagons, riders, people marching on foot. A whole bloody lot of them." He leaned in closer. "The queen is with them. And your son. Sir Geoffrey's family too."

Geoffrey watched as the Tower's eyes widened like a wild creature cornered in a hunt. His jaw set and his body tensed like a war bow at full draw. The change that came over him was sudden and drastic, and Geoffrey was certain that should the entire army of the Guardians charge at them now, they would find in the Tower, a foe that was more beast than man.

"Something has happened," Beledain said. "Something terrible."

No sooner had the words escaped the Tower's lips than Geoffrey felt it too, felt it deep within his bones. Something was wrong. Even the air seemed to suddenly grow colder, the wind strengthened, and the weak winter sun disappeared behind a cloud.

"For them to have reached us so soon, they would have had to have left no more than a day or two after we marched," Horn said.

"But what cause would they have to leave the safety of the city?" Val asked.

Thom Reaver's face was grim.

Geoffrey sucked at his teeth. "I suggest we go to them then and find out."

"But the Guardians?" Horn said. "The battle?"

Beledain's brow narrowed. "Marguerite," he began, "Ready the flag of truce. We need to parley. Now."

"Aye, sir," she said. "I'll fetch it at once."

Bel nodded and turned to the others. "Will the Warlord still honor it? Despite all of this?"

Thom Reaver pursed his lips. "I believe he will."

Val gave a nod. "Pronet and Gurney won't," she said, "but based on what I know of him, Thom is right. Rood is a man of honor and since the majority of the men who remain answer to him, the others will have no choice but to stand by his word."

Geoffrey turned his gaze to the Guardian camp. "Then we need to hurry. We may have survived one storm, but I fear before this day is done, we'll weather several more."

CHAPTER 40: THE ARMY OF THE DEAD

It took all of Beledain's willpower to resist charging off at once when Horn appeared with news of the queen's arrival. He somehow managed to realize that to do so would have been a complete dereliction of his duties; however, in that moment of alarm, the beast within him, the beast born from a lifetime of witnessing the horrors of war, cried out in panic and dread. No sooner had Sir Geoffrey finished speaking, however, before he spurred Tempest to a gallop, leaving Val, Marguerite, and the others behind him.

The great searoan clearly sensed his rider's urgency, sure-footedly navigating the battlefield toward the wagons of the baggage train that lie beyond the pavilions of the army camp. There, the attendants, camp followers, and hangers-on deemed unfit (or unwilling) for battle awaited the outcome of the day's bloody work.

As Beledain surveyed the sight now, however, he saw that the numbers had swelled and that far into the distance to the south and east, a disparate mass of wagons, carts, and folk on foot trailed into the distance.

"Lord Tower!" came a shout. Bel turned to see Freddy, Geoffrey's son and squire riding toward him. *He rides well*, Bel thought absurdly, *and he already seems to have forged a strong bond with his horse...*

"This way, my lord!" Freddy said. "The queen and my mum and sister are this way with Sir Armel."

"Is my son with them?" Bel asked, straining to keep his voice steady.

"He is, my lord."

"Lead on."

With a nod, Freddy spurred his horse and Tempest followed, through the camp, past the newly arrived peasants and livestock to where he spied a large wagon drawn by a pair of draught horses flying the banner of the Winter Rose.

At once, Bel urged Tempest onward past Freddy to the wagon. No sooner had he reached it than he slid from his saddle. Marina was waiting for him. She was not dressed in the finery of a queen at court, but in the simple, rustic clothing of a commoner for whom work and the necessities of life would not permit weathering the winter months at the side of a cozy fire. A small cluster of figures stood behind her, warmly insulated in blankets and skins. At a glance, Bel recognized Geoffrey's wife and daughter as well as Marcus and his nurses. Sir Armel too sat upon his horse beside them overseeing the small squad of horsemen he commanded as part of the queen's household guard.

"What is it?" Bel asked, striding up to her. "What's happened?"

Marina reached out to gently take Bel's gauntlet and he couldn't help but notice the grotesque antithesis of cold steel alongside the warm softness of her hand. He instantly became conscious of the oppressive weight of his armor—splattered with mud and blood and violence —as if it were a layer of hoarfrost or a leper's sores. His heart yearned to hold Marcus, but he felt so dirty, so diseased, so vile.

"We're fine," the queen said, gently turning his chin to hold his darting eyes with hers. "But Pridel is lost."

"Lost?" Bel's blood turned to ice. "What do you mean lost? How? When?"

Marina held out her hands placatingly. "I will tell you what I know," she said, "but we should speak to the Shackle for the whole tale."

"The Shackle has returned?"

"He has. It is because of him that we are here."

"Where is he?"

"He's here," she said gently, "but...he's not well. Quite frankly, I'm amazed that he's still alive."

"He's wounded?"

"Gravely," she said, "but he's been holding on so as to speak to you."

Bel gave a slow nod. "I will go to him," he said, "but tell me again, once and for all, are you and Marcus are safe?"

"Yes," she said. "I'm safe. Marcus is safe. Geoffrey's family is safe."

The tightening in his chest eased, but he still felt the sting of her news. "Where is Shackle?"

"In the wagon," she said. "This way."

Bel followed Marina past the others of the little group. He received kind smiles from Annabelle and Greta, a resolute nod from Sir Armel, and polite curtsies from Marcus's nurses. They held Marcus out to him as he neared and his heart melted at the sight of his son's face. The little boy reached out for him, but clad in his cold, lifeless metal, Bel instead leaned forward to let his son touch his face. The little boy's hands were slightly damp as they clutched at the coarse whiskers of Bel's beard, and when Bel pressed his lips to his son's chubby cheek, he felt again the compulsion to lift Marina and Marcus onto Tempest's saddle before him and ride for the horizon never to return.

He knew, of course, that such a thing was an impossibility, a flight of manic fancy, but it was there, defying his duty and tempting him with the beautiful lie of a life free of darkness and war.

With a heavy sigh, he pulled away from his son's grip and continued on to the wagon and his dying friend.

The Shackle reclined upon a pile of skins and blankets, a clay jug of forester's mash at his side. As Bel approached, he noticed red and brown stains soaking the coverings and heavy dressings and poultices upon the Blackguard's shoulder and along the side of his scalp. His sickle lie upon the bed of the wagon beside him, but it was missing more than half of its chain.

"Sorry I'm late," the Shackle said with a grin. "I wanted to look my best."

In spite of the gravity of the situation, Bel gave a smirk. "You know we don't stand on ceremony."

"Fair enough," he said, "but I'd rather not bleed out in front of the children—or the queen."

Marina smiled. "My dear Blackguard, I may not be a warrior myself, but I'm no stranger to wounds and war," she said. "I've certainly seen my share."

"Call it dignity then," the Shackle said. "Let me at least keep a shred of it here before I pass on."

Bel felt the familiar weight of grief settling upon his shoulders like a mantle of stone. From just beyond the limits of his vision, he sensed familiar voices beckoning to him. He ignored their woeful calls.

"Is there no hope then?" Bel asked.

"Not for me, I'm afraid. Not unless you know how to properly care for innards once they've become out-ards," Shackle said, his scarred face twisting into a ghastly grim. "But I needed to hold on long enough to see to it that while I might pay the ultimate price, I might buy time for you and yours. Just don't look under the blankets here."

Bel held his face impassively. "What..." he paused, "What about your title?"

He shrugged. "I think it best if it dies with me," he said. "Shackle is an appropriate name for this business, don't you think? I'd hate to lay that burden on someone else. Anyways..."

Bel gave a weak nod. "What did you learn?" he asked, "and what is it that gave you these wounds?"

The Shackle's smile faded from his face. "From what the queen has told me," he said, "You already know."

"You mean?"

"The boy—Thom Reaver—he weren't lying."

Bel's eyes widened and he exchanged a glance with Marina. "The Army of the Dead?"

The Shackle nodded. "After that lord from the Brock—the fish man— after he put me to shore along the coast, I headed for the Lighthouse. I passed a few villages and homesteads along the way, but by the looks of it all, everything was deserted—empty. It was as if the people just up and walked away leaving everything behind. Gone. All the while, though, I couldn't shake this unnatural feeling that someone was there. Of course, it wasn't until I got close enough to the Lighthouse itself that I actually saw them."

Bel gave a nod. "We ran into a few of them here as well," he said. "A Keeper was sent to track down Thom and recover the Key."

"Well, good thing then that it's far away from here in the hands of that fish lord. I'd hate to think of what those bastards at the Lighthouse would want it for." He cleared his throat and coughed. Red blood stained his scarred

467

lips. "There were hundreds of them. Maybe thousands. They stay indoors during the day, but at night they assembled in the streets like statues carved of wood. The Keepers then walk along with carts full of random weapons and armor and dress them like dolls. Anyways, I knew I had to get back to warn you. Only, that's when it got worse."

"What do you mean?" Bel asked, "and how did you end up with these wounds?"

The Shackle grimaced against some inner pain and wiped the blood from his lips. "The mountains," he said. "When I left the town to begin the trek back here over the mountains that separate the White Wood from Castone, I saw them. As many as Thom said lie hidden in the empty buildings, as many as I myself saw, there were that many and far more in the mountains. It's as if that's where they were hiding them, storing them, keeping them at the ready." He scoffed. "Brethren only know how long those things been right there on the doorstep of the White Wood without us ever knowing. Thousands of them. A whole bloody army, but one that don't need to eat, or sleep, or worry about the cold. They just...wait." He paused. "At least, they did. Now, they march."

"I was able to avoid them, mostly, until crossing the peaks to reach the western slopes. I thought surely they'd not crossed over to us yet." He gave a sardonic snort. "I was wrong."

Bel thought of the Wrathorn he had faced with Geoffrey. If the dead soldiers were dangerous enough for two warriors of title, what hope would there be for the common man? "And you say they march on Pridel?" he asked.

The Shackle gave a nod. "Feyhold is already overrun."

Marina touched Bel's arm. "We ordered all who remained to evacuate," she said, "but they attacked before we could get everyone out. Armel and the guard did what they could, but..." She paused. "What you see is all that remains. The others fell fighting so as to give the rest of us a chance."

Bel paused at the sound of voices raised in delighted greeting and he knew that Sir Geoffrey had arrived to be reunited with his wife and daughter. He glanced back toward them and saw Armel in deep conversation with Horn and Welmsey. Their faces were stoic, concerned. Again, Bel felt the heavy burden of command. He returned his attention to the Shackle.

"Do you believe they'll follow you here?" he asked.

"Sure as anything they will," the Blackguard said. He paused to cough and wiped red spittle from his lip. "It weren't like a normal sacking—not at Feyhold anyhow. There was no plundering. No ransoming. None of the usual horrors, for the dead have no need of gold and silver. There was only death—slaughter—with the only survivors being those who were fast enough to flee."

"And Pridel?" Bel asked Marina.

The queen lowered her eyes. "From what I could tell, it was the same."

The Shackle took a deep breath. It was clear that the conversation was taxing him. He was trying to hide it, but Bel knew that his friend was not long for this world. "When they broke Feyhold, they were led by a man in purple robes and a great beard. From what I could tell, it was he as had command of the dead army, but there were others like him as well. The Keepers." He gave a great, staggering sigh. "I'm sorry. I wish I could have done more."

Beledain shook his head. "You have nothing to regret," he said, taking his friend solidly by the arm. "Whatever chance we have of surviving this, it's you who has bought it for us."

"Then don't waste it," the Shackle said with his grotesque grin. "Cost a pretty price in blood."

"I swear I won't," Bel said.

With that, the Shackle lay back in the wagon and shut his eyes. Bel offered his friend one final look, then turned back to meet his men. Marina joined him, followed by Sir Armel.

"My lady," Geoffrey, Horn, and Welmsey said.

"I'm relieved to find you all well," Marina told them. "So where do matters stand?"

"Briden is helping Marguerite with the old flag and Val has gone off to inform the Talon and the other lords of Whitemane that we mean to parley," Horn said. "The rest of the Nivanus army has withdrawn and the wounded are being seen to while Sir Norton and the Malets reform the lines from the men still fit to fight."

"You mean to parley?" Marina asked Bel.

"I do," the Tower said. "All the more so now."

"I will come with you," she said.

No one disagreed.

"Horn," Bel said, "We need riders stationed on the path to Pridel watching our rear."

"To guard these folk?"

"And to warn us when the enemy finally appears."

"Your brother has allies in the south?" Welmsey asked.

Bel and Geoffrey exchanged a glance. "I fear greater threats than the Guardians and the Plague King come for us now," the Tower said.

The brows of the other men creased in consternation, but they nodded all the same.

"If there is nothing else, then we should waste not a minute," Marina said.

"Agreed," Bel said. He heard Tempest's heavy breathing just behind his shoulder and he turned to climb up into his saddle. "We need to have all of these people take shelter along the edge of the western wood," he said, motioning with an armored gauntlet. "But tell them not to make camp—not yet. Until we know what follows us, I want them ready to run."

"Aye, sir," Horn and Welmsey said together.

"And..." His voice fell. "Take special care of Marcus and Sir Geoffrey's family."

"I'll guard them with my life, my lord," Welmsey said.

"And the Shackle...let me know if..."

"Yes, lord."

Freddy appeared with Geoffrey's horse and together the father and son clambered into their saddles.

"Give me a moment to arrange proper transport, your majesty," Sir Armel said with a bow.

"Thank you, but there's no time," Marina told him. "I'll just ride Tempest behind the Lord Tower."

"No," Bel said, offering her his hand, "You'll ride before me."

With a gentle pull, he lifted Marina up to sit in front of him just behind the saddle horn. Bel wrapped his arms around her and gripped Tempest's reins while Sir Armel mounted his horse beside them. Sir Geoffrey and Freddy ambled up alongside them mounted as well.

"Now let's have a word with this Warlord," Marina said.

Sir Briden, Marguerite, and Thom Reaver were waiting with the old flag of Montevale when they returned. All three of them were mounted and ready to ride out to meet the enemy commanders. At the sight of the queen herself, however, they all bowed their heads and leaned forward in their saddles. "They're deciding whether they should dismount and kneel," Bel said quietly.

"Now that would be silly," Marina said.

"It's a sign of respect."

"I know, and I appreciate the thought, but now's not the time." She held up a hand to stay them and Bel called out. "Marguerite, to me. Briden and Thom, join the line."

"Aye, sir," Briden said, finding a place beside Armel while Thom guided his mare to follow Geoffrey and Freddy. Bel knew that, like the Shackle, Thom preferred to fight on foot rather than mounted, but for the sake of the situation, he had found a horse, probably from among those wandering master-less throughout the field.

"If you look there, my lord," Briden said, pointing toward a trio of riders approaching from the town, "Lady Val has called on Lord Talondaire to join us, and I believe that other man might be Sir Allard, if I know my heraldry."

Bel smiled to himself. If there was one thing Briden knew, it was his heraldry. "What about the Guardian camp?" Marina asked. "Have they seen us yet?"

Bel peered across the field toward the enemy reserve. Sure enough, the Warlord was clearly visible seated upon his great white destrier. Beside him and his attending steward were two other heavily armored Guardians as well as a man in white robes—a preacher or the like—and another dressed in the crimson finery of an Andochan nobleman. Rounding out the party, were the two vanquished leaders of the Nivanus army, Lord Pronet and Sir Gurney.

"Are you ready?" Bel whispered to Marina.

"I am," she said. "Are you?"

Bel nodded. "Of course I am," he said. "I'm afraid that in life there is little more to me than this."

"We both know that that's nonsense," Marina said. "But I suppose it would not do to call you out in front of your people."

The other riders began to trot toward the center of the field. "Your majesty," Sir Armel said. "It appears they ride."

"Thank you, sir," Marina said. "Lord Tower?"

"Together as one," Bel called out, and with but a touch of his heel, Tempest sallied forth across the cold, sodden ground.

In the center of the blood-soaked field, the three groups of riders met beneath the banner of truce. Val, Talondaire, and Sir Allard were the first to arrive and Bel could see from the Talon's Ashen complexion why he had not taken the field. Still, as was his way, the young lord sat his horse with a haughty expression that betrayed no loss of dignity.

"It's good to see you, Tally," Marina said aloud, "and to finally meet you, Lady Valerie."

"You as well, my queen," Lord Talondaire said. "I apologize that it has been so long."

The Warlord's party approached and at once, Pronet and Gurney exploded in fury. "There you are, you traitorous dog! You sat at the king's table only to stab him in the back!" Pronet snapped.

"Aye, Tally, how could you let this bastard get to you?" Gurney said, motioning toward Bel. "I mean, we're to be family! How could you choose them over your own?"

"Silence!" Dandon Rood commanded. He removed his helmet and held it within the crook of his arm. "Lord Tower, I'm told the flag you fly is the traditional banner of truce. What do you mean by this parley?"

"Originally, I called the parley in hopes of negotiating a cessation of hostilities," Bel said, "However, it is Queen Marina herself who brings news of a more pressing matter." Carefully he lowered her to the ground and she stood, chin held high, unafraid before the steel-clad enemies of the rebellion.

Rood bowed his head. "Apologies, my lady," he said. "In the midst of this bickering and hot speech, I did not see you. Please, forgive me."

"There is nothing to forgive, Warlord Rood," Marina said. "This is, after all, a battlefield. If anything, I am a trespasser in your domain."

"The only natives to a battlefield are the wounded and the dead, my lady. It is not a place any good man calls home."

"Then I fear we may all be trespassers soon enough," Marina said.

"What is it you mean?" the Warlord asked.

Marina took a deep breath. "Now, before I explain, I want you to know that I am aware of how peculiar, how far-fetched what I am about to say might sound. Yet, it is the truth."

"Then as a courtesy to you, my lady, I will endeavor to keep an open mind."

Marina smiled. "After Marcus Harding fell, I did not believe I would ever meet a man of such high honor among the Guardians of Andoch, particularly after aligning themselves with one so nefarious as the Plague King," she said. "I am glad to be proven wrong, my lord."

"Harding was without equal, my lady," Rood said. "Not only was he a good man, but to me, he was as a younger brother."

"Then 'tis a shame we find ourselves at such cross purposes, for as I understand it, he was to Prince Beledain, an elder brother."

Pronet gave an impatient sigh and Gurney picked at his teeth and spat upon the ground. The Warlord raised an eyebrow at them to show his displeasure, and returned his attention to Marina. "What is your news, my lady?" he asked.

Marina took a deep breath. "There is no sense bandying about," she said. "Warlord Rood, my presence here today is not out of a desire for diplomacy or because I am…bored or in need of entertainment."

"I did not believe it to be as such, my lady."

"My presence here today is due to the danger that now threatens all the lands of Montevale, whether they be loyal to myself or to Reginal. In fact, it may indeed represent a threat to the entire continent." She took another breath and cast a quick glance up at Bel before continuing. "Warlord Rood," she said, "I am speaking of an enemy that has not been seen for thirteen hundred years, since the days of St. Aiden, since the days of the founding of the Order." She paused. "Warlord Rood, I fear that the enemy we now face— all of us—is the army of the Warlock. The Army of the Dead. It is an enemy that requires us to set aside our differences in order to face this new and greater threat together!"

Silence reigned as Marina finished speaking. Bel watched the reactions of the others gathered around, both friend and foe. As he expected, his cousin Val simply nodded. She was a soldier through and through and she would fight any enemy who threatened her land and her people. Lord Talondaire's face betrayed a certain skepticism, only for Bel to realize that his face nearly always wore the selfsame expression. Sir Allard, the chosen representative of the remaining nobles of Whitemane who had chosen to stand with Talondaire, seemed in this as well to simply defer to the will of his lord.

Strange, Bel thought, that for thinking creatures, men were often so willing to wash their hands of the privilege of choice. Regardless, for whatever reason, it appeared that Talondaire and Whitemane remained committed.

The faces of the Guardians and the lords of Nivanus told a different story.

"You truly expect us to believe this nonsense?" Giles Pronet asked. "You called a parley in the middle of a battle to tell us that an army of corpses is marching northwest from Pridel?" He laughed. "You're bloody mad. Were your faces not so stony, I'd think you were taking the piss! Holy Brethren! You've all lost your minds!"

Gurney laughed along. "Tally, you were never this much of a fool," he said. "Have you really gone and allied yourself with...whatever this is?"

Bel's eyes panned to Dandon Rood and the other Guardians with him. With the exception of the Warlord, they seemed torn between concern and levity, like an adult after hearing a child share the content of a bad dream that woke them in the middle of the night. It was a levity touched with condescension to mask an undercurrent of fear.

They can feel it—Bel realized—*feel it in the same way that Geoffrey and I did when the Keeper first appeared at the inn. They know that something is amiss, but they refuse to admit it!*

Still, the men of the Order remained silent, unwilling to voice either their opposition or their support. On either side of the Warlord, the pair of men in plate armor frowned deeply, exchanging uncertain looks with one another, while the preacher in white muttered an orison under his breath, and the courtier in crimson eyed Marina skeptically. Rood himself remained silent, but his brow creased and he chewed upon his lip.

"My lady," the Warlord said at last. "While I mean no disrespect and I do not for a moment believe that you intend to deceive us, you'll understand my hesitancy."

"I understand how it must sound, my lord," Marina said.

"And as we stand here now upon this ground—made recently bloody by such a hard-fought and deadly battle—on *both* sides—the idea of a sudden alliance..." He sighed. "I imagine it would be a hard thing for many men to accept."

"Your bloody-well right it would be!" Gurney snarled. "Fucking traitors and tarts can line up to kiss my ass before I stand beside them!"

On reflex, Bel's hand tightened upon Spire and he prepared to run its point through Gurney's throat. His eyes blazed with rage and in spite of the cold, his blood grew hot.

Before he could act, however, the Warlord exploded with abject fury.

"Sir Gurney!" he cried, whirling upon the nobleman, "You will keep a courteous tongue or you will keep your foolish mouth shut! I would remind you that upon the field that surrounds us lie the bloodied corpses of *your* command—the Great Army of the Nivanus—reduced now to little more than a boneyard! And those few who didn't meet their end here today flee into the bloody wilds like chaff on the wind!" He heaved a great breath. "Why our King chose to ally himself with such wretched curs as all of you is beyond my understanding. You speak of standing a line? Kin keep us! Every moment I am forced to do the Plague King's dirty work, I feel my honor congeal like pus in a festering wound! But such are the consequences of abandoning wisdom! Such are the consequences when men glorify war and scorn peace. Perindal's Sword!" He choked down his anger and simply glared—at Gurney, at Pronet, at the men of the Order at his side. When he spoke again, his voice was low and calm, but carried with it a clear undertone of menace.

"You will conduct yourselves appropriately or you will remain silent! Am I understood?"

Gurney, beneath the glaring watch-light of such public humiliation, pressed his lips together in sullen silence.

The Warlord would not allow it. "Am I understood?" he shouted again.

At this, Gurney, Pronet, and the Guardians gave a clear, if reluctant, affirmative and Bel felt his tension ease.

"My apologies," the Warlord said to Marina. "Where were we?"

"I proposed a type of...armistice while we combat the greater threat."

"Ah yes." The Warlord turned his gaze upon Bel. "And you say you have fought these...creatures?"

"I have," Bel said, "as have a few others." He paused. "A friend of mine lies dying of wounds sustained while bringing us word of their movements."

The Warlord chewed his lip as he considered Bel's words. Suddenly his eyes settled upon Thom. "You were in Reginal with Lord Talondaire," he said. "The scribe."

"I was," Thom said.

"But that is not the first I have seen you."

"No, sir," Thom said.

Suddenly, the Warlord's eyes lit up with shock. "You're one of Rastis's boys, aren't you?"

Thom nodded. "I was. I am."

"By the Brethren, I knew I recognized you!" Bel watched as myriad emotions fought for expression on the old soldier's face as he struggled to make sense of all of the strange and seemingly unlikely pieces of information that had all fallen into place. At last, he shut his eyes and took a deep breath.

"This is a great deal to take in," he finally said. "I'm afraid I must beg time to consider all of this."

Marina gave a nod. "I understand," she said, "but I'm afraid that time is a luxury that we do not possess."

"All the same, I must have it," Rood told her.

At length, Marina gave a nod. "So be it," she said, "if you must, you must. However, do not take overlong. They are coming."

CHAPTER 41: LOCK & KEY

The courtyard inside of the main barbican of Galadin had become a veritable charnel house of blood and gore. As Brigid led the way down the stairs and along the battlements of the city walls, the cries of the dying kingsmen was a nightmarish chorus of agony punctuated with the intermittent screams of horses. It had been such a simple plan, such an obvious deception, yet by taking advantage of the enemy's flaws, their overconfidence, it had proved remarkably effective.

With a resounding clash, a sound like an avalanche sliding down a mountainside momentarily drowned out the din. Satisfied with the size of the Andochan horde caught within the walls, Adolfo gave the order and a great pile of wreckage—remains of carts, wagons, and broken stones—toppled from where it had been restrained by ropes along the inner side of the barbican, effectively blocking the passage inward and cutting off any retreat.

But it was not over yet.

"This way!" Brigid called, leaping from the battlement to the stone stairway that in turn led toward Hounton. Fergus hurried to join her in the lead while Lughus, Pike, Alban, and the others followed behind.

As they hurried along in pursuit of Harlow and the Guardian-King, the sounds of the battle fell away and were replaced by the sounds of smaller skirmishes spilling over into the Hounton streets. In the clear morning light, the damage caused by the bombardment of the trebuchets filled Brigid's mind with memories of Cragbarrow and while she was relieved that—at least for now—the devastation was nowhere near as extensive, she knew that the poor townsfolk would need a great deal of aid piecing their lives back together.

Through Hounton they hurried, down the cobblestone streets through the Trade Quarter and onward toward the Saint's quarter. A strange sensation overcame Brigid as she realized suddenly that she was following the very same path that she and Geoffrey had once taken as they fled the Hammer and his disguised kingsmen. However, whereas on that day she was the hunted, today she was the hunter, and the great golden hound that she had sought for safety now loped merrily at her side.

What a strange thing this life is! she thought to herself. *How twisted and turning is this path we call fate!*

At the archway that marked the boundary from the Trade Quarter to the Saint's Quarter, she paused to allow Lughus and the Galadin guardsmen to catch up. Fergus stood loyally at her side, his nose in the air as he sniffed aloud for any unfamiliar scent, any sign of their enemies. A low growl sounded from the depths of his throat and Brigid knew at once that they were close.

"Any sign of them?" Lughus asked, when he and the others had reached her.

Fergus gave a snarl and paced on ahead before turning and sounding a short, staccato bark.

"That's not the way to the grotto," Lughus said.

"No," Brigid said. "It's the way to the cathedral."

"Why would they be headed to the cathedral?" Pike asked.

"Maybe to steal the relics?" Tonkin asked.

Lughus's jaw set. "Whatever they're doing, it cannot be good."

"Then we should waste no more time here," Brigid said.

Lughus nodded. "Lead on," he said, "but stay sharp everyone."

Affirmative grunts sounded from the men of the guard as they took up positions around their lord. As before, Brigid and Fergus led, followed by Lughus, who was flanked on either side by Tonkins and Sedge. Behind him,

Pike and Alban followed with two others, Madren and Dross, bringing up the rear.

Somewhere, streets away, a skirmish raged on and Brigid wondered if Sir Beric and his men had managed to waylay the panicked knights who had fled the killing floor of the gates for the narrow streets of the city. She tried not to think about whether the occasional screams and whinnies of horses were evidence of the Galadin soldiers victorious or being ridden down. Either way the thought quickened her pace, for she knew that should they succeed in subduing the Guardian-King, the rest of the Andochan army would surely stand down.

From the archway, they navigated the streets of the Saint's Quarter past vacant shops and town houses, tiny shrines and green spaces, until finally the great Cathedral of St. Aidan loomed before them in all its grandeur. Miraculously, it bore no damage from the trebuchet fire and stood completely and utterly unharmed.

As Lughus and the others caught up to her, Brigid eyed the cathedral curiously. A strange feeling gripped her heart and sent a chill coursing through her limbs. For while the cathedral had become a place of quiet contemplation for her these past months, she now sensed something...ominous. She could not quite explain it, but it filled her with a sense of heightened caution and pervasive dread. It was the same sensation she had felt upon fleeing Blackstone, lost in the listless darkness that was all she could recall from her flight with the Falcon as she lay upon the brink of death.

It was clear from his expression that Lughus sensed something too.

Before she could remark upon it, however, the clatter of hoofs followed by angry oaths and cursing brought her mind back to the present and the battle. A pair of heavily armored horsemen rode up and down the cobblestone street in pursuit of roughly a dozen Galadin soldiers, men of Sir Beric's squad. Beric himself was nowhere to be seen, but his men had not yet given up the fight, for no sooner would the horsemen run down one man than another would attack from the side with pike or spear, forcing the rider to cease his pursuit in order to defend himself.

Still, in the few moments that Brigid stood looking on, she sensed at once that both riders were anointed Guardians, and as they drew closer, she recognized them as two of the great knights—justiciars—who attended the parley.

"Blood and fire!" Lughus grunted, his gaze passing back and forth from the knights to the cathedral.

Brigid's brow furrowed. "What do you want to do?" she asked quietly. "There's no time to waste."

Lughus grimaced. Despite their valiant efforts, Brigid knew as well as he did that a mere dozen foot soldiers were no match for a pair of the Warlord's justiciars.

"Pike?" the young baron said at last. "Take the rest of the men and help them."

The sergeant's face fell. "But, my lord, what about you and Lady Brigid?"

"We still have Fergus," Lughus said with a smirk.

Pike gave a reluctant nod. "Be safe, my lord," he said.

"You as well," Lughus said. He grasped the man by the arm and cast his glance around at the others of the Galadin guard. "All of you."

With a final nod, the group disbanded, heading off along their separate paths. The guardsmen ran to join their fellows in engaging the riders while Brigid, Lughus, and Fergus hurried to the great cathedral.

"When this is all over, I'll see them all knighted," Lughus said as they approached the great carved doors, "assuming we all survive."

"One step at a time, darling," Brigid whispered as the ominous feeling deepened in the pit of her stomach. "One step at a time."

Lughus gave a forlorn nod and for a brief moment their eyes met, the world fell away and there was only the two of them, two souls, two hearts, drifting together as one in the endless expanse of time and eternity. Whatever was about to happen, whatever lie on the other side of the great carven doors, Brigid knew that they would face it together. Come what may.

"Ready?" she asked.

Lughus gave a her a quick kiss upon the brow. "Yes."

"Hang on," Brigid said, and with a grin of defiance against death and sorrow, she wrapped her arms around his neck and kissed him deeply upon the lips. At once, she felt the tension within him ease and he enveloped her in a tight embrace. To feel him so close, to feel the intensity and truth of his love for her was all she ever wanted, all she ever needed, and as her heart beat strengthened in defiance of darkness and fear, she knew that for him it was the very same.

"If Death comes for us," she said when they were forced to part for want of air, "we face him with a smile."

"I love you," Lughus told her.

"And I you."

With a deep breath, they slipped from the embrace, steeled themselves for what might come, and with Fergus at their side, pushed open the heavy doors of the cathedral, ready to face the Guardian-King.

The once-bright colors that seeped in through the intricate stained glass windows seemed somehow drab and subdued in the frigid winter light, and the cold, unlit sconces and braziers contributed to a greater chill throughout the lofty expanse. Under normal circumstances, Brigid would appreciate such heavy silence, would find it comforting, encouraging even. The cathedral had become her refuge for quiet reflection and thought.

Yet that peace had become tarnished, corrupted, for in the very heart of the vaulted chamber, a darkness had seeped in like a burr beneath the saddle or a stone lodged in a hoof. It was a taint that spoiled the solemnity of the whole.

There they were, the invaders, the encroachers, the bringers of blight and darkness. They stood gathered around St. Aiden's tomb like flies upon a dung heap. The Guardian-King, the Hammer, the pair of guards, the little harlequin with his bundle, and the strange pallid man named Natharis Tainne.

"Ah, so you've arrived at last," King Kredor said as they approached. They paced together side-by-side down the center aisle with Fergus in tow. For a fleeting moment, Brigid imagined a different scenario, a more pleasant scenario where she and Lughus might have walked this path together. A dagger of fear pierced her innards as she wondered now if that other vision would ever come to pass.

"I have to hand it to you," the King said. "You made a good show of it out there. Were we allies in the manner of our ancestors, none would dare to oppose us."

"Were we allies in the manner of our ancestors," Lughus said, "you would not have threatened us with tyranny and war."

Kredor offered them an exaggerated eye roll. He leaned casually against the great tomb of St. Aiden with his arms folded across his chest. Beside him, Willum Harlow stood with a type of reverent attention that reminded Brigid of the showy deference that had been common among Alan's friends. Of course, whereas Alan had been a joke of a warrior, Kredor was clearly an accomplished killer. A brute and a boor, yes, but a killer nonetheless.

"What you call tyranny, I call order," Kredor said. "The Protectorate will help me to achieve that, and what we do here today will all but guarantee it."

Brigid's eyes darted past the brash King to where the Natharis Tainne stooped beside the tomb of St. Aiden and she watched as he traced a thin, claw-like finger along the small, strangely shaped depression in the stone. At once, he leapt to his feet and his strange eyes blazed with the dark fire of the Abyss. "It's here!" he cried, his voice echoing throughout the cathedral. "I knew it would be here!"

An inexplicable sensation of panic gripped Brigid's heart and icy water flooded her veins. Her eyes darted to Lughus and she saw from the way in which all color had drained from him that he felt it too. Even Fergus seemed to know something was wrong. His lips curled and a low snarl sounded from deep within him.

Kredor offered Lughus and Brigid an arrogant smirk and turned toward his advisor. With a wave of his hand, Tainne indicated the odd depression and Kredor paused to rub his thumb against it. "Alright, Paddock, bring it here."

Lughus cast Brigid a quick glance and strode forward, raising Sentinel. "What are you doing, Kredor?" he asked. "Have you not committed enough sacrilege for one day?"

At once, the pair of guardsmen with their tower shields stepped forward to place themselves between the young baron and the King. Behind them, the little man in motley knelt at Kredor's side and raised his cloth bundle before him with an air of maniacal glee.

"Here you are, your majesty!" the little man croaked.

Kredor drew back the cloth wrapping the bundle to reveal the scepter of the realm, the Key of Salvation, freed from the enormous silver reliquary. With a self-satisfied chuckle, the King raised the scepter before him and turned to his advisor. "You're certain, Tainney?" he asked. "The one who holds the scepter is granted mastery over the Beast?"

"Such is the belief of the Keepers," Tainne said.

"What?" Lughus uttered. "The Beast?"

Brigid's eyes flashed. "You cannot be serious?"

"When Aiden Galadin fought against Kalius Wrogan, the Lady of Light granted him the Key of Salvation not as a means of imprisoning the beast, but of commanding it," Tainne said. "And out of a peasant's fear and superstition, Galadin rejected the Lady's boon and instead chose to hide it, to allow the suffering of generations, centuries. War, cruelty, evil—all of this could have been prevented if only a righteous king—the Guardian-King— wielded the power of Dibhor's Beast."

"This is madness!" Lughus shouted. "Kredor, you cannot possibly believe this! Have you fallen so far from the path of wisdom? Are you so blinded by ambition that you would put your faith in this nonsense?"

Kredor gave a snort. "Same old superstition," he said with a chuckle. "You Galadins and your ignorant self-righteousness! You believe yourselves higher than the Order, higher than the Guardian-King!"

"Their arrogance knows no bounds, my liege!" Harlow added. "Let us not forget! Baron and Baroness Galadin have chosen to embrace the heretical legacies of the Marshal and the Blade!"

"Oh Harlow," Brigid said with a grin, "you say that like it's something we should be ashamed of."

Fergus barked and the sound echoed throughout the vaulted emptiness of the cathedral.

Tainne was growing impatient. "There is no time to waste, your majesty," he said. "Quickly, place the Key in the Lock and a new day will dawn!"

"Don't be a fool, Kredor!" Lughus snapped.

"I won't," the Guardian-King said, and with a sardonic sneer, thrust the scepter into the strange depression and with as much strength as he could muster, gave it a turn.

On reflex, Brigid readied her blades, certain at once that something terrible was about to come to pass. Lughus raised Sentinel and cast his gaze around while Fergus readied himself to pounce.

But nothing happened.

Again, Kredor turned the Key, then turned it back, and twisted it again. Nothing.

With a frustrated sigh, Kredor eyed his acting Loremaster. "What the fuck, Tainney?" he snapped. "You said it was supposed to open!"

Tainne breathed a sigh and his eyes blazed in the drab light. "There is one final requirement," he said. "It is the reason we needed the Galadin boy alive…"

Kredor's jaw tightened. "Oh yes," he said. He left the Key twisted in the lock of the tomb and drew his great sword, Testament, from the baldric across his back. With a cold stare, he leveled the blade at Lughus. "The blood of a Galadin sealed the Beast away!" he said, "and now the blood of a Galadin will free it."

The storms in Lughus's eyes flashed. "You call me self-righteous, yet you would profane the tomb of the Blessed Saint with violence and bloodshed?"

"I would piss on the tomb of the Blessed Saint if it gave me what I want," Kredor snarled. "Take him!"

At once, the pair of armored warriors charged, leading with their great shields. With an easy hop, Brigid leapt up onto a pew and slashed at the nearest of the warriors in passing. Sparks flew as her blade scraped across the metal pauldron, but did no damage.

With a quick step, she leapt to the next pew as the shield-bearer turned and lashed out at her with his heavy mace in a flurry of strikes. She was far too quick, though, and beneath the weight of his armor and shield, the man only succeeded in tiring himself out. With a grunt, he wound up and struck at her with a blow that would have shattered stone, but with the grace of a dancer, she simply sidestepped around him, and plunged her dagger through the seam of his gorget. A torrent of blood spewed forth in a great fountain as the man dropped his shield, fell to his knees, and collapsed in a widening lake of crimson.

Meanwhile, across the aisle, Lughus and Fergus made quick work of the remaining shield-bearer. The great hound met the man's charge low, knocking him off balance long enough for the young baron to slip Sentinel through the weak point under the Andochan's arm. He collapsed in a heap among the pews.

There was no time to rest, however, for no sooner had Brigid made her way to Lughus's side than the Hammer and the Guardian-King were upon them.

With a great stride forward, Kredor slashed crosswise with Testament, forcing Lughus, Brigid, and Fergus to leap backward to avoid the heavy blade. Lughus turned his wrist, rocked back on the ball of his foot, and attempted a quick riposte, but found his strike intercepted by the shaft of Harlow's mace. The Hammer's lips spread into a wide leer, and Lughus withdrew his blade just in time to turn aside a second blow from the Guardian-King.

At this, Brigid made her move, slipping in close to the king's side, and striking with both of her blades. Whisper touched the breastplate of the king's armor and was turned aside with the hiss of steel on steel, but Shade found its mark, piercing chain and quilt to find royal flesh below. However, before she could drive the point home, Kredor, grimacing with rage and pain, reflexively lashed out with a gauntleted hand, and she had to leap away.

No sooner had she found her feet, though, when she was forced to quickly bound backward again when the motley fool appeared from hiding among the pews and darted at her with a dagger of his own. He grinned maniacally, scoring a light slash along her right shin, but while painful, it was not serious and when Fergus suddenly pounced at him, hackles raised and teeth bared, the little man screamed in terror and scurried for safety beneath the benches.

Again, King Kredor raised Testament and struck, though this time, Lughus met the blow with Sentinel straight on. The clash of the storied blades echoed throughout the cathedral like a church bell. Again and again, the blades met in a deadly dance of parries and ripostes. While the warriors were nearly a match in height, Kredor's Testament was the longer of the swords, forcing Lughus to step in closer to the King if ever he hoped to land a blow. The Marshal, however, had the advantage of speed, and while his simple hauberk did not afford him the protection of Kredor's steel skin, he did not suffer from its encumbrance either.

With Fergus hunting the harlequin, rooting through the pews like a terrier after a rat, Brigid focused her attention on the Hammer. Harlow may have lost his signature weapon and his hand long ago, but he was still a deadly warrior, as crafty and quick in combat as he was in causing strife. With swift steps and deft strikes, he kept her on her toes, using his false hand like a buckler to deflect her counterattacks.

"Your cousin had much to say about you, Lady Blade," the Hammer said, casting aside her dagger and forcing her to leap out of reach of his riposte.

"Oh Willum," Brigid said with a wicked leer. "Surely you spent enough time with him to know that when the gods made Alan, they confused which end was meant to speak and which end was meant for spouting shit."

Harlow gave a snort. "True enough," he said, "but if you have the time—or the imprisonment—to sift through all of the refuse, you occasionally stumble upon a grain of truth."

"Such as?" Brigid feigned an attach with Whisper, side-stepped to the right, and slashed with Shade. Harlow fell for the feint and lunged to intercept an attack that never came, but at the last moment, used his false hand to turn aside her blade and prevent her from opening the side of his neck.

In the depths of Harlow's eyes, Brigid discerned the briefest flicker of fear, but when he spoke, his voice still carried the selfsame arrogance that she was accustomed to.

"He said you were a killer even before you became the Blade."

With a whirl of his arm, Harlow swept his mace around and before she could fully parry, struck her a glancing blow upon the left shoulder. It wasn't enough to do real damage, but it threw her off balance and she fell backwards over the back of a pew. At once, Harlow leapt forward and struck from on high, hoping to finish her, but she rolled out of the way of his attack, curled to a crouch, and sprang back to her feet. The Hammer followed her movements with his mace, lashing out in maddened pursuit, but she was far too quick for him. At last, with a whirling swipe, she knocked his mace to the side across his body and with her off-hand, slashed a deep gash the length of Harlow's cheek. Blood poured from the gaping wound, and wide-eyed with terror, the Hammer pressed his hand to his neck for fear that she had opened more than just his face.

"I killed a man who sought to rape me," Brigid said, her voice crisper than the winter air. "I killed a man who believed his birth and his station granted him the privilege to force others to bend to his desires." She advanced, her knuckles white as she gripped her twin blades. "I killed a man in the name of justice and because I refused to bow down to tyranny and fear!"

In a flurry of cold rage, she launched herself at the wounded Hammer, slashing and slicing and stabbing with the force of a hailstorm. Harlow did his best to parry and dodge, but he could not compete with the fury of the Blade and when finally, her energy spent, Brigid leapt back out of reach of any desperate counter, the Hammer could barely keep his feet, bleeding as he was from a score of wounds.

"You'd have made a decent constable," Harlow said with a ragged cough, "had destiny chosen otherwise." He slumped to the floor, rested his head back against the side of a pew, and shut his eyes.

A flood of emotion hit her at the vanquishing of such a longtime foe, but Brigid had no time for it, for a sudden scream echoed through the chamber she whirled around, desperate to find the source. Her gaze found Fergus. He had finally succeeded in catching the Harlequin between his slavering jaws and now shook the little man like a rag doll.

Meanwhile, Lughus and Kredor continued their deadly struggle at the foot of St. Aiden's tomb. The King swung Testament with the force of a gale, putting such strength behind each strike as to cleave the young baron in two, but Lughus was faster and his parries and counters far more precise; however, while he might penetrate the King's defenses, he could not pierce through the solid steel of Kredor's great armor.

Perhaps together... Brigid thought as Lughus and Kredor clashed again, their storied blades pressed together in a desperate contest of strength.

"You know you can't win this, boy," Kredor said with a smirk. "I was slaughtering Wrathorn by the dozens while you sat at Rastis's skirts listening to bedtime tales."

Lughus grimaced as he slipped Sentinel free, made a half-turn, and struck a resounding blow against Kredor's gorget. The King's eyes widened in shock and fear at the nearness of death.

"If you had done the same, the Order would still stand as a beacon hope and honor instead of tyranny and blood!" Lughus said. He reset his guard and prepared for Kredor's counter. "You are no king. You are but a pawn of the servants of Dibhor!"

"Superstition and rot!" Kredor shouted as he charged. He brought Testament down from on high, and stepped back to avoid Sentinel's riposte. "All that matters is a man's will—the will to power, the will to lead. The emperors of Calendral understood that, even Kalius Wrogan understood that, and with the power granted to me by what resides inside that tomb, the glorious days of the past will return again!"

The King raised his blade to strike, and seeing her chance, Brigid leapt into the fray, slashing quickly beneath his arms as Lughus parried the attack.

Kredor grunted when Whisper found its mark, its tip passing through the quilted undercoat to pierce the royal skin beneath. Yet it was only a trifling wound, more inconvenient than lethal. His armor was too well-made, too strong to penetrate.

With a quick step, Brigid leapt back to stand at Lughus's side and from among the pews, Fergus loped to join them, his maw stained red. Together they tensed and prepared to attack.

"Surrender, Kredor," Lughus said. "Stand down and you may yet live."

Kredor stood tall and defiant, fixing them with an arrogant sneer. "Despite what you may believe," he snarled, "my purpose here is just and good. With the power of the Beast, with a unified Termain, there will be no strife, no war. There will be only order and peace. It will be a golden era of prosperity and empire!"

"Only a fool embraces darkness believing it reveals the light," Brigid said.

Fergus growled low and Lughus readied his guard. "Surrender," he commanded, "else if you fall, your title will end and the entire line of Guardian-Kings with it!"

From the far side of Aiden's tomb there came the sound of derisive laughter that sent a shiver down Brigid's spine. Moments later, Natharis Tainne appeared, his strange eyes ablaze with a zealous gleam. The Keeper stood beside the Guardian-King. "Bloody Blackguards," he chuckled. "Those favored by Dibhor need fear nothing!"

"Then perhaps a lesson is in order?" Brigid sneered.

Lughus raised Sentinel into a high guard. "Kredor, this is your last chance."

In answer, the King offered them a malicious smile and leveled his great sword. "I have no need of chance," he said. "My victory is certain."

With that, the combatants converged. Again, the sound of metal on metal resounded through the cathedral as Testament rang against Sentinel. In the backswing, Fergus roared and leapt for Kredor's wrist, but before the his great jaws could find their purchase, the King lashed out with his steel gauntlet and struck the hound squarely in the skull. Fergus fell to the flagstones and the King whirled his weapon around, ready for the killing blow. In desperation, Brigid crossed her blades and with all the strength she could muster, braced herself to ward off the King's heavy blade. To her great surprise, she succeeded, though her arms fell numb from the impact and Whisper and Shade slipped from her grip.

The King raised his blade again and Brigid rolled backward out of harm's way, allowing Lughus to step in and parry the attack. With a swift repose, he forced Kredor to take a step back against the tomb, whirled his blade around, and knocked Testament from the King's hand. The heavy blade clattered to the floor. Before Lughus could position himself for a finishing blow, however, Kredor lunged, catching the young baron by the arm and grappling with him against the tomb in a frenzy of punches, kicks, and holds.

Brigid shook her arms, willing her hands to regain their grip, while Fergus whined incoherently at her feet. Kredor gripped Sentinel's blade in one gauntleted hand, throwing punches into the young baron's mailed shoulder with the other. At the same time, Lughus fought to free his sword, using his offhand to try to pry the steel-clad fingers back. Both men growled, snarled, and cursed in the midst of the desperate struggle, knowing that the one to emerge with the upper-hand was sure to be the victor.

At last, her arms still aching, Brigid rolled across the flagstones to where the King and the baron grappled and lashed out with her feet. With every ounce of strength she had remaining, she kicked Kredor squarely in the back of the knee. It was not enough to cause any real damage, but the sudden impact forced his leg to buckle and as he began to fall, Lughus was able to free Sentinel, recover his stance, and take a high guard.

The King's eyes widened as he saw death draw near.

Lughus inhaled deeply and Brigid forced herself not to look away.

But the blow never came.

Instead, Brigid watched as Lughus lurched forward and Sentinel slipped from his fingers, clattering to the floor. His eyes widened and they turned away from Kredor and found hers.

"Brigid..." he whispered.

Horrified, Brigid's glance traveled from his face to the odd, curved blade that protruded now from the young baron's side.

"No!" Brigid screamed, wrath and anguish flowing through her like a lightning strike.

With a steady stride, Natharis Tainne paced along St. Aiden's tomb and tore the curved dagger from Lughus's side. A fresh spout of blood poured forth and frozen with fear, Brigid watched as the young baron, her heart's other half, fell in a heap upon the floor. She screamed and the Keeper smiled.

"And now," Tainne said, turning his back upon her, "we find out if this prophesy holds any truth." Without haste, he made his way to the fallen King and extended a hand to pull him to his feet.

With the blade withdrawn, Lughus's blood flowed freely, pooling upon the floor beside the tomb. As Brigid fought to overcome her shock and despair, Fergus stirred beside her and attempted to rise upon his quivering limbs. The great hound whimpered mournfully and Brigid's vision clouded with tears.

"Brigid..." he said as she gripped his hand, his lips moist with crimson blood. "You must run...Take Fergus...and run..."

"I'm not going to run, you bloody fool," she wept. "We stand together. Come what may!"

"No," Lughus managed. He closed his eyes and with what little strength remained, he kissed the back of her hand. "Something is...happening. Something I...can't explain..."

"What are you talking—"

Before she could finish the question, however, she noticed that from where she knelt beside Lughus, his blood flowed slowly in a thick channel to collect around the stone base of the tomb. An eerie light began to emanate from the place where Tainne had inserted the Key, strengthening with each passing moment until it shone with an ominous gleam.

Taine and Kredor stood watching it, the King's face alight with curiosity, the Keeper's a horrid mask of maniacal glee.

"What now?" Kredor asked.

Tainne knelt down to wash his hands in Lughus's blood, then gripping the Key of Salvation in both hands, again, attempted to turn it. To the Keeper's surprise and Brigid's horror, there came a definitive click.

Kredor's lips twisted into a satisfied leer. "It worked!"

With uncontrolled excitement, Natharis Tainne picked up Sentinel from where it had fallen upon the flagstones and waving Kredor to him for assistance, the two men used the Marshal's blade as a pry bar to raise the top of the tomb. The eerie light grew stronger, more intense, and the air grew thick with mist and smoke-like fog.

"Lady save us!" Brigid said aloud.

Lughus squeezed her hand. "Brigid!" he said desperately, "Brigid! Run!"

"No!" she cried, "Lughus, no! I'll not leave you!" With desperate effort, she began to drag him as best she was able away from the tomb and up the center aisle. Fergus did his best to assist her, gently pulling the young baron by the shoulder. Barely had they made it a dozen feet, however, before the thickening fog began to darken like smoke and the pulsing light deepened to an ominous red hue.

"Aiden's Flame!" an airy voice gasped from behind her.

Brigid's eyes widened like a cornered fawn and she turned to see the Hammer, his face pale as eggshell, coughing out his last. His red-rimmed eyes betrayed his horror and a devastating shame.

Brigid's blood burned with sudden rage and her hands, beyond control, reached for the chief constable's throat.

"You did this! All of you! Do you see now the prize for your ambition!"

Harlow gave a weak nod. "And I shall pay for it, surely," he managed. "But while you stand here cursing me, you forget—" He paused to cough and blood seeped from the corner of his lips. "You forget the Gift!"

Brigid's eyes widened. "The Gift?"

"I've never known it to be used upon another Guardian," the Hammer said, his gaze falling upon Lughus, "but it may be the only way to save his life!"

"Why do you care?" Brigid sneered. "You've done nothing but seek his death from the very beginning!"

"That may be so, but this is...different. Do you not feel it? Do you not sense the vile darkness? The evil? The affairs of men are one thing, but that—that!"

A sound like thunder broke with a deafening roar from the tomb, though Brigid could barely make it out for the thickness of the dark smoke and flashing lights. It was as if a thunderstorm had somehow emerged from within the stone sarcophagus and was steadily expanding to fill the entirety of the cathedral's vaulted expanse. Maniacal laughter echoed from within the shadowy gyre and it felt as if the very ground itself had begun to shake.

"Hurry!" Harlow murmured. Blood ran in a pair of rivulets from the corners of his mouth and down his chin. "The blood of the Saint cannot fade. Not now!"

Brigid could not think straight for the overwhelming flood of emotions—grief, fear, nausea, anger, sorrow. She ground her teeth and shook her head. Lughus's grip was weakening around her slender hand.

"Damn it, girl! Hurry!" the Hammer cried.

Her blue eyes flashed and her chest heaved against the acrid smoke. Before her in the widening darkness, she began to discern the outline of some enormous, serpentine creature shrouded in an unnatural gloom. It was as if the shadows themselves had somehow gained substance and were now clinging together in defiance of the light in order to assume some monstrous form.

The Beast of Dibhor!

"Hurry!" Harlow cried yet again. Even Fergus seemed agitated beyond reason. He paced back and forth to lick Lughus's face before returning to nudge her side.

"I'm trying!" Brigid cried aloud. She tried to think back to how she had done it at St. Golan's when she had taken on the suffering of the children wounded in their flight. Yet it was suddenly impossible to think straight. Between the horrors of the tomb and the magnitude of her own grief, her hands shook and her vision was obscured by tears. All sense had left her, all sensation…but the feel of his hand in hers.

Focus on that! a voice spoke in her mind, a voice that was neither hers nor one that she knew. *Focus only on that and remember! Remember that through the bonds of your love for each other, your hearts beat as one!*

With an effort, she focused her mind—her will—upon her fallen mate. She forced her breathing to remain calm, and her heart to remain steady. She was vaguely aware that outside of her, the noise of the shadow storm had grown deafening. Fergus stood protectively at her side, shielding her with his great body and sounding his defiant bark.

Do not give in! said the voice in her mind. *Where love remains, there is always hope!*

"I will not," she said aloud through gritted teeth. "I will not submit! I will not give in! I will defy the Darkness and stand for the Light!"

No sooner had she finished speaking, than she discerned a sudden flash of otherworldly luminescence within the billowing cloud of shadow and the ground shook once more tearing deep fissures in the stones of the cathedral and shattering the stained-glass windows.

"I will not submit!" she cried out once more, and this time—*this* time, she was rewarded with a sharp pain in the side of her abdomen, just below her ribs. She tightened her grip on Lughus's hand and ground her teeth against the sudden torrent of agony. "*We* will not submit! We shall stand together—hand in hand—and welcome a new dawn!" She tasted blood and felt the cloth of her tunic growing wet and warm. "This, I swear," she cried, her vision fading. "Come what may!"

A deafening roar echoed from the center of the storm, a screech that bypassed the ears to tear at the mind with claws like a thousand rusty needles. Still Brigid fought against her fear and sorrow, her overwhelming horror and despair. She fought against her fading consciousness, against the agonizing pain in her side…

But in the end, she too fell to darkness, swooned, and saw no more.

CHAPTER 42: THE LAST STAND

After the Warlord and his attendants departed, the queen, the Tower, and the remaining captains stood together in the field, their faces grim. Thom sat uncomfortably upon his borrowed horse. He had quite forgotten where he had last left his own mount, but ever since Reginal, the very sight of her brought thoughts of Sparrow and he just couldn't handle that right now on top of everything else.

"We need to decide on a plan ourselves, regardless of whether the Warlord agrees to join us," Beledain said. "Of course, I'd rather have him with us than against us, but for the sake of our people, we need to prepare for the worst."

"Agreed," Queen Marina said.

"Are we completely certain that Pridel is lost?" Lord Talondaire asked. "As I recall, it was a mighty fortress."

"So was Feyhold by the time we finished with it," Sir Armel said, "but according to the Shackle, it has returned to ruin."

"Could we withdraw?" Sir Briden asked. "Ride south and meet the enemy in the field?"

"Our people are exhausted," Bel said, "and many are wounded."

"There are the common folk and burghers to account for as well," Marina said.

Sir Geoffrey chewed his lip. "What about the Brock?" he asked.

"What do you mean?" Armel asked.

"Well, you heard the Warlord. We defeated the great Army of the Nivanus. It stands to reason, then, that the pass to the Brock should be clear." Geoffrey shrugged. "If we march west through the pass, we will reach the barony of Helmstead where the forces of several of the barons have been mustering. What good is an alliance if you cannot call upon your allies in a time of need?"

"The narrow pass would certainly slow the advance of an army in pursuit," Val said. "It would also make for an easier defense."

"Hang on, though," Lord Talondaire said. "I am still not completely clear on this Army of the Dead business. What do you mean an *Army of the Dead?*"

"It's exactly as it sounds, lord," Thom spoke up. "Dead men risen to fight again. Like puppets or…beasts more like. Trained beasts where the Keeper simply has to point and command them to kill."

Lord Talondaire sighed. "Nonsense."

"Tally," Marina said, "I know how it sounds, but regardless of their nature, I can promise you that an army larger than both of those who took the field today marches for us now, and while I would not have you abandon your lands, I would ask you and your people to join us—if only for the sake of your lives—until we can discover a better way forward."

The Tower breathed a sigh and Tempest stomped impatiently at the ground. "Look, the longer we stand here, the less time we have to gather what common folk we can and make for the pass. We must make haste."

Sir Armel shook his head forlornly. "We fought so hard and accomplished so much only for it to matter so little. I am so sorry, your majesty," he said to Marina. "We have failed you."

"Of course not," Marina said. "No one could have accounted for this." She eyed Beledain. "Lord Tower, what would you have us do?"

Thom watched the general as he studied the horizon from the south through to the west and not for the first time, Thom was glad to have never been forced to bear the heavy burden of command. He could barely keep himself alive half the time, let alone all of these other people.

Finally, the Tower took a deep breath. "We will march for the Brock," he said. "We'll assemble the column and send the light cavalry to every farm and village that we pass along the way encouraging them to follow us. The infantry and the rest of the heavy horsemen will form a type of rear guard to protect the common folk, the children, and the old from any pursuit. Sir Geoffrey—" He paused. "Will you guide us?"

Sir Geoffrey gave a sturdy nod. "Of course, Lord Tower, though I'll need someone to show me the way."

"I will walk beside you, Sir Geoffrey," Marina said.

"It would be my honor, your majesty," Geoffrey said with a bow.

"And where my queen goes, I follow," Sir Armel said, nodding to Sir Geoffrey.

"Good," Beledain said. "Meanwhile, I will lead the rear guard and confound any enemies who pursue us."

"I will ride beside you, cousin," Val said.

"As will I," said Sir Briden.

Thom remained silent.

Quite frankly, he had no idea what to do. He was not accustomed to fighting on horseback and he had no real skill wandering the wilds either. Once again, he was adrift, just like it had been with Magnus, and he wondered now if perhaps that was part of his lot now as the Reaver—to wander, to fight, to ride the wave of destiny and fate wherever it might carry him.

He was still contemplating these matters when the others finished speaking and they broke off to see to their urgent duties, leaving him to find his own way.

What are you thinking now, Crusher? he heard Magnus ask from the recesses of his mind.

"I'm thinking the world is strangely easier when you're fighting for your life," he said aloud.

Look at that! You're learning! Magnus laughed.

"Shut up."

Sorry about that Sparrow lassie. She seemed a good one.

"I only wish I knew her better."

Thom stood alone in the center of the plain and gazed over at the Guardian camp. He could no longer see the Warlord or any of the other enemy leaders, but he was certain that they were in deep debate with one another over whether or not to accept Marina's offer of a temporary truce.

In fairness—objectively—the whole notion of an Army of the Dead was madness and had he not seen it with his own eyes, he imagined that he would have a hard time believing in it too. However, men of the Order, he realized now, were no strangers to the unnatural—even magical—qualities of the world. The whole nature of the Anointing and all of that demanded it. Besides, wasn't the very concept of faith dependent upon a belief in such fantastical things as that? How could they claim to be believers in St. Aiden and the Church of the Kinship and then deny the possibility of its existence now?

Thom breathed a heavy sigh and then inexpertly worked to turn the borrowed horse around. With a touch of his heels, he urged the beast onward toward the queen's camp, his heavy thoughts no less a frustrating burden. By now, the orders had been given and the soldiers hurried about here and there packing up the camp, stowing gear, and seeing to the wounded. It always amazed Thom how quickly and efficiently such a massive force of men could be organized and set to work at a common purpose. On *Sigruna*, it took a steady stream of threats and cursing for Magnus to get the men moving, and even then, there were often fights and shouting matches. Here, there were still occasional shouts and reprimands, but far more appeared to be accomplished in a far shorter amount of time.

Slowly, he found himself in the part of the camp where the common folk were beginning to collect in large groups to march. He watched as they went about here and there, their faces hollow with fear. Families huddled together with livestock and baskets of goods or tools. A few of the luckier ones led wagons or carts. Dogs and cats hung about, curious and unsure. A rooster crowed, lambs bleated, and a cow mooed.

When he reached the rear of the developing column, he dismounted and passed the horse off onto a nearby soldier before heading south a ways along the road. From his vantage point, he could make out the movement of riders—scouts—as they kept watch, hoping to provide as early a warning as possible should the Army of the Dead appear. The afternoon sun shined weakly through wide, gray sheets of cloud, and in the pit of his stomach, Thom felt with absolute certainty that it was only a matter of time. He recalled the fight at the Lighthouse, the teeming mob of dead men and women, of the blazing red eyes that shone from their sunken eye sockets, and the maddened cackling of the Grand Keeper Huskarn. At least the Key of

Salvation was safe. The Key to the Kingdom. The Key that kept the Darkness imprisoned and brought about a brighter day.

As Thom continued his quiet introspection, a tendril of darkness rose suddenly in the distance followed by another and soon another. They marred the horizon some miles off like claw marks. In his mind, he heard Magnus.

Look alive, Crusher. Smoke on the horizon.

Moments later, the riders on watch began to return, galloping at full tilt to make their report. The sense of urgency that had characterized the Montevalens now edged upon panic.

They're coming, matey.

Thom nodded. "If only I had your strength," he said aloud.

Magnus chuckled.

You don't need it. You've got your own.

From behind him, the thunder of hooves and the beating of a drum drew his attention back to the camp, the soldiers, and the battlefield. He spied Sir Geoffrey riding towards the banner of the Winter Rose and hurried after him.

"The folk of the town are still making ready," Lady Valerie told the Tower. "Talondaire's men are assisting them as best they can, but many of the other lords of Whitemane have fled to return to their own estates."

"They wish to see to the safety of their own families," Beledain said. "We can't begrudge them that."

Val nodded. "Allard said that they will attempt to join us at the Nivanus if they can."

"Kin keep them," Geoffrey said. "What's the Warlord say? Any word?"

"Not yet," Beledain replied. "I'm about to ride over to ask. We need to know if they agree to stand beside us and fight or if they intend to retreat and warn those lands loyal to Dermont of the threat."

Thom paused to catch his breath and leaned over onto his knees. "I can go," he said.

The others glanced down at him from the backs of their horses.

"You lot are all busy getting all of this in order," he said. "I'm standing around with little else to do. Let me go ask the Warlord. Besides, I suppose you could say I know him. Might make him more inclined to help."

Beledain offered Thom a quizzical grin. "You never cease to surprise me, my friend," he said.

Thom shrugged. "To be honest, I often surprise myself," he said, "though I suppose it's not hard to do if you never have any idea what you're doing."

Sir Geoffrey chuckled. "I know the feeling."

"Alright," Beledain said. "Tell the Warlord that we intend to form a line across the valley to block the southern road so as to buy as much time as we can for the queen and the common folk to flee westward. He is welcome to join, but if he chooses not to, we would request that he not interfere."

"Aye, sir," Thom said. He turned to shuffle off, but the Tower called him back.

"Thom!"

"Yes, Lord Tower?"

Beledain raised his spear in a warrior's salute. "Be safe, my friend," he said.

Thom gave a nod and then trundled off, a lone figured marching across the bloodied plain.

A short while later, he arrived on the edge of the Guardian camp to be challenged by a cluster of kingsmen on watch. Almost at once, he was turned away as a vagabond, but when the exchange nearly came to blows, word somehow reached the Warlord and the man Thom recognized as Rood's steward arrived to escort him directly to the Warlord's grand pavilion.

"Your name is Thom, if I recall correctly," the Warlord said. He sat at the head of a wooden table surrounded by the other great men of the Order who had attended the parley. Pronet and Gurney, however, were nowhere to be found.

"It is," Thom said, "but now I am also known as the Reaver."

The man in white robes scoffed. "Another Blackguard," he said. "It seems they appear like maggots to feast upon the wounded flesh of this corrupted world."

Thom ignored the comment. He could tell by the man's clothing that he was a prelate of the Hierophant's Tower and while it was the prerogative of such men to serve the religious needs of the faithful, none were more skeptical of the miraculous than they.

"I come with a message from the Tower," Thom said. "Smoke rises from the south and it is only a matter of time before the Army of the Dead reaches us. The Queen intends to lead the common folk westward to safety while Prince Beledain and our army defend their rear. He requests that—if you are unwilling to join us—that you do not interfere."

"Prince is he?" said one of the armored men. Thom eyed him carefully. His dark hair was cut short and a thick black mustache curled around his lips. "I was under the impression that he was forced to give up all of that when he became the Tower?"

"I'm not sure how much that matters right now," Rood said.

"Then what *does* matter now?" the prelate asked.

"I'd say that life is fairly important," Thom answered.

The prelate and the man with the mustache exchanged a look and shook their heads. The remaining men, the other armored knight and the man dressed in the red finery of a commissioner, remained silent.

Thom sighed. "I mean, you lot are anointed, correct?"

Warlord Rood waved a hand around the table. "The Arm, the Boot, the Cooper, and the Mortar."

"Well," the Reaver continued, "wouldn't you say it's the first obligation of the Guardians to stand and fight evil?"

"The prelate—the Boot—rolled his eyes grandly. "There is far more to the Order than fighting," he said. "Surely as an apprentice you would have learned that."

The commissioner in red, the Cooper, folded his hands. "My lord," he said to Rood, "with all due respect, why do we not attack? Our enemy is weary and wounded. They will be preoccupied with the defense of their common folk. If we strike now—Kin willing—we might even succeed in capturing the rebel queen and bringing all of this Montevalen nonsense to an end."

Rood waved a hand. "Using women and children to press an advantage is hardly honorable," he said.

"Perhaps not," the mustached man said, "but it is effective." He was the Guardian warrior known as the Arm. Thom vaguely remembered his name appearing from time to time in one of the books Lughus used to read."

The final man, the Mortar, leaned upon his fist. "The Guardian-King sent us to assist King Dermont in securing the realm. Our duty is to the King, and as far as I am concerned, honor is the direct result of duty."

Thom felt a sudden flash of annoyance. "Yeah, that's a load of shit, that is," he said aloud.

All eyes snapped to him. "Excuse me?" the Boot gasped.

"No wonder there aren't more bloody Blackguards with the way you all think," Thom continued.

"What would you know of our ways?" the Cooper said. "Whelp of the traitorous Loremaster, your whole tower—"

Rood slapped his palm on the table. "Do *not* speak ill of Rastis Glendaro in my presence," he said coldly.

The men fell silent at once.

Rood breathed a heavy sigh and rubbed at his eyes. "Blood and Fire," he muttered. "This bickering is so tiresome."

Thom was about to agree when he heard a commotion from outside of the pavilion—the heavy tramp of boots, a horse's whinny, and shouts of command. Behind him, the flap of the pavilion opened and a red-cloaked kingsman entered and removed his helmet. "Warlord Rood!" he cried.

"What fresh bollocks is this now?" Rood grumbled.

The man did his best to stand straight and dignified, but his agitation was clear. "My lord, a great army has appeared upon the southern road. The enemy has maneuvered to defend against them, but as of right now, we do not know their origin or their purpose."

"Lady save us!" The Warlord grunted as he stood and strode around the table to the flap of the pavilion. "Come, boy," he said to Thom as he passed. The others at the table followed as well.

Out across the plain, Beledain and the remaining forces of the Queen's army had indeed positioned themselves in a line facing the south with their backs open and exposed to the kingsmen. Part of the infantry had readied themselves to form a shield wall while others set spears and pikes against any charge. The heavy cavalry clustered together, preparing to run down the approaching mob, the majority of whom were on foot.

However, in spite of their quick action and maneuvering, even a cursory glance was enough to see that the queen's forces were heavily outnumbered.

"My lord," the Arm said to Rood. "Now is the time! We should strike!"

Rood's jaw set as he stared out across the plain. "Galen!" he called to his steward, "fetch me my blade!" Around them, the men gave a hearty cheer.

Thom felt a queasiness in the pit of his stomach. "I will return to my friends, my lord," he grunted. "Kin keep you."

The Warlord gripped him by the shoulder. "We will go together."

Thom's eyes widened. Besides the warlord, the other leaders of the Order eyed one another in a mix of shock and disappointment. "My lord!" the Boot said, "You mean to stand with them? Our enemies? Traitors and Blackguards all?"

The Warlord's lips spread into a thin line. "Do you not feel it?" he asked the other anointed men. "Have your titles so weakened over the generations that you can no longer sense the darkness that stands upon your doorstep?"

The men remained silent, but it was a sullen silence and Thom felt the cold resentment of their stares. He ignored them and as the steward reappeared, limping beneath the weight of the Warlord's great sword, Duty, he slowly readied his axe.

"It is the first duty of the Guardians to fight the forces of Darkness and to stand for the Light!" Dandon Rood said. "Regardless of land or station. The Order defends! The Order protects! The petty squabbling of nobles and kings matters little against the battle between good against evil! I, for one, will not stand idly by and allow such worldly matters to dissuade me from doing my duty! If you would do the same, then follow me. If not, then stand aside!"

With that, the Warlord drew his great blade and strode through the camp, stern and resolute, and Thom hurried to keep pace at his side. Behind them, a great tide of red-cloaks began to form as men took up their arms to follow them.

"I owe your master much and more," Rood said lowly to Thom. "For he was my friend and when he alone spoke the truth, I failed to heed him. Now I make amends."

"My lord," the Boot said, shuffling up alongside him. "Even combined, this new enemy is larger than both our own forces and those of the rebel queen combined!"

"Then I suggest you run, sir," Dandon Rood said.

Like a swarm of locusts, the new army had arrived and met with the Tower's forces in an echoing clash of arms. It was still too far away to clearly make them out, but Thom knew that the newcomers would be a strange amalgamation of peasant, sailor, and warrior. Some would be armed with proper weapons and armor, while others may be clad in rough-spun rags and sailcloth. Yet, as had been the case at the Lighthouse, it would not matter. For the dead neither felt any pain nor did they bleed, and thus would keep on fighting so long as their hearts and their heads remained intact.

Thom felt a shudder run through him at the memory of those luminous red eyes and the insatiable hunger for violence. He tried to ignore it, steeling himself for what was to come.

You've got this, Crusher! Magnus's voice sang in his ears. *Show these bastards who Death calls lord!*

Ahead, the dead men threw themselves at the shieldwall and refused to break at the mounted charge. Still, in the chaos of the melee, Thom could make out the figure of the Tower, the tip of his great spear, Spire, shining in the winter light. Together with the great stallion Tempest, he cleared great swathes of warriors, scattering them and pressing them back. A hurricane upon the battlefield, wherever the fighting was the thickest, they soon appeared with the force of a gale and the suddenness of a white squall.

To the Tower's side, the Warlord led his men. Like a crimson wave, they crossed the open field and joined the queen's ranks. As Thom met the enemy, the song of battle stirred his blood and beat with the steady timing of his own heart.

"For the Light!"

Shouting his battle cry, the Warlord entered the fray, his legendary great sword cutting down waves of risen dead wherever they stood in his way. Thom fought beside him, chopping and slashing with his great axe until the red-light faded from the dead men's eyes.

"By the Brethren!" he heard a voice cry. "They *are* the dead!" He risked a quick glance to see that it was the Mortar, standing but a few feet behind him.

Thom grinned and spit upon the bloody ground. "Believe us now?" He snarled, and split the skull of a fallen warrior.

"Madness!" the Arm shouted. "The King should hear of this!"

"Aye, he should." The Reaver scoffed. He raised his axe and brought it down, cleaving a dead man from the shoulder to the center of his chest. He watched the red light fade in the dead warrior's eyes, wrenched the axe free, and readied himself to face the next foe.

On and on, the twin armies fought against their common enemy. Hacking and slashing, blocking and bashing whether in the shieldwall or from the height of a mighty war horse, the Tower's forces and the Warlord's kingsmen fought the relentless dead. Together they cut down rank after rank of dead warriors like ripened wheat at Harvestide, and the bodies piled up to form walls and hills of bone and flesh.

At length, the armies of the former enemies converged, and Thom found himself fighting between the Warlord and the Tower upon the great stallion Tempest. It was a sight to behold. Tempest was a juggernaut of muscle and steel barding, running down whole ranks of dead men or casting them aside with the force of a tidal wave. From his back, the Tower skewered the red-eyed enemies like a master of the ring joust, his spire collecting broken skulls around the vamplate like laurels at a tourney. Together, they were a paragon of horsemanship, the perfect union of man and mount.

Beside them, the Warlord proved beyond any doubt the merit of his name. In his bright plate, he stood as a mountain of steel, his great two-handed sword slicing through armor and bone like a plow through soft earth. None could stand before his might, driven by duty and righteous strength, hoping that with every foe felled by his hand, he might shake off the weight of his own self-assigned shame.

And then, there was Thom.

At the sight of the dead warriors, with their red-glowing eyes, relentless hunger, and skeletal forms draped in rotting flesh, he felt the familiar sense of icy fear coursing through his veins. He remembered the horror, the futility he felt at being trapped atop the Lighthouse where Magnus fought his glorious final battle. He recalled the desperation, the terror, and the pain of his ankle twisting beneath him. And for a moment, he nearly lost his nerve.

But then, as happened sometimes, he sensed within his mind the strains of a song, an ancient song to which there were no words, but that he somehow knew the tune. Steadily, it grew louder, warming his blood and setting fire to his heart. His fingers tightened upon the haft of his axe, and with the strange battle fury that he could neither articulate or understand, he began to fight. With wild, reckless abandon and unrelenting force, Thom threw himself behind each stroke, carving a path through a wilderness of dead men like a woodcutter in a forest of bone. Magnus's laughter, merry and warm, echoed through his ears, and only later did he realize that it was not his Wrathorn friend's mirthful voice he heard, but his own.

Yet, despite the dozens of dead that their combined efforts returned to the grave, there were always more. At least, Thom thought, they had bought enough time for Geoffrey and the queen to escape the field and begin the long flight to the Brock. With any luck, they would be well on their way before the defenders broke or were overrun and the dead army could continue its pursuit, wantonly murdering any man, woman, or child unfortunate enough to be caught in its path.

But what if they were not well on their way? For the dead had no need of rest like the living. Nor were they affected by hunger or cold. Was it even possible that without the rearguard to defend them the desperate exodus to the Nivanus could hope to escape certain doom? No sooner had these thoughts crossed Thom's mind than he spied the Warlord split a dead man from neck to navel, wrench his blade free, and call out.

"Prince Beledain!"

On Thom's other side, Tempest reared up and crushed the helmeted skull of another enemy with a mighty hoof. "Warlord Rood?" the Tower replied.

The Warlord leaned upon his blade, his chest heaving with the effort of his breath. "It has been no less an honor to fight beside you than to stand once more with the Tower," he said, "but now is the time for you to join your people. Go and live to fight again!"

"What?" the prince's eyes went wide. "With all due respect, my lord, the battle is far from over," he said. "I will not abandon an ally in such dire straits."

"I'm afraid you must," Rood said.

Beledain shook his head and again made to protest, but the Warlord held up his hand. "You *must* defend your people," he said. "Without you, without your men, I fear their corpses will serve to replace those we have defeated here as they make war upon the living."

The Tower's brow furrowed, but he abandoned his protestation.

"Go!" the Warlord said with a resolute nod. "This fight belongs to the Guardians, for our failure to heed Wisdom, and our only hope of redemption."

At length, Beledain breathed a sigh. "Kin keep you then, Warlord," he said, raising his spear in a salute. "And know that whatever comes, my people owe their lives to you."

"Farewell, Tower," the Warlord said.

"Farewell," Beledain said. He turned to the Reaver. "Come, Thom."

Thom chewed his lip, and for reason he could not quite put into words, he shrugged. "Oh," he said, "I'm staying too."

505

Beledain fixed the young Reaver with his green-eyed gaze. "Are you certain?"

Thom chewed his lip, the strains of the Reaver's song still sounding in his ears. "Yes," he said at last. "I am."

Beledain sighed heavily. "So be it," he said. "May the Lady of Light protect you, my friend, and may we meet again."

Thom smiled. "Go," he said. "Protect the queen."

With one final nod, Beledain raised his spear and shouted orders to his men. The young girl who served as his standard-bearer raised the banner of the Winter Rose high and at once the soldiers of the queen's army began to form together into a defensive column. Thom turned his attention back to the battle. Beside him, the Warlord's face was grim.

"You should go with them," he said.

Thom shrugged. "Probably."

The Warlord gave a forlorn smile. "Well, if this is to be our end, then may it be glorious."

"Aye, sir," Thom agreed. "A song worthy of a thousand bards!"

Yet not all of the Guardian forces shared that sentiment. Barely had the forces of the Winter Rose begun their tactical withdrawal when the Arm rode to the Warlord's side, his mustache bristling with rage. "What is the meaning of this?" he cried. "The traitors escape while we fight on? This is madness!"

"It is the duty of the Order to fight this foe!" Warlord Rood replied. "This is our sacred purpose! Our first mission! Even this man—a young man whom you would disparage with the name of Blackguard—stands and fights! If you wish to run, then by all means go, but know that you will forever carry within you the greatest of shame!"

The Arm's jaw set and his eyes widened with rage, but he choked down his anger and drew his weapon. "Curse you, Rood!" he said. "Just know that when you stand before the Brethren to be judged, that it shall be you who bears the responsibility for any and all of our honored dead."

"I can live with that," the Warlord said, "or die with it."

On and on they fought, long after the Tower led the queen's forces from the field. Thom's arms and shoulder ached from swinging his axe and he could feel the burn of blisters on his hands and fingers. Yet still he fought on, taking pride in the knowledge that when his end came, it would be shoulder to shoulder with a warrior like Dandon Rood. His only regret was that he should not be able to tell Lughus about it, and even Royne. To be able to tell them how Ol' Thom Fatty had finally found his nerve.

Another rank of dead men marched forward to meet the Andochan line. At a shout from the Arm, the kingsmen locked their shields together to meet them, though it was clear that they were growing weary of the fighting. Many had already fallen and most of those that remained were wounded, but at the urging of their officers, continued to fight on. Thom's experience of the kingsmen had mostly shown them to be little more than boorish brutes; however, they had certainly shown their mettle against the unceasing horde.

Countless scratches, scraps, and bruises marred Thom's body as well, though he had yet to suffer any truly grievous harm. He knew that the uncanny power granted to him from his title allowed him to endure much more punishment than the average man, but there were certainly limits—as the Warlord was beginning to prove.

While Rood continued to cut down wave after wave of dead warriors, his armor was marred with red smears and stains of numerous wounds. While many, if not most, were superficial after the manner of Thom's, the way the old man winced and grimaced as he fought spoke of deeper, more severe injuries.

Yet, still, the Warlord fought on.

Finally, as the sun, at last, touched the horizon in the west, the commanders of the Army of the Dead finally made their appearance. Clad in the immaculate purple robes of their profane sect, the Keepers of the Lighthouse, the devotees of Dibhor the Dark Brother, rode forth. The red eyes of their unholy steeds shone brighter in the fading light, while exposed bone and pallid, dried horseflesh appeared in stark contrast to their ebon trappings and caparisons.

Together in one great assembly, the Keepers trotted at an unhurried pace, sonorously chanting a hymn to the coming darkness and filling the kingsmen with dread. Even Thom, for all his newfound bravery, could not escape a sense of cold fear, particularly when he saw that leading the vile procession was the Grand Keeper himself, Riggilo Huskarn.

"That's him!" Thom told the Warlord as they fought to catch their breath. "The Grand Keeper!"

"Then we must defeat him," Dandon Rood swore. Beside him, an assortment of minor men of the Warlord's Tower—cadets, partisans, and his loyal steward—men who flocked to their lord's side over the course of the desperate struggle—eyed one another grimly and exchanged a final, resolute nod.

The Warlord raised his storied blade as if in silent oath and with one final cry of "For the Light!" led his men against the servants of the Dark.

Thom was with them.

For all their martial prowess and for all their storied fame, the Warlord and his men met their match against the greatest, most skilled and armored dead men whose sole purpose in rising again was the defense of their profane masters. Without weariness, without pain, the dead defenders met the Warlord's charge, sacrificing themselves in order to bring down the Order's elite. Thom fought harder than ever before, swinging his bearded axe like a gale, but all around him, the Warlord's men died—cut down, beaten, or torn apart—until at last, only Rood remained, standing over the body of his loyal steward.

"I'm sorry, my lord," the man choked as blood poured from his side.

"Do not be, Galen," Rood said. "There's still a chance I might save you."

"Lady save us!" Thom cried. He swept a dead man's arm off, cut low to shatter the leg of another, and hurried to reach Rood's side, for he had a sense of what the old man had in mind and he knew that—even if only for a moment—he would be unable to defend himself.

But before he could make it to the great man's side, he saw the line of dead defenders part and the Grand Keeper, on foot with five of his subordinates, converged like phantoms upon the Warlord with palms outstretched, shouting praises to the Dark Lord Dibhor.

Horrified, Thom watched as their grasping hands clutched at the Warlord's armor, clothing, and mail, until the Grand Keeper himself placed a hand upon Rood's brow. Again, they began to chant in low tones, and this time Thom could not shrug off the icy daggers of fear. Before his very eyes he watched as the Warlord's skin turned white as linen and his eyes faded until the color all but disappeared.

He was dead. Dandon Rood, the Warlord, Greatest General of the Order of the Guardians, was dead. And his title with him.

Thom cried out in grief and anger. With a flurry of strokes, he cut down a pair of dead warriors and engaged a third, so desperate was he to reach the

Keepers and to bathe his axe head in their blood. "You bastards!" he shouted. "I'll kill you all!"

He gazed across the melee to find the strange, serpent eyes of the Grand Keeper upon him. At once, Huskarn's face contorted with unbridled savagery and he pointed a gnarled finger at the Reaver and screamed at his minions to attack. The risen warriors turned and followed his command, ignoring now any of the other Guardians and kingsmen for the sake of following the Grand Keeper's will.

A year ago, the old Thom would have shrieked in terror, thrown himself on the ground, and curled into a whimpering ball of blubbering as he resigned himself to his fate.

But not now. Too much had happened. Forged along the path of adventure under the mad tutelage of Magnus Bloodbeard, he had become anointed under the title of the Reaver. He'd seen friends die, innocents suffer, learned to take beatings, and to dish them out. He was not the child he once was, the child who had abandoned his best friend—his brother—out of selfish fear. He was a warrior, a Guardian, a Blackguard. Never again would he cower before the Darkness. He would stand and fight for the Light.

With a deep, bracing breath, he stared into the eyes of the Grand Keeper, raised his great bearded axe high, and smiled.

The risen horde prepared to strike, to overwhelm him in a swarm of savagery and death. Thom was vaguely aware that at his back, the Arm, the Mortar, and the other anointed men were shouting at the remaining ranks of kingsmen to fall back, to leave the bloody Blackguard to his fate. The sun continued its slow descent in the west—when without warning, a great shadow appeared overhead.

Thom had just enough time to leap for cover as an enormous creature dove from the sky, scattering dead warriors and kingsmen alike. The ground shook as it touched down and Thom covered his ears in a vain attempt to block out a deafening roar. Like a snuffling boar, he scurried along the ground, uncertain whether it was safe to stand, and rolled onto his back to see what was happening.

Instantly, he regretted that decision.

It was a creature unlike any he had seen before. Enormous, serpentine, with great, bat-like wings that stretched so far across the plain as to block out the sun. Its body was covered in sleek, black scales that shone like shards of obsidian. Its very flesh appeared to draw in the light, ensconcing the creature in an aura of darkness and shadow.

Atop its long neck, its head was the stuff of nightmares. Two enormous horns curled upwards along the line of a massive jaw that bristled with teeth like a graveyard of swords. A great cloud of sulfurous gas bloomed from its nostrils with every exhale and a low, rumbling growl sounded continuously from the depths of its dreadful throat.

Worst of all, however, were its eyes—great, white orbs the color of curdled milk and bone. Each marred by a single pupillary sliver of darkness that seemed a dread portal, a window to the Black Abyss itself.

Despite his newfound bravery, Thom could not resist a crippling sense of fear and despair.

The Beast of Dibhor! he knew, *The great creature of darkness banished by St Aiden and the Lady of Light!*

When the overwhelming shock of the creature's appearance slowly sank in and time once more began to march onward, Thom watched as one by one the Keepers fell to their knees in reverent genuflection. A type of ecstasy seemed to consume them and they shock and cried out in profane joy, then slowly, with an adoration born from a lifetime of zealous devotion, Riggilo Huskarn, the grand Keeper, strode forth and bowed.

"Lord Dibhor!" the Grand Keeper cried with a maddened cackle, "Praise you! Praise you, Lord Dibhor! The Beast of Dibhor has returned to restore order to the chaos and bring about a Golden Age!"

Huskarn's face beamed with zealous radiance and he knelt again, casting his hands upwards in beatific praise, his rheumy eyes tearful with the sight of the legendary Beast.

It was the last thing he would ever see. For with a darting motion and a sharp snap, the Beast's jaws closed around the Grand Keeper's middle and tore him in half.

Lady save us! Thom gasped as the Grand Keeper's stringy entrails hung in grotesque vines from the Beast's wretched maw. With a swift flick of movement, it swallowed Huskarn's upper half and dipped forward to finish the meal.

The remaining Keepers were too arrested with fear, reverence, and shock to move or speak.

It was then, however, that from behind the Beast's great horns, another man, also clad in the bright purple robes of a Keeper, climbed down to the battlefield and raising his voice, began to speak.

"Keepers, kingsmen, and Guardians alike, hear me!" he began. "My name is Natharis Tainne, Keeper of the Lighthouse in the First Degree, Loremaster of the Order of the Guardians, and chief advisor to Kredor Drude II, Guardian-King! Hear me!"

Thom glanced around him. To his surprise, the dead army had fallen still and now stood silent as a tomb. Behind him, the remnants of the Warlord's army also stood motionless, the four Guardian leaders—the Arm, the Mortar, the Cooper, and the Boot—assembling at the head of the army to hear Tainne's address. It was clear that they knew of him, and while Thom couldn't quite grasp the nonsense about this man calling himself Loremaster, Keeper, and friend of the King, he seemed to carry enough credibility that the fighting had—for now—ceased.

Tainne continued. "With the blessings of my Lord Dibhor and at the behest of the Guardian-King, I am here to inform you all that this fighting, this war is over! For after thirteen hundred years, the Order of the Guardians, the Church of the Kinship, and my lord, Dibhor, are once more at peace."

Thom shook his head. *What?*

"In the beginning," Tainne said, "in the days of Old Calendral, Dibhor too was regarded and respected as one of the Kin! But following the fall of the emperors and the heresy of the Warlock, humanity rejected Brother Dibhor and instead of veneration, they treated him with only scorn."

"But not anymore!" Tainne continued. "For through the wisdom of the Guardian-King and through the power granted to him through the Protectorate, the whole of Termain now stands united under the blessings of the restored Kinship! For the first time in thirteen hundred years, peace and unity shall reign!"

"So fear not, warriors of Andoch! Fear not the servants of Dibhor! Fear not the legendary Beast! By the power of the reunited Kinship, all bow before the Guardian-King!"

When Tainne finished speaking, his voice echoed throughout the silent battlefield. Thom felt his heart hammering against the wall of his chest like a war drum. For what seemed an eternity, nothing moved and the light of the setting sun became red as blood. The eyes of the dead warriors glowed brighter, but they remained still and quiet as the grave.

At last, from the Guardian shieldwall, the four anointed men stepped forward and turned to face the line of kingsmen.

"The power of the Guardian-King has saved us!" the Boot intoned, his white robes blazing crimson in the light of the sunset. "All hail King Kredor, Champion of Dibhor, Tamer of the Legendary Beast!"

At once, the other Guardians drew their weapons and raised them above their heads. Echoing the prelate's cry, they too shouted out across the plain, inviting the kingsmen to join them. "All hail King Kredor! All hail Lord Tainne!"

Before long, the entire battle line of red-cloaks was cheering in unison and beating their weapons against their shields. The remaining Keepers raised their voices in a sonorous hymn, and Lord Tainne stood in stately satisfaction. With a wave of his hand, the creature threw back its head and let loose a triumphant roar.

Crouching low to escape notice, Thom stood hidden among the statue-like corpses of the army of dead. All of the sudden, he felt a light touch upon his ankle and he looked down aghast with alarm. It was Galen, the Warlord's steward and sword-bearer. Blood streamed steadily from the corners of his mouth and with a listless gesture, he beckoned Thom to him.

"You of all men know better to believe him," the steward whispered. "For my Lord Rood often said that it was your master, Rastis, who alone foresaw the dangers of Tainne and the Guardian-King."

Thom's breath caught as he stared into the eyes of the dying man. "What would you ask of me?'

"Go, Thom Reaver. Warn the others—the Tower, the Vanguard, the other apprentices..."

"The Blackguards?" Thom felt his eyes burning with anguish and tears.

The young man nodded. "Hurry now while they are distracted," he said.

Thom nodded and made to move, but the young man held him back once again.

"Remember the last stand of the Warlord!" He grimaced. "And when men speak of what happened today, tell them that he met an honorable end!"

"I will." Thom said.

The steward fixed him with a stern gaze and offered him one final resolute nod. "Bring the Dawn, my friend."

Thom gripped the man's hand and held it tight as he shut his eyes and breathed his last.

"Bring the Dawn," Thom repeated, gazing into the distance at the setting sun. "Bring the Dawn."

CHAPTER 43: CODA

When Lughus awoke, he saw only darkness, an endless expanse stretching before him for eternity. His body ached, his mind felt broken. He wondered vaguely if he had passed beyond the veil and been banished from the sight of the Brethren to perish in the nothingness of the Black Abyss. For he had failed. He knew it. And with his failure, all Termain would suffer under the tyranny of the Guardian-King and the Beast of Dibhor.

No.

It could not end like this.

He would not let it end like this.

If ever there was a way to return to the realm of the living, he would not rest until he found it. It was his duty to protect the people, to fight the Darkness, and to safeguard the Light. A shared duty that belonged to him and to his love.

Brigid…

He had to find her, stand beside her, so that together they could usher in the new Dawn.

He gazed back into the bleak expanse, his vision steadily clearing with the intensity of his resolve. In spite of the pain in his body and the despair that hid within the shadowy corners of his mind, he steeled himself to defy the darkness. Come what may.

And there, dim and perhaps dying, and certainly far off, he discerned within the vault of blackness, a fragile pinprick of light. A single, lonesome star. Yet the longer he stared at it, the more its light grew and grew. His body regained its sense of feeling and while he felt an intense pain in his side, mere inches from his old crossbow wound, he also felt a warmth, a comfort. To his great surprise and relief, he recognized it as Brigid, lying beside him, her head upon his shoulder, her slender hand tightly clenching his.

We live... he thought as the memories of the battle in the cathedral began to trickle back to him. *We yet live...*

A great sloppy wetness passed along the length of his face and he winced as he instinctively tried to lurch upright to sit.

"Fergus!"

With a happy bark, the great hound rushed him, licking his face and whimpering with joy. Beneath the sudden onslaught, Lughus felt Brigid stir.

"Lughus!" she gasped, her breath cut short by some inner pain.

"Brigid!" he whispered, surprised now by the hoarseness of his own voice. He pressed his lips to her forehead and was alarmed to see the crimson stain it left behind.

"Thank the Brethren," she whispered, her voice near to breaking. "It worked."

Lughus felt his vision growing misted again as he held her. "What worked?"

"The Gift of the Guardians," said a voice.

Against the pain of his wounds, Lughus lurched upright, conscious suddenly that Brigid appeared to be suffering the same wound. To his utter surprise, they lay in the center of a great, circular ruin filled with broken stones, splintered timbers, and shattered glass. It was the Cathedral of St Aiden, he realized, though little enough remained that would identify it as such.

And there, seated upon a pile of rubble, was an old man, gazing into the heavens seemingly without care or concern.

"Well done, Blade," he said. "You brought the Marshal back from the brink of death. It takes an iron will to balance the healing of a wound without assuming it completely—particularly when healing a fellow Guardian."

Lughus's eyes met Brigid's and his throat felt thick with emotion.

"I'm afraid that in this case," the man said, "You will both forever bear the scar you share." He chuckled quietly to himself. "But I suppose there is a certain poetry to that."

For the first time, Lughus realized that in spite of the stranger, Fergus was completely calm. Brigid seemed to notice it as well and with furrowed brow, she asked, "Who are you?"

"Ah," the man said, and as he turned toward them, Lughus noticed the lute that hung from the strap across his back and the milky whiteness of his blind eyes. "My name," he said with a sonorous lilt, "is Sigmund."

"Sigmund?" Brigid repeated.

"Though it might well be that you may know me by another," he said.

"And what might that be?" Lughus asked, for already the name Sigmund summoned up a vague sense of familiarity. He had heard the name before—he was sure of it—long ago during his journey with Crodane.

The old man's lips spread into a forlorn smile and with a slight inclination of his head, he leaned forward at the middle, offering them a polite bow.

"The Bard."

THE TERMAINIAN CALENDAR

The Termainian calendar contains thirteen months, each month consisting of four weeks of seven days each for a total of 364 days a year. However, the thirteenth month, Harvestide, contains one extra day (Harvestide 29), known as the Feast of the Father, and is traditionally celebrated as a holiday. People across Termain either refer to the months with the suffix "tide" or by simply saying "the Month of the Bear" or "the Month of the Sun."

Seasons and Months:
Spring: Beartide, Stonetide, Salmontide
Summer: Suntide, Stagtide, Falcontide
Harvest Month: Harvestide
Autumn: Houndtide, Oakentide, Horsetide
Winter: Moontide, Wolftide, Owltide

Days of the Week:
Alanday
Perinday
Tengday
Galday
Kalladay
Aidenday
Kinday

Some Holidays of Note:
Beartide 1—Awakening (the first day of spring)
Salmontide 12—Lover's Night
Suntide 15—The Feast of St. Aiden
Harvestide 29—Harvest Day
Houndtide 15—The Feast of Perindal
Oakentide 20—The Feast of Tengale
Horsetide 28—The Feast of Galdorn
Moontide 15—The Feast of the Lady

DRAMATIS PERSONAE

The Nation of Andoch and The Order of the Guardians

- Guardian-King Kredor Drude, Lord of Titanis, Protector of Andoch
- Rordan Baird, the Chancellor
  - His followers in order of rank: Commissioners, Constables, Counselors, Courtiers, Pages
  - Willum Harlow, Chief Constable, bearer of the Guardian Title of "the Hammer"
- Hagan Shawn, the Grand Hierophant
  - His followers in order of rank: Hierophants (Provincial), Prelates, Ministers, Celebrants, Acolytes
  - Provincial Padeen Andresen, Provincial Hierophant of Baronbrock, High Cleric of the Cathedral of St. Aiden, bearer of the Guardian Title of "the Breath."
- Dandon Rood, the Warlord
  - His followers in order of rank: Justiciars, Cavaliers, Gallants, Partisans, Cadets
  - Gallant Galen Pine, his steward
- Lord Natharis Tainne, the Loremaster, boyhood companion to King Kredor, Keeper of the Lighthouse of Castone in the First Degree
  - His followers in order of rank: Sage, Seer, Scholar, Scribe, Apprentice

- Lord Marcel Pryce, Viceroy of Grantis in the Name of the Guardian-King
  - o Marcel Pryce the Younger, his son

The Nation of Dwerin and the Castle Blackstone

- Archduke Darren Beinn, formerly the Lord Sheriff of Dwerin
  - o His wife, Archduchess Josephine Beinn
    - ▪ Her maid, Livonia
  - o His son, Alan Beinn, called the Young Sheriff
  - o Lord Padraig Reid
    - ▪ Wilfred Barrow, captain of Lord Reid's scouts

The Nation of Montevale

- King Dermont Tremont, Lord-General of the Armies of Valendia, called the Plague King
  - o Kurlan Malacco, his seneschal, Warden of Reginal, called the Death Knell (deceased)
  - o Inen Vilnois, Warden of Whitemane, called the Golden Garron
  - o Vaston Delon, Warden of Roanshead, called the Boiling Sea
  - o Wilmar Danelis, called the Sundering Hand, Warden of Tremontane Castle (deceased)
  - o Lord Giles Pronet, Warden of the Nivanus Mountains
  - o Lord Jarrett Harren, Warden of the White Wood
  - o Canton, Dermont's chief of spies (deceased)
  - o Lord Talondaire, called the Young Talon, kinsman of King Marius on his mother's side
  - o Sir Gurney, called the Knight of the Rooster
- Queen Marina Tremont, called the Winter Rose
  - o Prince Beledain Tremont, Lord-General of the Army of the Winter Rose, called the Silent Prince or the Prince of Bells, bearer of the Guardian Title of "the Tower"
    - ▪ Marcus Tremont, his son

- o Sir Armel, called the Stone Thistle, seneschal to Queen Marina
- o Sir Welmsey, called the Knight of Verse
- o Sir Norton Wherling, called the Standing Stone
- o Sir Umbert Malet and his son Sir Guy
- o Sir Briden Sheradan
- o Horn (Harold Half-Wrathorn)
- o Sparrow

The Baronies of Baronbrock
- Lord-Baron Perin Glendaro, son of Harlan Glendaro and nephew to Loremaster Rastis Glendaro
  - o Imanie, his wife
  - o Millicent, Rosamon, and Alyson, his three daughters
  - o Sir Dalton Griegg, his seneschal

The Barony of Galadin
- Lughus Galadin, Heir to Arcis Galadin, former Apprentice of Loremaster Rastis Glendaro, bearer of the Guardian Title of "the Marshal"
  - o Fergus, a spirit hound of Perindal
  - o Sir Owain Rook, Seneschal to Arcis Galadin
  - o Horus Denier, his steward
    - Jergan, the master of the wardrobe, and his wife, Willa
  - o Randal Woode, Abbot of the Monastery of St. Golan the Ram
- Brigid Beinn, daughter of the late Archduke Danford Beinn and the current Archduchess Josephine, bearer of the Guardian Title of "the Blade"
- Geoffrey of Pyle, former farmer in the village of Pyle on the Spade, bearer of the Guardian Title of "the Vanguard"
  - o His wife, Annabel
  - o His eldest son, Karl (deceased)
  - o His youngest son, Frederick

- o His daughter, Greta
- o His father, Amos
- Sir Faden the Weaver
- Sir Adolfo the Madder

The Barony of Marthaine
- Baron Roland Marthaine
  - o His wife, Morgana
  - o His son, Gaston Marthaine, father of Lughus (deceased)
  - o Sir Ulfric Gond, his seneschal
  - o Guy Marthaine, Lord of Silverlake

The Barony of Nordren
- Baron Leoric Nordren
  - o Sir Theobold Nordren, his son

The Republic of Grantis
- Royne, bearer of the Guardian Title of "the Loremaster"
  - o Conor Vendik, his steward
- General Cornelius Navarro, the Gray Wolf, Commander of the Fifth Legion
  - o Captain Denaron Velius, Navarro's Second-in-Command
  - o Petran Gigas, Navarro's valet
- Salasco the Wall, a Blackguard

Other Folk of Note
- Thom the Apprentice, bearer of the Guardian Title of "the Reaver"
- Riggilo Huskarn, Grand Keeper of the Lighthouse of Castone

ACKNOWLEDGEMENTS

As another installment of The Bard's Heresy comes to a close, I wanted to take a moment to thank everyone who has taken the time to read my story and support me along the way. In particular, I want to highlight a few individuals.

To anyone who has taken the time to leave me a rating or review on Amazon, Goodreads, B&N, or any other bookselling platform, thank you so much. In this world where there are so many wonderful stories calling out for your attention, I am so grateful for you not only recognizing mine, but also leading others to my work.

To Warren Ashbrook, thank you for your encouragement and your beautiful pottery. They are my first pieces of fan art and I will cherish them always. And don't worry—Book IV is already underway.

To John Hudson, my father-in-law, thank you for your support, advice, and encouragement in this and beyond. I hope that you've enjoyed the adventure, particularly the evolution of Thom.

To my grandparents, though you never had the chance to read these books, there are pieces of all of you in these pages in ways that even I was unaware of and that I had never even intended. It's been a joy to discover them along the way.

Finally, as always, thank you to my wife, Dominique, and to my children, George, Heidi, and Bastian. The green "shield book" is finally done! I hope that one day when you read it, it makes you proud. I love you always.

ABOUT THE AUTHOR

For as long as he can remember, Justin Bello has always been a lover of adventure stories. As a writer, he likes to create morally ambiguous worlds full of characters who struggle to fight for good even when faced with seemingly insurmountable evil. He enjoys reading, writing, drawing, tabletop role-playing games, and more hobbies than he realistically has time for. A full-time English teacher, he lives in Pittsburgh with his wife, Dominique, and three children. Visit his official website at justindbello.com or follow him on Instagram @justidbello_author

www.ingramcontent.com/pod-product-compliance
Lightning Source LLC
Chambersburg PA
CBHW060240030726
47493CB00024B/1402